MOONLIT NIGHTS

-A Novel-

Jacob Parr

Moonlit Nights

Jacob Parr

Print Edition, 2013

Copyright© 2012 Jacob Nathanael Parr

ISBN-13: 978-1484195932

ISBN-10: 1484195930

Author's Note:

This book is a work of fiction. Names, persons, locations, police departments, government agencies, websites, and groups are the product of the author's imagination. While most cities and locations are imaginary, others are existing places that have been used and have been altered to fit this story. Geography, topography, history and other details of these places mentioned in this novel are either fictitious or used fictitiously.

This book is dedicated to Lora, My Lil' Coconut

Without you in my life I would never have had the support and love I needed to make this book a reality.

And

To my editor and mother, Gina

A woman who never gave up encouraging my literary dreams…

"He who makes a beast of himself,
gets rid of the pain of being a man."
Samuel Johnson

"The beast in me is caged by frail and fragile bars."
Johnny Cash

"No one who, like me, conjures up the most evil of those half-tamed demons that inhabit the human beast, and seeks to wrestle with them, can expect to come through the struggle unscathed."
Sigmund Freud

Prologue:

October 26th

It had been a long day for Sara Moulton, a long week to be exact. There had been plenty of stress weighing down on her lately, and with the deadline she was facing at work, the days seemed to be coming to a close faster than she anticipated. The month long project that the graphics firm she worked for was dealing with was winding down, and the last meeting she had had with her boss Melvin Brooks, had caused her to have to push up the schedule.

It seemed that Metropolitan Crossroads, a local charity group had moved up the grand opening of their latest downtown location, and Sara's firm was handling all the marketing. She had less than a week now before they had to turn over all their materials to the Metropolitan Crossroads PR people, and her design team was just not ready. They had been working double time over the last two weeks as it was, and now with the new, upcoming deadline, she was putting in more hours than she could imagine.

Of course this was not what Sara had imagined she would be doing at this time in her life, but until she could get herself financially stable enough to start her own advertising firm, working under the" 'Master of Delegation", Melvin Brooks, was where she had to be. At the still young age of twenty-seven, Sara had initially felt that landing the lead marketing job for Thompson Graphics and Design would be a great stepping stone to launch her own advertising company, but lately she hadn't had time to even think of branching out into the field on her own. In fact, at this point it seemed like her temporary stay at Thompson G&D was far from temporary.

Exhausted and weary, Sara had been putting everything she had into this project, and looking down at her watch she could feel all the pressure and lack of sleep catching up to her. She had to squint slightly to read the small hands and let out a sigh of disgust when she realized it was almost midnight.

It had been a good thing she had left the office that evening when she did, or else she probably would have missed the last train home. The metro didn't have any running from Metro Center down her leg of the Red Line towards Rockville station after midnight, and having to catch a cab this late from downtown would cost a fortune.

She had already had to do that twice this week, and she knew that her checking account couldn't handle anymore of those charges for the rest of the month. She would be lucky if she wasn't already in the red.

Still this is where I wanted to be, making a name for myself in the big leagues, and then going off and being able to have the top tier of clients coming to me for their creative needs and wishes. If only this is where I'm really headed and not doomed to Thompson Graphics and Design forever! She thought as she sat there.

Sitting silently on the hard Metro seat, she rested the side of her blond head against the smudged window and watched through the rain streaked glass as the silhouettes of buildings flew by as the train coasted past the backside of some rundown retail stores and then entered another underground tunnel, leaving the cold, rainy night behind for the time being. The tunnel lights passed by so quickly that they appeared to be a single bulb floating in the darkness blinking at her every other second.

"Brooks better not expect me in early tomorrow," Sara muttered as she blew a piece of hair from out of her face and closed her eyes for a moment. She wished she had some Tylenol left in her purse, but had taken the last few caplets at the office earlier. There was a slight pressure behind her eyes, and the aching just didn't want to abate. A warm breath escaped her mouth and fogged the window lightly, reminding her how cold it had been getting this last week. Waiting for the train at Metro Center had been chilly enough, but the walk home was not going to be fun.

The train had been moving for a short period, and soon began to decelerate as it made its way into the next station. Sara readied to stop. As the train began its coast into the above-ground station, she saw that the weather had grown worse than when she had left work. At least her jacket had a hood.

Of course I had to forget my umbrella at work.

Finally, the train arrived at the Rockville Station platform, pulling to a low, squealing stop and the doors opened with the perfunctory hiss. The recorded message chimed once again over the speakers, and by now Sara was up and pulling her purse strap over her shoulder.

"ARRIVING AT ROCKVILLE STATION. NEXT STOP SHADY GROVE. END OF THE LINE."

Sara picked up her work bag from the adjacent seat and stepped up to the open doors. A damp, musky aroma met her nose as she stepped off the train and onto the waiting platform. Puddles of water were forming as rain slid off the roof above, and Sara tried to hide her purse and canvas work bag underneath her coat as she looked towards the set of stairs and escalator that led down from the platform to the actual station.

Taking a quick look around, she realized that she had been the only rider to get off at this station. In fact, other than her, the platform was deserted.

The worried feeling in her stomach began to grow, and her thoughts continued to keep her on the edge. Suddenly the train doors closed behind her, startling Sara as it pulled away, leaving her standing there alone.

Geesh girl, get it together. It was just the stupid train doors.

She watched as the train that had just departed was swallowed up by the darkness and rain of the night, then turned back to look around her. There was no noise on the platform other than the continuous drip of rain running off the roof above, and the wind whipping about and tossing her hair around her face. Pushing strands clear of her eyes, Sara finally decided to head towards the escalators.

As she stepped onto the first moving step, she took one last look behind her at the desolate, dark platform as it slowly disappeared from view. Beginning her descent down into the station. Sara watched the station come into view, a vast concrete chamber with walls that loomed up to meet a tall arched ceiling, making a single person feel small in such a cavernous station.

A place that seemed even bigger now that there were no crowds of commuters moving back and forth through the large, iron gates during the daily hours. It was too quiet, with not a single soul inhabiting the metro station at this eerie hour. Once she reached the bottom of the escalator, Sara stepped off, her heels clicking hard and echoing loudly around the chamber. As she walked along the cold, tile floor, she had to stop briefly to look over her shoulder one last time for reassurance. The hall and top of the escalator was empty, but the shadowed corners and dark halls past the gates ahead seemed to be hiding something.

There's nothing there, it's just late and you need sleep!

Sara took a deep breath, her heels continuing to click loudly as she approached the gates and turn. The worried feeling that had been growing continued to tighten in her stomach. Something was there, keeping to the shadows and masking its true intent.

Sara's eyes darted back and forth trying to watch and listen for what might be hanging around in the last tunnel that led out into the East parking lot, but the sound of falling rain echoing through the station and her own heavy breathing masked whatever it could be.

Quickening her pace, Sara slung her work bag and purse over the shoulder and broke out into a brisk trot. Her heels continued to smack down on the tiles, bringing a loud reverberating clickity-clack rhythm each time her feet hit.

The information desk sat in the center of the station, no Metrorail employee occupying it this late at night. She reached the stations turnstile, SmarTrip fare-card ready in hand, and placed the plastic above the round electronic reader. A small beep acknowledged the fare-card was read, and the blocked gate slid open as she slid through to the stations exit.

As she moved down the tunnel, the dark, rainy parking lot appeared ahead of her. Thirty more feet and she would at least be out of the concrete confines of the station and into the open night air. Reaching the stand of coin-operated, newspaper machines on her right, Sara stopped to catch her breath and try to calm herself.

See it's fine— there was no madman waiting to grab me in the station, mom!

The dark, lonely setting was just like something out of one of the mystery novels sitting on the nightstand next to her bed at home. A woman coming home from work late at night with no one else around, the perfect setting for a murder. She could just imagine the headlines and news reports; there would be no witnesses, no one to hear her scream and run to her rescue at this midnight hour. She even fit the part perfectly; young, blond-haired, with a tone figure. Her face was just the type that a person would see printed and displayed in the newspaper machines that had yet to be filled with the next morning's edition.

Suddenly Sara let out another breath, feeling a sense of calm come over her. What was she doing? She was working herself up over nothing, being paranoid over the smallest details.

Or is it? No, stop it, you're causing this to scare you!

Looking around at the gloomy metro hall behind her, she quickly tried to regain her composure.

Taking another breath then pulling her bag and purse underneath the folds of her jacket, Sara set out into the dark, stormy night. Rain quickly poured down upon her, hitting her hood and shoulders like a steady thrumming beat. At least next weeks forecast was calling for somewhat decent weather. It would still be cold, but with the temperatures continuing to drop as winter drew closer, the rain just added an extra annoyance to deal with. They were even calling for the possibility of snow at the end of next week! That had Sara convinced it still wasn't too bad out here.

Walking across the dimly lit parking lot took no time at all, but once she reached the end of the fenced in area there would be even less light to see by. Sara followed the sidewalk running parallel with Stonestreet Avenue, the glow from the parking lots streetlights began to fade away, only to be replaced with the occasional, dim lamp post running along the various roadways and streets.

Tonight's moon didn't seem to be much help either with rain clouds masking the overhead sky and stars above her. Once she reached the sidewalk, she didn't even need to check her watch to know the time. The traffic lights at the intersection she was about to cross were blinking. That meant it was past midnight.

Sara quickly glanced both ways up and down Stonestreet Avenue, and then took one last look over her shoulder to the empty Metro parking lot she had just come through. It was empty, the only cars on the premises probably belonging to passengers who had left them there overnight. There was nothing else there, but the uneasiness was still present.

Hurry up and get home. You're almost there! Just get through the park and then a soft bed will be waiting!

Making her way through the intersection, Sara quickly turned down the first street off the main road. This was the usual route she took home during her daily commute, but tonight everything seemed darker and more isolated down Howard Street.

Reaching the bottom of the steep hill, Howard Street intersected with another small neighborhood road, and Sara crossed it continuing further down the street. The houses grew closer together, the small two- story houses crammed together to fit as many as they could down to the bottom of the street. At the end was the small entranceway to Croydon Park that she had to cross through to get home.

Okay, at the park at last. Hurry up!

Sara hurried down the last stretch of Howard and entered Croydon Park through the small gravel entrance way. She was fully tense by now, and her breathing had been getting shorter. She couldn't get the feeling of being followed out of her head. And with the rain pouring down upon her, and the wind whistling through the trees that grew along the fence line at the top of the grassy hill to her left, she knew that she was even more isolated than she had been before.

The park wasn't large, but the sidewalk that she was following ran down the middle of the wide open grounds, and fences and trees blocked the nearest houses from view. The last streetlight she had passed under had been at the end of Howard Avenue, and once she had entered the park, she had little light to guide her along. Along with the rain, it was actually pretty hard to see anything clearly in the darkness of the barely moonlit night. She knew that she was about halfway through the park and could actually make out the two individual children's playground sets on opposite sides of the path coming up ahead of her.

Pulling her work bag and purse strap higher up on her shoulder, she ran her hand into the purse and felt around the cluttered bag for her keys. The more she thought about the darkness, the more she realized how it was always the woman that was being followed by the knife wielding maniac at night, and just when they thought they were safe is when the killer would appear. Fantastical and fictional stories ran through her head as she replayed the various scenarios in her crime novels over and over in her head. Sara turned once more, staring back towards the entrance to the park and the last of the real streetlights she had to see by.

As she continued along, her hand closed firmly around the can of pepper spray at last. Sara pulled the keys out and held her finger close to the tab at the top of the mace. Her heels still brought a loud clicking tap with each step, but in the open area of the park and with the rain falling all around, it was much less of a noticeable attention grabber. Any masked murderers on the rampage out in this downpour would also be in for a surprise if they tried to sneak up behind her. A face full of mace was a powerful deterrent, and that idea calmed Sara down a bit as she continued through the darkened pathway leading through Croydon Park.

She could see individual lights up ahead glowing in various home windows as she wound along the sidewalk. Sara was now halfway through the park and almost to her street. On the right the first playground set became somewhat visible as she continued on, a set of children's swings and a tire hanging from a rope, and it was in that moment that she heard a snapping noise ring out softly behind her.

What was that?

Spinning quickly with her arm raised and can of mace ready, she found herself staring out into the rainy darkness with nothing but the faint silhouettes of trees and hills behind her. There was no one there. No crazed killer wielding a knife, no bogeyman, no anything.

Or is there? Can I just not see them and they've been following me this whole time?

Now she knew she was being paranoid, and her imagination was starting to get the better of her. There was nothing behind her, but the dark, empty path she had been following and the outline of the children's swing set she had just passed.

As she started to walk further, the second playgrounds shape appeared on her left. Now she was almost home, the last playground set being only fifty yards from her street. Suddenly there was another snapping noise and a quick swishing noise as if something had brushed past her.

Swishhh

Startled, Sara turned towards the outline of the children's slide and the other shapes of equipment that rested atop a small hill a few yards away from the path. She stared hard at the lines of the various multi-leveled platforms and connecting slides trying to make out details in the rain.

It was dark and she could barely make out much of anything. But she had heard something, felt something, or had she. Sara began questioning the state of her mind again. Her hand loosened the grip on the can of pepper spray as she went to turn back towards the sidewalk. That's when she saw the movement out of the corner of her eye.

It was quick. Something had moved, slinking along the backside of one of the playground platforms. With very little light she couldn't make out anything other than another movement as whatever was there was keeping low and to the darkness. Swiftly, the shape moved again and all Sara could make out were two fierce, smoldering red eyes.

She opened her mouth, but never had the chance to scream…

Chapter 1

The morning sun was invisible, struggling to break through the overcast sky, unable to bring warmth to the gray, fog covered streets below. This cold October day was starting out to be like most in this dreary week as a cold front had brought a miserable, wet climate that blanketed the city of Rockville, Maryland and most of the Eastern cities and towns over the last few days. The streets glistened with a dull shine that recent rain had deposited onto the wet asphalt, adding to the damp cold that seemed to be sucking all hints of the hindered sun's warmth away.

The hour was still early and dark enough that the tall street lamps lining the street were still on, making a small attempt to break through the thick fog that curled around their bases like a rising cloud of smoke. Visibility was minimal, the morning already starting to look like it was going to be another long, bleak day as rain came down in a light mist before the oncoming thunderstorms began later in the afternoon. The quiet silence of the morning was slowly broken as the roar of an engine reverberated through the air.

A beam of headlights became visible at the top of the road as a dark, 1970 Dodge Challenger rose over the top of the hill and began driving down the wet street marked with a sign identifying it as South Sybil Lane. The street ended at the bottom of the hill, houses lining both sides and a small community park sitting across from the last row of houses before the paved, circular cul-de-sac at the end.

The dark blue, Challenger coasted down the last part of South Sybil and pulled over behind the line of Rockville City Police cruisers parked along the community park side of the street. The fog illuminated with a spectral glow as the silent, rotating blue and red lights atop the squad cars flashed around in a timed cadence with each other, adding extra illumination to the weak glow of street lamps overlooking the grounds.

Strobes of color flashed across the fronts of houses and the windows of these residences where curious neighbors could be seen glancing out at the scene before them. Other more daring onlookers had made their way out of their homes and were beginning to crowd the street on the opposite side of the police vehicles where a couple officers were keeping them from crossing the yellow tape barrier that had been strung up to keep the nosy bystanders at bay.

Necks craned and people peered out from under umbrellas as the mist like rain continued to drizzle down upon them, questioning voices calling out as the crowd grew larger opposite the marked off crime scene.

More and more people came walking out of their homes, bundled against the damp, wet air with hastily thrown on garments and jackets to attempt to see what was taking place across from them inside the sealed off corridor of Croydon Park.

Stepping out of the recently arrived vehicle, Detective Aidan Preston took a moment to survey the quiet scene taking place twenty yards before him, before shutting the door to his personal vehicle, and pulling the hood of his black jacket over his head. The low static like patter of rain echoed a little louder as the drizzle grew harder, and a cold blast of wind whipped across his skin making him pull the jacket tighter around him. So far everything seemed to be quiet and the scene appeared to be under control.

Two young officers were handling the crowd of onlookers, and keeping them in a small, manageable group, but no reporters had arrived yet so there weren't cameramen to worry about crossing the police tape. It seemed that the crime scene was still being cordoned off, which meant the news vultures hadn't arrived as quickly as he had to really make the younger officers work to guard and enforce the line.

Of course he had been at home when the call had gone out half an hour ago, and he lived only a short drive away, and earlier when the dispatcher had called units out to the small, East Rockville neighborhood, hardly any details had been known. The last few calls that had gone back and forth over the police channels added a little depth into the severity of the call, and it wouldn't be long before one of the local news teams picked up on it, if they hadn't already.

Aidan Dean Preston, Homicide Detective for the Montgomery County Police Department was technically still on a leave of absence from the force, but when he had heard the call over the police scanner in his kitchen that morning, he decided to check it out since it was close to his house, and figured it wouldn't hurt to lend a hand to the local Rockville boys. The initial call had come in around 7 am.

The 911 Operator patched it through to the Rockville Police Dispatcher who sent out the first, responding vehicle five minutes after that. The first responding police cruiser reporting in over the scanner was what Aidan had initially heard while just waking up for the dreary day. What caught his attention at first was the location, 401 South Sybil Lane being only a short drive from his small, one story house off of Lincoln Street about three or four blocks away, but hearing there was a reported murder was what brought him out this dreary morning to look into it.

On the other side of the cul-de-sac, wooden posts jutted from the ground and prevented vehicles from being able to cut through and onto the opposite street which ran west along the right side of the old Croydon Park Pump House. The area of the park that was now an empty grass field used to be the site of a large water tower that had been torn down over a decade ago. The old pumping station, which was housed in 401 South Sybil Lane was turned into a meeting place and then a community center for various events.

Sitting on Croydon Avenue, another police cruiser was parked to the side along with a large, Rockville Police Mobile Crime Scene Unit where a couple of CSI technicians were moving back and forth from the park entrance behind the pump house, where police had also barricaded the area with a few, wooden sawhorses and more police tape.

As Aiden approached, one of the young officers began to turn towards him, raising his open hand to stop him from crossing. Before the officer, a young rookie with a badge acknowledging his last name as Westmore could speak, Aidan Preston stopped at the tape line and pulled the hood from off his head.

"Detective Preston, Montgomery County Homicide," Aidan said extracting his badge out from beneath his shirt, the chain it dangled from around his neck dripping a few cold drops of rainwater down his skin, reminding him of just how cold this morning seemed to be.

The rookie officer glanced at his badge, then at the man before him. Aidan Preston was slim yet athletic looking. He had a square jaw, a days growth of beard stubble outlining his features, piercing gray eyes, and shoulder length, dark hair. He was wearing a black t-shirt and jeans underneath his leather rain jacket, but it wasn't his lack of uniform that apparently had the officer look at his badge again. He was apparently surprised to see a homicide detective on the scene from Montgomery County Police so early.

"My apologies Detective, the officer in charge of the scene is back that way," the young man pointed back behind him, towards the faint silhouettes barely visible in the dense fog about thirty yards away, "You'll want to speak with Lieutenant Garza."

"Appreciate it."

Aidan ducked under the police tape, his jacket skimming the line and dropping a few more icy drops of rain down the back of his neck. If he wasn't fully awake after the quick cup of coffee he had downed in his kitchen earlier, then this weather would certainly do the trick.

As he stood erect, he straightened his jacket and pulled the hood over his slick, dark hair. Aidan paused for a moment to look over towards the group of people gathered towards one corner of the park, their shapes in the low light of the early morning and the miserable weather conditions seemed to point to there being four men crowded together discussing something, while a few shapes moved about the fog-covered ground near what looked like a playset, collecting items and putting them into clear evidence bags.

As he drew closer, he noticed the men's conversation stopped for a moment as they turned their attention his way.

"Mind identifying yourself over there?" one of the men called out from the group.

"Detective Preston, MCPD." Aidan hollered as he continued his approach towards them.

"Preston, Preston— Aidan that you?" a familiar gruff voice asked.

"The same, Jones."

"Well what the hell you doing out here?" replied the voice again.

Aidan came within view and could see through the fog, the large stocky form of Detective Mack Jones, an old friend from years ago. Jones was short with a large stomach and shoulders that made his neck seem almost nonexistent, while his goofy smile amid chubby cheeks and squinting eyes made him look almost Asian in a Buddha type way instead of the Italian heritage that he always claimed.

He was wearing a drenched trench coat that seemed a size too small and a tight, blue suit that was almost black due to the rain that had soaked through, but as far as Aidan could remember, Jones never seemed to have a set of clothes that fit.

Aidan stepped towards the figure and with an outstretched hand, felt Jones' large palms clasping over his own, and giving them a good, hard shake.

"Damn, how you been Aidan?"

Looking Jones over once more, Aidan smiled and clasped the large guy on the shoulder. He wondered what Mack had been doing recently as well, but he also knew exactly how official his status was at this crime scene at the moment.

"I've been good Mack, how is Angela?"

"Good, good, you know she just graduated last May from Montgomery College up at the Takoma Park campus!" Jones said with a smile that stretched proudly from ear to ear. Anytime someone brought up his oldest daughter, Aidan knew that Mack had some important announcement to make.

"That's great to hear," Aidan said returning the man's smile, "Oh and Jessica?"

"She's doing good too, just trying to make their daddy proud!"

Aidan removed his hand from Mack Jones' shoulder, shook a bit of water off it, and replaced it into the folds of his rain jackets pockets.

"So when did you get back on duty?" Jones asked.

Remembering that he was standing in the middle of a crime scene and that Detective Garza was somewhere around, Aidan glanced at the other three hooded men standing there in the rain, realized he didn't recognize any of them, and stepped to the side slightly to make the conversation a bit more private. He glanced around to the sides while he was at it, deciding he would prefer not to run into Garza if he could avoid it as well.

"Actually I'm not officially back yet," Aidan said, taking another quick look around them.

He noticed one of the investigators walking past them and heading into the fog in the direction of Croydon Avenue and the parked crime scene van. The man was carrying a clear bag with a dark crimson smear coating the sides of the plastic and concealing whatever contents the bottom of the bag held.

The other men started back into their original conversation, not really paying attention to Aidan and Jones anymore. Jones watched the guy pass then looked back to the original three members of his group, seemingly to wish they had a little more privacy. Mack studied Aidan for a moment, the rain trickling down his rounded features, and then said, "Well you're looking a lot better than you had the last time I saw you. So unofficially, what brings you out here?"

"Thanks. I actually still live a few blocks down from here and heard the call go out," Aidan said looking down for a moment and then back towards the other three members of Jones' group. "Figured I'd just swing by and check it out for myself."

"Hey well you know I'd never mind you giving some input into one of my cases, but unfortunately we're all down here on Garza's watch. He's the one formally in charge of following up this incident." Mack said with a sour look pursing his lips.

Jones had a way of letting it be known how it really was, and Aidan knew that Jones hated being called up to work alongside the infamous Sergio 'Pit bull' Garza. Garza had earned the name as he came up through the ranks. He made a reputation for himself working narcotics back in Queens, New York, and had made a few lucky busts that got some people talking about how, 'once Garza got his teeth into a lead, he didn't let go'.

It was a stupid nickname, one that Aidan knew the man didn't deserve, especially looking at his record once he transferred down to Maryland and took a job with the small Rockville Police.

A move that most people say transpired because his wife 'wore the pants in the relationship' and decided to take a corporate lawyer position in D.C., wanting to live closer to the capital for the commute. Since being with the Narcotics Division for a short bit and not making a name for himself there, he transferred over to Homicide hoping to add to his resume. Now, half the Detective's around couldn't stand the guy, and Mack Jones was certainly no fan.

"Oh by the way, did you hear about his last little show for the press over that Mayor's Aide ordeal?"

Aidan thought a moment, trying to recall the last couple months of local news. Unfortunately, the last few months hadn't been great for him, and he actually had spent some time away from the city up in the Appalachian Mountains to get away from everything chaotic going on in his life. It had actually been a suggestion that his psychiatrist had given, and after mulling it over for a bit, he decided to try it out.

"Nope, I was out of town for a bit up until recently," Aidan said not wanting to get into any further details.

Jones could see it in Aidan's face, the way his eyes seemed to show that his mind had wandered off for a bit, and decided to let it go. He had known Aidan for the last ten years, and knew everything he had been through over the last year wasn't something the guy was going to be discussing just yet.

"Well it doesn't matter if you heard about it or not. Let's just say that the Mayor's Aide, pretty young thing, checked out early, and Garza tried to make himself the darling hero for the media! Ha, it was a joke if you knew the shit he missed in stringing his little theories together for the press," Mack Jones laughed with a hearty gust as he recalled the event in his mind. "You know how they just feed into his ego!"

Aidan gave a small laugh and made a mental note to look into the case when he got a chance.

"Well speak of the devil," muttered Jones, as his rain-slicked face turned and squinted to the left.

Following Jones' line of sight, Aidan looked through the mix of fog and rain, and could see a pair walking towards them, rain running off their darkened forms as they came closer. Approaching out of the mist, Garza, dressed in what looked like an outfit straight out of a New York gangster movie, fedora and trench coat included, walked up to them with a look of annoyance on his face.

"Well well, if it isn't Detective Preston," Garza muttered as he stepped in front of Aidan. The man following him stopped at his side, folding his arms and looking Aidan over.

"Or is it still Detective? Last I had heard you were suspended pending an investigation into some nasty little business out of your jurisdiction." Garza gave a slick little smile as he glanced over to the man at his side, who responded with a little laugh of his own, then back to Preston.

"Actually Sergio, it's called a medical leave." Aidan said, punctuating each syllable of his first name. He had heard through the grapevine that he hated people using his first name. Had something to do with an old Captain in his old force back in New York hazing him as a rookie years ago. 'Pit bull' Garza glared at Aidan for a moment, having to take a small breath before replying. Aidan knew it had gotten to the creep.

"Either way, I don't believe you have any reason to be here at my crime scene. Jones, please make sure you help Detective Preston here to his car."

"Right away sir." Jones replied, managing to hide a brief smirk from his senior officer.

"Good, as for you three, I want you all over to the opposite side of the park right away," Garza snapped at the others that Jones' had originally been talking to when Aidan had arrived.

"I have some things for you all to do other than standing here chatting away. There are reporters arriving at this moment and I need this area secured until the CSI's can finish. I will handle the press."

Aidan shook his head slightly as he turned away, dragging a sleeve across his face to wipe some rain that was running down his forehead off. Jones followed suit and started to lead Aidan away before Garza really got on him.

"Now that the news crews are starting to show up, Garza's gonna have his hands full playing to the cameras. I've never seen someone so media hungry when the cameras come out," Jones muttered as they walked. "Puts the Chief to shame, and you know how he likes the publicity. Of course if Garza ever took his eyes off the cameras, he might actually solve a murder here or there.

The two walked along a small sidewalk that seemed to lead off into nothing but more fog, but as they continued, the path and more of the park continued to be revealed. Aidan continued glancing around into the darkness towards the flashing lights of the parked police cars about forty yards away.

He could see the crowd had grown in size since he had first arrived and now there were a few news vans parked at odd angles at the base of the hill. Aidan stopped for a moment and turned, looking over the crime scene more out of habit than anything else.

"So what happened?" he asked after waiting a minute just observing the motions of it all. He had a knack for this and paying attention to details was something he had always done. He also wasn't afraid to get his hands dirty, but really it was the thought he put into his cases that helped him solve the majority of the files that had landed on his desk over the years. That intuition, that attention to detail was something he found harder to focus on as of late, but even this being another police force's case, he was a homicide detective first and foremost.

"You really want to know?" Standing there in his soaked jacket, Jones looked down at the ground and dug the toe of his shoe into the muddy grass. "I figured with you still being on leave that you wouldn't want to be filling your head with this stuff right now."

Aidan looked over at his old friend, realizing that Mack didn't want to bring up anything that was too fresh to talk about, and Aidan appreciated that side of the gruff old man. "No, I've had enough time focusing on other things, sitting around not working isn't as glamorous as you might think," Aidan said as he watched a group of men working over near a swing set picking something up off the ground and bagging it. "At least not to me."

"Okay, just making sure. Of course, If I was on leave, I'd be somewhere sunny, not out in this shitty day on my own time. Maybe Florida. I guess I wouldn't really though, what with my next girl about to enter college now. Even community college is expensive, so you won't be seeing my ass out on a beach somewhere sipping one of them tasty, sugary drinks."

"Mack," Aidan said, looking the large man in the eyes. "Just fill me in."

Jones took a moment to look around and make sure they were alone. Everyone's effort seemed focused a little ways off, and now that the media was here, Garza was off his ass for the moment.

The fog was also helping, being that visibility was piss poor due to the inclement weather, it was hard to see anything clearly past a dozen yards. When he had first arrived it had been even earlier and made it that much harder to see what they were dealing with in the dark other than what the witness had reported in the initial telephone call.

"Dispatch put the call through to the responding unit around 7 this morning. It took them less than ten minutes to arrive since they were in the vicinity. The man who called it in was hysterical, dispatch had a hard time getting him to talk coherently and get him to speak clearly enough to send someone out in answer to the call. Spent part of the call on the phone calming him down enough to get him to stop puking his brains out.

'He was delirious. Seems he was up early starting his daily jog. Left his house and entered the park from the Sybil Lane entrance. Fog was so thick that early he apparently didn't see anything until he fell over something and landed in a slick of blood. Poor guy had tripped over the victim…

'…Or at least part of her."

Chapter 2

Aidan had been focusing on the dark shapes continuing to be illuminated by the revolving, police lights, and now video camera lights and flashes added to the scenes surreal foggy atmosphere, when the last part of Jones' statement registered in his mind.

"Wait what did you just say?

Aidan's attention was no longer on the parade of commotion in the distance, but fully focused on Mack Jones grim look. Jones nodded his head slightly in reaction to Aidan's questioning look.

"Yup, you heard right. The victim was discovered torn to pieces. Mutilated and dismembered."

Taking a moment to let that sink in, Aidan glanced around and noticed the closest, evidence-marking cones and numbers barely visible scattered about on the ground in multiple places throughout. The ones he could see were spread a good distance all from each other, marking various items to be photographed and collected. Looking towards the closest technicians, he could see how sickened their faces looked as they went about their work. Detective Mack Jones took the momentary pause to pull out a small notepad from a pocket in his pants. The paper was already damp, and Jones tried to shield it a little more with his hand as he flipped open the steno and scanned the pages.

"Victim's name was Sara Moulton. Age twenty-seven. She worked downtown for a marketing agency, one Thompson Graphics and Design. Seems she was on her way home from work late last night when she was attacked. Garza has the CSI guys bagging and tagging everything, but he's pretty sure it was gang related. Thinks that she ran into a group of MS-13 waiting for her. They killed her and hacked her apart. Then animals got to the pieces."

Aidan stood there, rain falling off his head and shoulders like a tiny rock at the base of a waterfall. He tried to take the whole scene in, the layout of the park, the location of the playground equipment and basketball court set over to the side near a wide field. He couldn't see much due to the weather, but knew the chance of not having any evidence compromised through the night was slim. It had been raining for hours so any residue or blood seemed pretty hopeless of being recovered uncontaminated.

"Animals?"

"Yeah, like a pack of stray dogs or something that came upon the body after she was killed. Looks like they scavenged what they could and dragged it around. Anyways there trying to pull up what they can on the victim. Looking for anything that can tie into any gang involvement or maybe it was just a case of wrong place wrong time.

'You know how its been lately. Prince George's County started having a big influx of El Salvadorians, Guatemalans and Hondurans a few years back, and there's been reports that their numbers have continued to grow throughout Montgomery County and Anne Arundel as well. There was an incident involving a few gang members a couple months ago and Garza seems to be using that as his basis for the conclusions he's reaching here. The frequency of gang related incidents including some pretty brutal murders over the last few years has increased. There's a little Italian restaurant up near the movie theater on the other side of the Metro Station, at night it turns into a Spanish nightclub. Anyways, apparently these guys got drunk, were fighting and attacked each other with machetes. One guy lost an ear. Another almost had his hand amputated."

Aidan continued to stand still, observing the wet, muddy grass around his feet. The rain didn't seem to be about to let up, and due to the fog, he knew this crime scene was going to be a mess.

Could a bunch of gang members have done this, or was it something else entirely?

"Mara Salvatrucha," he mused, thinking of some of the dealings he'd had with gang activity growing over the years. It used to be simple; guns and knives, but now there were certain cultures that were immigrating into the metropolitan area that had brought the brutal, guerrilla fighting to the states. Machetes, baseball bats, and other instruments had begun to grow in popularity as if they were still fighting in the jungles. Preston was thinking of the good old days of dealing with crime in the ever growing Rockville area when Jones caught his eye.

"Looks like Garza's about to head back over here and show us what he thinks of you being on his turf still." Jones said with a quick smile as he gestured towards the scowling form beginning to make its way towards them.

"Yeah, I'd better get out of here before you have to hear anymore of it from him as it is. Anyways, it was good seeing you, how about after this we can grab a coffee or something, get out of this weather." Preston said continuing to walk away from Garza's pursuing presence. He definitely didn't need to hear any more from that pompous ass.

"Yeah I'll give you a call once I'm done here."

Aidan saw someone pull Garza to the side for something and took the break he was given. Something was off about this whole scene. Something just didn't feel right. There was an eerie presence overshadowing the park, and Preston knew it didn't have to do with the creeping fog and overcast sky. Something was off and he didn't know what it was just yet.

Sliding back under the police tape, he made his way up the street towards his parked car. Looking back once more over the crowd that had gathered, he saw the usual mix of confusion, shock and horror that a body being discovered in a residential area usually brought upon the neighborhood. All it takes is one to get them riled up wanting answers, and if this miserable morning was any clue, it would be a hard day for everyone.

Right as Preston was about to turn back around, he caught a glance at the news van that had set up shop in the middle of the mayhem. Two people seemed to be running about attempting to get their establishing shots and equipment set up, while the talent was probably safely tucked away out of the rain and getting ready. Glancing back at the van, Aidan realized that it was one of the local stations, News Channel 5, and as soon as he realized that, he knew deep down exactly who would be out here this early chasing the story.

As if just thinking about him could cause him to appear, Aidan heard his name called out from the crowd. Looking towards the voice, he saw Ted Hanson, rushing through the crowd of onlookers, making a dedicated effort to get through and to Aidan. That was the last thing he needed as he turned around and continued to his vehicle, pretending to have not heard the reporter calling him. Unfortunately Hanson had zeroed in on Aidan, and even if he wasn't a part of this investigation, he wasn't about to be let off that easy.

I don't need this right now!

"Detective Preston! Detective!"

Ted Hanson was the epitome of the aggravating news journalist. Scratch that — he wasn't a journalist. He didn't deserve that esteemed title for the dirt he was responsible for reporting. Hanson was the type of guy who would pull one over on his own mother if it meant getting the story first, and that was something Aidan had firsthand knowledge of. Hanson was a slug. A slug that dragged itself around the city's streets, leaving nothing but a slimey trail where he had been, and purported to expose the ridiculous garbage he drudged up.

Hanson's grating voice broke over the steady pouring of rain just as Aidan was almost to the safety of his car. He heard the splashing of water behind him as he knew that he hadn't had enough time to get away before the leech, Ted Hanson came running up to him, rainwater pouring through his slick hair and rushing off his shoulders. Before he could get his keys out, Hanson was upon him.

"Detective Preston! It's Ted Hanson with Channel 5 news! Could you take a moment and speak with us?"

Aidan looked up just in time to see Hanson break to a stop at the back of his Dodge, a moment later a man toting a camera came up beside him and swinging it up onto his shoulder readied to start filming.

"Look Hanson, I have nothing to say to you, this is Rockville City's scene." Preston said hoping to get into his car before the camera began rolling. The last thing he needed was having to see his face on the news at a crime scene that he wasn't even supposed to be at. That last part caused him to cringe slightly as past memories surfaced about the last time he had been in the media's spotlight. It had been almost nine months ago, but the pain those memories brought was just below the skin.

Aidan knew he had to watch what he said to this man, him standing there in his expensive looking suit barely shielded by the elements with his jacket. His arm held out a small microphone towards Aidan, and he watched as Hanson switched into his 'on-air' mode.

"Yes, but I saw you coming from over there, and was wondering if you could shed some light on this incident for our viewers?" Hanson asked taking a few more steps towards Aidan; the microphone still held out towards him like the reporter was presenting him a trophy.

"Sorry can't help you out."

With that Aidan slid his keys into the door handle and was quickly into the seat of his car. He could see the angry look that crossed over Hanson's face as he waved the cameraman back towards the action. At least he hadn't pushed it. Not this time.

Good, at least I don't have to worry about being on Channel 5 tonight.

"You know Detective; I hadn't heard anything about you being back on duty since that event last May?"

What is with this guy?

Aidan tensed, his hands squeezing tighter onto the steering wheel before him. He let out a breath, deciding not to get involved with providing that rat any words from him and quickly turned the key in the ignition, and with a roar the engine shot to life.

"So are you back, or is this just a hobby for you on your time off?" Hanson yelled as Aidan put the car into gear and shot up the street, leaving the reporter out in the rain.

Ted Hanson, which was the last person Preston had hoped to see today. That man knew how to dig to a person's limits and then keep digging! As he drove up to the top of Sybil Lane, Preston pulled up to a stop sign and thought about what he needed to do next.

He let out a breath, watching his windshield fog slightly from the temperature difference. Mack would probably be busy for the next couple hours at least, and thinking about the odd scene of events he had just been witness too, decided he needed to look into things a little more on his own. After all, this was his neighborhood as well.

- -

Nick Austin Haley had just entered the offices of The Informant, the largest local paper the city had, when he spied Danielle Woods dropping off a stack of papers on his desk. Danielle was new to the paper, and had just recently gained an internship there to complete a requirement for her college major. As he slid out of his jacket and ran his hands through his long, damp hair, she saw him approaching and gave him a smile.

God she's pretty.

Nick thought, returning the smile and making his way past the few empty cubicles scattered around the main office area of the newsroom and got to his desk. Glancing at the rows of clocks up on the wall, each set for a different time zone as if they really needed to be reminded of the hour in every corner of the world for their small time paper, and saw it was just before 8. He was surprised nobody was in yet. Well nobody but Danielle.

Danielle had started working for the Informant just a few weeks ago, but already she had made a big difference in the atmosphere around the office. She definitely turned a few heads when she entered a room, and the Informant certainly could use the younger blood in its midst. It seemed to Nick that since he had been with the paper over the last few years, the staff continued to age and dwindle along with its subscribers. Of course, what did someone expect in today's world. Everybody had access to the Internet via there computers and cell phones, and the paper medium seemed to be a dying art form. Just like calligraphy and books. Pretty soon a printing press would be something little kids stared at behind glass in a museum or from the screens of their mobile devices. He could imagine it now — Mommy what is that big thing? Oh Honey, people used to actually use paper to give people information, instead of watching it or reading it online! Can you imagine that?

Nick broke away from the future outlook playing in his head to look back to Danielle. She was thin and toned, obviously spending hours probably on the treadmill at home while she watched the news of the day on television like so many other people for the up-to-the-minute breaking headlines. Yes, she was definitely pretty.

There was something that Nick found quite attractive about the bright eyes, full lips and small pixie-like nose that was framed by brown bangs that seemed to always be perfectly pulled away from her forehead. Her small elfin qualities made her even more enchanted looking, on top of the fact that she wore outfits that seemed to highlight the athleticism of her body and especially her legs. Realizing he was ogling her, he quickly averted his eyes up to meet hers.

"Morning, anything good come in?" he asked as he laid his wet jacket on the back of his chair and plopped down. Setting his damp shoulder bag down by his feet, Nick took one last look at Danielle then turned to the task at hand. His desk was a mess. There were papers in no discernible order strung about all over the workspace, and the files he did have organized were shoved into folders bulging from the amount of clutter that had accumulated over the last month. Even though it had been a slow month so far, there was still plenty he could hurriedly write up and get into his editor to keep him from complaining about the lack of crime related news happening in their bustling suburban city lately.

Giving him a moment to settle in, Danielle dropped off a few papers at a desk across from his then made her way back. Sitting herself on the edge of his desk, she gave him a quick once over as if his ruffled look was something new. That adorable smile brightened on her face again and Nick wondered what she found so amusing.

"Nothing really. Oh, Marty's in and said he wanted to see you when you arrived." Danielle mentioned, picking up one of the sheets she had put on his desk moments before, and looking it over.

"Looks like the records you wanted regarding the Mayor's accounting issues came through."

Nick sighed. That was at least something. He had been waiting for the Mayor's financial records to come in for a few days now, and had to keep stalling Marty from running with the story until he had the evidence he needed. It appeared that over the last few months the Mayor had been setting aside funds from a city authorized account and had been receiving a noticeable increase in an altogether different fund. It just so happened that the separate account was easily accessed by the Mayor's wife. She had also seemed to be splurging on some things lately.

Hopefully now I can wrap this story up.

"Yeah this is what I was waiting for. Thanks." He said as he scanned the pages Danielle had just delivered. There was a credit card bill highlighting a few recent purchases at some high end stores in the new Town Centers shopping district, and it looked like Mrs. Mayor had a weakness for designer shoes in particular.

These documents were exactly what he had been waiting for. Now he could hopefully get Marty off his ass.

Well well, Mr. Mayor, looks like I might just have to stop by later for a friendly interview, and get your public opinion on your wife's shopping exploits!

Nick set the paper down and looked back at Danielle who was still perched on the end of his desk, a small smirk pulling the one corner of her mouth up. She really was beautiful, and not in that skinny, super model way but in a girl next door type of fashion. Sensing that she knew he was staring at her, Nick cleared his throat and rifled through the other papers Danielle had brought him. Most were either story proofs that had been submitted and accepted, but towards the end Nick found a fax addressed to him that had come in that morning. Looking at the time-stamp at the top of the page, he realized that the fax had arrived just before he had entered the building.

Reading the message over twice, Nick quickly stood up, surprising Danielle who seemed to be lost in her own thoughts. He slid the fax into his pocket and set off for the stairs.

"What is it?" she asked as he started to make his way across the floor of the newsroom and towards the steps leading to Editor In Chief, Marty O'Finns office.

"It looks like the crime section might have just livened up!" he shouted back to her as he ascended the stairs towards the closed door above, overlooking the soon to be active newsroom.

Nick reached the top of the stairs just as the short, scrawny form of Marty O'Finn became visible from behind his closed office door. Just as he was about to knock, the door opened to reveal the stick-like form of his boss.

Marty O'Finn was just what you would think of when most people picture a newspaper Editor. He was thin and overworked, looking like he didn't know what the definition of a vacation was. His beady eyes stared out from a wizened face, with a graying mustache that had been combed and waxed with deliberate care. In fact that was the only tidy part of Marty that Nick had ever noticed working for the man over the last few years. Other than that, the man appeared constantly agitated as if the constant chain-smoking and cups of black coffee weren't enough to keep him going, he had to be constantly fidgeting with a toothpick or some other fixation.

"Thought I heard your voice. You know that story you've been having me hold is due" The man said, pulling the toothpick out of his mouth and pinching it between his nicotine stained fingers as he looked Nick Haley over.

"You ever get a good night's sleep?" he asked staring at the rumpled shirt and tie that Nick had pulled out from under his futon just this morning.

"You know how the saying goes Marty," Haley replied with a smile, "There is no rest for the wicked, and it looks like something wicked might have just transpired."

"What the hell are you talking about?"

"I just got a fax from a friend over at the Rockville Police Station, and it looks like my department might have just gotten a new story to breathe life into the pages. I still have to get a rundown of what's going on, but it looks like there was a pretty awful murder that just happened a few blocks from the Town Center this morning."

Nick pulled the fax out of his pocket, and handed it over to his boss. This was surely going to put the article he was working on hold, since he knew Marty wouldn't pass up the chance to get the details of a murder in their own backyard before the competitors. Hopefully, he'd see the priority that the document presented and give him a little more time on the Mayor's finance article.

Marty Lang, with deep, pock-marked cheeks and dark, graying hair that was swept well away from a receding forehead, squinting slightly as he left his reading glasses on the top of his head, perused the paper then looked up at Haley.

"This for real?" he asked, taking another look at the fax and handing it back to Haley. Tucking the paper back into his pants pocket, Nick could see the look that had come across his bosses face. He had seen it dozens of times over the last few years, every time Marty seemed to have to make a judgment call on postponing a certain story while one of his staff had to chase another. He had to decide which story to follow through with, and he took this decision like it was a matter of life and death. It didn't matter to him that subscription requests were down again this year and continuing to drop, he was a newspaper man through and through. Nick just nodded his head, sure that his source was golden.

"Okay, I want you to get out there and see what you can dig up. Don't forget to follow up with your other duties as well. This may be some big news, but it's only one story, and I've got other pages to fill as well!"

"No problem, I'll have the Mayor's story in by the end of the day, at least what I have so far, but I'm going to have to be out most of the morning looking into this." Nick said patting his pocket where the fax lay.

"Whatever Haley, just get on with it. Oh and give Thomas a call and figure out where the hell he is. His old lady said he was sick from food poisoning or something, but if he doesn't get in here within the hour, it looks like you'll be the only journalist with anything for anyone to read tomorrow!"

Nick took a look down at the floor and saw that Mike Phillips and Dave Shreck had made there way in finally and were looking up at him, trying to not stand out. They were both over an hour late, and Nick knew they were probably both still hung-over from the night before. As if Marty knew that they were listening from down below, he stepped over to the rail at the top of the steps and yelled over.

"You two hear that? Everybody's about to be out that door if you don't get your assignments in on time!"

Heading back down the stairs as Marty continued to yell orders and threats down at the newsroom floor, he just shook his head wondering how long he'd be able to keep this up. Sure jobs were scarce right now, and he would love to get in with one of the bigger papers, but for now the Informant was a reliable source of income, and with the economy always having its ups and downs, he just needed to focus on the work at hand.

"And remember Haley — copy needs to be in by five!" Marty yelled just as Nick made his way past his desk.

Grabbing his jacket from the back of his chair, he slung his arms through and was out the door and heading down the long granite staircase outside the Informant's main entryway. This story was definitely something he could use to pump life back into not only the crime section of the paper but his own fledging career. Pulling his cell phone from his pocket, Nick scrolled through his contacts and quickly clicked on a name. As he put the phone to his ear, he only had to wait for it to ring twice before being answered.

"Hello?" the voice answered on the other end.

It was show time.

Chapter 3

Aidan Preston was planning on heading back home after leaving the crime scene ten minutes before when his cell phone started ringing. It was still early in the morning and he had hopes of scrounging up something to eat before getting into his planned activities for the day. Reaching over onto the passenger seat, he picked up the phone and looked at the screen. The caller ID showed that it was from his boss, Chief Russell Stone.

This wasn't going to be good.

Flipping the phone open, he turned the window defroster down on his car's A/C just as he answered the call.

"Hello," he uttered, keeping his left hand on the wheel of the car and with his right the phone to his ear.

"Preston, I need you to swing by my office today," Stone said in his normal, deep growl.

Aidan had a pretty good idea what was on his chief's mind, and it probably wasn't going to be pleasant. Pushing those thoughts from his head, Aidan let out a sigh and responded.

"Sure Chief, I can get over there around noon if you want."

He could almost hear Russell Stone chewing the notion over. The image of the large, imposing man sitting behind his wide, oak desk becoming clear as the man grunted into the phone.

"No I've got a lot going on later today, you'd better get over here now so we can talk." That was it, nothing more seemed to be needed to be explained.

Aidan hesitated. His Challenger slowed to a stop at a red light, as he weighed his options. His hopes of getting home and getting some breakfast were quickly vanishing. Flipping his right hand turn signal on, he edged his car into the turn lane and checked to make sure the intersection was clear. Traffic was light. His windshield wipers moved back and forth slowly over the windshield expelling the excess water that was pattering down from the bleak sky, and he turned onto the cross street that aimed him away from his own neighborhood and in the direction of police headquarters.

"I'll be there in about fifteen," Aidan said clicking off the phone and turning the defroster back on to warm the insides of his car for the longer drive.

It took him a little closer to twenty minutes to pull into the parking lot of 101 Research Boulevard with traffic having been trickling along the streets due to the low visibility available that morning. Fortunately the sun seemed to have at least broken through the cloud cover and the frigid morning was warming up. The only problem on a morning like this was that it was a constant reminder that winter was almost here.

Police headquarters was a large office building that the police maintained as part of a lease agreement for multiple buildings in the county. It's large enough to house not only the main offices for the police department's staff, but also included lab space for forensics, computer-crimes divisions, and homicide investigations. The surrounding parking lot that Aidan now circled around was sparsely scattered with off-duty vehicles and unused squad cars. Selecting a spot in a near empty row close to the back entrance, he parked and looked around for a moment. His gray eyes studied the familiar parking lot and entranceway architecture to the building he had made a daily commute to up until a few months ago.

Now on administrative leave, Aidan didn't find himself nearly as immersed in the daily routines he was used to. He had hated the break from work immediately, restless without the purpose of solving crimes. However, he knew he needed the break physically. Even though his mind had clung on to the rush and need of constant action, his body was a different story.

Rotating his right shoulder slightly as he removed his seat belt, Aidan felt a wince of dull pain trickle through his upper arm and neck. It felt like a strain in the muscle, but he knew that wasn't it. The doctor's had called it a phantom pain that resonated from the injuries he had sustained almost a year ago today, but whether the pain was real or not, the trauma had been. Taking a deep breath to calm his worked up nerves, Aidan rotated his arm once more, attempting to work out the imaginary kinks. Counting out the breath and then releasing it, he opened the car door and stepped out onto the slick asphalt surface.

Here I go.

"Well look who finally made his way in," Detective Andrea Wilkes said with a smile as Aidan walked through the door and into the offices of the Homicide division. Wasp thin, with a permanent tan that covered her already olive colored skin, Andrea Wilkes was a stunning yet powerful reminder of what a woman wearing a badge could be. At a little over five feet tall, she was small yet strong.

Aidan knew that appearances could be deceiving and had been on the witnessing end of having seen Andrea in action. It was always a sight to watch her man-handle a perp twice her size and have their face in the dirt before they knew what hit them, especially when they pissed her off. She was certainly not one to back down from an engagement, and Aidan knew that in this line of work, female or not, he would choose Wilkes to have his back going into a situation in a heartbeat.

Giving a brief smile, Aidan took a look around the room. "Yeah well I guess you couldn't keep me away forever," he stated taking a moment to nod at the other plain clothed detective in the office. Tim Melvin sat in the back corner of the room, his desk a tribute to his dedication to the job. Every piece of paper and every file were organized to detail and had its home in its corresponding place. He was not the type to sit idly by while paperwork could begin to pile up, no matter how crazy the office could get.

"I heard Stone is waiting for you." The rookie detective said waving his fingers in mock horror as a smile broke out on his clean shaven face.

"Is he in his office?"

"Oh yeah, but you'll have to wait to get in there. A call came through a little bit ago and it seemed pretty important. He's been shut up inside since then with his door closed. It's good to see you Aidan." Tim said standing up from his desk and coming over to Preston.

Preston caught the young detectives hand in his and gave it a solid shake. It was good to be back in the office. He hadn't been in in a while and he definitely had things to do here that he couldn't from home. E-mails and messages could be checked, but reports and other paperwork that filtered through the various offices was something he had to actually get through by coming in.

"Good to see you too kid." Preston said removing his hand from Tim's and clasping him on the shoulder. Tim took the opportunity to lean in and whisper, "Oh and you can definitely say that Wilkes has been feeling abandoned by you."

Preston glanced over at Andrea who was eyeing the two of them and saw her roll her eyes.

"Oh yes, poor little me, just doesn't know what to do when the boys are out of the office! Can it Melvin!" Andrea stated shaking her head at the two of them standing across from her. "I'll show you what I can do with your abandonment issues," Andrea whispered to them, tapping her red polished fingernails on the holster of the Glock situated at her hip.

"Easy girl, easy," Tim jokingly warned taking a few steps back and motioning for her to calm down with his arms, "You know you're the last person I'd want to tangle with in this office."

"Or perhaps we could lose the guns, and I'll just use my handcuffs instead," Andrea purred taking another challenging step closer.

Tim's worried eyes flashed from Aidan's and back to Andrea's before a large smile broke out on Andrea's face as she closed the distance between them. She stepped right up to Tim, toe to toe and the height difference was glaringly evident. Tim stood a good eight inches taller than the small, compact hornet. However, if it came down to it Preston's money would definitely go to Andrea.

"Don't worry boy, I don't bite...hard." She said patting him on the cheek and turning to walk back to her desk, her hips moving ever so seductively as she slipped away and began to laugh. The confused and worried look the young detective had been sporting cleared from his face as he added a chuckle to Aidan and Andrea's own laughter.

"Haha, real funny Wilkes," Tim muttered, but Aidan knew Tim had probably been close to squirming when Andrea had first came upon him.

Just as Andrea got back to her desk, the phone rang and she plucked it off the desk and slid back into her chair, ready to get back to work.

Aidan took the time to walk over to his own desk across from Andrea's. The room was pretty big for the number of detectives they actually had working in the department. With most of them having varying schedules that ran throughout the week, most days the office was only half full. There were six main desks taking up the majority of the floor space in the center portion of the room. Each of these was assigned to one detective and every two desks were positioned to be facing the other. In all there were three main stations in the center, with various other tables and filing cabinets around the rest of the room.

This was the Homicide divisions work area, where they compiled all the data and evidence they had for each case the detectives were responsible for, and tracked and logged their information. On the off chance that something big happened like a mass murder, there was a separate conference room off to the side of the main office area, but that was used mostly for non-hostile interrogations and information gathering.

Aidan sat down at his desk, taking a moment to look over the room he had spent so many long hours over the past few years following and solving multiple cases that had ranged from all over Montgomery County. The wide grounds that he and his fellow detectives were responsible for covering was a large area, and sometimes it seemed like it would make more sense to let the local boys handle their own homicides when they took place in their area. However, Rockville was part of the county, and that meant if it was a homicide, they had ultimate jurisdiction.

Running his mouse up into the corner of the screen before him, the computer hummed to life and before long asked Aidan for his login information. Quickly typing in his username and then password, the system turned on and he was in. Taking a moment to click on his e-mail, he quickly perused the various interoffice memos and mail that had come in since checking the system from home this morning. It didn't look like there was anything of importance, and he quickly made his way through the final last clicks and then turned his attention to the mail stacked on the corner of his desk. There had to be at least two weeks' worth of letters and envelopes piled there.

Had it really been that long since he had made an appearance in the office? He guessed so. Being on leave certainly affected the daily routine. As he picked it up the first envelope, he noticed a letter underneath addressed to him from the Internal Affairs Department. Before he had a chance to open it, Chief Stone's deep husk of a voice broke assailed him. "Preston, is that you? Get in here will you!" Stone's words echoed through the office as Preston pushed away from his desk and headed to the Chief's office.

Chief Stone's office was half the size of Homicides entire work area. It was a large, imposing space, filled with various mementos and awards covering every shelf and desktop. Not like the man needed all this space, but when it came to the higher-ups in county government, it seemed they always had to try to top each other in office space. There were a few framed pictures of the Chief with various local politicians and even one of him standing out on a golf course with the Mayor and two other individuals. Other than that, the rest of the décor was strictly professional. There were multiple framed diplomas and accommodations hung about the walls to remind everyone of Stone's police orientated background, and even the plain name plate on the desk seemed to scream simplicity by the book.

"Morning Chief," Aidan said walking up to the large oak desk that Stone had seated himself behind.

"Morning, yeah, seems like you've had a busy morning already." Stone's penetrating, cold gaze hung on Aidan as he sat down across from the man, the grim look on his face showing him that this morning had not been a peaceful one for the man responsible for handling all severe crimes and homicides in the entire county.

Even with the body discovered this morning technically residing on a Rockville city street, it was Stone's business and no one in the county was going to pull a case out from under him. Aidan had no doubt the important phone call Stone had been on before he had walked that Tim Melvin had referred to earlier had probably been either the Mayor or Governor or somebody making sure that Stone was handling everything the way it needed to be done.

Taking a sip from a mug of coffee on the corner of his desk, Stone placed the cup down and then seemed to release some of the tension from his shoulders.

"Okay Preston, let's start over. How are you doing?" he asked, leaning back in his chair and placing his hands around his steaming mug. He appeared to be trying to clear the air of any chance of this conversation heading the wrong way. Stone was a good Chief, and while Aidan knew he had his share of problems butting with the man's superiority complex, he knew what he was doing, and in the long run of getting things done by the book that's what made the cases stick. Things being done right.

"I'm doing fine Chief, pretty much good as new."

"Well that's good to hear, I was worried that the time you've spent away from the action might be wearing on you. You're a good cop and I know these periods of leave can wear a man thin. Heck, It'd drive me crazy being away from this office for more than a few hours. At least thats what the wife believes, and with the hours I put in, I can't say I blame her. But your different Preston."

"Appreciate it Chief, but I've been keeping busy."

"Good, good, now what's the rehabilitation schedule look like? When are you going to be ready to go before the medical review board and get that evaluation out of the way? With everything that's been going on especially as of today I need every last badge I've got out there."

"I've got an appointment with the physical therapist this week, then after that I'm looking at being able to clear the board by the end of the month."

"'Bout time, those evaluations can be a real pain, but I need to know that you're mentally ready before I can have you out at crime scenes." At that last remark, Stone took another drag of his coffee and leaned back into his chair, his large form creaking against the worn plastic of the past its prime executive chair, and folded his arms across his chest. "Especially before your out at any scene."

Aidan studied the man for a moment, wondering exactly who had told him that he had been seen at the scene earlier today. Did Garza really have his panties in a bunch over something so simple, or had their been some other source, he wondered. Either way there was no denying it.

"Want to tell me what you were doing out there this morning? Captain Garza over with Rockville wasn't too happy seeing you visiting his scene."

Garza, there it was! Goddamn prick was a control freak.

"To tell you the truth Chief, I heard the call go out over the radio and happened to be at home. Guess I got tired of being cooped up and decided to check out what was all the fuss since it was near me." Aidan said shifting the position in his chair to get a little more comfortable against the stiff plastic back.

"Yeah well, we're definitely on top of that case, even though I have Garza leading the investigation. Something that screwed up just isn't going to slide in this county, that's for sure." Stone said, seeming to be weighing how much he was willing to share with his detective, off duty or not.

"Of course like I said before, until you've cleared your evaluation and boards, you can't be showing up at a scene of crime. It ruffles feathers to put it delicately."

"I'm sorry Sir, I had no intention of stepping on any body's toes, but this morning I was pretty much just a concerned citizen."

Stone snorted, "Concerned citizen, I like that, haha, yeah just like you. Either way though, things have to be done a certain way, protocols followed, and with your current designation I can't have you out there."

"Understood Sir. If you don't mind me asking, does this look gang related or what?"

"Officially we don't know what we've got other than a potential goddamn public nightmare!"

Aidan knew it was still too early for all the facts to be in, but from the bystanders that had gathered on the street earlier and the presence of Channel 5's one-and-only Ted Hanson, wasn't going to help matters. Just then the phone on the Chief's desk rang interrupting any further info he was going to gather from the man at the moment.

"This is Chief of Police Russell Stone," he said snapping the phone up from his desk before it could ring again. Stone's thick eyebrows knitted together in a mix of concentration and frustration as he listened to the line. With a nod of his head towards the door, Stone dismissed Preston. Apparently any further questions he had regarding this morning would have to be directed elsewhere. That was fine with Aidan, he didn't like being stuck in the big dog's office any longer than he needed to be.

Closing the door behind him as he left, Aidan took a final glance around the war room. Tim was on his own desk phone, busily typing something into his computer and juggling back and forth between reading off something from a printout spread out before him. He looked like he had his hands full. Aidan didn't deny that that was one part of the job he didn't miss at times.

The constant gathering of information and chasing down leads. No homicide was devoid of paperwork, and there always seemed to be some new procedure or additional way of handling things that the paper pushers down the halls deemed necessary to get the same results as before, sans the shorter amount of time it used to take. At that moment Andrea walked back into the room.

"Hey Tiger," she said with a sexy wink as she slid back around her desk.

Aidan watched her set the energy drink she had retrieved from the kitchen area down the hall on her desk and pop it open with a hiss. She took a short pull of the clear liquid, and just before Aidan could respond his phone rang from inside his jacket. Fishing it out, he checked the screen and answered.

"Preston."

"Hey it's Mack, you got some free time?"

Aidan glanced at the clock on the wall. It was already ten and Aidan knew that he might as well give up all thoughts of breakfast at this point.

"Yeah what do you have in mind?"

"Figured we could get together. I wanted to get your opinion on some things from this morning."

The muscles in Aidan's stomach tightened and he knew that he was definitely not going to be eating anytime soon.

"Yeah that could work. I'm at county headquarters right now, where did you want to meet?"

Aidan took a step over to his desk scooped his mail up and stuffed the envelopes into his pocket for sorting through later.

"Well I'm on my way over to the Medical Examiner's office down in Baltimore — figured we could meet over there," Mack said, the sound of his driving being visible in the background.

Hesitating, Aidan said, "You know I'm not back officially."

"Well then it'll just have to be unofficial."

Aidan glanced at the clock once more. If he was going to be able to get down to the ME's office to meet Mack he'd have to leave now, and even then there was no guarantee it wouldn't take him a good forty five minutes to get down there.

Yeah, breakfast is as good as gone.

"So are you in?"

"Yeah, I'll head out now, meet you there."

"Okay swell, I'll see you in an hour."

"Did you really just say swell?" Aidan asked imagining Mack Jone's big kid-like grin on the other end of the line.

"Yup, it's making a come back, I'm telling you! Before long all the kids will be saying it!"

"Alright, I'll see you there." Aidan clicked off the call and slipped his phone away just as Andrea looked up from her drink.

"Leaving me already?" she asked, a sultry, pouting look coming over her dark exotic features. Aidan wished he had the time to see where this was going.

It wasn't just a fleeting feeling he had for a woman like Andrea, but he just wasn't sure where a relationship might take them. Especially once he was back on duty. "Unfortunately I have somewhere I gotta get to," he replied not wanting to reveal any more than that of his plans to follow up on the morning's murder. He especially didn't need Stone overhearing it after their short little talk a few minutes ago.

"I suppose I'll just have to catch up with you later than, perhaps once my shifts over," she said, her mischievous grin reappearing.

Where could this lead? Is there something worth pursuing? Aidan wondered as he zipped his jacket up in preparation for the weather outside.

"Sounds good, give me a call."

And with that, Aidan exited the Homicide Division offices and made his way towards the parking lot.

Chapter 4

The drive from police headquarters to the Medical Examiner's office in Baltimore, Maryland was definitely not something Aidan enjoyed. It had taken forty five minutes just to clear the highway since there was road work that had closed down two of the south bound lanes heading towards the harbor. After miles of stop and go movement, the rain continually pouring down onto the cars and trucks awaiting to get over onto the toll bridge into the main stretch of the city, Aidan finally found his way across the bridge and onto the short, one-way streets that Baltimore was famous for. He had never known a more frustrating city for vehicle travel. Baltimore was unlike anything else.

Thriving in part due to its proximity to the Potomac River, Baltimore is located in north-central Maryland on the Patapsco River close to where it empties into the Chesapeake Bay. Located between the Piedmont Plateau and the Atlantic Coastal Plain, the city is divided into 'lower city' and 'upper city' segments.

These lower and upper halves encompass the majority of city geography making it not only the largest cultural center of Maryland, but the largest United States seaport in the Mid-Atlantic region. As such, Baltimore contains a wide and unique demographic that is unrivaled by any other large city in the country. It also happens to be the place where Montgomery County Homicide outsources its Medical Examiner work to.

Taking the streets a little faster than he had originally meant too, the Challenger cruised over the slick roadways, skidding around each corner and turn as Aidan attempted to make up the time he lost on the highway. Manholes poured steam into the wet, damp air, adding a life to the streets of Baltimore that Aidan knew all too well it had. That was the problem with Baltimore, and one reason Aidan was glad the city fell into its own county for police assistance. Montgomery County had its share of issues, but adding to them would only increase if the crime ridden streets of this wharf like town were among his share of responsibility.

Recognizing his turn up ahead, Aidan slowed his car to a reasonable speed as he approached the street and pulled past the main entrance to the Baltimore Morgue and into the small fenced in parking lot near the side of the building. The crowded, poorly lit parking area was reserved for county vehicles, and ended up as a reserve lot for the Baltimore County Highway Administration trucks. Seeing Mack Jones' Impala parked under one of the dim, dome lights spread throughout the lot, he slipped into a spot near the Rockville Detective's own vehicle and threw his car into park.

Emerging once more into the cold day, Aidan was grateful that the rain seemed to be coming to a close. Zipping his jacket up as he got out, he double checked the doors to his own car were locked tight and headed towards the stairwell leading to a side entrance door in the decrepit looking building.

The Baltimore City Morgue was located in an old factory building a few blocks from the harbor. It had once been used as a shipping company, many years before the turn of the 20th century when the waterways around Baltimore were filled with trade ships and barges constantly flowing in from the Atlantic. Now the old building, its architecture still standing from a time long passed fit right in with the rundown look of the city. Taking the steps two at a time, Aidan reached the door just as it opened from the inside. Mack was standing there waiting for him.

"Twice in one day, boy am I lucky!" he said with a smile as he held the door for his long time friend to enter.

"Yeah, sorry it took so long."

"Don't worry about it, I knew traffic was going to be a bitch with them working on those wonderful new road improvements down the last stretch of I-495."

Aidan stepped through the door, the smell of disinfectant and formaldehyde powerfully assailing his senses, all thought of his missed morning meal disappearing as they walked down the long, empty hallway towards the elevators at the end.

"So I heard Garza's officially on the lead with this," Aidan mentioned as they stepped into the first empty elevator and Mack pressed the down button. The doors slid shut with a groan and the ancient car began to lower down the rickety shaft with a constant whine of old gears turning.

"Yeah he's got his teeth into it for now, but we'll have to see what the ME's got, cause there was something bothering me about that scene." Mack admitted as the elevator slowed to a stop. With a ding announcing their arrival, the two men stepped out into the bright, fluorescent filled outside waiting room of the Medical Examiner's office.

Aidan shielded his eyes from the bright glow that harshly lit up the outer hallway they found themselves in. The scent of chemicals was stronger here, the walls and floors seeming to permeate with the harsh mixture of embalming fluids and death. A set of solid steel doors upon rusted hinges sat before them, the tell-tale signs of years of abuse from gurneys and other wheeled carts having left their mark over the ages.

At that moment a uniformed officer wearing the Baltimore City PD insignia on his jacket appeared from down the hall, his attention on a clipboard in his hands.

"Is the Medical Examiner in?" Mack asked as the young black man headed towards them. He was thin, the outline of his bulletproof vest filling out the bulky jacket he wore as he noticed them. Close cropped hair made his ears stick out much more noticeably than would be otherwise, and Aidan had the impression of a gawkily teen just out of the academy and proud to be serving and protecting the streets of Baltimore rather than lying on them, just another casualty in this city's growing urban struggle.

"Uh, yeah, Dr. Phillips is through those doors. He's currently in the middle of an autopsy," the officer said looking over Mack and Aidan as he withdrew a keycard from his belt. Placing it against a sensor next to the double doors, a small click sounded and the doors swung open to allow them entrance into the cavernous basement morgue.

"Appreciate it," Aidan said following Mack and the uniform through the doors.

The main examining room was a sparse, wide open area with four stainless steel tables set up under bright track lighting running the course of the ceiling. Against the far wall was a set of storage freezers, humming amongst the other electronic whirs and beeps from computers and other recording equipment spread along the outer walls. Two of the tables were occupied, the forms of two African American males, naked except for a white sheet over their genitalia, their dark skin glowing faintly purple under the bright lights from above were laid out. ID tags hung from their toes, and the only identifying marks distinguishing the two men were multiple tattoos, some gang affiliated designs that Aidan noticed were popular among the youth of Baltimore's streets.

Gangs; could Sara Moulton's mutilated corpse be the result of such a mentality?

A second set of doors opened off to the side of the main room and a flustered, older gentleman with crisp white hair and a gray goatee came bustling in. His cheeks were red from exertion, and the man walked with a slight limp, aided by a wooden cane. Dressed in a pair of blue scrubs, the man's abundant waistline was visible under the loose uniform. He reminded Aidan of a thinner version of a shopping mall Santa Claus. The man who appeared to be in the middle of running about, had the rosy appearance of wisdom and jolliness which was hinted at by the warm yet cautious eyes that sat behind a thick pair of glasses perched on the end of his nose. Aidan had an image of the white haired man pulling a watch from his pocket and gasping at the time, as if there weren't enough hours in the day to accomplish all he had to do.

Taking a pen to the ID tag on the second John Doe, the Medical Examiner added a note to the slip and then turned towards the two new visitors in his domain, examining them with thick heavy brows from behind his gold rimmed spectacles.

"Can I help you gentlemen?"

"Yes, I'm Detective Mack Jones with the Rockville Police Department, we are here in regards to the remains of Sara Moulton that was brought earlier this morning." Mack had flipped out the badge and ID from his wallet like a television detective, waited a moment for the elder Medical Examiner to take a quick glance and then slipped it away. Aidan knew that since he had made Detective a few years ago, Mack was the proud type that wouldn't be dropping that habit anytime soon.

Yeah Mack Jones, a real Columbo, Aidan thought as he extracted his own badge and displayed it for the Medical Examiner.

"Montgomery County Homicide as well, yes that's just as well," the man said taking a step back and supporting his weight onto the cane. "Unfortunately I haven't been able to process the body yet, as you can see we're pretty busy around here." He gestured to the two bodies currently on display on their respective slabs.

"And I've already spoken to Chief Stone about the current lack of personnel around here to handle the intakes, he's just going to have to wait. Darrel Tyson is the only other surgeon we have on staff here and he's out for the week due to a family emergency, two technicians are out for who knows what, so as you can see as well, we are currently short-staffed and backed up."

Aidan had been through this routine before with other people in Phillips position. They were usually underpaid, overworked and suffered from a superiority complex that put their skills above those of the average county or government employee. Such are those that fill the court appointed positions. Fortunately in Aidan's experience they were also easier to be compelled to see the logic of reason after a few simple prods in the right direction. Aidan decided to play to the man's ego a little and see if he could make Mack and his long drive worthwhile.

"Dr. Phillips, we were hoping that you would be able to do a cursory evaluation in regards to the remains while we wait in hopes of answering some questions that could lead us to gaining anything from your irrefutable knowledge. I'm fully aware of Dr. Tyson's talents and have worked with him in the past, but we would be eternally grateful if you could assist us with something at least general to garner."

Mack turned to Aidan and gave him a curious look, then realizing what his partner was doing, gave a brisk nod and added, "Yes, any light you could shed on this case could be invaluable and would certainly aid both our departments greatly."

Dr. Eugene Phillips seemed to consider this a moment, shifting his weight from the cane to his legs and then turned towards the storage freezers near the back. Mack and Aidan followed, watching the man hobble over to where he needed to be. It looked to Aidan like this man was used to things being done at his pace and not a moment sooner.

"Very well, you gentlemen can remain and be present while I see what we can gleam from our poor victim. What time did the subject arrive?" he asked stopping at a small computer table and withdrawing a logbook from the top drawer. He flipped it open and began scanning the entries.

"She would have been brought in a little over an hour ago," answered Mack who shot Aidan a grateful look at how easily he had handled the good doctor. Aidan Preston had definitely been around the block before in his ten years on the police force. He had started out like most green-eared rookie cops walking the streets and working a beat, but showed through hard work and dedication that upon being promoted to Detective, he had what it took to get the job done. That's what had attracted him to Homicide. It was a constant changing game where you had to keep your skills sharp to compensate for the ever-changing criminal mind. Of course there were still the simple, heat-of-the-moment violent crimes, but no place was immune from the snaking tendrils of murder.

The Medical Examiner had spent a minute looking over the records, finding the right page and recording something onto the log. "Aha, here she is, # M-315."

He set the logbook down and walked over to the matching storage locker. Gripping the metal door, Dr. Phillips twisted the handle and pulled the door open. A trail of cold air escaped the climate-controlled chamber, and the man took the end of the sliding table and gave it a hard tug. With a grunt he slid the sealed remains out from the cooler, exposing a black body bag sitting atop the built-in gurney. Along with the body bag, there were several smaller containers, in which Aidan assumed contained the individual pieces of the victim that the Crime Scene Technicians had collected.

"Oh my, this doesn't look good," Dr. Phillips muttered in response to the appearance of the multiple bags before him. He checked the corresponding tags to confirm all the remains were accounted for, then looked to the two detectives awaiting his help.

"Well let's get started," he said pulling on a pair of latex examination gloves and beginning the process of opening each bag and extracting their contents. After what seemed like an eternity standing in the corner of this sterile, bright room, the mixture of smells mingling together to form a strong, pungent odor that Aidan couldn't seem to ignore, Mack broke the silence.

"Hey let me talk to you for a second outside," he muttered, gesturing towards the exit doors.

Aidan nodded, following Mack out of the sterile environment, glad for the chance to breathe in a dose of the stale, filtered air being pumped through an ancient HVAC system that ran the entire length of the long, empty corridor. The uniformed officer was nowhere to be seen, but Mack continued towards the elevators.

Retracing their steps they didn't stop until they walked out the side door of the building that led to the parking lot. The rain had ceased, and the cold air was a godsend after being deep down in the bowels of the morgue for any period of time. Aidan breathed in deeply of the salty sea air that rushed off the harbor, zipped his jacket up to his neck, then once he had adjusted to the change in climate, turned to Mack.

The color in the man's cheeks seemed to go from a pale, drained hue to a rosier shade as he took a couple of deep breaths and wiped his forehead with the sleeve of his jacket.

"Sorry bout that, I just needed to get out of there for a minute. After seeing that poor girl torn apart earlier, then being down in that basement, I was starting to feel sick."

"No problem," Aidan replied, just as glad for the break from the fumes. "So what did you have on your mind?"

Mack's round face took in the parking lot as they stood at the top of the steps, his cheeks continuing to regain their lost color before he glanced at his meaty hands, then brought his eyes up to meet Aidan's.

"This case. There's something wrong with it."

"What do you mean?"

"I don't know, just a feeling I guess, but you've known me long enough to know that when something stinks, I'm usually right."

"Yeah, I used to chalk that up to you being part bloodhound," Aidan joked.

"Bloodhound and a few other things mixed in. Hey I can't help it if I was born a mutt. What can I say, my mother loved them I-talians. Not everybody could be graced with your genes, buddy boy." Mack shot back looking at Aidan's strong Celtic features in the overcast light of the morning. "Tall, dark and handsome, sure beats my short, big and jolly description any day."

"Okay, okay, so I'll rub your belly for good luck before the day's through, but what is it about the case that has you bothered?" Aidan asked as Mack put his thick hand over his stomach, patted it gently and eyed his friend through doughy, half closed slits.

"You leave my belly out of this, it's my nose that's got me questioning earlier anyways." A twinkle of humor seemed to flirt across Mack's face as he shoved his hands deep into his coat pockets.

"Well, you're gonna have to fill me in. My presence at the scene this morning and here now still hasn't been cleared, so you should probably catch me up to speed."

"Yeah I keep forgetting you're still on leave not to mention a whole different police force than we used to be, huh. Either way, you're the only one I'd be sharing this with as it is since Garza's got the investigations green light."

"What do you mean?"

"Well remember how earlier I mentioned the gang theory going around at the park?"

"Yeah, MS-13. What about it?"

"That's just it. This looks all about escalation, the way that poor girl's body was ripped apart. As far as we can tell though, she had nothing to do with any gang life, yet the way her body was mangled, this looked personal. Garza's got everybody chasing after anyone with Hispanic ties in the neighborhood. Thinks the girl might of pissed off the wrong homeboy."

Aidan imagined the park from this morning. Trying to remember what he could about the layout and location of things that he had seen. Unfortunately, he couldn't clearly picture anything that was helpful at the moment.

"I don't know, between the fog and Garza, I didn't really get a good look at much in the way of evidence or what took place." Aidan admitted.

"Well, I appreciate you coming down here anyways, and I'll try and get you a copy of everything from this morning so you've got the background, and we'll just have to go from there."

Nodding, Aidan placed his hand on Mack's big shoulder and said, "Sounds good, but for now let's go see what light the ME can shed onto our victim's last moments."

"Hopefully I can keep my breakfast down having to look at this mess again," Mack muttered and reached for the handle of the door.

"Fortunately I missed out on breakfast," Aidan mentioned as they once again entered the glum, rundown Baltimore building.

"Lucky for you." Mack said, holding a hand to his stomach in preparation and stepping inside.

Aidan and Mack made their way back down to the morgue's exam room. Dr. Phillips looked up from his task as they entered. Having arranged the pieces like a man completing a simple jigsaw puzzle, he finished and took a step back from the table where he had assembled the remains of the victim onto a vacant examination slab.

"Gentlemen, I give you one Sara Moulton."

The woman's remains were almost white from blood loss and the amount of damage to the various limbs and exposed sections was quite clear. The bluish-gray body had been situated as if it was whole, each bloated piece sitting where it would normally be found if they were attached.

In the time that Aidan and Mack had been gone, Dr. Phillips had set up a small tray of instruments next to the table, and positioned a microphone at head level, hanging above the body to record his findings. The Medical Examiner motioned towards a locker across from them where Aidan and Mack could find a set of scrubs to wear, and once dressed in the surgical outfits, they appeared at the older mans side, ready to begin.

Aidan looked the body over, memorizing the horrific details for later retrieval. From years on Homicide, he knew that the smallest observation could be key in answering a multitude of questions, and he was not going to let the nausea sweeping through his rumbling stomach divert his attention from the task at hand. Somebody did this to this poor woman, and he was going to make sure they were caught whether he was officially on the case or not. He was thankful that Mack had asked him to join him today. This woman had met her end in his neighborhood, a street that he lived near, and he was not going to rest until he figured out what had happened.

"Okay gentlemen, I'm going to start the recorder, if you could please state your names and ranks into the microphone after I begin so that everything is documented, then we'll see what we answers we can come up with in this preliminary autopsy."

Reaching up to the device hanging between them, the ME flipped a switch and a red light glowed to life on the recorder.

"Subject #M-315, Preliminary autopsy performed by Dr. Eugene Michael Phillips of the Baltimore County Medical Examiner's Office. It is 12:36 p.m., Thursday October 17, 2011. I am joined by..." Dr. Phillips paused and looked from Aidan to Mack, awaiting their response into the microphone.

"Detective First Class, Aidan Preston, Montgomery County Homicide."

"Detective Mack Jones, Rockville City Homicide."

After providing their names for the record, Dr. Phillips nodded then returned his gaze back to the body before him. He reached out and picking up a small scalpel from the tray, brought the blade to the corpse and began by slicing a small sample of flesh from the neck wound, scraped it slightly and placed the skin cells he had extracted onto a separate dish for observation later.

"I have already recorded body temperature, 92.5 degrees Fahrenheit which allows based on exposure to elements and time, we are looking at time of death around Midnight of the previous night to 12:30 p.m."

Aidan looked at the horrendous wounds the body had suffered. The victim's right arm and leg had been completely torn off from the body, resulting in massive damage to the bones and ligaments. Her throat appeared to have been ripped out, dried blood and other foreign substances congealed all around the neck and upper chest. Then as Aidan watched Dr. Phillips move the head slightly to the left, studying the damaged neckline, he noticed the marks that ran along the backside.

"Are those scratches?" Aidan asked, motioning towards the lower back of the neck. Dr. Phillips slowly maneuvered the head to the side and raised the torso at an angle to reveal what appeared to be four deep gashes that had been raked across the victim's back. Whoever had done this, it had been cruel and painful, Aidan was sure of that.

What kind of person could be sick enough? He asked himself, then shaking the thought out of his head, looked to the medical examiner for information.

"They do appear to be scratch marks, however the space between them suggests they would have been inflicted by an object rather than a hand. The span between marks would rule out the average, adult hand, leading me to believe it was probably done with a tool or weapon of some kind repeatedly dragged across the victim's skin to create this pattern. I'll know more once I get some of the various fibers and other samples analyzed that were recovered with the body, but from experience, I'd say some sort of knife, sharp, but not straight either."

"What do you mean, 'not straight'?" Mack asked, looking up from taking a few notes in a small notebook he kept on him.

"If the blade was sharp and straight-edged, without any defect in the tip, it would have cut from one end of the flesh to the other without producing these gouged pieces throughout, leading me to recognize it was a different type of tip that had been dragged across the victim's back, catching and ripping deeper into the skin at a few varying places."

Aidan watched as the Medical Examiner demonstrated a swiping motion with his one free hand, while he rested his hip and other arm on the examination table. He swung once with a fluid motion, then again with a jerking, ripping motion. "So it looks like the victim was grabbed and jerked around while the weapon was put to the skin." Dr. Phillips said with an embarrassed grin, stopping his charades for the benefit of the detectives and returning to the autopsy.

"Now this is interesting—"

Aidan and Mack both stepped forward, each taking up on one side of the man as he bent in close and examined the arm that had been severed. "It appears that we have multiple bite mark patterns covering a few different locations on the victim's body." He ran a gloved finger over an indentation mark on the inside part of the arm, then over to another similar mark a few inches away.

"Initial discovery of the scene, officers reported that it looked like a pack of dogs or one very large dog could have gotten into and disturbed the body," Mack said taking a step back and jotting an additional note onto his pad.

"Yes well, the only problem with that, is that these marks appear to have been inflicted both post-mortem and while our victim was still alive."

"You're telling me that whatever sick bastards cut this poor woman up, also set a dog onto her as well?" Mack asked, his rounded, gentle features hardening as he gazed at the body before him.

Aidan felt his own stomach knot and knew that Mack's stomach was probably fighting the urge to revisit with its breakfast contents as well. Who the hell would have done this to a person? Aidan couldn't see past anything other than the fact that this woman had been alive for most of the wounds she had received. That meant there was somebody out there, someone who had got off on torturing a poor, innocent woman on her way home from work, and that would just not do.

This gang or individual had to be caught, and Aidan knew he wasn't going to stop until he found out what had happened.

Chapter 5

Nick Haley stepped out of his old, rusted Oldsmobile, double checking to lock the doors even though he knew there was nothing important for someone to break in and steal. He kept everything he needed in the bag he now slung over his shoulder in preparation for his next stop along this morning's ever growing road to information. He had already stopped by the neighborhood that the murder had occurred, spoken to a few neighbors who either hadn't left for work yet, or stayed at home all day every day anyways.

Then without gaining anything new to work with other than the same old story about the police not letting them past the barricades and telling them they would release the information to the public when the time came, same bureaucratic bullshit he was used to, Haley decided to swing on over to News Channel 5 and see if he couldn't help running into an old acquaintance of his that happened to have been at the scene earlier.

Mike Jeffries was a cameraman for News Channel 5, and he also happened to be out on location with Ted Hanson that morning. That meant he probably had seen more than most people, and Nick knew that Mike had a soft spot for him, or at least Mike's wallet enjoyed their perfunctory run-ins. Checking to make sure he had an envelope with a couple twenties stuck in it that he always carried for emergencies, along with his tape recorder, crumpled pack of Marlboro's, and notebook, Nick closed his bag and headed for the door to News Channel 5's receiving area.

The station was housed in a tall, lone building that rose up into the sky high above the trees and shrubbery of its poorly landscaped grounds. High atop, Nick could make out the radio towers and satellite dishes that were constantly sending and receiving information all over the world, the news that filtered through them being analyzed and reported by the local station or sent to its subsidiaries in other counties or cities. Luckily being located in the Washington Metropolitan area meant that this news hub for Channel 5 was a large and complex building with many workers bustling about daily, and no one would realize he didn't belong.

Walking into the reception area, Nick headed straight towards the staircase past the elevator banks and next to the phones. He picked up one of the handsets to the pay phone and pretended to insert the required amount.

The secretary in charge of monitoring and recording who came and went was too busy making sure her nails weren't chipped to notice Haley move from the phones and through the door marked, 'stairs'.

Taking the stairs two at a time, Nick made it up to the third floor. He let out a little sigh of relief as he pulled on the door, it was unlocked and he walked into the editing area for Channel 5's news team. Sitting with his feet up on a desk, a slice of pizza dangling from his mouth, Mike Jeffries looked like a big kid, fresh out of high school. Of course, Nick knew the backwards cap and shaggy, brown hair in the eyes was just a look that the young man worked hard on keeping. He always said he had to 'live young to stay young', and that meant dressing and acting the part as well.

Mike swung his feet off the desk and taking another bite from the greasy pizza in his hands looked at Nick quizzically. As his feet hit the floor, he leaned forward and took a quick glance down the hall to make sure they were alone. "What the hell are you doing in here?" he asked, a facial tick giving away his unease. "You trying to get me fired?"

Nick slid the door behind him closed, giving them a little more privacy in the small office. For a world going digital, Jeffries workspace looked like it was out of the past. Old fashioned video cassettes were mixed among the many smaller, digital tapes littering the tables and spread out on the shelves. There were papers everywhere, the largest pile underneath the cardboard pizza box that had been just set down, uncaring what the greasy box could stain. There were soda cans filling up a recycling bin marked 'For Paper Only', and Nick noticed a small soda spill on the table near one one of the half-buried computer consoles where Mike did his editing work.

"I take it that spring cleaning is not 'in' this year with the college kids?" he asked as Mike finished the slice he was working on, chewing quickly and wiping his fingers off on his faded jeans.

"Since when is cleaning ever 'in' for any age?" Mike asked, a sheepish grin breaking out on the clean-shaven face that stared out at him from under the New York Yankees baseball cap twisted on his head.

"You really are a mess."

"Hey fortunately the station manager keeps off my back about my work area. What can I say, they don't want to impede my creative flow!" Mike joked, expanding his arms to encompass the whole, filthy room.

"Yeah, King of the Crap, that's you alright. So listen I need something from you." Nick stated, taking a look out the window blinds and glancing up and down the hall on the other side of the door. The coast appeared clear, but Nick wasn't going to take any chances. He didn't need Mike getting in trouble for talking to him, especially since he was one source of information he chose to keep. It didn't matter that Mike was a slob trying to relive his missed youth or whatever it was his life goals were aimed at, the man was reliable and thanks to his working at a competing news outlet, had access to things that Nick didn't.

"Man my boss is supposed to be by in a little bit for a completed segment that I'm trying to finish putting together for tonight's show, what is it you need?"

"That's okay, this won't take long. I just needed to know about the murder you filmed this morning, and was wondering if you might be able to get me a copy of the tape you took."

Mike studied the man before him, then leaning forward in his chair, his elbow almost landing in the pizza box, he put his palm out waiting. Nick knew the drill and without hesitating, pulled the envelope from his work bag, and slipped it into the cameraman's dirty hand. He opened it and quickly flipped through the bills before sealing the contents shut and stashing it away from prying eyes.

"That's a start, but I'm gonna need more than that. Ted Hanson and my boss Emily are looking to this murder to be one of the bigger stories at the 6 o'clock time slot. They find out a rival reporter got the scoop, I could have pressure on my ass! And believe me when I say Emily is not a woman you want getting on your back. She's a real mean S.O.B!"

Like you wouldn't jump ship to save your sorry ass the moment a fire broke out, Nick thought with a smile as he withdrew his wallet and took the last remaining bills from it and handed them to the waiting man. He really was a rodent when he had to be, but that didn't bother Nick as long as the intel was golden. Not bothering to count the money, Mike just looked it over and shoved it into the same pocket the envelope had disappeared to. A smile then broke out across his thin lips and he turned towards the computer monitor lying half buried under random trash and papers.

"That'll do, now allow me to show you the crazy ass shit we came across this morning!" Mike pushed a pile of papers off the counter and into a waiting chair below, then began typing onto his keyboard with quick strokes, waking the sleeping computer up now that his lunch break was over. Amazing how much work you could get from a man, by paying him extra to do what he's already supposed to be in the middle of working on, Nick mused, watching with interest as Mike's thin fingers flew over the keyboard and then quickly began inserting and flipping other controls on a separate machine at head level. To Nick it looked like some kind of recorder. Probably able to synchronize and aid the station in changing between recording in various formats. It was about the size of a VCR, but the tapes that Mike was interchanging into the machine were much smaller and obviously digital.

After a moment of working and typing, Mike sat back and motioned to the computer screen. "Okay this is what I got from Horners Lane this morning when we arrived." He slid a small knob on the control keyboard and the picture on the monitor began speeding up. Nick watched as they arrived at the street, dealt with police, attempted to get around the barricade, and other shots of the crowd and various footage as the video continued to speed along.

"Alright, this is where it gets good," Mike said with a look at Nick as if he was preparing him. "Oh and don't worry the copy I'm making you will have all the unrated features for no extra charge!" a short giggle escaped the cameraman's throat at his own joke, as he began to reel the knob backwards and slow the frames on the monitor. Once it was around normal speed, Nick looked at the screen and watched with repulsion at the scene playing out before him.

The camera panned across the park, fog making visibility almost impossible in parts, until it stopped on one item in particular. As the lens was focused and the shot became clear, Nick realized he was staring at a head. The woman's throat was almost completely torn away and the face seemed to be frozen in a state of fear. This was just sick, this poor woman. Who would have done something like that? It was brutal, beyond words and Nick had the strange feeling as he looked at the frozen mask of pain that was portrayed on the monitor that this was just the beginning.

Oh yes, this was just the beginning!

- -

Detective Andrea Wilkes found herself daydreaming at her desk towards the end of the day, and upon realizing how tired she was, she finally finished typing up the report she was working on decided to call it a day. Heading home on time, which for her was early, she figured she had a good chance of avoiding most of the rush hour traffic as she pulled off the highway and onto the street leading into her neighborhood. Her thoughts kept returning to Aidan Preston and the image of him, his rugged good looks and athletic build sweeping into the office earlier that morning.

There had definitely been something different about the man whom she had known over the last few years. Having worked with him on countless investigations, Andrea had always been impressed with not only how smart he was, but lately his actions had begun to pull at a part of her imagination that she tried to keep buried. He was handsome, more than just handsome; he was downright sexy with his beautiful gray eyes that seemed to just let you swim in them, and with him being on administrative leave, he seemed to have stopped caring about his personal upkeep as much. Instead of being wide eyed and clean shaven, he had entered the Homicide division earlier with a full days growth of dark beard that she found quite appealing on the older man.

It really gave him that almost James Dean, bad boy look that had always captured her heart. It was the same thing that had led to her initial relationship with her ex Robert Wilkes.

Pulling into the numbered parking space that was assigned to her with her townhouse, she parked her Nissan hatchback and grabbing the dry-cleaning she had picked up before work this morning from the backseat, made her way up to the small, welcoming entrance to her home. She noticed the perennials were starting to die that her neighbor had given her last spring, winter only a stone's throw away now, and pretty soon the rest of her small garden would be dead as well thanks to the colder weather approaching. Unlocking the deadbolt on the door, she nudged the door open, her arms full of the plastic bag of clothes, and entered into the kitchen. Hearing music playing loudly from down the hall, she set the dry-cleaning on the back of a kitchen chair and walked towards the source of the loud, booming tunes.

Amy her seventeen year old daughter was dancing around her bedroom, wearing a provocative outfit that was too short for her to have gone to school in. She was busy throwing her dark, chestnut hair around, bobbing to the 'beat' as she gyrated to the music, unknowingly in front of her mother's watchful eyes. Having seen enough, Andrea rapped her knuckles on the door frame, sending the pretty girl spinning around in shock.

"Oh God, mom!" she squealed in surprise, her cheeks flushing embarrassment as she regained her composure.

Amy looked just like Andrea had when she was that age. Beautiful and slim, her dark hair highlighting her thin neck and maturing curves. She was wearing a thin t-shirt that barely covered her smooth, flat stomach and a small pair of denim shorts that cruised low on her hips and barely covered her unblemished thighs. She had a pair of pink crosstrainers on, the thick bottoms adding a few inches to the short girls frame. Amy was co-captain of the high school cheerleading squad, and a member of the school counsel. At seventeen she had the looks and the brains to make something of herself, and that was something Andrea was proud of.

"Hi sweetie, can you turn the music down?" Andrea asked, watching her daughter skip across the room to her cluttered nightstand.

"What?" the girl yelled, looking at her mom and shaking her hips in time with the music.

"The music—can you turn it down?!"

"Oh, oh yeah, sorry. It's a new mix Didi just gave me," the seventeen year old said turning the volume on the radio down to a much more acceptable level.

"And do her parent's know she's listening to that stuff?" Andrea asked nodding to the radio and crossing her arms over her chest like a strict sentry standing guard.

"Oh yeah, believe it or not, but most parent's are actually becoming quite hip lately!" Amy said with a smile as she crossed the room and gave her mom a hug. Andrea squeezed her daughter back and then held her at a distance with her hands on the smaller girls shoulders.

"Please tell me you didn't wear that to school?"

"Oh mom, relax! I changed when I got home from cheerleading practice."

"Good, because I'd hate for you to lose out on winter break coming up by being expelled due to your clothing choices. It's bad enough your brother thinks he's changed races." Andrea said, thinking of her youngest child's desire to dress in nothing but FUBU and Sean John. What is it with kids these days? If they don't have a celebrities name on the label, they might as well not make it.

Amy walked over to the desk that sat in the corner of her bedroom and picking up a sheet of paper brought it over to Andrea. Looking at the permission slip in hand, Andrea saw that it was from the school. Oh God what did they need now? She was used to receiving notes from the guidance counselor frequently about her son Jeremy and his attendance issues, but Amy had so far been able to stay clear of that problem. Andrea attributed that to Amy being more like her, and Jeremy unfortunately seemed to have gotten more of her husband's genes.

Ah, Robert, what else can you manage to screw up without being here? Andrea wondered as she thought about her ex who had just up and left her and their two kids a few months ago. He said he needed time to find himself, some bullshit about a mid-life crisis, but Andrea wasn't buying it. She knew that the man had a wandering eye, and no matter how successful their marriage had been at the beginning, she just wasn't enough for him. He was probably out at some club, chasing girls half his age while she was stuck holding down the fort and trying to raise two teenagers by herself.

"I need your signature for a class trip next week." Amy said, breaking Andrea's thoughts from her current life issues and bringing her back to the present.

"Where are you going?"

"Mrs. McCallister is taking the entire senior World History class to the Washington D.C. She wants us to have firsthand knowledge of the monuments and buildings for a report we have to write by the end of the semester."

Andrea thought it over. At least it was a school sanctioned trip, and not some excuse to ditch class. Not that she usually had to worry about that from Amy, but at that age, you never know when they might look for some trouble. After all, Andrea and Robert had been high school sweethearts and look how that turned out. Hopefully, Amy continued to use her head instead of what had lead to Andrea having two kids before she was finished college. That had been a mistake. At that moment, she heard the front door bang open.

"Yo I'm home!" her son Jeremy's voice called out from past the kitchen. Taking the permission slip from Amy's hand, Andrea turned and followed the commotion coming from her son's arrival.

"Hey Jeremy," she said, watching the boy drop his backpack on the floor and head straight for the refrigerator. Pulling a soda out from the box on the shelf, he pulled the tab open and began chugging the cold beverage.

"Can you close the fridge while your doing that?" Andrea asked, watching her fifteen year old son, the spitting image of his father, glance at her then back at the fridge.

"Uh, I'm about to get something else out," he muttered, setting the can down on the counter and rummaging about inside the half filled shelves of the refrigerator.

"So how was your day?" Andrea asked, grabbing his backpack from the middle of the floor and tossing it into the living room. Jeremy continued going through a few cabinets and containers, before selecting a granola bar and closing the fridge door behind him.

"Same 'ol," he shrugged, taking a bite of the snack and picking his soda up off the edge of the table.

"Did you make it to all your classes?"

The boy stopped, seemed to think the question over and then nodded, continuing his path for his bedroom down the hall. Before he could reach the door, Andrea put an arm out and caught the boy by the shoulder.

"So I'm not going to have any calls from the school on the messages today?"

Once again he shrugged and Andrea knew that there was going to be something awaiting her on the answering machine sitting in the kitchen.

"Jeremy?"

"What?" he asked, taking a sip of his soda and trying to slink by her. "I might of been late for first period, but that's it."

Before Andrea could ask anything else, the boy broke her simple grip and slipped into his bedroom.

"Late, you're driving now, how could you be late when you have your own car?" Andrea called out, but he had already closed the door to the room. Feeling the anger rising up in her, Andrea let out a breath and counted to five. She was not going to let the boy's lackadaisical attitude screw up her evening. She had enough on her mind.

At that, the image of Aidan's rough, masculine features clad in his dark shirt, jeans and leather jacket from earlier entered her mind. Now why couldn't she get him out of her head? She'd worked with the man for years, and now that he wasn't around daily, she seemed to be even more enthralled with him when he did make an appearance.

He was flirting with you too, she told herself as she thought about him at the office that morning.

Yes, he had been flirting hadn't he?

Ignoring the closed door to Jeremy's room, Andrea walked to her own bedroom and closed the door behind her. She pulled the scrunchie from her hair and let her long, dark locks fall across her shoulders as she moved across the room to her own vanity. Slipping her gun from its holster she double checked the safety was on, and placed it into the nightstand next to the bed. Aidan Preston, maybe she should give him a call and see what he was up to? It was still early in the evening, and both her kids were in for the night, at least she hoped they were, so maybe she should follow up on the feelings she had felt earlier.

She stretched her neck back and forth, working a kink out, while she sat down on the end of her bed and slipped her shoes off. Working her foot in between her hand, she rubbed the sore digits as she stared at the phone on the nightstand. Either way, she had to check the messages for the day, and she wondered if there was anything important. Maybe Aidan had called, looking to catch her up on her offer earlier. Picking the phone off the cradle, she dialed into her messages and lay back on the bed waiting for them to play. After a moment there was a beep, and the automated tone informed her she had three new messages. Who could have called her home phone instead of her cell?

As if in answer to her thoughts, the first message began playing.

"Hello Mrs. Wilkes, this is Rhonda Mitchell at Seneca Creek High School —," Damn it, it was Jeremy's Guidance Counselor. He wasn't late for first period, he didn't even make it to school until third! Andrea was perturbed, the anger starting to build as she listened to the rest of the message.

"…If you could give me a call back at the school tomorrow, I'd like to discuss this with you," Rhonda finished saying and her recorded voice was then gone with a beep. Andrea pressed the related key to save the message and move on. The next message began playing and she immediately froze at the all too familiar voice echoing over the line. It's deep, southern drawl was unmistakable.

"Hey Andrea, it's me…," Robert's voice said, images of her ex-husband filling her mind as she listened to the voice drone on. "I was wondering if you wanted to get together sometime this week. I'm in town on business, and I was talking to Jeremy and thought it would be a good idea for all of us to get together at some point."

Andrea could feel her face flush with anger. He had been talking to Jeremy! That creep had no right to walk out on them and then keep in contact and show up when it was convenient for him! Trying to keep the anger from building up, Andrea sat up against the headboard of her soft bed and deleted the message before it could finish playing, sending the voice of her ex off into exile in the vast barrenness that al deleted recordings went to.

That'll teach him to call! Andrea fumed. How dare he, after months of not hearing from him, call her and want to 'get together', like some big, happy family reunion! Andrea would rather be tied down and tortured than let that man back into her and her children's life. That she was sure of.

Chapter 6

"The relationship between early human beings and wolves is one of great mystery and intrigue. Early man viewed this symbiotic relationship with fear of the unknown, and due to this way of thinking, hunted these pristine animals to the brink of extinction in a short period of time. The long-standing relationship between wolves and humans is rooted in their similar life roles of hunter-gatherers and as scavengers.

The wolf-human interaction developed into a close and almost intimate relationship during the course of domestication that led to the creation of a much needed and new relationship that arose between the two classes, allowing this bond to increase the need and reliance both species held for each other. Cooperation is at the core of canine social organization and fundamentally has led to this new creation of interactions and beliefs between the two, that of wolves and humans.

'We consider canines to be 'man's best friend' and an integral part in our evolution as a species. However, analyzing the cause and effect of this domestication shows how not only we have changed the species to be of more beneficial uses to us, but how these changes have affected the wolf population as a whole. By studying the communication of wolves through their actions and vocalizations, we can define the needs these creatures truly require, and how we as the dominant species on the planet can put defenses in place to allow us to keep the dwindling wolf population from facing another possible extinction and solidify their standing in the order or nature." Lisa Marie Davies, wildlife zoologist with the National Zoo in Washington D.C., and native wolf expert, finished her PowerPoint presentation and turned towards the large, oak table across from her.

She hit a small button on the remote she held in her hand and the lights to the room were raised, revealing the faces of the occupants around the table. Four pairs of eyes had followed her through her twenty minute proposal on the new gray wolf habitat she was working on completing, and now the owner's of those set of eyes were staring directly at her as she wrapped up her speech. Dr. Wesley Ashton, Director of the National Zoo and her boss rose from his seat, his natty, worn tweed suit hanging off his thin frame as he stood and adjusted the glasses perched on the end of his aquiline nose, then turning to the other three sitting beside him said,

"Thank you Dr. Davies for the update, I'm sure I speak for everyone present in saying that we are truly looking forward to the work you and your team will be doing towards the new housing facilities and exhibit. I for one cannot wait to see all these months of hard work bloom and let us enter a new phase here at the National Zoo.

'In the meantime I believe you have answered everyone's questions and concerns regarding the requested budget and funds allocation you wish to put towards your research." He finished with a nod to the three other people that were sitting at the table with him.

In attendance at this presentation, Lisa noted was the Smithsonian Chairman Bill Morris, Kathryn Morris, wife to Chairman Morris and the Zoo's leading wildlife researcher and Nancy Regal the woman in charge of the Zoo's public relations and budget committee. They were gathered together in this board room located in the Smithsonian Conservation Biology institute's main administrative building to discuss the upcoming project that Lisa was heading. As the resident wolf biologist and research expert, she was not only being heralded by Dr. Ashton as a huge addition to the staff of such a prestigious facility, but as a godsend as they began the final construction phase on the recent remodel the zoo was undergoing.

The Smithsonian National Zoological Park located in Washington D.C., is not only one of the nation's leading research facilities, but one of the largest structures and national landmarks on the East Coast. Commonly referred to simply as the National Zoo, it is one of the oldest zoos in the United States, and as part of the Smithsonian Institution, does not charge admission to the many hundreds of thousands of visitors that flock to its downtown location yearly.

Founded in 1889, its mission overview is to provide leadership in animal care, science, education, sustainability, and visitor experience. The National Zoo has two campuses. The first is a 163-acre urban park located in northwest Washington, D.C. The other campus is the 3,200-acre Smithsonian Conservation Biology Institute in Front Royal, Virginia. The SCBI is a non-public facility devoted to training wildlife professionals in conservation biology and to propagating rare species through natural means and assisted reproduction.

Altogether, the two facilities contain over 2,000 animals of 400 different species. About one-fifth of them are endangered or threatened. Most species are on exhibit at the Zoo's downtown, urban campus. It is best known for its always popular panda exhibit, but the Zoo is also home to birds, great apes, big cats, Asian elephants, insects, amphibians, reptiles, aquatic animals, small mammals and many more. Meanwhile, The SCBI facility houses between 30 and 40 endangered species at any given time depending on research needs and recommendations from the Zoo and the conservation community.

The National Zoo, as part of the Smithsonian Institution, receives federal appropriations for operating expenses. A new master plan introduced for the park in 2008 designs to upgrade the park's exhibits and layout. Part of that operating fund is what brought Lisa to the SCBI campus' main administration building. If all went according to plan, she would be given the financial grant she had requested, and truly show the faculty and overseers of the Smithsonian National Zoological Park exactly why she had been hired there in the first place.

Lisa Davies watched the four members of the Zoo's Board stand and gather their notes. Lisa pushed a strand of her black hair away from her face, a face that had high, strong cheekbones and full lips thanks in part to her Guatemalan heritage. The Mayan influence having infiltrated into Central American culture and blended the races to provide a prominent and unique look that included smooth foreheads, flat, round noses and it was that blending that gave Lisa her exotic look. Wearing a slim black dress and white blouse that hugged her curves in just the right places and accentuated her Hispanic roots, she wasn't normally inclined to dress up so much for a day at work, but today was special.

If everything came together like it was supposed to in the next few weeks, then she could be well on her way to staking out a claim for her name in the research for some of the most breakthrough information gathered regarding Canis Lupus, or the North American gray wolf. Her name would be synonymous with the field of research heightened and compared to the likes of world renowned wolf researcher L. David Mech and professor of vertebrate zoology and animal ecology, Dr. Luigi Boitani. At least that is as long as the Smithsonian Institute decided to give her the grant she had requested. Dr. Ashton stopped for a moment before following the others and exiting the room and placed a warm hand on Lisa's shoulder. She caught his strong gaze and smiled.

"Don't look so worried, you did great!" the aging director said in his warm, melodious voice. Dr. Ashton always seemed to know when she needed encouraging, and ever since coming to the East Coast had seemed to have been adopted by him and taken under his wing as a father-figure of sorts.

He was the type of man who held a warm spot in his heart for many, and he always kept his eyes out for those promising and talented enough to be brought into the folds of the staff that he treated like a family. He seemed to Lisa to be one of those kind, caring older gentleman whose face lit up on holidays when surrounded by their many generations of family and grandkids. It was a feeling that Lisa wasn't always used to experiencing, having come to this country as a baby after being adopted.

While her early childhood was as much a mystery to her as anything, Lisa did know that growing up in the Midwestern United States had truly made an impression in her life and guided her to the career she lived and breathed. From the earliest memories she could muster she remembered being outdoors, the great scope of the American Midwest stretched out before her like it was just waiting to be explored and have Lisa Marie Davies' name etched into a book somewhere for many more generations of young explorers to read about her adventures over such a pristine land and wildlife.

Other girls growing up wanted to be Disney princesses or fairies or some such nonsense, Lisa however remembered telling her stepmom that she was going to grow up to be like Davy Crockett! Fighting wild natives and taming new lands and beasts, yes sir, she was going to be Mrs. Davy Crockett!

Memories of her past aside, Lisa watched as the room cleared out leaving her standing in the conference room alone to clean up. She walked over to the slide projector and removed her flashdrive from the computer. Powering the machine down, she looked through the large room's window and out at the panoramic view below.

The building that housed the conference rooms and offices of the SCBI sat on a large hill that rose above the massive, wooded grounds of the Fort Royal, Virginia location and offered a view that Lisa always found to be reminiscent of those childhood days long ago out in the vast wilderness of the Midwest. The Smithsonian Conservation Biology Institute had been located here since 1974. Acquisition of the property to support the National Zoo's wildlife conservation programs was a colorful history with many events that eventually led to the facilities current purpose.

The U.S. Army obtained options for 4,200 acres of farmland and planned on developing a large facility for the breeding and training of horses and mules for the U.S. Cavalry. In 1912, construction of permanent buildings commenced and by 1916 the majority of the Ayleshire Quartermaster Remount Depot was completed. Grouping the buildings together to form a central post, eleven barns and stable complexes were constructed.

In its heyday, five blacksmith forges were busy daily, and staff of 400 civilian and military personnel carried on the business of breeding and training horses and mules. Mules and horses were also used for local transportation, and pulled mechanical mowers to mow the pastures and vast farm lands.During the cavalry's occupancy; nearly all of the woodlands on the property were converted to pasture at one time or another.

A second building boom occurred during World War II, when the Center served as a K-9 training facility and housed 600 German and Italian prisoners of war. Several temporary structures were constructed in the vicinity of the alfalfa fields, but today only the foundations remain. Most of the rock piles scattered about the property date from this period. The POWs were kept busy as laborers on various farms in the Shenandoah Valley, and many prisoners longed to remain in the U.S. after the war.

After World War II, the place of the cavalry in modern warfare was questioned, and in 1948, Congress passed legislation transferring the land assets of the Remount Service to the U.S. Department of Agriculture. In addition to the USDA functions, the Department of State used a portion of the Center's facilities as an Emergency Relocation site and a communications station.

The State Department equipped several buildings as offices in case of national emergency—enough for the Secretary and 700 State Department employees. By 1972, all that was left of this activity was the communication station. In the winter of 1973, USDA decided to close down the Research Station's operations.

Dr. Theodore H. Reed, the then Director of the National Zoo, had been searching for a captive breeding facility for over a decade when he heard of the possibility of obtaining the old Remount property.

The property was occupied by the Smithsonian in 1974, and title to the land was received in 1975. The facility was named the Conservation and Research Center, and was staffed with a dozen employees from various zoo departments as well as a handful of former Remount and Cattle station employees. The Center's mission has evolved over the years, but its focus remains true to the original concept--a center for conservation-related activities of the National Zoo and sister units of the Smithsonian Institution.

Breaking her concentration away from the window, she quickly finished packing up the materials she had brought and hurried out of the room.

The walk back to her research office was a short one that wound down across from the main zoo facility and actually up through the campus' heart, until she crossed the small intersection designed for pedestrians and golf carts and came to her home away from home. Designed years ago by the same architect who had built many of the other buildings scattered throughout the zoo's grounds, the Wolf Cave, nicknamed for the work her and her colleagues were doing there, was actually a newer building built during the zoo's last construction phase.

Old plans had been there all along to add the building to the original plots laid out when the zoo's second location was first built, but over time as the animal habitats and other projects grew and expanded, the Cave had never been added to the Washington D.C. location. Until now. During the latest construction phase, not only were they changing and adding to the layout of the main zoo, but they were adding space and buildings here at the Virginia campus as well. All in all, the Institute consisted of six centers: The Center for Animal Care Science, the Conservation Ecology Center, the Center for Conservation Education and Sustainability, the Center for Conservation and Evolutionary Genetics, the Migratory Bird Center and the Center for Species Survival.

Looking up at the large stone entranceway as she walked up to the glass doors below, Lisa felt a slight charge of excitement build up in her chest as she stepped underneath the large, statue standing guard like a sentry above the entry. Romulus and Remus, Greek sons and brothers originally believed to be the founding builders of the Roman empire were forever immortalized in myth and legends by the theme depicted in the statue before her.

While the statue was a replica of the thirteenth century medieval sculpture portraying the suckling of the two aforementioned legendary figures being suckled by a she-wolf.

The story as it was known to college students and academia of mythology around the world was a tale Lisa knew all too well. It told the tale of Numitor, a descendant of Trojan prince Aeneas, rightful king of Alba Longa. According to legend, Numitor's brother Amulius removed his kin from the throne, killed Numitor's sons, and forced Rhea Silvia, the king's daughter to become a Vestal Virgin.

In ancient Roman religion, the Vestals were priestesses of Vesta, goddess of the hearth. Among their many duties, they were sworn to a vow of chastity. By forcing Rhea into this sacred position, Amulius hoped to deprive Numitor's heirs from taking the throne that Amulius himself occupied. However, as the myth went, Rhea Silvia became pregnant thanks to the god Mars intervening in the mortals realm. Romulus and Remus were thus born. Hoping to kill the twins in infancy, Amulius left them to die, yet a series of miracles took place that would lead to the twins surviving and making their way into infamy.

After being abandoned and thrown into the River Tiber, a she-wolf rescued the babies and suckled them. A shepherd and his wife then fostered them and raised them up to be adults, prepared for life by their humble and fantastical beginnings. Once old enough, the twins returned to overthrow their wicked uncle Amulius, restoring Numitor back to power over Alba Longa. Having accomplished this feat the twins set out subsequently founded the city of Rome, an event that had its own bloody outcome and cost Remus his life at his brother's hands.

Looking up at the famous statue, an image that has been found throughout the world since the second half of the third century B.C., and been printed not only on coins from the region but engraved in multiple other artifacts over the years. Now, that same motif stood towering over her, reproduced in the form of a massive statue that sat overlooking the sidewalks and walking trails that criss-crossed throughout the zoo grounds.

Glancing briefly and taking the sight of the statue in as she passed underneath and entered the first glass door labeled 'Staff Only', Lisa felt a sort of kinship with the story of Romulus and Remus, the statue reminding her of the bond of a surrogate raising and nurturing a child that was not their own, yet suckling them and keeping them safe until they are old enough to go out into the world on their own and make a name for themselves. It was the same connection that Lisa felt with her own stepmother, a woman that had no blood relation to her, yet had raised her like her own.

With the sight of the statue out of view and now making her way quickly through the winding hallway that snaked through the Cave's extensive, main floor, Lisa reached her office door and unlocked it.

The first thing she noticed as she entered the odd shaped room was that her assistant Frank Siris was nowhere to be seen. He should of been here by now. The only other place she could think of that Frank might be would be the habitat. Just like Lisa, Frank's passion for wolves almost bordered on the obsessed. There just wasn't anything like being here at the National Zoo, surrounded by the animals that really fueled their research and being able to actually get paid doing it. Lisa walked over to her workspace and turned her computer on. She was curious to see if she had any new mail regarding the latest contact she had been talking to recently.

No more than a week ago, she had received a strange e-mail that had almost missed her when the Zoo's junk e-mail filter had marked it as trash. Luckily she had checked the deleted folder when looking for a different message when the subject line of the other e-mail caught her attention. It was from a man out in Northern Oregon who claimed to have stumbled on what he thought was an ancient animal graveyard located on one of his many acres of land. He hadn't reported the incident yet, afraid to let the story spill and have paleontologist and researchers trampling all over his land even if it could possibly be a an extinct boneyard, before he knew for sure what it was that he had found.

Over the last week Lisa had talked to him extensively, communicating via e-mail from across the country. Unfortunately until Lisa knew more, she couldn't validate leaving her job and flying 3,000 miles from one coast to the other on what could be a simple misidentification of remains and turn into a wild goose chase. That meant evidence of what the man had discovered. Chatting almost every day of the last week, Lisa had learned that Tyler Suffux, 56 years of age, was a lifelong rancher and what sounded like a dedicated husband to his wife Eleanor of 32 years. One day while he was out surveying a wooded plot of unused land, his dog, a German Shepherd had started digging at something that recent flood rains had uncovered in a small canyon far in the corner of his large, almost 200 acre property.

When he looked to see what had gotten the dog so riled up, he realized that the heavy rains had eroded the soil away from a wall at the base of one creek bed and there were a number of bones to be found sticking out of the ground like white, skeletal plants growing out of the earth. Unfortunately Tyler who hadn't gotten around to getting 'in touch' with today's technological world and had just recently learned to use the internet, only had an old 35 mm film camera to take pictures of the find. These with the help of his daughter he scanned onto the camera and had e-mailed Lisa with. Without the pictures being digital, the quality was pretty bad, but it was clear to Lisa that the old farmhand was onto something.

She had studied fossils, the skeletal structure and anatomy of almost every mammal in North America, and if what Tyler Suffux had unearthed on his property in Oregon, she knew they could be looking at the fossil remains of the extinct ancestor to the Gray Wolf, the Dire Wolf, an animal thought to be extinct since the Pleistocene Epoch, or as most knew the period as, the ice age.

While fossil records showed that the Dire Wolf's geographical range covered North and South American all those years ago, evidence had never been found in that location of the continent to suggest they were present there. This discovery if true could change the beliefs on migratory range of the canine and its ancestors for the history books. And from the last e-mail Tyler had sent her, he thought that he had uncovered more than a dozen various skeletons, and what he thought to be unfossilized remains as well. That right there was enough to get Lisa's heart skipping.

What if the Dire Wolf hadn't died out that many ages ago, or what if a common ancestor to them and the Gray Wolf had escaped classification and were waiting to be revealed. The evolution of the domestic dog is still a matter of much debate. Some scientists believe that the dog is descended from the wolf, while others think they are evolved separately from a common ancestor, possibly the same ancestor that spawned the Dire Wolf. Recently the American Society of Mammologist recommended that the domestic dog be reclassified as a new subspecies of wolf, Canis lupus familiaris. Since these findings seem to point to the modern day wolf and dog not only possibly sharing a distinct lineage, but if the finding of a more modern Dire Wolf or ancestor that could tie both species together was discovered in Oregon, it would change her entire world not to mention validate her theories on the relationship between canines and the effect human interaction played on the nearly wiping out of the wolf species!

After the last time they had talked, Lisa had gotten Tyler to agree to gently collect some of the fossils and send them to her for analysis. He had also agreed with her to keep his discovery quiet for the time being before she could authenticate his find by testing and studying the real-life samples and the next batch of photographs he was supposed to be sending along.

Lisa scrolled through her e-mail, double checking that she hadn't missed anything new, before turning her attention back to the work at hand. Frank still hadn't appeared and moving away from her computer, she decided to go out and check to see if he was at the wolf habitat.

The wolf exhibit was a newly constructed expanse of fenced in hills and mock cave system that allowed the family of gray wolves that the zoo had taken in to roam around more freely than the previous pens had allowed. Lisa loved that the wide acreage gave the majestic animals not only an environment that was more like the wild that these creatures existed naturally, but allowed visitors to the zoo to gaze on the wolves daily activities and get a better understanding of what they were really like.

Over the last two years the zoo's wolf rehabilitation plan had undergone a major overhaul, expanding their research from not only helping monitor and protect the ever decreasing Mexican Wolf population, but to incorporate a pack of five gray wolves, two adults and three pups into their own separate holding facility.

As Lisa exited the side door of the Cave and made the quick two minute walk to the wolf habitat, she saw that Frank was indeed down in the pen working with two of the pups. Adolpho and Lupa, two of the three gray wolf pups were leaping up and pushing their paws against Frank, their heads rolling against him as they played around. Spying Lisa walking up to the outer fence, Frank turned his attention from Lupa's searching nose and gave Lisa a wave.

"I was wondering where you were," Lisa said, watching Frank let Adolpho drop off him and then heading towards the enclosure's gate.

"Same place I always am. How'd the presentation go?" he asked, opening the gate once he was sure the two wolves were far enough away for him to escape without them being on his heels. The two wolves sensing their human interaction was over, hurried off, the younger Adolpho snapping playfully with his jaws at his sister as they ran up along a small hill and disappeared from view.

"The presentation went fine. I'm hoping that we'll hear something regarding the grant within the next month."

"Yeah, its ridiculous how drawn out the paper pushers can make something take," Frank replied, locking the gate and making sure it was secure. Even though only zoo staff had access to this part of the habitat, there was always the chance someone else could find their way back to the entry gates, and safety regulations required all gates to not only have visible signage old fashioned padlocks but newer electronic latches as well. Once he was sure the lock was secure, he turned to Lisa with a grin on his round face, the small goatee sparsely hanging off his chin the only sign that the young assistant wasn't still in high school.

"Oh your going to love what Zeeb did earlier!"

At mention of the older female wolf Lisa's attention and eyes shifted away from the pen and onto Frank's slightly husky form. Since coming to work at the zoo as part of his college zoology degree, the boy's appearance had seemed to change along with his attitude towards the unpaid internship. When he had first started he had been overweight and out of shape, slightly perturbed that the zoo couldn't afford to pay him for the time he spent working there and hesitantly completing assignments that would lead to his college education.

However, over the last half a year not only had his passion for the work truly broken through his rough outer shell, but the constant time he spent running around with the young wolf pups and monitoring their daily activities he had shed some weight and was beginning to lose the college-anointed beer gut that he had first arrived with.

Lisa was impressed by the young man. Not only was he working on getting healthier and the slimmer results would ultimately end up in his crush he held possibly being noticed by the girl who worked at one of the food stands in the zoo, but his interest in the work she was doing and wolves as a whole had really ignited something inside the boy just starting to discover what he wanted to do with himself for a career.

Lisa could remember being twenty one, and all the drama life can hold for a person at that age; relationships, partying, friends, love, jobs versus career, life altering decisions to be made, but she saw something in Frank that reminded her of her own passions. He truly loved working with the wolves here at the National Zoo, and while he seemed to have taken a special liking to the cubs they had recently acquired, he was a hard worker and that went miles towards impressing Lisa.

"So what did Zeeb do?" Lisa asked referring to the full-grown adult female that they held here at the zoo. Zeeb was a beautiful creature, with a coat of fur that held mixtures of grays, blacks and even some yellow streaking through her pelt.

While she was a little smaller than her mate Ulric, the female wolf certainly held her own when it came to securing her position in the packs hierarchy. She was certainly not going to let the younger cubs usurp her from her place as den mother, and constantly reminded them with the light snapping of her teeth and baring of her fangs and low attention grabbing growl she always demonstrated during feeding times.

"Here let me show you," Frank said reaching into his pocket and pulling his smart phone out.

Boys and their technology, Lisa thought as his fingers quickly scrolled across the phones screen, selecting the right choices and pulling up his desired target.

Handing the phone to Lisa, she looked down at the screen as a movie file began to play. Obviously Frank had been spending the morning recording the wolves onto his cell phone, and she'd have to remind him later about him spending his time more wisely when in the habitat. There were still plenty of chores to get done today before the zoo's thousands of daily visitors and tourists started to arrive once the gates opened in a little less than an hour.

Tilting the screen slightly to avoid the glare from the sun from washing the image out, she watched as the short video played. Zeeb was running, her legs carrying her swiftly across one of the long grassy expanses of the new habitat and quickly veered off from her original target, her legs slowing slightly as her eyes or ears caught sight of Frank recording her.

She charged towards the camera, Lisa watching as the image began to become a little rough and out of focus, obviously Frank had started to question moving out of the way of the charging animal instead of filming its approach. However, he remained where he was, the picture becoming steadier just at the moment that Zeeb came flashing up into the screen, colliding with Frank and sending him sprawling onto the ground.

The phone fell, continuing to record and Lisa gasped at the sudden turn of events. Her eyes glued to the small screen, she watched as the phone having landed on its side focused again this time on the image of Frank's body lying in the dirt. Zeeb was standing on top of him, her front paws firmly pressed into his chest and she was licking him crazily as Frank laughing and the wind knocked out of him, struggled to get the 100 pound wolf off him.

"Serves you right," Lisa said with a smile, handing the phone back to Frank as he switched out of the video mode and slid it back into his jeans. "What did you use to draw her attention to you like that?"

"I brought the tape recorder out and when I saw her sprinting along the upper part of the cage near the visitor observation post, I turned it on and played that latest wolf vocalization recording you got." Frank explained.

"Well it looks like it definitely worked; it'll be interesting to see how they respond to the general and specialized vocals." Lisa shook her head, thinking back to the footage of Zeeb clobbering Frank. A smile formed on her lips and she just looked at the boy, shaking her head slightly.

"What?" he asked sheepishly.

"Oh nothing, just imagining what would of happened had Ulric knocked into you like that! He's a good thirty pounds heavier than Zeeb."

"I would of been minced meat!" Frank hollered, the smile appearing on his face highlighting light freckles splattered across his nose and cheeks and the small dimples that formed whenever he was happy.

"That's for sure." Lisa said, then looking at her watch realized how little time they had to get ready before opening this part of the facility up for the important visitors that would soon be arriving. Even though the SCBI campus wasn't open to the general public, they still received certain groups that toured the facility or grounds. Most of the time it was visiting professors or researchers, but occasionally there were the wealthy benefiters of the Smithsonian who wished to see behind the scenes at what their donations were going towards. Giving herself a mental reminder to set up the wolf vocalization CD she had received from a colleague this past week, she gave one last look to this side of the habitat, then turning her and Frank made their way back towards the Cave.

Lisa knew she was going to want to check her e-mail once more before opening time, just in case she had received anything else from Tyler since last looking. It had been a few days since his last message and before that they had been talking every single day online. She just hoped that he had got the samples and pictures sent on their way before he went out there and tried to dig everything up himself to get all the glory. That was the last thing a possible scientific find like that needed was to have a local rancher unknowingly destroy fossils and other relics that could possibly be responsible for rewriting the history books.

Yes, she'd definitely send Tyler another e-mail when she got back to her office, see if she could find out where he's been hiding the last few days. Oh she had some many things to do. Pushing thoughts of the possible Oregon find aside, she focused on what needed to be done today, here on the East Coast of the country. Let Tyler and his wife Eleanor worry about their coast, between the grant proposal and starting the new field research on wolf vocalizations, her day was already as full as she could handle. Add to that the new gray wolf enclosure they were constructing at the National Zoo's urban park in D.C., and it was enough to topple the most organized individual.

Lisa was certainly going to be in for a long day, that much she knew for sure, yet no matter how hard she tried to focus on what needed to be done right now, her thoughts kept drifting back to the puzzle unearthed in the American Northwest. What exactly had Tyler Suffux stumbled upon?

Chapter 7

"Hey leave some for me!" Megan yelled, reaching out to grab the bottle of Grey Goose vodka from Tony's hand before he could finish downing the last drops.

Tony took another quick sip before letting his lips off from the bottle and handed it to Megan as she slipped away from him, taking a quick gulp herself. The liquor burned going down her throat and she felt the heat rise in her chest as the alcohol warmed her, standing there in the cold, night air with one of the cuter boys from her high school. Tony wrapped his arms around her thin waist and pulled her to him, kissing her on the neck as she leaned in against his lean, taunt frame. The muscles in his arms were hard, and Megan watched as they stretched across his young, tattooed skin.

"Oh baby, what a night!" Tony roared, the alcohol he had already consumed causing his words to slur slightly as he rocked Megan against him in the silver glow of the moon shining down through the ancient maple and oak trees around them. The night air was cold, a light wind rustling up through the tall trees and blowing a scattering of leaves across the gravel lot the teens were partying in. The abandoned quarry was the perfect spot for teens out late at night, looking for a little privacy and a lot of fun. Being a ways off the beaten path, the empty lot was the choice place for young adults to break out and party. The quarry's natural layout provided the perfect cover for those visiting the local lover's lane, a small, unused gravel drive leading up to the large excavation site, with untouched woods on all sides thanks to the current housing market being down the tube and new developments on the back burner. And with construction having been halted at the site since early last year due to permit problems, the abandoned construction site was the perfect place to steal away on a weekday night for some adult fun.

Tony ran his nose into Megan's neck, causing her to squeal a little and look over to the other people they were sharing the space with. Scott and Becky were a few feet away, sitting on the hood of Scott's Mustang, a few empty beer bottles laying on the ground around them as they made out, so self-absorbed in their actions that they might as well have been alone. The way those two behaved, especially once they were well into the party, they didn't care who was around to witness their transgressions. PDA was something they were definitely not ashamed of! Scott ran his hands down his girl's back, squeezing her jean clad butt and bringing a low moan from her as they continued kissing.

Megan tilted the bottle of Goose to her mouth once more and drained the last of the stinging liquid down her throat.

God alcohol sure got her feeling right!

"Let me get some," Tony said reaching for the bottle, then realizing it was empty, he gave Megan a proud smile and tossed the bottle off to the side. "Looks like it's time to open up the Jack."

Tony broke away from Megan, stumbling over to the back of the Mustang.

"Break it up you two lovebirds!" he cried, making his way past Scott and Becky and into the cooler. He pulled a new bottle from the rear of the car, and cracked it open. Before he took a swig of the whiskey, he reached over to the radio and cranked the knob up.

"I love this song!" he cried out as the music blared from the car's stereo. The deep rhythmic thump of Kiss' 'Party All Night Long', erupted into the night as Tony made his way back to Megan, cradling the bottle of whiskey like a newborn baby. Tony's baggy pants hung low on his waist, working on falling off his butt as he crossed the gravel, dragging his feet and kicking stones as he walked. He was tall and thin, his sleeveless shirt open revealing tattoos covering every inch of exposed skin on his arms and chest. While Tony wasn't the type to play sports or participate in extracuricular activities sanctioned by the school, Megan knew he kept in great shape from the way the light portrayed his pale skin. The metal studs that filled his ears and lip reflected the pale moon cascading down upon them through the trees surrounding the quarry, and noticing she was watching him, he stuck his tongue out revealing a piercing that he waggled up and down like a snake.

What was it about the punk look that got to her so? Megan wondered. It was probably the fact that Tony, with his piercings and tattoos and his hair shaved short on the sides and long in the middle sporting a dyed blue mohawk was so unlike most of the boys she knew. While he ignored the social acceptance that high school placed on those that fit it, Tony rebelled from being expected to conform to the 'clicks' and made his own way. That or it could be the fact that Megan's parents were horrified by the boys appearance and actions, and they didn't want their sweet, innocent angel being tainted by the boy's wicked charm.

"Where did you guys get all that?" Becky asked, looking at the bottle Tony had opened and was now downing in long gulps. Scott pulled away from her and walked over to the others in their group.

"Tony's got an I.D." Megan provided, watching Scott and Tony trade gulps from the whiskey.

"Wait, where did he get a fake?"

"Who said it was fake?" Tony asked giving Becky a queer smile.

"Then how—?" Becky began to ask, before Megan answered, "He used his brothers!"

"Oh," Becky muttered.

"Don't worry babe, it's only illegal if you get caught!" Scott called out as he walked back towards his waiting girl. Scott was stocky and short, a defensive tackle on their high school football team, with just enough brains to keep him from not failing out. He was a born jock and that was what made him and Becky such a great fit. She was on the cheerleading squad, and for some reason that stood the test of time, they were the two types of people that wound up together before they were all old enough to head off to different colleges, their lives forever distanced no matter what bond they held in high school.

Megan knew that her and Tony were one of those. She knew it was nothing serious that they shared, and once the year was out, they would probably both be headed in completely opposite directions. Oh well, at least she could have her fun while it lasted! Megan thought as she picked up a still cold beer she had set down earlier from the ground and sipped from it.

"It's a shame Amy couldn't get out tonight," Becky said as she hopped off the hood of Scott's Mustang and walked over to be enveloped in the boy's arms. His larger build seemed to absorb Becky's smaller, lithe size like she was hugging a life-sized teddy bear.

Yeah those two made a cute couple.

"Yeah well, that's what happens when your mom's a pig," Tony muttered as he lit a cigarette and blew the smoke out through his nostrils.

"I know, that would suck. I hate cops as it is, I can't imagine living with one!" Scott cried out, grabbing Becky and swinging her around in a circle.

"But we'll just have to have enough fun for Amy as well!" he continued twirling her, until they were both dizzy and Becky collapsed on the dirt with a cry. "Oommpph!"

The group's drunk laughter filled the night air, mingling with the music blaring out of the cars speakers. Scott helped Becky up, her hands wiping dirt from her legs and rear as she regained her balance. Megan watched the two come together, their mouths meeting as they kissed drunkenly yet passionately. Maybe those two would end up staying together after high school, Megan thought watching their hands explore each other feverishly, the bottle of whiskey sitting on the gravel beside them.

"There you go, get it Scott!" Tony chanted, pulling Megan closer to him as they watched the two make out in front of them. Megan could tell that the alcohol had loosened Becky up, the girl usually more timid when it came to such public actions. Of course, they were all pretty drunk by now, most of the whiskey Tony had opened now floating in each of their stomachs as they danced around the quarry. After a few minutes, Tony pulled her close and whispered, "What do you say we sneak off for a little bit?"

Megan knew where his mind was heading, and with how good she was feeling now, she wasn't about to argue, Not bothering to tell their friends where they were going, she took Tony's hand as he led them further from the car and into the darker corner of the lot. They passed around a large pile of gravel, and made their way into the tree line near the west end of the quarry. It was darker here, and feeling Tony's hot breath on her neck, her blood raced through her body, warming her even more. The anticipation of what was to come made her even hotter, her skin no longer feeling the cold as she slipped her jacket off and dropped it to the ground. They wound their way a little further from the car and their friends, the music being barely audible to them once they came to a stop.

"Wait, don't you think they might come looking for us?" Megan asked, taking a look behind her and seeing nothing but darkness covering the path they had taken.

Tony took her hands in his and pulled her against him, the warmth of his own body covering her as he ran his hands up and down the small of her back, feeling the goose-bumps rise on the skin underneath her thin shirt. He leaned back against one of the many old trees that surrounded the land the quarry was on, trying to slip his hands under Megan's shorts.

"Don't worry about it. They want privacy just as much as we do," he groaned, his hands grabbing onto her rear and pulling her tight against him. She could smell the mixture of vodka and whiskey on his breath as his mouth met hers and their tongues danced around together. He pushed his body against hers, bringing his hips tightly against her own and ground his pelvis around lightly. A soft moan escaped Megan's lips as she opened her eyes and pulled Tony tighter. Her arms were wrapped around his neck and her head was against his, the light prickles from the stubble of his mohawk tickling the side of her face. As they held together like this, Megan could feel the passion in her loins rising.

She wanted Tony right then and there, but wasn't sure she'd be able to. What if Scott and Becky came stumbling upon them in the heat of the moment? She'd just die! Then again, if she didn't keep going with what Tony had started, she might die either way.

Tony's mouth continued nuzzling against the soft flesh of her neck, lightly nipping at her throat as his hands continued exploring her body. Megan took a deep breath, exhaling slowly as she felt her head swim from the mixture of passion and alcohol.

Boy if her parents could see her now, she thought, picturing the shocked expressions on their faces if they were to see their daughter with this anti-government, teen punk, his pierced and tattooed body running against her own. The thought seemed to add to Megan's delight as Tony's tongue ran along her neck, eliciting a shock from her body.

Her eyes shot open and in that moment, the darkness of the woods around them, the tree they were leaning against, the soft music floating through the night air, and her body tight against his all seemed to mix together in an alcohol fueled vision, her breath coming out of her body and visibly warming the cold night air. Yes, this was perfect!

It was at that moment that she thought she saw movement out of the corner of her eye. She tried to turn her head but Tony was too busy holding her and planting kisses across her delicate clavicle. Twisting slightly in his grip, she heard Scott groan, obviously annoyed at her sudden movements and change of pace.

"Wait— wait, Tony I thought I saw—," she started to say, but Scott just kept up his oral attack on her neck, sucking her sweet flesh into his mouth and running the stud of his tongue up to her cheek. Megan suddenly caught sight of something further back in the woods, this time she was positive! "Scott!" she yelled, trying to push the boy off of here for a moment, his advances continuing to be persistent.

Finally Megan twisted out of his grip, Tony huffing loudly, "Ughh! What is with you?!" Megan just pulled away from him, bringing her finger up to her lip and attempting to quiet him. "Shush, I thought I saw something!"

Megan's eyes searched the darkness splayed out before them. The forest seemed dead silent, the always present chirping of crickets and nightlife absent, an eerie calm having settled over the woods. It was too dark to see very far, the trees forming a canopy that the moonlight couldn't seem to pierce. She had seen something, hadn't she?

Tiring of waiting, Tony reached out for her only to find her pull away from his reach again.

"Dammit Meg, what is your deal?" he asked, his mood quickly going dark as he pulled his cigarettes from his pocket. Muttering to himself he lit the end with his lighter and took a deep drag. As he breathed out, he heard a loud snap from somewhere behind them.

Megan's eyes widened and a chill swept through her body as she suddenly felt quite exposed out here in the woods. She thought back to where he jacket was, and realized she had dropped it as they had walked to their secluded spot. Now the cold night air was ever more present and she wished she hadn't tossed the coat aside.

"It's probably just Scott messing around!" Tony said, exhaling another stream of smoke into the air and leaning off the tree. "That you buddy boy?" he called out into the pitch black void.

"I don't think it was them, I thought I saw—" Megan began to say, her lips barely breathing the words.

"Thought you saw what? The boogeyman? Haha, yeah that's what it is, the boogeyman's come to scare us away so he can probably get down with his own girrrrlllll!" Tony shouted, the slur of his speech drowning out the last part of his rant.

Megan wished he would just be quiet. She couldn't see or hear anything with Tony acting like such a drunk ass. Then she heard another noise. This time it sounded like it was closer. A sickly snap of a branch or something cracked out from the forest depths.

"Tony, please..." Megan whined.

"Oh stop being such a baby— Scott is that you? Becky?" Tony yelled, stepping away from the tree and taking a few steps towards the source of the noise. Megan walked quickly up to him, dreading what could be out there, the primal fear of not knowing causing her blood to thicken and her skin to grow cold. At least Tony was there with her. He may not be much in the athletic department, but he would protect her from the unknown. Wouldn't he?

Maybe it is just Becky and Scott messing around! God I'll kill Becky!

Tony took another step towards the dark woods then stopped. He took another puff of his cigarette then turned towards Megan, a shrug raising his shoulders. Just then she did see movement off to the right, behind a series of trees about thirty yards away. It looked like a group of people running through the forest. That wasn't Scott and Becky then! Megan raised her arm to point, drawing Tony's attention back behind him and he glanced around the still forest, struggling to see what had got Megan so hyped up.

"Girl, I think your seeing things, how much did you have to drink?" he asked with a annoyed look crossing over his face.

"I swear to God, I saw something out there! It looked like it was a group of people running around!" Megan shouted, the strange feeling of being watched coming over her, and the hairs of the nape of her neck began tingling.

"Yeah right, it's the damn forest! You probably saw a squirrel or fox or something!"

Megan just stood there shaking, her arms wrapped tight under her breasts. She could feel her chest rising in quick, shallow breaths as her eyes scanned the darkness before her. She knew it hadn't been some small animal. It had been people. A group of at least four of them!

"I want to go back," she said, the shaking of her voice evident in her tone. Tony just looked at her with a mock look of surrender. Obviously the night wasn't turning out how he wanted it too.

"Fine, fine, we'll head back to the others!" he bitched, turning away from Megan and stalking off in the direction of the car and their friends. Megan hurriedly caught up to him, almost tripping at one point when a rush of intoxication flooded through her, her stomach churning ever so unbalanced. She reached out a hand to steady herself, the spinning of the woods taking a moment to stop, and at that moment they both heard the bloodcurdling scream.

Looking at each other with wide eyes, Tony and Megan heard a loud sound of something being broken apart from up ahead, and before they could do anything, a shape appeared in the darkness up ahead. Unable to move, Megan just stood there, her mouth open in silent horror as the image of Scott came stumbling into view. He looked lost and bewildered, his hair a mess, and his head swinging around wildly as he stumbled at them.

"What the hell?" Tony cried out as Scott almost collided into them, his mouth mumbling some incoherent nonsense that Megan couldn't discern over Tony's hysterics. When he turned to look at her, his eyes catching onto Megan's, she saw right then and there the most terrified look she had ever seen deep in those hazel orbs.

Scott reached out and grabbed hold of Tony's arm, mumbling something that sounded like 'Becky'. Becky? Where was Becky? Megan suddenly realized her friend hadn't arrived with Scott and that before the boy had come running out of the darkness, both her and Tony had heard a terrible scream.

"Oh my God!" Tony suddenly cried out, backing away from Scott as the boy dropped onto the ground, his arm clutching tightly to his stomach. That's when Megan saw the dark, crimson stain that was seeping through the young football player's shirt. Scott's head lolled to the side, his breath coming out in gasps as he writhed around on the ground, reaching out and trying to grab anything with his free left hand. Blood continued to seep from his stomach and Megan watched as the ground began to run red with the liquid.

Dear Lord! What in the hell?

Megan stood there paralyzed. She didn't know what to do as Tony, seemed to be about to pass out from shock. He was dancing about, looking back and forth from down at his friend's dying body to the blood that were now covering his own hands. Then Scott's ramblings seemed to halt and he took a deep breath. Coughing violently, blood seeped up from his throat, gurgling up and out the sides of his mouth like overflowing creek.

His eyes began to roll back into his head as his swinging arm finally caught hold of Megan's wrist. With a painful effort he pulled her down to her knees beside him. Megan could feel the tears welling in her eyes and begin to fall across her cheeks as she looked at the sight forever seared into her memory.

Scott turned his head towards her and with one last gasp, blood pouring freely from his stomach and draining across the rocky ground, muttered, "run!"

Megan and Tony both looked at each other, blood smeared over their arms and clothes as a loud snap erupted from behind them. Tony didn't have time to turn his head and look, but the fear he saw in Megan's own eyes was enough to let him know they were both about to die!

Chapter 8

    Aidan Preston awoke the following morning like he had after most of the nights he suffered through over the last few months. Sleep was scarce, but every night it was the same. He would awake with the covers of his bed thrown off him, his body covered in a sheen of sweat that caused the crumpled sheets to stick to him as he stared around the dark bedroom, attempting to gain his bearings.

    It was always the same with the recurring nightmare he had been having. His doctor told them that as he neared full recovery the memories would hopefully begin to abate, but so far there didn't seem to be any sign of them letting up. He was just going to have to power through it like usual.

    Reaching out to the nightstand, he found the lamp's knob and clicked it on, sending a soft glow of light across the room. His eyes took in the setting, the barely furnished room with bed and nightstand in one corner and a dresser with his various keepsakes crowding the surface.

    There was a framed picture of him, taken years before that showed his father and him standing in the foreground, a banquet taking place in the background all from an age long ago. The photo was ten years old, collecting dust as it sat on the dresser top and reminding Aidan of how life used to be. His father had been so proud of him that day. It was when he had been promoted to Detective First Class with the Montgomery County Police Department, and like his father before him had joined the ranks of the Homicide Division. It had been a truly special day, and Aidan remembered it was one of the only times he had ever seen his father shed a tear.

    The only other moment in his life that he could remember that had choked the old man up so was when his wife, Aidan's mother had been killed. She had been an innocent bystander, out shopping for the week's groceries when a man had attempted to rob the store she was visiting. The cashier hadn't wanted to give over the money they man had demanded, and three unarmed people had lost their lives due to the event. That was the day Aidan had decided he wanted to follow his father into a career in law enforcement. He felt he had to right the wrongs that were done that day, and work hard to make sure no one ever felt the loss he himself had been witness too.

    Of course it wasn't just murders that Aidan was responsible for, but a whole slew of crimes that were investigated by his division. Everything from vandalism and car jackings to armed robbery and domestic abuse fell into the folds of his job description.

At first he had enjoyed the work. The long hours and constant attention put into the cases as they were worked from beginning to end. The only problem was it was still a job. Sure there were good times that usually outweighed the bad, but eventually it all just began to feel overwhelming. Like no matter how hard you worked, there were still plenty of people out on the streets ready to stick up their neighbor, or mug the store down on the corner just for a couple bucks to go towards their next 'high'.

No matter how hard you strove to keep the streets clean and clear for all the honest, law abiding citizens out there going about their day, there always seemed to be those other levels of society that worked just as hard to bring it all down.

It was this constant up and down of memories and contradicting feelings of making a difference that had led to Aidan letting his guard down bringing him to this point in his life. Sitting quietly in the semi-dark bedroom, the soft tick of the alarm clock on the nightstand the only sound other than Aidan's breathing that could be heard; he realized he didn't know how much longer he could keep this up.

Weary from the lack of a restful night's sleep, he slid his legs off the bed and sat on the edge for a moment, the sheets completely off him as he reached up with his left hand and touched the scar that ran along his upper chest. It was a thick and ugly memento, having healed unevenly and still causing him to experience pain every so often. Whether the pain was real or not was something constantly in debate whenever he would see his doctor, but the side effects were certainly present along with the memories.

Aidan shook the drowsiness from his head, stretched his neck and then stood up. He felt the worn carpet under his bare feet as he stepped across the room and to the dresser. Pulling the top drawer open, he reached inside and removed a prescription bottle from behind a pair of socks. Twisting the cap off, he shook out two of the white caplets and tossed them into his mouth. Walking out of the bedroom and into the small bathroom off the main hall, he ducked his head under the sink and ran a splash of cold water into his mouth.

Taking a long sip, he threw his head back and swallowed the pills. After feeling the caplets run down his throat and disappear into his stomach, he turned the water off on the sink and stared at the image reflecting back at him. Need to shave, he thought as he looked at the dark circles under his eyes, No, I need a vacation. As he realized he was having an inner dialog with himself he laughed. Yeah right a vacation from what? You've been on administrative leave from work for months now. What do you need a vacation from? Yourself?

Standing there, looking at his features in the mirror, he reached out to grasp the sink with both hands and lowered his head in disgust.

What the hell happened to me?

Aidan didn't want to think of the answer to that question right now. It was already working its way constantly behind the scenes and he didn't need to face it this morning. That's what a shrink is for! A shrink that he had to go see this morning for the department. This day was not looking like it was going to get any better.

Turning the faucet back on and making sure it was cold, Aidan grabbed a handful of water and splashed it onto his face. The sharp cold temperature of the water stung slightly as he ran his hands over his face, then turning the sink off again and wiping his wet hands dry on his shorts, left the bathroom.

Taking a look at the clock hanging in the kitchen as Aidan entered, he noticed he only had half an hour to get to his doctor's appointment. With as much as psychiatrists charged by the hour, he wasn't planning on being late. Even though while currently on leave the MCPD provided him with a county shrink, he preferred discussing his issues with someone not affiliated with the department. No matter how private and confidential the topics brought up with a psychiatrist were, when they were ultimately being paid by the county, and the county had to be sure you were mentally fit enough to return to active duty, Aidan knew that certain things could be revealed to the powers that be. He had enough riding on his past that worried him about clearing the medical review, and he sure as hell wasn't going to lose out on being reinstated because he saw the wrong meaning in a picture with ink splattered all over it!

Slipping a pair of worn jeans over his legs and tightening his belt, he pulled a t-shirt from his dresser and threw it over his head. Not bothering with taking the time to shave the dark shadow of beard that had appeared on his face over the last two days, he tossed a pair of shoes on and then went to his closet for his leather jacket. Once dressed, he scooped his ID, wallet, and car keys off the dresser and headed out the door. He'd grab some coffee on the way so as not to be late for his visit to Dr. Harper's office.

"So how has your week been Aidan?" Dr. Steven Harper PhD, asked as Aidan sat on the same worn sofa in the modern, yet welcoming office that he had grown used to visiting weekly over the last couple months. The room was carefully decorated, allowing a little peek into what Aidan assumed were the expensive yet tasteful eccentricities of someone in living and cavorting in Harper's wealthy circle. While some psychiatrists offices seemed to remain bland and uninspired, possibly to make every patient feel welcomed and at home in the safety of this inner sanctum, Dr. Steven Harper let his own fascinating collection of curious decor and items spaced around the room create a glimpse of the man's own mind.

The floor was a polished, stained hardwood with the center covered by a beautifully and intricate Persian rug. The dark green chair, its cushions wrapped in a worn leather that was a testament to how many people had come before and would still come hopefully long after Aidan had left the good doctor's care. Meanwhile, a low coffee table the color of deep red that almost appeared black under the lamp light radiating from all corners of the room was sitting before the chair.

Across from that was Dr. Harper's own dark shaded chair. It was large and plush looking, the softness of the frame seeming to allow the man to sink slightly into its covers. Aside from the rich, dark colors of the floor and furniture, the walls were an eggshell white that seemed to stand in stark contrast to the rest of the feel of the office. Then of course there were the various trinkets displayed on a shelf against one corner and on the top of the wood desk that was off to one side. Dr. Steven Harper seemed to have an interest in old aboriginal art.

Lining a small, recessed shelf above the doctor's desk and on the corner of the neatly kept table was pottery. The old, ceramic pots and bowls were each carefully crafted by some artisan and culture unknown to Aidan, but appeared to be African or possibly Native American influenced. While none were exactly the same, the patterns and pictures carved or painted onto their surfaces were reminiscent of an ancient, simpler time.

The most prized of the pots seemed to be the ones sitting on the shelves lining the walls, but there was also a bookcase set against the opposite wall where the closed office door was that had other pieces displayed on it. Most of the books on the shelves were what Aidan assumed would be in a psychiatrist's collection. Tomes on psychotherapy, PTSD, the human mind and many more books referring to the subject of analyzing various issues filled the levels, but there were also a few catalogs that touched on the doctor's obvious love for this antique pottery.

"Has your sleep improved since the last time we talked?" Dr. Harper's deep baritone of a voice asked as he studied Aidan from his chair. His fingertips were tented together and barely touching his lips as he sat back and watched his patient with cool, attentive eyes. His whole attitude was relaxed, like a man about to slip into a deep sleep or state of meditation, yet he was alert and listened to everything Aidan said.

"To tell you the truth it hasn't. I tried taking the pills you recommended an hour before bed, but so far no luck actually getting past the dreams and having anything I'd call a rest full night's sleep." Aidan said, shifting slightly in the chair until he found a more comfortable position to sit.

Dr. Harper studied his movements, the restlessness of his actions. Aidan felt like a bug being examined under a high-powered microscope. Except it wasn't just some random person doing the studying, but a man who had the power to allow him to return to his place on the police force, or keep him under observation as the administrative leave dragged on for who knew how long.

Yeah he had his share of problems, and ever since coming to this man, he had opened up more of his soul than he would have liked, but what right did he have to keep him from the work he was born to do. His father had been a homicide detective, and his grandfather had been on the force for 28 years before retiring, long before Aidan was even a twinkle in his father's eye, so what qualified this man with his many degrees from places like Cornell and Harvard to be the sole barrier between him and his life. Sure things had taken a sharp turn almost a year ago and Aidan had been forced into an unthinkable situation, almost losing his life in the process, but he was healed dammit! That had been almost a year ago and he had the scar forever decorating his skin to remind him of that event.

So why did he have to relive it constantly with this man in his expensive office and colorful pots!

It's because of the dreams! Aidan heard his mind yelling. That's why you aren't ready to move on to the next step, because you can't close your eyes at night without seeing HER face!

Aidan knew from past talks with Dr. Harper that most police officers deal with both the routine and exceptional stresses faced in their jobs by using a variety of situational adaptive coping and defense mechanisms, such as repression, displacement, isolation of feelings, crass humor and generally toughing it out. He had learned that in the United States, two-thirds of officers involved in shootings suffer moderate or severe problems and about 70 percent leave the force within seven years of the incident. Police officers are admitted to hospitals at significantly higher rates than the general population and rank third in occupations in premature death rates.

He could recall Dr. Harper's voice telling him that, 'Moreover, the sheer magnitude and shock effect of many murder scenes, and the violence, mutilation, and sadistic brutality associated with many serial killers, especially if they involve children, often overwhelm the defense mechanisms and coping abilities of even the most seasoned officers.'

So what if 70 percent leave within seven years? He didn't care about seven years from now, he cared about now, today even. All he had to do was clear the mental health evaluation the department required of him to pass and he could be back out there on the streets, gun on his hip and badge hanging from his chest, protecting the public and doing his civil service. The service he was born to do. Yet, he knew he wasn't ready to be released into society just yet.

Working with Dr. Harper over the last few months it had been clear to Aidan which form of 'adaptive coping' he employed in his attempt to deal with the events of this past year. He had thought he could repress everything enough to just tough it out, but the dreams wouldn't let him!

"So tell me about the dreams?" Dr. Harper asked.

The dreams? He really wants to know about the dreams? Aidan took a moment to stare into the searching, intelligent gaze of the man across from him. Well if anyone could possibly hope of helping him understand the recurring nightmare his mind seemed plagued with nightly it would be Dr. Harper. Taking a deep breath and then exhaling, Aidan leaned forward in his seat, placed his hands on his knees and began telling his doctor about the dreams.

"It starts out the same way every time. I'm standing outside of a building. It's dark, yet the sky seems to have an iridescent, ethereal glow to it. Like it's alive almost. Anyways, I'm outside of this building, this warehouse that seems to stretch for miles on either side. Like it has no beginning and no end. It is just there. And so is the door," Aidan said, his voice low and his eyes staring at the hands he braced on his knees, his mind slowly remembering every detail of the dreaded nightmare from memory. As he continued speaking, he closed his eyes imagining every detail as he came about it.

"The door isn't so much a door as it is a mouth. An entranceway to some deep, dark forgotten place, a place filled with the unknown. And even though I don't know what's inside, for some reason I know that it is filled with pain. Pain and evil!"

Dr. Harper sat there, his fingers never moving from his lips as he just sat perfectly still in his large throne-like chair, absorbing everything Aidan had to say.

"So I'm standing before this door, this dark portal to some level of what I can only assume is hell and that's when I hear the crying. It's faint and calling to me from inside this darkness. It's begging for help. Help that I want to provide if only I know what I need to do, but I don't know what I have to do. In fact, at first I can't even get through the door. The more I try, the more it seems to distance itself from me. Like a tunnel with me at one end and this door at the other, but no matter how hard or fast I run I don't seem to get any closer to reaching it. It's frustrating, and the entire time the voice continues to call to me, wailing and begging for help, for salvation, but I can do nothing! Nothing!"

Aidan stopped talking for a moment, opened his eyes and realized that his hands were clenched, the grip just above the knees restricting the blood flow to his legs he was pressing so hard. He tried to breathe and found that with his eyes now open and the memory of the dream not as vivid that his breathing was beginning to normalize.

Jesus what was wrong with him? It was morning and he was sitting in Dr. Harper's office, yet recalling the dream that had been visiting him every night for the past few months he had felt almost like he had been transported away from this place. Like his mind had transferred to this unreal, ethereal realm while his body remained in the old, worn leather chair of his psychiatrist's office.

Yes, that is where I am. I am in Dr. Steven Harper's office. I am not standing before an endless warehouse with a door that seems like a portal to the underworld!

Slowly his breathing began to return to normal, the tightness that had begun to form in his chest began to loosen.

Yes, I am sitting here in a simple doctor's office. Just sitting and talking. That's it. That's it.

"Aidan?" Dr. Harper's voice called out to him, yet it seemed like it was far away. It wasn't as loud as it would be if it had come from the man sitting only four feet away from him. Suddenly Aidan looked up startled.

"What?" he asked. His eyes wide, Aidan reached up to his forehead and found a thin layer of perspiration coating his skin. He rubbed his fingers together, feeling the sweaty moisture between the skin of his thumb and finger. When he realized he was staring, his eyes transfixed on his fingers rubbing back and forth against each other, he realized also that Dr. Harper was talking to him. There was a look of concern that had changed the doctor's stoic, calm demeanor into that of worry.

"Aidan, are you alright?" Dr. Harper asked, sitting forward and placing his hand on Aidan's shoulder. Aidan's eyes jerked up to meet with Harper's. His cool gaze having turned to a look of turmoil.

"I'm...I'm...fine," Aidan finally mumbled, suddenly alert and aware of exactly where he was and why he was there.

"Yes, I'm fine," he repeated, more to himself than to the psychiatrist.

Dr. Harper reached towards the table and picking up a pitcher and plastic cup, he poured a glass of water for Aidan. Aidan took the cup he was offered and quickly downed every last drop. He hadn't realized how thirsty he was and how parched his throat had become until the cold, refreshing liquid was down gone and he allowed the doctor to refill his cup. Drinking the refill a little slower, Aidan watched as Dr. Harper's face resumed some of its normal characteristics and then set the empty cup onto the table.

"How are you feeling?" Dr. Harper asked.

"Better. Much better."

"Good. Listen Aidan, it seems to me that we might not have been taking care of these dreams you've been having as well as I hoped. Over our last few sessions I had believed that I was able to gauge the effect the incident that brought you to me was being handled. Unfortunately I don't think that is the case."

"Wait a minute doc..." Aidan began to say but Dr. Harper raised his hand up and cut him off.

"No, please let me finish," he said, waiting a moment to make sure Aidan was going to allow him to proceed. With a nod for approval Dr. Harper continued.

"It seems that even all the work we have done over the last few months, deep down you are still fighting your inner demons. You are continuing to struggle with the decisions you made and the consequences that followed. Until you are able to face those cold hard facts and learn not to repress them but instead to face them, you will not be able to get to the meaning of this dream and overcome the obstacles that have arisen.

'The dimensions of the building, the description of the door, the inability to reach it and the cries of pain and torture are all symbolic to you in those forms as a metaphor of sorts that keeps you from obtaining complete closure to your past. Everything you witness in these dreams you've been having can be taken apart piece by piece and analyzed into all sorts of answers, but it is all really portraying one simple issue."

"And what is that?" Aidan asked, watching the psychiatrist take a moment before answering.

"Hopelessness."

"Hopelessness?" Aidan repeated, turning the statement into a question.

"Yes, hopelessness."

What the hell is this guy talking about? What does any of that have to do with what happened to put me on leave, or the hospital or to these weekly sessions?

"I can tell by the look on your face that you are not following." Dr. Harper stated.

"I'm just trying to see the connection."

"The connection is simple. Ever present when you understand what it is that is fueling these dreams."

"Which is?"

"That you are a trusted public servant. You have sworn to uphold the law and protect your community. However, the night you responded to that call that led to everything else, you were left with the sense that you could have done something different and that is what gives you this feeling of hopelessness. While there may or may not have been a variety of different things that could have been different, a million possibilities that could have played out that night, there was only one way that it did happen.

The pieces that fit together to create the happenings of that night have already passed. The incident went the way it did, and there is nothing you can do to change that. It is the past, and you can only alter the future since it has not taken place yet. Because you have no control you feel hopeless. Hopeless that you didn't do something differently and hopeless that the outcome is what it is."

Aidan sat there listening to Dr. Harper explain his interpretation of the dream. Could it really all be that simple? Could the incident be the connection between the dream and everything else going on in his head? As the psychiatrist kept talking, Aidan thought back to that fateful night almost a year prior to today.

The night had started out like any other. He was working Homicide and was responding to a scene where there was a report of shots fired. The responding officer had shown up at an apartment complex in one of the slums scattered throughout the county. It was a rundown, low-income housing development where all sorts of police issues were always being sent out to investigate. Everything from domestic abuse and kids selling dope, to home invasions and murder.

When he had first arrived, the rookie officer had attempted to control the scene but had failed to secure it first. Upon entering the apartment where the call had been sent to, Aidan had discovered the body of a woman that had been shot multiple times in the chest. Her dirty, lifeless form laying in a pool of her own blood. It ended up that her boyfriend and her had gotten into an argument and he had killed her. What Aidan didn't know was that the rookie officer that was still downstairs trying to keep the onlookers back, he had not located the boyfriend or the gun yet.

It just so happened that the boyfriend was hiding in one of the tiny closets the apartment had. He was armed and he also had his seven year old daughter by the throat. The girl was terrified, tears streaming down her cheeks as she she had seen her mother's corpse and all the blood everywhere. Aidan had raised his gun the moment the perpetrator had exited the closet, but using the girl as a shield, the boyfriend ordered Aidan to leave. He was strung out, his eyes darting back and forth wildly, and the gun he held in his hand was shaking as the barrel was pressed against the girl's temple. Aidan tried to reason with the man but he was not listening. Thinking that he could take the guy out if he just had the right opportunity, he kept his weapon trained on the man and his innocent, human shield.

When the man had finally provided Aidan with a clear target, he fired twice sending a bullet into the assailants chest and head. The power of the rounds and the closeness of the subject sent the the man flying backwards, blood splattering the walls and floor. Unfortunately just when he thought it was over, the man's gun had dropped to the floor and a round had discharged.

That bullet, a freak accident that Aidan should have been prepared for or not risked opening fire, hit the little seven year old girl and paralyzed her for life. She was doomed to live out the rest of her life in a wheelchair all thanks to Detective Aidan Preston. That was something he would never be able to forgive himself for. Because of him a little girl had been crippled and it was all his fault.

Chapter 9

Nick Haley had watched the copy of the video Mike had given him at least twice. He couldn't help not looking at the gruesome footage, even though it repulsed him. He could feel his stomach was still knotted up the way it had the first time he played through the footage. He had hoped the second time would be better, that he'd be used to what he had seen and that his nerves might loosen up. However they hadn't and his stomach still felt like it had been torqued out of alignment.

What kind of a person could do something like that to someone? It just wasn't right.

Pushing the rewind button on his VCR, he heard the machine hum lightly as he sat back into the chair he had set before the television setup. Wanting to get to work on any leads he could gather right away, he had decided to stop at the first place he could to watch the unedited footage that News Channel 5 had recorded. Running a hand through his messy, long hair, he placed his hands on his knees and stared at the television screen, attempting to think of what to do next.

He had already had to waste part of the morning running back to Channel 5's building to pick up the copy of the tape Mike had made him. He couldn't get it the day before because the watchdog of a boss that the cameraman had to deal with had walked in on their impromptu meeting. Fortunately, Nick had been quick enough with an excuse about just happening by the station to meet his friend for lunch to keep the floor director from becoming suspicious. The pizza box being preset had helped, and Nick knew the wiry, weasel looking man that Mike had referred to as Don probably wouldn't investigate further.

Nick's only saving grace was that unlike television, his face was unrecognizable. A person couldn't tie his face to that of him being the journalist responsible for the Crime column over at The Informant. Thankfully, Don had just given Nick a stern look and yelled at Mike about paying attention to the Network's rules about visitors in the building. Having escaped that scene relatively unscathed, Nick had decided to wait until the next morning to retrieve the tape.

After picking up a copy of the unedited shots Mike had filmed and a copy of the broadcasted version he had stopped at a bar that a buddy of his owned to borrow the office and use their old TV equipment. He could have gone home or to the office, but the small pub was just down the street from Channel 5's building, so he had opted to head there instead. The tape's progression slowed and then there was a click as the tape finished rewinding and ejected from the machine. Pulling it out, he taped the edge against the palm of his hand repeatedly as he let his mind slip into its brainstorming mode.

He needed to find out what he could about the victim and get his story written before Ted Hanson could run another piece on the 6 o'clock news. Last night he had caught the segment when he had gotten home from interviewing a few other sources for his article. Now having watched the tape again, Nick stood up and walked over to the desk in his friend's office. Thankfully the owner/bar tender, Bohdan Chaplinsky, a friend from his college days, had been busy taking care of some things and had been able to leave his managerial office in Nick's hands.

Commandeering the desk and office, he had spread his notes out onto the top of the table, his eyes wandering across them as he tried to think of where the witness' statements, the video footage from the scene of the crime and the little bit of information he had been able to collect from a friend inside the police force were pointing him towards.

So far he still had to get copy into Marty by closing time for it to appear in tomorrow's edition. The only problem was he still didn't have much to go on. Thinking about everything that was laid out before him, his eyes took it all in and then he began thinking harder. There was something here, staring up at him from his jumble of notes and interviews, but for some reason he wasn't seeing it. What was he missing? He wondered to himself, his fingers beginning to drum rapidly on the desk top. Just then his cell phone rang. Pulling it out from his work bag slung over the office chair he checked the caller ID. It was a local call but he didn't recognize the number. Flipping the phone open he placed the device to his ear.

"Nick Haley," he answered.

"Is this the reporter?" the hushed female voice asked. Nick didn't recognize the voice, but replied anyways. In his line of work important information or news could come from anywhere, and that was one reason The Informant was quick to give out his cell number to anyone that contacted the paper and inquired about it.

"Yes, I am a reporter with The Informant. How can I help you?"

"My name is Katherine Childs and I work for the Rockville City Police. I had caught the news last night about that woman who was found murdered in the park, and then this morning I saw your article briefly mentioning it."

Nick knew exactly what she was talking about. He had gotten a short piece into Marty late yesterday afternoon to run in this morning's paper, but unfortunately without much to go on, it had really been a vague and poorly rushed article. What did Marty expect when he rushed him to get something, anything in by the end of the day. Only having visited Mike for that brief interlude the day before and working off the interviews he had conducted with the neighbors he could find home around the Croydon Park pump house, he had written a broad account of the few remaining facts he had. Hopefully once he had more to go on, he'd be able to write something worthy of his talents. He just needed to get to the bottom of the story, and this new caller might just be able to help him do that.

"Yes I did have a short article in the paper this morning. You mentioned you work for the police department?"

There was a slight hesitation before Nick heard Ms. Childs voice over the line.

"Well yes, now you don't have to put my name into the paper or anything right? I can remain anonymous so I don't get into trouble?" she asked, the small bit of worry in her voice piquing Nick's attention.

It was the same drill all the time. Someone comes forward with information and worried about getting into trouble or fired isn't sure if they are doing the right thing by going to a reporter with their information. Nick however, wasn't about to let this woman get away. She could be the lead he had been looking for, the source to guide his article in the right direction and get his editor Marty off his back.

"Of course. I can quote you as a source inside the police department. No names ever need to be used, and no one can give you a hard time for aiding the public by informing them of what is happening in their backyard and in searching for the truth."

The hesitation in Katherine Childs' voice seemed to dissipate after hearing that, as it did with most sources Nick was used to handling in his quest for a story. "Okay good," she stated.

"So why don't you help me out and start at the beginning for why you called," Nick suggested, the phone tight to his ear as he pulled the chair up and sat down at the desk. Pushing aside a few notes he had, he reached into his satchel and withdrew a small notebook and pen. Flipping the book open to a blank page he hunched over the writing surface and let the woman continue, hopefully to answer the question itching at the back of his mind of what she had to do with the investigation and how good this lead was going to be.

"Like I said before, I called because I had seen the news last night after I got home from work and then this morning when I read your article in the paper. I called the paper's phone number listed online and they gave me this number. Anyways, I already mentioned I work for the Rockville City Police…"

"And what do you do for the department?" Nick interjected, quickly jotting down notes as he listened.

"I work the dispatch board, taking the emergency calls, logging them and routing them out to the appropriate response teams and services. Well yesterday I was working my board when the first call came in. There are usually two of us who handle all the calls coming in for help during our shift, and since I was taking a call from a store owner who had reported a case of some teenagers vandalizing one of his store's windows, Debbie Robinson, the other woman working at the time fielded the call for the East Rockville call.

'A man, near hysterical had called 911 and she sent the first responding officer out to the park. Since we are in constant contact with all the emergency services teams over the radio, we get pretty involved in the different calls. Since it started out as a slow day, once I had finished sending a uniformed unit over to Marlo's Eatery to handle the broken storefront window and the teenagers who were fighting with the owner, I didn't have another call to distract me from listening to Debbie work. Just like the reported on the news yesterday, it was a terrible tragedy. That poor woman's body being mutilated like that!"

Nick continued scribbling, his quick notes recognizable only to himself as he wrote down everything pertinent that Katherine Childs was saying.

"I hope they catch the sick bastards that did this!" she was saying, the unease in her voice quite evident.

"You said 'bastards' as in plural? Are the officers investigating thinking that there may have been more than one perpetrator?" Nick asked. Now he was getting somewhere! Looking at the half page of notes he had written, he kept his pen poised and ready to keep taking down everything this woman had to say.

"Well yes. From everything Debbie and I could hear it sounded like the detective in charge of the scene believes there was more than one assailant."

This was perfect! Now he had something to write, and if what this woman was giving him was as golden as it sounded, he would definitely be ahead of Ted Hanson and Channel 5's reporting, securing The Informant and himself into the people's minds when they thought of their source of media coverage regarding the murder. Thank the heavens!

"Do you know who was in charge of the scene?" Nick asked, the contempt smile forming on his face widening as he wrote.

"Detective Garza was the one issuing most of the orders yesterday. He was the one in command and he was the one calling in over the radio for the different responding units and technicians. We obviously record every call and radio transmission that comes in through the City Dispatch, and when I listened to it this morning looking to get some answers for myself I was able to look at the typed transcripts and Garza was definitely in charge down there."

"Is there anything else you can think of regarding what the police are looking at doing to solve this murder?"

There was silence for a moment on the line as the Rockville City Police Dispatcher was obviously thinking about what she could and couldn't reveal about an active police investigation. Finally she spoke.

"Well I know that even though the murder took place in the city limits, because of the nature of the crime involved, it's really the Montgomery County Police Department who is running things. It's their investigation, but to avoid any jurisdiction issues and to not appear to be stepping on anyone's toes, they are allowing our department to pursue the active investigation, providing assistance when needed since they have wider resources than we do here at the Rockville City Police. And like I said, they don't think the woman was killed by the just one crazy lunatic, but possibly multiple unknown subjects." Katherine Childs paused for a moment, then saying in a quieter tone, "Look I have to get off the phone. I left the dispatch board with the excuse of going to the ladies room to call. I have to get back to work before anybody realizes I'm gone."

"Can I contact you later if I have any other questions regarding this story? I appreciate everything you've been able to provide, and thank you for realizing the public has a right to know what is going on," Nick asked.

He listened to the woman hesitate again, obviously worried that she might get in trouble for everything she had already told him, and quickly gave him the number to her home phone. She told him that he could call her after work and she would see what else she could dig up. Thanking her again for taking the time and risking the trouble her call could have caused her, he wrote her number down and promised her he would call later this evening once she was home from the office and alone.

Once the call had ended, he laid his phone down on the desk, his hands picking up the notebook as he reread his notes, committing everything to memory as he began planning out his next move. This story was definitely turning into something more than a simple murder.

The horrendous violence afflicted to the victim that he had witnessed on the tape was evidence of that. Add to the footage the information that the police thought there could be more than one person responsible for the sick mutilation this poor woman experienced and he was looking at a story that could really rock The Informant's readers to the core, get Marty to possibly give him the leeway he needed to expand his writing choices, and to show the public just how in depth his own journalistic endeavors could be.

But first, he had to look into a few more things for clarification. Was there some disturbed group haunting the streets of Rockville, looking for other victims to express their sick fantasies? Was the general public in danger? Who were these dark perpetrators that had prayed on a weak, innocent life, and would they strike again? Yes this was definitely a story that could get him somewhere in his recently less than stellar career, and he, Nick Haley of The Informant wasn't going to let some other journalist beat him to the finish line. This was his story and he now knew exactly what he had to do.

Pulitzer Prize here I come! Nick thought, collecting his notes and the video tapes and stuffing them into his work bag. He shoved his phone into his pocket and slipped the shoulder strap of his satchel over his arm. It was time to get this story moving, and he knew just where to start.

- -

Detective Andrea Wilkes' morning had been pretty hectic. After waking up she had to wait to get ready for work until her daughter Amy had finished getting ready for school, taking over an hour to shower, dress and apply her makeup. That was the price she paid for only having one bathroom in the small town house her and her two children called home.

Hopefully if everything went well during her next performance review, she just might get that raise she had been looking forward to and could start looking for somewhere other than the ever rising costs of Montgomery Village to live. However, until then they would just have to manage with the tiny, three bedroom one bathroom townhouse. At least Jeremy didn't take as long as his sister in the mornings.

Once she had got going for the day, eating a small breakfast and two cups of coffee, Andrea had headed into the office. She arrived a little bit before the other detectives in the Homicide Division, and sitting at her desk began to pour her attention into her the day's work.

This week had been a busy one for her. She had two domestic disturbance calls she had to follow up on in two different parts of the county, a case of armed robbery that had appeared to be open and shut but upon closer examination seemed to be not as simple as it first appeared and now the murder that the Rockville Police were heading up and her boss Chief Stone had told her to give them whatever assistance they needed. As if she didn't have enough on her plate with everything she was already handling.

Looking at a folder that she had opened before her, she skimmed the pages of the police report for the armed robbery incident. Abdul Parzian, a forty three year old immigrant that had moved to the United States about two years before and opened a small, delicatessen was working last week during the lunch hour, serving his usual 'Thursday Special' of chicken with green curry to a couple customers over the last hour. The deli's usual clientele was a mix of Indian and other Middle Eastern cultures that frequented the store on a daily basis.

However, at 2:15 p.m., that Thursday, a white male, aged approximately in his late teens entered the deli and approached the counter. Thinking nothing of the hooded individual and assuming he was just another customer coming to order, Abdul Parzian had appeared at the counter, his usual smile etched onto his face, and asked the man what he would like. At that instant, the youth pulled a large hunting knife from the waistband of his pants and jumping the counter of the deli, forced Abdul to hand over all the cash in the register.

To make matters worse, the deli's other patrons were completely unaware of the threat happening twenty feet from them and never got a good look at the perpetrator. With cash in hand, the young, white male dashed out of the deli and disappeared down the street. Video surveillance footage from the store across the street would have provided Andrea a perfect image of the escaping criminal's face had it not been out of order for the last month due to a faulty wire. It was just her luck that it wasn't going to be as simple of a case as she had hoped.

Reading through the store owner's description of the robbery and what he could remember of the young man's face, she also began looking for similar crimes where the perpetrator's description matched that of this case. Chances were that this wasn't his first time committing a crime. While she didn't have much to go on, she had still compiled all the latest robbery and drug related incidents together and was working her way through each file. She had a feeling that the motivation behind the robbery probably had to do with drugs. That was the unfortunate and most likely scenario that fit into the circle of events. Most than likely the offender was an addict who because of his addiction was forced to steal from his fellow man just to make ends meet and score his next 'high'. It was a sad world when so many people's lives were affected by something as ruining as drugs.

The worst part to Andrea was that it wasn't the illegal drugs that were having such a devastating effect on society but the medications being prescribed by doctors to deal with pain and other diseases. Andrea was glad that her own daughter Amy hadn't seemed to have gotten mixed up in that.

Her sweet 17 year old girl: still a baby in her eyes. That was a path she was not ready to go down with so much already on her plate as a single mother. That thought led into Andrea remembering the message her ex had left on the answering machine the night before. That was a whole other issue she did not need right now. When Robert had walked out on her and their kids years ago, Andrea didn't know how she was going to survive, but survive she had. It had taken a bit of time and more than a few bottles of wine over the first few months, but Amy, Jeremy and her had pulled through, and she was not going to let their deadbeat dad Robert ruin the progress they had made by trying to step back into their lives now.

Over my dead body, Robert Carl Wilkes! Andrea thought, pushing the image of her kids deadbeat father out of her mind. Looking back on it now, she couldn't believe that their marriage had lasted as long as it had. She kept telling herself that the only reason after their initial attraction that kept them married had been the birth of their kids. Amy had been expected, Robert and her in that early stage of love and marriage where there thoughts kept turning to starting a family.

It was the American way that that early infatuation brought upon people as they readied to move into after first becoming engaged. Children were just the first step towards completing the picture, yet there had been issues appearing in the relationship shortly after the honeymoon period had worn off. Andrea was a cop and her job came with not only its share of stress but danger as well. Robert's job at a local construction company wasn't paying enough to provide the ability for Andrea to quit her job and raise a newborn baby. That and she didn't want to quit her job. She loved being a cop.

Sure times were hard back then, but they made them work. They were young and 'in love' and had a family now. Then Andrea found out that Robert was cheating on her behind her back. Through counseling they were able to hold everything together at least for Amy's sake. Then as things continued to slide down hill she found herself unexpectedly pregnant again, this time with Jeremy. Robert didn't want her to keep the baby when he found out, but Andrea was not going to extinguish the life they had created. They continued to stick it out through the pregnancy and by the time Jeremy was born, Andrea thought things might be getting better.

Robert had gotten a promotion at work and was now the foreman of a large construction project, and it looked like they might be able to move from the one bedroom apartment they were renting and into a townhouse. But those were just fantasies! That was when Andrea found out about Robert's latest affair. She was devastated and knew she would never be able to forgive him and take him back. It didn't matter that she had two young children and had a full time job with no other family around to help her in her time of need. Andrea made it work, for her kids she would do anything!

Thinking of Amy and Jeremy and all the struggles they had overcome together, Andrea found a smile stretch the corners of her lips up from their hardened, stern concentration. That's when she realized her phone was vibrating on her desk underneath one of the case folders she had been looking through.

She completely forgot to turn the ringer back on when she had got back from the records room. Moving the folder aside, she saw that she had two new voice messages and a list of missed calls. What the hell? Who could be trying to reach her over and over? What could be wrong? Andrea picked up the phone and scrolled through the list of missed calls. They were all from her daughter Amy.

Why would she be trying so hard to reach her? What could have be so important? With her thoughts centered on the bad feeling she was experiencing for her daughter's wellbeing, Andrea ignored taking the time to check her voice messages and dialed her daughter's cell phone directly. After two short rings Amy answered, her voice hollow and the hitch in her throat a tell-tale sign she had been crying.

"He— hello?" Amy said through tears. "Mom— mom, oh my God, mom!"

Andrea was mortified. She had never heard her daughter sound so broken and defeated.

"Amy what's wrong? What is it baby?" she asked quickly, hoping to get to the bottom of whatever horrible event was torturing her daughter so.

"There dead mom, the school just pulled some of us into the office and told us that they're dead!"

"Who Amy? Who's dead?" Andrea asked, her heart heaving inside her chest, her fingernails pressing deeply into the palm of her free hand while the other held the phone clutched to her ear.

"My friends!" she sobbed, a heavy weight racking her chest.

Andrea felt like she had been delivered a blow, her chest tight like she had the wind knocked out of her.

"Amy— listen to me Amy. Tell me which friends. Tell me what happened."

Over the tears and sniffling, Andrea sat straining in her chair waiting for Amy to calm down enough to explain what was happening. She wanted to bolt right up and rush over to her daughter's high school, pull her from the office and hold her tightly, not letting her go for anything or anyone in the world.

"The Principal, Mrs. Russo pulled me and a couple other kids out of first period earlier. When we got to the office— we didn't know what was going on. Then we saw the police officers. We didn't know what was going on…" Amy cried.

"It's okay baby, I'm going to come get you and Jeremy as soon as I get off the phone with you. Do you know the police officers names that told you about your friends?"

"I— I don't know. They're Rockville City, I don't recognize any of them."

"Okay Amy, Okay. Listen, I'm going to hang up now. Okay? I'm going to hang up and head straight to the school right now. Have someone in the office pull Jeremy out of class if they haven't already and I'll be right there. Do you understand sweetie?"

Amy was hesitant, her voice sounding so frail and destroyed when she finally spoke again.

"Mom, Jeremy's not in school today. He ditched with some other kids."

"What?!" Andrea couldn't believe it. Of all the dumb things Jeremy could do lately and he decided to play hooky from school. Raining her temper in, Andrea decided to focus on Amy first. She needed her right now and she would just have to deal with Jeremy later. He was going to be sorry he decided to skip with his so-called friend, especially after today! Focus on Amy, she needs me now, Andrea reminded herself.

"Okay I'll find him later, you just wait right there. I'm leaving now!" she said moving away from her desk and heading out the door.

Before she could get out of the building though she ran into Detective Tim Melvin heading towards their office.

"Hey I've got to get over to my daughter's school, can you let the Chief know when he gets in?" she yelled as she rushed down the corridor that led to the parking lot.

"Uhh, yeah," Tim said a look of surprise appearing on his face as she flew past him like a bat out of hell. "Does this have anything to do with the new murders they uncovered this morning?"

What? How was Andrea the last to know about this? She was Montgomery County Homicide for Christ's sake!

"When did you hear about this?" she asked as she broke to a halt and studied Tim's awkward gaze.

"I just got off the phone with Rockville PD. This ties into the murder from the day before, same MO it looks like, and Lieutenant Garza is the one leading the case. It's all their scene, we're just providing resources for now."

"The hell we are! Tell Stone where I'm heading when you see him, I need to get my daughter. The people murdered were apparently her friends!" Andrea seethed. Tim had never seen her this mad.

"Oh man, I'm sorry," he muttered, the look on his face was one of a man unsure of what to say to that news. As a cop you dealt with your share of informing loved ones of family and friends deaths, but it was always different when it happened to someone you knew and worked with.

"Just tell Stone— I gotta go!" she yelled and was out the door and heading for her car.

What the hell was going on when her division was the last to know about something this serious? It didn't matter if Stone was trying to not step on toes by letting Rockville run the investigation. People were dying!

This wasn't just about one poor unfortunate lady being killed. Multiple deaths meant they were now looking at a serial killing, and with the short time frame between the bodies being discovered it looked like it was escalating!

Oh dear God, just let me get to Amy!

Chapter 10

Aidan Preston was leaning against the driver's side door to his Dodge Challenger, the cold of the October afternoon straining to penetrate his leather jacket as his hands folded the slip of paper he had received from Dr. Harper into a smaller size. Once the prescription was the right proportion, he slipped it into his wallet next to the few small bills of cash he had in the worn accessory.

The prescription was for another medication the psychiatrist wanted him to take. He believed it would aid him in finding a way to deal with the chemical imbalance in his brain that was producing the massive amounts of stress he was being racked with. Could this really be what he needed to get past the nightmares he was having and get a good night's sleep for once. Well it wouldn't hurt to try. Anything that could dull his senses and the vividness of the dream he kept experiencing night after night was okay with him.

The wind whipped around him, his hair pushed back from his stern face by the force of the strong current. It was almost November, and if the weather now was any indication of the coming months, then the city was going to be in for a brutal winter. Putting his wallet back into the rear pocket of his jeans, Aidan was about to get into his car when his phone rang. He answered quickly, Mack's voice greeting him as he hopped into his car to get out of the cold afternoon air.

"Hey, thought I'd let you know first since you've been unofficially aiding me in the investigation." Mack's gruff voice said, his call coming in clearer now that Aidan was out of the wind and inside his Challenger.

"Let me know what?"

"I'm on my way over to that abandoned quarry they have off River Road. Where they stopped construction a few years back on that new condo development that fell through. It looks like we have another crime scene."

Aidan felt that same feeling he had originally felt when he first heard the call go out for the incident at the park. This time however he wasn't sitting in his kitchen, but was behind the wheel of his car. He could be over there in no time. Chief Stone's words of warning echoed through his head as he started the engine. He knew he was supposed to be staying away from any active investigations, but he just couldn't sit by and do nothing, even if he was on administrative leave. Ignoring the feeling building in his stomach, he tossed the car into gear and drove out of the parking lot for Dr. Harper's office. River Road was only a ten minute drive from his current location; he could be there in no time.

"What happened?" he asked as the Challenger's wheels left the parking lot, spinning a little out of control as he whipped around the corner and headed down the street.

"It's another bloody nightmare is what it is," Mack said, the repulsion in his voice letting Aidan know that what he was about to see wasn't going to be pretty.

"Same MO as before?"

"Similar. The crime scene techs just arrived and are beginning to process the scene. Fortunately Garza's not here yet, so I'd figured I'd give you a call and see if you could get down here before him."

"Appreciate it. So what's the rundown?"

The Challenger slowed down at the last minute as Aidan approached a red light. Then seeing the intersection was clear, slapped the small police bubble he kept in his glove box for emergencies onto the top of his car. Pushing the power cord into the cigarette lighter, he flipped the light, its blue light flashing as he laid on his horn and sped through the intersection, blowing right by the red light.

"Same type of mutilation, but this time there was more than one victim," Mack's voice said over the cell phone connection. Aidan continued to feel the strange gut instinct that he got when something was up. He called it his cop's intuition, but really he didn't know why it happened.

"How many?" he asked, the feeling in his gut solidifying. Yes, this case was definitely not going to be getting better any time soon, and official or unofficial, Aidan was not going to stand by while his city was terrorized by some unknown threat.

"Why don't you just worry about getting here sooner rather than later, preferably before Garza gets here and I'll fill you in and you can see for yourself."

Aidan agreed, clicking the phone off and turning his attention fully on the drive ahead.

Arriving much faster than he had thought possible, Aidan's Challenger spun onto the gravel driveway that led up to the fenced in quarry. There was already a collection of emergency vehicles and police cars stationed around the main dirt field, and spying Mack's Impala at the end, Aidan pulled in next to it. Before he had the chance to get out of his car he saw Mack's burly, unmistakable form trudging towards him. Out of the car before the last notes of Green Days 'Bullet in a Bible" song had finished playing on the radio station he had left blaring as he raced over here, Aidan looked to Mack's face and realized he actually looked visibly shaken.

"That bad?" Aidan asked as he closed the door to the Challenger. Mack just nodded and using his chin pointed towards the end of the gravel drive. Even though he had never been to this desolate looking patch off near the edge of the city limits, he remembered reading about the failed land development deal that the city had eventually let lapse.

It had been a big deal awhile back when a company bought up the unused city acreage. People had complained about losing the little bit of old forest Rockville had left covering the northern city boundary. Past the area, Rockville ended and the city of Gaithersburg began. Unfortunately due to a large influx of real estate development deals Gaithersburg had lost its old time charm as it moved into the future and looked to leave its agricultural past behind and expand its idea of a larger, modern cityscape. When the conservationists couldn't protect the farmlands and forests in Gaithersburg, they fell back and worked even harder to halt new condo and apartment complexes from eating up the last of Rockville's green space.

While Aidan knew he didn't really care one way or the other what happened to the land, the development company and the city had reached a stalemate over the use of the acreage and after too much time had passed, the deed where the new construction project had begun was snatched up by the city and the apartments were never finished. Fortunately for those who were afraid the land would be ruined, the majority of the old maples and oak trees still stood, forming a small forest that surrounded the rock quarry they had dug when they first broke ground at the location.

It was this quarry that would now be shaded by a new and darker history to be recorded into the books of Rockville's past. It was now the scene of a multiple homicide, the lives lost were those of families and friends of people from all over this city and that was something that stuck in people's memories of a place. They were lives that were snuffed out far too early than they should have been and Aidan was not going to let that loss be in vain. He was going to figure out who was terrorizing his city, his home.

Aidan followed Mack as he headed towards the center of action. The crime scene technicians were working away quietly, the mood over the crime scene seeming to belay the gray, cloudy sky above. As Aidan crossed the drive, the gravel crunching under the soles of his and Mack's shoes, he realized the ground was still pretty wet from the heavy rains they had experienced what was only a few nights before.

"How's the weather treating the evidence collection?" he asked as they crossed a small footpath and began walking towards a red Mustang parked near the center of the quarry. It was certainly a secluded spot, the perfect place for teenagers to sneak out to and try to liven it up.

"The crime scene techs are making due. Obviously all this rain has degraded some of the samples, but once we get closer you'll see that there is plenty for them to collect and choose from. It's not nearly as bad as the park location, which from some of the reports I just checked this morning coming in aren't looking too good in the forensics department. Garza is pissed and had them double checking everything just in case they missed something minor. I'll get you a copy of the reports later if I can't sneak you into the precinct and show you the files yourself."

"I'd appreciate it," Aidan said, there short talk bringing them up close to the abandoned car. The first thing Aidan noticed was that the tires were slashed and there appeared to be a pool of blood smeared across the hood. The windshield was cracked and one of the tech's was dusting the Mustang for prints while another man was snapping away at everything that could be seen, taking the time to make sure he had plenty of documentation from multiple angles.

"Just remember, if anyone questions why you're here, tell them to check with me," Mack whispered as they walked up to a third technician who was pouring a mixture of white colored paste from a bucket onto the ground. Aidan nodded his head in agreement as the man looked up at them hovering over his shoulder.

"Can I help you?" he asked looking a little annoyed and Aidan assuming he was the type who didn't like to be micro-managed, watched the man finish slopping the goop onto the ground and then stand up.

"Yeah Sam, how ya doing?" Mack asked sticking his hand out towards the tech. The man reached out and shook Mack's thick hand, the quick movement causing Mack's excess weight to jiggle a little on his large frame. The tech was small, but obviously worked out.

"You know Detective Jones, we have got to stop meeting like this. Twice in two days, my wife might start to get jealous," the built black man said with a smile that exposed a brilliantly white set of teeth that contrasted sharply with the man's dark, ebony skin color.

"Shit, yours and mine both! What can I say though Sam, 'once I went black I just couldn't go back!'" Mack said with a devious grin.

"Ha, that's a good one Detective! Haven't heard that in a while. What can you say though, I'm just too good lookin' for my own good!" the tech jokingly said, his smile seeming to brighten even more to Aidan's eye as he watched the two full-grown men act like a couple of children. Clearing his throat to get Mack's attention, the tech's smile disappeared as he realized he didn't recognize Aidan and didn't need it to be someone to get him in trouble for his behavior while on the clock.

"Sorry 'bout that," Sam the crime scene technician apologized, giving Mack a quick, questioning look.

"Don't worry about him, he doesn't realize how you cope with the shit you see out here at these scenes," Mack said to ease Sam, who was keeping his mouth closed as he sized Aidan up.

"Yes, don't mind me, I'm just here to get some background on what happened," Aidan finally said hoping to not bother someone working towards the same goal he was. After what seemed a full 30 seconds of obviously deciding Aidan was alright, the tension in Sam's posture relaxed.

"Okay my brotha, don't mind the first impression, I'm as serious as a heart attack when it comes to the work I do in the field." Using his hand, Sam motioned towards the drying white sludge he had deposited on the ground. Aidan knew it was some kind of plaster the man was using, but what he was trying to cast was unknown.

"So what are you casting?"

"The only good thing about the storm we had the other night is it made the ground pretty wet. The moisture that was present in the dirt all around here was enough to give us a pretty good amount of footprints and other tracks to attempt to pull casts from. Most of the prints seem to be from the victims. It looks like they were out here for awhile last night judging from the jumble of imprints everywhere and the empty beer and liquor bottles that were left all over. Because of the footprints left we have a general idea of how the scene played out, but so far its just a general diagram since we are still collecting evidence and processing the scene."

"How many victims?" Aidan asked, realizing Mack had already been at the scene when he called him, so he was a step ahead in the information gathering phase.

"Four."

"Can you tell how many assailants there were? Are we looking at one or possibly more perpetrators?"

"At this time it's unknown, but from the look of the initial sweep we made of everything I'd say there were multiple un-subs."

"Can you take me through what you think happened based on the footprints and location of the bodies?"

"I can't right now since I've got to finish with the work I've still got left."

"Okay, well I appreciate you taking the time to talk with me," Aidan said as he extended his hand to the tech.

"No problem-o. Any friend of Detective Jones is a friend of mine. Name's Sam McNabb," the black man said shaking Aidan's hand. He was right, the man was powerful and had a strong grip too.

"Alright Sam, I'll catch up with you later," Mack said and he turned away from the guy who was already starting back to work, this time he was setting up numbered cones next to important places or evidence that needed to be marked before it could be photographed. He would return to the footprint cast after allowing it time to harden. Aidan followed Mack past the Mustang and they began walking along another gravel path, this one leading off towards the woods surrounding the quarry.

All along the path, Aidan could tell there were spots where the gravel had been recently disturbed, occasionally seeing what appeared to be drops of blood that was heading in the same direction they were. The pattern was chaotic there being various amounts of blood scattered in different areas along the path. It was as if the owner whose blood this was had stumbled along, bleeding out and losing either a little or a lot of the dark liquid as they stopped and started walking.

"So what do you know of the linear time line of events?" Aidan asked.

"Pretty much like what Sam said. This early we've got an idea but that's all it is. It's a working theory that may or may not be accurate."

"Okay, well let's hear this theory."

"Four teenagers were out here last night. From the look of the area around the car they were partying. There's enough empty beer and liquor bottles that they all must have been pretty intoxicated."

"Jesus— four victims?"

"Yeah. They've already been identified and their families notified. Turns out they all went to the same high school." Mack pulled a little pocket notebook from his jacket and flipped it open to a page somewhere near the middle of the well used steno. He scanned it as they walked ever so carefully down the gravel path to their next stop in this nightmare they were both living.

"Becky Strausberg 16, Scott Burrows 17, Tony Caprello and Megan Rhodes both 18. They are all seniors at Rockville High School except for Becky Strausberg who is a junior."

These cold, hard facts were a violent dose of reality for Aidan.

They were just kids, probably hadn't even figured out what they wanted to do with their lives after high school, and now they would never have the chance. Four lives ended before they even began. The thought sickened Aidan. Coming around a small little bend in the path, they were soon at the forest edge. The tree line was like a natural barrier, the shaded interior making the woods look like they were a separate world from the look of the rest of the quarry.

To think that if the land development deal had gone through those years ago, he wouldn't be standing before a dark, shrouded world of green that was as far distanced from the straight lines and perfect angles of the steel and concrete of modern society as possible. If sleek, new apartment buildings and condos stood in this spot would he even be here right now?

Of course he would, and if not here then this mess would have just happened somewhere else. That was the problem with so many people crammed into so small a place as a city. It didn't matter if it was a sprawling metropolis or just a quaint suburban neighborhood, you would always have crime and murder. Just not as much when the statistics were working against you. If one out of every fifty people had the makings of a serial killer, fill a place with an ever increasing population and that was just that many more nut cases ready to crack.

Standing amid the beginning of the tree line there was another crime scene photographer, camera in hand and busy snapping away. His attention was focused on a tree where lying against the side, invisible from the way Aidan and Mack had approached the scene was the corpse of one of the teenagers. The body was crumpled at the base of the tall oak, the boy's mohawk adorned head almost smashed beyond recognition. The head was dangling down, eyes wide open with the chin resting on the boy's chest, the neck twisted and torn open.

It looked like someone had placed a hook into his throat and then pulled it out rapidly, the skin exploding out, blood and gore having dripped down the body and collecting in the boy's lap. It looked as if he was sitting against the tree, his throat having been torn out, he appeared to be trying to keep any part of his insides from touching the marred ground around him.

The grass and dirt had been trampled down during the skirmish before the victim had been killed, and there were clumps of dirt leading away from the tree and off in another direction.

Well here's one. Three more to go, Aidan thought as he looked around forest for a sign of any of the other bodies. Spying a shoe laying on the ground twenty yards from the first body, Aidan made a straight path to the next victim.

The second victim was in even worse shape. The body was obviously female from the shape, but Aidan was unable to tell what her face had looked like or what color of hair she had being that her head was missing. The bloody neck was just a sickly stump, a massive amount of blood having drained onto the ground from the missing appendage. Other than that fatal wound, the girl's body had deep gashes that had ripped through her clothes and stripped her flesh down to the bone.

There was a second massive wound in the chest, the mark right where her heart should have been. Instead there was an empty cavity in the torso, the organ not inside.

You've got to be kidding me! Her heart was literally ripped out of her chest! This was getting worse and worse by the minute and Aidan knew now why the CSI from earlier, Sam, had alluded to there being plenty of evidence to collect and analyze. It was a veritable smorgasbord of various torture techniques that had been exercised by some truly disturbed individuals.

They ripped her heart out!

Aidan looked to Mack who had pulled a handkerchief from his jacket pocket and was dabbing the sweat from his forehead despite the day being too cold to produce sweat on its own.

"I shouldn't have eaten a big breakfast this morning," Mack said as if in answer to Aidan watching him.

"It doesn't matter if you ate a lot this morning or not. This case is horrid enough to cause a person to be sick even if there stomach was bare empty. Where are the other two?"

"I'm not sure yet. This was as far as I got earlier before I called and waited back at the quarry for you to get here," Mack stated, turning towards the photographer off to their left.

"Hey where are the last two victims located?"

The photographer looked up from the view finder of his camera and pointed with his left arm. "You got to walk that way for about another fifty feet or so. You can't miss them."

"Thanks! Come on," Mack muttered as they hiked the last stretch of dark forest floor until they came upon the last two victims. Aidan tried to swallow but his throat seemed too busy attempting to gasp for it to work.

"Jesus H. Christ— What do you think?"

Aidan didn't know what to think. The last bodies, one male and one female were both mutilated beyond imagination. They both had received deep scratches that had pierced skin and pulled interior organs and other body parts out. The male body was the worst, but that wasn't to say that the girl's death hadn't obviously been painful.

Dear Lord, what had these four kids been subjected to?

All his years on the force had not prepared him for anything like this. He began to think that the nightmare he had been having, the one that was keeping him from getting a peaceful night's sleep, was a happy yet odd experience compared to the carnage he was witnessing here.

Never had he seen something like this. It was deranged and spoke volumes of the murder or murderers roaming the streets of Montgomery County. He/she or they had to be stopped before the public picked up on this new massacre.

The press would have a field day if they got wind of this, and that was the last thing Aidan knew the city needed. He remembered the last time the Washington Metropolitan area had been subjected to an atrocity anywhere near the number this case seemed to be closing in on. As if reading Aidan's mind, Mack said, "Looks like we're looking at another serial killer in these parts."

"Yeah, and this time it's not one victim at a time. This time the killer or killers went from one unlucky victim to four! They've escalated their spree and I have a feeling they are enjoying this too much to be stopping any time soon."

Another serial killer, Jesus it hadn't been that long since the last one. Why was it that some cities or areas around the country get all the wackos while others never have to face the terrifying feeling of helplessness as the place they live is plunged into a period of tragedy and terror.

Aidan's mind went back to the fateful day back in 2002 when him and his fellow citizens were plunged into a nightmare. It had been the incident the media had dubbed the 'Beltway Sniper Shootings'. In October 2002, Montgomery County and the Washington Metropolitan area entered into the most dangerous killing spree and largest manhunt the country had ever seen.

It was three weeks of agonizing and grueling police work, a time where the public was mortified to leave their homes, adults not going to work and children staying home from school as two men traveled the city and county roads of Maryland, Virginia and Washington D.C., and built a terror spree that had never before been witnessed in the history of this country. Government agencies and law enforcement personnel all over came together to investigate an almost month long investigation that would stain the pages of history with the blood of innocent people.

And now, it looked like it was happening all over again. A dark, evil presence had settled over the city of Rockville, Maryland, and it seemed like its long-reaching claws were continuing to spread over the streets and neighborhoods, victimizing those who were unaware that it had arrived. Aidan would not let the place he called home fall prey to another indeterminable threat. A threat that could unhinge the safety citizens had come to rely upon. He had sworn an oath to protect these people no matter what and he was not going to re-neg on that promise. No matter what it cost, no matter what he had to do, Aidan was not going to fail.

No, failure is not an option! Aidan thought as he pushed the feeling he had in his gut aside and decided how to proceed. The one thing he knew for sure was that he had to find the killer or killers responsible for these atrocious acts. He didn't know how he was going to do it just yet, but he was on the move.

Chapter 11

So far there hadn't been any response to the latest e-mails Lisa had sent to Tyler Suffux farmer and resident of Portland, Oregon. She had inquired of him any news he could give her regarding the package he was supposed to be sending her. If he had already gotten the samples and photographs together, then shipping it across the country wouldn't be a problem. She had even offered to pay for the shipping herself in a hope of getting the package sooner, but Tyler had refused, saying that he could handle paying the charges himself.

The last e-mail she had received from him assuring her that it wouldn't be a problem to get the samples boxed up and shipped across the country to her office at the SCBI campus.

Through the advent of DNA mapping and sequencing, scientists were able to perform genetic drift studies that could take a species or certain animal and by finding repeating links, discover similarities between them and other animals. DNA is a nucleic acid that contains the genetic instructions used in the development and functioning of all known living organisms.

The coded DNA occupying a given position on the chromosomes of an organism are called alleles. An individual's genotype for that gene is the set of alleles it happens to possess. Lisa thought of the example one of the professors back in her college days of attending Arizona State University had used. To better get his class to understand how allele's fit into the grand scheme of DNA genetic drifts, he drew their attention to a flower he had produced from his desk drawer.

He explained that an example is the gene for blossom color in many species of flowers. A single gene controls the color of the petals, but there may be several different versions or alleles of the gene. One version could result in the flower having red petals, while another might result in the flower sporting white petals. These alleles present in every organism on the planet are transferred to the next generations of animals in a subsequent line. It is from this that characteristics and traits are passed down, and when performing a genetic drift census, you can work your way backwards to discover the originating organism.

In the case of the gray wolf, testing showed and was able to reaffirm that the gray wolf shares a common ancestry with the domestic dog. A number of other gray wolf subspecies have been identified, though the actual number of subspecies is constantly being debated as new discoveries are made each day in labs and out in the real world.

Most scientists and researchers seemed to agree that the domestication of dog took place around 10,000 B.C., and that the animals we know today that have grown into a large collection of various breeds and differing characteristics came from either the actual domestication of wolves or a common ancestor. Through micro-evolution and the passing of time, animal's behavioral traits and appearance have changed from what they once were to what we see today.

Even after Darwin discovered the new species of birds and reptiles in the Galapagos Islands, science has found many other examples of creatures adapting over time and because of geographical variants, and Lisa believed the wolf was no exception. In the case of the scientific classification of the family Canidae, dogs and wolves received much of the same traits and these coded allele's had been passed down through the lineage from a common ancestor. Of course, this was all pointless if what Mr. Suffux claimed to have found turns out to be nothing more than some old, dog or common wolf graveyard and not actually as old and significant a find as the bones of a dire wolf would be.

Clicking out of her e-mail, Lisa leaned back in the sturdy office chair and looked down at the work she had spread out before her. It was time to focus on finishing her initial report on the mornings vocalization tests. With the help of her intern Frank, she had hooked the CD player up to the speaker system that they had installed throughout the wolf habitat. They had spent a few hours in the large holding pen with the pack of wolves making sure all the speakers were placed correctly. Thankfully Frank was highly technologically minded, a characteristic Lisa knew most of the youth of today's modern generation were fluent in thanks to the easy availability of small computer tablets, smart phones, and social networking sites.

Today's youth were so absorbed in the latest and greatest gadgets that it had become a way of life to them to not leave home without their phone or laptop in their possession and constantly tweeting or posting their 'status' multiple times throughout the day. It was a new dawn of civilization, one that Lisa still hadn't found time to wrap her head around even though so many of her own colleagues were using the networking sites to keep up to date with current projects and research. While she used and checked her e-mail from her work computer, and had a cell phone like everyone else these days, she still couldn't see the need to let a person know what you were thinking or doing every hour of the day. That just seemed silly and a waste of time to her.

Picking up the CD that was sitting on the desk among her various papers and printouts, she pressed the 'open' button on the computer tower and the DVD-Rom drive slid open. Inserting the CD into the slot, she pressed the button again and the computer accepted the new media. While the CD's contents loaded, Lisa looked at the stack of data she had compiled before her.

Vocalizations were key she believed in truly taking the next step in the full-on study of wolf behavior. She looked at the basic facts she had written down and thought about the next step to testing her hypothesis. Lisa believed that because wolves senses were so much stronger than a humans, that people weren't truly understanding how important a role speech and the vocal cries and howls that these animals use to communicate was truly being understood for how important a role they played in the animal's behavior. Lacking the vocal cords that a human has to enable them to produce words and talk to his fellow man, wolves vocalizations seem to make use of the varying frequencies sound can reach.

Wolf's ears are triangle shaped and rounded across the top; they are much broader and shorter than a coyote or foxes. Wolves tend to have shorter/darker fur on the backside of the ear, with a lighter, somewhat longer fur along the inside. They are able to fold their ears back against their head, move them from side to side, and forward independently of each other. This range of motion like aiming the concave dish of a parabolic listening device assists the Wolf in detecting the direction of sound quite precisely.

Hearing is a Wolf's second most developed sense, following only after its ability to smell. It is thought that domestic canines can hear sixteen times better than human beings. It is believed that a Wolf's ability to hear is even better than that but there is no method currently to test the full range that a wolf can experience. Experts believe that Wolves may be able to hear frequencies far above the limits of human beings. The upper limit of human hearing is about 20 kilohertz, a Wolf's upper limit has been estimated at between 25 and 80 kHz. Depending on a clear line of sight, with no trees or other obstacles interfering, a wolf is thought to be able to hear another wolf's cry from six to ten miles away.

Wolves howl to assemble their pack, to provide warnings to one another, to distinguish where they are located in relation to each other, and to communicate across great distances. A wolves howl consists of a fundamental frequency which lies between 150 and 780 Hertz, and consists of up to 12 harmonically related overtones. The pitch usually remains constant or varies smoothly, and may change direction as many as four or five times.

While wolves from different geographic locations have different forms of howls, almost like the varying dialects or accents that people experience from different countries around the world, the howls of European wolves are much more protracted and melodious than those of North American wolves, whose howls are louder and have a stronger emphasis on the first syllable. The two are however mutually intelligible, as North American wolves have been recorded to respond to European-style howls made by biologists.

Wolf howls are generally indistinguishable from those of large dogs. Male wolves give voice through an octave, passing to a deep bass with a stress on "O", while females produce a modulated nasal baritone with stress on "U".

Pups almost never howl, while yearling wolves produce howls ending in a series of dog-like yelps. Howls used for calling pack mates to a kill are long, smooth sounds similar to the beginning of the cry of a horned owl. When pursuing prey, they emit a higher pitched howl, vibrating on two notes. When closing in on their prey, they emit a combination of a short bark and a howl. When howling together, wolves harmonize rather than chorus on the same note, thus creating the illusion of there being more wolves than there actually are. Lone wolves typically avoid howling in areas where other packs are present. Wolves do not respond to howls in rainy weather and when satiated.

It was this large amount of information that Lisa Davies had gathered over the course of her passionate, wildlife biology career that led her to believe that by using a CD of prerecorded wolf vocalizations, she could in fact get to the basics of the wolves language and communicate with them. And here at the SCBI campus of the National Zoo with access to a pack of North American gray wolves, she could test her theories and possibly add to the knowledge that the academic world has compiled on these beautiful creatures. This was Lisa's passion, her calling in life, and if she was able to backup her recent findings with hard data then the Smithsonian would have no reason to not give her the grant she had requested.

Clicking on the computer icon for the audio program, she heard the computer tower make a low humming noise as the CD's audio content loaded. Adjusting the desktop speakers to a set level, she heard the first track begin to spill out of the computer. A low, guttural howl began, its sound sending a tingle of awe over Lisa's body. No matter how many times she heard a wolf arching its head to the night sky and sending its low cry out into the wild it still gave her goosebumps, just like it did when she was a little growing up in the vast wilderness of the Midwest. The low vibrating howl ended like a song coming to its final stopping point and then she heard a slight yip of the wolf taking a breath and letting loose with a longer, more defined cry.

Beautiful, absolutely beautiful!

Lisa dragged the pointer of the computer mouse across the screen and selected a second file. Moments later a different howl drifted through the speakers, filling the office with the sounds of the wild. She was lost in her own memories as the various recorded howls continued to pour out from the computer. She remembered a birthday long ago, she believed she had just turned eight, her stepmom taking her camping for the weekend up in the foothills of the Rockies. It was a surprise trip she would always remember.

Her stepmom Laura had actually pulled her out of school for that Friday so they could hike up into the mountains to a scenic plateau overlooking a beautiful open expanse of forest. At the time, being in third grade and her mom taking her out of school for all things a trip had been huge.

Now thinking back on that wonderful birthday memory, Lisa could definitely see what had influenced her to become a wildlife biologist later in life.

She loved the great outdoors and usually tried to take a week off each summer to go hiking and camping somewhere around the country by herself. It was like a soul clearing, medicine walk that the Native American's used to perform in rituals. Except instead of finding an answer to who she was, she was just hitting the refresh button yearly and reminding herself of why she found this land so wonderful. It was a vacation that everyone should do, just to see what else was out there in life other. There was more to living than the tiresome repetition of going back and forth to a boring 9 to 5 job and the crowded, dangerous city life. There was a land filled with pristine beauty and life unmarred by the smog-filled metropolises of human society. Out in the wild you felt free!

Leaning forward in her seat, Lisa opened her eyes to see Frank breeze in through the doorway. His eyes meeting Lisa's and a smile forming on his thin lips.

"Okay I got all the speakers throughout the enclosure set up. We should have no problem controlling the vocalizations sources through each one and upping the frequencies when needed," he said, slipping into the chair next to Lisa.

"Great, I'm just about finished syncing them up on the computer for the first test phase."

Lisa moved the cursor along and dragged a few files into the computer program's audio time line. It was a simple program almost like editing a home movie digitally, except she had many more controls and settings she could tweak than the average home user. The software had actually been designed by a colleague of hers who had been using prerecorded wolf vocalizations to study if they could actually keep wolves out of certain farm lands where farmers were worried about wolves attacking their livestock.

If successful, the audio recordings could be used to actually mimic a pack's presence near farmland and keep the real wolves at bay. It could lead to the first non-lethal tool in a ranchers arsenal for protecting their sheep and chickens or any other livestock that wolves usually preyed on.

All it would take is the simple addition of speakers setup around the farms to create a zone where this technology could be tested and running the prerecorded vocalizations out into the surrounding forests to keep the presence of wolf packs from stepping into what they would think is another packs territory. It was an ingenious idea, and Lisa knew it would go a long ways to protecting wolves from hunting and execution if farmers didn't feel like they had to shoot to kill and protect their own property.

Frank pulled up his chair next to Lisa's and stared at the screen. As she finished layering the various audio tracks into the time line, she finished and waited for the rendering phase of the program to create one endless loop that would play in the wolf habitat.

"Looks good. I can't wait to see what kind of results we get," Frank said, the excitement in his voice quite evident. Lisa was glad that the college kid had kept with the internship here at the zoo. SCBI could be an imposing place to work and not being paid could put a person through some financial hardships with the amount of hours some of their research could take.

She was just glad they were paying her. Even though it wasn't much due to the fact that the scientific community worked largely off grants and donations and SCBI was no exception. They may be one of the biggest research organizations in the country possibly even the world with the amount of different projects they had spread into all corners of the globe, but that just meant they also had the largest expenses and operating costs to go with the prestige. You couldn't do the work if you didn't have the money and Lisa sure didn't have enough of her own saved up to ever hope of being able to be fully self-sustained and funded.

She wasn't like some of those in the scientific community who were fed with a silver spoon from birth, she had to work to get where she was, and that meant going through the various, low-paying positions as she ascended the ranks to becoming a member of SCBI's faculty. As the lead wildlife biologist on staff working with the new addition of the gray wolf population they had acquired, Lisa was looking forward to showing not only SCBI what she could do but the entire scientific community as well.

"Just remember, we're looking to get general results first. If everything goes according to plan we might just be able to secure that research grant I've been pursuing."

"Yeah that sure would help."

"I know what you mean, believe me! If we had the resources, I could actually talk the Smithsonian's director into hiring another assistant to help us. That could also mean your unpaid internship could become a paid assistants position."

"You mean I wouldn't be stuck having to eat Ramen noodles every night of the week?"

"You don't eat Ramen every night," Lisa said eyeing the heavy kid with a squinting gaze.

"Yeah well, it's not steak and seafood either!" Frank muttered with a playful grin.

Lisa laughed, "Haha yeah, steak and seafood. I wish I was eating lobster even if it was just on the weekends. Besides I've noticed you've been spending more time lately on your lunch breaks at the zoo's eatery, and I don't think it's the Gorilla Burgers you're going there for!"

Frank's face seemed to blush as he turned his head away quickly.

"I don't know what you're talking about."

"Uh-huh, why don't you just ask her out already?" Lisa prodded. Frank was a good kid and she felt for him. She remembered what it was like to be his age and in love, and she'd like to see his infatuation with the girl at the eatery turn into him actually saying something to her instead of just spending every minute of his break there and pining over her.

"I don't know, I think she has a boyfriend," Frank said, the blush on his cheeks fading away as he looked back at Lisa.

"Well you won't know unless you talk to her."

"Yes mom, geesh aren't we supposed to be adults working here. Not a couple of kids gossiping like it's middle school?"

"Oh sorry Mr. Sensitive. In that case, get back to work. I'm not paying you to sit around and gawk at the Eatery girl."

"You're not paying me!"

A smile broke across Lisa's exotic features, her dark eyes sparkling.

"Touche!" she said and ejected the CD from the computer. It was time to test out her thesis. Hopefully the results they were able to obtain would point towards confirming her theory. If they could harness the secret language of wolves they could possibly discover a whole new utility of the man-canine relationship. It wouldn't be a matter of dogs just being man's best friend and trusty servant and companion, but people would be able to understand their motivations and body language that much more. The applications could be endless, and it all rested on these tests they now had to perform.

Picking the CD up, she set it on the pile of her work and scooping it into her arms, headed towards the door to the adjoining work space in the next room, Frank following her slim, fit figure as she walked. Lisa, not one to dwell on her own beauty and looks, never realizing his eyes were on her rear as they walked.

"Alright, let's do this!"

Nick Haley couldn't believe his luck. He had been on his way over to check in at the office and speak with Marty about the story when he had gotten another call from 911 operator and dispatcher, Katherine Childs at the Rockville Police Department. He was barely on the phone a minute with the woman who had quickly taken a break from the switchboard to tell him about another murder site that had been found this morning. He couldn't believe how fortunate he had become by getting this new source who was able to access relevant, inside information from the department. Yes, Katherine Childs had been a Godsend.

With the information she had provided he had actually been able to get over to the latest murder scene before any other news outlet had even heard about the four teens massacred the previous night. Even though a uniformed officer had tried to stop him from passing the yellow police tape that blockaded the gravel road, stopping anyone from going any further into the carnage that seemed to flow from the place, Nick had eventually gotten through when the cops attention was turned to help the Medical Examiner's van pass the barricade.

Slipping past a small break in a fence that was further up the drive, Nick sprinted across the field and out of view of the watchdog of a cop. The man was thick, bulging biceps that strained the police windbreaker he wore over his uniform, and a thick neck that seemed to hardly be existent as it joined to his marine corps crew cut. The short, grunt turned police officer was not someone Nick wanted to get into a confrontation with, so he decided to avoid him at all costs and disappear towards where the real action was.

Taking one last look over his shoulder to make sure the cop hadn't seen him, he followed the rocky driveway a little ways before seeing the action taking place ahead.

There was a large police presence at this scene, and the curiosity that drove Nick to question everything, a needed trait for a journalist, was sending warning bells clinging in his ears. Yes, something terrible had happened here and Nick Haley and The Informant were going to be the first and possibly only media presence to report to the public about what was happening on their city streets.

This is my chance to really show Marty and the readers of the paper what I can do! He thought as he stepped off the gravel path and approached two men standing a little ways from the multiple crime scene technicians busily attempting to log, photograph and bag every last piece of evidence that could be important in solving this crime.

As he walked, he watched the two men standing there. They were not facing him so they had no idea he was approaching, but that gave him time to size these men up and get a general idea on how to proceed with getting some answers for him and his readers.

The closest man was almost too large to be a cop. When people often joked about cops sitting in their squad cars and munching on donuts, Nick knew that it was guys like this who probably started that misconception that had followed the image of police 'working' from the cruisers or staking out a subject.

Yes he was big, his round, large cheeks reminded him of a puffer fish, but with his small, beady eyes that were barely visible under a heavy brow and thick dark eyebrows, Nick could almost picture of Buddha wearing a trench coat and chewing on an unlit cigar with his meaty lips. The big man had coarse black whiskers sprouting from above his lip and they attempted to establish a mustache, but Tom Seleck he was not. In fact Nick couldn't recall having ever seen anyone who had ever been able to grow a 'stashe like the good ol' bandit from Smokey and the Bandit. That man's facial hair was impressive.

Drawing closer the large man shoved his thick hands into his pockets, a light wind blowing his trench coat open to reveal he had a pair of suspenders stretched tightly over his impressive gut. With his imposing, heavy size and Buddha like facial features, Nick had a feeling he just might be able to get something from the guy. Another ten yards and he would be side by side with them. He took the last distance slowly, letting him have time to try and break down the other man he was with.

Over the years of listening to everybody from liars, thieves, crooked politicians and many more, Nick had acquired a gift at being able to read people. This was another trait he used to his advantage in his profession. 'You can't bullshit a bullshiter', was how the phrase went and Nick was an expert at how to bullshit to get his story.

The second man standing next to the big guy was about as different as they came in regards to looks and body language. The man was tall and well built, wearing a dark t-shirt, jeans and boots. Over this he head on a worn, black leather jacket that had obviously seen better days, but still fit perfectly and when open, allowed the athletic musculature of the man's chest and stomach seem to be all the more noticeable under his shirt.

While Nick prided himself on keeping his own weight in the average range, this guy just seemed blessed with a strong physique and powerful attraction. Nick was pretty sure the solid chin covered in a light growth of dark hair and piercing gray eyes didn't hurt this guys chances with the ladies. They all seemed to find the tall, dark and handsome Bad boy look to die for, at least the ones he always tried to pursue in bars that ended up with him buying their drinks and then them heading off with someone who looked more like this guy.

Shaking his shoulder length brown hair out of his face as he reached the men, he was just about to say something when the thinner, dark haired man he was sure woman would describe as 'sexy and dangerous', turned towards him and caught him in his piercing gray stare.

"And you are?" Bad boy said, his gaze studying Nick's somewhat rushed appearance. He hadn't had time to change into anything new this morning and so as such he was still wearing his rumpled suit and tie from the day before. His hair was slightly mangled, in desperate need of a comb, and his own usually clean shaved face was starting a five o'clock shadow.

"Nick Haley," he said, and sticking his hand out, was surprised to find the man's grip was strong but not the type to crush your wrist and embarrass you when he shook.

"Haley, nope sorry, doesn't ring a bell," the man in the leather jacket said shaking his head and thinking. There was something about this guy that Nick found recognizable. He had seen him from somewhere but couldn't place the who or where. He thought it might have been at some other crime scene that he was sent to cover for The Informant over the last couple years, but that just didn't seem right.

"Well Haley, I'm Detective Mack Jones," the larger man said to speed up the pleasantries, "And this is Detective Aidan Preston."

Nick looked up at the faces and adding the names to who he was looking at he now knew why Detective Preston had seemed familiar. He had been the officer involved in that terrible tragedy down in Silver Spring about a year ago. Yes that's him alright, that's why he looked so familiar, Nick thought eying the man over once more.

I can't believe he's back on duty already!

Yes, now the event and news stories from the last year were coming back to him. He could even remember the possible court trials the guy had almost had to go through after that little girl got paralyzed. Some had called him a hero for saving her life, but others thought he was just trying to be a hotshot and save the day, and that carelessness cost an innocent girl the means to ever be able to walk again. Yes, he was the same Detective Aidan Preston.

"Mind if I ask what you're doing out here?" Mack finally said, not liking the strange look that had come over Mr. Haley's face as he had been starting at Aidan.

"Oh sorry," Nick said digging into his bag and pulling out his The Informant press badge and handing it to Mack. Mack studied it for a moment then handed it back.

"This is a closed scene until my Lieutenant clears it, so no reporters or TV crews are supposed to be out here. How did you get past the barricade?"

Nick decided to play it safe, after all he didn't want the grunt standing guard back at the police tape getting in trouble for letting him sneak past. He could just imagine that man's massive arms coming at him to choke him for all he was worst.

"Look Detectives, the truth is I'm here for the same reason you guys are. There have been four murders last night and another two days ago. That's five people! The public has a right to know, they need to be made aware of what is happening so they can do what they need to to keep them safe. So I'm here to gather information to inform and protect the citizens of this city, just like you guys are."

"Listen Mr. Haley, I'm afraid that this is a closed crime scene and you are not allowed to be here…" Mack was saying before the journalist cut him off.

"Detective, these killings are continuing and you can't tell me that the public doesn't have a right to know! If there is a serial killer running amok in this county, then my God, people have to be warned!"

"Calm down son. The investigation is still early in the initial information gathering phases and at this point we cannot say that the events of this last week are related until all the facts are in. In the mean time, once we have gathered the proper details, the Press Release Agent will issue a statement to the public regarding our findings."

"That's absurd and you know it! A woman was mutilated and murdered in Croydon Park of East Rockville two nights ago. Then last night four more people were massacred in the same violent way. You're telling me that they aren't connected?"

"No, what I'm telling you is that I can't have you here stirring up a hornets' nest of panic based off just a few similarities when we haven't even finished processing the scene yet. It is far too early to be jumping to conclusions and providing the public with anything you may have seen here so far would be premature and cause a panic!"

Before Mack could say anything else, or Nick had anything to add, a loud, gruff voice called out through the cold afternoon air.

"Dammit Jones! What the hell are these people doing here?"

All three men turned to see Lieutenant Garza tearing straight for their location. He almost knocked a technician over who was lifting one of the victims arms and looking for marks as the furious man in charge sped towards them. Without waiting a moment for a response, Garza's tirade continued.

"I want your guests out of here immediately! This will not do! If I wasn't short staffed as it is with everything going on, I'd have your fat ass kicked off this case!" He paused for a moment to take a breath then looked straight at Aidan. "And what the hell are you doing here? This is an active investigation being led by the Rockville Police Department! The last time I checked with Chief Stone, you weren't even back on duty! He's going to love hearing about this!"

Pausing again to inhale and prepare his lungs for more verbal abuse he was about to release, he turned to the last man standing next to Mack.

"I don't know who the hell you are and I don't care! Get the hell back to your vehicles and clear out. I see either of you two again at one of my scenes then you can both kiss your access to any investigation goodbye! I'll make sure you never work another homicide again! Is that understood— NOW GET OUT!"

Aidan gave Mack a supportive slap on the shoulder as he started to walk away, Nick Haley jogging to catch up. As they walked away they could hear Garza continuing to yell at Mack who just stood there looking at the ground like a big, ashamed bear.

"You were supposed to be the lead investigator on the scene until I arrived. Instead I see you've been talking to two people not even a part of this investigation! And what's the deal with the other guy? He had a badge around his neck, is he a reporter for Christ's sake?"

Eventually Garza's yelling grew quieter as they walked back to the vehicle staging area and they were far enough away to not know if Garza was still out there flipping his lid.

"Hey so look— I'm going to be writing this story whether I have all the facts or not. The public needs to know about the dangers they could be facing. I've already got most of my article written, and once I get back to the office I'm going to turn it in before the deadline. That means it's going to be in tomorrow's edition," Nick explained.

"I don't suppose there's anything I can do to stop you from running with the story?" Aidan asked as they approached the parking area. The big, burly guard from earlier was keeping a small group of onlookers back behind the ropes, the serious expression on his face enough to keep anyone from trying to get too close.

"No, but if there's anything that you can clarify for me or a different direction you can head me towards then I don't have to speculate or reach for any straws. I mean come on— it sounds like the way that guy back there exploded your doing the same thing I am. You're working around the system to get to the bottom of these killings. You aren't even on the force anymore are you?" Nick asked, and with that comment he saw the pain in Aidan's eyes as he looked straight at him.

"I'm still a Detective, I'm just not active. I'm still on administrative leave, but yes, I want to get to the bottom of these killings and stop whoever if doing them," answered Aidan.

"So help me out. You've got a lot more to go on that I do, and I've got resources you don't. We could work together to solve this thing and bring the bastard down. You can tell me what ever you want, and if there's something you don't want me to write, I swear I won't."

Aidan stood there, having reached the cars and stepped up to the side of his Challenger.

"Nice car, is that one of the original, performance models from when they first released them?"

"Yeah it's a 1970, Dodge Challenger R/T. Two-door hardtop, E-body frame and leather interior. I had to replace the Rallye instrument cluster with the speedometer, tachometer and oil pressure gauge, and the overhead interior consoles light was busted, but other than that, she's all original. She's got a 3-speed manual transmission with the optional 425 bhp, 426 cubic inch Hemi engine. Let's just say she's my pride and joy! Restored her myself. I had a lot of time on my hands a year ago."

Nick just nodded, understanding the detective didn't want to talk about his past. That was fine with Haley as long as he could utilize the Detective's current hobby.

"What do you say— partners?" Nick asked, pulling a business card out from his wallet and sticking it out for Aidan to grab. Hesitating a moment, Aidan finally plucked the card from his fingers and slipped it into his pocket.

"If we're going to do this together, we're going to have to do it my way."

"Hey you're the expert when it comes to homicides, whatever you say!" Nick said with a smile. He could tell by the look of the man's face that he was still trying to decide if this was a good idea. Truth be told, Nick wasn't sure it was in his best interests to work with the suspended Detective. Yet, there was something about the man who made him feel like he could trust him.

Oh well, shit happens— I'll just have to see how this plays out!

Chapter 12

The sun which had been hidden behind the gray, somber sky for most of the day was beginning to set. Occasionally, the red-orange clouds that could pierce the overcast sky were beginning to fade to darker hues as the sun disappeared from the horizon. Streaks of deep blues and purples were slashed through with fiery reds and yellows as the sun melted away and darkness began to settle over the city.

Detective Andrea Wilkes had raced over to her daughter's high school earlier and picked the girl up. Amy looked terrible. Her eyes were puffy from crying and the little bit of mascara she had applied before school had smeared down across her cheeks. She looked rough.

My poor baby, oh Amy!

When she had first walked into the Principal's office and saw her daughter and two other kids sitting in the chairs lining one wall of the main room, her teeth clenched and her heart nearly stopped. Amy was hunched over in the hard, plastic chair, her arms crossed over her stomach and her elbows against her knees. She looked like she had been rocking back and forth in that position like a woman who had just lost her baby. Her backpack was sitting at her feet, and even with the makeup the girl had put on earlier, her skin appeared to have been drained of color.

Having heard her mother rush into the office, Amy looked up at her, her red, moist eyes making Andrea's heart break. No one should see their child like this. The poor girl. Andrea walked right up to her and taking the empty seat beside her, she wrapped her arms around the petite, 17 year old girl and held her tight, whispering into her ear as she rocked her gently in her arms.

"It's okay sweetie— Mommy's here now. I'm here Amy," Andrea said in a soft whisper, her mouth planting reassuring kisses onto her daughters scalp as they just sat there.

The two other kids that had been called to the office looked about as heart-wrenchingly lost as Amy did. While they both seemed visibly shaken, they had obviously not been as close to the kids that had died since they were nowhere near Amy's catatonic state.

It took a few more minutes of holding her, before she was able to get her daughter out and into her car. She helped her buckle her seat belt, then sliding in behind the wheel, pulled out of the school's parking lot and headed home.

Once they were in the car, Amy just slumped back in her seat, her body seeming to not be able to put the effort into sitting up. Andrea didn't blame her. She couldn't imagine what her daughter was going through. On the way to pick her up she had gotten the information on the murders from one of the Detectives who was present at the scene. While it had been too soon to provide her with much details, he was at least able to give Andrea the names of the victims.

While she didn't know many of Amy's friends, she recognized Becky and Scott since Becky was on Amy's cheerleading squad and Scott played football for the high school. Andrea remembered their faces and she couldn't help remembering how young they were the first time she had met them at one of the school's football games that Andrea had attended to watch Amy cheer. She also remembered hearing Amy talk about them at various times over the semester. They had seemed close, and that meant this loss was tearing her daughter apart.

After getting home, Andrea helped Amy into her room, where she just crashed on the bed and asked to be left alone. Andrea consented and spent the time using her cell phone to find out what else she could about this latest four count homicide. Fortunately Tim had been sent out to the scene to aid the Rockville boys so he had a full knowledge of what was going on.

"So how bad was it?" Andrea asked as she began preparing a cup of tea for her daughter. As the water boiled in the kettle she had picked up the phone and called Tim Melvin's cell. A first she hadn't gotten through and just when she was about to leave a voice mail, he called her back.

"Pretty messed up, that's for sure," Tim said, his voice slightly distorted over his cell, probably from the interference of the area he was calling from.

"Does it look like it could be tied into the first murder two days ago?"

"Yeah. These bastards are sick. You won't believe the mess that the CSI boys are having to go through. They've spent most of the morning and afternoon processing the scene and they're still not done. They had to set up work lights out at the quarry just to be able to see everything now that the suns going down. They'll probably be out there for another hour or two."

"Is that pompous ass Garza still running the show?"

"Yeah, but with this continuing to get worse, I've heard talk about Chief Stone about to pull the rug from under him and assign a task force to investigate. Oh and guess who was here earlier before Garza threw his butt out?"

"Who?"

"Our pal Preston."

"Wait, what? What was Aidan doing there?"

"Not sure, but Garza was not a happy camper. He blew a gasket and chased him and some other unknown guy off before laying into Detective Mack Jones about procedure and keeping a secure crime scene or some such bull."

Andrea thought about what she had just heard. What was Aidan doing at another crime scene. He needed to watch out or Stone was going to try to crush him under his heel for insubordination. Aidan, what are you doing? She wondered as she thought of the handsome, still young Detective who had been getting to her emotions lately.

"From what I could gather, Jones was the one that called Aidan out and was walking him around at the scene." Tim added to break the silence that had entered between them as Andrea's mind wandered with thoughts of Aidan Preston.

She didn't know what was going on with him, but she knew that having seen him recently, he had sparked something inside her that she hadn't felt in years. There was some connection, an undefined attraction that seemed to be drawing her in and making her want to find out more about the man that she used to work daily with. Ever since he had gone on leave, there was something about him. Something he seemed to be hiding deep down from everyone, possibly including himself. Did he have some deep dark secret that he was protecting? Could the events of his past changed him into someone different? These were just some of the questions she wanted to uncover, but first she needed to check on her daughter.

Quickly wrapping her conversation up with Detective Melvin, she placed the phone of the counter and got the stove just as the kettle started whistling. Removing it from the burner, she poured the steaming liquid into a mug and dropped a green tea bag in, stirring it around with a spoon. Once the cup of tea was complete, she grabbed a small tray from under the sink and carried the beverage to her daughter's room.

As she entered the room, Amy groaned slightly and rolled over to face her. She had the coves of her bed pulled up to her neck and there were small moisture marks on her pillow case from her crying. Setting the tray down on the stand by the bed, Andrea ran her hand through her daughter's dark hair and then helped her sit up.

"Here you go sweetie," she said, handing the steaming cup to her daughter. Amy took the mug and blew lightly on the surface to cool it slightly. After waiting a moment she took a small sip to taste the temperature. Finding it wasn't too bad she took another sip, this time a longer one.

She handed her mother the cup of tea and let her head fall back against her pillow, her dark hair spreading out and framing her pretty face. Even with the red, puffy eyes and dried snot that had crusted on the insides of her nostrils, Amy was a beautiful girl.

She really did get her looks from me, Andrea thought as she sat pulled her daughter's desk chair next to the side of the bed and sat. She couldn't imagine going through something like this when she had been Amy's age. In fact, it didn't matter what age you were. Nobody deserved to find out that their close friends had been torn apart and mutilated.

Fortunately the Rockville Police officers who had arrived at Amy's school that morning to alert the school faculty and the interview Amy and the other two students about the last time they had seen or talked to the four victims, they hadn't provided any of the horrid details that stuck out in the case. For the most part they had given them very little information other than the fact that the four teens had been killed and suffered a gruesome fate.

Watching Amy lay there, her eyes closed and head pointed towards the ceiling, Andrea wondered what she could do for her precious child.

"Do you want to talk about it?" she finally asked as Amy lay there prone, her bed spread rising and falling lightly on her little frame as she took deep breaths to calm her overworked nerves. Amy lay there with her eyes still closed and just shrugged her shoulders slightly.

"Okay, well I'm going to go see about making something for dinner."

"I don't feel like eating. I really don't have much of an appetite."

"That's fine, you just rest," Andrea said tapping her hand onto her daughter's shoulder and leaned in to place a kiss on her forehead.

Stopping in the doorway, Andrea leaned against the frame and took one last look at Amy. Poor kid, facing something like this could probably lead to all kinds of issues. Maybe she should look into finding her some help. Possibly a psychiatrist or group she could go to to express her feelings and not bottle them up. First though, she'd give her some time and see how resilient she was. She knew Amy was a tough kid, she took after Andrea after all, so she might just be able to pull through.

You can do it sweetheart. I know you can.

"I'll check in on you again in a little while. I'm going to go see about locating your brother." Then with that said, Andrea closed the door to Amy's bedroom and headed for the kitchen.

Jeremy, where is that boy? I'm going to kill him! Andrea thought as she headed into the kitchen to retrieve her cell phone. It was bad enough he had been slacking off lately, grades slipping and missing curfew, but now ditching school put his behavior into a whole new category. Andrea was not going to let him start down the slippery slope that his father had tumbled down early in life. It was bad enough that Jeremy was like her ex husband Robert, but with everything going on lately she couldn't take the added stress.

Reaching up into a cupboard, she withdrew a wine glass and set it on the counter. Then stooping down to a lower cabinet near the floor, she pulled out a bottle of white wine. It was a moderately priced brand and year, Pinot Grigio being her favorite, and finding the corkscrew in the utensil drawer she pulled the cork out and poured herself a glass. She didn't stop pouring it until the amber colored liquid was near the rim. This was why she couldn't spend the extra money anything too pricey. The way she went through wine on days when she just needed to take the edge off of things and relax, an expensive bottle would just not be financially sound.

One glass wasn't enough, so Andrea usually found herself cracking open a new bottle every other night. Placing the cork back into the bottle but leaving it out on the counter for refills, she picked up her glass and headed into the living room.

Andrea kicked her shoes off and padded across the soft carpet until she reached the sofa. Plopping down gently enough to not spill her glass, she placed her feet up on the armoire and filled her mouth with the first mouthful of the sweet liquid. Taking a few more sips in just as many seconds, Andrea felt the warm tingling feeling of the alcohol entering her body. She let out a yawn and leaned back further on the couch, the sofa cushions sucking her in. This was definitely what she needed.

Having left work to go straight to Amy's high school, the thought of returning to the precinct to finish up the files and cases she had been working on was the furthest thing from her mind. She would just have to file today away under one of her many saved up vacation days, since taking care of her family and allowing herself some time to unwind was the most important task right now. She contemplated running a bath and soaking herself for as long as possible in the warm waters, but decided since it was still somewhat early then she might as well start something light for dinner. Amy probably wouldn't have an appetite for anything heavy, and she'd have to check the fridge to see what ingredients she had, but she was pretty sure she could whip something up that would fit all the requirements she had just made.

Draining the last of her glass, she stood up and walked back towards the kitchen. She was about to pour herself a second helping of the Pinot Grigio when she realized the indicator light on the answering machine was blinking. Now what? Who the hell could it be this time?

Pressing the 'play' button she went through the various command prompts until she reached her inbox. The first message that came through was from Amy's guidance counselor at school.

"Mrs. Wilkes, this is Rhonda Mitchell, Amy's counselor at Rockville High. I just wanted to touch base with you regarding a matter of some importance. There has been a tragedy regarding a few of the students who attend here and we are trying to get a hold of you to see if you could please find time to get down to the school.

'Amy is fine, but we would prefer to release her into your care since due to the circumstances the principal and I feel none of the students who drive should be doing so at this time. Once again, if you could just call me here at the school and let us know you received this message and will be able to come get your daughter, that would be greatly appreciated. Thank you for your time…BEEP."

Andrea pushed the delete button and waited for the next message to start. Well that answered her question of why she hadn't received any calls from the school this morning on her cell. They probably didn't have that number and that's why the let Amy call from her phone.

The next message began as Andrea was finishing topping off her second glass of wine. She was certainly feeling the effects of the first glass since she hadn't really eaten much in the way of breakfast this morning. Then with the detour she had to make to get Amy, taking a break for lunch had vanished as quickly as she had thought about it. She was just setting the bottle down on the edge of the counter when her ex husbands voice cracked through the machine.

"Andrea, what the hell is going on? I just got a call from Amy's school. Is she alright? What happened…" the unexpected surprise of hearing Robert's frantic voice caused her to miss the edge of the counter and the bottle went crashing to the ground.

"Dammit!" Andrea muttered as shards of glass and the remainder of wine that had been in the bottle were scattered across the linoleum floor.

"…Anyways, I need to know what's happening with my kids. Call me back as soon as you get this!"…BEEP…END OF NEW MESSAGES…" the automated voice rattled off before going into its selection of options.

Ha, your kids? They will never be your kids Robert!

"…PRESS '7' IF YOU WISH TO DELETE THIS MESSAGE… '9' IF YOU WISH TO SAVE IT…"

Andrea reached over to the phone's base and pressed the '7' button, and once again she found herself having to delete another call from Robert and it hadn't even been twenty four hours yet. What more did she need to deal with right now?

Grabbing a dishcloth from next to the sink, Andrea dropped onto her hands and knees and began picking up the pieces from the shattered wine bottle. Starting with the glass shards first, she dumped them into a trashcan and then began soaking up the spreading liquid with the towel.

What right did Robert have to call here?

They were divorced, and since then she had heard from a friend that he had gotten married to that bitch he had abandoned his kids and her to pursue.

Through perseverance they had made it through the separation and divorce, and at the time the custody case had been the only thing they could agree on and settle with ease. Andrea got the kids and there wasn't a single judge anywhere who probably wouldn't have disagreed with the court's decision. Even though Andrea was going to have to raise two children on her own while working a full-time career as a police officer, her lawyer was easily able to provide enough documented proof that Robert Wilkes was not fit to have custody of two children no matter what age they were. He had spent the last few years going from job to job, never seeming to last very long at any of them, until he finally settled back in Maryland just recently.

That was one reason she didn't like him calling the house number and leaving messages. She didn't want her kids to find out that poor excuse for a father was back around.

Couldn't he just stay out of their lives?

Just then the phone rang in its cradle. Taking the soaked dishrag she had used to absorb most of the wine, she placed it in the sink and reached for the receiver. Before she could say hello, Robert's voice was screaming over the line. Why couldn't he seem to get the hint that they didn't need him for his help?

"Jesus Andrea, where have you been? I've been calling over and over and left you a message on your work and home phone! Is Amy alright? The school called, but before I could get any answers out of them they said you were already on your way. What happened?" Robert shouted, his high-strung voice cracking from the constant abuse his was putting his vocal cords through. Andrea could hear the anger seeping through his tone and she was not about to let this man blame her for what had happened.

"Robert— Calm down!" Andrea yelled into the phone as she brought it back up to her ear to make sure that he wasn't still yelling. No point in letting him destroy her ear drums, after all, he had already destroyed so much in her life. Waiting for her ex husband to regain his composure, she finally filled him in on what had happened. Once she was done reciting all the relevant information that had just passed over the course of the morning and afternoon, she realized she had a question for Robert.

"Robert, how did you know about the problem at Amy's school?"

"I told you, they called me this morning and as soon as I got the message and called them back, they told me you were on your way. After that I'd figured I'd just try to find out the facts from you."

"Okay, but the school shouldn't have called you," Andrea said reiterating her point.

"Well I'm still listed as one of Amy and Jeremy's emergency contacts, so when they can't reach you, then they call me."

"Well I'm going to need to change that. You left us Robert, and can't just step back into our children's and my life after being gone for so long and destroying the faith they had in you."

"Look things are different now, I've got a god job going for the time being, and I've managed to clean up my act. I would really like to visit you guys this week if there's some time. Especially to check in on Amy and Jeremy. I'm sure Amy is having a rough week and its only going to get worse before it gets better."

He 'cleaned up his act', yeah right. Andrea knew that that was probably the furthest thing from the truth and that was another reason she didn't want her deadbeat addict of a father spending time around them. They were still young and impressionable, and with Jeremy already starting to slip in the wrong direction lately, having Robert there wouldn't be the best thing for the family.

"No Robert, I don't think that's such a good idea…" Andrea was saying but Robert quickly cut her off.

"Look I'm coming down to the city in a few days. I want to see you all and would love if we could do something together, maybe see a show, or a movie or something. What do you say 'Dre?"

She hated it when he shortened her name and called her "'Dre", and warning signs were going off inside her head telling her to just get off the phone, she just needed to hang up.

"I don't know if that's such a good idea. Maybe in a couple weeks, but right now is just too hectic with work and the kids, and now with Amy and this whole mess. I don't want them to get the impression that your back in their lives, just to crush their hopes when you vanish again. And I especially don't want you around if you're using again!"

"Look Andrea, I swear on my mother's grave that I'm not. I've been getting help and going to meetings and haven't touched any dope in four weeks!"

Andrea stood there staring at the second glass of wine she had poured before the bottle had shattered on the floor. She picked up the crystal glass and downed the whole glass in an instant. God help me for what I am about to do!

"Okay if your down in the city this week, we'll meet up as a family."

Was she doing the right thing? Should she really be giving this man a second chance? A man who had hurt her and her children continuously by abandoning them for some other woman he was attracted to. Andrea wondered if the only reason he called was due to him needing something. Was his latest marriage not working out as he had hoped? Or could it be that he was using again and hoped to be able to manipulate Andrea or even worse her kids into getting him money to support his habit.

"Great, you won't regret it! Oh and tell Amy and Jeremy I said hi and that I'll see them soon! Goodbye 'Dre," he said, the hope in his voice seeming to be genuine, but with Robert you never know. After all she was married to him for years and after all that time and the tests and tribulations they had gone through, he had proven you never know a person's inner flaws until they become evident.

Shifting her thoughts from Robert as she grabbed a roll of paper towels to finish dabbing up the last of the spilled wine, her head flooded emotions of men and relationships and much more, Andrea found her mind slipping back once more to Aidan Preston.

Was there something there that she might be able to follow through with? Could all these years of knowing the man, working side by side with him, learning how he thinks and works be leading up into the accumulation of there being some little nugget of hope that she should possibly study some more. Maybe there was something other than the obvious sexual attraction she felt towards him. Could this truly be worth exploring?

Andrea wasn't sure, but she would certainly look into it. She just had to keep Aidan and Robert apart. The last thing she needed to be was playing both sides of the field. Other woman could do it, so why can't she?

Picking up her cell phone she scrolled through her contacts and selected Jeremy's number. She listened to it ring over and over again before finally his voice mail picked up asking her to leave a message. Frustrated at the boy, she tried calling twice more and then on the last attempt, she waited for the beep and left a message.

"Honey it's mom. I talked to the school because you ditched your classes today and we need to talk. Where are you, and why aren't you answering your phone? You need to call me as soon as possible. Some pretty bad things have happened and I need you to get home so we can talk as a family." Having left the message, she set her phone down and opened the refrigerator. Pulling a few various ingredients out, she set them on the sink and began to prepare dinner. She just hoped that by the time she was done, Amy would have some form of appetite.

The girl needed to eat to not only help her stomach but to also get over the vivid images of her friends losing their lives.

Come on Amy, I know you can do it. Don't worry sweetheart, I'm going to find out who did this and make sure justice is served. Don't you worry about that my sweet Amy! No one is going to terrorize my family!

Chapter 13

The National Zoo had been much livelier earlier in the day, but now as the evening approached, the animals all seemed to be sleeping or just lounging around in their habitats. It probably had to do with the lack of activity going on around the urban park. The best time to walk the various paths the led to the many, enclosed animal habitats and animal houses was in the morning.

With the animals just waking up and eating their various breakfast time meals, they were much more active than as he day grew longer. You had a better chance of being able to interact with the animals before the heat of the day and all the excitement of the many visitors moving around the park, shouting and running about, children and adults of all ages emerging on the urban location daily. Tens of thousands of tourists flocked to the large Smithsonian landmark each day and with so many people coming and going the animals seemed to become much more sluggish as the day dwindled on. As the outside temperature dropped due to spring ending and the colder months on its way, the animals would continue to become less active as winter approached.

With the Zoo normally closing around sunset, Jeremy looked up to the sky to see that the orange and red hues that splashed across the clouds now that the glum, overcast clouds from the afternoon was fading away. These streaks of light spilling across the horizon began to shift in color and be replaced by deeper blues and purples. Jeremy just sat there for a moment, enjoying the cool October breeze whipping around him and making him pull his coat tighter against his arms and back.

"I love the sky when it looks like that," Jeremy said to his friend sitting across the picnic table from him.

"Yeah whatever, so its got some streaks of color running through it. Before long it's gonna be dark and then we won't be able to see shit," Tommy muttered, then taking a sip from the large soda he had bought at the Zoo's eatery, finished the beverage with a loud, draining slurp and shot if into the air and towards an open trash receptacle.

"It is getting late. What time was your brother going to be here?"

Tommy just shrugged, then began finishing off the plate of fries he had laid out before him. They hadn't eaten this morning since they skipped out on first period and decided to go check out what Tommy's older brother was doing at work. It was really just an excuse to get some free food with his employee discount, but neither of them were going to pass up the food. Their server had been a cute, blonde college girl who had put their orders together and Tommy had whispered to Jeremy that this was the girl his brother was secretly crushing on.

Jeremy had met Frank a couple times and even though they were related, they were as far apart of the spectrum that unless you knew them, you'd never know they were brothers. That was fine with both of them as they both got annoyed by the other pretty quickly.

While Tommy could care less about attending college and pursuing any goal no matter how easy, a trait that had unfortunately been wearing off on Jeremy, but Frank was different. He took schooling seriously and was using that to advance himself into the field of his dreams. Once while over at Tommy's house after school, they had gone into Frank's bedroom to check for a stack of nudie magazines under his mattress, but instead found all kinds of books on biology, wildlife studies and nature.

The majority of these magazines and books were geared towards the research and conservation of wolves. While Tommy could care less about any animal, Frank had noticed the interest Jeremy had shown upon seeing his collection, and today after Frank had found out his brother was ditching class, he had called Tommy and told him and Jeremy to get over to the zoo around closing, and once he was off for the day, he would give them a behind the scenes tour of the place after hours.

While Tommy fawned boredom and really only wanted to check out the Reptile House, the large building that housed the many snakes, turtles, alligators and more scaled creatures, Jeremy wanted to go with Frank and see the wolves. The last few times Jeremy had seen Frank, he had come up with dozens of questions regarding the captive animals. Frank had explained through conservation enterprises the National Zoo only had Mexican wolves and maned wolves at the Zoo currently. However, when he told Jeremy about the pack of gray wolves they had at the campus Frank worked at, and that eventually once construction was complete here at the urban park, the gray wolves would be moving to the Zoo's new habitat. Jeremy couldn't wait.

As they sat there waiting, Jeremy's phone started to vibrate in his backpack. He retrieved it and checked the screen before forwarding the call to his voice mail. "Shit it's my mom for like the thousandth time," he muttered, sliding the phone back into his bag.

"She probably found out you skipped today. You're going to be in so much trouble!" Tommy nagged.

"Oh stuff it. I wouldn't be out here if it wasn't for you."

"Yeah right, you just wanted to meet up with Frank so he can blow your mind with all the crap he's been doing with around here. I mean what a joke. He spends most of his time here and doesn't get paid! You wouldn't catch me dead doing something that stupid. If I'm doing work then I'm getting those dollars son!"

"Whatever, he promised me he'd take me on a behind the scenes tour of the new wolf habitat. Besides I wouldn't mind working at a zoo."

"Yeah so you can go around cleaning crap up after the animals? There's a way to spend your life— scooping up elephant shit all day!"

"That's not just what they do here! They do research and keep the animals healthy, they work on helping the endangered species from being wiped out..." Jeremy started to defend his feelings on the subject.

"Woah there dingleberry, what crawled up your shorts? Geesh, how is it you know more about what they do here than me? I mean Jesus, Frank's my brother but the way you two talk I'd think you were lovers!"

"Oh can it!" Jeremy said, throwing a half eaten french fry at the mocking teen. Tommy batted it out of the way right before it would have hit him in the head.

Just then, Jeremy's backpack began to vibrate. "I hope that's Frank, it's getting late," he said as he opened the bag and looked at the phone.

"Well?" Tommy asked, the boredom in his voice showing he was tired of hanging around the zoo any longer. It was almost closing time now that the sun was almost set, and Frank still hadn't arrived to pick them up.

Jeremy ignored Tommy's pestering as he checked the new text messages on his phone. He scrolled through a couple, shaking his head as he looked to his friend.

"Nah, it's my mom again. She's freaking out and wants me home right away. Says we need to talk about something," Jeremy said as he deleted the most recent text messages from his mom.

"She's probably going to ground you for skipping school today."

"I'm too old to be getting grounded anymore, I mean geesh, I'm almost sixteen!"

"Yeah right, I've met your mom remember. She's a cop! She'd probably slap a pair of handcuffs on you and toss you into your bedroom for the rest of the school year like your own personal solitary confinement," Tommy said with a sneer that turned into a jesting laugh.

Jeremy looked around the empty eating area located near the panda house exhibit. The few shops and food places had already closed up for the day, metal shutters pulled down and locked over the windows of the buildings. In fact, for the last twenty minutes that they had been waiting at the Eatery, neither boy had seen another person anywhere.

"Maybe we should take the Metro back," Jeremy finally suggested. He knew he was going to be in hot water with his mom, and he really didn't want to make it any worse than it was going to be.

"Why? Frank was on his way, you heard so yourself," Tommy muttered, then with a mischievous smile added, "Besides, didn't you hear about what happened to that woman the other night who rode the metro home?"

Jeremy turned on his feet quickly, almost knocking into Tommy who had been following him away from the Eatery.

"What happened?" Jeremy asked, the intrigue oozing in his voice.

"Where have you been lately? A couple of kids were telling me the other day before school— oh wait you've been ditching the last couple of days to avoid that ass, JP Mathews."

"I have not!" Jeremy cried out defensively. "That wannabe bully doesn't bother me. I'd kick his ass if it came down to it!"

Now it was Tommy's turn to respond. He burst out laughing, kneeling over slightly like he had just heard the funniest joke in the world.

"Hahaha, yeah that's a good one, you kickin' Mathews ass— that guy us like 6'2" and weighs as much as some of the big guys on the varsity football team! If he hadn't flunked a few times and been held back two grades, he's probably be off playing ball in college somewhere."

"Or jail," Jeremy suggested.

That last remark brought a smile to Tommy's face. His grin was wide, and then it disappeared, only to be replaced with a look of relief. "Well look who finally made it," he muttered as he reached down and picked his own backpack off the ground, slinging the strap over his shoulder as Jeremy followed his gaze.

Frank, Tommy's older brother was walking down the path towards them, his arm waving back and forth to catch their attention.

"Hey!" he called out as he approached the abandoned zoo eating area. "Hope you guys weren't waiting too long."

Jeremy told him they hadn't, while Tommy just shrugged and brushed past his brother.

"Sorry it took so long for me to get over here. Since I work out of the campus in Virginia, traffic can sometimes be a real exercise in futility," Frank explained as he waited for Jeremy to gather his backpack and the trio headed out the way Frank had arrived.

It was a short walk to get to Parking Lot A, one of the lots used for many of the staff and volunteers that worked at the zoo's urban park. One the way, Frank not getting much out of the two teens about how school had been, switched gears and told them about the project he had spent the day working on.

"So once we get all the data compiled, we should know if we have a valid set of parameters to test Lisa's theory on the application of vocalizations to aid in the understanding of wolf communications," Frank explained to a captivated Jeremy while Tommy just rolled his eyes.

"Sounds like you're using a bunch of big words to try and sound smart," Tommy uttered as they reached the car.

Before Frank could say anything to his younger sibling, Jeremy broke in. "Well I think it sounds cool. I wish I could be doing something like that and working with wild animals all day instead of being expected to go to a school where the most interesting thing we get to do in Biology class is cut open frogs."

"Yeah well you have to start somewhere. Believe me when I say I didn't like high school at all when I was your guys age," Frank stated as he unlocked the doors to his beat up station wagon and they got in.

"Sure, Mr. Honor Roll— Mom and dad are always going on about how you were the one that got the brains in the family," Tommy guffawed from the back seat.

"Oh yeah, and what did you get then?"

"Please sucka, I got the good looks. The ladies love me!" Tommy cried out bringing laughter from the entire car as Frank pulled out of the zoo's main entrance and turned onto Connecticut Avenue.

"I appreciate the ride Frank, my mom's been on me all day to get home," Jeremy admitted as the station wagon drove down the dark road.

"Oh don't do the crime if you're scared to do the time!" Tommy hollered from the back.

"No problem kiddo," Frank said, flipping on his headlights as the sun-streaked sky had finally seemed to slip below the horizon. Tommy was quiet for a little bit before finally coming up with something to spout out.

"We were just going to take the Metro home if you took any longer to get there bro."

"Oh you don't want to take the Metro after what happened the other day," Frank replied, checking his rear view mirror before switching lanes.

"Ha, see I told you something went down a couple nights ago on the Metro!" Tommy hollered, slapping the back of Jeremy's headrest with his palm as he bounced in his seat.

"Wait, you were weren't joking? What happened?"

"You know, for a kid who's got a cop for a mom, you sure live a sheltered life. No wonder your acting out and skipping classes. The rebellious phase has begun!"

"Shut up Tommy," Frank said, giving his brother a stern look in the rear view mirror. "And if anything is leading to Jeremy skipping classes, I'd put my money on you being the bad influence responsible."

"Yeah yeah college boy, why don't you stay out of it while I fill my corruptible apprentice in on the latest, gory murder to grace our fair city!" Tommy said, leaning forward and putting his head in between Frank and Jeremy's seats.

Ignoring his loud-mouthed, younger brother, Frank followed Connecticut Avenue a little further before taking a turn in the direction of Jeremy's home.

"Anyways, I can't believe you hadn't heard about the murder two nights ago!"

"Will you just get to the story already," Jeremy said, anxious to hear the story before they arrived at his house and he had to face his mother's wrath.

"Okay, okay. So two nights ago some woman was riding the metro home late at night and at some point some crazy wacko attacked her and cut her to pieces. From what I heard from a guy who lives near the park they found the body in, he said the were body parts all over the place. Can you imagine that?"

"Bullshit! You're making this up," Jeremy said but the look on his friend's face told him he wasn't.

"Your mom's a detective, she didn't tell you anything about it?" Tommy asked with a look of skepticism.

Jeremy glanced back from the passenger seat and looked at the teen. He was about to tell him to 'cram it' when he realized that his mom did work homicide. Why was this the first time he was hearing about this?

"No she didn't," he finally admitted. "She usually doesn't talk about the cases she's working on."

"Well if one of my parents was a cop, I'd be all over the latest gossip. I mean— who knows how many crazies and wackos there are walking about every day. And, they don't even catch them all. Most of them wander the streets killing people and never getting caught. Imagine that! What if someone you knew was a psychopath with a closet full of victims. Could be anybody, even the people living right next door!" The interest in Tommy's voice continued to grow as he spouted his opinions to the rest of the car.

"I'd put my money on Mr. Feldman."

Jeremy shot him a questioning glance, his face showing that he clearly thought Tommy nuts. "The janitor at school?"

"Hell yeah! I mean look at the guy. Everybody's seen the way that creepy old man stares at the various girls as they walk down the halls. I bet he probably tricks them down into the school's basement where his workshop is and molests them. Feldman's probably one sick bastard— and with the weird stub of an left hand, it looks like it was mangled in some machine!"

As the boy continued to expand on his theories, Frank finally cut in.

"Enough already Tommy. Mr. Feldman's been working at that school for years and no girls have gone missing. As for his hand, I heard he nearly lost it years ago when the high school had an old boiler room and some rusted pipe exploded. The guy was lucky to keep his arm, let alone his life."

"So, that clawed hand is still freaky! It's like a claw or hook or something. And the reason nobody's found any bodies down in the school's lower levels where the guy creeps about all by himself is he probably gets rid of them in the old furnace. Probably even keeps mementos to remember his victims by!"

"You've been watching too many horror movies," Jeremy said, rolling his eyes at Tommy before turning back around in his seat.

"Whatever. All I'm saying is if I had your mom, I'd be all over her to find out what kind of crazy shit is going on in this city. It's boring enough around here, we need something to stir things up, just like the murder in the park."

"Well she's probably just trying to shelter me and Amy. Doesn't want us to know all the details about every crazy roaming about. Besides, if something important did happen, I'm sure she'd tell us. She probably just doesn't want to talk about work when she gets home after dealing with all those 'crazies' each day!" Jeremy said a little too defensively, and he hoped Tommy hadn't caught the edge in his voice.

Ever since his dad had walked out on them, his mom had been the only thing keeping their family together. He knew she had to work hard to provide for them, and she had every right to not want to drudge up the seriousness of her job when she came home at night. She put in so many hours a week as it was, he knew she liked to come home and just unwind. Usually her favorite thing to do was grab a glass of wine when she got in from a long shift, plop down on the couch and channel surf for a couple hours as the wine bottle got lower and lower. It wasn't like she was an alcoholic, and Jeremy had read somewhere that police officers had a higher susceptibility to becoming drunks and addicts due to the stresses they faced in the line of duty.

As Jeremy looked through the windshield turned back in his seat, he saw that Frank was just turning the wheel of the car, and the station wagon pulled to a stop in front of his house. The porch light was on and Jeremy knew his mother was probably standing inside the kitchen just waiting for him to walk in before she laid into him. He should have returned her texts and at least let her know he was okay, but he also didn't feel like he needed to be checking in with her every few hours. After all he was almost sixteen, practically an adult!

Here goes nothing, he thought to himself as he climbed out of the car. He saw the blinds in the kitchen window move and he knew that she had seen him arrive.

Great, I can't wait to hear this!

Saying goodbye to Tommy and thanking Frank for the ride, he shut the door to the wagon with a thud and turned towards the small, townhouse.

Well it's now or never, he thought as he walked up the little cement path and reached the front door. He knew his mom was on the other side just waiting for him to enter. With one last fleeting thought of hopping back into the car with Frank and Tommy, realized he'd have to come home eventually, and went in.

Getting back to The Informant's building had taken a little more time than Nick would have liked. He had placed a call to the paper and was fortunate enough to reach Danielle at her desk. He asked the cute office intern for an update on if there was anything going on over there that he should be aware of and she had told him that Marty was looking for him. Apparently the Editor in Chief was spitting blood about Nick not having turned in any proofs so far and with the late hour, he wasn't going to be holding the presses for much longer.

Nick told Danielle to tell him he'd be there shortly, and once off the phone, he stepped on the gas pedal and shot towards downtown Rockville to try and make up some lost time and get his latest article in on before Marty ran a substitution piece. If that happened he would never hear the end of it.

He had already gotten his boss to postpone the Mayor Finance Scandal article he had been working on to allow him to focus on the murders, but from what Danielle had said over the phone, it didn't look like Marty had much patience left for excuses. Fortunately for Nick, after leaving the latest murder scene this afternoon, and getting Detective Aidan Preston on board with his mission to discover the murderer's motives and hope to stop them before they struck again, Nick had gained an invaluable ally.

After driving out of the quarry, his old car almost breaking down twice as he made it back to a paved road away from the quarry's abandoned area, he had stopped by Starbucks to use their free wi-fi connection and pull up what he could on the good old Detective Aidan Preston.

Nick remembered the man's name and face from a while back, there had been something big that had happened with the guy, but he couldn't quite put his finger on it.

Being a journalistic reporter, he delved in deep with the stories he was assigned, but once they were no longer news, he didn't really pay much attention to the events that transpired afterwords. That is unless the aftermath of a certain event or individual warranted the new interest.

His job and world revolved around reporting the news and keeping the public informed of what was happening in the world. Since his designation was the crime and politics section, working for a smaller paper like The Informant, meant that he didn't usually need to focus his attention on the stories that affected people outside of the paper's smaller market space. If he wrote for one of the bigger guys like the Times or Post then he might have a little more to give back to his readers, but since that wasn't the case, he just had to make do with The Informants smaller circulation and hope that eventually he would break out into the bigger arena.

Pulling his laptop from his workbag hanging on the back of his chair, he pulled up his internet and connected to the coffee shop's wi-fi server. Within a minute or two of looking he had found what he was looking for.

The headline read, 'Cop Kills Armed Murderer, Innocent Girl Critically Wounded During Standoff'.

Nick's brain went working into overtime as he scanned through the article quickly, scrolling through the pages until he came to a photograph of Detective Aidan Preston. It looked like it had been taken a few years ago, the Detective's hair had been shorter, and he seemed to not have the weary, troubled look that he had seen on him at the quarry earlier.

Nick continued reading through the article, the whole time he had the sense that the Detective was still haunted by his inner demons. Nobody should have to go through that, he thought, and quickly reading through a second article he had pulled up, began looking for anything more recent. It took him a little longer to find what he had been searching for but on the third page of the computer's search engine results he came to an article that had come out a couple weeks after the first articles he had found. This one answered the questions he had been wondering after being chased off from the crime scene by that one loud-mouthed, arrogant bastard who had shown up.

Detective Preston was chased off the scene because he wasn't on active duty. Interesting, Nick thought as he perused the last of the article and then sitting back in his chair, nursing the cup of coffee he had bought when he first entered the coffee shop, he thought about what he had learned.

So the detective was on administrative leave due to the way a possible violent scene had turned out. It sounded to Nick like the guy had saved the girl's life, especially since the cop who had first shown up hadn't secured the scene and cleared the apartment. That rookie's mistake had led to not only the suspect being killed, but Preston being shot and the little girl he was attempting to save being crippled for life. What a tragedy.

An incident like that would make him think twice about his line of work, but here Aidan Preston was, obviously recovered from the bullet he took to the upper chest, but no doubt carrying a load of guilt and anger, and he was still out there, whether his bosses wanted him to or not, and he was following up with the murders.

Nick had to hand it to the guy. He was one touch son of a bitch and it seemed like he took his job seriously. Detective Preston might not be working this case in the lines of procedure and protocol but that wasn't going to stop Nick from taking advantage of their possible partnership.

Pulling his cell phone out from his pocket, he quickly dialed a number and waited for the person to pick up. After a couple rings, Danielle's soft voice came over the line.

Nick was already standing, stashing his laptop back into his work bag and heading for the door of the coffee shop when she asked, "Hey Nick, what's up?"

"Darling, I was wondering if you could do me a favor," he stated, tossing his half drank coffee into the trash and exiting the store.

"For you— anything," Danielle breathed out in a low breathless whisper like she was trying to imitate an old movie actress attempting to seduce the main star of the film. Maybe Marilyn Monroe, Nick thought picturing Danielle's sexy figure and blonde head of hair. Yeah, she did remind him of a younger Monroe.

"Appreciate it," he said as he headed for his car. He looked at his watch as he walked across the street to the adjacent parking lot. It was a quarter to five. If he was going to be able to get everything he needed to do before this day was over he was going to need help.

"Okay, do you have a pen to write this down?"

"Yup, go ahead."

Nick began telling the pretty intern what he needed her to do. He just hoped she'd be able to pull it off in time. Well, guess he'd just have to see.

Chapter 14

The results of the initial vocalizations testing were looking good. So far the pack of gray wolves had responded incredibly well to the audio cues they had initiated with the help of modern technology.

The Sony outdoor speakers were small and portable, with a rugged, waterproof exterior they were capable of being placed in any number of normally inaccessible locations around the wolves' habitat and surviving in the outdoor elements for any period of time they were needed. Built into the speaker's tough shell was a small rubber coated antenna that allowed the speakers to operate wireless when receiving the audio transmission from the stereo setup attached to the computers audio-manipulation software. This increased the practicality of using them for the purposes at the zoo since it would be painstaking work to try to run wires all throughout the habitat. The only other option would be to bury the cords, but then they risked the wolves digging the cables up and biting into them. Just like a dog tearing a yard up in pursuit of a bone, wolves were known to be notorious diggers.

Studying the observations Frank and her had written down in notebooks earlier, Lisa Davies turned her attention to the most conclusive data she had recorded. According to the reaction of the wolves and how they had responded to the prerecorded vocals and other sounds they had played through the speakers and into the habitat, her theory on wolf communications seemed to be close to coming to fruition.

The wolves, especially the adult two, Ulric and Zeeb, seemed to have the largest response to the sounds as opposed to the three siblings. Lisa believed the difference could be due in large part to the individual animals they had to test. The two adults had been born and raised in the wild, experiencing a world far different from the simulated environment of a zoo. Once they had been captured, the wildlife refuge that originally had been caring for the pair of gray wolves realized that the female Zeeb, was pregnant. Her children, Adolpho, Lupa and Raze were thus born into captivity and eventually due to the size of the new family, they were moved and sent across the country to what would finally become their home here at the Virginia campus of SCBI until their permanent habitat was finished and they were moved permanently to become the first gray wolves housed in the Smithsonian National Zoological Park's downtown urban park location.

Checking off a few notes on her clipboard, Lisa looked up just in time to see a figure through the glass of her office door. A subsequent knock sounded as the unknown figure on the other side knocked three times on the closed door. Not bothering to stand, Lisa set the clipboard down and turned in her chair.

"Come in," she called.

The Director of the National Zoo, Dr. Wesley Ashton opened the door and strolled in to the office, his light tweed jacket complete with patches on the elbows reminded Lisa of a odd-looking college professor instead of the man responsible for running the largest zoo in the country.

Stopping for a moment to shut the door behind him, he turned and with a smile, walked over to Lisa. Standing up, she hugged the kind faced man, his graying beard tickling the side of her cheek as they held each other in a tight grasp. Finally the older gentleman broke away and with a smile said, "Ah my dear, you look beautiful as ever."

Lisa was used to the man she had grown to see as a father over the years appearing at the most random times, always checking in on her to make sure she was okay and see how she was doing. The look in his deep eyes, set behind thick bifocal glasses, was one of caring and love. Ever since she came to work for SCBI, Dr. Ashton had been at the forefront of those she could go to for help or questions. He believed that a research facility or a zoo were only as grand as the people you had working behind the scenes to do the actual massive amount of daily work being done at this organization, and because of that he hired the best he could to round out the faculty and staff of both the SCBI building and the Zoo's urban park facility.

In fact it was his need to scour the country for the best and brightest minds that had led him to discovering Lisa Marie Davies in Teton County, Wyoming. At 28, she was the youngest wildlife biologist on staff at the Yellowstone National Park's research outpost. While former colleagues used to joke that it was Lisa's beautiful Mayan looks that had attracted the aging Director to her, she knew it was the work she had done on the conservation of the gray wolf population's dwindling size and need for protection that had really gotten her the job offer to come to the East Coast and work at SCBI. That had been six years ago and even though Lisa missed Yellowstone Park's exquisite beauty and the amazing open expanse of wilderness, the opportunity presented to her by coming to Virgina was something she couldn't pass up.

"Thank you Dr. Ashton, you're as kind as ever. How can I help you?" Lisa asked, turning away from the work spread out before her and turning her full attention to the Director of the institute that she called home. All thanks to this man.

SCBI was a chance in a lifetime to work with amazing talent and like-minded individuals with the same goal of protecting and learning about the animals that make up the vast world on the planet Earth. Nowhere else in the known galaxies of space is there hardly viable proof of other living organisms, yet when it comes to Earth, there is a multitude of diverse species that inhabit every ecosystem and environment spreading to every corner of the world.

"Well my dear, I wanted to talk to you about your presentation and the upcoming Board meeting."

Lisa nodded her head and waved to the spare seat beside her.

"Don't mind if I do," the older man said, pulling the chair up and sitting his small frame down. A small wince quickly vanished from his face as he sat and rubbed his knees lightly. "It isn't so grand trying to get around this place every day when the doctor's keep telling me I'm not getting any younger." A smile appeared and Lisa returned the expression.

"Anyways, as you know, the Board of Directors meets at the end of each month to discuss everything from budgetary restrictions, department spendings, new proposals and such. That includes grant requests, which we both know you have turned in and If I do say so myself, made a passionate plea to justify the allocation of the Smithsonian's funds to your cause."

Lisa nodded again and feeling slightly flattered at how he always seemed to dwell on her actions and achievements like a proud father, a figure she never had in her own life, felt her cheeks blush. Fortunately for her, her darker, Spanish skin color helped hide the fact that she was blushing and Dr. Ashton didn't seem to notice as he continued talking.

"Just between you and I, I believe you shouldn't be worried about anything coming between you and your research. I have a feeling that your department is going to get the funds you need in order to really provide you with the monetary and research fundamentals required to continue your groundbreaking theories. To tell you the truth, one of the main reasons I fought so hard to get you here is my childhood fascination with wolves myself."

This glimpse into the man she had known for six years and who was not only her boss but a mentor of sorts made her attention focus even more on his words. She was getting a peak at the man behind the prestigious title of Director, an image most people never got the chance to view.

"Really?" she asked.

"Oh yes, like many boys growing up I enjoyed the study of things like the long-extinct dinosaurs and the creepy, crawly forms of bugs and spiders, but wolves were always one of my favorites. That is one reason I have supported the past projects we started like the conservation efforts established for the Mexican Wolf Reintroduction Program. It has been a much needed program long overdue, and is a perfect example of what the SCBI was founded for. After all, we serve as an umbrella for the Smithsonian's global effort to conserve species and train future generations of conservationists. You have to remember one of our four main goals in the latest strategic plan released by the Board.

'We are here to 'advance understanding and sustaining a bio-diverse planet', and the scientists we have here working for the National Zoo are pioneers in the field of conservation biology. We have long been leaders in the study, management, protection, and restoration of threatened species, ecological communities, habitats, and ecosystems," Dr. Ashton continued.

Lisa just sat there watching the man give his speech. It was one he had obviously perfected over the years of his being Director of the National Zoo.

"Just remember what we do here at the SCBI. As the benefits of conserving biodiversity becomes more clearly defined, we will allow Smithsonian scientists to be recognized as leaders in developing ways to stem the loss of the multitude of diverse species and aid in the recovery of endangered species and habitats. It's through our conservation efforts, that we not only advance research and scientific knowledge in conserving wildlife, but through the demonstration of animal care, science, education and sustainability that we showcase, we provide a model that other institutes strive to achieve.

'Not only are we leaders in the field, we teach and inspire others to protect wildlife, natural resources and animal habitats. Here at the Smithsonian and I believe that with the last renovations and new exhibits wrapping up, the grand opening of our first ever gray wolf exhibit. After all we are the Nation's Zoo! Not only do we provide the highest quality animal care, we advance research and our scientists are world leaders in conservation biology who work all over the globe! Our research ensures the health and well-being of animals in captivity and in the wild."

The look of excitement on Dr. Ashton's face was quite clear to Lisa. She was excited to ever since she learned about the zoo's plans to expand and construct new areas for the introduction of species of animals they had previously not shown at the zoo.

"Anyways, I spoke to the Board earlier regarding the next phase of exhibits we have been building and they think, which I agree with, we should have the opening before schedule. The enclosures are completed in the new section and there's really no point to wait all the way until the new year. If we're done ahead of schedule, then we believe we should allow the public access to the new improvements as soon as possible."

Lisa just sat there taking it all in.

"The Moonlight Trail walking path is finished and by the end of the week we can begin transporting the animal's from their holding facilities and to the zoo in time to have the opening celebrations," Dr. Ashton finished with a wide, gleeful smile.

"How soon are we talking?"

"We won't know until we reach an agreement at the Board meeting, but the initial talks are looking at setting the opening gala in December."

Lisa sat forward in her chair.

"But that's only a little more than a month from now— there's only a week until November as it is!"

Dr. Ashton seemed to think this over for a moment and then put a calming hand on Lisa's own.

"Yes it is sooner than we planned, but imagine the waste of time and money if the enclosures and trails were to remain closed up until the originally scheduled grand opening. It really makes more sense to give the animals more time to acclimate to their new environments before the new year begins. There would be less chance of any issues arising if we can take care of everything before winter sets in. It would just make it more of a problem trying to deal with the move without having to deal with the snow as well. It's supposed to be a pretty harsh winter this year."

Lisa sat there thinking everything she had just heard over. Was there enough time to actually accomplish it? Would moving the wolves, her wolves from the SCBI campus to the zoo interfere with the research she had been doing lately? Would the change in their environment, the home they had already adjusted to and become comfortable with, make it so she would have to postpone her audio vocalization tests? Question after question flooded her mind as she sat there listening to Dr. Ashton drone on. Normally she would be attentive to whatever the man had to say, but for now she was lost in her own thoughts.

Dr. Ashton noticing that he had lost Lisa into her own world, gave her a moment to regain her composure. He knew she'd go along with the change in dates, she just had to warm up to the idea. That was another reason he had hired her. She wasn't dumb. She could view the big picture and realize that this change was in the best interests for all concerned.

"Lisa?" he asked finally drawing her eyes to him.

"Yeah?"

"Thought I lost you for a moment."

"No, well yes, sorry. I have a lot on my mind with everything we've been working on here, and then with the grant and now the possibility of a new opening date for the Moonlight Trail, I sort of just zoned out for a minute," Lisa explained.

Dr. Ashton just waved her apology off.

"Don't worry my girl, don't worry. It'll all work out. Like I said, nothing is official yet, I just wanted to give you a heads up. We won't know anything for sure until the Board meets this week"

"Well I appreciate you taking the time to let me know."

"Of course my dear, like I have always said, the Smithsonian is a family, and as such, I believe I have to look out for all interests involved. And you are one of those interests that matter greatly."

Lisa smiled.

Having said what he came to say, Dr. Ashton stood from his seat, his arthritic knees causing him to groan slightly as he got up. His eyes took a look around the office, taking in the various lab space and work tables dedicated to the work Lisa was pursuing.

"Well, I'm off. Other faculty to check on, other research proposals to catch up on. It's a glorious time for the scientific community with great minds like yours leading the way in conservational studies!"

"Take care Wesley," Lisa said as she watched the man slip out of the room and with a cursory look down each hall, he made a left and disappeared from sight.

Lisa leaned back in her seat, the padding of the chair pressing into her lower back. She would never understand how some academics could spend most of their days sitting in chairs like these, hunched over desks for long hours under the harsh glow of fluorescent lighting and working on their dissertations to submit to the various scientific journals. No, that was certainly not how Lisa would survive living long enough to make a difference in the world of science and discovery.

She tried to focus back on the recorded notes her and her assistant Frank had jotted down earlier. Unfortunately, Frank had to leave early to go pick up his younger brother and a friend from downtown. Normally she would have minded him cutting out from work early, but he was a hard worker and since he was unpaid for the time he put in around the lab, Lisa didn't mind letting him ditch out a little early. She could finish going over the notes herself. However, after the Director's surprise visit she had a lot more on her mind than her current research project. She kept finding herself thinking about the zoo's latest renovations.

The latest exhibit to open at the Washington D.C., urban location had been the new American Trail. It was home to a wide range of North American animals, including beavers, river otters, bald eagles and ravens. In addition to those enclosures, the American Trail was also the location for the new seal and sea lion exhibit. Lisa had walked it a few times on her multiple visits a week downtown to the Zoo, and was impressed with the way they had designed the walking path and animal enclosures.

As a person walks down the trail, the landscape and flora of the local Rock Creek forest that runs along one side of the Zoo follows the path then gives way to the faux rocky shores of the coast. Walking along, the large Oak and Poplar trees eventually give way to evergreens and various ferns pepper the landscape.

Continuing along, visitors hear the sound of water and when looking for the source, realize they have arrived at the river otter's section. Then nearing the end of the American Trail, an underwater sea cave offers an extraordinary view of life below the habitat's waters. This trail was originally the home of the zoo's Mexican Wolf collection, but they were replaced with another atrium for the expanded bald eagle exhibit.

Now her thoughts turned to the news she had just received from the Director of the National Zoo, Dr. Ashton. If what he said had any truth behind his words, then the latest exhibit and newest constructed walking trail that the zoo had built was going to be opening in almost less than a month.

She remembered all the hard work she had put into the planning and designing of the new trail with the Board, other SCBI and Zoo faculty and the contractors and specialists who were to bring this dream to life. It had seemed like a long shot just two years ago when the idea had been brought up in a meeting, but since then, Ashton ran with it and with Lisa's help, they were about to see the Midnight Trail come to life!

Designed to best accommodate the animal's needs, the new exhibits would create an enriching environment for the occupants to be able to roam freely through larger enclosures that will better mimic the outdoor territories they are from. Every exhibit and facility throughout the Midnight Trail had been constructed using sustainable, eco-friendly materials to follow through with the conservation message. Viewing spots for the visitors were spread out frequently throughout each enclosure and the way they had been designed, it allowed for the maximum amount of visitors to the Zoo to be able to see as much of the open grounds as possible.

Built into each habitat using real rocks, trees, bushes and creek beds, every animal enclosure was designed to optimize the feeling of being out in the forest along with the animals themselves. State of the art fencing and viewing ports were added so that tourists could get as up and close and personal with the various creatures without the Zoo having to worry that they would be disturbing or distracting the animals from their daily, natural routines. Specialized glass walls followed the entire length of the winding path, creating the feel that as a person walked from one end of the trail to the other that they were not viewing wild animals trapped in cages, but that the animals could actually be roaming about alongside them. The walls were coated in a special film so that visitors on their side of the walkway could see perfectly clearly into the habitats, but if a person looked through the other side they would see nothing but dark glass.

This new addition to the walls was implemented so that humans could not disturb the animals in their enclosures and instead would go about their daily activities as naturally as possible. Planted all along the walls and walkways down the trail, large oak and maple trees rose high above the ground, adding to the darkness of the forest that the trail was supposed to be mimicking.

The Midnight Trail was going to be one of the most advanced zoological exhibits in the country, the entire winding walk actually making a person feel as if they were in the woods themselves. It was the next closest thing a person could do besides getting into the enclosure with the captive animals. And, captive or not, they were still wild and the animals that were to call the Midnight Trail home wouldn't take to kindly to obnoxious visitors in their domain.

This was where Lisa's family of gray wolves would be moved to in just a few weeks, possibly sooner if the Board decided to open the trail up ahead of schedule. However, for the time being they were currently enjoying the wide open space provided to them at the SCBI campus. While the gray wolves would be the main attraction with the possibility of them adding an additional three adults to the pack, the new area would be dedicated to the zoo's current resident Mexican and Maned Wolf population.

Lisa thought about the conservation efforts they had already been working on at the National Zoo. It was a program that started long before she came to work at SCBI, but it was certainly a much needed plan to keep the animals from becoming extinct. The National Zoo, she knew was working with more than 40 other zoos and breeding facilities around the country to save the Mexican wolf. To keep the population genetically healthy, breeding efforts are carefully managed under an specialized survival plan created to provide the Mexican Wolves with the best chance of survival from extinction.

Before settlers arrived in North America, gray wolves could be found throughout most of what is now the United States as well as Canada and northern Mexico. As early as the 17th century, people offered wolf bounties to protect their livestock. Bounties were common across the country by the 18th century. Both private citizens and government agents used traps, poisons, and guns to kill wolves. And they were highly successful. Additionally, forest clearing dramatically reduced their habitat.

By 1900, wolves had been removed from the northeastern area of the country as well as much of Canada. By the early 1980s, it looked like the subspecies of Mexican wolves, native to the southwest, were extinct in the wild. However, a handful of Mexican wolves survived in zoos and other breeding facilities. These, and five wild wolves caught in Mexico between 1977 and 1980, became the foundation for a breeding program. Lisa could recall how big of an event that was in the scientific community.

The Mexican Wolf Rehabilitation Program was the last hope for saving the subspecies. She knew that Mexican wolves, which were added to the federal list of endangered species in 1976, are protected by the Endangered Species Act, and are being reintroduced into the wild as part of the Mexican Wolf Recovery Plan, and that because of the efforts of SCBI and their affiliates, other gray wolf subspecies had made a comeback as well.

Lisa wasn't sure how much she liked the idea of moving the grand opening ceremony up ahead of schedule, but then again it wasn't her call. She may be responsible for the care and studying of the wolves in her charge, but when it came to matters of the National Zoo and their plans for progress, she was nothing.

I hope I can finish collecting my vocalization tests before this all happens. I'm just going to have to work harder at it, make sure it gets done before the big move.

Turning back to the reports and notes Frank had left her to go over, she began scanning the pages for the finalized results. As she correlated the findings and began the monotonous task of transferring the data into the computer spreadsheet, she looked at her watch and then leaned back in her chair, arms over her head as she stretched her back and yawned. It had been a long day so far and she was contemplating calling it quits, and picking up on the data transfer with the help of Frank the next day. However, before she could head home for the evening she wanted to check her e-mail one last time.

Logging into the Smithsonian's e-mail server, she scrolled through her inbox. She had a few memos that had been sent out to everyone who worked for the SCBI, another was from a colleague looking to meet up for coffee next week to discuss some work he had going on, but as she continued to read through the messages, she realized that Tyler still hadn't responded back to her.

That's odd, I wonder what could be keeping him from contacting me back?

Lisa double checked her inbox and then made a cursory glace through the junk folder to make sure it hadn't been misplaced again, but no, there were no new e-mails from her latest West Coast pen pal. They had been writing back and forth to each other for days and everything had seemed to be going well on Lisa's end. He had promised to package up the samples she had requested and the newer photographs his daughter had taken for him to replace the hardly recognizable ones he had taken, and then he was supposed to ship it across the country to her office at the SCBI campus.

Where the devil are you? Lisa wondered as she pulled up a new e-mail message and began typing another message to Tyler.

Hope he doesn't mind me filling his inbox constantly, she thought. Then again he should have responded to her last inquiries. It wasn't like the man she had been constantly talking to online for a week straight to just up and disappear, not bothering to have the decency to respond to her many messages.

As she finished typing her e-mail, she took one last look at the message she had typed out and then pressed send.

Come on Mr. Rancher Man, let me know you sent me those bones!

Chapter 15

Setting the thick, file folder Mack had provided him down on his work desk and leaned back in the stiff chair. The office was quiet since he had arrived half an hour earlier. Detective's Tim Melvin and Andrea Wilkes were both out of the building. He had learned from Mack that Melvin was actually assisting down at the crime scene at the quarry that Garza had run him off of earlier, and when he had inquired about Andrea, the secretary down on the first floor said she had flew out of the building early this morning due to some emergency that involved her daughter.

Siting in the hard, wood chair in the warm office, the building seemed to have had the heat kick on due to the colder temperatures outside, and now Aidan found himself sitting at his desk with his forehead slick with perspiration, his shirt starting to stick to his back as he prepared to go over the case files on the murders that Mack had compiled for him. Before he opened the folder and began to go through it, his thoughts turned to Detective Andrea Wilkes and he wondered if everything was alright with her and her family.

While they had known each other for years, working many of the same cases together and solving a large percentage of crimes, their relationship had always hedged on the professional. Sitting in the hot office alone with his thoughts, Aidan began to think about what he knew of the woman's life outside of the police force. He knew she had been married years ago, and through some fault of her ex husbands, they had never reconciled. He also knew she had two kids, but for the life of him he couldn't remember their names at the moment. He did recall that they were in high school. They attended Rockville High and he was positive the oldest was a senior preparing to graduate and go off to college.

As Aidan thought about how different his life would be if he had kids at this point in his life and they were old enough to be in high school. Not wanting to dwell of failed goals, he pushed his own dilemma out of his mind and thought of Andrea again. Yes she was a beautiful woman, and any man in their right mind would probably be willing to drop everything they had going to snatch her up. However she was a cop, and a damn good one at that, and from personal experience, Aidan knew how their choice of careers affected relationships and loved ones. Just starting out, the statistics didn't look good.

Suddenly his day dreaming was drawn back to his previous train of thoughts. Wait a minute— Andrea's daughter was a senior at Rockville High School! Wasn't that where those four teens discovered earlier had attended? And now Andrea was out of the building for some 'family emergency'? Something wasn't adding up, and a sense of worry shot through Aidan as he pushed the crime scene folder across his desk and reached for the phone sitting in the cradle on his desk.

What if something had happened to Andrea's daughter? Andrea may be one tough Detective and had proven that to Aidan many times on various police busts and investigations that didn't go as planned, but if the knot in his stomach was an indication or some form of gut-instinct, then the woman he had been proud to call his partner many a times needed his help! He was just beginning to dial Andrea's number when the door to Chief Stone's office swung open, and from the look on the imposing man's face, Aidan was about to have his tail handed to him.

"What the hell is wrong with you?" Stone demanded as he brushed out of his office and into the Homicide Division's work area. "Are you just trying to get kicked off the force due to insubordination?"

Yes the man was angry, and the recent events of everything happening lately probably wasn't helping the Chief's high blood pressure one bit. His face was flushed and Aidan could see his eyes looked bloodshot from lack of sleep and no doubt the pressure certain political parties were putting on the Chief to wrap these murders up. City elections were coming up in November and the Mayor and most of the city council were either going to stay in office or be replaced by the other candidates through the people's votes. That meant that Stone couldn't let this rash of murders plaguing Rockville all of a sudden spread out of control.

A serial killer on the loose did not look good and ease the voters' minds when they hit the polls to elect the people responsible for keeping them safe. Obviously the Mayor was adding just the right amount of pressure to keep Chief Stone in a constant state of stress. The man's reddened, serious expression looked like he was suffering from a hernia.

"I'm sorry, could you be a little more specific?" Aidan said as he watched the man stomp towards him, the sour look on his face belaying the anger that had probably been rising up inside him all day.

"Dammit Preston, you know exactly what I'm talking about. Lieutenant Garza has been lighting my phone up with complaints about how we're handling the joint cooperation into these murders. I've been letting the Rockville PD run with this case since it was in their backyard, giving them aid when they wanted it, but Garza is pissed off that he's got officers hanging around his crime scenes when they aren't officially cleared to do so.

'And as if you being there isn't enough, he told me Detective Jones had invited you there and you both were talking to a reporter! Jesus, Mary and Joseph— like that's what we need right now with everything going on— a damned reporter snooping around the investigations and providing the public the fuel it needs to start a major pandemic!"

Aidan just sat there letting the Chief express his anger. He knew that to interrupt the man now would just rile him up further.

"City elections are in a week and I've got the Mayor and now the Governor on my ass to find the killer or killers that are responsible for these murders, and frankly, we don't have a lot to go on. There have been talks about bringing the FBI in and setting up a taskforce to hopefully get to the bottom of this thing, and current investigation aside, I cannot have you out playing Detective when you're still suspended! Do you understand me?"

"Yes Sir. In my defense though, Detective Jones did authorize my presence at the scene, and I was just helping add a fresh perspective to the investigation."

"Detective Jones is not the lead investigator handling this case, you would need to be cleared by Lieutenant Garza, and to tell you the truth, that man does not want you within half a mile of his investigation! He's already asked me to bring you up on a preliminary suspension for interfering with his case and talking to a Goddamn reporter before the scene had even been processed fully, but since your still on administrative leave, that seems pretty pointless now doesn't it?"

The color in Chief Stone's face seemed to be dissipating slightly, and Aidan knew he was loosing steam the longer he hashed out his displaced anger. Obviously the murders were getting to him, and political pressure aside, Aidan could understand where the man was coming from. Having a Detective muddling around in an active investigation wasn't exactly kosher, and Stone was certainly by the book when it came to these things.

"Look Chief, I'm sorry I got involved in the case and went to the crime scene. I'll steer clear of Garza and his investigation until I get cleared to be back to work. Sorry if I caused you any trouble," Aidan said, the sorrow he felt for the man's latest responsibilities evident in his apology.

"Fine, it's fine. Just don't let this happen again or else I will be forced to bring you up on charges for interfering with an active investigation. Until you are officially reinstated, you need to head home and stay away from this case altogether."

"Understood Sir," Aidan said, standing up from his chair and beginning to gather the newest mail and reports that was stacked in his file box in the corner of the desk. Then he remembered something the Chief had mentioned during his ranting. "Oh Chief?"

Stone was walking back towards his office when he heard Aidan. Spinning on his heels, he faced the man with a questioning look on his face.

"What is it now?" Stone asked.

"You mentioned the FBI a moment ago. Are we really setting up a taskforce and joining forces with the Feds this early into the investigation?"

"I've got five dead and mutilated bodies down at the Baltimore County Morgue, and I agree with the Mayor that we need all the help we can get on this one." Then adding as an afterthought, "However, just because we need every available officer we can get working on solving this thing, you are not to be sticking your nose into it. For the time being I want you just treading water until the Medical Board clears you to be back on the force, then you can snoop around all you want and hopefully put your talents to good use.

'Truth is I could use you on this one, but rules are rules, and I do not need Garza or anybody else questioning my judgment during this case. I'm under the microscope as it is with bodies continuing to turn up in my county, and I'm not going to have you of all people add to my frustrations!" Stone said, and with that he turned and disappeared into his office, slamming the door behind him.

Aidan just stood there for a moment, looking in the direction the Chief had gone, his brain running through everything he had just learned. Sure the Chief had asked him to sit this one out until he was off administrative leave, but Aidan wasn't one to sit idly by when people were being murdered, especially if he could do something about it. As he ran the last few parts of Chief Stone's lecture through his mind, he realized something wasn't adding up.

There must be more to this than five dead bodies if the FBI was getting involved. Usually there had to be some sort of requirement for the boys out of either the main headquarters in Washington D.C., or the specialized field office in Quantico, Virginia, with their somber black suits and serious expressions to hop into their black, SUV's and other matching, government-issued vehicles and show up wherever they were called into assist. Of course when the FBI was involved they usually liked to run the show, their feelings of the 'local' law enforcement being below their pedigree. In Aidan's experience of dealing with the 'Hoover Boys', it usually took some extraordinary circumstances to get the Feds involved. Normally they didn't step into an active case until either the murders took place over multiple state lines, it was a matter of national security or possibly terrorism, or there were things taking place behind the scenes that required the government to get involved.

Being headquartered at the 'J. Edgar Hoover Building' in Washington, D.C., the Bureau operates 56 field offices in most major cities across the United States. The FBI also maintains over 400 resident agencies across the United States, as well as over 50 legal attachés at United States embassies and consulates. Many specialized FBI functions are located at facilities in Quantico, Virginia, as well as a "data campus" in Clarksburg, West Virginia.

The FBI Academy, located in Quantico, Virginia, is home to the communications and computer laboratory the FBI utilizes. It is also where new agents are sent for training to become FBI Special Agents. The Academy trains state and local law enforcement agencies, who are invited to the law enforcement training center.

The FBI units that reside at Quantico are a vast collection of the latest in law enforcement techniques and include; the Field and Police Training Unit, Firearms Training Unit, Forensic Science Research and Training Center, Technology Services Unit (TSU), Investigative Training Unit, Law Enforcement Communication Unit, Leadership and Management Science Units (LSMU), Physical Training Unit, New Agents' Training Unit (NATU), Practical Applications Unit (PAU), the Investigative Computer Training Unit and the "College of Analytical Studies."

Over the course of his police career, Aidan had worked with the FBI on a couple of cases. He had even attended and completed a certification on basic criminal behavioral classifications a few years back that Chief Stone had thought would aid the detectives in the Homicide Division to better understand and predict a killers motives and possible subsequent targets before they were able to strike again. While the information gathered during the two-week seminar included mock cases with actual serial killer profiles built into the scenarios and exercises to make the training as realistic of a real world investigation as possible. Of course nothing could prepare a person for dealing with the daily pressures and feelings involved in a real life homicide investigation.

Having worked over the years with multiple agents, many the stereotypical 'man in black' image that most American citizens conjured up when thinking of the denizens of the federal agency, Aidan had learned that most of them didn't like to take 'backseat' in an investigation, especially one that could have a major media response following its every step. The last time he had been involved in such a situation was a care that would stick in his mind for the rest of his life. It was the Beltway Sniper Shootings from a few years back. Aidan thought about the incident that had been such a major nightmare for all law enforcement involved. He had been on the case as well as every other detective, police officer, emergency services responder and anyone with a law enforcement background in not only Montgomery County, but every town, city and federal organization within a hundred miles of the shootings.

While the investigation was publicly headed by the Montgomery County Police Department and the Chief of Police that was Chief Russel Stone's predecessor, the event ended up bringing in the aid and assistance of The Bureau of Alcohol, Tobacco, Firearms and Explosives (ATF), the FBI, the Secret Service, the Virginia Department of Transportation and the police departments in Maryland, Virginia and Washington D.C., where the shootings took place.

	None of that mattered anyways though. This was Aidan's baby, and he was going to make sure that he was kept in the loop of everything going on.

	Every little detail…

Chapter 16

Walking out of the back door of the station and onto the paved lot where his Challenger sat waiting, Aidan glanced around at the mostly empty parking area. The parking lot did have a few county maintained vehicles and spare police cruisers, but the majority of the on-duty officers and various other police personnel worked out of the various police substations spread throughout the county. Since the Homicide Division was located here at police headquarters, there weren't a lot of staff who worked late at night to be present at this hour. The mass of people working at this location were the regular nine to fiver's, who after there shifts were done for the day, headed home to be with their families and catch the latest sitcoms and sports programs on the television. They finished their duties and putting work behind them, headed off to enjoy life. That was something Aidan Preston just couldn't do. He was a Detective and in his line of work he found that he was always on call. The bad guys didn't clock out and take the night off, so neither could he, administrative leave or not.

He began to think the last few days over as he pulled his keys out and unlocked his car door. Things were beginning to get complicated and he was risking a lot if he was going to ignore Stone's orders and continue to follow the leads in this investigation on his own. Climbing into his car, he turned the engine over and sat there waiting for the car's heater to kick on and begin the slow process of warming the frosty interior. With the sun having set already and winter just around the corner, the weather was getting colder by the minute. Rubbing his hands together and breathing on his knuckles to warm the skin quicker, Aidan thought about his old partner and fellow Homicide Detective, Andrea Wilkes and decided he should check up on her and see if everything was okay.

Aidan didn't have any definitive details about what had happened earlier, but he had heard from the front desk secretary that she had rushed out of work earlier due to some 'family emergency'. While Andrea was a tough woman and could definitely take care of herself, there was something about her that made Aidan feel like he was obliged to take the time and check up on her. He felt he owed it to her.

Yes, there was something he found irresistibly attractive about the petite yet strong female Detective. It wasn't just her obvious beauty. Andrea Wilkes could turn the heads of any man when she walked into a room, especially when she wasn't in uniform. No, it wasn't that. There was something else that seemed to be distracting his thoughts of the murders and causing him to conjure up her face in his mind's eye.

With long, dark hair that she usually kept tied up on the back of her head in a bun when she was on duty, Aidan could picture her slender neck that led to strong shoulders that sat atop of body that most women would kill for. He knew that Andrea was one of those women who when they weren't working, was out jogging daily, eating right, and maintaining a physique that aided her in tussling with men twice her size when the job required it.

	The last time he saw her the day before when he had stopped by the office to pick up his mail and check the latest messages on his computer, he had almost forgotten how sexy the woman was. With her deep brown eyes and full, bee-stung lips, Andrea Wilkes reminded Aidan of that one actress from those tomb raiding films. In fact, if Andrea hadn't gone into law enforcement, Aidan was sure she would have been perfect for the movies or the runway. There was an element about her that he couldn't quite place, but the woman seemed to exude sex appeal.

	And had it been his imagination or had she been flirting with him yesterday as well? Aidan had been preoccupied with catching up on everything that was going on in the office since he hadn't been there in so long due to his mandatory leave, in fact he hadn't even been checking his e-mail as regularly as he usually did since getting out of the hospital and recovering from the being shot. Then again, he had been staying away from anything police related over the last few months until just two days ago when he heard the call go out for the first murder that just happened to be a few minutes of a drive from his house.

	Yes, she definitely was flirting— no doubt about it! So where does that leave me now? Should I see how far she is willing to take it?

	With the car finally warm enough to drive, Aidan shifted it into gear and pulled out of the parking lot. He remembered that Andrea lived in a little townhouse up in the Montgomery Village area of Gaithersburg, and turning onto the street he needed, he decided to take the highway to get up there sooner.

- -

	Andrea had just finished giving her son Jeremy the longest, harshest speech of her life. It was bad enough that he had skipped school on a day where his sister Amy's friends had been found murdered, but then for him to ignore the million calls and texts she had sent his phone, all for him to saunter into the house after being dropped off by a car she didn't recognize, and then act like SHE was overreacting!

Overreacting? She'd show the fifteen year old teenager what overreacting was! Andrea had had enough. She had thought she had figured out how she would handle the situation with her son during the time Amy had been sleeping in her room, and Andrea had fixed herself a glass of wine to try to soothe her nerves and think. She had expected the volume of missed calls and texts she had sent her son to give him an idea of the urgency which he needed to get home, but there had been no such luck.

As irresponsible as his father!, Andrea thought as the boy stormed off to his bedroom. Before she could yell anything more, the sound of wood crashing against a frame echoed from down the hall as Jeremy slammed his door shut, hoping to hide out in the sanctity of his own room.

No, he's not getting out of this that easy!

Andrea stormed down the hall after him, preparing to rip the door off its hinges if he had dared to lock it. When she reached the door she was about to pound her fist when the door further down opened and Amy's washed-out, pale image appeared leaning against the door frame. She looked awful.

"Mom?" the girl asked, her voice little more than a harsh whisper.

"Yes Amy?"

"Please don't be mad at Jeremy."

The look in her daughter's eyes made Andrea's tightened shoulders slump. It was a look of defeat— like she didn't have the will to take anymore stress. Andrea felt her temper settle as she passed her son's door and took Amy into her arms.

"I'm sorry sweetheart, I was just frustrated. I hope we didn't wake you."

"No...I couldn't really sleep too well. It's just..." Amy seemed to be struggling to find the words to express her feelings.

"It's okay, why don't we go sit down in the living room. I'll make you some more tea."

Andrea led her daughter into the living room that extended off from the small kitchen. There were two sofas both pointing towards the television set in the corner of the room and a small coffee table in between them.

Andrea's recliner with the footstool sitting in front of it was off to the side a little from the other furniture, her excuse for trying to make the cramped room seem as open as possible. Guiding Amy to the soft recliner, she let her sit and after making sure she was comfortable enough, Andrea entered the kitchen to make another cup of tea.

As she filled the kettle up with water from the sink, she heard the television click on, the noise filling the whole level of their townhouse as Amy reached for the remote and lowered the volume a few notches to a more appropriate level. Andrea felt another brush of anger slide through her as she knew they never set the television's volume that high when they watched it.

The only reason it would be that loud is that Jeremy had been home earlier instead of going to school, probably having come in right after she left for work, and been watching music videos on MTV or something. That boy, she thought, trying to push the anger down again so she could be there for Amy. She didn't need anything else to be worrying about right now, and her mom and brother starting World War 3 was the last thing to cause any good.

Once she had set the kettle on the stove to boil, she returned to the living room to find Amy watching the television with an eerie intent. Andrea looked at the screen and saw that it was on Channel 5. The news reporter identified on the screen's captioning as 'Ted Hanson', was describing the events that had happened the night before.

"...as you can see behind me, police and paramedics arrived to the scene to discover the remains of four local teenagers who had become the latest victims in the devastating rampage just so recently afflicting our city..." the reporter was saying, and Andrea recognized the abandoned quarry that they were filming at.

"Honey, maybe you shouldn't be watching that," Andrea said walking into the living room, her own eyes glued to the screen.

"No mom...I have to...I need to hear what happened to my friends," Amy said, her voice choking up twice as she turned her gaze from her mother back to the TV.

Andrea didn't argue. Since she had left work to attend to Amy earlier she hadn't heard much about what had happened at the incident either. She sat down on the edge of one of the couches and watched Ted Hanson continue his report.

"...Police have been reluctant to answer any questions regarding these murders and have withheld the identities of the young victims from the press. However, we must ask the question, are we really safe? Are the police doing enough to protect the citizens of this city from the brutal crimes being inflicted on the innocent? With local Mayoral elections coming up in less than a week, we have to ask— are the people we vote for to lead us in this upcoming term, willing to do what it takes to keep the average man and woman safe? Or, could our families be devastated by the loss of a loved one at the hands of this monster that is right at this moment walking our fair streets? I'm Ted Hanson with Channel 5 News, keeping you informed."

After that the screen took a moment to clear and then the image was replaced with the Channel 5 news team sitting around a large desk and ready to continue on to the next story.

"Thank you Ted," the older, male news anchor stated to the camera as he picked up his the notes on the desk before him and stacked them neatly, "...And if you are just joining us, that was Ted Hanson, one of our field correspondents who was just relaying the latest in the growing murders that are mounting in the city lately. You can follow us online as we continue to bring you the most recent information on this story as the events play out, and don't forget to check back in for the News at 11 to find out the latest. Now it's time for the weather..."

Andrea just shook her head in disgust. It was amazing how the news channels were so quick to capitalize on the depraved and senseless acts o violence and other issues in society just to get their ratings to go up. Everything was a competition for them, and if something truly awful happened then they were on the scene like vultures circling a carcass, each one of them just waiting for the opportune time to pick apart whatever juicy morsel they could.

She hated TV reporters, and working Homicide, she had had her fill of dealing with the parasites. Especially Ted Hanson. He was a parasite in his own special league. Andrea could recall one time a few years back when she was working a double murder-suicide and Hanson had shown up at the scene to try and get the exclusive coverage of the incident. He had annoyed the hell out of her as he hovered about, having his cameraman film her and continually prodding her with questions. She didn't know how many times she had to turn away from him and utter, 'no comment', until he seemed to realize she wasn't going to be offering him any info. Then to make matters worse, he started trying to hit on her, asking her out on a date like he was Don Juan and he had come about to rescue her from every other man in the world. The nerve of that creep!

Now that the news had switched off and some new game show that Andrea didn't recognize was beginning to play, she headed back to the kitchen to turn off the stove before the kettle boiled over. Grabbing another mug, she walked back into the room and handed Amy the second cup of tea. Amy removed her hands from the afghan blanket she had draped over her as she lay back, snuggling tightly into the recliner, and accepted the mug from her mom.

"So do you want to talk about it now?" Andrea asked, sensing her daughter's mood had improved a little from the near catatonic state she had been in early this morning.

"I don't really know where to begin...I just can't believe they're dead," Amy muttered, taking a sip of the tea and staring into the mug like the water held her mesmerized by her reflection.

"I was supposed to go out with them that night you know?"

Andrea's head twisted violently towards her daughter, the look of shock quite clear on her face. "Wait, what?" she demanded, attempting to keep the worry out of her own voice.

Amy just sat there continuing to stare at her tea. A moment stretched by and then finally her red, puffy eyes looked over at her mom.

"Yeah, they had asked me to go out with them that night. I was going to go, but had a paper I was working on for school so I canceled on them," Amy admitted.

Andrea couldn't believe her ears. A knot seemed to form in her stomach as her mind immediately pictured what she would be doing differently this moment if her daughter had carried out her plans and gone out with her friends the night before. Andrea felt like she was going to be sick. She couldn't believe how close she had come to losing her daughter.

Studying her daughter sitting there, she attempted to memorize every detail of the young girl sitting on the chair, blanket wrapped around her as she sipped from the steaming mug. A strand of her dark hair, hair just like Andrea's hanging down across her forehead. Andrea silently thanked God for the opportunity her daughter had been presented and the choices she made. Because of her using her brain and focusing on a paper she had to write as opposed to hanging out with her friends late at night, her daughter was still with her, alive and well.

"Oh baby, I'm so sorry about your friends," Andrea said, then admitted, "I'm just so grateful that you are here. If I had lost you— I don't know what I would have done."

"I know mom."

"Amy you are so special to me, the thought of losing you would be just too difficult."

Amy sat there quietly, obviously something weighing heavily on her mind.

"I feel so bad for their parents, especially Becky and Scott's parents. They must be devastated. I knew them, and I feel like I should go over and see them— see all the families of the four who were killed even though I didn't know Tony all that well. Megan was on the cheerleading squad with me too."

"If that's what you want to do, of course we can. I'm sure they just need some time right now with everything being so fresh and all. Why don't we plan on doing it once they've had time to let everything sink in. I'm sure they are all taking it incredibly hard and need time to mourn."

Amy seemed to think about this. While she was still not her bubbly self, she did seem to be coming out of the funk she had been in earlier. Andrea just hoped the mood continued to improve. She hated seeing her daughter so down.

"Yeah, I guess we should probably give them a couple days. I know Becky's mom is probably taking it the hardest. She never seemed to be the happiest woman, especially after she got divorced last spring. I just hope she doesn't do anything drastic," Amy said, the tone of her voice radiating with worry.

"What do you mean honey? You don't think she's suicidal do you?" Andrea asked worriedly.

"I don't know. I just know that she's been going through a rough time, and now with Becky…with Becky being killed, I just don't know how she might react."

Andrea decided she'd look into the parent's of the murdered teens and pay special attention to Becky's mom. They were all going to need help over the next few weeks, and Andrea's background with the police taught her to watch out for the warning signs that someone might try to hurt themselves. Of course, Andrea wasn't so sure she wouldn't think the same things if she had Amy and Jeremy stolen away from her like that.

"Well, I'll let someone down at the station know to check up with Becky's mom and make sure she gets any help she needs. Don't worry about that. I'll handle that call personally, first thing in the morning."

"Thanks mom," Amy said with a slight smile that barely brightened up her face.

I know it's hard baby, but it'll get better, Andrea thought as she watched her daughter turn her attention back to the TV screen. Obviously she needed to get her mind off things and what better way then to watch the mindless drivel that poured out of televisions everywhere. Andrea decided to give up trying to help Amy with any other emotional issues right now, and resigned to let her lose herself in the program she was watching.

Suddenly the phone rang. Andrea got up to head to the kitchen. Picking the receiver up from its cradle she was about to answer when she realized it wasn't the home line that was ringing. Where was her mind at? Reaching for her purse, she extracted her cell phone and looked at the screen. No wonder she hadn't recognized the ringtone. She had set various tones up for most of the people she talked to on a regular basis, but the person's name that was flashing on the small screen was someone she didn't talk to regularly, or at least she hadn't talked to him that often in the last few months up until the other day.

She put the phone to her ear and answered.

"Hello?"

"Andrea?" Aidan Preston's low voice asked over the line.

"This would be she," Andrea said, a slight tingle of anticipation and a strange yearning at hearing his voice reverberated through her.

"It's Aidan."

"I know, they do make a thing called caller ID you know."

"Oh yeah, right. Anyways, I had heard that you left the station earlier and—well I was wanted to check up on you and make sure everything was okay," he admitted.

Andrea felt a hitch in her throat before she could reply. He had called her to see how she was doing! He had been worried about her! Quickly pushing her thoughts aside and ignoring the fact that her mind was acting like some schoolgirl crush was filling her imagination she answered.

"Well I appreciate you looking in on me. To tell you the truth, it's been a pretty rough day."

Aidan seemed to be listening intently, waiting for her to finish talking before he began.

"I see. Is there anything I can do to help? You know I'm always here if you need a person to listen to."

"Actually, that would be great. After today, I'd be willing to hire one of those ridiculously priced, self absorbed shrinks to diagnose the problems I'm having! Anymore and I might end up a basket case!"

Aidan laughed, his strong voice sounding comforting to Andrea as she listened to him through the phone.

"Well, I certainly charge less than those 'shrinks' you referred to, but for the record I don't think they like that term, at least mine doesn't."

Andrea froze. That's right, Aidan was having to see a psychiatrist for the shooting he was involved in. That's why he was on leave! How could she have been so stupid and forgot? As if Aidan sensed her hesitation and realized she was beating herself up for her choice of words, he said, "Don't worry about the 'shrink' comment, it's a mandatory thing, and to tell you the truth, the guy's not half bad."

"Okay, well sorry anyways. I didn't mean to sound like I was judging you because you go to a psychiatrist," apologized Andrea.

"No problem. I guess we're all a little nuts anyways. Some just a little more so than others." Aidan responded.

Andrea smiled. It had been too long since she had worked with Aidan, she had almost forgot how endearing he could be. Not to mention his sense of humor. It was somewhere in between charming and dark, but there was something about that edge that got to Andrea.

"So, how about we go get a drink and you can tell me all about the problems you're having. That is if you're not too busy," Aidan offered.

"No I'm not too busy, but I don't think I should leave my daughter alone tonight. Her friends were the four kids killed out at the abandoned quarry last night."

She could hear the gasp over the connection as Aidan realized what she had told him. He was speechless for a moment.

"Oh wow, I'm so sorry to hear that. Is she alright?"

"She's pretty shaken up, but she's a strong kid and she'll pull through," Andrea admitted, but even as the words left her mouth, she hoped they were true and that this incident hadn't scarred her daughter for life.

"Well instead of going out to get drinks, I could come over to check on you" Aidan finally stated.

Andrea couldn't believe her ears. Was he actually asking to come over to her home? They had worked together for a couple years, ever since she had transferred to Homicide from Vice, and sure they had gone out for drinks a couple times after work, but back then it was just like she was one of the guys. This was different. This seemed to be something else, like he was looking for an invitation to take her out. Her heart fluttered slightly as her mind remembered their back and forth at the office the day before. She hadn't read to much into that, playing around and being flirtacious was just how she usually found herself reacting around a man that intrigued her. Aidan Preston just happened to be such a man. Was he that concerned for her?

"You know Aidan I am a grown woman, I can usually take care of my self."

"Oh I know it. Remember I've seen you in action," he admitted.

Where was this going? Could he really be interested in her? She thought of his thick, dark hair and thin, strong build. He was most certainly a handsome man and Andrea loved the darker, dangerous side his attitude seemed to portray. He was cool and collected and wasn't one of those guys who tried at it. It was just a part of who he was. Yet, Andrea was still hesitant. Was it a good idea to possibly start something with someone she had to work with once Aidan was reinstated? Of course there were still plenty of avenues they had to explore before any relationship could even be considered. He could just be trying to be a considerate friend, Andrea told herself, even though she didn't think that was true.

"So what do you say?" he asked after a minute of her not saying anything. She had been to absorbed in her own thoughts to realize how distracted she really was.

"Sorry, my mind's wandering. Um— yeah, how about you come over and we could talk," she finally agreed.

"Okay, I can be over there in probably about twenty minutes, will that work?"

Andrea looked at the clock hanging on the kitchen wall. It was a quarter to 7 already.

"Yes that'll work," she said, and with that Aidan told her he'd see her soon and hung up.

Standing in the kitchen with the phone in her hand, Andrea wondered what she was thinking. She had invited Aidan over to her home while her kids were home.

She definitely found him attractive, but to make matters worse, she suddenly realized that her ex husband Robert, would also be stepping back into her life in a couple days to check on their kids. She wouldn't be able to avoid him.

Was this really the best time to be looking at a new relationship? She wondered.

Oh hell, guess there's only one way to find out!

Chapter 17

When Aidan arrived at Andrea's townhouse he had to circle the block twice to find a place to park. Unfortunately all the spots vacant in the developments parking lot were either occupied or assigned and reserved for the various home owners. All the unmarked, guest spots were filled, so Aidan ended up parking out on the street about a block away from Andrea's townhouse.

The distance from the car to the house gave him time to rethink his actions. Here he was telling himself he was coming here to check on a friend in a time of need, but his mind kept hinting at there being a deeper reasoning to his decision. Andrea was one of the strongest women he had ever met, and showing up with the excuse of coming to comfort her in a time of need seemed a little lame to him as he approached the townhouses door. Once he stepped up onto the small landing, he wrapped his knuckles lightly on the wood, and then waited. After a minute of no one answering, he stepped back slightly to view the house number to make sure he was at the right house. Seeing he was indeed at the correct address he reached up and used the brass door knocker to announce his presence.

Finally he heard the sound of footsteps approaching the door and the small view plate in the door grew dark as someone was obviously looking out at him from the other side.

"Andrea, it's Aidan," he said, and then he heard an unrecognizable male voice come from the unknown person on the opposite side of the door,

Just then, Aidan heard the sound of the deadbolt being undone and the unknown individual who had been studying him through the peephole came into view. He was barely older than a child, and Aidan assumed the boy was probably around fifteen or sixteen. Still a child according to the state, even though the boy looked like he was knowledgeable beyond his years. That was how it was these days in society. Kids were growing up too fast, drinking and experimenting with drugs, having sex earlier and earlier and learning more about life due to people's changes in the way things used to be.

Without bothering to introduce himself, the boy just opened the door wider and stepped to the side. Aidan walked in, taking in the layout of the room when the teen broke the silence.

"Mom, you've got a visitor!" he yelled, and even though Andrea was not visible in any part of the first floor, the boys loud announcement echoed about the entire two-story townhouse and was sure to reach its intended target.

A moment later, Andrea appeared and assured her son he could go away and that she was expecting the visitor. The boy gave Aidan a suspicious look, but turned and disappeared off into the house.

Aidan looked the woman standing before him over, taking in her beauty and appearance in a quick glance so as not to make it obvious he was staring. Normally she had her dark hair up and in a bun, but now her long locks were loose, hanging down to her shoulders and framing her heart-shaped face. She stared back at him with those deep, brown eyes set apart by her smooth, exotic complexion, and her full lips turned formed into a smile.

"Well that didn't take you very long," Andrea said, stepping past Aidan and closing the door to avoid the chill of the evenings air from entering the house.

"No it didn't, but parking was a pain. I had to leave my car out on the street about two blocks away."

"Oh no, you could have parked in one of the visitor spots."

Aidan shook his head in disagreement.

"Nope, they were all filled up, but hey, it's no big deal. The walk gave me some time to think and enjoy the night air."

Andrea eyed him cautiously. Here was Aidan Preston, a man who had expressed feelings of worry for her when he found out she had left work this morning, and now here he was standing in the narrow foyer of her small, townhouse, his rugged good looks and dressed down appearance causing some long forgotten urges to rise up in her. What is it about this man you find so fascinating Andrea— what is it about him that's so damn sexy?

She had been grown accustomed to living on her own, raising her two kids by herself for so long now, she had forgot what it was like to rely on someone else when times got tough. And now, here was Aidan, his strong, defined chin covered in a fine stubble from not shaving over the last few days and his intense gray eyes that seemed to just be drawing her into him.

"Can I take your jacket?" Andrea asked as she led him through the foyer and past the small walk-through kitchen.

"No I'm fine, still trying to warm up from being outside too long."

Finally arriving in the cozy living room where Andrea offered him the recliner as she sat down on one of the couches, but Aidan declined and sat on the couch she had chosen. Even though it was a three cushion couch, and there was the middle cushion between them, Andrea still felt her heart's rhythm speed up at the close proximity of this man to her.

"So why don't you tell me what you've been going through. Let me see if I can help," Aidan said in that oh so familiar voice that Andrea had grown accustomed to hearing every day back before, when Aidan was working as a Detective, solving crimes alongside her, back before his hospitalization and the subsequent issues that followed.

She felt bad for him, knowing that he held a lot of guilt over what had happened that day almost a year ago. Yes, he had healed from the bullet wound when the suspect shot him, and yes he had saved that little girl's life, but when he had returned fire on the suspect, when he thought he had a clear shot even though he was bleeding from the bullet lodged in him and losing a good amount of blood, when the bullet took the killer out and his gun dropped, it was that one piece of the puzzle that he blamed himself for. When that gun discharged as it hit the floor and the little girl screamed and collapsed, Aidan had changed.

There was a deeper, brooding side to his personality that Andrea had noticed in the weeks following the surgery to remove the bullet from his chest. He was racked with guilt, and Andrea knew that it was through that incident that she had first realized how much she cared for the man she had been partners with in the Homicide Division for two years. Up until now she had never made her growing feelings known, other than the occasional flirting at the office, but now, here he was sitting in her home, no more than a couple feet from her, and she couldn't help feeling like she was a young girl first being noticed by her longtime crush.

Andrea took a deep breath, trying to keep the butterflies in her stomach from interfering with her recounting of the days events. After all, she had to remind herself, that's why he is here in the first place. Not because deep down he loves you and had to rush over and see you, but because you were partners and he was just a friend being there when another friend needed help!

"I had just gotten into the office this morning and was working through some case files that had been piling up on unsolved homicides in the area. I was looking for anything that we might have missed in the initial investigations that could shed some light on things nowadays," she said, stopping for a moment to just study Aidan, her mind trying to think of what was really relevant to why he was here.

"Go on," he encouraged.

"So anyways, I was going through the files, checking everything out like I said, and I realized I had accidentally left my phone on silent. When I looked at the screen, I realized I had about twenty missed calls from my daughter, Amy…"

Andrea took the next ten minutes recounting the events of the day as Aidan sat patiently and listened.

When she was finally done, he sat forward and reaching over, placed his hand on top of hers. The gesture itself was almost enough to make Andrea's heart pour open and tell him how interested and attracted she was to him. Yet, reality kept her cautious, and she knew that it might not be such a good idea to start dating someone you work so closely to. She didn't know if she was ready for that step and definitely didn't even know where she fell on Aidan's scale of things that mattered deeply to him.

"Listen, it'll be alright," he said, giving her hand a little squeeze and then pulling it back to his side of the couch.

She wished he had left his hand there, the electricity she felt when their flesh had touched had definitely been a sign to her that there was something between them worth exploring. But does he feel the same way? she wondered as she looked deep into his gray eyes. There was just no way of knowing and she wasn't about to come right out and admit her feelings for him. He had just recently stepped back into her life now that he had started coming into the station to get his mail and check his messages. Then of course there was also the rumor she had heard from Tim Melvin about Aidan showing up at both of the crime scenes in the company of Detective Jones with the Rockville PD.

"So now that I've caught you up on my life's drama, tell me what's been going on with you?" she asked, slipping her long leg over the other as she turned on the couch to face him better.

Aidan had watched Andrea reposition herself, his eyes instantly drawn to her jean clad legs, his mind racing with thoughts of the woman in a little less clothing. Wow, she really was having an affect on him! He had never realized it before when they used to work side by side, but now that he was officially away from the work and demands of the job, he was beginning to see Andrea in a whole new light. To make matters worse, he was loving what he was seeing.

"Well what do you want to know?"

"Why don't you start with why you've been looking into these murders recently. I've heard through the grapevine you've pissed Lieutenant Garza off pretty well, and that the Chief had to tell you to steer clear of the investigation."

"That's true," Aidan admitted, a sheepish smile appearing as he thought about how furious Garza had been. "He was spitting blood, and the Chief wasn't all too happy about my freelancing either."

"So why are you stirring up trouble? Has your life gotten so boring being away from the action that you decided to jab a stick into a hornet's nest just for fun?"

"No, nothing like that, but I will tell you that being on administrative leave all this time really does wear on a person. I'll be lucky if I make it to the Board's review to pass and get reinstated."

Andrea seemed to think about this for a moment, then added, "Well you look like you're doing pretty good. Do you think the medical review might not go so well?" Andrea asked, her thoughts returning to the situation Aidan had survived and she could only imagine what he must be going through, faced with the decisions he made and the results of his actions. Knowing Aidan, she was pretty sure he blamed himself for the girl's loss of her legs.

"I'm not sure how the reviews going to go. I can't even go before the ruling Board until my psychiatrist clears me."

"Will he not?"

"No, he will, it's just that he thinks I might need some more time to work out some issues I've been having. You know 'shrinks', they get you hooked into a schedule of sessions, and even after you're through the originally planned allotment, the next thing you know, they're wanting you to add more weeks because you're not deemed 'healed', and the whole time they're lining their wallets with your hard earned cash," Aidan announced, shaking his head back and forth in amused annoyance.

"Wow, sounds like you really appreciate the mental health community," joked Andrea with a flash of that gorgeous smile.

What is it about this woman that's getting to me so? Aidan wondered.

Before he could finish that train of thought a soft, feminine voice called out from behind him.

"Mom?"

Aidan turned around on the couch to see a young girl, wearing an over-sized t-shirt as a nightgown and a pair of athletic shorts underneath that rode up high on her long, tan legs. The girl was the spitting image of Andrea in a younger, less defined way. Aidan had to take a look from one to the other before accepting that he wasn't just deluding himself with faint similarities. No, they were almost identical, the young seventeen year old almost an exact duplicate of her mother.

"Oh I'm sorry, I didn't realize you had company," the girl said when she spied Aidan sitting on the opposite end of the couch.

"That's okay, I was just leaving," Aidan said, standing up and offering his hand to the girl.

She looked curiously from her mom to Aidan before accepting his strong hand and giving it a light shake.

"You must be Amy," Aidan stated as he let go of the girl's hand stuck his both deep into his jean pockets, his casual care and down to earth appearance seemed to emanate from him.

"That's right," the girl said, giving her mom a quick mischievous look.

Andrea just rolled her eyes, knowing what was on her daughter's mind. No she was not seeing this man. She would have to explain later that they were just co-workers and nothing more. At least not yet, her inner voice whispered hopefully.

"Amy, this is Detective Aidan Preston. He works Homicide with me," Andrea explained.

"Oh okay," Amy said, her features expressing that now she understood, but still thought her mom was hiding something. "Well it's nice to meet you. You should come over again some time, maybe my mom could cook."

"Amy?" Andrea blurted out at the openness of her daughter's rash keenness.

"Haha, no it's fine," Aidan said, defending the girl who had been through so much today. He could see the lines under her eyes and the tell-tale sign that she had been crying earlier. "Anyways, I do have to get going to meet up with someone." Then looking at Amy, said, "Perhaps I'll have to take you up on that dinner offer. I get pretty tired of eating microwaveable dinners for one most nights."

"Great!" Amy announced and then turned away and left the room.

Andrea had walked over to Aidan and placed a hand on his shoulder.

"Sorry about that, I don't know what got into the girl," she explained.

"It's no big deal. Maybe I will have to stop by again this week sometime," he said, the anticipation obviously evident in his tone. Yes there was something going on between them. Whether you wanted to call it a chemical balance, or a spark or just plain old romantic interest, Andrea Wilkes was certainly a woman he would like to get to know more of.

Walking him to the door, they said their goodbyes and Aidan had even leaned in and given her a quick brush of his lips on her cheek. Andrea had felt her heart stop almost as his prickly cheek slid across her own soft skin, and she felt that yearning again.

As she watched Aidan walk out into the cold October night, the wind whipping around with a sharp bite to it, Andrea heard the soft pad of footsteps crossing over the linoleum floor of the foyer behind her. Turning, she saw Amy had come back out from wherever she had disappeared too while her and Aidan said there goodbyes, and was now standing next to her mother in the door frame watching the silhouette of Aidan Preston vanish into the night.

"So, what's the 'story' with you two?" Amy asked making quotations in the air with her fingers when she said the word story.

Andrea just looked at her daughter as she shut and locked the front door.

Andrea felt a smile tugging at the corners of her mouth and just shook her head, barely saying, "I don't know just yet."

Of course she didn't know what the future held for her and Aidan, and even if there was some connection between them that needed to be explored. It was all too early to tell.

After all, she just didn't know.

As he hit the last key, adding a period at the end of the sentence he had just typed, Nick Haley leaned back in his chair and glanced around the main floor of The Informant's newsroom. It was already past quitting time and most of the staff had gone home. He had just finished typing up his latest article on the recent murders that were being committed on the streets of Rockville, and the only people left working were the ones responsible for getting all the last layouts and copy together to get tomorrow mornings edition out.

Nick had knew he had pushed his luck for probably the last time when he showed up at the building ten minutes to quitting time, his article on the latest murder at the abandoned quarry off River Road not even written. Marty had given him an ear full, the thin man's face turning beet red as he let loose with a tongue lashing that made everybody on the main floor turn and watch. It was the third time in the last two weeks that Nick's late articles had held the following mornings newspaper from going to the printers on time. That meant more money hashed out to keep the people responsible for running the printing presses, and more money meant Marty was less happy. In fact he had ended up on the verge of possibly strangling Nick when he showed up ten till 6 o'clock with nothing in his hands.

Sure he had the story of the decade, these murders becoming a huge boost for the newspaper's circulation, but Marty expected Nick to obviously work magic. He had shot over to The Informant's offices, pushing his little hatchback as hard as the engine would go, straight from the scene of the crime. The same scene he had met Detective Preston, and after gathering a little inside details into the investigation from him and Detective Jones, soon found himself and Preston kicked to the curb by the arrival of Lieutenant Garza. Fortunately for Nick, he had already seen enough to be able to give his readers an up close and personal account of the crime scene.

Take that Channel 5 news and 'wonder boy', Ted Hanson!

By the time he had left, he had seen two news vans driving down River Road in the direction of the quarry, but he knew that once they got there, that one massive police officer that looked like he could life a car would be watching the arriving reporters and curious onlookers like a hawk.

He was sure that Lieutenant had probably flipped his lid on the cop guarding the barricade for letting him and Detective Preston in and he felt bad since the guard had actually attempted to stop him. Nick had just had the right moment to slip by unnoticed. However, Hanson and whatever other news channels were at the scene right now were obviously being left in the dark and there was no way they were going to have the information that he had. When he had explained that to Marty, he realized that was probably the only reason he hadn't been strangled in front of his coworkers.

Now with his article finished he looked over to the desk furthest from his and spied Amber currently hard at work completing the favor he had asked of her. As if sensing he was watching her, she looked up and Nick gave her a thumbs up to indicate he was done with the article. As he got up from his desk, he pressed the 'Enter' key on the keyboard and a message popped up saying his document had been successfully submitted. It was now someone else's worry about getting it in to tomorrow's morning paper.

Strolling casually over to Amber's cubicle, he took the time to check the young, sexy woman out. Today she had her hair pinned up with a large, leopard print hairclip, but a few strands of her light blonde hair were hanging down onto the back of her narrow neck. His eyes traveled over a firm, hourglass shaped frame covered by a simple, white blouse and a tight black skirt with a slit that rode up the outside of her thigh exposing more of her pantyhose clad legs. Once he was within a few feet of her area, she sat up, pushing her chest out slightly as she acted like she was just sitting there without a care in the world. The pose pushed her large chest out towards him and he knew she was attempting to tease him. Hell, she drove most of the men in the office crazy with her form fitting outfits and the way she slid around the office, slinking like a sexy cat sneaking up on its prey.

"All done?" she asked as he stepped up to her.

Resting his hips on the corner of her desk, he folded his arms across his chest and said, "Yup, now Marty should be able to cool down. I thought he was going to have a stroke earlier."

Amber giggled. It was a cute, innocent sound, but Nick knew the girl was far from an angel. He could just see the darker side in those sparkling blue eyes when she stared straight at him, her eyes seeming to be just devouring him alive the way they took him in. The only problem was that in some of the long talks they had since she had come to work at

The Informant, there had been mention of a boyfriend. While these references had been few and far between, and from the way Amber carried herself around the office, Nick assumed it wasn't anything serious. Of course, he couldn't be sure since he had never asked her outright about any man in her life.

"So were you able to get all that info I asked you for earlier on the phone?"

"Yeah," Amber answered, pulling a manila file folder she had sitting on one section of her desk and handing it to him added, "Oh and you owe me— big time."

Nick took the heavy folder, stuffed with content and slipped it under his arm. Placing a hand on Amber's shoulder he leaned over and said, "I really do."

Then with a peck on the cheek he headed off towards the stairs that led to Marty's office. It was time to enter the dragon's lair. Hopefully, he'd had time to cool off. If not, then the folder he was carrying wouldn't be of much use.

"Here we go," he muttered to himself as he started up the stairs.

Marty, wait till you see what I've got for you!

Giving the door a hard knock, Nick hardly waited for the Editor in Chief to answer before swinging the door open and stepping inside. Marty looked up from a piece of paper in his hands and narrowed his eyes at Nick.

"What the hell do you want? And, you better have submitted that article or else I'm taking the overtime I have to pay the boys working the printing press out of your paycheck!"

"It's done."

"Bout damn time!" grumbled Marty. "So what the hell do you want now?"

Nick hefted the folder in his hands and handed it to his sullen, irritable boss who had just half an hour earlier almost murdered him from rage.

"What's this?" Marty asked as he took the manila folder from Nick and opened it up.

He took a moment to scan through the contained papers, pausing a couple times to look up from his reading and give Nick a quizzical look, his eyebrows raising up each time he did, then falling back down into their almost permanently pissed off looking place. Having gained his bearings on the papers he had quickly rifled through and knowing time stood still for no man, especially the Editor of The Informant, Marty quickly brushed the papers together and handed them back to Nick.

"So what's this all about? You're supposed to be working on the murders story and followups, not chasing some bizarre— what?— fluff piece for the local section?"

"I think the two are related in some fashion," Nick stated, trying to figure out how to explain his theory to the man and get him to approve his running with the article without making it seem completely off the wall.

Amber had done him the favor of pulling all the information he had asked for that she could find in their archives and online. He knew the girl hated having to go down to the lower level of The Informant's basement level, where it had a subterranean feel to it.

It was dark, and dusty and old. Amber had once referred to the archives and the hermit of a man who worked down in them as giving her the creeps, and made the comparison to that of the lair of the Phantom of the Opera. All that was missing she informed Nick was a large pipe organ and the reference could be complete. Thinking about it, while Nick knew it wasn't nearly as bad as Amber's imagination made it out to be, he had to concede that it wasn't a place he enjoyed going down to spend the required amount of time it would have taken to find the information he wanted. While most forms of media and records seemed to be online nowadays, The Informant, thanks to Marty's tight budgetary concerns, had never gotten around to digitizing many of their old back-stories and editions from years prior.

That's where the basement level of the building and Nick's 'favor' had Amber spending most of the afternoon looking into the information he requested and then copying it all into a folder for him. Nick pictured the custodian of records Dmitri Poleski, a strange, recluse of a man who doubled as the building's janitor and handyman. He seemed to have been working for The Informant since the days just after the Cold War, and probably had some ties to the Red Nation. He was a constant presence in the old building even though nobody actually saw most days since he stayed busy down in the archives.

At night, once most of the staff were gone he would come up to clean and take care of minor repairs needed around the place. Nick even wondered if the odd, Russian 'phantom' actually lived down there. It wouldn't surprise him one bit if her found out Poleski had retrofitted one of the downstairs closets into a bedroom and never actually left The Informant. He wondered if Marty even cared, or if he just left the man alone to his own devices, calling upon him whenever his services were needed.

Either way, Amber had ventured into the underworld-like depths of Poleski's realm and gotten the hermit of a man to help her in pulling all the records and past articles Nick had asked for. This collection of material was what Marty had just finished looking through and seemed waiting for a response to what it had to do with any of the stories Nick was supposed to be working on. That's where Nick hoped the Editor in Chief would connect the dots and once he began explaining his idea.

"Okay, follow me on this…" Nick started and began rummaging through the folder to find the right pages he needed. Once he had located the photocopied pages, he handed them to Marty who studied them as Nick began explaining himself.

"Quite a number of years back we did a story on a couple that had been mauled to death by a pack of wild dogs. I think it was spun into a community awareness piece due to the nature of the problem back then of free-ranging canine packs that were roaming America's city streets and backcountry roads.

'Since they lingered on the edge of domestication, living in dilapidated buildings, old cars, sewers and anywhere they can find shelter from the elements and a ready source of scraps and food they could scavenge up. Some are abandoned pets, others born to the streets, and in order to survive, these social creatures form packs, scavenging garbage or kill livestock, using their numbers to their advantage.

In the United States we lead the world in the domestication of pet dogs, and with the economy and financial issues facing so many American's like the loss of their jobs, and other factors like having to downsize their living arrangements or moving into rent-controlled facilities where pets are not welcome, the number of animals becoming homeless is growing exponentially. Even though they're considered man's best friend, when financial difficulties press down on the owners of dogs, they prefer to abandon them rather than face euthanizing the, thinking it's kinder and better for the animals."

Marty just sat there, his eyebrows knit tightly as he tried to figure out where Nick was going with all this. "Okay?" he stated, moving his left hand in a circular motion to signal Nick needed to wrap it up.

Time was wasting, and time to Marty, meant money. Nick continued, swapping one article from Marty's possession and giving him another sheet to look at.

"In 2009, the ASPCA estimated that one million dogs and cats would become homeless in the United States due to economic hardships. That was then, before we had the economic crisis and the issues with the stock market that we've had in the last couple years. That means the numbers have increased. Four million dogs and cats are being put down each year by shelters. They say it is impossible to accurately record how many dogs are actually out there on the streets, feral and running about.

'From the research Amber did for me, I learned that selectively bred wild foxes produce puppies that have domestic characteristics, in both nature and appearance, within two to three generations. The opposite is also true. As dogs are forced to fend for themselves, they will breed with other dogs that display survival traits and produce offspring with these same characteristics. This happens most often within the first or second generation. That means that within a year, one dog can become a skilled hunter and contribute to the numbers of wild animals in a homeless pack."

Marty looked flustered now, obviously the statistics Nick was providing him were going over his head, and the look he was giving him told him all he needed to know. He had to wrap this up.

"Okay the point is, an old article we had published in the paper a few years back was about this local couple that was mauled to death by a pack of wild dogs," Nick stated, watching as Marty seemed to be starting to put the pieces together in his head.

"I think I recall that one. Didn't the woman report the strange group of mixed-breed dogs wandering around her home over near the Aspen Hill area of Rockville. Her and her husband were taking an evening stroll when they were attacked and killed?"

Bingo— Marty was starting to follow along!

"Exactly! Susan Reynolds and her husband Chaz, both in their mid-sixties, were out one night taking a walk through their neighborhood and decided to stop by the little, wooded playground and park that was down the street from the local swimming pool. The husband Chaz had gone into the woods apparently, although their were no eyewitnesses so the Rockville Police weren't sure of the actual chain of events. Anyways, when their oldest son realized they hadn't come back from their walk and got worried, he set out on the same path they took every night in search of them.

A shredded piece of shirt that the son was able to identify, some strands of hair and a bloodstained patch of ground was all that was found at the site where the couple were attacked and killed. Upon further searching, the authorities were able to locate the bodies of the wife and husband by following the trail of blood and drag marks deep into the wooded area off from the children's park.

Their bodies were torn apart and mutilated, but because there were no witnesses they weren't able to confirm how many animals had been a part of the pack, though they suspect there were around twelve based on analysis of the paw prints discovered at the grisly scene. Sound like anything you've heard of happening around here recently?" Nick asked, watching Marty's eyebrows unfurl as recognition dawned on his stern face.

"The murder at Croydon Park!" Marty exclaimed, the look in his eyes one of deep interest now as he studied the papers Nick had handed him more carefully.

"Yes. Some of the details are just too similar, and from a source I just met that's pretty damn close to the investigation in the Rockville and Montgomery County Police Departments, they told me the Medical Examiner found what appeared to be bite marks on the first victim's body, "Nick added.

Now I've got him hooked, Nick thought watching his Editor finish flipping through the pages of the file rapidly.

"What about the second crime scene, the one you were just at?"

"They're not going to know anything until they get the bodies to the morgue and finish processing the scene. They were still in the middle of collecting evidence when I got there, but from the horribly mutilated bodies of two of the four victim's that I could see, I'm willing to bet they have bite marks somewhere among their many wounds. I'll just have to wait for them to get the autopsy back, and hopefully my source will be able to let me know."

Marty was definitely following him now, so Nick pulled the next piece of research Amber had dug up from the folder and stuck it out for Marty to read. He took the copy of the article, one that had ran in The Informant's pages a couple of years ago. Nick watched as his eyes darted over the material, and Nick continued explaining his ideas while the man read the clipping.

"Now the police have ruled the first incident a murder, despite the fact that there was evidence some animal or animals were involved. I think the killer or killers might have used dogs that were possibly trained to be violent and attack on command, and let them loose on the victim when they assaulted her. As you can see from the article in your hands, it's not as far fetched as it might sound. It's happened before," Nick said, taking a moment to stop and let Marty finish reading the paper.

The article from April of 2009 was titled, "Street Gang Uses Trained, Ferocious Dogs to Attack Rival Gang Members, Leading to the Death of Three". The story went on to explain that the owner of the two pit bulls, used the two dogs as a weapon to chase down and attack three rival members of a different gang when he spotted them in the territory he and his companions claimed as their own. Three members of the Lincoln Park Crew died from the wounds they suffered from the animal's vicious, initial attack and from the twenty-three year old, Ray Jose Gonzalez originally from Silver Spring, Maryland, having stabbed them multiple times in the chest and throats.

Once arrested the gang member and owner of the dogs would only say that the three victims had provoked him and he had set the dogs on them in a case of self-defense. The accused expressed he was not sorry for his actions, and that because of his 'pets', he had saved his own life from being taken by the gang members. Nick remembered the prosecutor's grave recounting of the event, and his statement that had made it into the article.

He was quoted as saying, "The most unique aspect of this horrible tragedy is that dogs were used to level the odds in favor of the accused, and that because of the violent nature that these animals were subjected to, they were turned into nothing more than a cold weapon for Mr. Gonzalez to utilize in ending the lives of these three men."

Marty finished reading the article and returned it to Nick who was waiting impatiently to hear what his boss thought. Clearing his throat, his eyebrows knitting together again in stern concentration, Marty leaned back in his plush office chair and asked, "So you think this scenario might be what similar to what happened in these latest murders?"

"Yes I do. Like I said before, the similarities that fit these latest murders and the facts from the articles I was able to find are quite shocking. I think whoever murdered the first victim, Sara Moulton, and the four teenagers over at the quarry, might be getting his kicks from setting his dog onto the victim and watching them be mauled, before he goes about finishing killing them."

"That's just sick if you ask me," Marty admitted.

"I agree, but if you had seen the bodies at these scenes, you'd know that the police are looking for a sick individual!"

"Well follow this up and make sure you keep digging into the research. Have Amber continue to help you. Tell her I'm pulling her from working with Terry Cartwright on the upcoming political elections coming up this week. I want her working with you full-time on this. This story is getting big play, and readership is up. I want to capitalize on this attention while we can, and if you keep getting the scoop ahead of the likes of Channel 5 and the other media outlets than you're going to make me one happy man! I might even give everyone that Christmas bonus people are always asking about!"

Nick laughed. It was a long-running joke around the newsroom of The Informant that Marty was as tight with money as Ebeneezer Scrooge from A Christmas Carol. And every year around the holiday season, Marty seemed to encompass the role without even realizing it, and become increasingly difficult and obnoxious to work for during a time when people were supposed to be joyous and celebrating. Of course, Nick knew the Christmas season was really one of the most depressing times of the year for most people. It was the complete opposite of heartfelt and warm for many of the people who were alone for the holidays.

"Okay, we'll I'm going to go get started to the preliminary write-up for the article, and see if I can find out anything more about the victim's injuries or what the police are thinking."

"You do that," Marty said as Nick took all the papers from him and stuffed them back into the manila folder.

He headed for the door, but stopped short as Marty called, "Oh and Haley…" Nick turned, the file stuffed under one arm, his other reaching for the door knob, and waited for his boss to finish his sentence.

"...I don't care how big this story gets or if your hunch about the animal involvement turns out to be right, I don't want any more late copy coming in! You know the deadline, and you've had your last time of pushing the presses later than they should be kept waiting. I've got a paper to run, and if you can't keep up with the schedule, you might want to think about a career change!"

Once Marty was finished releasing the last of his pent up anger from earlier, Nick slipped out of his office and headed down the stairs to the main floor. He had a lot to do, and for just one moment he questioned whether his hunch was a good one.

Of course it is you idiot! The patterns are too similar between the different events. Maybe the psycho out there killing people got his idea from the old news story, maybe he's a copy-cat and taking it to the next level.

Nick didn't know for sure, there were still so many questions to be asked and so much work to do. He reached the bottom of the stairs and headed for Amber's cubicle.

I've got a story to follow, the truth is still out there— and it looks like Amber and I are going to be spending some quality time together.

Nick wasn't sure if her was pushing his luck, but then again, there was only one way to find out.

Chapter 18

It's too early for this shit, Detective Mack Jones thought as his bulky frame was seated in the large, spare conference room across the hall from the Homicide Division's offices on the second floor of Montgomery County Police Headquarters. Resting on the table before him were his big hands with thick fingers wrapped around the half empty Styrofoam coffee cup he had been drinking from. Already he was on his second cup of the cheap, burnt tasting liquid and the meeting he found himself here for hadn't even begun.

Goddamn Feds! He silently cursed, as he looked down at his shirt, the material stretched tight across his gut and straining the buttons, and realized he had spilled something down the front of him. Using on hand, the other still on his coffee, he brushed the residue from a powdered donut he had wolfed down quickly on his way in this morning. All that rushing around so as not to be late and the head honchos wasn't even present yet.

What, do they have better to do then catch a serial killer?

Mack took the opportunity to lean back in his flimsy chair, the seat groaning slightly under his weight as he surveyed the people and faces who were also present for the meeting. In attendance for this impromptu gathering were people he had worked with over the years, some he could put names to, others he couldn't. There was also a few new faces he had never seen before.

Lieutenant Garza was the one who caught Mack's eye first. The man was a restless ball of energy as he paced back and forth from one corner of the room to the other, stopping occasionally at the large window panes that looked out from this second floor vantage point and onto the traffic moving along Research Boulevard below. Garza was anxious and Mack had a feeling he was not looking forward to hearing what Chief Stone had to discuss this morning. Of course nobody was going to hear what the Chief needed to get off his chest until their federal guests arrived. Garza had been all too happy run lead on the investigation into the murders when they first began. He was looking to make a name for himself here in Rockville, and even when things progressively got worse and the body count rose, Stone for some reason known only to himself, kept the egomaniac in charge.

That was the first mistake of this investigation.

Stone should have let the people who were trained to do this sort of thing handle the preliminary murders. Mack himself had a hell of a track record for solved murders and other vicious crimes, and if Stone was going to let the Rockville Police Department have the lead on the murders, he would have gladly volunteered to run the show.

However, Stone had gone with Garza and that had irritated a lot of people not only in Mack's division but over at Montgomery County Homicide as well. Speaking of the Chief, Mack leaned forward in his chair and glanced out into the hallway. Where the hell is he?

Stone had been in his office when Mack first arrived at the building. He was going to say hello since it had been some time since he had seen the Montgomery County Chief of Police. Then again, that's how it was when he had his own Chief, Captains and other hierarchy to deal with over at the Rockville PD. He had only to deal with his own higher ranking officers. When he had first arrived, he saw the Chief was busy talking to some people in his office, and the look he received as he had approached told Mack that he didn't have the time for a friendly 'hello' and didn't want to be disturbed. Instead, Mack had made his way to the small county kitchenette and helped himself to a leftover pot of weak coffee that had probably been made sometime during the night shift hours ago. He had contemplated making a fresh batch when Detective Tim Melvin had strolled in, looking as tidy as ever in his neatly pressed suit and polished, dress shoes. Mack had always assumed Tim was gay, no straight man spending that much time on their appearance and color coordinating their attire.

Then again, Mack wasn't one to really get on someone about their appearance. He was overweight by at least fifty pounds, and his loving wife was constantly worrying and asking him to work on shedding some of the extra pounds. Even though he hated it when she nagged him about his unhealthy lifestyle, chalking it up to the constant fast food and sitting around a desk that his duties for the Rockville PD kept him swarmed with, he did know that he really ought to diet. His clothes were certainly snugger than they had been last year, and he had to add a new notch to his belt to keep his large pants from falling down.

No wonder Aidan always joked about him looking like one of those damn Buddha statues. Being short and stocky, the extra weight seemed to have gone straight to his midsection, and when it came to shopping for clothes, the sleek designer brands never seemed to come in his measurements. So instead he was left with shopping at the local Big & Tall, where everything he got that fit him in some areas was either too loose or skin tight in other spots.

Maybe the missus is right. Maybe I should start working on losing some weight. Sure would help keep me from tiring out as fast with everything that's going on right now. After all, the hours are just going to keep getting longer until we catch this bastard.

Mack spotted another stain, this one on his jacket and began rubbing it with his thumb. Once it was as clean as he was going to get it, he looked to see who else he knew that had arrived.

In addition to Garza and Tim Melvin, Mack recognized Trisha O'Mally, a computer specialist who worked full time for the MCPD. Her responsibilities included not only being fluent in all the latest technology and equipment needed to run a mobilized command center from any location, but she was a valuable asset in that she was a magician when it came to being able to locate whatever information she needed on a person.

With just a name or suspect's description and a few other minor details, Trisha really could work magic with a keyboard and pull up every dirty little secret they had if it had ever been digitized at some point in time. This made her the go to technology expert anytime Stone wanted to put together a crack team to accomplish something.

Other than the three familiar people, there were two other men who Mack had seen around before, but couldn't place a name to the face or which department they were from. There were about fifteen people sitting around the large conference table, and with the many officers, specialists and various technicians the local agencies had at their disposal, it was hard to keep track of all the latest job titles for people who needed the extra entitlement and the faces that belonged to those positions. The two possibly forensic science geared men were both busy talking among themselves at one corner of the table, obviously not caring to socialize with the rest of the room until they had to.

Oh well, to each his own, Mack thought as he shifted in his seat and heard the chair groan some more. Better not break— crappy county budget can't afford decent office furniture!

Running his chubby hand through his straight, greased black hair, he looked up just in time to see a group of people walking towards the conference room. In the lead was Chief Stone, whose entourage included two serious looking men wearing crisp, black suits that could have come off the same factory assembly line and a slim woman with curly, auburn hair and pretty green eyes and wearing a dark business suit. Once they entered the conference room, Chief Stone motioned for everyone to take a seat around the large rectangular table in the middle of the room. Once everyone had sat, the man of the most importance in the group of new arrivals sitting directly next to the Chief, Stone took a moment to look around at each of the men and women assembled before him.

"Ladies and gentleman, I thank you for taking the time to meet on such short notice and at so early an hour, but as we begin to get rolling right away with the topic at hand, I'm sure you will understand why there is such an urgency to assemble this joint task force as quickly as possible. Those of you who find yourselves in this room have been handpicked by myself, based on the needs of this group, your overall skill sets and the need to have at least one representative from each agency involved to help facilitate clear communication among all concerned," Stone said, meeting every person's gaze at least once as he spoke, then continued.

"As of now we are working towards the goal of identifying and putting measures into place that will lead to the capture of the unknown suspect or suspects responsible for the gruesome murders that have been continuing through the city over the last week. We are joined by FBI Special Agent in Charge, Jim Poole who has been sent to us from the Quantico, Virginia field office to aid us in our pursuit of the wanted assailant. He is a member of their Behavioral Analysis Unit and has worked on over twenty serial killer cases throughout the country over the last twenty years. Now, without wasting any more time, let me introduce you all to Special Agent Poole."

The man who stepped up next to Stone made the imposing bull of a Police Chief seem tame. He was tall and well-built, his head bald and smooth and the deep facial lines creasing his face pointed to him being close to his fifties, yet due to his solid build and the probability that he hit the gym every day, his skin was pulled taunt over his muscled features and toned body.

He appeared to have spent his early years in the Marine Corps, and even though that had probably been twenty years before, he still carried himself upright and with an air of confidence and control about him. Overall, Mack thought, he was one tough S.O.B., he didn't want pissed off at him. That was the problem with some of those boys from the bureau. They were a completely different breed of law enforcement agents, and operated within the safety of the most powerful government in the world, the United States of America.

The stern, penetrating look that had been on the man's face as he scanned the room, taking in every little detail of those before him with the swiftness of years of practice and training. Standing up from his chair, he ran one long hand down his suit, smoothing non-existent wrinkles away as he then standing perfectly straight and tall, clasped his hands behind his back and began to speak.

"Thank you Chief Stone. As you all have just been informed, my name is Special Agent Shepherd Harris, and I am here because these murders are not a federal matter due to the severity of the circumstances. While this is to be a joint task force involving those of you with the Rockville and Montgomery County Police Departments, I just want to make it clear that every piece of information and decision goes through me and my team before being considered approved. I'm not looking for any show-boaters or lone wolfs on this team, and everything will be cleared through our agency first.

'We have investigative jurisdiction over any violation of the more than two hundred various categories of federal crimes. In case some of you were under the misconception that the FBI cannot be granted jurisdiction due to these murders not crossing any county or state lines, I just want to remind you that falling under one of our top investigative priorities at the Bureau, is that we are not only here to support all local law enforcement agencies when requested, but to combat significant violent crimes. And, what we have here is certainly to be classified as a 'significant violent crime'. I have spoken to the other agencies around the surrounding areas and those closest to the two known crime scenes, and we will have full cooperation and resources not only from them, but from your own departments as well."

Mack watched the impressive man basically tell everyone they work for him, no if-ands-or-butts, and there wasn't a single murmur or complaint from anyone in the room. Not even Garza had let his displeasure with the current situation slip from his big mouth. This guy sure knows how to lead a team, Mack thought as he studied the bald, striking presence of the commanding, Special Agent Poole.

"Now, the first thing that needs to be taken care of is that we have to get a handle on the media so as not to go starting a panic among the citizens. I'm sure most of you remember the Sniper Shootings and how some people had become so afraid, they would not leave their houses. We can not allow the public to feel terrorized by these murderers, and will do everything within our power to make sure that the suspects are brought to justice as quickly as possible. So far the sites our UnSubs, or unknown subjects if you're not familiar with that term in your area, have chosen for their attacks have been centered in the city limits. However, we believe that there may be other similar attacks and corresponding murders that we are currently compiling a list of that crosses the country over the last few years at the bare minimum. That is the real reason the Bureau has shown an interest in these murders. We do not wish to swoop in and tell those of you how to handle your own local law enforcement issues, but if these murders are linked to the same perpetrators."

Special Agent Poole took a moment to let his words sink into the crowd of fifteen law enforcement officers that had been gathered for this briefing. Noticing a hand go up from one of the man sitting across the table from him, he nodded and allowed him to ask his question. The man was obviously a technician of some sort. The type that worked behind the scenes to accomplish his work in aiding the Detectives and officers in their continual pursuit of answers and the finding of the forensic evidence needed to make sure the investigators findings stuck in court.

"Yes, so just to be clear, we are looking at multiple assailants?" the man said, pushing his coke bottle-like glasses back onto the bridge of his nose with a finger and staring wide-eyed at the agent.

"I'm sorry we haven't had the time to get to formally go over everybody's names, but Mr....?" Poole questioned.

The thin, thirty-four year old forensic technician sat straight in his chair, all eyes on him. "Oh...sorry, my name is Dr. Henry Cushings, and I'm the lead Forensics Technician for the crime lab and actually the whole Department," answered Cushings, as he fidgeted about slightly, obviously not used to being the center of attention, and preferring to work in the solitude of the forensics lab along with a few other technicians.

"Well Dr. Cushings, to answer your question; yes, we believe the murders you have been subjected to in this city are being committed by more than one UnSub."

Another hand shot up, this time from a rough, uniformed officer near the other end of the table.

"Yes?"

"Officer Desmond Okeke, Sir," the tough-looking, black man said, sitting cool and quiet in his seat like he was a statue or on guard duty. The only movement the man made came from his large, fleshy lips that parted to reveal a set of teeth where one was missing from near the front of his mouth. He gave off the appearance of having grown up with a hard life on the streets and his deep voice was colored by his thick Brooklyn accent.

"I thought serial killers worked alone usually, I mean— you hears 'bout the likes of Bundy and Dahmer, and they didn't have no partners," Officer Okeke stated.

A smile formed on Poole's face as he glanced quickly around the room, obviously impressed by the basic collective minds that had been assembled before him, and then turning his attention back to the uniformed officer's statement, he said, "Yes, normally the type of criminal mind that fits the profile of a serial killer is that of a loner. In the past the most famous cases, some of which you just mentioned and were the precedent of the image we think of when we imagine a person capable of multiple homicides. However, that isn't always the case," Poole paused and took a moment to look around the room again, making sure everyone's attention was centered on him.

"Based on the forensic reports that your departments have been able to furnish us with, we were able to compare the initial findings with other unsolved murder cases around the country that fit the same modus operandi, and realized that there have been other locations where murders matching the description of the case here are far too similar to be coincidental. I am currently having my team pull all the police reports from across the country that seem like they could have been committed by our boys.

The heaviest volume of unsolved murders matching the forensics found at the two murder sites here in Rockville are actually further west, the majority being situated around more rural areas in the Northwestern United States. We have multiple reports of extremely violent deaths where the victims were assaulted and the bodies mutilated, in some cases beyond identification."

Mack watched the crowd of people gathered around the table exchange worried glances and humorless expressions among each other. Yeah, he had a feeling there had been something off about these murders the moment he had arrived at the first scene only three days ago. Jesus, has it really only been three days? He couldn't believe how much had happened in that short amount of time, let alone five victims being nearly torn to pieces, their body parts just strewn about like ravens picking at an animal carcass.

Thinking about the sites where he had been working on gathering information for his report to Lieutenant Garza, he remembered Aidan when he had first shown up. It had been good to see his old friend out and alive after everything he had been through over the last year. Even though he was technically not an acting Detective due to his administrative leave, Aidan was the type of guy who was dedicated enough to the job that it actually fueled him and breathed importance into his life. He was a great cop and an even better investigator, but unfortunately Garza had made sure that Aidan couldn't really be looking into the murders, whether Mack would have liked the second set of eyes and Aidan's impressions of the events to aid him in cracking this case. He remembered the old days when Aidan and him used to work together.

That was before he had transferred to the Rockville City PD because it didn't look like he would be making Detective at the County any time soon, and he needed the self-worth the promotion would have brought him. Luckily, the RCPD had just had one of their Detective's retire, and Mack jumped at the opportunity. All though he missed the dedication and late hours Aidan poured into his work when trying to solve a case, Mack had a family and needed to be home more when his work was done for the day. Suddenly, Mack heard the tail end of something Garza had been saying, and quickly attempted to pick up on the question the Lieutenant had asked.

"…just as you said, but I still don't see how you can jump to conclusions on this investigation based on half-baked theories!"

Mack watched the irritated Garza smack his hand down on the table with a loud thud as he finished his ranting. Mack kicked himself mentally for not paying attention to what had been being said. He couldn't believe Garza was actually arguing with the feds in the middle of the briefing. Poole must have said something to question how the investigation had been handled at the beginning, the blame obviously falling on Lieutenant Garza since he had basically forced Chief Stone to let him be the lead investigator.

Once Garza was finished, Mack turned his heavy frame towards Special Agent Poole. The federal agent was standing there, still in his stiff, military like posture, but instead of the confident steely gaze he had held moments earlier, his thick, dark eyebrows were pinched and drawn down, the bald head of his showing a vein throbbing in time with his heart beat as he seemed to be taking Garza's outburst into consideration.

That or perhaps he's deciding whether he should just pull out his government issued sidearm and shoot the guy, Mack thought with a smile forming on his chubby face.

Now that would be something to see!

Poole leaned forward and placing his hands palms down on the table, looked straight at Garza's spineless self. The anger that seemed to be welling up inside of the agent made the whole room silent as they waited to see how Poole would respond to Garza's statement. Finally, taking a small breath of air, Poole answered the arrogant Lieutenant with a response the entire room was waiting to hear.

"You, were the lead investigator on the scene at the first murder were you not?" Poole asked, the clipped tightness in his voice evident to all.

"Yeah I was, and I don't think we need the Feds to come rolling in here like we're a bunch of clueless simpletons who don't know how to tell the difference between a jaywalking offense and a mass murder! I had everything moving along smoothly when I was running this investigation. And as far as I'm concerned we don't need you and your buddies…" Garza motioned to the two additional FBI agents seated near Poole, "…to come in here like you own the place and start telling us how it's going to go down! These murders happened in the city limits, that means it is the responsibility of the Rockville Police Department to investigate these crimes, and if and when we might need your 'assistance', then we can involve you and your team!"

Mack was stunned. He couldn't believe Garza had the 'stones' to tell Special Agent in Charge, Jim Poole to basically sit back and let Garza run the show. Chief Stone was about to say something, but Poole held up his hand and motioned for the Chief to set still, that he would handle this situation himself. Locking eyes with Garza, Poole leaned his weight forward on the table some more and the whites of his knuckles began to show as his knuckles rested on the smooth surface.

"Lieutenant Garza," Poole began. "It seems we have ourselves a little problem with the matter of jurisdiction in regards to this case."

"You're damn right we do!" Garza replied explosively.

"As I have already explained, these murders and mutilations of people recently are not an isolated incident, let alone anything new. I have also already informed the group gathered here in this room that I have my field office compiling reports on all the missing and unsolved murders that fit the criteria of possibly having been committed by our UnSubs. Now, while that information is put together and shipped here to this building, which by the way will be our temporary base of operations either until we catch these sick bastards or find a more suitable command center to coordinate everything through, we at the bureau will be aiding in all of this effort. However, my assistance does come at a price!"

Garza seemed to be losing some of the steam from his sails as Special Agent Poole continued explaining what was currently taking place.

"My services and the services of the Bureau are provided to you in the hopes that we will stop these madmen before they can strike again. However, any illusions you had that you would be running things, possibly looking to make a name for yourself with the local media and earn your fifteen minutes of fame, all these ideas need to be locked back up in your mind. You might as well throw away the key once you do that, because I am in charge of this investigation, and I have the full weight of the United States government behind me.

'So, if you can't handle sitting on the bench when it comes game time, you might as well get off the team, because there is no room on this task force for childish illusions of grandeur! We have a group of people roaming our great country, attacking and mutilating innocent victims! So if you aren't going to be able to get that through your head, the door is right there and I suggest you use it!"

The room was so quiet that you could hear that the majority of the people surrounding the table had literally stopped breathing.

Holy crap, this man is good, Mack thought as he watched the look on Garza's face go from angry to that of a little boy who had just been spanked for some wrongdoing. Mack would have burst out laughing seeing that jackass Garza put in his place, but then he too might become the object of Poole's attention, and that was one man he didn't want to piss off.

If I was Garza, I'd probably have pissed myself!

Chapter 19

The recessed bolt action on the new, Remington Model 700 was a beautiful piece of craftsmanship. It slid smoothly under little pressure, slipping the Premier AccuTip, polymer-tipped big-game bullet easily and snuggly into the chamber and allowing the precision designed ammunition to explode out the end of the stainless steel barrel and hit a target with devastating accuracy. And, with a thicker jacket and harder lead core regulating the weight retention, the rounds provide optimal penetration of the intended target with enough power coming from the rifle's firing mechanism to ensure whatever is hit stays down. Designed and built to master the most extreme conditions, the rifle features Remington's armor-tough, new black matte TruNyte Corrosion Control System on its stainless steel barreled action and stock, and with the X-Mark Pro adjustable Trigger with it's super-tight tolerances and mirror-like surface finish, the rifle was definitely the perfect choice for any hunting needs a man could have.

To add to the overall package, the Mark 4 MR/T Riflescope, a coveted yet expensive addition to the Model 700, gave the shooter a serious boost in magnification and accuracy to get any job done, covering everything from 50 to 700 meters thanks to the scope's intricate sights and adjustments.

All in all, it was one hell of a gun. Jack Morgan was proud that he had saved up, setting aside a little bit from his paychecks each month until he had enough to purchase the new hunting rifle. It had cost him over a grand, but with quality and craftsmanship like the Remington he know held in his hands, he knew it was worth every penny. Of course, now the only problem was that it wasn't hunting season around these parts, and that meant he had to be careful where he and his buddies went out to score a deer or two.

Jack Morgan was forty-three years old, and had grown up hunting his whole life. He would be damned if he was going to let some little thing like not having a valid hunting license or tracking and shooting deer on protected woodland stop him from trying out his new, favorite gun. Dressed head to toe in an all camouflage outfit complete with a dark green baseball cap and his trusty, Gore-tek hiking boots, his two best friends, Keith and Lucky, dressed in similar gear and sporting their own expensive hardware, though none as nice as Jack's, had driven up in Lucky's 4x4 truck to the concealed spot they parked their vehicle at.

They covered the truck in a large, camouflage-printed tarp, making it pretty much invisible amongst the trees unless you knew where to look. They would be back for the vehicle in a day, once they had successfully bagged their desired trophies.

"No point in making it too noticeable that we're out here," Jack said as they unloaded their gear and supplies and set off for their final destination for the base of an access point to the Appalachian Mountain range that they used frequently.

The Appalachian Trail or simply the AT, is a marked hiking trail in the eastern United States extending between Springer Mountain in Georgia and Mount Katahdin in Maine. It is approximately 2,181 miles long, and passes through the states of Georgia, North Carolina, Tennessee, Virginia, West Virginia, Maryland, Pennsylvania, New Jersey, New York, Connecticut, Massachusetts, Vermont, New Hampshire, and Maine. The majority of the trail is in wilderness, although some portions traverse towns and roads, and cross rivers.

The Appalachian Trail is famous for its many hikers, some of whom, called 'Thru-hikers', attempt to hike it in its entirety in a single season. The Appalachian Trail, the Continental Divide Trail and the Pacific Crest Trail form what is known as the Triple Crown of long distance hiking in the continental United States, and it stretches so far that an unofficial extension known as the International Appalachian Trail, continues north into Canada and to the end of the range, where it enters the Atlantic Ocean.

Maryland has 41 miles of the trail, with elevations ranging from 230 to 1,880 feet. The trail passes through several different biomes from south to north, and the climate changes significantly, particularly dependent upon elevation. In the south, lowland forests consist mainly of second-growth; nearly the entire trail has been logged at one time or another. There are, however, a few old growth locations along the trail, such as Sages Ravine straddling the Massachusetts-Connecticut border and atop higher peaks along the trail on either side of the same border, the Hopper, and "The Hermitage", near Gulf Hagas in Maine.

In the south, the forest is dominated by hardwoods, including oak and tulip trees, also known as yellow poplar. Further north, tulip trees are gradually replaced by maples and birches. Oaks begin to disappear in Massachusetts. By Vermont, the lowland forest is made up of maples, birch and beech, which provide spectacular foliage displays for hikers in September and October. While the vast majority of lowland forest south of the White Mountains is hardwood, many areas have some coniferous trees as well, and in Maine, these often grow at low elevations.

It is this massively diverse geological makeup and untouched forests that makes this point a hunter's paradise, and that was exactly why Jack and the two Sampson brothers, Keith and Lucky were hiking into the forest depths in search of the 'big score'. They were looking for a buck that they could shoot and bring back home that would rival any of the white-tailed deer population that people scored during the legal hunting season. Of course with it being almost November, they also had to look forward to the startup of wild turkey season, which ran from October 29 through November 5.

It had taken them a good hour hike up through the woods until they knew they were far enough from civilization that nobody would spot them hunting illegally, and they had almost reached their final destination. They didn't need to be discovered out here, especially with each of them carrying guns. That was one set of hassles Jack could do without right now.

He still had to pay off that fine he received for killing a red fox last spring with a crossbow. The Park Ranger had confiscated the expensive bow and given him thirty days to pay the ridiculous $500 fine. To make matters worse, he didn't even get to keep the damn animal. Costing him that much money, the least he could of done was had it stuffed and mounted. Not that a pathetic little fox would mean anything to his collection. Since he was a teenager when Jack used to go out with his father hunting, he had learned the importance of his Second Amendment right and would 'bare' his gun to anybody who tried to tell him when and where he could hunt.

It's all them damn eco-friendly, PETA loving conservatives fault, he thought angrily as he trudged up a small hill and turned to wait for his companions.

"Will you hurry the hell up Lucky!" Jack called down from his higher vantage point as he watched the two brothers he had known since childhood lumber along the trail. From this small outcropping of rocks where the trail forked and headed deeper into the thick woods of Rock Creek Park, he could look out through the trees in his line of sight and see that the sky was beginning to darken. Damn, they weren't going to be able to hike much further once the light from the sky was gone until the moon came up. Fortunately for them, when Jack had checked the local forecasts on the radio that morning he had learned that tonight was supposed to some pretty decent visibility thanks to the cloud cover not going to be so thick. Nights like tonight, the moon would be able to light their way without having to rely on their flashlights as much. You never know when them damn them Rangers with the National Park Service could be out snooping around, Jack thought, hoping they were able to stay clear of any other people on their trip.

Fortunately they had nature giving them the advantage over being discovered. Being one of the oldest national parks in the country, the main section of Rock Creek Park runs for 2.75 square miles along a valley of the same name. Due to it being considered a large, 'urban natural area', hunting had been banned from the insides of the forest for years.

It's massive wooded expanse runs over 2,000 acres, the major portion of the area north of the National Zoo's land, and it spreads out until it reaches the mouth of Rock Creek, the large creek that the national park is named for, where it feeds into the Potomac River. In 1933, Rock Creek Park, along with other National Capital Parks, was transferred to the jurisdiction of the National Park Service, and it became the duty of the United States Park Police to maintain order across the land.

The Appalachian Trail is relatively safe. Most injuries or incidents are consistent with comparable outdoor activities. Most hazards are related to dangerous weather conditions, human error, plants, animals, diseases, and fellow humans encountered along the trail. Violent crime, including murder, has occurred on the trail in a few instances. Most had been crimes by non-hikers who crossed paths relatively randomly with the victims somewhere on the AT. Jack remembered reading in the paper quite a few years back, sometime in the mid-nineties, that two women had been abducted, bound and murdered near the trail in Shenandoah National Park. The primary suspect was later discovered harassing a female bicycler in the vicinity, but charges against him were dropped, and the case remains unsolved.

Creep could still be out here, snatching hikers off the trails and having his way with them! Jack thought as he stepped over a long tree branch that had fallen across the path at some point during a recent storm. He knew there were all kinds of crazies that shunned the cities and flocked out here to be alone with the solitude of the forest. Most of the time they were never heard of, occasionally only being caught for their crimes if they slipped up and made a mistake. Of course, out in these vast woods, if you were smart, you could stay hidden from the authorities and their rules.

Jack knew that if they didn't want to be found out here, they wouldn't be. Back in 2002, after a year of being missing that Prison Intern that had been all over the news had finally been found out here in Rock Creek Park. He couldn't remember the woman's name, it was Chandra, or Kendra or something, but either way, it just went to show a person that if you knew what you were doing, you could live off the land and never be discovered until you were ready to. His father had taught him everything he knew about hunting, tracking, fishing and surviving in the Great Outdoors, and Keith and Lucky were just as good. Who knows, Lucky might even be the best of all three of us, Jack thought as he remembered the time Lucky had earned his nickname.

Back when they were all in middle school, they had decided to head out one night and sneak into Old Jeb Wilson's barn. The ancient geezer had had an illegal distillery stored in one of the barns on his property where he made a moonshine concoction that had appealed to the boys when looking for some adventure one night. That was back before Maryland actually was an agricultural staple, unlike today where every piece of farm land had been bought up and turned into homes.

Jack could remember it like it had happened yesterday, even though in reality it had been over thirty-some odd years ago. Once it was late enough and each of their folks had gone to bed, the boys snuck out of their houses and met at the edge of Jeb Wilson's property. Their plan was simple. They were going to make sure the tough, racist old man was sure to be asleep, then having drawn straws, Lucky had been chosen to go into the barn and steal a jug of the powerful 'hooch', then bring it back so they could all slink off into the woods and enjoy their conquest.

It was supposed to be a simple plan, getting into the barn being the hardest part. Of course that's when things began to fall apart. Lucky had slipped into the barn through an old plank that had rotted away in the side. It was just big enough for the scrawny boy to squeeze through. Once Lucky was inside, the darkness of the enclosed building made it impossible to see. At one point he tripped over something and the next thing Jack and Keith knew was there was a crashing noise from Lucky having knocked into the still and sending the whole things toppling over. Jeb Wilson's dog had heard the commotion and began to start a ruckus that would have woken the dead.

Before Lucky could find his way back to the hole in the barn wall, Old Jeb was out of his house, pants halfway around his ankles and a shotgun cradled in the nook of his arm. Knowing they could do nothing for Lucky, Jack and Keith had dashed into the nearest tree line, fearing they'd be spotted, they lay on the cold dirt ground and didn't stir a muscle. By that point they heard Jeb Wilson entering the barn, and after turning on a kerosene lantern, found his distillery had been trashed.

Jack remembered hearing the old man cussing with such ferocity he thought he would have a brain aneurysm. As the minutes ticked by and Jack and Keith lay frozen like statues, they thought Lucky was surely either dead or been beaten unconscious by Jeb.

Minutes continued to stretch by, Old Jeb continuing to do whatever he was doing in the barn, and from right behind them, they heard footsteps approaching. Keith had looked like he was about to scream until upon turning they saw the wide-eyed form of Lucky standing there in one piece, a large, glass jug held tight against his body. Jack and Keith were speechless. Lucky was alive! The three of them quickly vanished into the woods, not stopping until they were as far from Jeb Wilson's property as they could get. Once they had stopped, the boys collapsed on the ground, passing the moonshine among themselves and listening to Lucky tell his story.

It seemed that after he had knocked into the distillery and heard the dog start barking, he had tried to make a break for it. However, he faced the problem of not being able to see where he was going. When Jeb entered the barn and went for the kerosene lantern hanging on a post about ten yards in, Lucky had slipped by him and right out the main doors to the barn. Old Jeb had been none the wiser, and Lucky had been able to grab a bottle of the prized liquid as he dashed away.

Since that day, Jack would swear to anyone he met that the boy was the luckiest boy alive. Of course that had been a long time ago, but to this day, Lucky continued to have things continually go his way.

Stopping to take a sip of water from the canteen he carried attached to his belt, Jack let Lucky and Keith catch up to his position. Keith was heavier than he or Lucky, and that usually meant Lucky stayed back to help him along whenever he had trouble keeping up. Jack blamed it on how unhealthy Keith was. The man smoked two packs of unfiltered cigarettes a day, drank like a fish every night and the only exercise he seemed to get when away from the mechanic's shop him and Lucky co-owned was when they headed out to do some illegal hunting. Jack hated the term 'poacher', since he figured the animals out in these woods were put here for man to rule over. He was pretty sure that's how it was in the Bible about the Creation of the world, but Jack wasn't really religious anymore and couldn't remember the exact words. Either way, it was something along those lines.

Once Keith and Lucky had caught up to him, Jack offered Keith a pull from his canteen, even though Keith had a CamelBak hydration pack strapped in between in shoulders on his back, the small tube to draw water from positioned right near his mouth. The man ignored Jack's offer and with a grin, pulled a small flask no doubt filled with alcohol from his camouflage vest. Shaking his head at the sight, Jack turned to Lucky and asked, "You think we're going to get anything tonight?"

Lucky took a drag from a cigarette he had lit and shook his head up and down quickly, but before he could say anything, Keith broke in.

"Course we're gonna get lucky. 'Sides you got that sweet new rifle to play with, so we're gonna have to find something. Maybe we'll even come across something bigger than that 10-pointer we bagged last week."

"Yeah that would be nice. I can't wait to see what this baby can do," Jack said patting the Remington slung over his shoulder.

"Well not all of us can afford such pricey toys whenever we want," stated Lucky.

Jack knew that he probably made more than Keith and Lucky combined. During the week he worked for a large company called Deacon Construction Group, and the size of the contracts he got correlated to the commission he received each month, and the last couple of months, business had been booming. That's why he had decided to spend the extra cash on the Remington Model 700. Since the three of them were out in the woods every week, he figured it was a solid investment.

"Sure got dark quick," Keith muttered looking around at the twilight like atmosphere that they were surrounded by now that the sun had vanished from the sky.

The moon was just as bright and visible as the weather report had predicted, but with the thickness of the forest canopy, it was still pretty dark. Jack pulled a small led flashlight from his pocket and clicked it on.

He scanned the area, looking for the path that would lead them to the concealed hunting blind they had set up a month before. Using mesh netting and branches and leaves from the woods, they had been able to cover up all the gear they needed on their weekly excursions. Without having to haul all that extra weight up the steep hills and valleys that littered Rock Creek Park, it made it much easier to hike deep into the area and get a head start on their hunting.

The spot they had found a few years earlier and continued to visit frequently was a perfect place to hunt and be left alone to the thoughts in your head. That was why the three men came out here. They didn't mind stashing the truck and hiking the hour long trail to get to this point, at least the majority of them didn't. With Keith being out of shape and letting his health really go downhill, it took an extra twenty minutes to get to where they had to.

"Come on, let's get a move on— I got a feelin' we're gonna rustle us up some big, ol' beauties!" Jack said, turning and treading carefully over the small hill.

Once they had reached their destination, Jack unslung the Remington from his shoulder and took off the pack he was carrying on his back. The backpack was a Coleman brand, backpack with heavy duty frame and pockets that could hold everything he could need for this little excursion into the woods. He kept the trusty pack filled with a mixture of various odds and ends that could come in handy during their two days out in the middle of nowhere. Other than the essentials like camping gear, spare clothes, waterproof matches, firelogs and water treatment tablets, Jack also stocked his gear with a first aid kit and extra ammunition for the Remington and the additional firearm he carried strapped to his waist.

The second gun was a backup and his weapon of choice in case they stumbled upon anything that could give them trouble. Jack believed in being prepared, after all he was a boy scout when he was little, and their motto was that very phrase. You never knew what you would find when you left the safety of civilization and journeyed out into the wild. Even though Rock Creek Park was somewhat more urbanized that say the Appalachian mountains, it was still a large forest that had its share of dangers. Bears were the only thing Jack could really see needing the .357 Magnum revolver for anyways. They frequented the woods all through the East Coast mountain ranges and forests, and he didn't plan on stumbling upon one without the firepower provided by his pistol.

If they did come across a full-sized black bear, an animal that could is the largest mammal native to Maryland, and can reach a height of eight feet standing on its hind legs and weigh over 800 pounds, he wouldn't hesitate to drop it with the Federal Premium HydraShok ammunition he kept loaded in the cylinder of the Magnum.

The black bear is a species native to Maryland that was once distributed statewide. Bears were historically abundant because of the excellent habitats provided by Maryland's native woodlands, meadows, swamps, and coastal plain. The black bear population suffered, though, as European settlers colonized Maryland.

By the early 1900s, loss of habitat had restricted black bears to the western portion of the state. Maryland's last black bear hunting season took place in 1953. By the mid 1960s, the black bear population was nearly extirpated and was restricted to the more remote mountainous areas of Allegany and Garrett counties. In 1972, the status of the black bear was changed from that of a "forest game" animal to being listed on the state "endangered species" list. Even though recently the black bear had been reclassified as 'forest game', the rules and regulations restricting the shooting of a bear made it damn near impossible to legally claim it most of the time.

Of course, Jack and his buddies weren't out here for the bears. He had his .357 Magnum locked and loaded as a precaution. The last thing they needed to do was accidentally stumble upon a black bears home, especially if there were baby cubs around. In that case, the mother bear became a massive, deadly presence that would rise up and charge a man down, shredding them to pieces with their massive claws and powerful jaws, all as a result of protecting her offspring.

As the three men began unpacking their gear and setting up their base camp, Jack decided to take a little excursion by himself off to check out the woods and look for any new game trails that might have formed since the last time they had been out there. Grabbing his canteen and the Remington, he took one last look at Keith and Lucky busily setting up the tents and other supplies, then without bothering to give some worthless excuse, he disappeared down one long, winding trail towards a perfect location to set up a blind that he had found the last time he was out this way.

Let them get the tents and cooking stove set up, I did most of the work the last time, Jack thought as he trudged along through the woods, finally reaching his secret spot after about fifteen minutes of walking. He had used the Bowie knife he kept strapped to his leg the last time he was here to carve a notch high enough in one of the large trees in the area to mark it for later recognition. Seeing the cut in the bark about six feet up the large tree, he looked up and saw that the small hunting chair he had setup suspended ten feet above the ground was still tethered to the tree with the strong adjustable bands he had used.

Making sure his rifle was secure over his shoulder; he found a decent foothold in the tree near the ground and began his ascent. With little effort he climbed the short distance and slipped quietly into the camo-patterned metal seat. He looked out from his spot, surveying the dark forest for as far as his eyes could see. It was quiet. He could hear the chirping of crickets and other insects sounding off into the night, and from somewhere off in the distance he could hear an owl hooting, calling out into the dark as its eyes probably searched for a mouse or other small animal to claim as its dinner.

Taking a sip from his canteen, Jack then laid his rifle across his lap and began tightening and double checking the various knobs and levers that were part of the highly sophisticated, Mark 4 MR/T Riflescope. Once he was satisfied that the rifle was set to his chosen specifications, he raised it up, cradling the butt of the matte black stock against his shoulder, and looked placing his cheek softly against the cool metal of the Remington, he stared through the scope and scanned the soft glow radiating from the trees of the moonlit forest around him. It was a perfect night; the clouds non-existent, and the large, pale body of the crescent moon looking like the bright, new sliver was cradled in the arms of the old. It seemed like a portent of things to come that night.

Jack wasn't superstitious or anything like that, but the feeling he had sitting in his hunting blind, the light of that big bright fragment coming down through the trees and casting a pale light upon the forest caused a small shiver to run down his back. It was a beautiful night, and with the forest being lit up so well in some areas thanks to the aid of the white, heavenly slice above, Jack had a feeling that tonight he was going to be pretty damn lucky.

Who knows, after tonight, maybe I'll have earned the nickname Lucky, and he'll be back to just plain old Dale, Jack thought as he imagined bagging a huge buck that would set a record for the area. Of course he wouldn't be able to let people know, if the media got wind of it he'd be in hot water with the police for illegal poaching of deer in the off-season, but still, he'd know what he had bagged and so would his two buddies.

If it's big enough, maybe I'll have to have it mounted for my study, he continued thinking, knowing he should have tried to find something to replace that pathetic little deer he had hanging there now.

Yeah, I need a big boy, something that will make people gawk with their mouths open when they enter my place!

As Jack scanned the surrounding forest, his eye staring out through the high-powered rifle scope, his left hand fiddled with the knobs on the top and side of the Mark 4's sights. He twisted the knobs to change the elevation and focus. Once he had the sights zeroed in accurately for around 200 yards, he stopped messing with the settings.

Of course at 200 yards, he didn't even need the powerful scope, that was just overkill for so simple a shot that would normally not require Jack to even use a scope, but at night, it would aid in picking out the image of a deer clearer than without using it. That and he was anxious to try out his new Remington and all its bells and whistles.

Peering slowly around from his vantage point up off the ground, Jack payed special attention to any slight movement he could pick up in the forest and trees. He had had that feeling he got when something was around, and when he noticed a slight rustling sound somewhere in the distance he swiveled his body towards the direction of the noise and slowly scanned the area. Yes, there is something out there, he told himself as he steadied his excited breathing like he had been taught by his father when he was a boy.

The forest seemed to lose all sense of being alive, and Jack's attuned his senses to everything that was going on around him. His eyes were looking for the slightest movement to be seen through the telescopic sight of the Remington Model 700, and his ears were attempting to filter out the chilly wind rustling through the trees and rattling the leaves as he strived to locate his prey. As he studied his surroundings, he suddenly found it strange that the forest had seemed to grow eerily silent. No longer were there the chirping of crickets or the hooting of an owl or any other nighttime creature. It was as if the nocturnal world of the forest had gone into hiding.

What the hell? Why is it so quiet?

Jack continued to look through his scope, moving the rifle back and forth over the forest floor below in a switchback pattern, working his way from closer to farther into the forest. He wasn't liking the sudden absence of sound, the woods having taken on a quiet, unreal silence. It was like something was spooking the animals and insects, but what?

"Damn it," Jack muttered under his breath as he realized why the forest had suddenly gone dead.

Goddamn Keith or Lucky must be out there wondering where I got off to!

He looked around, continuing to study the trees and bushes for any sign of one of the brothers. Even though he couldn't hear or see anything, he knew there was somebody out there.

Where they hell are you, you damn dip-shits! You're scaring away the damn deer!

Even though he was pretty sure that one of his two buddies had stumbled upon his secret spot, he kept quiet just in case he still had a chance to rustle up a buck. He figured that maybe one of the two idiots out tramping about the woods would scare one out of hiding, and using that to his advantage, score the first kill of the trip.

Suddenly he the silence of the area was shattered by a loud noise off to Jack's right. He spun quickly in his seat, the shooter's nest shaking slightly as his quick action shook the cables holding the chair to the tree, and he stared through his scope. Ready for anything, his finger barely lying against the trigger, he tried to figure out what the hell had just caused that explosion of noise.

It sounded like someone had came barreling through a grouping of bushes, and staring through the magnified sights of his rifle, he could see a few branches that were swaying far too violently to be moving by the little breeze there was. Jack was sure something had came through that way, and was now somewhere in the tree line about fifty yards from his current position.

Swinging around in the seat, he kept the rifle braced tightly against his shoulder and attempted to find the source of the earlier distraction. The chair he was on shifted slightly from his movements and he stopped fussing about so as not to have one of the cables slip from the trunk they were supported from.

Were Keith and Lucky messing with him? Jack wasn't sure, but he wasn't about to call out and reveal his spot. He was still holding onto the hope of nailing the first kill of the night. If one of his buddies was out there, they had better knock it off, or they were likely to get a bullet in the ass for their shenanigans. The thought of them returning home from this trip, Keith unable to sit from a bullet grazing his ass due to their stupid pranks brought a smile to Jack's lips.

That sure would teach them— what the hell?

The second Jack had swept his rifle past a certain span of trees, he was sure he had seen something slipping quietly into the next group of wild growing bushes that were only about thirty yards from him. It had been too quick to make out what it was, but he began to have the feeling that it wasn't Keith or Lucky. It had moved too quickly for one of them. Maybe it was a coyote, Jack thought, knowing that the woods were full of the mangy animals.

As he attempted to focus on the bushes he was sure the animal had run into just moments before, he suddenly felt his whole body thrown forward as he nearly toppled from the shooter's nest. Grabbing onto one of the cables to keep himself from falling the ten feet to the ground, Jack realized he had lost his grip on the Remington and the rifle must have fallen to the ground.

What in Christ's name was that?, he wondered as he leaned over slightly, looking down towards the ground to see if his rifle had fallen down there.

He couldn't see the gun, and in fact he couldn't see anything down below that would have attributed to the tree shaking so violently that he was almost thrown from his perch. Jack felt a cold sweat trickling down the back of his neck. Something wasn't right, and pulling the .357 from the holster on his belt, he cocked the gun prepared to take another look below.

Grabbing a tight hold of the cable that was wrapped around the large tree trunk with his left hand, he set his feet solidly on the chair and leaned over for another look. He felt the beads of sweat on his forehead tingling from the cool night breeze and his fingers wrapped around the handgun were clammy from a sense of dread.

What the hell is going on?

As Jack took a glance down towards the ground, he once again could see nothing but the base of the tree and the ground covered in its mixture of leaves and other plants. As his eyes scanned the forest floor he thought he saw the butt of his Remington half covered under some of the vegetation and leaves. Before he could reposition his feet and look over on the other side of the shooter's nest, there was a loud, crashing frantic sound like a bear charging through the woods. The only problem was it sounded like it was directly under him and the scurrying noise he could hear echoing out into the eerily silent night air sounded like claws scratching deep into wood, wood like the tree he was sitting up in!

Jack tightened his grip on the powerful Magnum, ready to squeeze as many rounds as he could at whatever it was that was coming for him. However, before he could look down the other side of the chair he was standing in, he felt a sharp pain in his lower leg and he cried out in surprise.

"Ahhh!" Jake yelled as the explosion of pain reverberated through his whole left side. Looking down he saw that a dark arm, covered in bristly, coarse fur had broken through the base of the chair he was standing on, the long, razor-sharp claws at the tips of the fingers of the unknown hand were surrounding his lower leg, the claws slicing through his pants and puncturing deeply into his calf muscle.

Pain continued to flow through the lower half of his left side as Jack swung his Magnum towards the assailing appendage and prepared to fire. However, before his finger could squeeze off a round, he felt the powerful arm yank down on his leg and before he knew it he was toppling head over heels and came crashing to the forest floor below. He hit the ground and felt the air knocked out of his lungs from the violent impact.

Wheezing and trying to pull air into his chest, Jack's head rolled back and forth quickly as he looked for the creature that had upended him from his shooter's nest and almost ripped his leg off. Thinking of his leg, he looked down at the bloody mess, the skin and muscles had been ripped away and the bone was visible in multiple spots. He winced in agony, feeling hot tears spilling from the corners of his tightly closed eyes. He couldn't bare to look at the damage and blood that was flowing from his body.

Bear— it had to have been a bear— what else is that big— It climbed the tree! It pulled me down and mangled my leg!

Jack forced his eyes open, avoiding looking at his destroyed limb, and pulling harsh gasps of air into his lungs. Then he realized, It still has to be here, it wouldn't give up now that it has me out of the tree!

He frantically looked around him, and then realizing he had dropped the .357 in the fall as well, he was unarmed and alone.

Oh dear God, please help me!

Jack was just in the middle of sitting up, propping himself up onto his elbows when he heard the loud snap of a tree branch being broken from directly behind him. Eyes widening in fear, he tilted his head back just as a shadow fell over his helpless form.

As his eyes settled on the the thing he knew now was going to be responsible for his death, the only thought he could think of was, The fangs are so sharp!

Then with a loud and final crunch, the jaws of the beast snapped down over Jack's head, the long, sharp teeth puncturing through flesh and bone, and that was the last Jack knew as he entered the darkness.

Chapter 20

In the first-floor zoology lab located in the Cave, Frank finished transferring all the hand-written data and notes that he and Lisa Davies had taken over the last two days. It had been an enormous amount of work to compile the hours of watching and logging of video and their own eyewitness reports of the testing they had done in the wolf habitat. Frank leaned back in his chair and let out a long yawn, stretching his arms over his head and trying to wake himself up a little. He dropped his arms down to his sides and stared at the computer screen sitting before him. All that data and the hours of testing they had put into the last two days, and they were finally beginning to get somewhere with the being able to correlate Lisa's theories into real-world mechanics.

Frank pictured the beautiful, wildlife biologist and his boss, and thought of how lucky he was to have the chance to not only be working here at the National Zoo, but to be working with someone as brilliant as Lisa Davies. It was an honor to have been chosen to be her assistant, and to be completely honest, he hadn't thought that he would have been selected for the zoo's internship program. Sure he had pretty good grades, but they weren't stellar, and Frank knew that to have a chance at working at such a prestigious organization as the Smithsonian, that he had to bust his butt to show them he belonged among their ranks. Even if his rank was at the bottom of the pecking order, he still pushed himself everyday to continue to try and impress Lisa, and it finally looked like it was paying off.

Just the other day, Frank recalled, she had mentioned that if the grant proposal went through they'd have more money in their department to work with, and Lisa had hinted at him going from intern to full-fledged assistant. Frank was ecstatic. The sometimes grueling hours and the massive amount of work they had to do between just the two of them, and now it looked like his dedication was about to pay off. Of course, he knew that none of it would be possible if it wasn't for Lisa and her brilliance.

Thinking of the tall, raven haired zoologist, her darker, Hispanic complexion and killer body all wrapped up in one hell of a package that was complete with a brain that could change the scientific world one of these days. Yeah Frank had a slight crush on the woman, but while the thirty-four year old was only ten years older than him, she was more of a mentor and he knew she'd never be interested in him. That she was too kind to ever say that was just another one of the woman's remarkable charms.

Of course, while Lisa Davies may be out of his league, there was always Tammy over at the Eatery.

Frank saved the data he had entered and pushed away from the desk. Standing up he thought about heading over to the food court like area where the cute, blonde and just turned eighteen year old girl worked serving burgers, fries and a whole other mixture of fast food like food to the workers and visitors that came were present daily at the campus. He could really use the break to go visit her and grab a diet coke, but Frank knew that Lisa was hopefully going to be back soon from the board meeting that she had left a few hours ago to attend.

Figuring he didn't have enough time to make it over to see Tammy and grab some caffeine, he tiredly headed for the small kitchenette that was down the hall from the lab. As he stepped inside the dark room, a motion sensor captured his presence and the bright, efficient CFL bulbs in the ceiling came to life, lighting the room as he entered.

Got to love the environmentally minded here at SCBI, Frank thought as he walked over to the coffee maker that was near the back of the small room. Other than a few basic appliances like the coffee maker, microwave and an EnergyStar refrigerator, the room only had a round, cafeteria style table and a few plastic chairs to sit in. While the Cave had around a dozen or so employees that worked in and out of the lab space and offices, most of them preferred to grab their meals at the Eatery with people from the other labs and buildings. It was usually the only time they got to see some of their colleagues aside from group lectures and the occasional educational seminars that the Smithsonian setup for the staff to keep them apprised of all the new advancements and natural scientific breakthroughs happening around the world, many of which were being performed by Smithsonian funded scientists and researchers.

Filling a mug with some water from the water cooler in the corner of the kitchenette, Frank poured it into the back of the coffee maker and flipped the machine on. He listened to it hum to life and walked over to the giant cork-board that hung on the opposite wall. The board was a place where anyone could hang information or flyer's that they might think others would be interested in for anything others might want to see or attend. Mixed among the general science and nature related pages, someone had even hung up a poster for their daughter's dance recital coming up in November. Frank perused the latest additions to the cluttered board while he waited for the coffee to brew.

One flyer caught his attention that he hadn't seen before. It was a inner-office memo that had gone out to all the buildings on the SCBI campus regarding this upcoming Halloween.

Geesh, how could I have forgot that Halloween was coming up?

Frank figured it was due to all the work they had been doing around the lab and inside the actual wolves' enclosure that had made him completely forget about the upcoming holiday.

It was in two days! He couldn't believe that October was almost over, and that November was about to be upon them. Then again, it sure was starting to get cold as fall seemed to be slipping ever closer to a quickly approaching and possibly harsh winter.

Frank hated the cold, and sometimes he wondered why he hadn't moved off to someplace warmer. He had a few friends who had decided to attend school in Florida, and whenever he talked to them online, they were sure to remind him of the beaches, girls in bikinis and the booze that he was missing. It sure sounded like a blast to Frank, but he had to keep reminding him that he didn't want to be some deadbeat, possible college dropout, but instead wanted to truly make something of himself. That meant buckling down and working hard here for the National Zoo.

By the time the coffee had finished brewing into the mug below the machine, the small room smelled strongly of the beverage. Frank stepped away from the corkboard and began looking through a cabinet for the sugar and creamers.

As he found the proper containers and poured the desired amount into his steaming mug, he heard a voice from behind him.

"Well if it isn't Mowgli back from spending time with his brother wolves," the southern drawl of an accent said.

Frank had just finished fixing his coffee and stirring the liquid with a plastic spoon as Marcus Wright entered the lab. Wright was twenty-six, an wildlife biologist. Lately he had been researching the 'History of the Wolf in Modern America'. As usual, Marcus was wearing faded jeans, a sweatshirt with 'Princeton ' printed on the front and his usual pair of cowboy boots. He had a small goatee that he kept trimmed short and long, dirty brown hair that was in need of a cutting.

Marcus eyed Frank for a moment, then with a smile said, "Just kidding Frank, I know your mother didn't abandoned you to be raised by the jungle, but the way you take after them wolves, you'd never convince the others."

"Haha, very funny, Marcus," Frank said while suppressing a yawn. He had come to expect this playful banter anytime he ran into the man. He just didn't think he could handle the 'Southern Gent's' sense of humor right now.

In the always moving and progressive world of constantly changing information and researchers continually trying to prove new things about the animal world and nature itself, many scientists and professors arguing over varying thesis's and differing views on a subject, the younger generation that had been recruited by the Smithsonian were constantly competing and trying to get 'one up' over each other. After having interned at SCBI for the last year, Frank was used to the constant ribbing his fellow colleagues could give, and Marus Wright was certainly one to try and stir up controversy wherever he went.

Marcus was working on an interesting theory in his field of study, the basis of myth and legend, and the effect these tales and stories passed down over the centuries have influenced human societies view on certain animals. His current source of study, which had brought him to work at the Cave for the last few months as he gathered his data for his thesis, had him researching the misconceptions people had regarding wolves and what perplexities these misconceived notions have caused. In general, he was writing what he believed would be a paper to get him into the latest Journal of Modern Zoology for the ideas he had regarding early civilizations and urban farm life and their troubles being able to adopt a co-habitable relationship between people and wolves in the world.

He believed that because of early settlers fears of the unknown, and the terrorism they attributed to wolves due to their lack of understanding the creatures, and the old tales passed on from previous generations of like-minded, unintelligent farmers, that humans caused wolves to rush to the brink of extinction, only to be brought back by conservation efforts now that people understand them better. His views are not only to focus on wolves, but that is the first part of his research and the depth of his main argument on the subject of the mass extinction of certain animals and species from this earth by human hands.

"Oh Mowgli, I get it— Jungle book," Frank announced after taking a sip from his mug, Marcus' reference just registering in his sluggish brain.

"Wow, you must really be logging the hours," Marcus said, shaking his head at the younger man.

Even though Marcus was only two years older than him, he always tried to act like Frank was a child playing in a grown-ups world. That was just the way Marcus was.

"Maybe you should try a Redbull instead of the coffee. That stuff's pretty awful," Marcus suggested as he watched Frank's face grimace as he drank the bitter liquid.

"That's what sugar's for," added Frank as he took the container down from the cabinet again and poured a large helping of the crystals into his mug. Once he was happy with the taste, he put the container away for the last time and turned towards Marcus.

"So where's Mrs. Mowgli?"

Frank just stood there staring at the man, obviously he wasn't going to stop until Frank engaged his ridiculous antics.

"You mean Lisa?"

"Yeah, how are you and Ms. Davies getting along?"

Frank wasn't sure if Marcus was trying to be funny and insinuate they were seeing each other just to annoy him, or if he was actually asking about their research. Frank had made the mistake during the first month he was interning at the Cave by thinking he had been befriended by Marcus, told him how attractive he had thought Lisa was. While Marcus obviously agreed, he still poked fun at Frank regarding the subject whenever he could. Figuring he'd play it safe, he decided to tell him about their work's progress.

"Actually we're doing fine. We were able to catalog the physical and auditory responses of half of the pack in relation to the audio vocalizations we're supplying them with inside the environment," Frank explained.

"Uh-huh," replied Marcus, his interest in someone else's research not nearly enough to get him to give his full attention. Instead he headed to the fridge and opening it up, then took a long moment deciding what he wanted. Frank just continued talking, giving the man the benefit of the doubt that he was listening.

"Anyways, so we're half was done with the initial testing. We still have to get the results from Ulric and Raze, but since Ulric is the alpha and Raze tends to be more of the loner of his brother and sister, we might need to spend more time with them to get a stabilized and accurate result."

"Right, right. Sound's like you're coming along," Marcus muttered as he finally stopped looking through the fridge and pulled out a microwaveable dinner to eat. He looked up and then with a look of seriousness coming over his tan, Southern features, he said, "Did you know that even wolves have their own folklore legends?"

Frank just stood there, unsure how to respond to this change in topics, as Marcus continued.

"It's true— In 1913, a wolf called "Old Lefty" is said to have killed over 380 heads of livestock. He got his name because he'd lost his right paw in a trap. Then in 1925, another wolf, this time named "Three Toes", who supposedly lost part of his paw in an incident with a trap as well was reported to have taken over $50,000 worth of cattle. They had a hunt that consisted of over 150 men to hunt down, find and kill the legendary animal. When he was found, the reward was supposedly a solid gold watch. Can you imagine that?"

Frank just stared at the man, unable to believe how one-tracked his brain could be. Frank could have just told him his mother had died instead of explained the research they were working on one lab over from Marcus', and the man would still have only been waiting for his turn to speak and rattle off whatever thoughts were filling his head at the moment. Instead of getting angry, Frank just chalked it up to the way Marcus was and said, "You're unbelievable."

As if Marcus had been waiting for that, he looked up from the meal in his hands and flashing a big smile that showed off his perfect, bleached teeth, said, "That's what the ladies tell me!"

Before Frank could say anything in response, he saw Lisa walking down the hall past the kitchenette. Taking that as his cue to break away from Marcus, he grabbed his mug of coffee and headed for the hall. "Sorry got to go— We'll have to continue this riveting talk another time," he called out as he reached the door.

"Go get her 'Tiger'!" Marcus called out as Frank exited the kitchen area.

Shaking his head at Marcus' sheer ridiculousness, Frank pushed the image of the young biologist aside and rushed to catch up to Lisa. He arrived at the door to the lab, and rounding the corner, almost ran directly into Lisa. She was walking straight for him and he had to swerve to avoid splashing his cup of coffee onto the both of them.

"Woah!" Lisa cried out, startled by the sudden appearance of her assistant.

"Oh crap!" Frank cried simultaneously as his coffee sloshed over the lip of his mug and spilled across the floor. Fortunately none of the steaming hot liquid hit either of them as they brushed into each other, each almost knocking the other over.

Lisa reached out and caught herself on the door frame just as Frank was able to get his coffee under control. The two of them took a moment to let out a breath, looking at each other and then laughing.

"Well that was close," Frank admitted, heading to find some paper towels to clean up the spill.

"Yeah, I was just coming to look for you. I just got back from the Board meeting," Lisa said, a large smile forming on her beautiful face.

"You got the grant?" Frank asked.

"We got it!" she replied, the smile still big and bright, and Frank could see that sparkle in her eyes. He just knew she was going to make a name for herself in the world of wildlife biology, and he was hopefully going to be there for the ride.

Lisa could hardly contain her excitement. The entire trip back to the Cave from the meeting where the Smithsonian's Board of Director's gave her the final verdict. Her application for an SCBI research grant on her thesis to 'study and discover specific communication patterns, and the applications of vocalization in wolf societies', had been reviewed and the SCBI's Natural Research Fund had bestowed upon her the funding her department needed to continue her research and prove her ideas to the world of natural sciences.

Now, having almost taken her assistant Frank out with her haphazard, over-excited actions as she had first arrived in her main office and found it empty, was rushing to find him and tell him the good news, and almost dropped him hard enough to make a hockey player proud.

Fortunately they had both seen each other at the last minute and were able to avoid the possibly dangerous encounter with a steaming cup of coffee involved.

Helping Frank clean up the spilled liquid on the floor, she tossed a handful of paper towels into the trashcan and turned to see him standing there with a smirk on his face.

What's so amusing? Lisa wondered.

She could tell that the confused look on her face must have caused him to think about his own facial expression and he dropped the smirk.

"Sorry," he replied.

"What was so funny?"

"Oh nothing, it's just nice to see you so happy. You've been a bundle of nerves the last few weeks waiting for the Board review of the grant, and now that you got it, you're like a whole new person," Frank explained.

"I haven't been a bundle of nerves," protested Lisa, but thinking back she knew he was right. She had been stressing far too much about every little thing.

Probably been giving myself ulcers!

"You're right. I probably haven't been much fun to work around have I?" she asked, hoping her anxiety hadn't been affecting the people around her. She didn't think she had noticed anything wrong with Frank lately, then again her mind had been in a million places.

"No, no, you've been fine," Frank said, then pausing and giving her another smile, added, "Well, maybe a little moody."

Lisa laughed and Frank joined in. It was good to see the mood around the place was finally lifting. Thinking back on the last week especially, she could see how sour she might have been, and the amount of work she had been pushing them towards completing. Having no control over the fate of the grant approval, she had been burying herself and her assistant under a lot of hours and continuing to push for faster completion times of their testing schedule.

Frank certainly deserves better from a boss. Maybe the first thing I can do with the new budget is get him secured into a paid position. He definitely deserves it— especially if he's been putting up with me and my bad attitude all week and this is the first time he's said anything.

"We'll all I can say is I'm sorry if I've been a slave driver lately. I promise we'll slow the testing phase down to something more manageable. Maybe you can even take a night off this week, see if that girl over at the Eatery wants to see a movie with you," Lisa hinted.

She knew that Frank had a major crush on the girl, and Lisa had actually met her a few times and they'd talked. She'd even tried to drop some hints about a 'wonderful intern' she had the pleasure of working with that the girl would probably love to check out. Yes she had been trying to help Frank out without interfering with his love life, but if he kept waiting for the right moment, he'd probably never ask her out. And, Lisa could tell from the way he was blushing now, he definitely had a thing for the girl.

Deciding to let him off the hook from having to respond or explain his colored features, she decided to change the topic of their conversation.

"Oh by the way— Figure I might as well tell you so you have a heads up, but the Board has moved the scheduled Grand Opening event for the Midnight Trail up to December. They just let me know today at the meeting, and since we're basically the ones 'running the show', so to speak in regards to the gray wolves, we're going to have to put the audio vocalization testing on hold for the time being and concentrate on the opening."

"December?" Frank asked, really more of a statement than a question.

"Yeah, which means we don't have much time."

"Well I guess it's a good thing I got all the data we've collected so far digitized and into the computer. At least we won't have to worry about losing anything now that the priorities of the lab are changing."

"Not changing, just shifting," Lisa clarified. "Since we got the funds, the research is still a priority, but the opening of the new trail and the enclosures is number one.

"Okay, well I guess I'll get to work. Sounds like I should get all the data backed up before we start on the game plan for the Midnight Trail. I can't believe they moved the launch day up, that's not much time."

"Tell me about it. Either way, we've gotta get it done, so yes, if you would start on the data backups, I'll get to work tying up my loose ends."

Frank nodded in understanding and agreement and headed off to his main workspace to begin copying the computer files and data logs he had entered onto the computer earlier. They backed up all major data and research onto removable hard drives that were stored in a separate storage vault located in the main building of the campus.

Every researcher and scientist no matter the field, had a certain protocol to follow regarding data safety regulations. All files and any other information deemed important to the work being done at SCBI was to be copied to these drives and then stored in a waterproof, fireproof storage vault that was kept locked to prevent any issues regarding research safety on-site. While not too many of the staff that worked every day on the campus was worried about their ideas or data being stolen, even by rival colleagues, other graduate students or competing academics, the measures were set in case something actually happened to the originals.

Every precaution needed to be taken when so much information and knowledge was at stake. If a fire were to break out in a building, a water pipe burst or leak, a power outage, total server crash or any other disaster took place in any one of the SCBI facilities, there was no worry of total loss.

Letting Frank get to work, Lisa sat down at her own desk and logged on to the SCBI server. Most of the computers were networked together in the various buildings all over the complex, and Lisa took a minute to open close out of the server and open her internet browser. When accessed to the server a person can check the SCBI message system, but restrictions on non-work related e-mails made it so all e-mail was interoffice only. Someone couldn't send a message to a personal account, they could only receive them. Unless of course the destination of the message Lisa had to send was to one of the computers on the SCBI campus. However, the account she needed to check now was not work related per se.

Having closed the link to the computer's server and using the web browser, she opened her Hotmail account. This was the account she used for her correspondence with her contact in Portland, Oregon. It had been a few more days since she had last heard from him and so the last time she had checked, he hadn't replied to her inquiries. She also hadn't had a package arrive for her from the other side of the country.

Where could he be? Why hasn't any boxes come for me, or at the very least, why hasn't he been responding to my e-mails?

Clicking on the link to her inbox, Lisa waited a moment before the page loaded. Scanning the latest messages she realized there was one from Tyler Suffux!

There you are— I'll be damned!, she thought, quickly moving the pointer to the message and with a fast tap of the mouse, opened it up.

She couldn't believe her what she was reading.

What the hell had happened?

She re-read the message again just to make sure she hadn't missed anything. Leaning back in her chair and letting out a deflated huff, she stared at the open e-mail on the computer monitor.

From: TSuffux5522@expressmail.net
Sent: Fri 10/28/12
To: LisaM_Davies1@homail.com
Subject: Re:Important fossil discovery. Need your help.

Ms. Davies,

I am writing this message to you because my husband Tyler is unable to. He had told me that he was in contact with you regarding the old bones he found out at the end of our property. He had been so excited when he found them. Wouldn't shut up about them. He was so glad you were going to be able to assist him in figuring out what they were. Tyler was convinced it was something big. Unfortunately, I hate to tell you that my husband has gone missing along with our dog. The police do not suspect foul play and believe he just ran off, which is absurd. I know my Tyler and he would have done no such thing. For the first few days they had search parties canvas our land. They believed he might have gotten hurt and lost somewhere out in the woods. I hope they are right and we find him, but the police have told me to not hold onto these ideas for fear of his body turning up, or that he took the dog and split. I know he didn't just up and leave. I pray every night since he has been gone, that he turns up. It has been a week now since he disappeared and I'm beginning to feel the worst has happened. I just wanted to let you know since you had been keeping in contact with my husband. If you do hear from him, could you please let me know, just so I know he is still alive. Thank you for your time, my husband believed this was so important that I just had to write you when I saw all your e-mails.

Sincerely,

Eleanor Suffux

Lisa sat back in her chair and closed her eyes tight. She tried to imagine poor Mrs. Suffux, worried sick about her husband disappearing, but because of how important his discovery had been to him, his wife had taken to responding back to her to let her know what was happening.

Poor woman!

Feeling like something just didn't add up, Lisa, with her eyes still closed, tried to picture Oregon— 3000 miles away, and the issue of a missing man.

Had something happened to him?

Lisa just didn't know. She now had the answer to why she hadn't heard from the man for so long. She hoped for his wife's sake that he possibly could have hurt himself so far from their home one night going to the site of the fossil discovery, that maybe he was just injured and unable to get back. Perhaps the police would come across him soon and he would be okay.

Of course, Lisa wasn't so sure she believed any of that. It wasn't likely a man and his dog were injured and not able to make it back to safety or be found by the search teams. Lisa also didn't believe he could have run off. Even though she didn't know him or his wife personally, from the small amount about him she had gathered from their communications, she could only see one possible reason for his disappearance, and she hoped she was wrong.

Please Lord, let me be wrong, Lisa said to her inner self, but for some reason she knew the worst had come to pass.

For a reason she could not understand, Tyler Suffux was dead.

Chapter 21

"To tell you the truth, this case just keeps getting weirder and weirder," Mack said in between bites of the greasy, bacon cheeseburger he was devouring.

Aidan Preston sat across from the overweight Detective, watching him consume the slab of beef and pig. Not taking his eyes off Mack's amusing food consumption, Aidan's own food sat before him growing cold. He had ordered an Italian cold-cut and a side of fries, but once the food had arrived, he found he wasn't that hungry. Mack however, was making up for the both of them.

The small booth they were sitting in was off to the corner of the diner, further away from the rest of the establishment's patrons. Aidan had asked specifically to sit in the empty section so that he and Mack could have their privacy while they ate. Taking a sip from his soda, Aidan set the cup down and said, "So tell me about the task force."

Mack had already explained to him on the phone that the FBI was now involved and running the show like they always did when they became involved in an investigation. Most of the agents Aidan had worked with in the past really did have an arrogance about them bordering on a God Complex. The felt superior to the local law enforcement agencies they come in to assist, and throwing a fit when they are left out of the loop on anything, seem to have a hard time extending the same courtesies to others that they expect extended to them. There was no proverbial handing of the olive branch when it came to working with the feds.

"Well the Special Agent in Charge they sent over is one tough son of a bitch. You should have seen the way he put Garza in his place at the meeting. I thought I had seen some ball-busters in my time but this Agent Poole is a whole different animal."

"How so?"

"Well for starters, he laid everything out there for everybody right at the beginning. No beating around the bush. This is their show and we're just there for the support," Mack explained, the anger in his voice trying to be contained.

"Look, so what if the feds want to swoop in and attempt to solve this thing. As long as bodies keep turning up here on our city streets, we've got just as much right to be involved. Or at least you do," Aidan said, having to remind himself once again about Chief Stone's warning about staying away from the investigation.

If he wanted to get reinstated back to Homicide Division, then he was going to have to watch his back as he helped Mack from the sidelines.

"So what new information do you have for me?" Aidan asked, hoping Mack had brought copies of all the incident reports and the Medical Examiner's autopsy discovery for him to look over. Since he had to stay away from the station, he couldn't be seen looking through the files of an active investigation or pursuing anything that Stone had told him to leave alone. That was one of the reasons he had met Mack at the diner. That and not surprisingly, Mack was hungry and wanted a burger.

As if it made it okay that the man was wolfing down a large, bacon cheeseburger with all the fixings and a plate of greasy fries, Mack had asked for a large Diet Coke to go with the meal. Aidan shook his head at the image of the look on the waitress' face when he had ordered the meal, like she thought it was ridiculous that he actually thought a diet soda would balance out the burger he had ordered. Mack's excuse was just that he liked the taste of diet better than the original. Aidan knew that wasn't true.

Even though his once long ago partner seemed like he didn't care about his health based on the upkeep of his body and the weight issues the big man had, he wanted to live as long as possible to see his treasured girls bring grandchildren into this world. That was the moment Mack was truly looking forward to the future for.

Thinking of how happy Mack Jones was, and how his life had changed from the wild bachelor he knew so many years ago when they were going through the academy together, to the more mature and level-headed individual who sat across the booth from him. He still had that childish side to his big, jolly appearance, but the man inside that heavyset body was a dedicated husband and father. It made Aidan think of his own life, and the emptiness he had inside when it came to romance. Sure he had dated over the years, shopping around for Mrs. Right, but so far when it came to the relationship department, he hadn't been so lucky.

In college he had been serious with a girl. Her name was Naomi Taylor and she had been in his Forensic Anthropology class at the University of Maryland. The college, having one of the most selective acceptance rates of any higher-education, public university in that less than forty-three percent of prospective students applying get in. It is a top-ranked public research university located in the city of College Park in Prince George's County, Maryland.

Founded in 1856, the University of Maryland is the flagship institution of the University System of Maryland. With enrollment consisting of more than 39,000 students, over 100 undergraduate majors and 120 graduate programs, Maryland is the largest university in the state and the largest in the Washington Metropolitan Area.

He was completing his third year of schooling, looking to securing a Criminal Justice degree as his major with a minor in Sociology, and she was a sophomore, attaining her Forensic Science degree with dreams of joining the FBI or CIA.

With the University of Maryland's campus so close to the nation's capital, the resulting proximity results in strong research partnerships with the Federal government. These partnerships coupled with the fact that the campus is also located on the East Coast not too far a distance from Washington D.C., and Quantico, Virginia, there are multiple resources for recruitment into divisions of the FBI, CIA, NSA, the Department of Homeland Security, the Department of Defense many other government agencies.

Naomi had been a bright student and Aidan had found himself drawn to her the moment they met. Things got serious pretty quickly and before they knew it, they had moved off campus together and we're acting like newlyweds. Unfortunately, the honeymoon phase of the relationship didn't last as long as either of them would have liked. It ended up, they had moved to fast and not really taken the time to get to know each other. Their relationship, as they began to drift apart they realized had been based on purely physical attraction at first. He had loved her curvy, model like body and wild side when it came to being together physically. He could still picture those bright, green eyes, and her long, curly auburn hair that highlighted her little, adorable face with her button nose. She had fallen for his rugged good looks and his athletic, lean body that he kept in shape with daily runs and a dedicated diet back in those days. All in all, they had been drawn to each other based on looks, and the emotional side just wasn't there for the long haul.

That had been a long time ago, and now sitting here in this diner with Mack, the murder case being the reason they had met up, Aidan found his thoughts drifting to Detective Andrea Wilkes.

What is it about the woman that I can't seem to get her out of my head?

Aidan realized Mack had just said something and he had completely missed it.

"What?" he asked, clearing his head and focusing on the task at hand.

"I said that this Agent Poole seems to be a hard ass, and I'm going to have to play it cool if I'm going to be able to keep you in the loop without anyone realizing that you're not official."

"Well I gotta tell you, from the way your describing him, you better play it as safe as possible. I don't want you getting in trouble for including me. The last thing we need is both our asses sitting on the sidelines waiting to be go before the review board to get reinstated. It's bad enough that I'm playing this so close to the ropes with Stone keeping his eye on me, I do not need your career in jeopardy because of me," Aidan admitted.

"Hey, if it came down to that and I got fired, me, Janet and the kids would just have to sell the house and move in with you. You got the room right?" Mack's face gave a quick smile before disappearing into the last remaining bites of his burger.

"Oh yeah, that's just what I'd need— roommates," Aidan muttered, "I had enough of living with someone else in college."

"Speaking of which, you ever kept in touch with that girl— what was her name?"

"Naomi," Aidan answered, "And no, I lost contact with her after college."

Of course that wasn't completely true. Aidan had looked up his old fling from his days at the University of Maryland, and found out that Naomi did eventually make it into the FBI just like she wanted. She had been recruited a few years after she graduated, and as far as Aidan had last known, she was working down at their headquarters in Quantico, working the forensics angle of the criminal mind for the Behavioral Analysis Unit stationed there. He had thought about trying to track her down when he had last been out there for a training seminar a few years back, but chickened out at the last minute. It would have been nice to see how she was doing, he thought.

She's probably married and got a kid or two anyways. Then again, Andrea has two kids, and he was certainly thinking about her an awful lot these days.

"So back to the topic at hand— serial killers on the loose— What do you have for me? Are these the reports from the boys down at the lab?" Aidan asked, picking up the few sheets of paper Mack had set on the table before their food had arrived.

"Yeah, the lab techs were able to get all the evidence analyzed from the first scene where Sara Moutlon was killed. Blood results, fiber analysis, and everything else. Add to that, the Medical Examiner up in Baltimore finished the full autopsy and that's included in the file," Mack said, wiping his fingers off on his large slacks, the grease from his food slicking the dark material with a slight shiny trail.

Aidan looked through the reports. Attached to the last page with a paper clip holding them together were a stack of photographs from the crime scene. Looking at the pictures, Aidan was glad he had hardly touched his meal. The graphic nature of the scene was enough to unsettle the toughest stomach, unless it seemed you were Detective Mack Jones. He appeared to have an iron stomach and strong constitution when it came to food.

As Aidan flipped through the various reports, his eyes studied the results and he felt a disappointment at the lack of evidence and results the lab was able to conclusively find. Turning to the ME's report, he found the same level of concern with the autopsy findings. Sara Moulton had indeed been alive for the beginning of the attack. The time of death based on the findings of the Medical Examiner seemed to be supported by the blood loss and tissue damage at the sites of the wounds pointed to her death being quick. Aidan could only hope it had been as painless as possible, but he knew she must have been terrified in her last moments.

Turning the page to look at the lab's analysis of the blood samples collected, he found that all the blood at the scene was AB Positive. It looked like it was all from the victim and none of the assailants hadn't been injured in the attack.

Reading the column where the data for the various bite mark analysis was where the report seemed to get weird. Under the heading of the description of the wounds, there had been no match for any particular canine tooth or jaw pattern that these marks fit. Why the hell not? As Aidan continued to read over the results he saw that the reports didn't seem to clarify anything up. The case was still a bundle of unanswered questions.

Why did the saliva samples come back as unclassifiable? Why wasn't the lab able to classify and type the forensics they found to any known type of dog? Had the weather from that night contaminated everything and degraded the samples to the point that the results of the lab's work was useless in providing them with any answers?

Aidan just sat there staring at the papers, becoming more and more worried that without the evidence they needed to point them towards the identity of these killers, the body count would continue to grow.

He saw that the body had been identified by her father Michael Moutlon, and Aidan knew that the man must have been devastated to see his daughter Sara lying on that cold, steel slab, her body mutilated nearly beyond recognition, and an officer asking him it that was his baby girl. It was a scenario no father should have to be put through, and it was the reason why this case mattered so much to Aidan. He was going to figure out who these unknown assailants were, and once they were safely locked away from the general public, would he be satisfied knowing why they did what they had done. First though, he had to figure out who they were.

You're going to pay, he uttered silently, imagining he was face to face with the unknown murderers. However, he couldn't quite picture their faces since he didn't know who they were looking for just yet, but they would, and once he did, that amorphous, blank silhouette would be replaced with the visage of the murderers responsible for the loss of five lives so far.

I will find you, he promised the dark silhouette in his mind's eye.

I promise…I will stop you!

Andrea had taken the following day off of work to stay home and keep an eye on Amy. After everything that had transpired the day before, her daughter finding out four of her friends had been viciously murdered, Andrea decided to let the girl stay home from school. There was no point in sending her in to relive the event with her fellow classmates, the halls of Rockville High School obviously being a buzz with chatter and gossip. No, she would let the girl stay home and grieve.

In the morning, after calling into the office and letting Chief Stone know she wouldn't be in and that he could take it out of one of her many, accumulated sick-days, Andrea let Amy sleep in and without making too much noise, dressed in her running outfit and slipped out for a brief jog. The chill of the morning air was quick to awaken her mind, and after running for about forty minutes through one of the many paths she routinely followed, she began to feel the frigid air burning in her chest and her legs started to cramp. Cursing herself for not stretching out properly before heading out, she slowed her pace and let her muscles and lungs start to cool down.

By the time she arrived back home, she had a thin coating of perspiration sticking to her skin and when the wind blew it caused the sweat to chill her even more. Unlocking the front door to her townhouse, she stepped inside and went straight to the kitchen. As she entered the small room, she kicked her running shoes off and padded across the linoleum floor in her bare feet until she reached the refrigerator. Opening the door to the old, bulky appliance, she reached in and pulled out a bottle of water. Twisting the cap off, she quenched her dry throat and was just about to go check on Amy when the doorbell rang.

Who the hell could that be?

Andrea wasn't expecting anyone since she would have normally been at work this early, and she knew Amy wasn't even awake yet. Walking back through the kitchen and to the small foyer near the entrance, Andrea was almost to the door when this time the unknown visitor bypassed the doorbell and gave the door a loud knock. Andrea jumped slightly, when the pounding started. She had just been in the process of leaning forward to look through the peephole when the banging of the visitor's knuckles surprised her.

Damn it girl, get your act together, she told herself, shaking off her momentary hesitation and looked through the round, fish-eye lens on the stained, oak door.

"Shit," she found herself saying as she the image of the visitor standing on her front step was revealed.

It was her ex husband. What the hell is he doing here? Andrea wondered, then remembered his phone call from the night before. He had told her he was going to be coming by to see her and the kids. She had tried to talk him out of it, but he had been adamant, and now here he was. Before she could even think of ignoring it, hoping he would just leave and go back to wherever he had come from, she heard his voice through the door.

"Dre, I know you're in there, I saw the shadow at the peephole. Besides your car's in the driveway." Robert Wilkes said, his so familiar voice one that Andrea wished she had never heard before in her life.

Why did he have to come by now? Couldn't he just leave her to look after their kids after a tragedy like Amy was going through occurred? After all, he had done it in the past!

"Andrea?" he called again, this time pressing the doorbell once more.

Dammit, he was going to wake up Amy!

Unlocking the door, she flung it open to reveal Robert standing there, his hands on his jean clad hips, his red flannel shirt sticking out from his pants and a dumb grin stuck on his face. He reminded Andrea of that Brawny guy on the paper towel rolls. Every time she saw them at the grocery store, her mind automatically pictured Robert and his manly, carpenter-like look. He had always been partial to wearing flannel shirts and jeans, and being a contractor, that was pretty much as close to a uniform as he got. Andrea always hated those shirts. Of course, over time she came to hate a lot of things about the man.

And now he's standing on my doorstep.

"What do you want?" Andrea snapped.

"Well it's nice to see you too," he said maintaining the grin, the amusement in his eyes at how she was dealing with his arrival seemed to be just dandy to him.

"I told you I didn't want you to come!" she said angrily.

"And I told you I was going to come when I talked to you on the phone yesterday," he fired back, the grin still there.

"Look, you said in a couple of days, not the very next morning, and I don't have time for this!" she protested.

Robert dropped his hands from his hips and crossed them over his chest, standing there as if he wasn't going to take 'no' for an answer. She knew that look, had seen it many times over the course of their marriage. He could be incredibly difficult to reason with, at times it seemed once he got an idea stuck in his head, he would do whatever it took to make it a point to prove he was right. Even if his perception of 'right', wasn't the best opinion of the matter. He studied Andrea standing there, letting a huff of breath escape through his thin lips in annoyance.

"Andrea, she's my daughter too, and if something like this happens, I have a right to be there for her."

That did it for Andrea. Now he was acting like he had rights to be there for the kids he abandoned?

"Rights— what rights do you think you have when you left and I was here raising her and Jeremy by myself?"

Andrea could feel the anger rising up in her as her ex just stood there like a sentry, unwilling to move or concede he was wrong.

Just leave already— that's what you're good at!

"Look, I know I wasn't there in the past, but in case you forgot, you weren't exactly sorry to see me go," Robert said dropping his arms and stepping closer to the door.

Andrea stood her ground, her body blocking the entryway to the house. She was not going to let him inside, he'd have to try and force his way in, and that was something the feisty female police officer was just dying to see him try. The thought brought a little smirk to her lips as she stood there keeping her body in the frame of the door.

He seemed to be studying her, his eyes roaming over her skin tight, sweat pants and the small, lightweight jacket she wore whenever she went out for a run. Andrea felt like he was undressing her with his eyes and the thought repulsed her. Yes, the man had seen her naked, an unfortunate side effect of them being married for years, but now that they weren't together, having been divorced for years, his leering attention to her body disgusted her and she felt self-conscious standing there in her tight running clothes. She tried to repress the memories of them together, the love they once shared having been brought to a painful end when she had found out about the other woman in Robert's life. He had tried to keep her a secret, but she had found out. He had been careless and had actually been talking to her constantly from the sanctity of their own home. The memory of her discovering he had cheated on her burned her like a scalding iron.

"I don't know why you thought coming here in the morning was going to accomplish. Especially after just calling me up out of the blue last night and telling me you want to see me and the kids. We'll Jeremy and Amy aren't here, there in school, and I have to get going to work. I'm already late as it is!" Andrea lied, hoping he'd buy it and just leave.

"I came because your job, the one you chose over our marriage and me had pulled our daughter into it. She's probably traumatized from her classmates being murdered, and I think I need to be here!"

She felt the anger boiling up in her. How could he try to pin this situation on her? Her job had nothing to do with what had happened to Amy's friends or the end of their marriage! Robert was just trying to put the situation onto her, like he always did. That's what had ended their rocky marriage— he had tried to act like everything that had gone wrong between them was her fault, when it was he who had cheated on her. Yes, maybe her job had taken up a lot of her time and she was dedicated to the work, but that was no excuse for him slinking off to be with another woman!

"My job had nothing to do with Amy's classmates being murdered, or you cheating on me and ending the marriage!" she said sharply, her blood boiling and she could feel the heat rise up and her ears and cheeks flush with anger.

"I'm sure it doesn't help separate the fact that you working as a cop is going to keep Amy surrounded by the memory of what happened. You live and breathe working Homicide, and that is not the atmosphere that Amy needs to be involved in. Her and Jeremy need to be kept away from these murders, I've read about them in the paper and seen the coverage on the TV. They do not need to be reminded that their mother is out there in harm's way, trying to find the serial killer that's running around this city. What if you get as involved in this case as you did in that one before?" Robert said, his voice matching her own raised tone.

Andrea knew what case he was referring to, and she didn't want that time of her life dredged up again, especially now. It was a long time ago when she had just started out as a Detective for Montgomery County. One of the first cases assigned to her ended up being the murder of an elderly couple who had there house broken into by a man looking to score prescription medications. The man had seen the victim at the pharmacy picking up his pain medication that he took for the pancreatic cancer that was ravaging his weakened body. Unknown to the man, the addict who had a history of drug abuse issues and home invasion charges had seen him pick up the medication and followed him home.

The resulting burglary went bad when the elderly couple wouldn't give the man the pills and in a fit of rage he killed them both, stabbing them with a knife he had taken from their own kitchen. When Andrea had been involved in the investigation into the murders and home invasion, she had discovered the identity of the assailant based on fingerprints that had been recovered at the scene. With the county and city police searching for the murderer, it took them two months to actually track him down. Once found, living homeless on the street, his addiction having robbed him of his job and apartment, Andrea had attempted to arrest him, but in the ensuing struggle, the man had gotten away. Andrea could still remember the wild, glassy-eyed look of the man as he swore he would find and kill her before escaping down a side street and disappearing into the crowd.

A week later, Andrea had returned home from work one night and found the man had broken into her and Robert's house. Fortunately her husband had taken the kids out to the movies so they weren't home during the event, but when Andrea had realized the man was inside, having stolen a kitchen knife just like he had from the couple he had murdered a month before, and waiting for Andrea to enter her bedroom.

Fortunately, she had realized something wasn't right about the feel of the house when she had walked in. Then noticing that the back door had been forced open, the small window above the handle smashed out and the glass scattered on the floor below, Andrea pulled her service pistol and searched the house. Not bothering to take the time to call for backup, she was worried her family would be home any minute from the movie theater, and she went ahead to find the intruder.

Upon entering her bedroom, the crazed drug addict leapt from his hiding spot in the closet and almost lodged his weapon into Andrea's arm. Fortunately she had been ready for him, and with a quick adjustment of her footing, was able to doge the attack and send the man sprawling into the floor. Not having to use her gun, she was able to wrestle the knife away from the man and subdue him. For good measure she remembered punching him hard enough to knock him out so that he was no longer a danger until backup arrived. That was the end of the event and the real danger that her job had brought into her family's life. Looking back on it now, with the man sitting in prison with multiple life sentences, she wondered if her not stopping the killer that first time in the alley she found him, had the situation played out differently, could her family have suffered from her mistake? What if they had been home when the madman broke in looking for her? Andrea pushed the thoughts from her mind. She had too much going on right now to dwell on the past, and right now her problem was the arrival of her ex husband, Robert.

Robert stood there, the wind picking up and blowing his thin, brown hair back from his forehead to reveal a receding hairline. The thought of a man like Robert, as vain as he was in regards to his appearance going bald was just the right illustration she needed to imagine to help the anger that had built up from his surprise arrival to lower a little. She was still mad, but now at least she was thinking a little clearer, not fueled by blind rage like she had been moments before.

Taking a breath to calm her nerves even more she looked straight into Robert's eyes and said, "Look, since Amy and Jeremy aren't home and I have to get to work, there's really no point in continuing this conversation now. I have to get ready. We've got a lot going on with these murders, and my boss is already expecting me to be arriving any moment. Obviously, it would be better if you left and came back when I'm expecting you, instead of you just showing up on my front doorstep."

Robert seemed to be thinking it over, his questioning glare telling her he might not be buying what she was saying. After all, she would never in her right mind have let Amy go off to school today, especially the way she was acting the day before. However, her only saving grace seemed to be Robert not knowing how serious the deaths had affected Amy.

"Okay," he finally consented, the look on his face one of defeat. "But, that doesn't let you off the hook for later. I'm coming by once your off of work and we're all going to talk. I want to know that Amy and Jeremy are okay, regardless of how you feel about it."

Andrea didn't feel like arguing anymore. She just wanted to get rid of him.

"Fine, call me later, and I'll let you know when you can come by."

"Good. Will do. I'll talk to you later Dre," he said and with that he turned and headed for the car parked on the street.

As Andrea went to close the door, he turned and added, "Oh and I'm staying at the Holiday Inn off Rockville Pike, just in case you change your mind about wanting to talk. I really would like to have an actual conversation about some things that have been on my mind."

Not bothering to respond, Andrea just let the door shut, the image of Robert standing there next to his car disappearing from view behind the closed door.

Like hell, she thought as she leaned against the door frame and let out a deep sigh. The last thing I want is to spend any time with you, Robert!

Picking herself up from her slouched position against the door, she wandered back into the kitchen and tried to clear her head and focus on what she was planning on doing before Robert had interrupted her morning. She remembered she wanted to check on Amy before calling back into the office and checking up on how things were going with the investigation. When she had talked to Stone earlier, he'd been perturbed about her calling out, his excuse that the joint task force was a priority. However, she was glad to remind him that her daughter had known the teens who had been slaughtered, and she needed her more. She could keep up with the investigation from home for at least today, then once she knew Amy was okay, she'd be back in to poor all her time and energy into her role in the investigation.

The one bit of good news she had learned from Stone was that Sergio Garza was no longer leading the search for the killers. She wasn't sure how she felt about the FBI stepping in and taking over, but it beat working under the "Pit Bull", as she had heard they called the Lieutenant over at his department.

Andrea went back through the kitchen and setting the bottle of water back into the fridge, she left the room and headed down the hall towards Amy's bedroom. As she neared the door, she could hear that her daughter was awake inside. The faint sound of sniffling could be heard through the door. Giving the door a light knock, she listened for a response.

"Come in," the strained voice called out from the other side.

Grasping the handle of the door in her hand, she opened it and entered her daughter's room. Laying on the bed, a box of tissues sitting on the nightstand next to her, Amy was sitting up with her back against her headboard, a wad of tissues crumpled up and lying on the messy comforter around her shrunken form. The dark circles under her eyes were enough to tell Andrea that the girl hadn't slept well the night before.

Andrea's eyes took in the appearance of the bedroom that was adorned with and reflected her daughter's youthful and innocent tastes. The walls were still painted a light pink color with purple accents that the girl had wanted when she was just ten years old. Andrea couldn't believe her and the kids had been living in this small townhouse that had been their home for the last seven years. Posters lined the colorful walls, pictures of some of her favorite bands like Green Day and Justin Timberlake having replaced the illustrations of Care Bears and American Girl dolls that used to grace the room. Gone were those childish relics of years past, and now the changing influence of 'growing up' had changed the decor of Amy's bedroom to reflect the girl's constantly changing tastes. She even seemed to want to change the colors of her bedspread and sheets and the layout of the room every few months to accommodate the latest trends affecting her tastes as she aged.

"Hey baby, I just wanted to see how you were doing," Andrea said, stepping into the room and taking a seat on the end of the bed by Amy's feet.

"Mom, I just don't know what to do. I can't get these thoughts out of my head. I can't stop dwelling on them," the girl explained as she put a tissue to her face and blew her nose.

She looked terrible, and seeing her daughter in this condition was heart wrenching.

Why did this have to happen to her?

Oh my poor, sweet baby.

All she wanted to do was get Amy's mind off the events of the day before, but she didn't know where to begin. How do you comfort a seventeen year old girl who has just lost four of her friends?

"Can I get you anything?" Andrea asked, placing her hand on the part of the dark blue bedspread where Amy's feet were positioned. She patted the lump under the covers and wished that she knew how to handle the dilemma she was facing now.

The arrival of Robert in their lives was enough to get her frazzled. Add to that, the fact that she was supposed to be working along side the FBI to solve the murders that had afflicted the city over the week, causing panic among the public and now, the crimes had hit much closer to home with the deaths of Amy's friends. How was she going to handle all these issues stacking up in her life? What did she have to do to get a handle on the situation and direction her week had taken?

Amy let a used tissue slip from her hand and join the pile lying around her weakened looking form. Her eyes weren't nearly as dead as they had been the day before, but they were still red and puffy from crying, and Andrea could see that she was still lost in her thoughts and emotions.

She would still need time to adjust to everything that had happened, and Andrea didn't know how long she could deal with seeing her daughter looking like this. It really was depressing and tearing at her soul.

She would do anything to protect her children, even though her job was important to her, they came first. No matter what. Looking at her daughter lying there in bed, looking so helpless and hurt, Andrea realized what she had to do.

The killers responsible for taking the life of Amy's friends had to be stopped. Yes, the joint task force was working on doing just that, but Andrea needed to get to work on the case as well. Sure the FBI was a powerful force to reckon with when it came to finding and tracking down serial killers, but so was she. She had a detective for a long time, and she was good at her job. Better than good, she was one of the best, and she knew that the best way to put her daughter's crushed spirit back into alignment was to find the bastards responsible for her friend's deaths.

Yes, it was time to get to work.

Those bastards are going down!

Andrea placed her hand on top of her daughter's and looked her into the eyes as she spoke.

"Don't worry Amy— I'm going to nail the bastards who did this, that I promise you."

Chapter 22

Aidan met Nick Haley for a cup of coffee at a local Starbucks in the Rockville Town Square's bustling new downtown shopping district. The entire area had undergone a major revival over the last year, millions of dollars being pumped into the city's town center to turn it into the largest, urban-renewal development that the Rockville had seen in years. Where there had once been a dilapidated shopping center with rundown and failing businesses, the rejuvenation that the restructuring and construction of demolishing the old site and rebuilding had accomplished, created a new wave of life for the growing city.

Rockville Town Square is Town Center's newest neighborhood, with 15 acres of shops, restaurants and residences. The area is the hub of county and city governments and home to residents, restaurants, and retail. Here, citizens can find specialty shops, barbershops, salons, and coffee shops, ethnic grocers, farmer's markets, and other retail ventures.

A person can take in a movie at the large movie cineplex boasting stadium seating and state of the art digital 3D projectors and then dine in from an eclectic mix of eateries and restaurants. All this taking place just a block from the Metro Red Line's Rockville Station, so that people can travel from all over the county to enjoy the sprawling shopping district.

Above the high-end, street level shops running the course of the new area, there are multiple condos and apartments that tower above the street-level shops, providing the new town center with plenty of housing and living options as the city continues to grow in population. There are a mixture of various priced options to choose from in the area, and people continue to move into and travel to the ever progressing Town Square.

This new shopping mecca is exactly where Aidan found himself seated in the local coffee shop, having waited for the reporter he had met recently at the latest crime scene to arrive, nursing a cup of coffee on the small, round table in front of him. He heard the chime of the Starbuck's door opening and looked up to see Nick Haley enter the restaurant.

He was dressed almost exactly how he had been when Aidan had first met him at the quarry crime scene the day before. With long, brown hair falling to his shoulders and a jacket pulled tight and zipped up to his throat to prevent the wind of the cold day from getting through, Nick Haley looked like the kind of image of the ever-moving, fully dedicated journalist that he appeared to be. He had on a pair of worn, black slacks and brown dress-shoes that were scuffed and had seen better days.

Spotting Aidan sitting at the small table, Nick waved and ignoring the look of the woman behind the counter, headed straight for the table.

"Sorry I'm late," he apologized as he slung the satchel-like bag off his shoulder and laid it down on the ground by his feet. Then pulling out a chair, he sat and looked at Aidan and the cup of coffee sitting before him. Steam rose from the cup and Nick could smell the strong aroma of the beverage, noticing a hint of some spiced flavoring added to the scent of coffee beans filling the air around the table.

Noticing the reporter's eyes on his cup, Aidan asked, "Did you want to take a minute and grab something to drink? I've already been here for a few minutes so I went ahead and decided to get something so I wasn't just taking up one of their tables reserved for paying customers."

Nick listened to Aidan explain, and shook his head. Taking one last look over at the counter and the menu board, he said, "No it's fine. I've already had two cups this morning. The life of a local reporter— finding yourself traveling all over the county for a story and living off coffee and energy drinks."

Aidan laughed and leaned back in his chair, his hand still on his cup as he waited for Nick to get comfortable. Once the reporter was ready, having taken his jacket and hanging it on the back of his chair, and pulling a small notebook from his work bag, he looked at Aidan carefully, seeming to judge how this new, mutual partnership was going to work. He had always been a loner when it came to working a story, that was just part of a reporter's job, following the leads and running with the facts. However, now he had a Detective who was as close to the investigation as any source Nick had had, and he was willing to work with Nick to solve these murders. That was just fine with him.

Nick pulled a copy of that mornings edition of The Informant and offered it to Aidan. Glancing at the paper, he reached down to the seat next to him and picked up his own folded up copy. Setting it down on the table next to his coffee, he patted it with one hand.

"Picked it up this morning so I had a chance to read your article just before you got here," Aidan informed Nick.

"And?" the journalist asked, curious to see what the Detective's opinion of the murders so far would be.

"I think you hit the nail right on its head. I appreciate you not putting the other stuff I told you into the article. I gotta tell you, at first I was hesitant to be working with a reporter on this, but you came through. I haven't had the best experience with your kind," Aidan explained.

"My kind? Please, you make me out to sound like a vulture preying on the helpless."

"Well in my experience that's exactly what some of you do."

"Fair enough, but since we're working this thing together, I'll stick to only putting the facts as you furnish them. I agree the public doesn't need to know everything about the murders. They have the right to be kept informed, but that doesn't mean we can't tone down the amount of information we feed them."

"See, I knew I liked you for a reason," Aidan said with a laugh.

Aidan took a sip of his coffee, surprised by how good the pumpkin spice flavored coffee tasted. It was the flavor of the month and the barista that took his order had suggested he try it. She had said it was their special blend that came out every October, and that it was popular all through the season. Glad he had taken the girls advice, he took a longer gulf of the steaming liquid, savoring the smooth kick the flavored beverage had. Pumpkin spice, just another reminder that fall was almost over and winter was coming up. Most places seemed to have some special variety of beverage during the various holidays, and he knew beer and the constantly growing micro-brew fad capitalized on these various concoction's.

Of course, the special flavor was also a reminder that Halloween was tomorrow night. That meant that tomorrow night was All Hallows Eve. The night and following day were always a curse for the various law enforcement agencies. It was at times like this where the crazies seemed to come flooding out of the woodwork, their skewed visions of these multi-faceted holidays always bring out the odd ones.

Most people didn't seem to realize that the evening traditions were just a prelude to All Saints Day which fell on the first day of the new month. Devil worshippers, satanic cults, and kids just looking to embellish the mixed traditions the holiday had grown to represent.

"Now here's another strange detail that's been kept from the media to help isolate anyone calling in to brag or admit they are the murderer. You'd be surprised how many nut-cases will flood to the station looking to get some attention or hoping to make it on TV for their fifteen minutes of fame," Aidan said pulling a photograph from the envelope and setting it on the table.

Nick leaned forward, picking the photo up and examining it. The picture was a closeup shot of the victim's torso, her shirt and jacket shredded and only staying on the body due to the stickiness of the blood that it was doused in. Chunks of ripped flesh dangled from the chest, some of the woman's ribs visible among the hunks of torn open skin.

"We actually almost missed it due to the severe damage that the body was inflicted with."

"Missed what?" Nick asked, his eyes taking in every detail of the horrific photo, but all he could see was blood, bloated flesh that looked like it had been stripped almost entirely from the bones, and a partial view of the woman's intestines that were hanging from the gaping wound lower on her body. Fortunately the photo was a close-up and the majority of the intestines were not visible.

It was bad enough looking at the detail this photograph provided. His eyes looked around a little more and then he looked up at Aidan, not knowing what the Detective was referring to.

Aidan stretched his arm across the table and with his finger traced a shape on the photograph's surface. His finger followed the lines of the deepest cuts that had been inflicted, and as he traced them, Nick began to see the pattern take shape.

"Oh dear Lord!" Nick muttered as Aidan removed his hand and watched the reporter's own finger touch the glossy print and move slowly over the lines in the same direction Aidan's had. It was certainly a pattern, a pattern carved into the victim's chest upon death. She had been marked by her killer. A calling cards of sorts! Nick traced the shape back and forth with his finger one more time to confirm the discovery, then he looked up and met Aidan's gaze.

"It's a pentagram!" he cried out, unable to wrap his head around what he was seeing. It was shocking to think that whoever had butchered and mutilated this poor woman, once he was done, carved a deep pentagram into her chest. It was a calling card of sorts, and Nick's brain began scanning every corner of his mind for some connection. Words began to fill his mind, Halloween— pentagram— satanic rituals. Could that really be the connection? Could these sick individuals be performing some form of evil dark arts and sacrificing the innocent victims in some bizarre performance?

"Yeah, I had the same look on my face when I saw this photo earlier," Aidan answered.

"Is it a calling card or something the killer wanted us to see? What about the other bodies? Do they have the same mark?" Nick was speaking quickly, the excitement of this flood of information hardly having time to filter and be sorted by his brain.

"Woah, slow down. They joint task force just realized this mark was there. The ME hadn't noticed it when he performed the autopsy because it appeared to just be massive multiple incisions cut into the torso It wasn't until another officer who had seen the photos was setting up Halloween decorations at his house and when putting up one of the many pentagrams, jack-o-lanterns and ghost decals, he realized the pentagram he was hanging looked just like the weird photo he had seen earlier but couldn't figure out why the cut marks didn't look random but somewhat familiar.

"So the killers are some sort of devil worshipers?" Nick asked, trying to fit these new pieces into the growing puzzle of these murders.

Aidan had been right about the photograph. It was just strange.Things continued to get weirder and weirder, and right now things were not looking like they were slowing down. There were continuing to be new twists and turns associated with these murders, and yet the bodies continued.

Could the other four victims have been marked just like the first woman?

So many questions.

Aidan could see Nick was wracking his brain trying to tie the various bits of information together. He knew how the reporter felt since he had been doing the same thing himself. In fact he had been beating himself up over it. Between the issues with sleeping nights and the feeling that he could do something about these murders, he felt the strain weighing him down. He felt like he was drowning, unable to tread water as the level of the liquid seemed to continue to try to suck him down. Except it wasn't water. It was the blood of the victim's who were continuing to loose their lives while he sat by unable to solve the case. It didn't matter if he wasn't officially on the investigation, he felt responsible for bringing it to a close. He wouldn't allow the helplessness that Dr. Harper had referenced affect him anymore.

"Here's something else," Aidan said, picking up another photograph and laying it on the table.

Nick looked down at the next picture, finding this one was even more grizzly that the last, he wondered if he was going to be able to look at them any further. The videotape he had watched that showed the scene from a distance had been almost too much for him, and now here he was sitting across from Detective Preston as the man laid out photo after photo of the victim's brutal deaths.

The next photograph was a picture of the majority of the victim's remains as they had been found laying against the base of the park's playground set. Blood was splattered over the plastic steps leading up to a children's slide, and the body was spread out, the one intact arm lying on the ground, outstretched as if the woman was reaching for the steps, no doubt trying to escape her attacker. Nick closed his eyes, wishing he wasn't a part of this story, but he knew that was a foolish thought. His job was to get to the bottom of these murders, and he was grateful that Aidan Preston, for all his work-related issues and on-leave status, was able to get copies of the case files from his friend Detective Jones and now sitting here in this coffee shop, share the details of the investigation with him.

"Pretty bad, huh?" Aidan asked, bringing Nick's eyes to open and look upon the man sitting across from him.

Aidan's expression was grim, having already looked through the files and photographs as he studied them for any sign of a clue to the serial killer's true identities.

"Yeah, it's bloody awful," Nick agreed.

"There's one more thing I wanted to show you and get your opinion on," Aidan said, drawing Nick's eyes from the photos on the table and onto his face.

"What's that?" the reporter asked, wondering what it was that he could help this man who seemed to have seen it all assistance with.

Aidan pulled the last group of photographs from the envelope and handed them to him. Nick took them and studied the shots. The first was a close up of the woman's severed arm. The bloated, grayish blue skin was mottled with dried blood and cuts going all the way around the appendage. The second photo showed her stomach, the ropes of the slimy lengths of her intestines mixed in a pool of dried blood with the mulch of the playground soaking up the crimson liquid.

The blemished and bruised vision of the torso was bad, but there was something similar between the two photos. That's when Nick noticed that the photograph of the stomach had the same indentations in the flesh that the arm had. What the hell were they? He looked up at Aidan for guidance, the puzzled look letting the Detective know he saw something but he wasn't sure what it was.

"The indentations that look like gouged cuts circling the arm and stomach in those photos and in a few others that were taken at the scene confirmed the same thing that me and Detective Jones saw at the Medical Examiner's office the day the body was brought in to be examined. Those indentations that follow in the form of a jagged line across the victim's flesh are teeth marks," Aidan explained.

"Teeth marks— Jesus somebody or something was eating her?"

Dear God, I hope it wasn't 'someone'!

"We don't know yet, but that seems to be the general consensus regarding the markings in correlation to the wounds. The victim's stomach had been ripped open and something took some bites out of the internal organs. Same thing with the arm and another wound that was located at her throat where the damage was also severe. The problem is, some of the wounds happened before she was dead!"

"Oh my God…" Nick muttered staring at the photographs, then suddenly ignoring the gruesome evidence the photos were revealing, he looked up at Aidan with a glimmer of something shining on his face, he said, "I think I know why she might have been bitten up."

Now it was Aidan's turn to be surprised. How could this reporter know anything about the teeth imprints that the victim had covering her body. That was one piece of information along with the pentagram carved into the chest, that had had not been revealed to the press. So far no one had much of an idea except that they thought a hungry dog or some other starved animal like a fox might have come across the victim's corpse before it was found that morning and disturbed the scene by taking advantage of the free meal.

Unfortunately, that theory didn't explain the bite marks that had been inflicted on the woman before she was dead. Those were the marks that Aidan was the most curious about.

A grin spread across Nick's face as he reached into his bag at his feet, and scrounging around through the messy contents he withdrew a folder of his own.

"I think I might have an idea of why the victim was bitten," Nick said, and then spent the next few minutes explaining the research he had a woman that worked with him pull up on the history of feral dog attacks around the country and the growing number of fatal attacks that were occurring more often than they used to due to animal overpopulation.

He then went into his theory and spent the next five minutes explaining to Aidan about his idea that the killers had used dogs to attack the person before they set themselves upon the injured victims themselves. Aidan sat there stunned and slightly disgusted by the theory that Nick reached, but as the reporter went on and showed him the printouts and copies of old newspaper articles, Aidan was surprised to see that the man might just have a point.

Those sick bastards who killed these people were not only carving them up and mutilating them in a tremendously horrible fashion, but they were engraving a specific mark into at least the first victim, Aidan would have to check with Mack about the last four, but then they were also possibly setting trained, vicious dogs onto them to create even more mayhem and destruction.

These people are sick! I have to stop them before they strike again, Aidan reasoned, because he knew deep down, they would strike again— if they hadn't already. He realized he hadn't heard from Mack so far today. He was probably tied up with his involvement in the joint task force, but he definitely needed to talk to him. He had to find out about the latest victims and if they also had the evidence of being bitten by inhuman teeth before death. The same with the pentagram. Could they be marking their victims with a token that held some symbolic significance to them? Were the people behind these murders some fantastical cult or group who worshiped the devil, or were they just trying to point the police in the wrong direction?

There were still so many questions to answer, and time seemed to be running short. Aidan knew it wouldn't be long before another crime scene was discovered, and who knew how many innocent lives would be lost this time?

Suddenly, Nick set the photos down and said something to draw Aidan's attention back to the present. He looked at the reporter questioningly.

"I said, I've seen marks that looked similar to this, at least the teeth marks before."

"What, where?" Aidan asked, feeling like this partnership with Nick Haley, reporter for The Informant newspaper, might just be turning out to be a good relationship they had started.

"A few years ago, you remember that incident at the San Diego Zoo, the one where a tiger escaped from its cage and mauled the visitors?" Nick asked, the look of excitement radiating through his features as he sat there all worked up by his newest revelation.

"Sounds familiar, what about it?" asked Aidan, trying to figure out where Nick was going with this train of thought.

"Well it was a big story that I actually got to write for the local public here. You know, domestic news unless it's politics, not being to popular around here since we're so close to Washington D.C.. Anyways, this tiger got out of its cage, attacked some zoo visitors and killed one of them, police thought these kids were provoking it, became a whole big investigation once the media got a hold of it.

'It was big news, hitting all the angles that a paper can present. It had everything— unusual circumstances, possible cover-up, the stalled police investigation, issues from the public and the families of the victims, I mean everything! Not to mention when word got out to all the animal lovers that the officers that went into secure the scene just opened fire on the animal and killed it on the spot. Well because it drew so much controversy because people were arguing about how the tiger got out, if the kids did actually piss it off and cause it to escape, what the police should have done differently, the media had a big part in all the controversy and I remember covering it all for the locals here," Nick explained.

Aidan was nodding his head, following Nick's recap of the event and once he took a break to allow Aidan a chance to respond, he said, "Yeah, it's coming back to me. That was a while back. Made the San Diego Zoo look bad and they had to redo the cages security measures. I remember because the National Zoo downtown actually inspected all their enclosures as well and there were a few police incidents that we had to go down and assist the District's Police to keep protesters from picketing down at the Zoo's exhibits. I remember this one group wanted people to setup shop at every zoo across the country and try to rile visitors up about the cruelty of keeping the animals in cages. Think PETA on steroids, these guys were extreme."

"Yeah I remember— I had to write a story on them as well. They called themselves "A.L.A.", the Animal Liberation Army, animal lovers with personal grudges against any establishment who thought that people should be allowed to keep pets or any other animal in a cage."

"That was them— "A.L.A."— damnedest bunch of wackos," Aidan said shaking his head. "So, what does the tiger attack in San Diego have to do with what's going on here?"

Nick thought about it for a minute, seeming to be grouping his scattered ideas into a cohesive thought before speaking.

"That's what these photos and the reports you brought seem to be reminding me of. A large predator attack!"

Aidan looked at the reporter then realized he was right. The wounds and bite mark patterns were similar to something he would imagine coming from a big animal attacking a person. Even the victim's at the quarry who had been massacred and mutilated had similar wounds that resembled something you might see from the brutality of a mountain lion or bear attack.

Maybe there was some other animal around these parts, or something that could have escaped from the National Zoo that would match the evidence of the crime scenes. So far the teeth hadn't been matched to any known animal, and the tracks that were cast were pretty disfigured from all the rain that had degraded them, but maybe they needed someone who wasn't familiar with human bite patterns and the violence they could summon up and inflict on a fellow human being.

He needed an expert on large, predatory animals, and possibly someone who was also familiar with what types were found in the mountains and woods that were scattered all through the Washington Metropolitan area. Obviously something weird was going on here with the pentagram carved into the victim's chest, making a human the man possibility for a killer, but what if this group of people was staging the scenes to resemble a animal attack?

Was that what this was? Some weird society or cult mimicking an animal's attack patterns and using this information to stage the crime scene's to resemble whatever creature they worshiped or meant something to them?

Dear God, this was the break I was looking for, thank you!

Aidan looked at Nick and began to quickly pick up all the papers and photographs he had spread out on the table and shuffle them together. Nick just watched the man work frenziedly, unsure if he should say anything or ask for clarifications. He was certainly a man on a mission.

Then Aidan looked up at Nick and asked with a smile, "You got some free time today?"

"Yeah, why?"

"I think it's time we got over to the Zoo and talked to an wildlife expert. Particularly, one who knows about large, predatory animals!"

Chapter 23

Ted Hanson was pissed. How could that bum of a reporter, Haley, have gotten the jump on 'his' story? These murders that were appearing all across the city, and he was the one the public should be getting the hard-hitting facts and breaking news from, not that rag of a paper, The Informant! Ted felt his face grow red, his ears feeling hot. Yes, he was mad that his boss Emily Erickson, that mean, hard excuse for a station manager was just wasting his talent out on the streets. He had proved his worth to Channel 5, and the TV News anchor job should have been his ages ago.

The only thing that seemed to be getting in his way was Emily Erickson and her loudmouth excuses that rained out of her big, black lips. He pictured the woman who was getting the brunt of his displeasure, and he wished he could go straight to the station owner and complain about the unfairness of the situation.

Maybe that's what he would do. Yea, that could work, he thought as he imagined skipping over Emily's annoying, useless existence and going straight to Barry Whitfield. Ted smiled as he imagined the scowl of an expression that would mark his bosses face if he went around her and straight to the main man. It would be priceless!

Emily Erickson had been with Channel 5 for what seemed like an eternity, and ever since Ted had taken the job of on-air reporter from his predecessor, she had been the bane of his existence there at the station.

Short and stocky, the light-skinned, African American woman with a chip on her shoulder and too much makeup covering face reminded Ted of a cartoon. She usually wore layers of mascara and green eye shadow that caked her eyes, and bright red lipstick that accented her large, full lips making her seem like a clown. That's exactly what she is, a clown! Ted thought, picturing the comical appearance of the woman, with her horrible fashion towards the cheap business suits she wore daily to work. All she needed was a water-squirting flower pinned to her big chest and a pair of long, red clown shoes instead of the high heels she wore that squeezed her fat ankles over the tight straps that wrapped her meaty legs.

Oh, she disgusted him!

Storming through the main studio, an area that consisted of the main stage where the 5 o'clock and the 11 o'clock nightly news was shot. Massive scaffolding ran up to the ceiling with large banks of lights and various colored spotlights hung suspended over the round recording area.

The large desk for the various anchors was center stage and off the side, a large green screen where the weatherman reported in front of. Large cameras mounted on movable gurneys so that they could be positioned wherever the floor director asked them to be moved were sitting around the outside of the main staging area, and the various cables and cords snaked across the slick floor as Ted rushed past.

There were a few technicians who were currently adjusting the various camera mounts, getting them ready the next news broadcast, while Don Cain, the main floor boss was shouting orders over to them about the proper handling of the expensive camera equipment. Absent from the main stage and not in the editing bay where he was usually found lazily pretending to be doing something important was Mike. Where the hell is that worthless bastard? Ted wondered as he kept up his brick pace through the various areas of the third floor. He wanted to confront the cameraman who he usually had the displeasure of being stuck with on his various in-the-field assignments. Ted had the sneaking suspicion that Mike was toying with him and had lied when he had brought up someone providing The Informant's garbage reporter, Haley with information on the story of the crime scene they had filmed their segment at that first day.

He wasn't sure, but he thought he had heard that Mike had a visitor in the office that day, and he was willing to put money on it being Nick Haley. Mike was always complaining that the station didn't pay him enough, and Ted knew he would do anything to increase the money he was making. The world was full of snakes and leeches, Mike was a conniving snake, and Haley was a leech. Thinking again of how Haley had stolen his story out from under him, Ted gritted his teeth and broke out through the set of thick, double doors that was supposed to keep the third floor off-limits from the general public, of course a lot of good they seemed to do the other day with Nick Haley, and hit the button on the elevators to go up.

Yes, it was time he and Barry Whitfield had a little chat!

Once the elevator announced its arrival at the third floor with a soft ding, Ted rushed into the car before the doors had even opened fully and was quickly jabbing the 'Door Close' button over and over with an angry pace. Once the doors to the car slid shut, he hit the button for the top floor and tapped his brown loafer clad foot on the carpeted floor of the elevator car as it rose higher and higher.

As the elevator reached the highest level of Channel 5's building, the door opened and he flew out onto the twelfth floor. This was where Barry's office was, the smart and powerful man who ran the station like it was his life, which in fact Ted knew, it was. He had inherited the station from his father Oliver Whitfield, one of the big-shots in New York who ran many of the CBN Network's affiliates and satellite stations all over the East Coast. Daddy Whitfield had given his son his first job straight out of college, where Barry had wanted to be a lawyer.

Of course that idea had pissed his old man off since he believed the entertainment and broadcasting market was the only job a Whitfield should have, especially his only son. Rumor was he forced Barry out of law school and made him take over the studio here in the Washington Metropolitan market, grooming him to eventually be able to take over the larger world of CBN's communication network in their New York marketplace.

Either way, once the old man was gone, Ted figured Barry Whitfield would probably not follow in his father's outlined plan for his life, and the man who enjoyed Washington D.C., and all it had to offer in the way of politics and everything else that Barry seemed to live for, but would instead keep his place running the daily in and outs of Channel 5 right here in the D.C. market.

Ted was relying on that passion for this studio to get the man to see that Emily Erickson was truly wasting a valuable asset by not promoting him to TV news anchor.

By God, I am the most recognized name at this goddamn station, and once this story goes National, something I'm damn sure going to make sure happens, they won't be able to say no— no matter how big a stink that pain in the ass, Emily Erickson makes!

Reaching the outer door to the twelfth floor's offices, he quickly straightened his ties, smoothed his hair down and brushed off his crisp suit. He needed to look like he could be the leading face that people associated with Channel 5 News, and that meant not rushing into the office of the owner of the station and looking like he just came from a jog around the office. Taking a deep breath to calm the anger he was trying to refocus to use to his advantage, he pushed open the door and stepped through to find himself face to face with Jessica Marfisio, Barry Whitfield's secretary.

"Is Mr. Whitfield in?" Ted asked, putting on his most charming smile and sliding up to the woman's desk. The pert brunette with her dark hair pulled back into a fashionable and no doubt expensive hairstyle was wearing a designer suit that revealed a shapely figure underneath.

I wouldn't mind her working under me, Ted decided with the devious verdict regarding the attractive woman adding to the grand smile he presented. Picturing her on his arm as he arrived at some grand function or one of Whitfield's impressive, monthly soirees he holds at his large Potomac home for his upper-class friends and guests. They were said to be a veritable who's who of the Washington area.

Jessica just looked right through his smile and gave him an annoyed look, like his presence here was a waste of her precious time.

"You don't have an appointment," she said in a calm and measured tone. Obviously he wasn't her type.

She's probably a Dyke! he thought, feeling the earlier anger he had towards the station and those who worked inside its walls building up inside him again.

"No I don't have an appointment!" he snapped.

"They I'm afraid Mr. Whitfield doesn't have time for you," she answered smartly.

That bitch!

"Look can you just tell him Ted Hanson is here and would like to see him for just a moment?"

"Who?" the secretary asked, infuriating him even further. Of course she knew who he was, she was just being daft!

"Hanson…Ted Hanson…I work here for heaven's sake! I'm one of this station's biggest talents!" he screamed. Now he was losing it, the heat in his face flushing his cheeks.

Before Jessica had a chance to respond, the door to Whitfield's office opened and he saw Emily Erickson standing there, her scrunched up, fat face just staring at him with disappointment. Behind her, sitting at the large, mahogany desk in the office was Barry Whitfield himself.

What the hell is she doing here? he wondered, thinking this whole idea was just one bad experience unraveling before his very eyes. He opened his mouth to say something, but Emily cut him off. "Hanson, get your scrawny ass in here!"

The look on the secretary, Jessica's face was one of glee. He hated her even more than he could imagine, the blood pounding in his ears he was so upset. Then his eyes fell upon Emily in her blue suit coat and black pants. She couldn't even bother to coordinate her outfit and she could get in to see Whitfield when he couldn't. Seeing the look on her face, he realized how bad an idea this had been now that he was standing here with an expression of being caught with his hand in the cookie jar. He had been yelling at Mr. Whitfield's secretary, acting like a pompous ass, and the woman he had come up to the station owner's office to talk about had not only heard his actions, but so had Mr. Whitfield!

Ted felt the anger slowly dissipate as he realized he was in trouble. Nothing good was going to come of his trip to the twelfth floor now that he had lost his cool. Add to that, the fact that Emily "Triple E" Erickson was going to be present as he was brought into see Barry Whitfield himself. That little nickname for his clown of a boss was one he had actually gotten a few of the other anchors and station crew to recognize and it was a moment he was proud of. "Triple E", because Emily Erickson was short, fat and ugly! Now of course, he couldn't bare to even look into her eyes as he took one last glance at the secretary's mocking smile, and made his way into the office, Emily closing the door behind him as he entered, trapping him inside the large, stately room with her and the owner of Channel 5 News.

Oh crap! he thought as he heard the door click shut behind him.

This wasn't going to be good!

Stepping into the office of the Homicide Division, Andrea could see the flurry of activity that had ensued over the short day she had been absent taking care of Amy. So much for coming back to something a little less hectic than the last twenty-four hours she had gone through. Amy had cheered up a little bit over the day, and by the time Jeremy arrived home from school, all though Andrea was just waiting for a call from his guidance counselor to say he had skipped class again, her daughter had returned to acting a little more like her old self.

Of course, things had seemed a little more normal around dinner, even Jeremy's attitude seemed to be evening out, and they were able to get through a nice family dinner that Andrea had whipped up while afterward Amy took a relaxing bath to calm her nerves and work out the stiffness she felt from laying in bed all day. However, the night didn't wind down gently from there.

Andrea was just finishing clearing the plates from the pre-made meatloaf she had served for dinner when the phone rang. Picking the wireless handset up from the base sitting on the kitchen counter, she didn't think about who it could be as she put the phone to her ear and answered, "Hello?"

She felt a chill run down her spine as the familiar voice she had already had the displeasure of hearing earlier came over the line.

"Hey it's me," Robert said in a cheerful tone.

Damn it all to hell!

Andrea waited a moment before responding, remembering she had told him to call and they would get together once her and the kids came home.

"Yes?" she asked, keeping her voice under control to make sure her ex didn't pick up on the distressed quality of her words.

"I figure it's late enough for you all to be home, so I just wanted to let you know I'm on the way. I should be there in about fifteen minutes," he said, the sound of his car driving down the road loud in the background of their conversation.

"I still don't think this is a good idea. It's not needed. Amy's doing much better."

"Look we already agreed on this. She's my daughter and I have a right to see her and Jeremy."

"Jeremy was talking about going out with his friend Tommy in a little bit."

"Well tell him I'll be there soon and that he can wait. I'm sure he'd stick around until I arrive since I know you probably haven't told them I'm coming," he said.

He was right. Andrea hadn't told them that their father was supposed to be stopping by, and she didn't know how they'd respond. They had both been through a rough time when Robert had walked out of their life years ago, and now that he was on his way, she might as well warn them. It was only fair.

"I'll let Jeremy know but I can't promise you he'll stay and be here once you arrive," Andrea announced, looking over her shoulder towards the living room where Amy and Jeremy were sitting on the couch together watching television. They looked like one, big old happy family just going on with their lives like nothing terrible had happened the day before. Jeremy had even surprised her by apologizing to her for his actions the day before. Andrea hadn't expected that from the boy, but had a suspicion that Amy had talked some sense into her brother's mind.

Taking a glance at the clock on the wall before her, she saw it was a quarter to six. She had wanted to have dinner early so they could all watch a scary movie that was going to be on TV in an hour. CBN was doing their annual '31 Days of Halloween' special, and they were playing one of her favorite horror films, "The Silence of the Lambs". She just loved the creepy, melodious accent that Anthony Hopkins uttered throughout the movie.

Oh well, looks like I'll have to be dealing with Robert now instead of watching the classic film.

"Okay, make sure you tell him. I'll see you in a little bit," Robert said, and then he hung up.

Once the line was dead, Andrea replaced the handset onto the charging base and turned towards the living room. It was time to deliver the news...

Reflecting on the night she had experienced and the issues that arose from Robert coming over, her brain mulled over the situation and the events that transpired. It had been pretty much how she imagined it would be. Amy had been okay with the fact that her father had arrived, probably because he kept reminding her that he had come into town to make sure she was okay. Jeremy on the other hand was not okay with the situation, the resentment he still held for his father evident in the way he avoided Robert's questions and comments and seemed to distance himself from the conversation altogether.

As soon as Tommy had arrived, having borrowed his car from his older brother, Jeremy was out the door, not so much as a goodbye leaving the boy's mouth.

Andrea now focused on the action happening since she had walked into Montgomery County Police Headquarters and saw that the investigation had certainly taken over, some of the offices and labs being transformed into the main operations center for the joint task force.

The office that she worked out of, Homicide Divisions work space had been shifted aside and was now dedicated to the search and capture of the serial killers plaguing the city. Having taken the previous day as one of those allotted for vacation purposes so she could tend to her daughter in her time of need, the entire investigation had progressed and Andrea worked to catch up on everything she had missed.

It appeared that all the facts were in regarding the first victim, Sara Moulton, but the lab was still working on sifting through everything from the second scene. With four murdered teens, there was a massive amount of evidence and forensic material to go through and analyze. Not to mention the area that the scene encompassed was pretty large and there had been a lot of square footage to cover.

The crime scene investigators had found everything from hair samples, fibers, various residues and a collection of saliva found in the bite marks that was awaiting DNA typing. So far only the preliminary reports of data had come in, but nothing appeared clear cut. The only thing that had been confirmed was the pathologist was able to determine time of death to be around eleven o'clock the night before the bodies were discovered.

Finding her way through the mayhem that occurred when multiple people were crowded into such a small space and expected to work in such an enclosed environment, she made it to her desk and pulled a copy of the reports up on her computer. As she scrolled through them, memorizing all the important details, she looked up to see Mack Jones standing across from her desk. He looked like he hadn't changed much since the last time she had seen him, his large gut seeming to have gotten a little fuller and his slacks and dress-shirt were tight across his heavyset physique. He was wearing a tie that hung too short, the end of the material a good six inches from his belt, but then again, it wasn't like the gruff Rockville Detective had much care put into his appearance. Wiping his forehead with the back of his hand, he extended the other to her.

Reaching out with her own, she shook the meaty digit, her small hand being swallowed up by his thick grip. Releasing her from the handshake, Mack gave her a small smile, the extra skin of his fat face creasing around his lips and his heavy brow and flabby cheeks made his eyes squint and appear almost closed.

"Hey Detective Wilkes," he said in greeting.

"Hey back Jones, how's it going?"

"Not too bad. As you can see it's pretty busy around here since the FBI was brought in."

"So where's the agent in charge?" Andrea asked, looking around the room at the various officers and other unknown faces of people either walking around completing some errand or those at the bank of desks set up in the corner of the room working diligently on paperwork and making phone calls.

The room had been set up in a format similar to the one that the Montgomery County police used back when they had their last task force working out of this building during the Beltway Sniper Shootings years ago. The main office where Homicide was located had been crammed full of extra desks complete with computers and telephones on top of each one. Every person in the task force was assigned a partner who shared one desk. So there was a total of six desks in three rows in the one corner of the room and the original four desks like Andrea's and Tim Melvin's that made up the last part of those dedicated to the serial killings. Two filling cabinets and an extra computer had been pushed into the room also, and all of the phones were tied into the same board so that all calls coming in could be monitored and recorded.

They had released a hotline number that people could call if they had any information to report regarding the murders and an officer was assigned to man the line at all times to filter the calls coming in. So far it had all just been the usual crazies calling in to report themselves or loved ones as the killers. It was amazing how many wives, girlfriends and other significant others called in to report their family and friends suspicious behaviors and other random information.

Andrea noticed the pretty woman in a dark black suit that was sitting at one of the desks, a phone to her ear as she talked adamantly with the person on the other end of her conversation. Andrea noticed she was very beautiful, and immediately compared her own features to those of the woman with her reddish-brown hair and sparkling green eyes that looked up and over at Andrea, who shifted her gaze so as not to seem impolite for staring.

Mack who had noticed Andrea's curious stare and said, "That's Naomi Cassidy, a criminal profiler with the FBI."

"Oh," Andrea replied, acting like she hadn't really cared who it was. The truth was she had a strange feeling like the woman posed a threat to her.

It was a ridiculous feeling obviously, she didn't know the woman and there was nothing she could foresee her competing with her for. Yet, the feeling persisted. Taking one last glance over at the woman still involved in her phone call, Andrea looked back to Mack.

"So who's the guy in charge?"

"That would be Special Agent Poole," Mack replied, looking around the room quickly, then having spotted his target, pointed with one heavy arm across the room to the direction of the man.

Special Agent Poole was standing before an African American officer that Andrea had seen before, Desmond something, and discussing a report in his hand, when a lab technician entered the room and walked up to the two men.

Andrea's attention was on the man who seemed to exude confidence and gave off the type of powerful attraction that people turned their heads and paid attention when the fit, bald man stepped into a room. He seemed like he had been around the block, and Andrea assumed that since he was with the Bureau and had been sent to run the task force, he certainly had the experience and know how to do it right.

She watched as he listened to the technician, then turned and with a loud, booming voice, said, "Attention everyone!"

All eyes in the room turned to him as he walked to the center of the office so he was visible to the many people present.

"Okay, we just got the analysis and lab work back regarding two of the victims from the second scene. You know the groups you've been broken into and the tasks assigned to each of you. I want this information gone over and every single one of you hitting this with every resource we've got."

There was a murmur around the room as the activity that had already been constant seemed to now pick up a frantic pattern as people rushed to their desks to pull up the information and perform the tasks they were given. Andrea wondered what her job would be since she had missed the first meeting being home taking care of her daughter. Then as if he had read her mind, she watched as the Poole walked towards her, his sharp, black suit crisp and sleek as it moved along his muscled form.

"Speak of the devil, here's the one you were asking about," Mack said and slowly faded away, off to handle his own workload as the bald man stopped at the side of her desk, his movements stiff and delivered with military precision as he looked down at Andrea. Deciding that it seemed more appropriate to stand in the man's presence, she slid away from her desk and stood at attention.

"Detective Andrea Wilkes," she said.

"Detective, I'm Special Agent in Charge, Jim Poole. I understand you had a family emergency that kept you out yesterday and I appreciate you being back to work. At a time like this we need all the hands we can get. I assume that Chief Stone filled you in on the current objectives while you were out?" he asked, his odd accent hard for Andrea to place.

"Yes Sir. I do however wonder what my assignment will be within this task force. I would have expected the Chief to…" she began but he quickly cut her off. She noticed his attention was on the woman with the auburn hair who had been on the phone only moments ago. She was waving him over to her with one hand, the expression on her face one of grave urgency.

"Hold that question right there— I'm afraid I will have to be right back," he said and quickly headed over to the other side of the office.

Well that was quick, she thought, slightly annoyed that she had been cut off and then dismissed so quickly.

What the hell could be so important to just walk off in the middle of a question? Andrea wondered as she watched the woman quickly speaking to Poole, and she could tell from the look on the two FBI agents faces that something big was going on. Something major. And then, as if in answer to her questions, Poole nodded to the woman Mack had referred to as Naomi and turned once more to address the group. This time however, the information was much more dire.

Andrea's stomach tightened.

"People— we've had another murder!" Poole shouted, and the room grew quiet as all eyes turned to the FBI agent.

Oh no, Andrea thought, that feeling she always got in her stomach when something bad was happening appeared right on schedule again, and she knew this wasn't going to be ending any time soon.

Not another one!

Chapter 24

Before heading downtown to visit the National Zoological park's D.C., location, Aidan had given Mack a call to fill him in on what he and Nick Haley had come up with so far. He explained their running theory on the killer's possibly attempting to emulate the attack patterns of a large predatory animal, having some sort of link The gruff Detective listened intently and then told him the news Aidan was afraid of hearing, however much it went towards validating their hypothesis regarding some form of cult or organized group of wackos with satanic motives being behind the murders. Yes, the other four victims had matching marks etched into their bodies in various spots, all of them resembling pentagrams. At first no one had noticed them among the many wounds the bodies were inflicted with, but once they had discovered the first one, the others weren't hard to miss.

Fortunately, Mack had saved them the time and energy of going downtown, by informing them that the FBI had already inquired of the Smithsonian regarding an expert on animal attack wounds. They had been informed that their best bet would be going to the Virginia campus of the Smithsonian Conservation Biology Institute. Aidan had also learned that while that was one source of information the joint task force was looking into, they had only just called the institute to ask for assistance of their researchers and labs in the investigation, and that hadn't sent anyone over or faxed the information they wanted analyzed. That was good news for Aidan as he and Nick climbed into his Dodge Challenger and speed down the interstate for Virgina, hoping to get to SCBI and retrieve the information they required from the wildlife biologist Mack had referred them to.

Getting to the SCBI facility took them a little more than half an hour. Their only saving grace had been that it was still early enough to avoid the lunch hour traffic that would have filled up the interstate and local roads with hungry workers out looking to enjoy their break from their jobs.

Pulling up at the main gate to the facility, there was a small guard station that was manned by a lowly rental cop. The man sitting in the little booth had his feet propped up on the counter inside, a crossword puzzle book in his hands as they drove up. He dropped his feet off the counter and he stepped out of the shack as Aidan rolled his window down and held out his wallet, displaying his badge and ID to the man.

"Detective Aidan Preston, I'm here to speak to someone at Building 15 about an ongoing investigation."

Taking a quick look at the items, he nodded his head and gave a little grunt of acceptance.

"Welcome to the Smithsonian's Virginia campus," the cop said. He was wearing a government-issued, security uniform just like the ones the officers who worked security at all the buildings downtown wore.

"Thanks," Aidan answered, reaching over and turning the heat up a little on the A/C since his window was now down and the cold air was filling the car's interior.

The rent-a-cop stepped into the guard station and came back with a clipboard. He asked to see Aidan's ID again, and quickly jotting down his name on the log, he nodded again and hit a small button that activated the gate. The long, metal gate slid open on well-oiled hinges, allowing access to SCBI to Aidan and Nick. Rolling his window back up to rid them off the penetrating cold that had tried to seep all warmth from the inside of the car in the short amount of time they had been occupied with the guard, Aidan put the car into drive and moved away from the booth and down the long paved drive that led into the compound.

Aidan was surprised at how big a plot of land the SCBI seemed to maintain. They passed building after building, and when there weren't buildings or other small connected sheds and breezeways, they found themselves winding through large spans of woods and hills. Sometimes there seemed to be fences separating various expanses of land, but most of the time the grounds were wide open. Every so often, Aidan even spied old barns that looked like they had been converted to other uses at some point in the last couple decades.

"I didn't even know this place existed," Nick said as they both drove slowly down the road that wound through the campus. "I just thought the Smithsonian did all their research at the actual Zoo. Who knew they needed this many buildings."

"Yeah," Aidan said, noticing a sign up ahead that had a listing of buildings with arrows pointing in the direction they could be found. He saw that Building 15 was straight ahead according to the sign so he stepped on the accelerator and quickly got moving.

This is no time for sight seeing, he reminded himself, and they soon made their way to a parking lot where they were able to park the Challenger. The parking lot was large, and yet it was full of cars. Obviously a lot of people worked here at this facility, and he guessed there was probably at least one other parking area to accommodate all the people that came here daily.

As they got out of the car, Nick pointed out the large building ahead of them. It was three stories and quite wide, and as they approached the reporter said, "It looks like that's the main building on this campus."

Aidan stared ahead and saw the large number one engraved on a plaque near the buildings entrance. Above the set of glass doors that led inside the structure was a sign that read, 'Smithsonian Conservation Biological Institute Headquarters'. Agreeing with Nick, they decided to head inside the main complex and ask for directions to Building 15.

There was a large, fountain that sat in the middle of a beautifully sculpted flower garden, a bronze elephant statue sticking out from the center of the water feature, its trunk raised above its head and water raining down onto its back and flowing into the main fountain.

As they passed through the garden and stepped inside the building, they found themselves standing in a large, wide open space that held multiple life-sized animals and other various artifacts that were spread throughout the lobby. It was a taxidermist dream, all the once live creatures positioned throughout the entryway, a symbol of the work being focused on at this center.

About ten feet further there was a reception desk where a man sat, wearing the same uniform that the guard at the entrance to the facility was wearing minus the heavy jacket since he was inside, and was occasionally glancing at a bank of monitors that was set up on the desk and reading a well-worn book that he was engrossed in. Aidan walked straight for the bored looking receptionist sitting behind the wide desk, catching the man's attention as he approached.

"Can I help you?" the man asked, seeming to remind Aidan of a walrus. The man was big, with a rounded midsection and a large, orange-tinted red, handlebar mustache and a thin head of graying hair that was combed over to cover a evident bald spot the man was trying to hide. It was amusing to Aidan that the man who worked here at the reception desk of the Smithsonian's campus dedicated to the study of wildlife appeared to mimic an animal himself.

"Yes, I'm Detective Aidan Preston with the Montgomery County Police Department," Aidan said, then motioning to Nick said, "And this is my associate Mr. Haley."

Nick nodded, not bothering to mention that he wasn't tied to the police but instead was a journalist for The Informant. Aidan figured there was no reason to point out the man was a reporter and had no official ties to a police matter. Of course, thinking about it, neither did Aidan.

The walrus seemed to come alive at the mention of the police affiliation, and from the look on his face, he was curious as to why a detective from Montgomery County was here in Front Royal, Virginia, at the institute's facilities.

"What can I do for you?" the man asked, and Aidan saw that he was wearing a name badge on his uniform.

"Well, Mr. Vincent, we're are actually looking for Building 15, and we were hoping you could point us to it," Aidan replied.

"Ah, the Cave, it's actually just a short walk from here."

"The 'Cave'?"

"Yeah, that's the term the staff here uses for Building 15. They do most of the research on wolves there, hence the nickname," Mr. Vincent responded with a shrug. Obviously he didn't seem to understand the mindset of the researchers and zoologists that worked at SCBI.

"Gotcha— well Mr. Vincent, could you aim us in the right direction, we're supposed to be meeting someone."

"Sure, sure," the guard said and quickly explained how they could get to Building 15.

Thanking the man at the reception desk, Aidan and Nick quickly headed back outside into the cold air and made their way to their destination.

As they approached the gray, modern building that was the Cave, Aidan studied the large statue that was situated high on the ledge of the roof sitting above the building's entrance doors. He had seen pictures of the statue before, and knew that it was a replica of a famous sculpture somewhere over in Europe.

"Remus and Romulus," Nick pointed out, commenting on the bronze sculpture as they slipped beneath the massive ornament and entered the glass lobby doors of the Cave.

They found themselves in a lobby, too small for their to be any need of a receptionist in this building. Besides the fact that visitors to the campus probably had no need of ever stepping foot into Building 15, since it was dedicated to research purposes only. Aidan looked around and spotted a sign at the beginning of a long hallway that led to the various labs and offices that were housed in the Cave, a separate hall running the opposite way from the junction. Running his finger over the sign, scanning the list of names and room numbers, he found the person he was looking for.

Wildlife Biologist Lisa Davies' office was located in room seven. Looking down the hall, he saw that the main hall that led furthest down the center of the building was labeled with even numbered offices, the odd running the length of the opposite hallway. Tapping his finger on the nameplate for Ms. Davies, Aidan turned to Nick and saw he was nodding his head in agreement. Yes, that was who they were supposed to be meeting.

She was the one Mack had told them had been suggested to the task force when they called the National Zoo's main number and asked for someone who could answer some questions pertaining to predatory animals of North America.

Heading down the hallway to the left, they followed the odd numbers until they reached the room with a seven stenciled next to the office's entrance. The door to the room was open and Aidan could see that it was a large space with multiple desks, computers, scientific equipment and other typical items he suspected a person would find in a research environment like the Smithsonian.

As they walked through the door, they were greeted by a young man in his early twenties. He was slightly husky, a Virginia Tech sweatshirt covering his slight belly and a pair of jeans that were worn and tattered in spot. He had a pair of dirty tennis shoes that looked like they probably needed replacing, and even his sweatshirt seemed to have a few tears in various spots.

The young man was sitting at one of the desks, busily typing at a computer and as they entered the lab, he looked up, brushing his medium length dark hair away from his rounded face and gave them a questioning look. Obviously they weren't used to getting many strangers walking into their labs.

"Um, what can I do for you? This space is sort-of off limits to the public," the boy said, his eyes taking in their apparent, unscientific appearance, Aidan being in his usual dark t-shirt, jeans and leather jacket and Nick wearing a cheap, rumpled gray suit and heavy winter coat, his worn work bag ever present strung over his shoulder and resting against his side.

"We were actually looking for Lisa Davies," Aidan answered while he noticed the journalist was busy looking around the room. He had found an erect skeleton of some animal on four legs, the bones attached together with rods so that the body was supported into a lifelike pose.

The young man who had been busy working at the computer when they had first arrived seemed to look over at Nick studying the skeleton and said, "That's Canis lupus, it's the main animal we are studying here at the Cave— well Building Fifteen, here at SCBI."

"Interesting, I thought it looked like a large dog of some kind," Nick said, his roaming gaze held on the skeleton, his attention set on the animal's skull, especially the jaws.

"Actually it's the North American gray wolf, not a dog," the kid replied, then adding, "And Lisa should be back any minute, she just went to Dr. Wilcox's office. He's just down the hall, so she'll be on her way back here momentarily if you want to wait."

"Don't mind if we do," Nick answered, his fingers tracing the teeth of the gray wolf skull, as Aidan stepped over to stand beside him and see what he found so intriguing with the skeleton.

"What's up?" Aidan asked.

"Oh nothing, just noticing how similar the teeth seem to be to the bite marks in those photos," he said continuing to run his finger along the tips of the lower jaw.

At that moment a striking woman entered the office, her silky black hair and Hispanic features making her dark brown eyes and full lips even more noticeable.

Aidan and Nick both turned away from the wolf skeleton as the woman looked up and noticed them standing there. She was wearing a white blouse that accented the deep color of her skin and a light blue skirt that hugged the toned, sensual shape of her body. She was definitely beautiful, and Aidan and Nick found themselves speechless at the woman's entrance.

There was something special and exotic that radiated from the woman's appearance.

"Oh, who are you?" she asked, those dark eyes studying Aidan and Nick as they stood there staring at her.

Aidan recovered quickly and nudged Nick with his elbow, the reporter standing there gawking at the alluring woman before him.

"My name is Aidan Preston, I'm a Detective with the Montgomery County Police Department," he said then gesturing to Nick who had finally shaken the stunned demeanor off his face, said, "And this is…"

"Nick Haley," the reporter finished, extending his hand and shaking the woman's appendage, noticing her delicate yet firm grip.

"Pleased to meet you, I'm Lisa, Lisa Davies, wildlife biologist here at the institute," she responded, her deep brown eyes moving from Nick to Aidan and then back to the reporter again as he released her hand.

"Well in that case Mrs. Davies, you're just the woman we were looking for." Aidan said.

"It's Miss, actually, I'm not married," she said, and Aidan could see Nick's eyebrows raise in slight intrigue at her correction.

"Sorry, Ms. Davies, then."

"That's right. How can I be of assistance?"

"We're here in regards to the multiple murders that have occurred in Montgomery County," said Aidan.

"Oh, yes— a gentleman from the FBI had called earlier asking a few questions about possible animal's that could have migrated into the city limits that aren't native to the area," she answered.

"Yes, he would have been calling for the same reason we came here today."

"Well, unfortunately like I told the agent on the phone— there have been no reports of any invasive species that aren't innate to the local ecosystem."

"What about non-invasive species? What kind of large predatory animals do fit into the geographical locale around Maryland?" Aidan asked, hoping that the zoologist was right.

"There's no wildlife that would be entering city limits, other than that which is already currently known and seen around the city. You have the usual suspects such as deer, squirrels, raccoons, rabbits and foxes being some of the most familiar mammals seen around. Six species of mammals are extirpated in Maryland and are no longer found in the state. Over twenty species or mammal fall under the category of either rare, threatened or endangered," Lisa explained, taking a pause from continuing when she saw a question forming on Aidan's lips. "You were about to ask something?"

"Yes, you said 'extirpated'— could you explain?" he asked.

"Oh, of course," she said as she thought about how to better explain what she was referring to for her two visitors. Then forming the right wording in her mind, she said, "Extirpation is also alluded to as 'local extinction'," then paused again, to make sure the two men were paying attention.

"It's the condition of a species which ceases to exist in a chosen geographic area, though it still exists elsewhere. Local extinctions are sometimes followed by a replacement of the species taken from other locations. The work we are doing to reintroduce the gray wolf to the area of Yellowstone National Park and eventually here in on the East Coast is an example of this. The six species that are no longer found wild in Maryland include the Gray wolf, American elk, Eastern mountain lion, Snowshoe hare, American marten and Eastern harvest mouse. Local extinctions mark a change in the ecology of an area, and sometimes that change can be good for location like in the case of an aggressive, invasive species, but other times it can actually harm the ecosystem. That is when conservationists such as those working here at SCBI research and work on methods to reintroduce the animals that were lost that can be beneficial."

"Okay, so what animals are around that could be responsible for maiming a person?" Aidan asked, trying to get to the point.

He was all for learning new information, but with these murders continuing, he had a deadline to meet. He just hoped that he wasn't wasting his time following this theory that Nick had first come up with.

It seems possible these maniacs could have some connection to, could be using animal attacks to pattern their murders after, or could they be off on everything? Please let this visit to this woman pay off, Aidan thought.

"Montgomery County contains a smaller selection of wildlife, especially larger creatures that are common to that generalized area rather than that of Maryland, so if we widen the scope of the possible subjects that could technically drift down into the area, like a rogue animal, then the number of subjects increases to encompass a wider range of fauna. The list of possible animals includes black bears, bobcats, Eastern mountain lions, bobcats, even foxes and coyotes could be responsible for attacking and mauling a person if the situation was right," Lisa said.

"If I show you some pictures from a crime scene, could you possibly tell us is you think the wounds resemble an animal attack?" Aidan wondered.

"I can try," was Lisa's response.

Reaching into his jacket pocket, he withdrew the envelope that contained the crime scene photographs from the first murder.

Hope she doesn't freak out on me, this is probably gonna make her puke!

He opened the envelope and slid the stack of photographs out.

"Why don't we take these over to my desk," she said, and the three of them walked across the large office and while Lisa sat down in her chair, Aidan and Nick borrowed two metal folding chairs from a table littered with various documents and notebooks and sat down across from the wildlife biologist.

Once they were seated, Lisa looked over to her assistant and introduced him to the men.

"Gentlemen, this is Frank, my assistant," she said with a wave of her hand, then asked, "Is this matter able to be discussed in front of him? If not, I can ask him to leave."

"It would probably be better if we spoke with you alone. This is an active police investigation," Aidan said, looking over at the young man who had returned to entering data into the computer before him.

Lisa nodded in understanding, then turning towards her assistant, said, "Hey Frank, why don't you go check on the pack."

The young man nodded and dismissed himself from the room without any hesitation. He seemed to understand his role around the place, and had no problem following Lisa's suggestion.

"The 'pack'?" Nick asked, his eyes unwavering from Lisa's face as he took in every detail of the beautiful woman.

"Yes, here at SCBI we have a holding enclosure containing a gray wolf pack of two adults and three pups, the pups being all siblings, and we are studying their traits and characteristics while performing other research, all until they are moved to their permanent habitat at the National Zoo's urban park in downtown Washington D.C."

"I see," Aidan said, then as an afterthought before he showed her the photos asked, "You wouldn't happen to have any missing wolves that have escaped recently would you?"

A smile appeared on Lisa's face and she shook her head in disagreement.

"No, I'm happy to report that all our animals are here and accounted for," Lisa said to Aidan's apparent disappointment.

Of course, it couldn't be that easy!

He then set the photographs onto the desk before the woman and spread them out like a deck of playing cards. There were six photos that he had chosen based on them having the clearest visual of the bite marks on the first victim. Unfortunately due to the severe nature of the woman's injuries, even thought Aidan had tried to choose photos that were also less graphic in nature, none of the pictures showing too much of the wounds other than the intended markings, they were still bloody awful.

Lisa made a gasp, sucking in her breath slightly as she looked down at the photos laid out before her.

"Dear Lord," she murmured as her eyes scanned the pictures.

"I'm sorry they are so graphic, but unfortunately these were the only photos I could show you to get your opinion on the apparent bite marks."

Studying the top photo for a moment, Lisa then sifted through the others, taking her time, the grave impression on her beautiful features hardening as she finished doing through the stack. Once she had came to the last one, she spread them all out in a row to see each all at once.

She's taking it better than I thought, Aidan thought as he watched Lisa Davies, wildlife biologist, study the pictures, her face seeming to soften a little as the time passed. Then finally she looked up and straight at Aidan.

"What do you think?" he asked, those deep, dark eyes meeting his and he could see the horror in them. He knew that she was appalled by the pictures, but he needed her help, and she seemed to understand that as she gave her initial assessment.

"Well in order to analyze the bite mark patterns there are a few basic guidelines that need to be followed to get a reliable match. For a physical comparison to be successful, normally an odontologist or pathologist at the scene would have to make sure the possible bite mark in question has to be accurately reproduced. It has to be created in life-size dimensions. Once this is done, normally the photos would be compared to known evidence like the person or animal you are trying to match the bite mark to."

Nick was scrounging around in his bag and pulled out a digital tape recorder. "Do you mind if I record this?" he asked Lisa.

She looked at him oddly for a moment then asked, "You're not a Detective are you?"

As if he had been caught in some red-hot lie, Nick hung his head and replied, "No, I'm with The Informant newspaper."

"I thought your name sounded familiar," she said, a smile appearing on her face as she realized she had just assumed he was with he police as the Detective was. That'll teach me to jump to conclusions, she thought, kicking herself mentally for not asking sooner.

"In that case, no I don't mind," she said and continued talking as Nick flipped on the recorder and set it down on the table in front of Lisa as she talked.

"Usually plaster casts are used to analyze similarities and dissimilarities in shape, size, positioning, and other distinguishing characteristics seen in the bite mark to be compared so that the photos can be matched to known evidence and a ranking can be assigned to either confirm or rule out a positive match. Other than using a casting of the teeth being studied, the other way would be to overlay a transparent copy of the recorded teeth over the photograph and judge how they line up. Some examiners use computer software like Photoshop to create the transparent films and then lay them over the scanned image of the victim's wound to tell if they match."

Lisa then went on to explain that the threshold variable in bite mark analysis is the fact that, in cases of physical assault having skin injuries, the anatomy and physiology of the skin, and the position the victim was in affects the detail and shape of the mark left on the body. The characteristics that hold the most weight in matching a bite mark are aided in the fact that a person's general dental characteristics vary upon such things as racial variations in skeletal anatomy, jaw width, tooth position and the depth of the puncture wounds.

While using a transparent overlay can give the person studying the markings an idea of how the wounds correlate to the proportions of the photograph, but they cannot judge depth and the condition of the incisions of the actual flesh. That is why, while the method of using photographs can help narrow down possible suspects that appear to be of the same dimensions and shape of the marks, but to get an undeniable positive identification, a actual cast of the jaws must be compared to the actual victim's body to confirm that there is a match.

Alternatively, some analysts ignore size comparisons and focus on similarities in class and individual features of the puncture wounds. In both situations, the possibility of error arises from the examiner's subjective methods and partial selection of the available physical information.

Being able to recognize these variables that can affect the positive matching of a bite mark, all forms of comparative techniques should be used by the crime lab technicians or odontologist who is the examiner.

The recent development of easily available digital imaging software and image-capture devices such as scanners and digital cameras have created an opportunity to better control these well-recognized variables and allows the forensic examiner to turn the computer monitor into a comparison microscope with the added benefit of the better control of image visualizations, being able to correct common photographic discrepancies with size and possible distortion and the fact that the data can be reproduced in multiple formats and saved and archived electronically.

This electronic backup is key in being able to keep the evidence of the wounds from being ruined as a the actual samples could be corrupted and destroyed, altering the results to be obtained. As a body decays, the physical evidence becomes transitory, fragile and eventually becomes useless for comparison, so these formats that the bite marks can be saved to will help the examiner reach the correct ruling and rate the findings. The depth of the bite marks can also not only rule out a specific animal or person based on size of the teeth and the direction, but also give a general idea of the bite force administered onto the victim's skin. The deeper the punctures, compared to the size of the teeth where they come out of the subject's jaw helps the examiner judge how powerful the bite was.

Aidan and Nick just sat there as the woman finished up explaining the basis of analyzing a bite mark. As Aidan looked at the photos on the table, he realized they might not be good enough to clearly identify who or what made them. That's when Lisa told them what Aidan had begun to fear.

"Because these photographs are not life-size, are taken at various angles without any two being similar and only having six to go with, each a photo of a different bite, I'm afraid I can't be too sure. Also, like I said before, I would need an actual casting to compare any similarities to any known animals, especially those native to the area," Lisa explained.

"Is there any way to at least gauge if they look similar to a specific animal based on generalizations? Aidan asked, his hopes being dashed by the lack of evidence he was able to bring with him. Such was the issue with not being on the case officially. He didn't have access to any of the actual lab results and forensic data collected

Then Nick chipped in his two cents, "Yeah, can you just assume the woman in the photos is about average size, or correlate the injuries on her to how they would appear on your own self. The victim was a woman, so using your dimensions as a base starting point, could you estimate the size of the animal or possibly what type of species it would be had it attacked you?"

"That's not a bad idea," Aidan said, surprise registering on his face as his hope was returned to him.

"Well, I suppose I could hypothesize."

"I'd appreciate any help you can give us," Aidan answered.

"No problem. I had read about the murders in the paper— it's just tragic that a woman could be murdered and left mutilated, but I didn't realize you were thinking she could have been attacked by an animal."

"Actually we know that the victims were killed by a person or persons, however as you can see from the photographs, they either had some unknown animal with them and used that to attack the victims also, or they attempted to make them look the murders were performed by a rogue creature."

"I can tell you from looking at these…," Lisa said, gesturing to the photographs still spread between them, "…while a person may have been involved, these wounds are definitely characteristics of a large predator, and it wouldn't make sense to try and create such a random pattern of wounds and bite marks. The amount of time it would take just to inflict these marks would have made the exercise extremely time consuming. I just don't see how it could be man-made."

"Well, that's why we're here— you're the expert on wildlife, and we could definitely use your opinion."

Lisa studied the photos more and then reaching into her desk, she pulled out a marker and began drawing circles on her forearm in the same location and drawn in detail to the same size as those in the photograph. Aidan and Nick watched the woman work, surprised and amazed at how quick her mind worked. She had chosen the photo of the arm because it seemed to show the wounds the clearest.

She quickly finished the marks on her arm, and then double checked that they were as accurate as possible. The black marks encircled her forearm, the spacing between the puncture marks seeming even larger in between the incisions seeming larger than anything she was used to witnessing.

"I wish I had a cast to gauge how deep these puncture marks are. That would help immensely in identifying if an animal attack is responsible for the majority of these wounds." Lisa said.

Just then, Aidan remembered he had a copy of the Medical Examiner's report which listed his findings, including how deep and the sizes of ever wound and cut on the body.

"I think I have something better than a cast," he said asking Nick for the folder he had given him to put into his bag, which inside the folder was the autopsy form. "I've got the report with the exact description and dimensions of every wound on the victim's bod.

After Nick got the folder out, he flipped through it until he found the report and handed it to Lisa. She took it and immediately began reading the document. Then pulling a ruler out from a drawer on the side of the desk, she measured the marks in the photo and attempted to multiply the dimensions in her head so they were correlated to the best of her ability.

Aidan and Nick had been watching her the whole time, silent as she worked diligently to make the markings conform as close to the original pattern that befouled the victim's arm.

Once she was done, she rotated her arm around, her eyes studying the lines she had transferred to her skin. A minute later she looked up from her appendage and her eyes met with Aidan's and Nick's.

"Well I can tell you one thing for certain…," she said, the sound of her voice belaying a tone of confusion. "…these are definitely bite marks, basing my findings on this rough replica, however, there's no species of animal, native or invasive to Maryland that could have made these marks."

Aidan looked at the woman's marker-covered arm, then his eyes traveled back up to her face. He was confused, having placed a great deal of hope in the fact that the bite marks could have come from a known animal like a coyote or fox that had stumbled upon the victim's remains. Now he knew this case was certainly becoming the strangest he had ever worked on.

"So it couldn't be a dog or something?" Nick asked.

"No," Lisa said shaking her head quickly, "These bite marks are too different from any dog I've ever studied. These marks were either man-made, which like I said would be entirely time consuming, or we're dealing with an creature that has a bite force and jaws that are much bigger than anything I've ever seen, and it's powerful. I don't even want to think about what could have inflicted these wounds, but if they were man-made, they did a hell of a job. They imprints and spacing look similar to a canines build, specifically a wolves, but like I said, the size doesn't match. I'm not sure what the hell did this."

Great, so there's either a freaking bear loose in the city that had come across the killers twice in two different spots to inflict their damage onto the bodies, which is completely unlikely, or whoever killed these people gets off on carving their victims up so badly that they take their sweet time doing it! What the hell had been brought to the streets of Rockville? Aidan didn't want to think of the answer.

It was scary— plain and simple.

Whoever had done this to these people was pure evil!

What happens when the next victim shows up?

Can I protect those who depend me me?

Aidan just didn't know, and he felt like he was drowning in helplessness.

Are the bodies just going to keep appearing?

Aidan looked at Lisa and Nick and they all seemed to be sharing the same worries.

What the hell is going on?

Chapter 26

Dr. Harper PhD, sat in his usual spot, the plush, comfortable looking chair that looked like the man would never replace it no matter how much time passed and money he made in the private sector, helping those facing serious psychological complications, or just letting those that were dealing with the twists and turns life can throw at a normal person, talk to someone else about their problems and get it off their chests. He was certainly a dedicated psychiatrist and from the diplomas hanging on the walls of his ornately decorated office, Aidan knew the man certainly had the background for the task of helping a person work out whatever deep-rooted fears or issues may be inflicting them.

Aidan took in everything as he sat in the dark green, leather sofa that he always found himself positioned in whenever he met the good doctor for their weekly sessions. It had only been a few days since he had last seen Dr. Harper, but a lot had happened regarding him and the case, and he had called the psychiatrist up and asked to be fit into his schedule at the end of the day.

Of course, even though his office hours for seeing patients were over for the day, Dr. Harper had made an exception and waited for the Detective to get back from Virginia, where he said he had been drawn to in regards to the latest murders. While Dr. Harper was hesitant to see Aidan pursuing the case so fervently, disregarding the possible department issues that could arise from his insubordination at a time where he was supposed to be on administrative leave, Aidan had been adamant about needing to speak with him and get his insight into some things that had him bothered. Naturally, Dr. Harper agreed to meet, the help of his patients always a priority in his life.

Now, the two men sat directly across from each other, the sleek, richly-stained coffee table between them with Aidan's copies of the police reports from not only the first victim, but the second set of murders as well laid out on the black tabletop. After parting ways with Nick Haley after their trip to the campus of SCBI, Aidan had met up with his Mack and was able to get the heavyset Detective to run a copy of the latest crime lab results and autopsy findings out to his car so Aidan didn't have to enter the building and risk being seen by Stone or anyone else who knew his unofficial capacity to be snooping around the investigation.

Dr. Harper had listened to Aidan catch him up to speed on the proceedings that had been taking place over the last week since the murders began, and then after reading through the police reports, the psychiatrist was attempting to answer the questions that had been gnawing at the back of Aidan's subconscious. Harper had to agree with the man, this case was full of strange facts and an even more bizzare undercurrent of something else that was lying just under the surface of the murders. He was now trying his best to make some sense of everything for Aidan.

"Have you ever heard the term 'Clinical Lycanthropy', Aidan?" Dr. Harper asked, his eyes studying the Detective softly from behind long tented fingers that were pressed together in one of the doctor's many habitual poses that he had come to notice whenever he was in a long, thought-provoking session with the man.

"Lycanthropy— you mean werewolves?" Aidan asked, the amusement in his tone, telling Dr. Harper that the man was missing the key relation.

A small smile pursed Harper's lips as he sat there studying Aidan from his seat of authority, leaning forward slightly, his elbows resting on his knees and his hands remaining clasped together almost as if he was praying, but his eyes were open and he began talking again, his slow, well-educated voice reflecting a hint of an accent that the doctor had held onto from his childhood growing up down south in Baton Rouge, Louisiana.

"No, not werewolves per se, but 'Clinical' Lycanthropy? Emphasis on the clinical not the fantastical."

"I don't believe I've heard the term," Aidan answered honestly, the skepticism in the doctor's statement making him wonder if maybe this man with his years of training and schooling in the study of the human psyche, might be a little off himself.

It was funny, his psychiatrist had never seemed one to go bringing up the likes of imaginary monsters and bogeymen. Then again, the things he probably heard from some of his varying clients could probably make you wish there were things that did go bump in the night, supernatural things that would mean the horrors that the human conscious could produce being monstrous enough for some.

There were some truly sick individuals out in the world, Aidan knew, and just like the case he was following of the recent murders, there were plenty of real monsters in society to have to rely on creating new ones. However, ignoring the detective's good humor, Dr. Harper continued his explanation, knowing that the smart Detective would soon see what he was getting at.

Werewolves, really? he imagined, stopping himself from laughing out loud before Dr. Harper had a chance to explain himself.

"Clinical Lycanthropy is a term we use in the world of psychology that does not get heard of by the general public very often. It is a rare psychiatric syndrome that involves a delusional belief that the affected person is, or has, transformed into an animal. It is named after the mythical condition of lycanthropy, the supernatural affliction you mentioned just a moment ago, in which people are said to physically shape-shift into werewolves. The word zoanthropy is also sometimes used for the delusion that one has turned into an animal in general and not specifically a wolf, and the behavior can also be described as therianthropy, however, for the case at hand and to help us diagnose the possible cause of the killer's behaviors' and actions, I will refer to the term that is generally accepted, that of Clinical Lycanthropy."

"Okay," Aidan replied, sitting up in his seat as the mention of wolves and beasts got his mind spinning, and he became intrigued to hear the doctor's outside opinion on the matter. He was an excellent observer, and knowing the mind of a person as well as he did, possibly he could aid him just like the FBI had their fancy criminal profilers.

Of course, when he talked to Mack earlier and found out that the lab results were finally in for the second crime scene and that over the course of his running between Maryland and Virginia, another crime scene had been reported, he remembered Mack telling him that the FBI had no leads so far on the killer's mindset. The new murder had happened up in the woods, a good distance into the forest bordering the area of Rock Creek Park and the Appalachians.

This time a poacher who was hunting illegally with his two buddies had been found dead, his body dismembered brutally like the others. The two half-drunk friends who had discovered the body thought a bear had been responsible, but once again the remains had a pentagram carved into the chest.

What is it with that marking?

Then, coming back to the task at hand, Aidan turned his attention to Dr. Harper as he explained his theory, and as the man talked, Aidan began to get that feeling he always felt when he was onto something.

"Individuals who are inflicted report a delusional belief that they have transformed, or are in the process of transforming into another animal, typically a wolf. It has been linked with the altered states of mind that accompany psychosis, the reality-bending mental state involving delusions and hallucinations, with the transformation only seeming to happen in the mind and behavior of the person experiencing these delusions. It's usually not until the person has a moment of clarity during these hallucinations or upon review of his actions at a later time that he reports that he sometimes feels like an animal or had felt like one but was now back in their human guise." Dr. Harper said, taking a moment to make sure Aidan didn't have any questions.

"So if it's a delusion of hallucination, then it's all in the person's head. Their just imagining it right?"

"Well, yes and no. You must remember that the human mind is a vast and complex organism capable of untold feats that researchers are still discovering. We have hardly tapped the outer layer of the brain's possibilities and are continuing to learn new things every day. So while the answer to your question of them imagining this transformation is yes, their minds are so completely enveloped in the idea that they are changing, their minds believing the delusions are real, that the person behaves in a manner that resembling the altered state of being, crying, grumbling or creeping, howling, scratching and a whole assortment of characteristics of the animal they imagine themselves to be."

"I see," Aidan stated, starting to see the direction the psychiatrist's examination was heading.

"Yes. Although Clinical Lycanthropy is a rare condition, it has been studied in depth over the many years and is largely considered to be an idiosyncratic expression of a psychotic episode caused by another condition such as schizophrenia, bipolar disorder or clinical depression. There have been documented cases that date back to the beginning of written history, cultures all over the world having some form of stories that speak of this condition, and are actually based on the supposed 'werewolf' actually suffering from this disease.

Using the technology available to us today, doctors have been able to actually record using neuroimaging, the activation of these changes in a person suffering from this ailment and have found that the areas of the brain that represent proprioception, or the ability to sense the position, location, orientation and movement of the body and its parts, that when these people say they believe their bodies are actually transforming, it is a real perception to them, as real as a healthy person sees his own body," Dr. Harper said, shifting in his chair and lowering his peaked fingers into a fist and laid them into his lap.

"So you believe that the people who are committing these terrible murders could be suffering from the delusion that they are in fact wolves, and that is why they victim's bodies are being mutilated and appear to have been purported by a large predatory animal?"

"Exactly!"

Aidan thought about what the doctor had said. It made sense, by God, it certainly fit everything that had happened and the basic facts of the case. Just then Aidan realized something else.

"But wouldn't it make more sense if the delusional assailants committed these crimes and acted out their fantasies as werewolves on the full moon only?" he asked.

Dr. Harper seemed to think about this for a minute, his eyebrows tightening in concentration, and then he said, "Not exactly. The person afflicted with this disease and these grand hallucinations of themselves as not a human, but a creature that has historically been tied to the full moon in the literature and legends of this mythological and fantastical beast might feel more inclined to act out their crimes the strongest when the moon is full, but I am of the opinion that any moon will do."

"That would explain why all the murders have occurred at night. The perpetrators we are looking for according to the Medical Examiner's estimation of time of death places all the victim's being killed at night! They are choosing their victims based on the fact that they are available to them at the right time of the evening, when the moon is out and they feel the most in tune with it!"

Dr. Harper looked at the excitement flowing from Aidan and smiled. It was good to see the brooding man that had entered his office an hour ago with so many unanswered questions weighing on his mind, start to be able to put this mystery to rest with his help. It was good for Aidan to feel like he was gaining the upper hand on the investigation even if he was risking getting into even more trouble by disregarding his commanding officer, Chief Stone, by continuing to follow the murders and working on his own to bring the killers to justice.

"Yes, I believe that is the scenario that makes the most sense," Dr. Harper answered, enjoying seeing one of his patient's issues improving. Now if he could just get Aidan to face the other underlying troubles the man had buried under the surface of his thick outer shell. Before he could sign off on him being back to functioning at a level to reenter his job as a Homicide Detective, the man needed to work on the problem of facing the demons that were afflicting him regarding the incident of the shooting and the girl being paralyzed that had first led Aidan to seek his care. That was the ultimate goal, and until they were able to deal with those issues, Aidan would continue to be on leave from the Montgomery County Police Department.

Aidan was thoroughly pleased with Dr. Harpers profiling and behavior analysis of the criminal minds behind these horrific murders plaguing the streets of Rockville, and now with the third crime scene stretching the width of the killing zone, they had to be stopped.

I'm one step closer to getting these bastards! Aidan thought as he processed all the information he had learned from his visit to Dr. Harper.

Then another question popped into Aidan's mind. Since he was already into Dr. Harper for who knows how much his after-hours session was going to cost him, he might as well get every subject that was itching at his mind answered before he left.

"One other thing…" Aidan said, and Dr. Harper leaned back in his chair waiting for Aidan to finish. "You said that Clinical Lycanthropy was a rare condition, yet we are looking at more than one suspect responsible for these murders. Could the killers both really be suffering from the same disease?"

"That's something we won't know until the FBI or this joint task force you mentioned catches the subjects. Normally as you know from your background in law enforcement and the courses you mentioned taking in criminal behavior and forensics, serial killers are typically lone individuals who stick to themselves and perform their unconscionable acts on their victims by themselves. Even in the casebooks where the killer's were actually diagnosed as suffering from Clinical Lycanthropy, the murderers have usually been individuals. However unlikely it is though, there is always the possibility that these people met and found themselves to be like-minded and suffering from these 'transformations', that they developed a pack-mentality and have found comfort in being a part of this suffering together."

Aidan nodded in understanding.

"These casebooks cover some fascinating history from all over the world, many old myths and legends dating back thousands of years. The werewolf had a wide-spread narrative that reached every corner of the earth and influenced many of the fairy tales and fables of those times. During the middle ages, especially in the span of the 15th to the 17th century, Europe fell under the dark shadow of ignorance and superstition. Towns were spread out, many surrounded by dark and unexplored forests, and wolves were considered a terrible scourge of the farmlands and people. Their attacks on the livestock that so many villagers considered essential to their existence caused the creatures to be feared, and exaggerated tales of their influence were spread from town to town.

'Amid these medieval times, many people were accused of being werewolves and they suffered the same persecution and eventual executions that people thought to be witches were exposed to. Obviously it was not as well-known an event as the Salem Witch Trials, but it was certainly as devastating," Dr. Harper explained, leaning back further in his chair. He glanced at his watch and noted the time.

"I'm sorry to be keeping you so late," Aidan apologized, looking at his own watch and seeing it was past seven, the sun having already set for the night.

Dear Lord, let this night pass without any incident! He thought, knowing in his gut that tomorrow morning there would be another crime scene and another victim somewhere in the Montgomery County.

"The time's no problem, I would just be home nursing a scotch by now— alas, it is my one and only vice other than a fine, hand-rolled cigar occasionally," the psychiatrist admitted with a shrug.

Then Dr. Harper straightened his posture a little more so as not to appear to be nodding off into his chair, resuming his half-closed eyed look that meant he was compiling his thoughts and actually listening intently despite the opposite his appearance would normally relay to someone unaccustomed to his habits. Fortunately, Aidan had been seeing the doctor long enough to know to expect this behavior and not be put off by it. Pushing the sleeve of his fine tailored suit over his wrist and hiding the watch from view, Dr. Harper continued his tale.

"The most famous werewolf and lurid werewolf trials in history took place in 1589 in the town of Bedburg, Germany. In this late 16th century time, the town was terrorized by a vicious and diabolical, evil beast who slaughtered the cattle of the townspeople and killed multiple women and children in unspeakable ways. The horrified people of Bedburg believed they were cursed by a bloodthirsty werewolf, a terrible and ravaging monster that victimized them all as it prowled the woods that circled the rural, country village.

'It ended up that a widower and the father of two young children, named Peter Stubbe, a wealthy farmer in the community was leading a double life. The townspeople knew him as a kind and pleasant man, but the truth was that he was a vile, depraved madman who satisfied the blood-lust that he hid under his false facade and only when he donned the skin of a wolf did this black, evil side was revealed.

'For many years, farmers around Bedburg were mystified by the strange deaths of some of their cows. Day after day for many weeks, they would find cattle dead in the pastures, ripped open as if by some savage animal, but this was actually the beginning of Peter Stubbe's unnatural compulsion to mutilate and kill. This insatiable drive would soon escalate into attacks on his neighboring villagers.

'Children began to disappear from their farms and homes. Young women vanished from the paths they traveled daily. Some were found dead, horribly mutilated. Others were never found. The community was thrown into a panic. Hungry wolves were again suspected and the villagers armed themselves against the animals. Some even feared a more devious creature— a werewolf, who could walk among them unsuspected as a man, then transform into a wolf to satisfy its hunger…"

"So Stubbe would put a wolf skin on like a shirt, and he then believed he transformed into a wold?" Aidan interjected, looking to Dr. Harper for clarification.

This is sounding more and more like what could be afflicting us here, but a modern day lunatic with the delusion of being an animal! Could it be possible? Aidan was beginning to think the answer was yes.

"Stubbe would cloak himself with the skin of a wolf when seeking out his victims, and once he was caught, he confessed at the trial that the Devil himself gave him a magic belt of wolf fur at age twelve that, when he put it on, transformed him into "the likeness of a greedy, devouring wolf, strong and mighty, with eyes great and large, which in the night sparkled like brands of fire; a mouth great and wide, with most sharp and cruel teeth; a huge body and mighty paws."

'When he took the belt off, he believed, he returned to his human state. This 'devouring wolf', as he called himself, was responsible for the deaths of thirteen children, two pregnant women and numerous livestock.

'The young women among his victims were sexually assaulted before he tore them apart, while the pregnant women, he ripped the fetuses from their wombs and "ate their hearts panting hot and raw," which he later described as "dainty morsels." Small children were strangled, bludgeoned and throats ripped open with his bare hands. Some were disemboweled and partially eaten, and the lambs and calves were ripped apart and devoured raw."

Dr. Harper stopped to let the details sink in before he continued. Aidan just shook his head, unbelieving that a man could be so depraved. Yet, he thought about the victim's bodies of the scenes he had seen already, and remembered how morbid the third, latest scene in the woods had been from Mack's description. Yes, a person could be so sick and twisted, but unlike back in the sixteenth century, these latest murders were being committed in today's society, and the graphic nature of the mutilation was rivaling that of any serial killer in the modern day world that Aidan had ever heard of.

To make matters worse, there is more than one perpetrator! That's at least two people that could be responsible for the death and destruction he had witnessed lately!

"Anyways," Dr. Harper said, "Perhaps his most fiendish murder, he reserved for his own family. Stubbe had incestuous relationships with his sister and his own daughter, whom he impregnated. He also murdered his son, the firstborn child born to him. Stubbe led the boy into the forest, killed him, then ate his brains."

"How was he caught?" Aidan asked.

"Stubbe thought himself invincible through the power of his magic belt. Yet, it was this belief that ended his reign of terror. When the limbs of several missing people were found in a field, the villagers were further convinced that a ravenous wolf was responsible, and so several hunters set out with their dogs to pursue the predator. The men hunted the creature for days until at last they saw him. But according to the account, they saw and chased down a wolf, not a man. The dogs chased the animal until they had it cornered. The hunters were sure that they were chasing a wolf, but when they came to the spot where the dogs had it cornered, there cowered the man, Peter Stubbe. According to the account of one man who later wrote about the event, George Bore recorded that Stubbe being trapped with no room for escape, Stubbe removed his magic belt and transformed from the wolf to his human form.

'Thought now to be a werewolf, Stubbe was arrested and brought to trial, and it was only under pain of torture on the rack that his confession to all of the heinous crimes came out, including sorcery, his consort with the Devil and the story of the magic belt. Stubbe was found guilty on October 28, 1589, and his execution was as gruesome as any of the crimes of which he was accused: his body was strapped spread-eagle on large wheel; with red-hot pinchers, his executioners pulled his flesh from his bones in ten spots; his arms and legs were broken with a large blade, his head was cut off."

"Jesus," Aidan muttered, closing his eyes and shaking his head slightly to clear the image from his mind. "But, this happened a long time ago, have there been more recent cases where the killer suffered from Clinical Lycanthropy?"

Nodding his head in sad agreement, Dr. Harper sat forward again and placed his long, tented fingers against his chin as he answered Aidan.

"The most recent case I can recall was in 1995. It was the case of Jack Own Spillman III. He raped and sexually mutilated two female children, and one woman, killing them all. He referred to himself as a werewolf to his cellmate, because he loved to stalk his prey, and he said he, "regretted not being able to store his victims in a cave." That was only

I'm surprised I didn't know about these things, then again, they're not exactly local cases that I would have been involved with.

This session has certainly been worth the time and maybe the department will cover Harper's bill when I get them this information, Aidan thought, knowing there was a fat chance in hell that Chief Stone would be pleased with him sharing case files for an active investigation with his psychiatrist, even if it was to be confidential everything they talked about. If Stone or the FBI Agent heading up the joint task force found out he had talked not only to his doctor, but was working with a reporter on the investigation unoficially, he'd be out of a job so fast he'd probably get road-rash on his ass as they threw him out he doors of police headquarters.

"What about the sudden startup of these killings, what could have triggered it?"

"That is also something that won't be able to be determined until the suspects are caught and are able to be studied by professionals to get a grasp on their reasoning and motives," Dr. Harper answered, then pausing for a moment as an idea struck him, he added, "Have you given any thought to what this week is?"

Puzzled as to what the doctor was referring to, Aidan shook his head no, and then Dr. Harper informed him, "Tomorrow night is Halloween!"

"Of course, I completely forgot about what was so special about this week. I should have realized they could be related. Do you think there is a connection?" Aidan asked.

"I think it's a possibility, but like I said, all of my impressions are just conjecture at this point until the authorities apprehend the murderers. Halloween has typically been thought of over the ages as the devil's holiday, but really it's history is deep with religious overtures and connections. However, I think the most important connection tomorrow night might have with these murders is stranger than you might think…"

Now Aidan was definitely sitting forward in his seat, waiting for Dr. Harper to finish his thought.

"On October 31, Peter Stubbe's body along with the bodies of his daughter and mistress, both of whom were convicted of abetting his crimes, were burned at the stake. By directive of the magistrate, a warning to other potential devil-worshipers was put in place for all to see.

'The wheel on which Stubbe was tortured was set high upon a pole from which hung sixteen yard-long strips of wood, representing his sixteen known victims. Atop that was the framed likeness of a wolf, and above on the sharpened point of the pole was placed Peter Stubbe's severed head— that was the final piece of information gleamed from the retelling of the tale of Stubbe's life and death. The officials wanted to make sure that any who did not worship or attend the recognized Catholic Church during this time, could possibly face the same fate that Stubbe's life had taken due to his unbelief in God."

As Dr. Harper finished speaking, Aidan's eyes widened at the revelation that this week had regarding the significance of the holiday.

What horrors would Halloween hold?

Aidan closed his eyes, not wanting to picture what would happen tonight or on Halloween. Tonight was also known as 'Devil's Night', and Aidan knew something wicked was still to come!

This murder spree was far from over!

Chapter 25

Nick sat perched on a tall stool, a whiskey and cola sitting on the long, oak bar counter before him. His fingers were wrapped around the glass, condensation from the ice cubes clinking around the concoction making the glass sweat. This was his second drink since he had gotten into the little bar. Having figured he needed something strong to get his senses from unraveling at how tightly wound they were from everything he had seen and done today.

After they had left SCBI, Aidan had dropped Nick off at his car. Climbing into his rusty Oldsmobile, he quickly turned the A/C on and hit the button to fill the car with warm heat. At first it came out as a cold blast of air not much warmer than the outside temperature, but after a short bit, the heat began to flow. That was much better. Then putting his car into gear, he pulled out of the parking structure in Rockville Town Square and headed off to get his story typed up and entered into Marty.

Nick remembered looking at his watch and seeing that it was already almost four o'clock. He only had an hour to get the story typed up and submitted. It didn't matter if he had the story of a lifetime, Marty was serious about replacing him if he tried to turn in one more article past the deadline. Of course, the skinny, over-stressed Editor-in-Chief who was probably at this minute still sitting in his office at The Informant, smoking one of his unfiltered cigarettes and stressing about some aspect of the paper's constantly shifting economic future. He had been in a great mood once he saw the story Nick had typed up and got in before the end of the work day. His trip to Front Royal, Virginia had been a blessing, adding plenty of material for the article, and the leads that he and Aidan Preston were following were coming along nicely.

And boy was this going to be one hell of a story!

He had the scoop of a lifetime, and this story seemed to be just picking up pace. Who knew, maybe he'd be able to turn this serial killer business into a steeping stone out of the stale, restrictive environment of The Informant, and get involved with a newspaper that provided a journalist with something a little more reputable in the way of recognition, like the Times or Post.

Having just enough time to get the article written up relaying all the information he had gleamed from Aidan regarding the second occurrence of murders at the quarry, the possible cult angle and the crazed animal that could be on the loose or being used by the cult was going to blow his competition out of the water tomorrow morning when people awoke to their newspapers and saw the latest he had to relay to the public.

Oh yes, this was going to be big, and it looked like it had no intention of slowing.

Nick lifted the glass to his lips and let the cool, sweetly strong liquid course down his throat. He felt a slight shudder in his throat as he poured the fiery mixture down into his stomach, the warmth spreading over his body and up into his face as the alcohol hit his gut. With a light smack of his lips he set the drained glass down onto the counter and motioned to the bartender for another. Whiskey and soda, what an invention, he thought. Just the right amount of sugary soda to cut back on the strong, alcoholic taste of the whiskey and provide the consumer with a drink that slid easily down their throats, providing the drinker with all the more reason to keep downing the mix.

As the bartender slid over to him from behind the counter and was about to pour the bottle of low grade whiskey and soda into his glass, his friend and owner of the little pub appeared from the back.

"Hold it Scott, I'll take care of that," the large, imposing form of Bohdan Chaplinski said as he walked up to the bar. The bartender Scott looked to his boss right before he had filled Nick's glass and looked up at Bohdan.

With a shrug he said, "Whatever you say Bo, you're the boss," and set the soda nozzle down and placed the bottle of whiskey on the counter. He then turned and headed over to take care of the other patrons at the far end of the bar.

Bohdan 'Bo' Chaplinski, was an imposing sight to behold even with his tall, solid form bent over and leaning on the counter in front of Nick. When he smiled, Nick could see the two gold teeth that Doug had put in years ago to replace those that had been knocked out in a bar brawl that the thick man tried to break up. Of course, the 6'4"— 250 pounds of bulging muscle that made up the man's thick frame. His neck and shoulders reminded Nick of a raging bull, the veins running underneath his skin, prominent as they intertwined with the muscles of the man's massive body.

Even in college, Bo's had been big into weightlifting, but it wasn't until after they graduated that he had really added bulk to his big truck of a frame. Bo pushed himself off the counter, taking the bottle of cheaper whiskey back to the shelf of bottles behind him and grabbed one from the top shelf. The good stuff! The few times a month that Nick did make his way into Bo's pub, his old friend always broke out the expensive whiskey and gave Nick a few drinks worth.

Hey when a friend wants to doll out the rich stuff on me, I'm not going to stop 'em, he thought, remembering exactly why the old, college buddy really enjoyed seeing him and never charged him when he did drink there. It wasn't like he took advantage of the free booze, since he only stopped in occasionally to 'The Dancing Bear', a funny gimmick that was as much a testament to the large Russian owner as it was to his off-the-wall humor.

Either way, back when Nick was writing up the Local column for The Informant, and Bo was just getting the pub off the ground, Nick had wrote a few reviews extolling the bar as, "a grand environment to socialize, grab a drink or eat some of the best bar food on the East Coast", and that helped the small establishment get off the ground and people to notice it. Of course, Nick always felt like Bo took the debts he believed he owed people seriously, even though he had insisted he hadn't done much.

'The Dancing Bear' was a nice place to go, and even tonight when the crowd was small, only a few people frequenting the homely pub tonight, and Nick took a quick glance around at the other patrons that Bo had. There were two men playing darts over in the corner, a small group of people watching a boxing match on one of the flatscreen TV's that hung in the corner and a a few others sitting on the stools at the bar where a second television was set to the local, CBN Channel 5, that sat on the wall above the bar counter. It was this screen that Nick had been barely watching as he had been nursing his drinks, figuring on having another glass or two and calling it a night until Bo showed up from the back.

"How's it hangin'?" the large Russian asked, his gold teeth sparkling in the light as he smiled and set Nick's refreshed drink in front of him.

Taking the glass, Nick took a sip of the high end whiskey that Bo had mixed in with his cola and let out a sigh as he said, "I'm telling you Bo, if I could afford to drink this stuff every night, then I'd probably die a happy man."

Bo let out a loud, rumbling laugh, the deep roar echoing in his chest and drawing looks from some of the patrons scattered around the bar. "Hahaha, oh Haley, that's why I like you— you know how to appreciate the fine things in life!" Bo said and then finished off with another deep uproar as he slapped his knee and then found his way back to leaning down on the counter, his voice lowering as he whispered, "Oh by the way, remember that broad Tiffany…"

Nick traced through his memories, trying to place a face to the name, then remembering a small, cute black girl that Bo had been hitting on one night when she had come into 'The Dancing Bear' with some friends, said, "Yeah, the college kid from the other week."

This brought a proud, smile to Bo's face as he whipped out a bar napkin with a number scrawled onto it in pen. He slapped the napkin down onto the counter and his smile grew wider. "Well just so happens she was in here earlier with some friends, turns out she's a senior 'bout to graduate from Maryland and she fell for a certain big oaf's charm tonight!"

Nick looked from the napkin to Bo's beaming face and smiled. It was good to see his friend so happy, and even though the image of Bo's massive dimensions next to what he remembered of the skinny, black girl who was no more than 5'2". It was an odd combination, that was for sure, but as long as Bo was happy and it worked out, then Nick was happy for the man.

"Well congratulations! Of course, you're technically robbing the cradle with that young thing— hope she's legal," Nick said with a slight jest.

"Oh no worries there man, she's even old enough to drink, believe me, or else she wouldn't be in my establishment!" Bo said with a serious look crossing his features.

Nick knew that was certainly true. Bo was a firm believer in not allowing underage drinking in his pub— no exceptions! The man may be a big softy when it came to most things in life, but when it came to following the law regarding his place, he stuck to the rules. Picking his glass up, Nick looked at Bo and raised his glass in mock salute.

"I'll drink to that," Nick said, and with a a quick tip of his wrist he downed the drink quickly. As he set the empty glass down on the counter he gasped, the strong and costly whiskey hitting home. "Woooh," he said, his chest on fire and he had the distinct taste of orange and vanilla that hit him hard as his face flushed .

"Haha— that'll teach you to down a glass with Macallan 30 year old Single Malt!" Bo rumbled, highly amused at the look on Nick's face.

"Jesus, I thought it had soda in it!"

"No way in hell I'm cutting Macallan with soda— it's $850 bucks a bottle!"

Nick hit his chest once with his balled fist and coughed. Yeah, the whiskey was good; good and sure as hell would knock someone off their feet if they weren't expecting it. Without a doubt, he hadn't been.

"Well next time, warn me before you go changing what I'm drinking," Nick said, still trying to get the fiery feeling inside him to dissipate. Moreover, he now knew to watch and make sure that when he was drinking a whiskey and soda and Bo was pouring, he better make sure he didn't forget the soda.

Although I appreciate him thinking I was worth a glass of $850 whiskey!

That was certainly something he would have not found himself drinking on his salary from The Informant.

What the hell, he thought, cracking a smile as Bo watched him and mimicked the expression, his gold teeth visible.

"Knew you'd come around— hahaha, shoulda' seen your face!"

Nick just shook his head, and then realized that the television screen above the back counter was just switching from the program that had been droning on in the background to the news.

Damn, it's already 11 o'clock, Nick realized as he watched the Channel 5 News team come onto the display. Looking over at Bo, he gestured towards the flatscreen.

"Hey can you turn it up?"

"Yeah sure, give me a minute to find the remote," Bo said, and began digging around under the counter. After a minute he came back up with a small object in his hand and pointing his massive trunk of an arm at the TV, he added a few notches to the volume coming out of the unit. "Anything in particular you're looking for?"

"I wanted to see if there was anything new on the serial killers," Nick answered.

"Oh yeah, I've been reading your latest pieces. Nice job— scary stuff happening, you don't think about that type of thing happening here in Rockville."

"It is certainly something new, but hey, gives me something to write about other than the latest drivel I've been stuck with. Nobody really cares about the Mayor's wife's shopping sprees," Nick admitted, truly glad that not only The Informant was doing well, its circulation up, and that meant more readers reading his headlines.

Just then, a shift in the news program drew Nick and Bo's eyes to the screen. The nightly anchors had mentioned something about the murders and the action on screen shifted to a correspondent in the field, reporting from a wooded site, where a collection of police cruisers, crime scene vans and a vehicle with the Medical Examiner's logo on the side were all parked at the entrance to a trail that led into the forest. Nick then realized that the footage had been filmed earlier that day, since the sun was still up and visible even under the canopy of trees all around, and then he noticed that the reporter wasn't Hanson but some other young up-and-comer they had.

Why wasn't Hanson on this story? When the hell did this happen?

Questions abuzz in his head, Nick tried to focus on the reporter's story, the words capturing the bottom of the screen let him know that the video had been shot near a trail somewhere in the vicinity of the Appalachian's on the Maryland side. Although, the Appalachian Trail could place this crime scene in one of almost too many possible locations due to the mountain range's size.

"Thanks Ron and Katie…I'm Chris Beckham with Channel 5 News, taking over for Ted Hanson…and I'm bringing you the latest on the murders that are sweeping across our Montgomery County. Earlier today, police were informed that the body of a local man had been discovered torn to pieces. The victim was first discovered missing by his friends while they were camping out in the woods here in the Appalachian Mountains. Police are currently looking into the two witnesses stories, believing their presence in the forest could be related to a rash of illegal poaching that has been thought to be occurring in the area according to a source with the Park Rangers.

'At this time, their reason for being at this spot unconfirmed, police are still considering the two friends of the victim as possible suspects. According to one of the friends who we were able to speak with briefly, the victim had been identified as Jack Morgan, a sales rep for Myncroft Pharmaceuticals.

Mr. Morgan had disappeared at some point when the group had first arrived and was setting up their base camp. A search for Mr. Morgan was begun shortly after his disappearance was noted, but due to the late hour and lack of light, the search was never completed until his mutilated remains were found the next day.

'The pathologist on the scene believes they were able to rule out the possibility of this attack being committed by a black bear, which are known to inhabit the area, but have not been linked to any human deaths in recent years. If this death is ruled as an actual homicide, this would be the sixth possible murder to be linked to the serial killer that has been plaguing the area over the last week. At first the killings seemed to be centered in Rockville only, but now with this sixth death, the radius of the assailant's reach has now been enlarged to encompass all of Montgomery County. We will continue to bring you all the latest on this shocking story as details continue to emerge. Once again, I'm Chris Beckham, Channel 5 news…Ron…" the reporter said, signing off and the camera switched back to a view of the CBN studio.

"Thanks Chris…" the news anchor began to say, but by then Nick had turned his attention away from the TV and saw Bo staring at the screen.

The big man seemed to be shocked by the latest news, and to tell the truth, so was Nick. He couldn't believe he hadn't heard from any of his sources about this latest murder. He would have to give Aidan a call and see what he could learn. As he glanced around the room, he noticed that the pub had grown quiet, all eyes glued to the TV as the pre-filmed clip had aired and the new Channel 5 correspondent filled people in. In addition, he had done more than just alert the general public to the latest details, he had missed out on his chance to have any information in on the latest killing so that the story wouldn't run in the morning paper. Marty was going to be pissed.

How the hell could I have missed that?

Nick was racking his brain, trying to think of what he needed to do, but regrettably he realized how late it actually was and that he had been drinking and his writing skills would probably be influenced by the alcohol. No, it was better to not dwell on the story until he had a chance to sober up some.

Ted Hanson was drunk. His impromptu meeting with Barry Whitfield and that bitch Emily Erickson had gone about as well as he had expected after he blew up on Whitfield's goddamn secretary outside his office and the two higher-ups had heard his ranting. Now he was suspended, them having replaced him with another, worthless reporter to cover the story he had broke. These murders should have been his big break that would take him from a lowly TV correspondent to a respected desk job as a Channel 5 News anchor!

How could that bitch have done this to me? I was putting CBN on the map with these murders! That story is mine— and they just suspend me, put that useless, brown-nosed Kevin Brant on my exclusive! How dare they!

As he had already been drinking down at Jonathon's Bar and Grille when that cunt of a bartender cut him off. Like she knew when he had enough— he had just gotten started. Unfortunately, the liquor store was closed or else he could have just grabbed a bottle there and gone home to his apartment to stew in his anger, drinking away the painful remembrance of the meeting he had in Barry Whitfield's office. Now though, with the liquor store closed and the bars open, Ted decided to be out in the public eye.

After all, my viewers deserve to see me walking their streets, them mere mortals compared to what I am going to become!

His hazy mind struggling to picture his dreams of sitting behind that grand desk, anchor of CBN nightly news with that gorgeous co-anchor Katie Collins at his side. He could picture it now. Yes, that is where he was headed. This suspension was just a small detour in his way, a wall he had to climb to get closer towards his final goal. Whitfield would realize how important he was to the network. That much he knew for certain. No matter how many Emily Erickson's stood in his way, he'd make it known that benching him was a mistake.

Reaching the door to a small pub he had barely noticed as he stormed down the street, his hands stuffed into his coat pockets, his face braced against the wind, he pulled on the handle and stepped into the bar, hoping he wouldn't have the same issue he had at the last place to interfere with his mission of getting wasted. He didn't want to remember this day for as long as he lived, and he knew exactly how to accomplish that. The key was alcohol!

As he entered the small pub, a place he had never bothered noticing or having ever frequented, he remembered the sign above the entrance saying it was called The Dancing Bear. That was a ridiculous name for a bar. Who the hell would name a place after some asinine act in a second-rate traveling circus?

With his mind still on the absurdity the owner's had named the place, he made his way through the almost empty bar, looking around to see if there was a chance there could be any women that didn't look half bad and might make the night a little more interesting. That's what he needed— more alcohol and a lady to replace the other memories of this day.

The bar was little more than a main room decorated in shades of red and black, with tables laid out around the floor, and a few booths sitting against the far corner. The tables and bar stools were all some hue of red, while the oak counter and floor were wood. There were black accents, and the theme seemed to not be as bad as the name of the place entailed. Well at least it doesn't look like the inside of a big-top carnival tent, Ted thought as he stepped up to the bar. He noticed the television behind the counter was on Channel 5, and the anger that he had been experiencing all day at his workplace started to rise in his body. He felt like he should order a cheap bottle of beer just so he could throw it at the television, ending its mocking existence.

A drunken smile appeared on his face as he thought of the amusing idea. Then he thought of the downside. He'd be out of this place and in the cold again before being able to add to the number of alcoholic drinks he had consumed in the last few hours. That was unacceptable, so that meant smashing the TV was out. A slight wave of disappointment washed over him as he sat down on one of the many unoccupied bar stools, having to grab onto the counter to avoid from falling. He had almost missed the chair! Maybe he was drunker than he thought.

Oh well, I'm here now so I might as well get my drink on!

The bartender, a young man with styled blonde hair that was held up with too much gel that it looked wet still even after what Ted assumed was a full day of work. Then again, it was a bar so maybe the guy had just gotten in to work. Somehow Ted doubted it, and soon found himself annoyed at the bartender just because of the way he did his hair. That fashionable hairdo, with his glob of styling gel and possible hairspray as well was truly irritating.

What the hell is wrong with people that they can't just have a regular haircut anymore?

Just then, as if to validate his theory on 'normal' hair styles, Ted glanced around the room, taking in the few other customers who were scattered about and checked out their heads of hair one by one. As his eyes traveled to the furthest end of the counter, he realized of all people to run into, of all nights for it to happen, that the 'news-hound' who worked for that ratty excuse of a paper, The Informant, was actually sitting here talking to one of the guys working there.

Of all the luck! Nick Haley is here on the same night I get suspended from the story we're both chasing! And, look at the size of that gargantuan he's talking to. He's an real life ogre!

Ted just stared, trying to figure out what to do, the anger continuing to build up as he watched Nick Haley just sitting around, joking and having a good time while he was miserable and halfway on the road to blacking out and forgetting this day ever happened.

Yes, that's what I need!

Turning to the younger man with the blonde locks of hair on his head, he ordered a drink, careful to not slur his words for fear of being denied service once again.

"Give me a scotch on the rocks…a double," he demanded and while the bartender just nodded and began fixing his order, he turned back in the direction of Nick and the juiced up bartender talking to him from the other side of the counter.

They seemed to be acquaintances, most likely good friends the way they were carrying on, little bits of their conversation drifting down the bar and Ted was able to pick up the occasional word or phrase. Even though there was an old-fashioned jukebox set in a far corner of the bar, an old classic from the heyday of rock and roll, Ted believed it was ZZ Top or Led Zeppelin— one of those ridiculous groups that were once referred to as 'hair bands', the song was playing loudly from the old machine, but he was still able to hear what the journalist was saying.

Once the bartender set his order down on the counter top within reach, Ted snatched it up and downed half the glass before setting it back down hard.

Damn it, did Nick just say something about the serial killer?

Ted strained his ears, filtering out the song playing and echoing around the enclosed space of the pub as best he could, and tried to hear a little more of the conversation Haley was having.

Damn wannabe reporter, he's nothing but a stain on the bottom of my shoe! I'll teach him what real reporting is! Ted thought, then scooping his half drank scotch up into his hand, he almost fell getting off his barstool, and stumbled along towards the journalist.

Yeah, I'll show him, then taking another big gulp of his drink, his erratic movements sloshing some of the liquid out of the glass as he moved closer to the end, he reached Haley with his back turned to him. *It was like he wouldn't even recognize Ted was there!* Then Ted's seemingly cotton-filled, fuzzy recollection reminded him that the man just hadn't noticed his arrival in the pub, but that just set off a while new set of problems for the drunken soul. *Well he should have noticed me enter…everybody should have noticed my arrival, I'm on TV…I'm a goddamn celebrity!*

With those last words echoing in his head, Ted reached out and with his free hand, shoved Nick's shoulder.

"Hey— I wanna talks to yous!"

Chapter 27

Nick felt the presence approaching when whoever it was had gotten right up behind him, but the reporter didn't bother turning around, assuming it was just another wandering patron who had strolled into Bo's establishment for a night cap or two. After all, that's why he was there. However, Nick realized his mistake when he felt the hard shove on his shoulder, and heard the slurred words of a drunken idiot assaulting him.

Turning around quickly on his stool he realized it was none other than the infamous Ted Hanson in the flesh. And from the looks of it, he was well worse for wear, the smell of heavy drinking just wafting off the man's skin and breath. Nick knew he hadn't seen the TV correspondent in the bar earlier, and even though he had a half-filled glass in his shaking hand, he knew it had to be new, Hanson having had to just arrived at The Dancing Bear.

Jesus, the man's wasted off his ass! Nick voiced silently to himself, watching the red-faced reporter struggling to stand as he accosted Nick verbally, his words coming out half incoherent as he swayed back and forth. Nick glanced over at Bo who had risen off the counter, his towering figure glaring at the drunken fool.

"You know this prick?" the large Russian asked, ready it seemed to Nick, to grab Hanson up by the scruff of his neck and haul him outside. Knowing Bo, he probably would too. Deciding to try and prevent any issues from arising from the drunk reporter's appearance, Nick looked at Bo and put a hand on the man's steel-like bicep and shook his head. "No, I know this guy, just give me a minute with him before you go trying to throw him out to the curb," Nick pleaded, watching the infuriated reporter continue to shift back and forth on his wobbly legs, and finally the man reached out and steadied himself by grabbing onto the polished counter top of the bar.

Well here goes nothing, Nick hoped, knowing full well that if he couldn't talk some sense into Ted and calm him down, that Bo would.

And then Ted would most likely be in worse shape than he started.

After dealing with Hanson, and being able to prevent a fight from breaking out with the drunken fool, Nick had offered to buy the guy a drink, but the offer was refused. Even though he had calmed down some, he was still hot-headed and had too much alcohol in his system. Nick would have liked to stay in The Dancing Bear, and watch the events fold out as when he had left, Ted was attempting to get Bo to supply his loaded body with another drink, but Bo seemed pretty stuck on his answer of 'No'. Moreover that just infuriated the reporter even more, and seeing that it was almost midnight, Nick decided he had better call it a night himself.

I've got a lot to do tomorrow to follow up on this new murder! Might as well head home and get some sleep while I still can…

That's when he was saying goodbye to Bo and doing his usual routine of offering to pay for his drinks, which Bo with a firm hand on his shoulder, the massive arm dwarfing Nick easily, refused whole-heartedly. He gave his usual speech of Nick being too good a friend to the old Russian that he wouldn't dare take his money. Shaking his head in defeat, Nick returned his wallet to his back pocket, then thinking better of it, pulled it out and removed a twenty dollar bill from the small fold of money he kept on him at all times.

"You better make sure he takes a cab home," Nick said, motioning with his chin towards the slouched form of Ted Hanson, who had found his way over to the jukebox after Bo warned him, "he needed to go chill out, and lose some of his steam".

"Yeah," Bo agreed. "He probably shouldn't be driving. It's bad enough he can hardly walk. But, then again it's a Hunter's Moon, it draws out all the crazies."

Nick's attention snapped back to Bo who was setting the twenty dollar bill under the cash register where he could get it out when the time came to pay the cab driver. He had already called the local cab company and they told him it would be around twenty minutes, which Bo had told Nick meant more like an hour with that company.

"Wait what did you just say?"

"Me? What…I mentioned how the moon draws out all the crazies. You know, it's almost a full moon. That's when the lunatics all seem to come crawling out and makes my life here at the pub pretty interesting— never a dull moment," Bo answered.

"Yes I got that, but what did you call the moon?"

"It's the end of October, the full moon is called the Hunter's Moon— haven't you ever heard it called that before?"

Nick thought about it for a moment then shook his head. He ran his hand through his tangled, shoulder-length hair, using his fingers as a comb as he did so.

Finally he replied, "No, I've never heard it called that. I know last month was the Harvest Moon. I'm pretty sure everybody's heard it called that, but no, I've never heard October's referred to as the Harvest Moon. I guess I didn't even think about all the other months having a name for the full moon."

"Yeah they each do. The names are all based on old Native American names, and have to do with what each month meant to them or what they did during that month. Obviously, the Harvest Moon came out and they knew it was time to harvest all their crops."

"Why was it called the Hunter's Moon exactly?"

"Lemme see, it's been quite a few years since we were in college, but as far as I can recall, they called it the Hunter's Moon because after the fields have been reaped for the harvest, the leaves begin to fall and the deer are fat and ready for eating. Hunters can ride easily over the fields' now open space, and the fox and other animals are more easily spotted. Back in medieval times they called the moon in October the Blood Moon, I think the pagans still call it that as well, but mostly it's known in the main cultures as the Hunter's Moon."

Nick couldn't believe his ears, and his mind was spinning at what felt like a hundred miles an hour. He quickly wished Bo a goodnight and headed out the door to get home. He had the basis of his new article on the tip of his tongue and he didn't want to forget any of it before he got to his ancient Oldsmobile and got home. However, even though he wasn't nearly as drunk as Ted Hanson had been, with the alcohol in his system he was worried that by the time he got the car's engine warmed up enough to get home, that he'd have forgotten the train of thought he had been working out in his head.

It was the perfect tie in to everything he and Detective Preston had uncovered so far, and it would make a great addition to the new piece he had to write, really tying the articles main points and theories up nicely, as if they were a present and had been finished off wrapped with a bow. Yes, the moon angle was definitely the right direction to go, and he could just picture the article in his mind's eye as he stood before his car, struggling to find his keys and get out of the freezing night air and away from the chilling breeze that was whipping past him as he tucked his head into his chest, hoping the wind would die down.

Then his hand closed over the ring of keys in his pocket and before he knew it, he was in well-worn driver's seat of his Oldsmobile, digging through his work bag for his notebook to jot down a few reminders before he set off for him.

As he jotted the ideas down, he realized how well they did fit into his and Aidan's theory about the murders. He had been wondering what relationship the time of year could have to the upstart of the killings, and now he thought he had it! It was the moons— the names they were given represented their usefulness as a reminder of the special time of the year and what could be accomplished then. As he pictured the various pieces fitting into place, he knew he was right about the correlation between the time of the year that October seemed to hold for these murderers attacking the citizens of the county he called home.

I can't believe I didn't see this sooner!

It was all about the moon.

He remembered that at first, they weren't sure why these events had begun when they did, the psychotic element of these serial killer's minds seeming a mystery to all, but thanks to Bo's offhand reference to the month's name, Nick could suddenly see things much clearer. He knew the moon's bright, ghostly orb held a powerful sway over various things on the planet. It was because of the moon that we had tides in the ocean, and thanks to that constantly changing pull, life existed. He knew that various researchers over the years had argued about the moon's actual role in life on the planet and how it affects things, many half-baked theories and possible reactions being thrown about as people strive to understand exactly what power that Earth's satellite controlled as it orbited the planet.

The word lunatic actually came from the association that the moon played on people's minds. Even though it was a widely argued theory, there seemed to be some truth to the moon having some power over the people that inhabited the Earth. He remembered the argument one scientist had made regarding the human body's reception to the forces of that galactic body comprised of dirt and ancient craters. While people would probably continue to argue the subject endlessly for years to come, Nick believed the idea held some relevance.

After all, it was a well-known fact that the moon controlled the tides of the ocean, that because the human body contained 75% of precious water, that it only made sense to believe the moon held some power over humans as well. After all, why wouldn't it? It was all beginning to make sense.

The theory in research calls the occurrence the lunar effect, and sitting there in the car as he waited for the engine to warm up, Nick used his phone to pull up some information online regarding the effect so he could make sure his notes were as accurate as possible. Sitting there quietly, his parked car in the small, lot across the street from The Dancing Bear, his notebook on his lap and his cell phone in hand, Nick began to read up on the interesting pseudo-scientific theories regarding the moon and life on the planet Earth.

As he read, he became enthralled in the ideas that encircled the moon and realized that common held beliefs in science may become classified as pseudoscience when they are not able to be readily defined by certain scientific measures. Without the validation of supporting evidence by submitting the claim or belief to the scientific method, these theories because they cannot be tested or confirmed possibly because they are not fully understood or there is no current test or technology to authenticate them, the theories are refuted and generally placed into the category of pseudoscience.

This pseudoscientific theory of the lunar effect is widely spread through many aspects of life including sociology, psychology and physiology, suggesting that there is a correlation between specific stages of the Earth's lunar cycle and deviant behavior in human beings. Every person's biological makeup being different, each person has a varying degree to which these effects can affect them.

The exact origins of this theory are ambiguous historically, because paleolithic moon artifacts from many cultures predate written history. This belief has been around for many centuries. The term lunacy itself is derived from Luna, 'the Moon' in Latin. The connection between the words lunar and lunatic can also be demonstrated in other languages, such as in Welsh, where these two words are lloer and lloerig.

Nick realized that there were a few articles on the subject, and then noticed a few that links to pages regarding other sources of literature on the moon's effects on the plants, animals and inanimate objects of the Earth. That's when he saw one link regarding the full moon and it's relation to werewolves.

Werewolves huh? Nick mused as he continued studying his phone's screen with a slight smile forming on his lips. Now there's a beasty to be worried about roaming the darkness, oooh! Little did he know that Aidan had already been down this road with his psychiatrist and reached a similar conclusion.

He continued to look around the various websites, his eyes quickly scanning the pages as he worked his way through each one. He saw studies on the moon and epilepsy, the moon and it equated to the number of police arrests and hospitalizations in the country. It seemed that the studies he was scanning and the information he was quickly digesting into his brain for later retrieval showed that there was a larger number of arrests and admissions during the phase when the moon was full, and it wasn't just a localized event.

Because these studies showed data collected from all over the world over various yeas, he knew that pseudoscience or not, there was probably a underlying truth to the theory, whether it could be proved or not.

There were however, like all studied events, the opposite found by other researchers and analysis of data, but that was to be expected. Whenever there were so many scientists and researchers testing the same idea but using different groups of variables, the results would be declared the opposite of other's findings. Such was the way of science, and Nick knew there would probably be an endless debate ranging for as long as people were alive on the lunar effect. All that mattered was there was some connection to the serial killers, and Nick believed there was.

The Hunter's Moon had lived up to its name this October, people being tracked down and murdered on the streets and in the woods that made up the geographical makeup of Maryland.

Yes the Hunter's Moon had been affected and just like the pagan's believed, the Blood Moon was truly floating high above, watching from its heavenly place in the sky, and the streets were running red with the blood of innocents.

What is going on around here— who are these bastards?

Just then Nick felt a strange, overwhelming feeling come over, like a dark, cold shadow had descended upon him. He tried to shake the feeling, assuming it was just the alcohol and cold of the October night getting to him, but for some reason that didn't seem right. It was something else, something he couldn't place his finger on at the moment.

What is it?

Why do I feel like something is wrong?

Nick looked up from his phone and studied the vacant street. Gone were the crowds and multiple vehicles that passed through the Town Center all day long, replaced by an eerie quiet that was only broken up by the occasional car speeding past the deserted parking lot. While there were a few other cars in the lot, there were no other people, and that feeling of loneliness was what Nick credited with his sense of unease.

As his eyes continued to scan the darkness around him, testing the A/C on his car to see if it was warm enough to be turned on high and get him home in some comfort, he spotted a group of men meld from the edge of darkness down the street and walk down the sidewalk on the other side of the street. The appeared to be headed for Bo's place.

Nick studied the group, finding his eyes drawn to their curious appearance in this weather. With winter almost upon them, Nick expected at least one of the the four men to be wearing a coat, but instead they all seemed to be wearing various shades of dark clothing. They reminded Nick of a biker gang, the way they traveled together seemed to just look right for this group, except they weren't clad in leathers and bandannas. Well, at least most of them weren't.

A car appeared down the road, turning onto the street at the intersection up a ways and the headlights blinded Nick. Covering his eyes from the blaring illumination, once the car had gone past, he noticed the group of three white males and one black individual had vanished from sight. He strained his neck to look down the various streets he could see from his position, but there was no luck— they were gone. Nick couldn't seem to shake the strange feeling he was stuck with, but by now the engine was warmed up and putting his Oldsmobile into drive, he pulled out of the parking space and onto the street.

Looking at the illuminated display on his dash, he saw it was a quarter to midnight. He really needed to get home. Adding a little more weight to the gas pedal, the Oldsmobile sped down the street as Nick made his way home. The entire drive to his apartment, he couldn't shake the feeling that something was wrong.

That something bad had happened.

But what?

Was it just his nerves? That had to be it. But the feeling didn't go away.

Aidan sat in his bed, trying to unwind and go over everything he had learned with Nick Haley at the SCBI campus earlier and while he was with Dr. Harper. It was a lot to process and Aidan felt the constant mental fatigue of working a case after so many months of being on administrative leave to be exhausting. Not to mention his chest and shoulder were beginning to flare up and bother him.

He wasn't sure if it was a result of the stress he was under or if he had done something to antagonize the old wound, but when he had arrived home for the night, he found himself going straight for his dresser drawer and the prescription bottle he kept hidden inside.

Although he had a valid prescription for the pain killers, he still felt guilty about taking them. He figured it was due to him knowing that he was still dependent on them and that when he went back to active duty he would have to be off them completely to clear the medical review and be allowed back to work. However, as of right now, he couldn't seem to shake his reliance from the strong narcotic.

Thinking back to a little over a month ago when Aidan had realized he had become addicted to the opiate-based pain killer, he had talked to Dr. Harper who suggested that until his life improved in quality and he worked on his other problems that he would continue to have an issue with his control over the little pill that both his mind and body craved at times.

That was the reason he had gone out to the seclusion of the cabin, he wanted to get away from the problems he was facing in his life and hopefully give himself the strength to quit his new habit before it became to severe. At first, his problem had seemed like it was an easy fix. All he had to do was get out of town for a week or so, away from the job suspension, the recurring nightmare and give himself the isolation from society he would need to quit the addiction of the prescription pills cold turkey. At least that had been the idea. During the first part of the week he was able to ignore the craving his body had for the little pill, telling himself he was strong enough to not be dependent on the pain killers, and that he could go a week without having to take them.

Of course that was how his vacation to the secluded cabin in the woods off one point in the Appalachian Mountains. He had attempted to pass the days of the week, clearing his head and doing things he hadn't done since he was younger. Being out in the great outdoors had been a wonderful experience when he was younger and his father had him join the Boy Scouts of America to experience the true beauty of the country's wilderness.

Trying to recapture those old memories, Aidan had rented a canoe the first day he was on the lake, and he spent a few hours of the morning on the pristine body of water, attempting to fish and hopefully catch his dinner. When he hadn't caught anything to go towards his nightly meal, Aidan just assumed it was for the best since he couldn't really remember how to clean and gut a fish to prepare it for dinner even if he had caught one.

That was the first day and it passed without incident. He was able to sleep for a few hours until the dream woke him up again in the middle of the night, and his chest was aching right where he had a freshly healed scar directly under his collarbone. Whenever he moved around or thought about the site of his bullet wound, his body was wracked with guilt and the feeling of helplessness, not to mention the phantom pain that seemed to shoot through his upper torso and neck whenever he moved his shoulder too much.

He had spent the day in a canoe, paddling with his arms as the craft had glided across the smooth, peaceful surface of Lake Needwood, and now he was paying for him overdoing it.

Having barely just finished the hospital-sanctioned physical therapy, he had overworked his muscles and the recovering wound site, and now he was in incredible pain as he tried to work the stiffness out of his joints early that morning. The sun hadn't even come up yet and he was sitting up in bed that first night in the cabin just like he was now, except now he was in the safety of his own home and he wasn't attempting to go off the pain killers without the effort of weening the drug out of his system. He had learned the hard way about how painful the withdrawals could be by trying to just up and quit from those days camping out.

After he had been up all the rest of the night, his shoulder causing major discomfort, Aidan had begun questioning his decision to come up to the cabin without having refilled his medication. He thought that by secluding himself and working on removing the stress of everything going on back in Montgomery County, that he could avoid having to get the new prescription filled, but soon realized how badly a mistake that had been. He was able to get through one more day before the withdrawal symptoms started, progressing worse and worse until Aidan couldn't take the pain anymore. It was felt like as the drugs left his system, they magnified the discomfort he was feeling where the pale, ugly scar ran along on his chest and the pain he felt in that part of his body.

Battling the constant night sweats and chills that seemed to ache throughout all hours of the day, and already having issues being able to sleep throughout the night, Aidan lasted three days before the nausea, aches and cold sweats finally got to him. He had driven into the nearest town, a forty-five minute drive from the secluded cabin and had his prescription refilled at the local pharmacy. Remembering how bad he felt that he had failed being able to will himself off the pain killers, telling himself he was weak and needed help before the problem grew any larger, Aidan had finished out the week in a sour mood with the help of the narcotics.

Picturing how sick he had been and his actions the moment the pharmacist gave him his refill, Aidan shook his head in disgust. As soon as the man had finished filling the bottle, Aidan took the container from him and popped two of the pills into his mouth, not bothering to get a drink to wash them down so that they could start working on getting into his system as fast as possible. He could recall the sad look in the pharmacist's eyes, probably from witnessing another soul lost to the addiction of the powerful drug. Yet, Aidan kept telling himself that it was okay because he was legally prescribed it by his doctor.

The only only problem was that instead of taking less and less as time went on and his chest wound healed from where he had been shot, instead of weening himself off the pills slowly, he found himself taking more and more. His tolerance had increased and he now needed more milligrams of the narcotic for it to get him to the same pain-free state as before.

It wasn't until about a month ago that with the help of Dr. Harper and their continued sessions that Aidan was able to tell the psychiatrist about his addiction. Harper, who had experience treating various patients for all sorts of dependency issues was able to help Aidan get back on track and work hard on getting off the evil pills. Through a detox program and self-help exercises, Aidan was able to start the process he should have been already working on over the last few months of getting off the pain killers. Nowadays, he seemed to be only taking the pills whenever the 'pain' seemed to get too noticeable and interfered with how he was doing through the day. Eventually he'd be off the pills and he knew that that day was coming up.

Before long, he had to go before the Montgomery County Medical Board to see if he was mentally and physically ready to go back to active duty.

The first thing he needed though was Dr. Harpers referral saying he was ready, and until he got to the root of the nightmares he was having, and kicked the habit of relying on the pain killers, Aidan wouldn't be able to go to the Board. And lately, it seemed like with him following the leads and interfering with the investigation that the joint task force was doing regarding figuring out and stopping the serial killers from murdering people around the county, he might not even have a chance to go before the Board if Chief Stone brought him up on charges of insubordination and hindering an active police investigation if he didn't play it safe and watch how noticeably involved he got in the case. That's where his inside help came into play.

Having Mack Jones on the task force made it easy to keep tabs on the investigation from the perspective of the FBI and the local police departments as the worked together on profiling and capturing the perpetrators. Then of course there was also Detective Andrea Wilkes. Just thinking about her made Aidan suddenly restless. Here she was, a woman he had worked with for a few years, a woman who up until recently hadn't shown too much interest in a relationship other than the professional one they shared working Homicide for the Montgomery County police. Now, here they were with him coming over to her house to check up on her, and then them making plans to get dinner together tomorrow night!

Aidan wondered if he was making the right decision. It was a tough choice to pursue a relationship with someone in the workplace, plus it wasn't exactly like she didn't come with a little baggage.

Aidan had never been married before and other than in college, he had never had a serious relationship with a woman. Andrea on the other hand, had not only been married for years and then divorced, but she had two teenage children as well. Thinking about the pros and cons of chasing a relationship with the woman he felt so attracted to, there did seem to be more issues that Aidan wasn't sure how they would figure in to the equation.

Could he and Andrea actually make a go of a relationship and have it work? The idea did seem to awaken some desire he had had buried deep inside him, where he kept himself sealed off from letting a woman get too close to his heart. When it came to relationships, Aidan hated to admit it, but he was afraid he might be a hopeless romantic who believed there was someone out there in the world that was perfect for everyone else.

Was Andrea Wilkes worth stepping into the unknown for, pushing all his worries to the side and just jumping off the ledge to fall head first into a relationship with a woman he felt so attracted to? Aidan thought about the questions racing through his mind as he sat on his bed, the sheets across his lap, and his eyes wandering around the room carelessly as he pondered everything.

Yes, the answer is yes, he told himself over and over.

Detective Andrea Wilkes— just the thought of the beautiful brunette with the tough no-nonsense police attitude that made her perfect as a partner, and the fun-loving, dedicated side that could make her a partner of a different kind.

Aidan thought about and knew his answer.

Yes, a personal relationship with Andrea was worth all the risks.

Chapter 28

Stepping away from the jukebox after selecting an old favorite of his, Michael Jackson's 'Thriller', Ted Hanson fell back into one of the empty booths and rested his tired legs. His head was swimming and his vision couldn't help but make the room appear to be spinning slowly. So much for drinking until he couldn't remember, he thought as he sat there taking a sip of the water the massive owner of the place Bo had brought him, wishing the giant had brought him some coffee instead of the tap water.

Tap water— what did he look like, a dog?

Ted tried to think of something else for fear of getting the owner riled up enough to kick him out into the cold until his taxi got there. At least he had a ride on its way, and of all things to come about today, Nick Haley, his nemesis on the serial killer story, was paying for it!

How do you like that, he pondered as he sat there, holding his head between his hands and praying he still had some Excedrin Migraine at home in his medicine cabinet. Just then, he heard the light chime barely noticeable through the loud music blaring from the jukebox of the outside door opening. As he looked up, he watched a new group of people enter the pub. At least it's starting to get more lively, he thought watching the group walk in, their demeanor seeming so serious as they took a booth across from him and sat. He watched two of the four pick up the bar menus and study them while the most stand out of the gang used one arm to motion the bartender.

The blonde-haired bartender with the wet looking hair headed over to the booth and began taking their orders. Ted watched as they all ordered an expensive round of shots and told the bartender to keep them coming.

What the hell did these guys do that they could afford to be drinking shots of aged whiskey like they cost nothing?

They didn't look like much to Ted, who had hung out with some of the wealthiest people in the Tri-State area using his public celebrity from being on TV to occasionally get himself invited to their parties or whenever they had large charity events. Those were his favorite, since it was more about the who's who of the Washington Metropolitan and how well-dressed they could get than the actual cause they were supposedly gathering for. It was all about dressing to impress their fellow socialites and the gawking at trophy wives and girlfriends who were garbed in rich fabrics and designer labels, yes, those were the society types who had money to order the most expensive beverage on the menu and drink to excess.

However, this group didn't look like that. They didn't act like that either. They were all wearing cheap clothes, nothing with a name brand designer that Ted could distinguish, and their manners as they sat around finishing off trays of shots faster than the blonde bartender could bring them were despicable. They appeared to look like those wandering bums who lived off their wealthy parent's trust funds, dressing down just to rebel against their families, and never accomplishing anything for themselves.

That must be it, Ted thought as he watched another tray of refills brought over to their table. They were trust fund babies, even though they all appeared to be older than the typical, losers who traveled around wasting their youth, never having to work for anything in their life, their every wish and desire just handed to them. The oldest of the four, the man that the group seemed to be centered around was dressed in a black t-shirt with a gold chain hanging around his neck. He had a pair of distressed jeans fraying in spots, and a heavily scuffed pair of steel toed work boots all appearing as if they were painted onto his well-toned, fit body. Ted couldn't see his eyes since he was wearing a pair of expensive sunglasses which Ted thought was odd.

Why do people think they look cool wearing sunglasses indoors? Ted wondered as he continued studying the man in the other booth.

The leader as Ted came to think of him from the way the others around him acted towards him, was rugged-looking and obviously athletic. His jaw was square, his nose straight, his lips thin and surrounded by a dark stubble as if he just didn't see the need in shaving everyday. Long, thick dark-brown hair ran down to his shoulders, framing his strong facial features even more. He reminded Ted of one of those models in a magazine advertisement for some manly cologne. He seemed to embody an appeal that was attained from just existing, like he didn't have to put any effort into his looks or being the dark, secretive leader of a group of ruffians—he just was.

"What you looking at boy?" one of the others in the booth growled, and Ted turned to glance at the owner of the deep voice that had called him out.

Ted didn't know what to say. His head was still swimming from the alcohol and the man suddenly seemed to just dismiss him as quickly as he had brought attention to Ted's actions.

"Freakin' queer!" deep voice said, and Ted felt a flash of anger at the mongrel who was obviously still watching him.

The first word that came to Ted's mind was 'mutt'. That's what the gruff man who seemed to be trying to instigate a fight reminded Ted of a mutt.

He was short and built, in fact all the members of the group seemed to be in incredible shape, making Ted self-conscious of his own looks. But, having to remind himself that he was a local celebrity and that that it wasn't like he was fat or anything, he just didn't have the large muscles with the defined cuts and 5% body fat content that these fellows had. He was Ted Hanson after all! I am somebody around here—this is my city! He took a quick glance at the ruffian and tried to dismiss him from mind, but he continued to stare at the booths odd occupants.

'Deep voice' was back to his own table's conversation and at one point he heard someone call him by name. So the mutt was named Fillin? What the hell kind of name was Fillin? Ted wondered if it was a nickname, or if the man's poor mother had just wanted to give the bastard something she could call him when she yelled and smacked him around as he grew up. This brought a drunken smile to Ted's face. As he sat there, his attention occasionally drifting back to the table with the four strangers at it, he watched the one black guy that was part of the group using a long finger nail to pick at something in his stained teeth.

There always has to be one, Ted thought, shaking his head back and forth sloppily. Taking a sip from his water glass, he studied the last two tough guys. The black guy had dread locks that went down half way to his waist and wore the only outfit that seemed to Ted like it should be their official uniform for such an unsavory bunch of hoodlums. He had a leather vest on, with a shirt underneath that looked almost like it was composted of millions of tiny metal links, like a chain-mail shirt. He had a pair of leather pants on, with a dark red bandanna tied around his neck and another around his wrist.

The last of the group was also the biggest. He appeared a good head taller than the others, and his wide chest and big arms looked like he could bench press Ted's leased BMW. He always believed that being successful was all about acting the part, and that meant looking like you belonged at those charity events and parties with those white collars and the filthy rich. In fact, he actually rented his beautiful house, not bothering to correct anyone who believed he actually owned the three bedroom, modern styled Tudor in Potomac, the same with his car. "Dress for Success", was a slogan he remembered hearing when he was young, and he applied that to his life now.

Suddenly he realized that all the alcohol and water he had downed was going right through him. His bladder felt like it was going to burst and he stumbled up from his seat and headed for the restrooms at the back of the pub. Unfortunately he had to pass right by the table of savages to get there. As he did, his eyes were busy watching the group's passionate discussion and he missed his footing due to his alcohol-induced balance issues.

Before he knew it he was falling, reaching out wildly to try and stop his fall. As he hit the ground, Ted's hand had smacked into the back of the man they called Fillin. He was in the middle of tossing back a shot when the sudden nudge caused him to smack the shot glass into his chin, spilling the whiskey down the front of him. The man jumped up with a uproar as Ted climbed to his feet.

"Sorry…my fault…" he muttered, his words slurring even worse as his dizziness from the tumble caused his world to spin even worse than before.

Fillin was up out of his seat and grabbed the back of Ted's sport coat, twisting him around quickly.

"Boy, do you know what you done?" he asked in that growl that emanated from deep in his throat.

Ted just stood there, staring down into the face of the shorter man, and before he realized it he was laughing. There was still a wet mark on the man's shirt from where the shot had splashed and Ted suddenly found it one of the most amusing things he had seen, especially after the anger he had been experiencing all day long. It was like a damn burst and unable to stop he was laughing in the face of this stranger who still held onto the back of his jacket, the anger in the man's eyes as they widened in amazement at the drunken fool in his hands. The man's dark eyes narrowed and Ted could see the fury in them. It was raw and of a pure animalistic nature. Ted tried to regain his composure, his laughter fading as he looked and noticed all eyes of the occupants at the table were on him and their friend, just waiting to see what he would do.

Before the man could do anything, Ted heard the loud voice of the pub's owner, that giant the size and thickness of a brick wall yelled out from back behind the bar. "There a problem over there?"

Ted had finally stopped laughing, the hatred in Fillin's eyes having seemed to sober him up to the realization he was a second away from probably having his ass kicked by the furious patron. Fillin held onto Ted, his grip tightening as he looked over at the bar owner, probably deciding if his wrath was worth dishing out on the drunk in his possession.

"I asked if there is a problem over there?" Bodham yelled, this time his hand smacking down on the counter, the loud crack drawing every eye in the bar to the scene progressing involving Ted.

"No, no problem over here…Fillin…let him be," the man in sunglasses said in a smooth, foreign accent that Ted couldn't place.

The short man holding onto Ted released his grasp on his jacket's collar, and with a pure hatred in his eyes, stepped back from him to return to his seat. He reminded Ted of a dog being called by his master, and Ted then stumbled back a few feet from the table, straightening his suit coat as he turned his attention away from the beating he had almost received had the pub's owner not stepped in, and continued on his way to the restrooms, the urge to piss even stronger than before. He had almost lost it when he saw that look in Fillin's eyes, but now he was safe and on his way.

He noticed that most of the patrons in the pub had returned back to what they had previously been occupied with before Ted had interrupted the peace and flow of the place. Reaching the restroom doors, he pushed through the one labeled 'MEN', and made his way to one of the multiple urinals against the wall. Quickly undoing his fly, he felt a flood of relief as he began urinating, the build up from all the alcohol and water he had drank flowing out of him in what felt like a never-ending stream.

As he finished up, his shoulder's slouched and his legs weak, Ted realized how tired and intoxicated he actually was. He needed to get home and sleep, sure that in the morning this whole day and night would seem like a distant memory. He zipped his pants up and headed for the sink with wobbly legs to wash his hands. Stepping up to the sink, he missed the knob the first time, then on the second try he was able to get the water running. Then, after squirting a jet of soap onto his hands from the dispenser on the wall, he began to lather his hands while the water ran.

Ted was busy, crouched over the sink and scrubbing his hands when he looked up and nearly screamed.

Jesus!

No, it was Fillin, the thug from out in the pub. Ted remembered the look of hatred that had been in the man's eyes minutes earlier, and spun around quickly to face the man who had appeared directly behind him in the small restroom.

"It's just you and me now queer!" he growled, reaching out and grabbing Ted by the lapels of his jacket.

Pulling him close enough that Ted could smell the stench of his breath, he noticed the look of hatred from before had been replaced. There was now what? What was that look? Ted's mind raced as he tried to answer the question, the nauseating closeness of the man, making him feel sick as his grip tightened and he pulled him even closer. It was amusement, that's what was in the man's dark eyes now. Amusement!

"Looks man...I donna want any troubles," Ted mumbled, his brain struggling to fit the words together in his hazy, intoxicated state.

However, Fillin just held him there, staring into his eyes like they were endless orbs. Then Fillin spoke in that deep voice Ted had first associated with the man. "Trouble— oh you have no idea the trouble you've found!" Fillin then shook his drooping form back and forth quickly, shaking the drunk reporter and causing him to draw his eyes back up to the hoodlum's.

That amusement was still there in his eyes, and Ted knew the man meant to do him harm. He hoped that one of the patrons or even the bar owner himself had seen the man follow him into the restroom, but realized that no one had seen anything and that he was all alone. If they had seen him followed, they would have already been there to stop this man from assaulting him.

"Looks…just lemme go…," he muttered.

"Go? After you embarrassed me in front of my friends? Oh no, I'm afraid it's not that simple," Fillin said, continuing to hold him close, spittle landing on Ted's face as he stood there in the man's grasp.

As another fleck of saliva landed on his face from the ruffian, Ted found himself grow angry. Reaching up and hitting at Fillin's hands, he tried to break the hold the man had on him. "Lemme go— get the hell off!" he cried out, but the man held firm, adjusting his grip to avoid having Ted's struggles cause the wasted reporter to break free.

"Oh no, I can't let go— I have a surprise for you!" Fillin said, shaking Ted around again violently and then with a powerful force, shoved him hard up against the restroom wall, his grip still tightly on Ted's jacket.

Ted struggled in the man's arms trying to force him off, but the man's grip was too strong and Ted was too drunk. "Get offa me!" he cried out again, hoping someone would hear his pleas for help. Yet, no one was coming through the door. He was all alone and the man assaulting him didn't seem to be stopping.

Pushing hard against the man's arms, Ted could feel the solid muscles under the man's shirt, unbudging no matter how much he struggled. Suddenly the man pushed up close to his face again, that look of amusement seeming to bring his eyes alive as a wicked smile appeared on his face. "Watch this…" Fillin whispered and then dropped back, keeping Ted pressed against the wall and at an arm's length from him.

Ted looked into the man's eyes again and that's when he noticed the change. Where there had once been a dark, lively amusement, now the man's eyes seemed to become cold and hard. They seemed to be penetrating deep into his soul, and Ted felt a chill run down his spine and a cold sweat break out on his skin. Trying one last time to struggle and break free, he found that the man had full control off him, and there was no use in escaping Fillin's hard grasp.

As Ted watched the man, his vision blurring as he struggled uselessly and exhausted himself, he suddenly witnessed something happening to his attacker. There was a change coming over him and his body seemed to stiffen. That's when Ted saw something he was unable to comprehend, but sent another chill coursing through his inebriated body.

That's when the man called Fillin began to really change.

Besides the stiffening of the man's muscular physique, a jolt seemed to pass through him as he shuddered uncontrollably for a second, closing his eyes tightly, and as Ted watched, the man's eyes flew open— gone were the dark irises and in their place were piercing black orbs with hints of red flecking through the pupils. The stare was cold and hard, and Ted sensed a hunger that radiated from those strange orbs.

Then he noticed something else as he felt his body slammed tighter into the wall, hearing the drywall crack from the force, the man's arms were beginning to sprout a fine, bristling patch of dark hairs that seemed to be flowing out of his exposed flesh. Ted felt his bladder release as the transformation continued, luckily he had urinated only minutes before and the wet spot that soaked through his pants was small and barely noticeable.

This can't be happening— dear Lord, what is he? Ted's mind shouted.

However, the man with the demonic eyes that shoved him harder into the wall, pieces of plaster raining down on them from the ceiling above, inhaled sharply through his nose, sniffing and looked down at the stain that had spread over Ted's crotch. Ted felt pain in his shoulders where the man was holding him against the cracked wall, and when the man named Fillin looked back from his crotch and their eyes met, the man smiled a cruel smile filled with razor sharp teeth.

That's when Ted tried to shut his eyes and block out the horrible transformation, but the man's hands tightened on his shoulders and he felt the fingernails begin to pierce through his clothes and cut deeply into his skin.

"Aaaahh!" Ted cried out, his eyes opening from the pain shooting through him and he saw the change taking place before his very eyes in quick flashes…

His attacker's bones seemed to be moving and stretching the skin from underneath, the wiry black hairs covering more and more of the reconfiguring form…

A lupine snout stretched out from Fillin's face, his jaw widening as his mouth shot open and a hot spray of foam flew onto his face, revealing a glistening set of long, deadly-sharp fangs that were positioned just inches from his face…

The t-shirt and jeans the man had been wearing tore as the dimensions of his body seemed to grow and bones could be heard snapping, muscles tearing and restitching themselves together as the fury, bipedal creature continued to hold onto Ted's shoulders, hard, sharp claws cutting through his flesh and digging into his shoulder blades, the nails nicking the bones in Ted's shoulders and sending what felt like jolts of lightning through him.

Oh dear God…make it stop!

Suddenly Ted felt himself falling, his body dropping away from the broken restroom wall as the creature, still in its final throes of transformation let him go and he hit the floor with a hard thump. Ted stared up through fuzzy eyes, the pain from his shredded, bleeding shoulders causing bursts of blinding pain to shoot through his head and cause his vision to continue to blur as the reporter began to slip in and out of consciousness. From his position on the floor, he watched as clawed feet ripped through the pair of boots only feet from his head and the dark fur had fully covered the transformed man, yet he was no longer a man. Instead, there was a wolf-like beast that looked like it had clawed its way out of his deepest darkest nightmare.

Ted looked up at the blood-thirsty creature standing on two legs before him. It had grown at least a foot taller and wider from the man's original size, and now in Fillin's place was a dark, furred creature from hell, it's furry ears pointing out from its head and the penetrating fiery, red-speckled eyes seemed to look deep into his soul as the creature's head tilted down and took in the sight of Ted's crumpled form laying there in pain, blood flowing from his wounds and spreading across the tiled floor of the restroom. Ted tried to push his body up and move away from the large, wolf-like creature, his breathing labored and coming out in gasps as he felt tears streaming down his face.

"No, no, no, no, no…" he kept muttering, the slurring of his words even worse with the pain and torment shouting through his brain, attempting to wake him up from this nightmare. However, no matter how hard he tried, he couldn't wake up— this nightmare was real, and Ted Hanson was about to die.

This isn't possible, this doesn't exist!

Ted opened his mouth to scream for help, but as he felt the first cords of his voice coming out, the creature thrust it's muzzle into his neck, the teeth closing down hard on his throat and he felt a burst of wetness explode all over his face and chest. As Ted's eyes closed he realized the splash had been his blood pumping out of his torn open throat, his scream having been cut off and silenced right as it began.

Then Ted Hanson's eyes closed for good, the river of blood flowing freely from the stump where his head had been moments before, the tiled floor slick with the vital pints of the dark liquid.

Chapter 29

The night seemed to call to them, the crisp chill of the cold evening had just enough bite to remind a person that winter was coming. Pale, iridescent light cast down upon the group from the growing orb of the almost full moon, the air feeling electrifying as the group slipped through the wooded grounds of the vast expanse of land that made up the sprawling, community property that connected to the forested, beginning of Rock Creek Park near East Rockville's city limits. The Civic Center sat on a rich tract of earth where the main mansion that sat on a historic, ornately-landscaped manor estate, complete with its rose gardens and fountains set among old stone ruins and pathways that twisted over the lawns amid well-trimmed shrubs, bushes and trees that were over a century old.

The group, led by Conall Peterson, had escaped from the pub a few miles away in the Town Center, leaving a bloody trail of death in their wake as they made it to the safety of the deserted grounds of the Rockville Civic Center. The moonlight glinted off the gold chain around Conall's neck, the half-dollar sized pendant with its pentagram laying against his thick, muscular chest as he walked through the trees, the cold air making the bare skin of his upper torso tingle, his pack trailing behind him as they took their time crossing a wide open area that eventually led them into the safety of the woods that surrounded the manor's estate.

Glenview Mansion, was a pillared, neoclassical, 19th century home sitting comfortably nestled among its gardens and stone walking paths up on the hill overlooking the large field that the home looked upon. It was this field the pack had just crossed, and now as they entered the sanctity of the hundred and fifty three acres of woods that eventually led to joining with Rock Creek Park. The many nature and hiking trails that wound through the Civic Center's grounds were the perfect place for Conall and his subservient followers would run the gauntlet of these miles of tree lined hills and peaks.

As Conall walked, he turned his head to look back at the pack of men following him swiftly through the woods, and said in a growl, "Sloppy, Fillin. That was sloppy!" The anger and disappointment that Conall felt towards the shorter man was clearly evident in his tone.

Conall stopped walking for a moment, turning around to face the other three individuals who were following him. Fillin had always been the wild one, hard to control at times, he was always chomping at the bit as he fought Conall's decisions time and time again. Yes, the man was difficult, but he was a member of the pack, and as such Conall allowed him to run free ocassionally, giving him a little room to maneuver and make his own decisions without Conall having to reel in the leash like he did with Tala and Fenris.

Altogether, they were a tight-knit group and no matter how much trouble one of them caused, they always had their pack mates backs if something was wrong or they needed something of the other, after all, Conall was the alpha and his word was law. He believed that all three of the men in the group served a purpose far greater than they saw in themselves. Their mission was one of grave importance, and Conall would not allow them to fail!

Their secret existence had already almost been revealed when that rancher back in Oregon had discovered the burial ground of their fellow brothers of the night. Conall had been a werewolf for over sixty years, even though he appeared to be no more than half that, and all that time no one had ever discovered their existence or came across the ancient burial ground where they honored their fallen brothers and ancestors and buried their bones.

Ever since Mr. Tyler Suffux and his goddamn dog had come across the graveyard, their presence not only disturbing the bones of the dead, but his human curiosity getting the best of him and him sending samples of one of their long dead cousins off to the East Coast where he hoped to have the unusual discovery confirmed and validated, before he revealed his find.

That was enough to chill the hot blood running through Conall's body. If the remains were allowed to be studied by someone who knew enough to realize that the skeleton and whatever else Suffux had sent was something more than just old wolf bones, then their hidden lives could very well be exposed to the world. A fact that had happened long ago when their ancestors roamed wild and free over the history of the world, eventually their stories passing into folklore and myth as they became smarter and looked to secrecy of their existence as a method to the survival of their species, but now all that was at stake.

That was why, when Conall had learned that Suffux had shipped a package containing who knows how much damning proof of their reality, he had gathered three of his most trusted brothers and they had set out for the East Coast, specifically the Washington Metropolitan area to hopefully intercept the package before it could be analyzed by the modern scientists of today's technologically advanced world

However, their mission hadn't been without it its fun. As they had quickly crossed the country on foot, traveling at night and resting by day, they had actually arrived faster than the package being shipped. It was pointless to try and intercept the remains at one of the many shipping facilities that the shipment had to be processed through, and decided to just wait for it to arrive at its final destination. Unfortunately, before they could discover which address Suffux had sent the package to, that hot-headed fool Fillin had ended his suffering too quickly and killed the man before he could reveal the information Conall required.

Now, they had to do it the hard way. Everything had been going fine, them being able to transform and hunt, staying off law enforcement radar all throughout their crossing of the country until they arrived in Maryland. Usually they traveled constantly, the life in the pack having them move to a different hunting ground every night, one separated by a large distance from the other so none of their kills drew too much attention.

However, being in Maryland longer than Conall expected as they had to wait for the remains to be delivered, the pack had grown restless and him being alpha male, had let them lose themselves to their animal side and the body count had begun to stack up. That was okay with Conall since once they had completed their objective, they would be on the move again, constantly roaming the continent like a roving band of gypsies, which they weren't too far from being as part of their survival skills.

Their species had been almost hunted to extinction the world over centuries ago when the fear of werewolves was at the greatest and the belief in their existence was widely accepted. Since then, being able to hide themselves better to prolong the chance of them surviving into the upcoming millenniums, had become a priority and their society had gone underground, welcoming the spreading of stories and old wives tales that made people think they would be considered crazy by their fellow humans to believe in the reality of werewolves. It was this fear of being locked away in a mental institute or just dismissed by society as a lunatic that helped Conall and his brothers keep hidden from the mortal world.

Of course they had to be careful now, the local police according to a news report he had seen a could days ago at a motel they had stayed at revealed that the Montgomery County Homicide Division was looking into the sudden murder spree that had inflicted them. Conall was not to thrilled that there was so much attention being placed on their actions over the last week. It was Fillin's fault that the pack had this FBI joint task force looking for them. The first night they had arrived in Rockville, Conall had been lax in keeping an eye on the pretentious young wolf and he had let him go off on his own. That error in judgment had led to Fillin attacking and killing a woman on her way home from work late at night.

He had followed her from the Metro station she had gotten off at, and as she wound through a park near the motel they had been staying at that first night, Fillin had changed and feed on the woman. It was this careless act that had brought the heat onto the pack's movements. The other victims had been pack kills, them killing to satisfy their blood lust. It was part of being a werewolf, that animal side that was so difficult to control when near so many potential food sources like a city provided. After all they were predators who lived for the hunt. They didn't discriminate when it came to their victims, but they usually expressed better judgment on Conall's part on where and when to feed.

Damn Fillin!— the wolf was only forty in their years, which meant that to mortal humans he appeared to be in his late twenties. Due to their genetic makeup, they lived twice as long as humans did, giving them a true taste of the world they inhabited. In his sixty years on the planet, Conall had traveled the entire world, visiting every continent including the birth place of their species, the country where the Mesopotamian poem, The Epic of Gilgamesh, first mentioned the existence of their kind back in 2000 B.C.

Widely considered to be the cradle of civilization, the land of Mesopotamia, translated from the ancient Greek meaning "land between rivers" is the area of the Tigris–Euphrates river system, largely corresponding to modern-day Iraq, northeastern Syria, southeastern Turkey and southwestern Iran.

It was here that the first werewolf was said to have been born, tales of their creation story being passed on from generation to generation by word of mouth and traditions that had been performed for thousands of years. They were a noble species, and that was why the inexcusable act of grave robbery by that fool in Oregon had to be righted. The burial site held a specific meaning to American lycanthropes, its history and use of the location for centuries since the first werewolf came to America and founded the spot known to their kind as The Calling Cliff, named so for the myth that had been passed down of when the first European werewolf came to this continent and began building their new domain in this new world.

There had been other shape-shifters on the continent already, but they were unorganized and more lone wolf than pack-orientated, so when the European wolf known as Lyall, who's surname meant wolf, came to the plateau that overlooked a massive, forested canyon, his howl bringing forth the many wolves that traversed the woods alone and formed a new pack for the protection of extinction that the place became known as it was today as the spot that the grandfather of their American brethren joined forces with the European wolves and formed a mega pack that would last through the centuries and continue to grow in pack sizes due to the laws that governed each individual pack.

While there was one ruling order for all the packs on their respective continents, there were hundreds of smaller packs that were made up of various sizes and types, but all governed by one alpha male. This was how Conall had come to rule his odd band of misfits, and now he had to not only look out for his species survival and steal back their ancestors remains, but he had to ensure his packs safety while the local law enforcement agencies attempted to hunt them down.

Of course, as long as Conall was in charge, he would let nothing happen to his pack mates. That much he was sure. Fillin may be a handful, but he is a brother, and us wolves stick together, he thought as they began their journey through the forest trails again, not stopping until they had gone many miles away from the scene of the massacre at the pub.

The cops would have their hands full tonight!

Conall thought of the taste of warm, coppery blood and the flesh of the two victims he had chosen as his own. As alpha he had first choice of the kill, and he had decided that once Fillin had killed the drunkard in the bathroom and drew the attention of the other patrons in the bar with the noise, Conall and the other two pack members had transformed themselves and finished off the rest of the possible witnesses in the place.

He remembered the massive, powerful form of the owner of the bar, he had been a worthy opponent, his size easily dwarfing Conall in his human form, but once in his animal form, it had been a true match of the giants.

The thought of burying his snout into the ripped open chest cavity of the fallen giant and ripping the heart out with his jaws brought a smile to his face as he recalled quickly eating the delicacy.

Oh yes, it had been a good night, and now that they were away from the prying eyes of any humans in the area, they decided to change once more in the safety of the woods, with the beautiful, moonlit night shining above and their running free and wild in the open.

Yes, it was time to run! Conall thought and felt the stirrings of the change coming over him, his eyes glued to the almost full moon.

Only two more days and it would be at its fullest!

A true Hunter's Moon!

- -

Detective Mack Jones had been home when the call came in on his cell phone. Rising in the dark of his bedroom and careful not to wake his wife, he had found that it was Special Agent Poole calling. Answering the phone as he stepped into the master bathroom for privacy and to keep the noise from bothering his spouse, he had answered it in a hushed tone. That's when the FBI bigwig told him that they had another crime scene, this time it was at a bar near downtown Rockville Town Square.

Jesus! Mack thought as he had gotten off the phone with Poole and dressed as quick as possible. Before he knew it he was standing inside The Dancing Bear, an odd little pub— one of many in the always expanding town revitalization project that encouraged small business owners to open up their stores and restaurants in the Town Center and peddle their wares to the thousands of people strolling through the area daily.

Now it was 2 a.m., and Mack was standing in the middle of the most disgusting display of butchery he had ever witnessed on his many years as a police officer and then the extra years as a Detective for the Rockville Police Department. The mess he was viewing, had certainly been committed by the same individuals who they were already looking for with no luck so far.

They had gotten lucky and recovered two human fingerprints at the second crime scene, but so far they hadn't turned up a match. That didn't mean they wouldn't, but if there was no record of a similar print in the IAFIS system, the FBI's master database, then chances were the two different individuals who's prints were able to be lifted from the scene, just had never been arrested before, served in the military or held a government job. If they had, AFIS would have their prints stored in the system.

IAFIS is the Integrated Automated Fingerprint Identification System. IAFIS provides automated fingerprint search capabilities, latent searching capability, electronic image storage, and electronic exchange of fingerprints and responses. IAFIS maintains one of the largest biometric databases in the world, second only to Mexico. IAFIS has over 66 million subjects in the criminal master file, and more than 25 million civil prints.

Fingerprints are voluntarily submitted to the Bureau by local, state, and federal law enforcement agencies. These agencies acquire the fingerprints through criminal arrests or from non-criminal sources, such as employment background checks and the US-VISIT program. The FBI then catalogs the fingerprints along with any criminal history linked with the subject.

So far, there hadn't been any 'hits' in the system, the program having already gone through millions of records in the last few hours. Mack knew that to get a match, a fingerprint technician scanned the print in question into the system, and computer algorithms are then utilized to mark all minutia points, cores, and deltas detected on the print. These are the lines and varying patterns that make a person's fingerprints unique from every other person in the world.

The fingerprint image processor will generally assign a 'quality measure' that indicates if the print is acceptable for searching, and with one of the latent prints that had been pulled off one of the first victims from the quarry murder site, the print had been assigned a quality measure of 'excellent', meaning all the varying points, cores and deltas on the print were of a clear and precise condition when the lab technician had pulled it from one of the victim's flesh.

Normally latent prints were hard to pull off bodies, but due to the perpetrator having carelessly touched the dead teenager's chest when they had carved the pentagram design into the flesh, the FBI and the joint task force now had at least one piece of valid evidence to use towards nailing these bastard's butt's to the wall, making sure they all got the death sentence for their murderous killing spree.

The bloody thumbprint had been discovered by the lead Forensics Technician, Dr. Henry Cushings. He had been studying the marking that had been branded onto each of the victim's bodies, when he noticed the imprint that had been pressed onto the skin, obviously due to one of the serial killers having pressed his hands onto the victim's epidermis when working on etching the symbol into their bodies.

Now what the hell did a pentagram have to do with these murders, and why did the UnSub as Special Agent in Charge, Jim Poole referred to the perpetrators as, choose this emblem to tattoo onto their victims? Mack tried to think of what he knew about the design that was ever present in cultures and among certain groups of people. As far as he could recall, the pentagram or five-pointed star, seemed to be used in various circles of dark arts and devil worship that went on even today.

Mack knew from some brief research he had completed regarding the symbolic design. Pentagrams had been used throughout ancient Greece and Babylonia, and even today was a used as a declaration of faith by many Wiccans. The symbol was worn and held dear like the use of the cross for those in the Christian religion and the Star of David in the Jewish faith. The pentagram had magical associations, many people who practiced Neopagan beliefs wearing jewelry that incorporated the shape. Even Christians used the five-pointed star to represent the five wounds of Jesus. It was even used and associated with Freemasonry and many other cultures and religions the world over.

The devil worship angle was the theory that Mack was interested in following. He had spoken to Aidan earlier and heard his psychiatrist's theories regarding the possible motives behind the killings, but Mack had a different idea. While Aidan believed these lunatics were getting their kicks imitating the attack patterns of a certain animal, thinking they even might be one for that matter as they mutilated their victims, Mack followed the evidence and to him, it seemed to be pointing to the devil worshiper's angle because of the pentagram. As far as he could remember, those types of dark and evil rituals practitioners of satanic guided spirituality invoked, it seemed obvious that the perpetrators they were searching for were obviously off in the head.

Taking a look at the crime scene he found himself in now, that demented, devil worship angle seemed all the more feasible to the heavyset Detective as he leaned against a door post and studied the mess before him.

Halloween was still a few days away, the day where children and even adults all over the country would dress up in various costumes depicting the various ghouls and goblins that had become such a part of the wide-spread history of the holiday. Even his own kids both far from being considered children anymore, would don the popular costumes that girls seemed to become during the festive night and go bar hopping, stopping at their favorite haunts to be a part of the individual costume parties and celebrations that the night ushered in, women usually dressing in sexy bunny costumes or various other disguises that oozed with sex-appeal.

Mack just hoped his girls wouldn't be dressed so risqué. With everything going on lately, he didn't need to be worrying about their safety anymore than he already did as a protective father.

The idea of his own kids wandering the streets at night while multiple real monsters walked the streets hunting for their next victims was something that Mack tried to push from his head. It was bad enough that here he was, standing on the outskirts of the bloody crime scene that had been discovered only an hour before, watching the pathologist and boys from the CSI department work at processing the horrid events that had unfolded in the small pub called The Dancing Bear. It was a place Mack had never been in before, but now having seen the mayhem and destruction that lined the floors and walls of the establishment, he knew he would not forget the place for as long as he could remember. Maybe he'd be lucky and get retro-grade amnesia, the only thing he could think of that would erase the images he had seared into his brain over the course of the week.

To Mack, it seemed like the murders could be escalating and there was a good chance the culmination of this killer's work could possibly be working towards the holiday that would fall upon the city in two days time. Mack was worried that if this was the big event that these lunatics were working towards, their killings continuing to grow in the number of bodies starting to pile up at the Baltimore County Morgue and in the sick, depraved way that the mutilations continued to become more violent, like the killers were amping up their nastiness each time they took a life.

Could Aidan actually be right about his full moon theory? He had heard some rubbish a long time ago about the moon's effect on the crazies in this world, after all, it did seem that thinking back upon all the years he had worked for the Rockville Police, that the more serious and depraved crimes happened around the full moon. Could it just be a coincidence? Mack wasn't sure, but he knew he wasn't willing to bet the serial killers wouldn't strike on the full moon. What was worse was the moon would actually be at its fullest Halloween night!

As if things weren't bad enough as they were, now no matter who's theory ended up being the closest regarding the UnSubs motivations for the murders, in two days time, they would have all the elements lined up in favor of their latest chosen hobby— the murder of innocent lives.

Mack turned and focused his attention on the scene before him. The quaint, little pub that had once looked like it might have been a good place to spend the night drinking away the day's worries was now a complete mess. Blood coated the walls and large pools of the crimson liquid had collected on the polished wooden floor, while tables, chairs and bar stools lay scattered around the room, many of the wood furniture broken and splintered, separated from the rest of the pieces that would make them whole.

The long, wooden bar with its black, polished top was cracked in the middle, something big and strong having smashed into the once-solid counter top. Positioned with his arms and legs spread eagle, and his once-imposing body mutilated to the point where he was only identifiable from the ID in his wallet, was the owner of the bar. His chest had been torn open, the ribs and breastbone having been ripped apart by what appeared to be a person's bare hands, yet the pathologist wouldn't know for sure until his examination of the body was complete.

Mack did know one thing for sure though. The body of Bodham Choplinksy had been seriously maimed before death, and his heart had been ripped out of his chest while he was still alive. That much the crime scene technicians had been able to tell him as he now stood back away from the action and let the boys from the lab do their work.

Closing his eyes and whispering a silent prayer for protection for the city he loved, and begging God to aid him in capturing the sick bastards who were responsible for adding seven more bodies to the growing list of victims, giving a grand total of 13 dead in less than a week.

The city was already in a panic, the joint task force working as hard as they could each minute of the day and tried to come up with clues that would lead to them apprehending the suspects, but so far nothing had panned out. This had quickly gone from a single horrible incident when the first victim was discovered to a case of epic proportions. They hadn't had a body count like this one since the Fall of 2003, when the Beltway Snipers had killed just as many people in a frame of time closer to a month. This had been done in a third of the time, and it wasn't over yet.

Mack pictured the image he had seen earlier when he first arrived with Detective Andrea Wilkes of the Montgomery County Homicide Division, and being the second officers on the scene to respond to the initial call, they had been the first to see the carnage up close and personal. Feeling sick to his stomach from the nauseating smell of death and the pungent odor of warm blood covering almost every inch of the pub's floor and walls, Mack remembered the sight he had seen when he first walked into the men's restroom.

He had been warned to expect an awful sight, but nothing could have prepared him for the devastation that had occurred in the bathroom. The man's torture and subsequent death were obviously the first incident to take place in the safety of The Dancing Bear's heavy, metal door that chimed when opened. Already, Mack had heard the soft bell go off every time someone new entered or exited the main entrance of the establishment. He wished he could just pull out his revolver and shoot the damn speaker.

Then again, now that Special Agent Poole was on site and directing the movements of everyone working, like a choreographer putting the finishing touches on a symphony orchestra performance, every person and instrument knowing exactly what needed to be done. The scene was a public-relations nightmare. A customer had entered the bar earlier looking to get a drink from his favorite watering hole, when the man stepped inside the establishment and saw the mayhem that had taken place. The shocked man had even stepped in a pool of blood and tracked it outside as he ran out of the pub to call 911. However, by the time the police arrived to secure the scene, the hysterical witness had already informed everyone he had come across about the bloody scene, and by the time Mack and Andrea had arrived, followed shortly after by Agents Naomi and Poole, a large crowd on curious bystanders had grown outside the pub.

There were officers from both Rockville and Montgomery County attempting to keep the onlookers back away from the building, but with so many people living in downtown Rockville, the crowd didn't seem to be getting any smaller despite the efforts of the police officers to get them to break up and depart from the incident. Now however, the media had become involved, camera crews and reporters mixing with the crowd as everybody tried to find out answers to what had happened under The Dancing Bear's roof. Fortunately for the police and FBI, they were able to keep the growing crowds back as the investigation continued. They had already been at it for an hour, and there was still a massive amount of evidence to be collected. Mack walked back towards the direction of the first victim, entered the men's restroom and bent down to examine the body.

The man was certainly a bloody mess, the amount of blood having flown from his wounds pointing to the fact that he was alive and his arteries were pumping the precious pints of blood through his body well into the mauling that he had been subjected to. Mack shook his head as he examined the body closer, careful not to get too close and possibly contaminate the scene. As he studied the body of the victim, he realized that the man seemed familiar somehow, like he had met him before. Staring hard at the facial features of the man who's body was lying in a lake of its own blood, the head having been separated from the torso at the neck, and the appendage was lying over a few feet from the body, at the base of the wall where a large hole had been created in the drywall, probably from something or someone being smashed into it repeatedly.

As Mack studied the head, trying to place the face from where he might have seen this man before, he noticed the chips of plaster and white dust in the man's hair. Taking a closer look, but careful not to step anywhere that still needed to be processed, he realized the powdery coating in the man's dark hair was bits of drywall from the broken restroom wall. So the man had been thrown into the wall at some point, causing the damage he had noticed and leaving the light coating of dust to appear on the back of his scalp and in his hair.

"Poor bastard," mack mumbled, as he looked over the scene, then realized why the victim's face seemed so familiar. When he had thought about the news reporters hounding the cops outside for access into the pub, he remembered seeing the Channel 5 News van parked down the street. However, when he had looked around quickly before going past the yellow, police-tape barrier and into the middle of the scene of the crime, he hadn't seen the usual Channel 5 correspondent chasing after the story, the scent of a major piece to be aired for thousands of nightly viewers that the usual guy he saw hanging around the crime scenes wasn't with his usual cameraman. The skinny guy with the camera on his shoulder, filming everything he could was the same, but the reporter was different. Younger and not as nicely dressed.

Oh shit!

That's when Mack realized why the victim in the bathroom looked so familiar! The victim lying before him with its head separated from its shoulders, was none other than that sleezeball, Ted Hanson! The prick that interfered with all sorts of police investigations, claiming he was doing it because the public had a right to know what was going on. Well now it looked like Hanson would finally be giving the public everything it wanted. The murder of one of the most infamous television reporters in the Washington Metropolitan was going to shock the general public even more than it had in recent days.

This wasn't good, Mack thought as he looked down at the now recognizable face of Ted Hanson. The man was certainly going to live up to the life he had expected of so many others, a victim of one of his own stories.

How ironic.

Looking back over to the body laying crumpled on the tiled floor, the clothes bloody and torn, Mack suddenly noticed something he hadn't seen before. Hanson had something clutched tightly in his hands! Mack dropped to a knee next to the body, careful not to get anywhere near the pool of congealing blood that had formed, and peered closer at the reporter's left hand. Squeezed tight in a fist that had become frozen in a statue-like grip was a collection of hairs.

Hanson must have grabbed a handful of his attacker's hair during their struggle! Mack pondered excitedly as he looked at the collection of wiry, dark hairs in between the man's clenched fist.

They had their first real chance at an uncontaminated source of possible DNA. They just might be able to solve these murders before another possible victim shows up before the killers are caught. Mack wished Aidan was here to see his discovery. Then Mack realized that the lab only needed a few samples to hair, possibly only one hair follicle to gather the DNA sample they would need. However, there was a whole assortment of hairs in the man's fist and he really did want to get Aidan's opinion on them.

The joint task force's lab and testing could take days with so much evidence to process, and since Aidan had been working on the case unofficially and now had a source of help that had access to a research lab in the Smithsonian, Mack realized that Aidan might just be able to get some results from the woman well before all the testing came back from the police lab's testing.

Taking a look to make sure he was alone and couldn't hear anyone approaching the men's restroom, Mack dug into his pocket and removed a small evidence bag he had tossed into his tight suit jacket earlier when he had first arrived. Slipping a new pair of non-latex gloves over his big hands, Mack plucked a few strands of the dark hairs from Hanson's palm and quickly sealed them into the bag. Without wasting any time, he placed the bag now containing the attacker's hairs back into his pocket and looked up just in time to see Agent Poole coming into the men's restroom.

"Find anything?" the agent asked as he looked down at Mack.

"Oh yeah, I was able to identify the victim, and look what he has in his hand," Mack said, his large form still crouched over the body as he pointed out the remaining hairs in the victim's tight fist.

"Well I'll be damned, looks like we just caught our second big break in this case," Poole whistled and looked at Mack.

Mack just smiled, knowing it was only a matter of time before they caught these perps!

Oh yeah, you can't hide from us— we've got a part of you now!

Chapter 30

Having almost given up hope on hearing from Tyler Suffux again, Lisa Davies had returned to the pile of work she had at hand, her and Frank having spent many hours working on the two main projects she had to attempt to complete as soon as possible. The deadline the Smithsonian's Board of Director's had given her for the Grand Opening of the Midnight Trail was official, and that meant Lisa and her department had less than two weeks to get the wolves ready to move to their new permanent habitat at the National Zoo in downtown D.C., and have everything complete and ready for .

To make matters worse, Lisa was still trying to find the time in their crammed schedule for her testing of the wolf vocalizations. Now that she had received the funding she had requested, she was all for getting to work right away on the project she held so close to her heart. Her research really could change the lives of the Gray Wolf in society for good, and give them a fighting chance to excel and grow in the conservation efforts that they were doing at the SCBI.

It was this work she was doing, when her office phone started ringing off the hook. Lisa grabbed the phone and putting it to her ear, answered, "This is Davies…"

"Hi Miss Davies, it's Max— over at Building One," the kind, old voice of the SCBI campuses main guard who worked at the reception desk, was one that contained a slow drawl that always reminded Lisa of the slow-poked tortoise always taking its time in the race against the fast-paced hare.

"Hey Max, what can I do for you?" she asked, twirling the phone cord around her finger as she sat there, her eyes traveling over the empty office before her as she listened to the old guard explain why he had called.

"Actually I wanted to let you know that a package came for you today, it's here at the reception desk. I haven't had time to send it over to your building yet since I'm the only one working the desk today."

Lisa sat up straight in her chair. Did she really just hear the man correctly?

"Wait, you said a package arrived for me personally, not just addressed to the department?" Lisa asked, her heart skipping a beat as she realized this must be it! Tyler Suffux's shipment must have finally come in!

"Yeah, that's right. It's addressed to you."

"I'll be right there!" Lisa said, slamming the phone down onto the receiver and leaping up from her desk. This was it— she could finally be on the verge of discovering something bigger than life!

If the remains Suffux had found on his large piece of land were more recent skeletons not fossilized from being in the ground for millions of years, then the supposed extinction of the Dire Wolf would be an amazing scientific breakthrough, altering the known history of the animal that was thought to have vanished from the Earth so long ago.

Lisa hurried out of her office and quickly slipping out one of the side entrances of the Cave, she made her way to SCBI's main building where Max was waiting with her package. The entire time it took her to make her way over to the headquarters, her mind was racing, trying to picture what might be in the box that Tyler Suffux had mailed her. His last e-mails hadn't really said what he was sending her other than it was supposed to be new photographs and hopefully some of the unfossilized remains the rancher had found in the corner of his property. The bundle of nerves was tightening in her stomach as she walked briskly to Building One, unable to contain her excitement.

Then she remembered Eleanor Suffux's e-mail about her husband going missing, and Lisa felt a small voice in the back of her head warning her about the mysterious situation regarding the man's disappearance. Yes, it was odd, but unfortunately being over 3, 000 miles away from Oregon, Lisa just couldn't picture the odd incident having any bearing on the package that had just arrived.

Stepping through the double glass doors and into the lobby of the Smithsonian Conservation Biology Institute's headquarters, Lisa saw the form of Max sitting behind his desk and when he looked up and saw her approaching gave her a quick smile.

"That was quick," he stated as he watched Lisa's lithe, beautiful form return the smile and step up to the big desk.

"I've been waiting for that to arrive all week," she said noticing the large box wrapped in UPS standard packaging sitting on the floor next to Max's chair.

Max's eyes followed hers to the package at his feet, and with some effort he hauled the large box up and set it on the counter. "Well, I already signed for it when it was delivered, so she's all yours," he said, sliding the box to her, then as an afterthought asked, "Do you want me to get one of those little handcarts so you can take it back to your lab?"

Lifting one corner of the box, Lisa realized it was pretty heavy. She wouldn't be able to carry it back to the Cave by herself.

"Sure, if it's not too much trouble."

"Oh no trouble, wait right here," Max replied.

Lisa stood there as the older guard took off from the desk and disappeared for a moment out of sight and into a small room that only the reception desk had access to. Lisa took the moment to look at the package, the box having arrived according to the printed shipping label from out of Portland, Oregon.

Lisa wondered if maybe that's where Tyler Suffux had disappeared to, leaving his wife to worry and call in the police to search for him and the dog. Could he have taken his German Shepherd and driven into the town to ship this package to her and then gone off maybe with some friends to have a good time, or maybe he had a lady friend he was seeing that his wife Eleanor didn't know about. Without knowing too much about the couple, having only talked to them online over the course of almost two weeks, Lisa was afraid all she could do was speculate. She knew practically nothing about the missing, older rancher and his distraught wife other than what she had learned from his e-mails, and that wasn't much.

Is that it Mr. Suffux? Do you have a woman on the side that your off with while your wife sits at home worried something awful has happened to you? Do you make it a habit of running off without telling her where you're going, leaving her to just assume you and the dog are out running errands?

For some reason, as Lisa stared at the large, heavy box and the meticulous handwriting that had been scrawled on the original delivery label, Tyler Suffux taking the time to make sure he spelled everything neat and orderly so that there would be no confusion with the package going to the wrong place, Lisa had the odd feeling that something was not right with the Oregon Police's assumption that the rancher had just pulled up his ties to his land, grabbed his dog and left his loving wife to take care of their massive acreage.

No, that doesn't make sense at all. Tyler Suffux was certain this find he had come across was something big and important, or else he would never have sent the box all the way across the country to Lisa for validation of his find. Something had to have happened to him! Lisa was sure of it, but the little voice at the back of her mind kept reminding her that she had no idea what could have happened.

Oregon was a long ways from the Washington Metropolitan area where she lived and worked, so who knows what kind of things could be going on out there. All she knew was that lately around here, the talk about the serial killers murdering people all over the Montgomery County Maryland was troubling enough. They had their own problems here on the East Coast without her worrying about one man and his trusty dog disappearing, yet there was still that feeling Lisa couldn't seem to shake.

At that moment Max returned pushing a small dolly for Lisa to take her package back to her own building.

"Well, here you go, sorry it took me so long to find the blasted thing, someone didn't put it back in the right place," Max said, shaking his head at the absentmindedness of his fellow guards.

"No, I appreciate you getting it for me."

"Say…" Max began, picking the package off the counter and heaving it as gently as possible onto the handcart below, "…what do you have in here, a set of weights for your home gym?"

Lisa smiled as Max finished settling the package onto the Dolley and stood. His cheeks flushed from the mild exertion. "Actually there hopefully bones," she stated, the hope in her voice evident. Max just shook his head.

"Doc, you might want to consider a vacation if you work all day in those labs, dealing with animals and bones and what not, then you go getting personal packages of more of the same," he said with another shake of his head.

"Ha— a vacation— after this next few weeks with the Midnight Trail opening having been moved up, on top of everything I have going on with my own research, I probably will need to take one," she said, giving the lonely guard another big smile as she pushed down on the dolly's handrail and tested the weight. It was much easier to move now. "Well thanks for all your help Max, I really need to get this back to my office now."

"Okay Miss Davies, you take care of yourself," he said, stepping back behind his desk and resuming his position in his chair.

"Alright, well thank you again for calling about the package and getting the handcart," she called out with a wave of her hand as she pulled the dolly through the lobby and out the doors, making her way to the Cave.

The walk back was nearly as quick a time as she had getting to Building One to pick up her delivery. She had rushed to get there and now that she had the heavy package, she was in a hurry to get back to her lab space and explore the contents that had arrived from Oregon.

As she sped along the sidewalk that led to the Cave, dolly rolling along the paved walkway as smooth as it could. One wheel seemed to be crooked and every time it turned one whole revolution, it caused the handcart to rattle and attempt to veer off course. Lisa kept a tight grip on the handle, correcting the direction each time the wheel threw it off and eventually she had arrived back at her office.

Shifting the large package off the dolly's flat shelf, she pushed the cart off to the side and stared at the big, brown box sitting in the middle of the floor. She felt like a kid again, waiting for her step mom to tell her she could open her presents on Christmas morning. It had always been an exciting time, her wide eyes traveling over the array of presents as she decided which to open first.

Usually she started with the biggest first then worked her way down to the smallest of gifts, her excitement and anticipation towards finding out what was in the largest of wrapped boxes being too much for her unchecked patience. Now, standing here looking down at the UPS package, she felt the same as she had those many years ago growing up in the Midwest, just her and her step mother, no other family but them.

Because Lisa had never had any brothers or sisters to compete for her step mom's affection, Christmas had always been a time of her being spoiled with a pile of presents, a tradition her step mom continued to keep up with, every year sending her multiple gifts throughout the holidays.

Finally, unable to put her curiosity off any longer, Lisa grabbed a small scalpel from a drawer of lab equipment and cut the corners of the package, peeling open the ends to reveal the contents. As she cut the last piece of tape from the box, she set the scalpel down next to her and then sat on the floor with the large delivery opened and awaiting her. Digging into the top layer, she found that the box had been filled with multiple wads of crumpled up newspapers, a cheap solution to having no packing bubbles or those inflated plastic bags that seemed to be being used more and more by companies these days.

Removing the old-fashioned protective layer, Lisa bent slightly at the waist and looked down into the box. Her pulse had quickened as she had been removing layer after layer of newspaper and now she had finally reached the contents of the package.

Her hands slid over the smooth skull, the small nicks and cracks of the carbonized bone visible from the unshielded effects of mother nature for who knew how many millions of years. She picked the fossilized head up in her hands, surprised by the size and weight of the object. It was like lifting a rock of the same size, so it was heavy!

Wow, Lisa thought as she rotated the prize before her eyes, taking in every square inch of the fossil as she sat there staring. The larger size and various differences in the remarkable skull were exactly what Lisa needed to see for herself. Photographs just couldn't relate how a certain object truly looked as you felt it in your hands, viewing it in real life and she tried to commit every last scratch and indent to memory.

Photos also couldn't give you an accurate size reference, the scale being affected by so many possible outcomes. No, you had to have the real thing to truly understand what it was you were looking at. This was amazing! Lisa took a few more minutes to study the skull before finally setting it down on a pile of newspaper softly to avoid damaging the ancient, skeletal head.

She couldn't believe this discovery had been found one day when a rancher was just out surveying one of the many stretches of land he owned, and thanks to a flash flood and his good old German Shepherd's obsession to dig things up, he had discovered what he had called a "bone yard of all these big skeletons", she also remembered how he had said that, "They're big, each one bigger than any wolf I'd ever seen!". At first she hadn't believed him, and she reminded herself that still had to see evidence that there were also bones at the uncovered site that were not fossilized, that would be a big discovery just in its own right! Yet, even if they were all just fossils in this animal grave site, the find was going to be huge.

Lisa leaned back and just stared at the skull sitting on the floor before her. Sitting there on the pieces of discarded newspaper, she imagined its eye sockets just watching her as she studied it back, and felt the rush of excitement she had experienced ringing throughout her body. She felt so alive right at that moment!

This is Dire Wolf! She thought, sitting there in awe at the fossil she now had in her possession. While many museums and organizations would love to have even a replica of the extinct prehistoric wolf from before the Pleistocene Era. This was the first fossil of Canis dirus to be discovered in this part of the country. The first specimen of a Dire Wolf ever found was by Francis A. Linck along the Ohio River near Evansville, Indiana in 1854, however the largest collection of fossils had actually come from the La Brea Tar Pits in California. Having a possible multitude of bones found in Oregon would alter the migration of the species, and Lisa felt that exciting chill course through her as she stared longingly at the skull.

It was a creature unlike any other species that ever existed. Although it was closely related to the Gray Wolf and other sister species, Canis dirus was not the direct ancestor of any species known today. Unlike the Gray Wolf, which is of Eurasian origin, the Dire Wolf evolved on the North American continent, along with the coyote, and co-existed with the Gray Wolf in North America for about 100,000 years. It was one of the abundant Pleistocene megafauna—a wide variety of very large mammals that lived during the era. Approximately 10,000 years ago the Dire Wolf was thought to have became extinct along with most other North American megafauna, but Lisa knew they'd have to date this new collection of fossils to see if that perception could be wrong. The Dire Wolf, Lisa now knew, could have just moved further North to survive extinction for a few more thousand years or so, and then passed away from the world of man.

It was a unique creature in that it exhibited hyena like characteristics. Like the hyena, the dire wolf hunted and scavenged for food. Researchers suspect that dire wolves, due to their scavenging nature, scattered the bones of animals they killed or that were killed by other prey. The dire wolf was not quite like any animal existing today.

The dire wolf looked fairly similar to the modern gray wolf, however, there were several important differences. It was larger than the Gray Wolf, being far more powerful and vicious. It had a larger, broader head and shorter, sturdier legs than its modern relative, with teeth that were much larger and more massive, pointing to a hypercarnivorous activity. A hypercarnivore is an animal which has a diet that is more than 70% meat, with the balance consisting of non-animal foods such as fungi, fruits or other plant material, so in essence it was a serious meat-eater.

It is believed the animal used its relatively large teeth to crush bone, an idea supported by the frequency of large amounts of wear on the crowns of their fossilized teeth, and the presence of a large temporalis muscle made its bite force much stronger than any wolf or canine species in existence today. The weak symphyseal region of muscles indicates it killed in a manner similar to its modern relatives the Gray Wolf, by delivering a series of shallow bites, strongly indicating pack hunting behavior.

All in all, the Dire Wolf was a formidable foe to any other large carnivore and to early man who would have probably stayed away from the large killing machine, and while there was still much to learn about the animal, this new discovery of a bone yard featuring their remains in the Northwest would possibly give them a whole assortment of new information on the species as a whole. Lisa was tingling with excitement!

Just then she realized she had been so absorbed with the fossilized skull that she had forgot to look and see what else might be in the large box. Pushing the skull aside for the time being, she leaned over and peered into the open end of the package. A strange, musty smell assaulted her nose and removing a few other pieces of newspaper from the inside of the delivery, she found a gasp escaping her lips and her eyes widened in utter astonishment. She reached inside the package, her hands shaking slightly as she brought the second item out and set it on the floor before her. She didn't know what to do

Can it really be? she wondered, her amazement causing her heart to feel like it had skipped a beat. No, it's not possible!

Yet, here it was, sitting on the floor as real as everything else in the lab. She was looking at a clear plastic bag that was wrapped up and tied at the top, but due to the transparency of the bag, she was able to see the contents. Inside the plastic bag was the source of the smell she had picked up when she had noticed the box might contain more things that Tyler Suffux had packed up and shipped to her.

It was a part of a lower leg, the large foot still attached, but the most amazing thing that had Lisa shaking with awe was that the foot was much larger than a Gray Wolves paw, that it had to be either from a Dire Wolf since it had been found in the same spot, or some other similar species that was linked to the them.

However, the most amazing and utterly impossible thing about this piece of leg and back foot was that it wasn't a fossil! In fact, it still had traces of flesh and fur on it!

Oh my God! Lisa thought as she stared at the massive paw, her jaw open from wonder and her mind racing to process what she was seeing with her own two eyes.

What the hell did Suffux discover?

Chapter 31

Nick Haley had slept soundly through the night, the alcohol he had consumed the previous night at Bo's place had helped him pass out, and now he had risen to find the sun shining through the blinds partially open on his bedroom window, the bright light filtering through and causing him to cover his head with the blanket he was wrapped in.

Oh, what time is it? He wondered, reaching around the small table next to his bed and searching for his alarm clock. He had obviously forgot to set it judging by how high the morning sun had risen. Nick didn't dare expose his eyes to the blinding brightness of the sun, his head aching fiercely from a nasty hangover. "Great, just what I need," he muttered to himself as he felt his stomach feeling like it was doing somersaults from the alcohol sitting in his belly.

Damn it, I'm probably late already, he cursed himself and his actions, finally feeling his fingers close around the clock and pulling it under the bedsheets to stare at the glowing red numbers. It was almost nine o'clock! He had slept in late.

"Ughhh!" he moaned as he slid the covers off him, his eyes welded shut to prevent the light from sending shots of red throughout his vision as he lay there wishing he hadn't drank so much. What the hell was he thinking? Finally, he opened his eyes slightly, feeling the burning of his retinas as he looked around the sun-filled room. Reaching onto the small table again to set the clock back, he then realized his cell phone wasn't there. He always put it right on the tabletop before going to bed, this habit having been instilled in him over the years as a journalist kept odd hours and had to be reached at any time when there was a story to be pursued. So where was his phone?

Opening his eyes wide, he glanced around the room, his hand running through his long, brown hair then going to his eyes to shield them slightly from the onslaught of sun coming through the window.

Alright, think Nick, what did you do with it last night? He tried to remember his movements from the previous evening, but it all just seemed to be a hazy blur. He could recall going to The Dancing Bear, and talking to Bo for some of the night, then he remembered seeing the news report on the latest murder in the woods. That was something he had to remember to check into. He also needed to call Aidan Preston; however, he was sure that this late into the morning the Detective had probably tried calling him. If only he could find his phone!

As he sat there, his eyes roaming the room to see if he had set it down somewhere else, he spied his pants and sports coat, the ones he had been wearing the previous evening lying in a pile at the foot of the bed. He quickly sat up all the way, reaching down to snag the clothes. Quickly rifling through the pockets, he felt the familiar shape of his phone, his search was over! Pulling it out, Nick was annoyed to see he had turned the phone off. Who knew how many people had been trying to reach him all morning, only to get his answering machine. Stupid, stupid, stupid, he told himself as he turned the device on and waited for its startup procedure to finish. Once the animated screen was done, he saw he had a couple new voice messages awaiting him.

Dialing into his account and entering his pass-code, he quickly went through the four messages, listening to each one and then deleting it. The first two were from Marty wondering where he was. The Editor wasn't a happy camper about not having any news in today's edition of The Informant regarding the latest killing, and he was pretty pissed off.

Oh well— I had no prior information to know about it, he thought, but knew that it was his job to be informed of any crime happening in the city. Instead he had spent the day running around with Aidan in search of information on the serial killer's reasons behind the killings. While it was a great article he had submitted, he knew that it was nothing compared to the breaking news of another victim being discovered in Montgomery County. While people did care about the behind the scenes look into a crazed, serial killer's mind and the reasons he murders and maims people, finding out they had struck again was just that much more important of a story. Nick was pretty upset he hadn't checked with his sources and discovered that little tidbit of information, instead of going out and getting drunk at a friend's bar.

The third message was from Katherine Childs, the Dispatcher for the Rockville City Police. She had some news she wanted to talk to Nick about as soon as he got a chance to call her. He automatically decided he wasn't going to remember to call her with the headache he had surging through his skull, so he quickly scribbled a note with her information on it into the spiral notebook he kept next to the bed. He made sure to underline the message, his notation for it being something important he needed to follow up with, then moved to the last message.

There was a beep as Katherine's message was deleted and then Aidan's voice came over the line.

"Hey Nick, I need you to give me a call right away. I already tried you at your work, but they said you hadn't come in yet. I need to talk to you regarding something pretty serious. I remembered when I dropped you off yesterday you had mentioned going to see a friend at his pub after you got your article in by the dead line or something.

'Anyways, I thought you had called the friend Bo, and I was just wondering if that was short for Bodham? If it was and you were at The Dancing Bear last night, I need to talk to you as soon as you get this. It's important. Call me back," and with that the message was over.

What the hell could be so important? Nick wondered, then realized he hadn't mentioned Bo's full name to Aidan the day before. How had he known Bo was Bodham Choplinsky, or what bar the man owned? Nick suddenly had an awful feeling growing in his stomach, and this time it wasn't the result of the alcohol. He didn't bother saving the message or deleting it, it would save itself as he exited the messaging service and began typing in the number Aidan had left him to call back. The feeling in his stomach was certainly getting worse as the line began to ring. On the second ring, he heard Aidan.

"Haley?" he asked, no time for a formal greeting or anything.

"Yeah, I just got your message— what's up?"

"Jesus Nick, where have you been?" Aidan asked, and Nick could hear the worry in his voice. Something was certainly wrong, and Nick had no clue of what could be going on.

"I've been asleep. My phone was off," Nick replied, wiping a piece of crust from the corner of his eye that was a reminder of his long slumber.

"So you're alright?" Aidan asked, the worry in his voice starting to fade, and Nick wondered immediately if the reason for the concern was that the Detective thought the reporter had come to some harm. What was going on?

"Yes I'm alright, what is going on?" Nick demanded, realizing afterward how sharp and blunt he had been.

His head pounded loudly in his ears and he couldn't deal with the waiting. He needed to know what was going on. He never knew how to have patience, it was one of the characteristics he had never learned and served him well in his career of chasing down leads for the stories he wrote. Aidan had seemed to pause, collecting his thoughts. It was driving him crazy, this waiting while Aidan thought about how to word whatever it was he had to say. Finally he spoke.

"There's been another killing spree," Aidan admitted.

Nick's stomach plunged as he began to connect the dots. "Where?" he finally asked, unsure if he really wanted to hear the Aidan's answer.

"The Dancing Bear, last night."

Nick's heart stopped. He had just been at Bo's the night before. That's how Aidan knew Bo's full name was Bodham, the serial killer had struck at Bo's place. Dear Lord, what happened? Nick wondered, and Aidan quickly filled him in.

"A customer walked in late last night and discovered that the bar was the scene of a murder. It was a bloodbath— no survivors. When Mack gave me the news, the name rung a bell and I remembered that you had spoke about going over to the pub last night. The team that dusted and printed the place, combing the whole bar for fibers and other forensic evidence, were pretty sure nobody had made it out from the look of things. Yet when I couldn't get a hold of you, and you hadn't shown up at work today, I started thinking you might have been there last night."

"I was there last night!" Nick said, his stomach performing what felt like flipping motions, bile rising in his throat. Turning his head away from the phone, Nick gagged and caught himself from puking all over his floor. His throat burned from the acidic taste and he coughed loudly. He couldn't believe what he was hearing— Bo's big smile, his gold teeth twinkling from the lights, then the vision faded and he realized he was still holding the phone to his ear and Aidan had been speaking. He hadn't heard a thing.

"Wait what?" he asked, hoping Aidan didn't have any more details for him right at that moment. His stomach couldn't take it.

"I asked what time you left last night."

"Um…it was around midnight, that's all I remember. I was pretty intoxicated," Nick admitted.

Aidan waited a minute and then said, "Look, how about I come pick you up. I can fill you in on everything that's happened over the last day and night regarding the killings, plus I think you should talk to my buddy Mack about you being at the bar last night. Who knows, you might have seen something and not realized it."

"Okay, okay— give me half an hour to shower and get ready," Nick answered. He gave Aidan his address and hung up, wishing he hadn't drank so much the night before and had accidentally turned his phone off. As he headed for the bathroom to shower and change, his stomach continued to ache as the leftover alcohol rumbled about, and he knew that he needed to eat something to help soak up the feeling and sober him up. Hopefully the shower would help clear his mind, because right now it felt like it was pounding and full of cobwebs. His thoughts turned to Bo's smiling face again, and as he pictured the image in his mind, the realization that his friend had been massacred filtered though his thoughts.

Jesus, what a night! he thought and entered the bathroom.

Aidan arrived in his usual dark Dodge Challenger, the car pulling up outside Nick's apartment and the sound of the powerful engine rumbling echoed through his head as he locked his front door and hurried downstairs to meet up with the Detective. The loud reverberating motor wasn't going to help his headache at all, but fortunately he had taken some pills he had left in his kitchen cabinet for migraines and wolfed down a piece of toast to get something into his stomach before Aidan arrived.

As he approached the car, Aidan leaned over the passenger seat and unlocked the door. Nick pulled it open and slipped into the vehicle, careful to make sure his feet and his work bag were in the car before slamming the door shut.

"Thanks for picking me up," he said, and Aidan just brushed it aside with a wave.

"No problem, after everything I'm about to tell you, and the sound of the night you had, I'd better do the driving this morning anyway."

"Well I appreciate it," Nick said as he ran a hand through his still damp hair from the quick shower he took before Aidan had arrived at his apartment. "So can you tell me about The Dancing Bear now?"

Aidan sat in his seat, his growth of beard seeming thicker than Nick had remembered. Obviously the Detective was opposed to shaving daily, a habit hat Nick found absolutely necessary as he ran his hand over his smooth chin and cheek. Of course, he also didn't have the rugged looks that a couple days growth could accent like it did on Aidan.

"Yeah, but first— where do we need to go? We can meet up with Mack a little later so he can ask you some questions about last night. I called him right before I got to your place and they were pretty busy at County Headquarters. Apparently the newspapers and television studios are starting to setup their antennas and mobile broadcasting vans outside there so they can keep up to date on everything going on with this. It's turned out that this is becoming a huge story, everybody's following it, and I heard talk they might be getting National coverage. I even picked up a copy of The Informant this morning to see what you had to say in your article."

Aidan pulled a copy of that morning's newspaper from under his seat and handed it to Nick. Unfolding the paper, Nick saw his headline in big, bold print across the front of the newspaper.

Front page, not bad! Thanks Marty!

The headline read:

"Possible Trained Animal Involved in Murders Terrorizing Metropolitan Area", and directly under the title was his name.

That was what he liked to see. Maybe this would help boost his career and help him get his foot in the door at another paper. He had been fortunate enough to get the article in on time, and using the information he and Aidan had gathered from that beautiful, female wildlife biologist that had taken his breath away, he had written a story he knew would get National recognition.

"Well speaking of articles, I guess I should stop by the office first before doing anything else, my Editor is probably spitting blood right now over me not being in yet. He had already left two messages on my cell."

"Office of The Informant it is then," Aidan said and stepped on the gas as they shot around a car puttering ahead in the passing lane, and made a sharp right, the powerful Hemi engine purring as they shot around the corner and onto the next street.

Slowing the Challenger down as they came to a red light, Aidan turned in his seat slightly so he could see Nick better. He must have thought it would be better for the man to hear about the death of his friend in a one-on-one type setting like this before they got to the police station later and entered into the mad world that could be associated with the investigation.

Fear and panic were starting to form in the mind's of the public, and Nick couldn't blame them. It seemed no one was safe in Montgomery County at the moment. Taking his eyes off the road for a moment, Aidan met Nick's stare and began telling him what he knew of the previous nights situation.

"Like I mentioned earlier, a customer had walked into the bar and seen the victims and the blood all over the place. Ends up he made it outside to puke then proceeded to call 911. By the time the police had arrived to look into the call, the guy was hysterical and had got quite a crowd forming on the street outside the pub. The responding officers were able to secure the area and do an initial check for survivors before the FBI led, joint task force arrived to handle the processing of the scene. They initially found six bodies, all male and an additional body in the men's room. Every single one of them had been torn apart like they were rag dolls, and the task force has been able to identify all the patrons of the bar, one bartender and the owner of the place, Bodham Choplinsky."

Nick just sat there quietly as Aidan drove through the light, having turned green, and made a left at the next intersection. They were on Maryland Avenue, and Nick knew they would reach their final destination in no time with Aidan driving. Fortunately, it would only take them a few minutes with the light traffic of that morning anyways. There didn't seem to be as many people out on the roads as there usually was on a weekday morning, and Nick had a feeling it had to do with people staying home in the safety of their own domiciles, just like the Washington Metropolitan area had done before years back during the Sniper Shootings.

Sitting among his thoughts, Nick couldn't face the realization that Bo had been killed. Thinking of the massive giant of a man, it seemed ridiculous that he could be taken down by anybody, much less a few crazed serial killers who were already out of their minds and busy hacking up six other individuals.

It just doesn't make sense! I've seen Bo pissed off, he's like a goddamn wrecking ball when he's mad. Nobody, nobody could have done that to him, especially with so many other people in the bar as well. Nick imagined Bo being like Schwarzenegger, able to take on a whole army by himself. But, the truth of the situation seemed to be echoing in his mind, the truth of the matter being that the big Russian had met his downfall, and he was now deceased.

Nick felt like he had just been punched in the gut, and quickly kept himself from getting nauseous. That was the last thing he needed right now.

"So you said you left around midnight right?" Aidan asked, trying his hardest to keep Nick in the conversation and to not lose the man in his own thoughts.

"Yeah, I had been there for a little more than an hour I guess, maybe closer to two. That dick Ted Hanson, you know from Channel 5 News had shown up out of nowhere, drunk off his ass, and I gave Bo twenty bucks to make sure he got home safely. Something about him getting suspended for pissing off his boss's secretary or whatever. Anyway, after that I took off. Ended up getting home, and then the next thing I remembered was waking up this morning, a splitting headache and last night being mostly a blur. I had accidentally turned my phone off and once I checked my messages, that's when I called you back," Nick replied.

Aidan glanced over at Nick, taking his eyes off the road for a second, and said, "I'm sorry about your friend."

"Thanks— so who were the other victims?"

"Other than Choplinsky, there was Scott Wales, bartender at the pub, three buddies from Maryland University who were apparently regular customers, two boxing enthusiasts who had shown up to watch the fight on last night, and good old Ted Hanson of Channel 5."

Nick stared at Aidan, who's attention was focused on watching the traffic as he turned at the next street and added a little extra peddle on the gas, sending the Challenger roaring off onto the empty street, then hit another turn without slowing and Nick felt his stomach rumbling with unease.

"Wait— Hanson was one of the victims as well?"

"Yup, he seemed to have gotten the worst of it, and from what Mack told me about the preliminary time of death taken by the pathologist at the scene, it looks like he was the first to die."

Aidan's words sunk into Nick as he pictured Hanson's temper and bad mood last night, coupled with the amount of alcohol he had obviously consumed, and just shook his head in disbelief.

"I can't believe it," Nick muttered as he no longer focused on Aidan's heavy-footed driving.

"Tell me about it. I was certainly no fan of the guy, he was an outright asshole, but nobody deserves what was done to him. His head was decapitated from his body!"

Nick just continued to shake his head, then realized he also knew very little about the other homicide, the one he had seen on CBN at the bar when he was with Bo. The thought of the big man caused Nick to wince as he once again remembered the Russian's fate.

Why were these killers doing this? How and why were they choosing their victims? Was it just that they were after one person specifically and the rest of the patrons at the bar just happened to be in the wrong place at the wrong time? Questions flooded Nick's mind.

"So tell me about what you learned yesterday— did you get a chance to talk to that psychiatrist you know about our findings?"

Aidan stepped on the brakes as they coasted up to a stop sign that led from the small roadway they were on, and onto the larger thoroughfare of the four lane Rockville Pike. About two miles down from there current location was The Informant's office building. Aidan took the rest of the time until they reached The Informant, filling Nick in with everything he had learned from Dr. Harper. The possible ties to Halloween and werewolves, the Clinical Lycanthropy possibility, everything he had discussed with the psychiatrist. By the time he was done, Aidan had just enough time to give Nick a rundown of the murder that had been discovered in the woods.

Once he was done, Nick just stared at Aidan, not saying a word. His mind was working on absorbing everything he had just learned, and the while the alcohol seemed to be working its way out of his system from the previous night, it was still a lot to process.

"Jesus Christ..." Nick muttered, his brain working overtime as he thought about the serial killers and realized how he could use the information to take him a step above the competition. No one had named them yet!

Aidan realized Nick was quiet and since they had arrived at The Informant, he was just sitting there in the passenger seat, quiet and seeming to be reflecting on everything.

Finally Nick had it— Yes, it was perfect!

He turned his head to look at Aidan and said, "I've got it!"

Aidan looked confused for a moment, then asked, "Got what?"

"The name the media needs to really get the serial killer story out there to warn people and get them to be cautious of going out at night until these bastard are stopped!"

"Well what is it?"

Nick smiled, then meeting Aidan's eyes, he said, "The Moonlight Massacres!"

Thinking about it for a minute Aidan seemed to agree, he nodded his head up and down and said, "It's certainly catchy…and accurate."

"Yeah, and if these lunatics really are some crazed wackos who find some comfort in performing their killings at night based on the moon, then it looks like we very well may have a 'werewolf' on our hands in Rockville," Nick added, his smile stretching from ear to ear and Aidan had to laugh.

"Right, werewolves— well Clinical Lycanthropy or not, I don't think we're gonna need silver bullets to take these crazies down. I think the good, old-fashioned full-metal jacketed hollow points should do just the trick," Aidan said patting his leather jacket and his trusty sidearm underneath. "If a .44 can't do the job, then we'll go shopping for some silver, but somehow I doubt we'll need it."

Nick just smiled and looked from Aidan

He and Aidan, Detective and reporter did make a pretty good team.

Guess it's time to go solo and face my own troubles now, Nick thought as he opened the car door and climbed out.

"Give me twenty minutes, then we can get a move on with our investigation," he said, holding the door open and ducking slightly to stick his head back in the car.

Aidan just looked at his watch then at him and nodded.

Twenty minutes— Time to go see Marty!

Chapter 32

The scalpel sliced a sliver of tissue from just below the ankle, the tiny sample of skin was then placed in a small petri dish where Lisa studied the dead flesh under a powerful microscope, looking at the object at 100 times magnification. She was studying it at a microscopic level, the tissue strange and foreign, she knew right away there was something different about the piece of skin she had removed from the piece of a leg that Tyler Suffux had sent her from his find in Oregon. Lisa still didn't know what it was, since the Dire Wolf was thought to have died out ten thousand years ago, there was no skin or hair samples to compare this discovery with.

It could be part of the extinct animal, however, Lisa wasn't so sure. The dimensions of the object which included about five inches of the lower leg and the whole padded foot of the creature, didn't fit any of the Dire Wolf fossils that had been found so far in the La Brea Tar Pits and in other locations across the country, the remains were too large. As she stared at the hair and skin of the piece of leg, she began to wonder if this wasn't something even more startling and amazing.

Lisa wondered if Tyler Suffux had come across an actual, modern-day descendant of either Dire Wolf, or if it was a different species all together. Excitement filled her, and she had pushed all the other things in her life out of her mind, focusing solely on the remains of the unknown creature she was studying. However, she knew that she wouldn't be able to divert all her attention to the remains, there was too much going on in her life lately Frank her assistant, was due back from the Gray Wolf habitat any minute from performing the latest batch of vocalizations testings with the pack and recording the results, and she still had to write up the proposals for the Grand Opening event the Smithsonian was preparing for regarding their latest construction project, the Midnight Trail.

Lisa just wished she could push all the other things on her plate off to the side until she had the time needed to analyze the remains and figure out what they were exactly. She could be holding one of the most amazing revelations to affect the natural world and the scientific research community in whole for the next few generations. An undiscovered animal that was either related to, or was the modern relative of the Dire Wolf, having escaped extinction by evolving and adapting to live in the region of the Pacific Northwest.

This has the potential to be huge! Lisa imagined as she backed away from the microscope and walked back over to the tray she had sitting on the lab table, a smaller tray holding an assortment of dissection tools while the main one held the actual leg of the unknown species.

She just wasn't sure if due to the time restraints she was facing with her other projects, if she would be able to perform the needed work to document and study these creature samples all by herself. In fact, she knew she couldn't, not with her own work with the Gray Wolves and preparing the final steps before they were moved from the SCBI campus to the National Zoological Park downtown.

The Board had chosen to move the opening of the Midnight Trail up from after the New Year to now before, and that meant Lisa had her days booked. Taking on another project that required this much dedication was out of the question if she relied only on herself. Fortunately, she had a friend over at the National Zoo who would be perfect to aid her.

She just hoped he wasn't too busy with his own work and research. Either way, Lisa knew that she could at least get started on the initial DNA sequencing and attempt to isolate what species this leg came from. Since she didn't want to reveal anything about this new secret project she had to anyone just yet, she figured she might as get as much work done now before her assistant got back.

Lisa picked up a sterilized scalpel from the assortment of instruments and approached her target. The leg was lying on the cold, stainless steel tray and as she brought the blade close to the old, musty remains, she noticed a strange marking on the skin under the fur that was right around the ankle. It was a dark blob that appeared to be on the skin in one isolated place, but not anywhere else on the darkened flesh. The pigments were certainly different, and Lisa used the scalpel and a pair of tweezers in her gloved hands to push the fur around at varying angles away from the spot so she could see it more clearly.

With the sample having been dead for a while, decomposition had set in, and the piece that had been exposed to the elements and Mother Nature had been picked clean. Fortunately for Lisa, the lower part of this leg had been buried at some point so that the skin, tissue and some blood were still visible mixed around the tufts of dark, wiry fur that was still slightly oily and covered in dirt. She wished she could wash the leg off and remove some of the debris, but she was worried she might remove something important or accidentally contaminate the sample before she had the chance to type its DNA.

Finding out the animal's taxonomical status was the most important step in figuring out it's background and species and to answering her inquiry into what exactly she had laid out before her. She wondered if it might be a genetic mix of two different species, but the question nagging at her was what two animals could have crossed together to form this odd, enlarged breed, or if it was even a combination at all?

The wolf-dog was such an example of species in the same taxonomic classification having specifically shared traits and genes to form a new species. The wolf-dog is a cross between a Gray Wolf and a dog, which some people refer to as a wolf hybrid. However, in the scientific community there was some disagreement on the potential confusion that could arise by naming this breed as such instead of more appropriately referring to the animals as wolf-dogs.

In 1993, Canis lupus familiaris known to the average person as the common dog, was reclassified in the internationally recognized publication, the Mammal Species of the World: A Taxonomic & Geographic Reference, under the species status of Canis lupus, or more widely known as the Gray Wolf. This falling under the genetic umbrella of the Gray Wolf were the subspecies the Timber Wolf, the Arctic Wolf and the dog. Because of its domestic status, some scientists believe the Canis lupus familiaris should be more specifically refeered to as a domestic variant of the Gray Wolf rather than a subspecies because of its domesticated status.

A filial number refers to the number of generations that an animal is removed from the pure ancestry of that species. The classification 'F1 hybrid', is a term used in genetics and selective breeding where the F1 stands for Filial 1, which is the filial generation that all animal offspring resulting from a cross mating of distinctly different parental types is classified as. The offspring of distinctly different parental types produce a new, uniform variety with specific characteristics from either or both parents. In animal species those parents usually are two inbred lines. An example can be found in many domestic hybrid breeds today. Certain domestic hybrid breeds, such as the dog, are classified by their filial generation number. It is this number and term that is used to distinguish the percentage that a creature has inherited from its family as each new generations moves the animal further from the original breed that it initially spawned from.

A wolf-dog has one parent that is a pure wolf, while the other parent is usually another wolf-dog or a common domesticated dog. The degree found in the rating of F2, refers to an animal that has at least one grandparent that is pure wolf. A wolf-dog that had at least one great grandparent who is a pure wolf would be considered and classified as being F3, since it is three generations removed from the original Gray Wolf. It is the same working classifications that go into human ancestry, a person continuing to get less and less of a percentage of relatives genes the longer the bloodline continues to change over each successive new generation.

However, in relation to wolf-dogs the documenting of these new generations only pertains to how they are recorded on paper. The real percentage of wolf or dog that an F1 or F2 wolf-dog/wolf mix has can vary among the litters of pups born at one time. For example, a litter of F2 animals could have more wolf like traits ingrained in their appearance while they act more tamed like a regular dog, or it could be reversed and one or more hybrid animals from the litter could appear to be dogs but have wolf like characteristics and behavior.

These pups from the same litter would genetically not be the same percentage, however, on paper they would all be classified as the same since their ancestry is the same.

In the case of Canis lupus, famed wolf researcher L. David Mech summed up the problems inherent in the taxonomic classification of the various subspecies of the Gray Wolf, claiming that "because of the interbreeding or integration of wolves, there is a melding of traits that are generally used to determine one subspecies from another. For decades, differences in the pelage, skeletal features, and behavior were used to distinguish among subspecies". In 1959, Raymond Hall and K. R. Kelson recognized 24 subspecies of North American Wolf, but other authoritarians on the subject disagreed because they were using a different classification system to distinguish the various ancestry and filial percentages that made up the different subspecies. However, L. David Mech, commenting on the problems with the current wolf taxonomy in 1970, noted that there were "probably far too many sub-specific designations . . . in use." It wasn't until Hall's publication in 1981 that the taxonomic division of Canis lupus into 24 subspecies became the single, most widely accepted classification system of North American wolves.

It was thanks to this system that Lisa would be able to remove a sample of DNA from the unknown animal's leg she had in her possession, and hopefully discover what lineage and what path its ancestry leads towards finding out the creature's taxonomic classification. Though Hall's taxonomy of gray wolves is still accepted today, in 1996, Ronald M. Nowak and Nick E. Federoff challenge it, narrowing the subspecies from 24 to five categories: arctos, lycoan, nubilus, baileyi, and occidentalis.

Research has progressed from pelage, skeletal features, and behavior to include statistical analyses of cranial morphology and the newer studies of mitochondrial and nuclear DNA that have arisen through technological and scientific breakthroughs over the last few decades and the most amazing achievement of the mapping of not only the human genome but many other species of flora and fauna from all over the world as well. While Nowak and Federoff cited various studies focusing on genetic evidence that indicated to some researchers that "there may be even fewer identifiable kinds of gray wolf", presently, both Hall's and Nowak and Federoff's classifications are widely accepted.

Lisa preferred Hall's more defined system, where it separated the various wolves known across the world to more subspecies that distinguished their individual characteristics more so than delegating all the subspecies into only 5 wider-ranging categories. Plus, if she was going to be able to figure out what ancestry and genetic traits this specimen sample had, she would need to be able to narrow down the results she got to as close to a genetic ancestor as possible. That was the only way to know exactly what animal this creature was related to and if it was some hybrid mix or not.

"What are you?" her voice no more than a whisper as she stared at the strange piece of animal remains laid out before her.

Yet, she knew the answer to her question would not be so readily revealed. She still had to collect samples and analyze them. Fortunately, since she worked here at SCBI, she had access to some great equipment, the right tools for the job ahead, and for the few things she wouldn't be able to ascertain from what she had at her disposal in her own lab, her friend over at the National Zoo would certainly have access to the equipment she did need. Yes, I'm going to get to the bottom of your mysteries, she thought staring at the hairy stump.

It was odd how similar it was to a Gray Wolves' paw, yet had such distinct characteristics and a much larger size than even the Dire Wolf. Could it be that she was indeed looking at the remains of a new species of wolf, one that had escaped extinction all together or adapted and evolved over the last thousands of years to form the creature that was missing this part of its leg. Lisa wondered if there was more of this body where Tyler Suffux's dog had dug it up. From his e-mails she knew he said that it was an area littered with fossils from long ago, and even some more recent kinds of animals. It was his inability to tell what kind of animal he was looking at that had been discovered on his property, and Lisa assumed he had only sent her this one small piece because it would have made the package weigh far too heavy to include anymore than the Dire Wolf skull, the photographs and this piece of a hind leg.

The photographs— how could I have forgot! Lisa just remembered Tyler's daughter was supposed to help him take clearer photos and send them with the package for Lisa to see the site and the uncovered fossils and remains herself since it was impractical to board a plane and fly 3,000 miles just to diagnose a possible archaeological dig-site with paleontological significance. Lisa quickly skirted over to the package she had left lying on the floor and began digging through the last of the scrap newspapers until she found an envelope lying at the bottom of the box. Tearing it open, a collection of photos fell out into her hand and she took them to her desk where upon flipping on the lamp, she sat down and started thumbing through the digital prints.

The first few seemed to be establishing shots that Tyler's daughter had taken, the content of the scene showing a deep valley surrounded by lush evergreens and wild grown bushes that needed to be cut back. The next photo was of the rocky path leading down into the small canyon, the rocks and dirt showing recent evidence of having a surge of water running through the natural creek bed that lay at the bottom of the valley. Years of water following this course, the natural rocks acting as a barrier to keep the flash floods contained to one portion of the landscape, clearing the bottom of the canyon of all vegetation and plant life. It stood in stark contrast to the lively wooded land that capitalized the area.

As she rifled through the photographs, she finally came to the last few prints. They were closeups of the rocky canyon floor and the exposed creek bed. Here there was no sign of life either, the waters of constant floods having eroded piles of dirt that had once covered the bottom of the valley, revealing a massive amount of bones that truly did look like bleached, skeletal plants rising up from the ground. Upon closer examination she could make out the various shapes of bones and skulls of multiple animals that had been fossilized. There was also a photo of one of the fossils that Lisa immediately recognized as the Dire Wolf skull that Tyler had sent her.

Yes, the photos were real and the site did exist! Tyler Suffux had discovered an animal burial ground of some sort where the remains of the extinct Dire Wolf would show that the creature had moved from the Midwest and Western States of North America and up into the Northern Pacific coastline at some point thousands of years ago. It was an amazing discovery, and Lisa was the one who could capitalize on it and use it to erase the believed history of these magnificent relatives of the Gray Wolf, and rewrite the history books and scientific journals of the modern natural world!

Flipping to the last photo, Lisa gasped. It showed a smaller section of the canyon floor where more recent skeleton remains seemed to have been dug up. The shocking part wasn't necessarily how recent these animals seemed to have died, although it would certainly speak volumes on the subject of a common ancestor linked to the Dire and Gray Wolves, but in the photo of the small corner of the creek, mixed among the pebbled and rocks, there was the image of not only what looked like human skeletal fragments, but the scattered remains of a creature that had part of its body that was originally stuck out of the ground that was as clean and white as the other skeletons.

The half buried section showed a part of a head and the spine of a animal that had the same black, wiry fur and appeared to be the size of something that could have been the owner of the piece of leg that sat on her lab table right now. Unfortunately, there was only one photo showing the mystery creature and with it still mostly buried in the rocks and dirt of the dry creek bed, only small parts of it were able to be captured in the picture.

What the hell was it, and why were there pieces of what appeared to be human bones lying among it? Lisa wondered and at just that moment a hand touched her shoulder and she jumped out of her seat with startling speed.

"What the hell is that?" Frank asked, his head pointed in the direction of the dissection tray with the leg on it.

Lisa took a deep breath, glad she hadn't screamed when her assistant had nearly given her a heart attack, and turned to face the young man. She could see he had dirt on his clothes, a tell-tale sign he had been playing around with the wolves again, and letting the breath out she answered his question.

"I don't know," she said, still trying to get her heart rate to slow as she walked over to the lab table, Frank following closely behind until they reached the table and the tray it held for anyone entering the lab to see.

Lisa knew she would have to be more careful in the past about leaving things of such a sensitive nature locked up or hidden until she could finish her testing and know what the hell it was.

"Um, Lisa— what is this thing?" Frank asked, the confusion quite evident in his voice as he stared down at the stainless steel tray and its contents.

"I think you better come take a look at these photos," she said and walked over to her desk to pick up the pictures she had dropped when Frank had almost scared her to death with his quiet arrival. She'd have to warn him about making some noise when he entered or exited the rooms, so as not to cause her to develop some medical condition like a weak heart. There was enough going on right now, that her health had to be the top priority to keep her strong and energetic enough to accomplish everything she had to do over the next month.

Handing the photos to Frank, she watched as he scrolled through them, taking a good look at each one, then moving onto the next. His attention was firmly on the photographs as he reached the last one and his face turned into a look of pure confusion.

"What the…" he stated.

"Yeah, that's about how I summed it up when I saw it. Damn strange if you ask me, but until we get it analyzed, I don't know what to tell you."

"It's definitely a wolf of some kind isn't it though?" he asked, his eyes glued to the last photo of the half-buried, half-decomposed, furry corpse with definite canine characteristics noticeable in the part of the skull that was visible in the photo. It was too bad Tyler hadn't dug this creature's skull out of the ground and shipped it to her instead of part of its leg, but either way, it was enough for her to get a DNA sample and figure out what he had come upon at the far corner of his property, on the surveying expedition with his German Shepherd almost two weeks prior.

The look of intrigue and wonder that was Frank's expression said it all.

Yes, he had no idea of what to make of the photos either.

"Want to help me extract some samples for the DNA analysis?" Lisa asked, and knew from the way Frank's face lit up that he couldn't wait.

"Oh yeah!"

"Well then let's get started!"

As Lisa added the final sample they had collected into the petri dish, she moved across the room and began setting up the various slides she had taken that held tiny pieces of tissue removed from the unknown creature's leg.

She had also pulled out some of the hairs and placed them into multiple, sealed glass beakers, labeling each with a marker to remember which part of the leg they had come from. Some of the hairs were from the top half of the padded hind paw, while others had come from the just below where the hock area of the leg would have been if the leg had been whole and was indeed a wolves. They went with the region of the animal's pelt where the most intact looking fur was chosen for them to study. She would keep some of the samples they had taken here at the lab, and the others she was sending to her friend Morgan over at the National Zoo for analysis.

Lisa was also able to withdraw a small sample of the creature's blood by sticking the needle up in between the pad of the animals paw, careful not to scratch against the long, razor sharp claws that stuck out of the digits of the foot. This blood sample they would use to get a DNA profile of the creature compiled. Since red blood cells do not contain DNA, she would have to try to type the animal based on whatever she could get from the white blood cells that had hopefully not been too degraded over time as the partial limb had started to decay. Its level of necrosis was beginning to cause the skin and cells to break down since the creature was no longer alive and blood had stopped flowing through the limb, and she was hoping too much time hadn't been wasted already in getting the sample sent to her.

The limb should have been packed in dry ice to keep the limb just cold enough to survive the 3,000 mile trip across country. On top of that, there was no telling how long it had been dead before Tyler Suffux had discovered it based on when it had been buried. Because of the condition it was in, it was hard to believe this limb that was in bad shape had died that long ago, or else there would be absolutely nothing left to it but bones. Even buried the tiny microbes and parasites plus the worms and other insects in the soil would have stripped it eventually down to nothing but its bone, so the fact that there was some hair and flesh still on it was a miracle.

As Lisa finished setting up the slides and then turned on the large projector attached to the table, a Micron Select AbGen FD electron microscope hummed to life and she stood back while the machine went to work zeroing in on the sample Lisa had placed on its digital reader plate. The big machine was the size of a child's school desk, and when it came to life, it filled the lab with a soft whirring noise as various plates and optics switched around and with the press of a wireless remote in her hand, she was able to bring the sample into focus and enhance the image projected onto the screen she had pulled down in one corner of the room.

An electron microscope is a type of microscope that uses a beam of electrons to illuminate the specimen and produce a magnified image. Electron microscopes have a greater resolving power than a light-powered optical microscope, because electrons have wavelengths about 100,000 times shorter than visible light, and can achieve magnifications of a sample up to about 10,000,000x, whereas ordinary, non-confocal light microscopes are limited by diffraction to magnifications below 2000x.

The AbGen EM electron microscope uses electrostatic and electromagnetic "lenses" to control the electron beam and focus it to form an image. These lenses are analogous to, but different from the glass lenses of an optical microscope that form a magnified image by focusing light on or through the specimen.

Now with the tissue samples they had spent the long hour of collecting, Lisa also took a beaker that Frank handed her and extracting a few pieces of the specimen's fur from the glass vial with a pair of tweezers, she placed the hairs onto the flat, glass like panel in the tray on the AbGen EM, next to the tissue samples. Both images were displayed on the wall and her and Frank were able to see both magnified to incredible degrees.

"Wow…I'm always amazed at technology these days," Frank stated as he looked at the clear images displayed against the projector screen's backdrop.

The hairs were magnified to the point where the various layers were clearly visibly seen, a needed step if they were going to attempt to compare hair samples in the database to those that they had taken from the leg. The same would be done with the tissue taken from the skin. As they both stared at the two individual images, Lisa was glad that the SCBI had spent a large amount of grant money to update some of the more widely used laboratories on the campus where they were doing hair comparison, species identification and DNA sequencing on a daily to weekly basis. The upgrade had made it possible for Lisa to get the older modeled equipment for her own lab, and while she usually didn't find a need for the instruments and various microscopes, sequencers and mega-data processors, she was certainly making them useful now.

There was a soft beep and a printer hummed to life in the other corner of the lab. Leaving Frank to work his way through the massive database of animal hairs that the SCBI had stockpiled for research needs, along with the job she gave him of preparing the control groups that he still needed to arrange for the tissue analysis. As Lisa began walking towards the other corner, she saw that the machine was slowly spitting out page after page of printouts that had been sent to it from the DNA sequencer where Lisa had run the blood typing and tests. The results had obviously finished from the expensive and almost fully-automated Seeder Plains 3000XP DNA Analysis System and the findings were being printed out now.

The Seeder Plains 3000XP DNA Analysis System is an automated unit capable of reading and analyzing DNA sequencing products that have been generated by incorporating WellRED fluorescent dyes into the DNA. The systems 650 nanometer and 750 nm diode lasers excite these dyes, which then fluoresce and are automatically detected and processed by the 3000XP DAS software. The system is equipped with an array made up of eight parallel capillaries, permitting electro-kinetic injections of eight samples at a time. This high throughput setup allows for 96 samples to be processed and analyzed by the system's software in 24 hours.

They are able to sequence multiple samples in a batch, or run, and perform as many as twenty-four runs a day. These perform only the size separation and peak reading; the actual sequencing reactions, cleanup and resuspension in a suitable buffer must be performed separately.

The presence or absence of a strand of DNA is then detected by monitoring the output of the detector. Since shorter strands of DNA move through the gel matrix faster they are detected sooner and there is then a direct correlation between length of DNA strand and time at the detector. This relationship is then used to determine the actual DNA sequence. What used to take a human operator hours to configure and assemble, now takes the machines a matter of seconds to process.

Lisa checked the printout and saw that the first run had finished. She looked at the pages and begin to feel like her and Frank had screwed something up. They had obviously contaminated the samples somehow. The result was showing that once the DNA had been analyzed, it had found genetic matches to a few different matches.

Leave it to the people who don't do this every day to mess it up! She thought looking over the first run and its initial findings.

They had obviously gotten some of their own cells into the mix that the 3000XP had analyzed. The results were showing that along with finding matches to a certain link of DNA commonly found in wolves, there were many unknown variants and genes it was unable to match. The most annoying one was that Homo Sapien was showing up in the list. That meant either the animal had human DNA as well as wolf and other characteristics, or they had screwed up.

Taking a deep breath, Lisa let it out, dropped the pages back onto the print tray and walked over to her desk. She needed someone who knew what they were doing to test the samples from the specimen they had removed earlier. The tissue, blood and hair samples all needed to be looked at by a professional, and fortunately Lisa had just the person in mind. Pulling her e-mail up, she saw that Morgan over at the National Zoo had responded to her inquiry. Clicking on the message, she waited for the e-mail to load and fill the computer's screen.

From: MorganG@nationalzoo.org
Sent: Fri 10/30/12
To: LisaM_Davies1@homail.com
Subject: Re: Can you help a friend in need????

Lisa,
Of course I'd be honored to help out a friend in need! Just bring the samples over tonight and I'll run them through our equipment and get you what you need. It sounds like you have quite an interesting find on your hands. Make sure you bring the hairs, tissue and blood samples so that I can run all the tests and cover all the bases. Just stop by once you're off work, I'll be here most the night catching up on some things. Until then...

Yours truly,

Morgan Garrett
Assistant Curator

National Zoological Park
3001 Connecticut Ave. NW,
Rock Creek Park, Washington D.C. 20880

Lisa felt a flood of relief fill her, knowing that Morgan could help her get to the bottom of the mystery of the strange specimen sitting in the freezer in her office was a heavy burden off her back, and bring her one step closer to answering her questions.

At least Morgan can keep this a secret, Lisa thought, and then looking and seeing that Frank was still hard at work comparing hair samples, she decided to go assist him so they could wrap up this phase and she could get over to the Zoo before they closed for the night.

Morgan was an odd man who worked all kinds of strange hours, so him being there by the time she arrived at the Zoo wasn't a concern. If he said he'd be there, he would. Plain and simple.

Thanks Morgan, I'll owe you! she thought as she closed her e-mail and headed for the other side of the lab.

"You won't believe this…" Frank said as she approached her young assistant.

Chapter 33

Jesse Vaughan hated working the night shift at SCBI. He had been assigned to the gig for the last week ever since Todd Blaski had come down with the flu or bronchitis or some such ailment, and so far, the job of guarding the large facility after hours, having to check each building multiple times throughout the late hours as he walked the preordained route that his rounds took him on through the vast campus, this job was certainly not why he had sought out a career in security. In fact, he had hoped that the assignment would be the much needed change he needed compared to the boredom he experienced working for the government as a guard for the Smithsonian Institute.

He had imagined it would be fun and exciting, when he first had taken the job back a few months prior, he had gone through an intensive background check and had to complete firearms training and become certified to carry the weapon he now had attached to his belt. Though over the last few months, the flashlight that dangled from his waist had seen much more action than the gun had. Moreover, he had never even had a reason to remove his weapon from its holster during any moment over the course of time he had been with the Smithsonian Institution's Office of Protection Services.

Instead, his normal daily routine had him tasked with normally protecting visitors, staff, property, and grounds of the federally-owned and managed Smithsonian Institution museums and research centers in Washington, D.C., New York City, at the 2,800 acre Smithsonian Environmental Research Center in Maryland, the Smithsonian Biological Conservation Institute in Front Royal Virginia as well as oversight of the security operations in the Smithsonian Facility in Panama.

Taking this shift when his shift supervisor had told him Blaski was sick and out for the week, he had hoped he would see some excitement. Images of him having to protect the facility in Virginia from rival research companies that were out to sabotage their competitors and steal valuable trade secrets to sell on the International Black Market filled his head.

Of course, now that he had actually taken the late-night shift, he saw how wrong he was. He realized the ideas that had been floating in his head of spies breaking into one of the many research labs or offices here at the SCBI campus was nothing but exciting plot developments from a movie. Nothing actually happened at the facility, and what made matters worse, was it wasn't even like any of his buddies even knew the Smithsonian had a place out in the middle of Virginia. They all were familiar with the various museums that they worked at downtown, or some of the lucky ones who got transferred out to New York, at least that city had a chance of bringing some livelihood to the job.

It wasn't even like he was a real police officer or anything, more like a rent-a-cop working at a shopping mall, but even they got to arrest people for shoplifting or other petty crimes every so often. Here at the Smithsonian, the federal guard force that consisted of over 850 officers, had limited special police authority to actually do anything if something did ever happen that could be considered not in the normal functions of the day's shift.

It wasn't like somebody was going to try and steal the dinosaurs from the Natural History Museum, or Dorothy's ruby red slippers from American History, or even a useless piece of moon rock from the Air and Space Museum! Jesse thought, annoyed that his career was stuck in a job that didn't appear to be going anywhere anytime soon, and the worst part was that here he was about to have a new baby with his girlfriend Stacy, that making two little dolls to crawl around, drooling on everything and smelling up their crowded apartment with their shit-filled diapers, and he was going to die of boredom first.

Life isn't fair! Jesse thought as he pictured his buddy Davey, just back from Afghanistan where he was killing towel-heads and truly protecting the American Dream! Why couldn't I have joined the military instead of taking this crappy job babysitting these old buildings housing their even older, useless exhibits of crap with a capital C!

Or, I could have tried for the Metropolitan Police Department again, Jesse heard himself reminding him as he walked along the outside of Building One, the main structure that housed the headquarters here at SCBI's campus. Jesse used to have the dream of being a cop, arresting the bad guys and getting into shootouts that he came out of the situation unscathed while the criminals were sent packing, his expert marksmanship having picked off each one with accuracy that he had perfected playing first-person shooters on his Xbox. Unfortunately, he had failed the entrance exam to be accepted into the Metropolitan Police Training Academy, Washington D.C.'s primary police force, and he was hesitant to retake the exam even though it had been over a year and he could.

Maybe Stacy's right. Maybe I should just be happy that I made it into some line of law enforcement, rather than being stuck working at his old job as a sales clerk at one of those giant retail stores.

No!...what am I talking about— I wouldn't call this crap working law enforcement!

Sure the Smithsonian Museum protection officers are security officers that have been designated as 'special police' under some US Code, Title 40, Chapter blah-blah-blah, but even though they had that 'police' designation and possessed limited police powers, Jesse considered it a joke to compare the two positions.

For his training to join and become a part of the Smithsonian's law enforcement services, he had to undergo forty hours of training, an amount that doesn't even meet the standards of the real, established police academies, and he had to show minor proficiency in firearm handling, arrest, handcuff procedures, and pepper spray use.

After that, they were assigned to one of the nineteen Smithsonian museums or research sites in New York City, Maryland, Virginia, or the District of Columbia. There is even a specialized K-9 unit with bomb-detection dogs that patrol the various museum grounds, but Jesse hadn't attempted to go into that field. It was bad enough he had another kid on the way, and one that sniffled and cried nonstop at nights that it was still hungry or thirsty, but what did it expect when it had crap coming out of it as soon as it ate! Yeah, like the last thing he needed was to be dealing with damn animals as part of his daily routine, they were just like a freaking baby!

No, I'll just deal with working this gig for now, and once Blaski's back, I'll think about taking that entrance exam for the MPD again. Maybe this time he could concentrate and spend the time he needed to to study and pass the damn thing. That would sure show Stacey that she wasn't dating a loser who was only capable of getting her pregnant and barely covering the monthly bills even though his hourly rate wasn't half bad for the work he was doing.

That's the only plus side to this shit, he thought as he reached the glass doors to Building One. They pay was pretty damn good for an hourly job— that and the benefits that came along with it being federal government meant that if the kid got sick they'd at least be able to take them to the doctor without it costing an arm and a leg, and heaven forbid he thought about how much Stacy's pregnancy expenses and the hospitalization when she went into labor with their second child were going to cost!

Jesse just shook his head as he reached out, grabbing the door handles and pulling. They came to a quick halt and shook slightly, the lock being engaged correctly. He then tried the other doors around the building and found they were all still locked as well.

"Go figure", he muttered to himself as he checked off the time he had reached the structure on the clipboard he carried, and looking at his watch, he saw his loops around the campus were starting to take a shorter amount of time as he got the hang of the layout over the last few night. Then concluding this night-shift was actually better than his normal, 8 to 6 gig at the Natural History Museum, where he worked the main entrance metal detectors, and was slowly being annoyed by how many people flocked to the museums daily and felt it was a violation of their constitutional amendments to be expected to follow security protocols upon entering the government building.

Goddamn yuppies, Jesse thought. He certainly didn't miss the crowds of idiots, and going over the things he did like about Blaski's guard shift here at SCBI, he realized that working late and not getting home until morning to his cramped apartment that he shared with Stacey and his son, he didn't have to deal with the little brat waking him up all night, disturbing him from getting a good nights sleep with his whining.

Maybe once Todd Blaski is back from his sick leave, I can convince him to switch shifts with me, Jesse contemplated as he continued along his route to the next building to be checked and made sure it was secure. Not like they never were, what with how many researchers and scientists seemed to be leaving the campus and going home when Jesse arrived for his shift each day of this week. There seemed to be a lot of people who worked at SCBI, and just once, he wished one of them would do something to make his life a little more exciting.

Perhaps a disgruntled scientist, one of them real crazy types like that one guy with the Albert Einstein-looking hairdo, would bring a gun into his lab and start shooting up his colleagues, then Jesse could step in and shoot him down in a rain of bullets, just like in the movies! He'd be a hero! Continuing to picture the make-believe scenario in his mind, Jesse smiled slightly at his imagined heroics and walked towards the next structure on his route, Building 15, or as he had heard some of the researchers refer to it, "the Cave".

What a bunch of weirdos that work here, he thought as the designated Cave came into view, complete with its odd statue that was displayed on the building's center overhang, out there for all who entered the small courtyard and entryway to the building to see and Jesse figured, question the architect's sanity. Who would want such a weird statue to sit on top of their place of work? What was it with these academia types and their weird fascination with history and animals? Sure it sucked when a certain animal was killed off, Jesse could remember reading a few years back how conservationists like the ones here at SCBI were working on saving the Bald Eagle from going extinct, but to save all the animals? Jesse thought that was a waste of time. There were definitely some creatures like bees or the termites that an exterminator had just found in his apartment, that could be wiped off the face of the Earth and he wouldn't mind. You wouldn't find him shedding and tears for the loss of such a pest. It was already going to cost him a fortune to try and get them removed from his home, and add the damage they had already caused to the foundation of the floor in some spots, and he was sure the world would be a better place without them.

Taking one last look at the large bronze statue of the she-wolf and the two babies underneath, some historical children who founded the Roman culture of something like that, and Jesse headed for the doors to check that they were locked.

As he approached, his mind busy with his latest grumblings about the lot that life had served him recently, he pulled on the glass doors and felt the same, sturdy nature about this entrance as all the buildings he had already checked. Yeah, the doors were locked, what an amazing occurrence, the campus was safe and secure! Turning to start in the direction of the side of the structure, Jesse suddenly heard what sounded like the soft patter of glass raining down onto the ground from a broken window.

"Shit, what was that?" he said, reaching for the flashlight on his belt and heading towards the source of the disturbance.

His mind raced as he pictured all sorts of varying scenarios that he might encounter, the excitement and intrigue flowing through him as he walked through the freezing night air, his flashlight's beam illuminating the side of the building as he continued on. He felt like this gig might jest be getting interesting, all thoughts on the different hyped up beliefs he had rushing through him as he made his way to the end of the building. Turning the corner, he looked towards the back entrance, seeing the cause of the noise.

A whole glass panel that made up the back entrance's exit doors had bee smashed in, the fragments of glass and debris littering the concrete covered ground and inside the small breezeway that divided the Cave into two separate structures. Jesse knew that the left side housed most of the research labs, while the right hall led to the offices and rooms designated for storage. As his light danced across the ground and the shattered window pane, pieces of glass caught the bright beam and sent the light reflecting off the fragments and into the dark night sky like a million little prisms laying about. Jesse ignored the comparison his mind was making to the effect his flashlight had on the glass, and he turned his attention to the fact that someone had gained access to the Cave's interior by breaking out the glass from this section of breezeway. There was an intruder somewhere inside!

Reaching back with an unsteady hand, he undid the snap that held his gun in the holster, and with one hand on the butt of the weapon and the other holding the flashlight up to see, he glanced around at the building's dark insides, Jesse swallowed hard, knowing this was the exact situation he had been dreaming about yet found a small bit of apprehension about entering into the unknown, then pushing the worries out of his head, stepped over he glass all over the ground and entered the Cave through the hole in the large window. It was now or never.

Sweeping his light down both hallways and listening for any other noise, Jesse found that it appeared to be quite silent inside, the only noise being the wind as it picked up and brushed across the outside windows of the building, rattling them slightly in their frames. Other than that, it appeared to be dead inside. Jesse could pick up no noise or see anything that would explain how the glass window had been broken and glass had been trailed inside as if by being stuck on the bottom of someone's foot.

Where the hell is the intruder?" Jesse pondered as his beam traveled over the various closed doors that led to each lab and office space, each one appearing to not have been forced into. Finally having cleared this part of the building, he began walking towards the East wing where the majority of the labs were contained. Hopefully, he would catch the person who had broken in to the building in the act, and be able to contain them until the real police arrived. What was he saying? This was his job to keep this place safe and he was damn sure not going to let the Virginia Police Department upstage him in apprehending a burglar.

As he walked down the abandoned hall, hand still firmly on the butt of his gun, ready at any moment to pull the weapon from its holster, his eyes took in everything, looking for anything out of the ordinary. Just then he heard a noise, what sounded like wood splintering and a door being broken off its hinged. Pulling his gun out and cocking it, he gripped it and the flashlight tightly and headed for the sounds. Little did he know that what he would find would not be some common burglar at all.

Jesse raced down the hall, his heavy belt shaking from the weight of the equipment on it as he ran. He had everything he could possibly need plus more on the bulky belt, its contents including pouches filled with all sorts of things, from two extra clips of ammunition for his automatic, to handcuffs, a selection of twist-ties and plastic flexi-cuffs, a small stun gun and extra cartridge, radio and his pepper spray. There were even pockets where he kept his car keys, cigarettes and wallet so they weren't taking up space in his pants and he could easily store things in those pockets if need be. The only thing he did keep clipped to his one main pocket on the front of his pants was a small, folding knife with a four inch blade. When folded, the knife was easily stored in this spot. Overall, he was prepared for anything, or so he thought.

Rounding the corner of the last hallway, Jesse found himself in the Cave's East Wing, row upon row of doors lining the hall that led to the various labs in the corner of the building. Close to the end, Jesse noticed that one of the doors had been smashed in, splinters of wood and screws from the doors hardware were lying on the ground. He felt his grip tighten on the objects in his hands, his sweaty palms threatening to cause him to lose his firm clutch on the flashlight and pistol. Past the broken down door, the office beyond was pitch black and Jesse aimed his light towards the frame, the damage done to the broken door becoming evident as he drew closer.

What the hell? He wondered as he eventually made it to the entryway, his footing taking the path slowly as he decided if he should call for backup. The heavy duty radio that was clipped to his belt wasn't even on, a break in procedure that Jesse just noticed. He had turned it off when he was sitting at the desk, tired of listening to the dispatcher on the Smithsonian's secure channel yak away with some other unknown person that went by 'Lou 32' on the other end of the radio. Now he wished he had left it on, at least so he could call for help if he needed to, but it was too late now. If he turned it on now, any chance of sneaking up on and surprising the intruder when that obnoxious beep sounded off and broke the silence.

Stopping at the entrance to the lab, he looked at the door and felt a shiver run through him. It had been torn from its hinges alright, and to make matters worse, there were four long gashes in the top half of the wood, they looked like claw marks and Jesse Vaughan felt scared— really scared for the first time in his adult life. Moving the beam of his flashlight from the destroyed door and into the office beyond, Jesse wished he had thought it through before quickly following whoever was in the building inside, without having radioed in the incident first. It had been his stupid wannabe 'hero' complex that had led him to rush inside, not thinking the situation over clearly.

The light illuminated the office, his body stiff and the shake in his hands noticeable as the beam trembled slightly, the areas he was shining it moving around and casting shadows on the walls. Taking a step further into the office, he was now fully inside, his eyes narrowing as he searched the dark corners of the room. He stopped when he noticed some of the equipment that had sat on one of the various tables set up throughout the lab, the scientific paraphernalia and things that Jesse couldn't identify even if they were together, were smashed all over the floor.

It appeared to be a set of beakers and test tubes that had been thrown down judging from the assortment of items that sat on the other counter tops. He had no idea what the material was used for, but someone had destroyed it. There was also a big piece of equipment that had been wrenched from the corner of the room, the marks on the floor from where it had originally sat to its current location, a tell-tale sign that the heavy apparatus had been thrown into the corner as it lay there smashed to pieces.

Just then, as Jesse's eyes turned towards the other side of the room, flashlight and gun aimed into the corner, the light was blocked from reaching the wall by a shape that had seemed to appear from nowhere and he saw the teeth and claws, almost squeezing the trigger and firing off a round!

Jesus! What the hell! Jesse thought as he saw that the object actually wasn't alive and in fact it was a skeleton of a wolf. It had been set up to appear life-like, and Jesse felt his heart beating rapidly in his chest as he realized he had almost shot at a simple lab skeleton. This was a research facility after all, they probably had all kinds of bones and skeletons laying around. Jesse remembered his high school anatomy class had a adult skeleton that sat in the corner of the class, his teacher using 'Billy Bones' for his lectures on the human anatomy and the skeletal structure. It was a common enough thing to find, and he assumed there were probably more dioramas and other animal remains setup, and that he'd have to be careful before he had to explain to his supervisor why he had shot at nothing more than an long dead animal! That was all he needed to be faced with now.

It was bad enough he hadn't followed the rules and called the break-in into the Smithsonian Dispatcher. After all, whether there was a real animal in the lab or not, he still had to remember that someone had broken into the building. That shattered glass from the window wasn't just from some kid who might have sneaked onto the property with a rock , looking to cause some harmless mischief, somebody had trailed the shards into this facility on the SCBI campus. After tonight he'd probably be removed from this position entirely, even if he managed not to get in major trouble and face suspension, he would still be back at the Natural History Museum dealing with the crowds of annoyed visitors who thought they were above being asked to go through security. Didn't anyone still remember September 11th and the fear that had followed that day? He was there to protect them so they could enjoy looking at all the junk the museum had to display and not have to worry about the likes of Al Qaeda.

As Jesse moved his light off the skeleton and the corner of the room it occupied, he went to check the last part of the lab and the small office that was directly off from it and through a doorway with no door to close off the two spaces. Obviously whoever worked in this lab wasn't afraid of their privacy being nonexistent as they worked with their peers. Suddenly, as Jesse was moving closer and closer to the office, his light trying to illuminate his way, he heard a noise that he didn't recognize coming from the direction he was headed. Whoever had broken in was still here and was currently in the office!

Jesse's fingers tightened on his gun, trying to push the fear aside that was eating away at him from the inside. He was careful not to add anymore pressure to the trigger, it was already as far back as it would go without setting the pistol off, and the last thing Jesse wanted was to shoot some kid, whether or not he was up to no good. As he took a step closer, he heard a strange, loud breathing that was coming from the office. It didn't sound like it could even come from a normal kid or even a man for that matter. It was deep and had an almost laugh like wheeze to it as the person was obviously exhaling. He kept his hand with the gun in it up and lowered the flashlight down some so as not to reveal himself as he almost reached the door. He didn't even think about the trespasser having seen his light when he was shining it around the lab.

His forehead was pouring sweat, his back soaked and he could feel his armpits had stained the pits in his uniform. Taking one more step closer, Jesse quickly jumped around the corner, his light coming up as he shouted, "Security— Don't move!"

The dark figure moved quickly, with lightning speed it lashed out at Jesse.

That's when everything went spinning around as he felt a powerful blow land across his chest and he tumbled head over heels into the nearest table, the equipment sitting on top of it going flying to the floor and crashing with a loud smash.

"Aaaahhhh!" he cried out as he rolled.

He landed hard, his back and shoulder aching as much as his chest did from the blow, and raising his arm up he realized he had lost his gun, but held onto the flashlight. Raising the bright light up, it fell upon his assailant. The blackness parted, and he was staring at a pair of hideously large jaws, saliva dripping onto the floor before him.

Holy shit!

The pain in his chest had started to dull, it burned to breathe since the blow had knocked the air out of his lungs, and he tried to pull big breaths through his mouth and nose to keep from hyperventilating. Jesse found it hard, but he knew he needed to move. Before the creature was upon him, a beast that was entirely too large for Jesse to think that even if he had his gun, it wouldn't be enough to stop the raving monstrosity. As it came straight for him, the creature walking on its back legs, the limbs bent forward reminding Jesse of a dog's legs, but it was bipedal, it's arms— yes arms— it wasn't some animal reared up on its back legs, it was freaking walking!

Jesse wanted to move but his body felt paralyzed except for the tremor of fear that was shaking him to the core.

"Oh dear God…" he muttered but before, he wanted to shut his eyes and block out the figure taking another step closer. He felt his heart pounding in his chest, and wondered if the beast could hear it thumping with it's elongated, furry ears.

As the creature stepped through the light and past the flashlight's beam, the creature's form was swallowed up by the darkness again, but Jesse knew it was still there. He could smell the musky, oily stink from the creatures body as it approached him. All he could see was the outline of the tall, broad shouldered monster, but by now his breathing was still erratic, he was unable to call out for help.

Jesse knew screaming was pointless, the beast was upon him.

The feeling of sharp talon-like nails piercing into his thighs as the creature came upon him shot through his head.

Then the feeling was gone, the creature was gone, and Jesse realized there was no light at the end of the tunnel when you die.

All that was there was that beast's demonic face and burning red eyes.

Then Jesse knew no more.

Chapter 34

Andrea tore the fax that had just come through from the machine next to her desk and studied it. It was a printout of the latest lab results from the forensic department regarding the evidence analyzed from the woods of the third crime scene. She quickly scanned the document, looking for the information she needed to memorize before her meeting with the FBI's Agent Jim Poole and Agent Naomi Cassidy. Andrea still felt like there was some competition from the pretty redhead with her cute button-nose and full lips, but she tried to ignore the feeling since she wasn't sure why it kept creeping up on her whenever she thought of the female FBI agent. Maybe it was just her natural instinct to feel threatened whenever a new woman entered the picture. It was like she felt intimidated by the woman's presence here, like she had invaded Andrea's work space and it was a competition that Andrea felt like she might lose to the attractive agent.

Ignoring the feeling tugging at her subconscious, Andrea directed her thought back to the work at hand and read over the faxed report. They had gotten the lab results back regarding the victim's wounds and once again it didn't make sense. So far, the Medical Examiner had stated in his notes about the different killings that the force exhibited by the unknown assailants was much too high to have been committed by the average male. The amount of strength needed to dismember the victim's limbs and inflict the various wounds had to have been a man with incredible size and power. He had to have been in amazing shape and that meant that one of the murderers was either a large bodybuilder or he was tapping into some hidden reserve of strength when he murdered the individual victims, just like a woman who due to the terror of losing her child is able to life a car off the ground to save the baby.

The human body was capable of some amazing things, but to think that at least one of the serial killers was able to tap into the adrenaline his body produces to allow him super-human strength to commit these crimes. Something wasn't adding up. Andrea finished going through the report and began to feel a sense of doubt at the way the investigation was leading.

Maybe when she sat down with Agents Poole and Cassidy, she could explain her worries about the direction the joint task force was taking, and they would have some new insight into the issues that were bothering her. Yes, something was certainly not adding up!

Adding the report that she had just received to her file containing the reports and photos from the multiple crime scenes, Andrea stood up from her desk and headed towards the conference room where Jim Poole was waiting. As she entered he greeted her with his normal, stiff military-like precision and shook her hand in a tight, strong grip before releasing it and offering her a seat at the large table that took up most of the room. Andrea sat, and without wasting time, she set the file folder down in front of her and quickly got to the point.

"I think we've been looking at these killings all wrong," she stated and began pulling various pages from the folder, while Jim Poole just stood there waiting for her to expand on her statement. She could see from his body language that he didn't like being questioned or having his leadership questioned, but with the body count continuing to rise on the streets, Andrea wasn't going to cater to this man's ego just to get along.

She noticed that despite his crisp white dress-shirt and expensively tailored and pressed black suit, his eyes betrayed the exhaustion behind the lack of progress they had made so far in the multiple serial killer case. There was a presence in those eyes, one that Andrea assumed was frustration.

He had circles under his eyes, the lines in his face seeming more pronounced than they had been just a day ago. The puffiness she could see added to the redness of the eyelids let her know that the man hadn't slept in days. She felt sad for him for a moment, unable to blame him for the stress he must be feeling with his superiors back at Quantico obviously passing on the anger the Mayor and Governor of Maryland were expressing towards the investigation. The problem was, they just didn't have anything concrete to go on so far. Andrea hoped to change that by going over some of the newest results that the lab techs had come up with, praying that they were afforded a break in the case. It would do everyone involved some good, and Andrea had her own worries besides the murders weighing on her mind.

She had received another call from Jeremy's guidance counselor that morning, informing her that her son had missed two classes the day before and today he had not even bothered to show up at all. That was all Andrea needed right now, and to make matters worse, Amy was still moping around, the depression she was experiencing from the loss of her friends seeming to be on the upswing again. That girl was a roller-coaster of emotions right now, and Andrea just didn't have the time now that seven more people had met their end at The Dancing Bear just the night before. Talk about bad timing, it seemed like the media was hosting an all out witch-hunt for the UnSubs as Poole referred to the perpetrator's, and with her ex Robert continuing to call and check up on Amy and Jeremy, she was at her wits end.

Did she really have to be dealing with that asshole of a man with everything else stacking up?

It seemed like if she had to balance one more thing on her plate, that her life would tip and everything would come crashing down to the ground. That, she did not need. Watching Agent Poole unbutton the lower button on his suit, he pulled a chair back from the long conference table and sat opposite Andrea. The female Homicide Detective knew it was time to rattle the cage.

"I think our profile is off regarding the UnSubs," she stated quickly.

"How so?" Poole asked, his eyes studying Andrea as she set out two documents from her file onto the table and pointed to the first.

"I think that based on the evidence, their motive for these killings doesn't make them behave like the average serial killer. In general, a serial killer's motivation for killing is usually based on psychological gratification. Often, a sexual element is involved in the killings, but as you know, the most common motivations an individual has to perform their acts include anger, thrill, financial gain, and attention seeking. The murders are usually attempted or completed in a similar fashion and the victims may have had something in common, for example, occupation, race, appearance, sex or age.

'The main issue is that there seems to be nothing that we can compare each victim to. Every one of them has no other discernible traits that distinguish one from the other. While the victims appear to have been chosen at random, no thought seeming to be put into whom or why they choose them, there has to be some underlying motive connecting them. It's the only thing that makes sense, but with our profile of the type of person we should be looking for so incomplete, the lack of evidence not aiding in narrowing down our search parameters, I think we may need to go through everything again and rebuild the profile from scratch," Andrea explained, watching Poole's facial expression as she talked.

He didn't seem to like hearing that all the work that had been put into the profile of their UnSubs was useless, but Andrea felt like they needed to reexamine the facts and each case to look for something they must have missed.

The pieces of this bizarre puzzle just weren't fitting together and the body count was continuing to rise. Poole let out a sigh, reached up and loosened the immaculately-fashioned knot on his tie and undid the top button of his tailored shirt collar, giving Andrea the first real look into the man and not the pristine, workaholic she had seen that held himself in such high regard with the passion he put into his strong appearance and incredibly tidy wardrobe.

Instead, now Poole looked just like the rest of them, his body seeming to relax a little from the stiff, military-like posture that was ingrained into him and his shoulders slumped slightly once the task of loosening the restrictive garment around his neck was complete. It made Andrea see him as more human, rather than the by-the-book, sharply dressed and unbreakable FBI Special Agent she had first met.

Once he seemed to have relaxed his tight muscles, he looked into Andrea's eyes with those bright, penetrating blue orbs of his and he said what was on his mind. It was something she hadn't expected to hear from the Agent in Charge of the joint task force admit. Agent Jim Poole didn't seem to be the apologetic type, but obviously the pressures leaning on him from his higher-ups and the local politicians were getting to him.

"To tell you the truth Detective Wilkes, the profile we had come up with so far hasn't been something I've been comfortable with either. It was my call to let Agent Cassidy, the Bureau's Criminal Profiler put together the list of potential traits and characteristics that we released to the media to hopefully help us get public input on the hotline, but the calls we've been getting and having to comb through for possible leads are far too varied.

' It's like we released a generic picture of the average American male and have every single person who knows the millions of people who the sketch could possibly be, calling in and telling us its every husband, brother or friend they've ever known. It's far too much information to go through and get a reliable lead, but unfortunately we don't have much to go on," Poole stated, leaning forward in his chair and bracing his elbows on the table before him. He looked down at the reports Andrea had laid out, his eyes traveling over them and then back onto Andrea.

"Agent Cassidy has already profiled the killers in a general sense based on what we do know, and it would seem like there has to be some connection, and if not with the people, than with the places chosen. Since the number of victims varies from one scene to the next, it would seem that instead of a copycat killer, one of the UnSubs might be more predisposed to kill than the other. Naomi thinks that explains the first and third crime scenes. In both of those cases there was only one victim. Moreover, in the second and the latest, there were multiple murders. She thinks that one of the perpetrators might be the most aggressive of the group and that the other or others are simply aiding the first when they are required.

Poole rubbed his hands over his eyes as if trying to waken himself up from a half-attentive state, then continued.

"We had four victims at the second scene and seven murdered at the fourth. Add into that the individual killings separating each one and it seems to point to one being the more deranged and the one who has lost touch with his impulses completely. Of course the main issue is we still don't have much to go on, so as of now, there is no way to figure out how many people we are actually looking for.

'We know that there has to be at least two, but Naomi thinks there might be as many as four based on the forensics and differences in wounds at the scenes where multiple victims were found. The latest Agent Cassidy has figured is that there seems to be no thought put into who they kill, just choosing the most opportune at the moment. They don't have a certain type of victim they go after like many of the more famous serial killer cases have in common. I think the motive goes beyond the ease of the kill, but we are looking for a type of person that kills on a whim; putting no thought on selection other than they were at the wrong place at the wrong time."

"That's an interesting theory but as you yourself said, we don't have much to go on," Andrea said, her eyes watching the slight nervous tick that Poole had developed from either the lack of sleep or the heinous details and pressures of the investigation, or both.

There was a slight winking motion that his left eye did, and Andrea had noticed it the whole time he had been speaking, it being barely noticeable unless a person was sitting here in the conference room, up close to Jim Poole and watching his every move with intrigue like Andrea was doing. She was trying to figure the man out, but he still seemed guarded of his actions, even in his semi-relaxed state.

"Do you think we should scrap the profile and go through everything again?" she asked.

Poole waited a moment, seeming to choose his words carefully before responding, "I think that if we don't figure out what it is these UnSubs are trying to accomplish, then we will never get any closer to bringing this manhunt to an end. The Mayor of Rockville and the Governor of Maryland have already authorized me to double the size of the task force and I'm certainly going to add experts to the team. I have three Agents with multiple years of experience as well as another Criminal Profiler who I'm bringing in to work alongside Agent Cassidy to hopefully create a clearer picture of who we are looking for. I've worked with him on some other cases with the Bureau and know he's a terrific asset that I don't want to waste. He has had many years working on and aiding some of the biggest serial killer cases in the country and at this point we need all the help we can get."

"Who is the Criminal Profiler?" Andrea asked, interested in knowing who she would be working alongside with as the team grew to incorporate the new agents and officers they needed.

"His name is Dr. Lincoln Crichton, and he's one of the best analytical minds in the world. He used to be a part of the Behavioral Analysis Unit out of Quantico, the FBI's top group in delving into the criminal mind and aiding local law enforcement groups their expertise in tracking down killers and solving crimes, but he recently retired from the Bureau and is now only a part-time consultant. He spends the rest of his time teaching at various conferences and seminars around the world on everything from Forensic Psychology to the Psychosis of the Mass Murderer."

"I thought his name sounded familiar. Me and another Detective with Montgomery County had attended one of his training seminars a few years back. Aidan actually utilized some of the techniques we had learned on the Beltway Sniper Shootings years ago."

Yes, I remember the case, although I wasn't stationed at Quantico when the FBI assisted the MCPD in the manhunt. You said there is another Detective here with experience in this field though? If that's true I'd like to get him involved," Poole said.

Just at that moment Detective Mack Jones' large form appeared in the doorway, Special Agent Naomi Cassidy right behind him. They were here for the small meeting that Poole had called an hour ago. Poole looked at his watch and saw it was time they got down to business, but first Mack walked into the room followed by the female FBI agent and said, "Unfortunately that officer you were just talking about isn't with the Department currently."

Poole looked up, surprised Mack had heard as much as he had of his and Andrea's conversation. "Oh, and why is that?" he asked, curious to know who he might be able to add to the task force from the multiple candidates he had available from the Rockville City PD and the Montgomery County PD.

"Because Detective Aidan Preston is on administrative leave currently, " Mack said, turning his head towards Andrea and meeting her eyes in his glance.

"Ah, that's too bad, he sounded like a promising resource, especially if he was familiar with the area and had the expertise and status you both seem to be bestowing upon him."

Suddenly Naomi broke into the conversation saying in disbelief, "Wait, Aidan works here?"

All three of the them looked to the surprised FBI Agent, and momentarily Mack froze and fixed her with a strange stare.

"What a minute— you're that Naomi? He asked, the sound of surprise in his voice registering to Andrea.

That Naomi? Who the hell was this woman and what history did she have with Aidan? Andrea wondered, realizing that catty, womanly feeling of protecting something that belongs to her seemed to reappear and she suddenly realized why she had been feeling threatened subconsciously by the female Criminal Profiler this whole time. It was because her and Aidan had some past involvement with the man she had begun to form an emotional attachment to, even though she wasn't sure how far she should be taking things with him.

Then she remembered they were supposed to go get something to eat later that evening, but instead, Andrea couldn't help but keep wondering what kind of friendship or relationship Naomi Cassidy and Aidan Preston had shared in the time before she obviously knew him.

Mack had known him for a good many years, and she decided to ask him about it when she could get the big man alone. She'd have to wait until after this meeting, then she could get some answers to her inquiries.

At that moment, Poole reined the odd, unrelated conversation in by getting right down to business. The two new arrivals sat down, joining Poole and Andrea at the long, conference table, each bringing their own files and folders to either take notes about what they discussed or to provide evidence on some point they were trying to make to the group.

"Okay, so what news do you have Agent Cassidy regarding the profile changes we had discussed this morning?" Poole asked and Andrea looked at him quickly.

He had already figured the profile was off, and had asked his Criminal Profiler, Naomi, to rework the profile? Why didn't he just say so when they had been talking earlier, Andrea wondered as Agent Cassidy opened one of her folders and took out three copies of a typed sheet of paper with information filling the page. She handed them each a copy and then began explaining the contents of the sheets.

"The motives of serial killers are generally placed into four categories that are used to generalize the reasoning they form in their minds to act out on their fantasies or needed outlets of frustration and commit the horrendous acts that we associate with them. These four, selective classes are visionary, mission-oriented, hedonistic and power or control. However, these motives are not completely one-sided and a killer may display considerable overlap among these categories," Naomi said, pausing for a moment to make sure everyone was keeping up with her.

She waited while Mack finished writing a note into the notebook he had brought in with him, then continued.

"Theories for why certain people commit serial murders have been advanced over the years and these hypotheses continue to be altered or changed as new criminals act out and become serial killers. It's not until they have taken the lives of either a few people over a short period of time or multiple victims in a longer period. As soon as a second victim is determined to be the result of an UnSub, we label him a serial killer based on these conceived notions.

'Some theorists believe the reasons a person eventually cracks and becomes a mass murderer are biological, suggesting serial killers are born and not made, and that their violent behavior is a result of abnormal brain activity. Unfortunately, there is no scientific statement that can be made concerning the exact role of biology as a determining factor of a serial killer's personality. It just isn't possible."

Mack continued to jot down notes as fast as he could, his stubby fingers holding the pen tight in his hand as he attempted to keep up with Agent Cassidy's speaking.

"The 'FIS' or 'Fractured Identity Syndrome' suggests a social event, or series of events, during one's childhood or adolescence results in a fracturing of the personality of the serial killer. The term 'fracture' is defined as a small breakage of the personality which is often not visible to the outside world and is only felt by the killer. 'Social Process Theory', has also been suggested as an explanation for serial murder. Social Process Theory states that offenders may turn to crime due to peer pressure, family, and friends. Criminal behavior is a process of interaction with social institutions, in which everyone has the potential for criminal behavior. A lack of family structure and identity could also be a cause leading to serial murder traits. A child used as a scapegoat will be deprived of their capacity to feel guilt. Displaced anger could result in animal torture and a further lack of basic identity.

'When the first victim was murdered, we assumed it might be a gangland slaying based on preconceived notions from the brutality of the mutilations. That pointed us to the possibility of it being a gang that could be comprised of members from a specific area of the world where brutal attacks or mutilations are more common. However, the first victim, Sara Moulton had no ties to any gang and was as far from having any reason for the killers to choose her and act so savagely towards her.

'While the morbid severity of the wounds would normally suggest a personal grudge towards the victim, I don't believe that has any bearing on this case," Naomi explained, pushing a strand of her auburn hair away from her face and focusing on Mack as he raised his hand, the opposite from the right which was furiously trying to keep up with her as he wrote quickly across the notebook page.

"Yes?" Agent Cassidy asked in acknowledgment of Mack's raised hand.

"You said that there were four characteristics or whatever that serial killers fall under— what are they and which one do our boys fit in?" Mack asked, noticing everyone's eyes went from him to Naomi as she answered the question.

"Visionary serial killers suffer from psychotic breaks with reality, sometimes believing they are another person or are compelled to murder by entities such as the Devil or God. The two most common subgroups are 'demon mandated' and 'God mandated'. The "Son of Sam", David Berkowitz falls under this category. He claimed a demon transmitted orders through his neighbor's dog, instructing him to commit murder, although later in interrogation the issue arose if Berkowitz had possibly just made the hearing commands from the dog part up.

'Mission-oriented killers typically justify their acts as ridding the world of a certain type of person perceived as undesirable. The list includes but isn't limited to such people as homosexuals, prostitutes, or people of different ethnicity or religion, however, they are generally not psychotic. They see themselves as attempting to rid the world of the ills that plague society.

'The hedonistic type seeks thrills and derives pleasure from killing, seeing people as expendable means to this goal. The main subtypes that psychologists have identified as being part of the hedonistic killer are lust, thrill and comfort. The last of the four categories was power, or sometime it is referred to as control. The main objective for this type of serial killer is to gain and exert power over their victim. Such killers are sometimes abused as children, leaving them with feelings of powerlessness and inadequacy as adults. Many control-motivated killers sexually abuse their victims, but they differ from hedonistic killers in that rape is not motivated by lust but as simply another form of dominating the victim. The example of Ted Bundy traveling around the United States seeking women to control and then kill is a perfect case in point of the power struggle a killer can feel," Naomi said.

She stopped to allow anyone to ask any questions about the large amount of information she had just provided them with. She had given them a crash-course in entering the psyche of a mass murderer, and the inner workings of their twisted minds, and as Mack continued to write down what she had just said, Andrea piped in with a question of her own.

"So what type does your profile attribute to the perpetrators we are dealing with and looking for?" she asked.

"I believe they fall under the category designated as being a hedonistic type They seem to derive their pleasure from the thrill of the kill, and with the amount of carnage they leave behind, it seems that they have escalated to having formed a sense of blood-lust that is insatiable to them, leading the UnSubs to continue to perform more gruesome acts on their victims than the last. The primary motive of a thrill killer is to induce pain or create terror in their victims, which provides stimulation and excitement for the killer. They seek the adrenaline rush provided by hunting and killing victims. Thrill killer's murder only for the kill. The attack is usually not prolonged, and there is no sexual aspect involved. Usually the victims are strangers, although the killer may have followed them for a period of time. Thrill killers can abstain from killing for long periods of time and become more successful at killing as they refine their murder methods. Because they derive such joy from the maiming and torture of their victims, it seems highly probable that this is the characteristic that best fits our boys."

"It sounds to me, that the first killing might not have actually been the first time they had killed. Maybe they have just gotten bolder, leaving their victims in higher profile spots to get off on the media and public terror they are creating," Mack added.

"Yes, it is very likely that these people have killed before," answered Agent Cassidy as she looked from each face around the table. Once her eyes met Poole's, the Agent who had been sitting quietly the whole time Naomi had been speaking, finally seemed to weigh in with his opinion on the matter.

"We will have someone at the Bureau start pulling up any violent killings that have been reported throughout the country over the last year. Hopefully we'll get a hit that might lead us to discovering who or where these suspects are from," Poole said, running his hand over his bald head, and then pinching the bridge of her nose between his eyes as if he had some ache in his head.

"That's a good idea. If we get any hits, we might be able to refine the profile based on a geographical location and the attributes that are inherited in the various parts of this country. After all, America may be a mixing-pot of races, but every coast and grouping of states still has its own accents, attitudes and general air about them. Look at the 'Southern Belle' stereotype that has ingrained itself into our minds about the way we expect people down South to act and behave. It's the same in every state of this country, all over the world in fact," Naomi added for good measure.

Andrea just sat there, writing a note down on her own papers and thinking about everything they had just covered. She was in the middle of trying to separate all the information and break it down into usable facts that would aid her in her part of the investigation, but as she finished writing her notes, her mind turned once more to the effect working the long hours this job was requiring had created in her own home. She didn't have the time to really keep up with her kids. She needed to have a sit-down with Jeremy and discuss his recent attendance issues at school, and Amy was still dealing with the loss of her friends. She had seemed better this morning than she had been the last few days, but the look she saw when she stared into the girl's dark eyes, her appearance one that reminded Andrea so much of herself at that age, that look was what was really dragging at Andrea.

If only we could bring these murderers to justice! she thought, knowing that the news could possibly have the effect of breaking the gloomy mood that was hovering over her daughter.

"Did you have anything relevant to add Detective Jones?" Poole asked, looking to the large man and nodding for him to begin.

"Yeah actually I do. As you know we sought out the help of a wildlife biologist that could serve as an expert on the investigation to help us with some of the evidence we had uncovered that pointed to an animal possibly being involved in some of the attacks due to the pre-death bite wounds and what the Medical Examiner has ruled as "possible, large claw marks" on some of the victims bodies. Now when we called the National Zoo in Washington D.C., we were referred to contact the Smithsonian Conservation Biological Institute and speak with one of their zoologists that is an expert in predatory animal wounds. I faxed the reports with the descriptions of not only the wounds, but the footprint markings that were recovered at two of the scenes as well," Mack paused as he sifted through his notes, looking for the right one, then once finding it, he pulled out the information he had received.

Andrea sat there quietly, her attention tuned into Mack as he quickly scanned the notes before him, preparing to make sure what he said was obviously as accurate as possible. When dealing with a case this serious, it paid to be certain of your facts and evidence or it could lead the investigation off into the wrong direction.

"The wildlife expert and zoologist for the SCBI facility located in Front Royal, Virginia, which is part of Warren County, is a woman by the name of Lisa Davies. She was able to take a look at the tracks we found and analyze them. This the result of her many years of experience and having worked at Yellowstone National Park, she has firsthand knowledge in regards to bear, wolf and large predatory cat attacks like mountain lions and cougars. Anyway, she compared the tracks found at the scenes to all known animal species that inhabit native North America and the closest thing she found was that they match a wolf in style and similar shape but they are too big to be related to any known native species in the country. That and the fact that there are no wolves in this part of the country anymore," Mack said.

"Then does the expert have any idea what could have made them— could we be looking for a large dog? I know some breeds can get quite large like the Mastiffs or the Irish Wolfhounds. Could the killers have had one of those with them, an animal they had trained to attack and be ruthless when initiating the murders? Sort of like a dog bred to fight, except in this case instead of fighting other dogs, the UnSubs released them on the victims. Maybe to help in evening the odds for the assailants when they were faced with multiple victims at one scene," Poole asked, but seemed to already know the Detective's answer before he could give it.

"The expert doesn't believe so. She said that "dogs are imperfect walkers", as opposed to what we're looking at in the crime scene tracks. She said that wolf and large dog tracks are similar, but reveal enough about the individual animals to allow identification. She said that wolves are hunters; they are "perfect walkers", approaching their prey carefully, often indirectly.

'Most domestic dogs don't hunt to feed themselves and their hunting technique is sloppy. Their tracks are erratic, showing signs of playfulness as they might become distracted by things like chasing birds or other small animals," Mack stated as he glanced up from his notes.

"So if it isn't a domestic dog that we printed at the scenes, then what the hell is it? Couldn't it be that one of the UnSubs has a wolf as a pet. I know it's not common, but it does occur. Even those hybrid mixes are becoming more popular, the ones that look like wolves but are much tamer and less likely to rip their owner's throat out," Agent Naomi Cassidy added, as confused by this information as the rest of the group.

Andrea knew the feeling, and Agent Cassidy's remark repeated itself over and over in her head… Then what the hell is it…what the hell is it…what the hell is it?

It seemed like every time they seemed to have some information that could reveal a clue to the killer's identities or how they mutilated their victims, the evidence was useless. Already, most of the hair and saliva samples had come back from the lab as useless, having been contaminated or degraded to the point where the samples were useless.

It was a frustrating occurrence that seemed to be happening over and over with this investigation. Andrea was tired of the body count rising, and each scene with its multiple victims and forensic evidence scattered all over the place being of no help. They needed a break in this case, and they needed it before the killer could strike again.

Mack had seemed to find the information he had been looking for and quickly reading it over, he leaned back in his chair, hands on the conference room table, and said, "A Gray Wolves track is about 10.5 centimeters, and they are a padded print with nail marks usually being able to be distinguished in the track because they are digging animals. Canines stride length usually exceeds the width as opposed to large felines like Mountain Lions, Cougars, and Bobcats where the length and width of their strides is equal. Due to us only being able to make copies of a few of the tracks due to the heavy rains at the first scene and the gravel and harder dirt at the second, the prints we have to work with aren't very good. However, Ms. Davies at SCBI was able to tell us a few other things about them."

"Which is?" Poole asked, the anticipation of good news weighing on his taunt facial features.

Even Andrea was hoping that Mack had something good to report. Looking around the conference room at the faces of those gathered, she knew they could all use some good news. Something to keep them all going.

Suddenly there was a rap at the door and they all turned to see Desmond Okeke, the dark-skinned Officer with the tough outer shell, standing in the door frame to the room. With all eyes on him, he didn't offer his usual smile that Andrea had noticed was a perfunctory action that she had come to expect from the Rockville Officer as they worked side by side the last two days in the joint task force's commandeered office area that had once been the space she knew as well as her own home, her departments headquarters for the Montgomery County Homicide Division.

Luckily there hadn't been much else going on in the County that required as much effort to look into as these serial killings. They were already stretched thin as it was, and the approval for Poole's reinforcements hadn't been issued to bring in some much needed, new blood into the weary investigation. Even though it had only been a week, the brutality and the body count was weighing heavily on everyone. They could all use extra assistance.

"We've got a report of a dead body that just came in from the Warren County Police Department— Mutilated just like the others," Okeke explained.

Andrea felt that tightening of her stomach like a restless swarm of butterflies had been set loose inside her. It was beginning to become a normal feeling for her every time she learned that the killer's had struck again.

"Where?" Poole asked.

"Warren County is the district that Front Royal, Virginia, is in. They had a call reporting a possible break-in earlier and when they arrived on the scene, they found their night guard had been killed. Same MO as the latest victims," Okeke answered quickly, knowing Agent Poole was in no time to wait for his answers when he got agitated by the news of another murder.

"Wait Front Royal— that's where SCBI is," Mack stated as they were all jumping up from their seats, gathering notes and reports, and preparing to head out immediately for Virginia, and the latest crime scene.

"Yes Sir," Okeke said, then added, "The break-in was at the Smithsonian Conservation Biological Institute's campus there."

Andrea watched as realization dawn on everyone's faces, and she herself felt like they had been slapped in the face.

What the hell? What kind of a coincidence is that? That's where our expert is aiding us from, and they have a break-in and a murder!

Something was not right.

No, Andrea thought, something was definitely not right!

Chapter 35

As Lisa pulled into her parking space in section C, the area reserved for SCBI staff in front of Building One that morning, she noticed that something was wrong. Instead of the lot slowly starting to fill like it usually did this early in the morning, it was already half full, an unusual occurrence when she came in before hours to catch up on work as she had. The atmosphere in the air seemed to be gloomy, and it wasn't the gray of the overcast sky that was giving her that feeling. The moment she had pulled off the main road and driven towards her destination, she had noticed the red lights that were flashing from atop emergency vehicles, painting the buildings closest to the parking area with their strobing pattern.

Near the end of the long, open parking lot right where the sidewalk started to lead up to the main structure that housed the SCBI's headquarters, there was a collection of police cruisers, an ambulance and some other van marked with the Front Royal, Virginia's County Government logo on it. The strange apprehension she had felt pulling into the campus just moments before, passing through the large, wooded grounds filled with tall evergreens of cedar and spruce as she had wound her way on the smooth, paved road that led to her place of work was still there, and now that she had seen the emergency vehicles, she knew something was certainly not right.

What could have happened? she wondered as she made her way past the cars and other vehicles filling parking section C, and started down the walkway leading to the main building. She looked up at the long structure sitting before her, its architecture reminiscent of the days of old when the campus had first been erected on the property. Now the trees that had grown up around the buildings seemed as if they were fighting to take the property back.

Every one of the multiple structures scattered along the many acres of land that the Smithsonian's research facility sat upon was overshadowed by the tall, natural giants, many of the maples and oaks that dotted the property beginning to lose their fall colors as the leaves fell to the ground and blew around the land in preparation for winter.

Lisa pulled her coat tight around her throat, keeping the whipping breeze from chilling her as she passed through the landscaped garden. The fabulous Koi pond that sat at the center of the courtyard, its permanent, bronzed elephant statue standing silently amid the water had been shut off due to the temperature dropping these last few weeks as November approached.

Making her way past the last of the flowered hedges and ornately-carved benches that made the beautifully accented area such a relaxing place to take a lunch break during the warmer months, Lisa began heading for the walking path that led to Building Fifteen, the Cave.

As she passed the entryway to Building One, she saw Max, the lonely security guard stepping through the glass doors and waving her down. She slowed to a stop, tossing her long, black hair over her shoulder with the toss of her head, hoping the wind wouldn't be too harsh on her appearance the longer she was outside, and waited for the older man to hurry over to her.

"Max, what's going on? Why are the police here?" Lisa asked.

"I'm afraid they haven't told me much of anything," the guard admitted, shifting his stance as he glanced in the direction she had just been heading, then added, "All I've heard so far is that there was a break-in last night."

"I noticed all the emergency vehicles, but why would they need an ambulance for a burglary?"

Max just shrugged, his eyes meeting Lisa's and she saw that he had a worried look in them, then after a moment he said, "All I know is that the police showed up about thirty minutes ago and cordoned off the area over by Building Fifteen."

"Wait, the Cave— someone broke into there?" Lisa asked quickly as soon as Max had mentioned the building she worked in. Immediately her thoughts turned to all the research her and Frank had been doing, but then she couldn't see how any of that would be worth breaking into a locked facility at night for.

Max just nodded.

"I noticed all the police cars weren't from Virginia, there were some from Maryland to. Why would that be?" she asked, wondering what reason a different state would have regarding a break-in at a Federal Government's research facility.

"Couldn't tell you. Like I said, they didn't tell me much. All I know was that I was told by Dr. Ashton and Mr. Morris to stop anybody from going that way when they showed up…" the old-timer said, gesturing with his chin once more in the direction of her office and lab, "…and to send them over to the Eatery. Everybody's been gathering there. They don't want anyone disturbing the area that way, so you're supposed to either take the long way around, or you can cut through Building One if you want."

"Yeah, I think I'll do just that. Thanks," Lisa said, taking one last look in the direction of her office and then heading back to the courtyard and glass doors that led inside SCBI Headquarters. Max seemed to be staying behind, probably so he'd have a quicker time stopping people as they arrived than he would if he had to run out from behind the reception desk inside Building One.

Making her way through the lobby and out the back exit doors, she turned right and followed the walkway that would take her the fastest route to the Eatery.

As she approached the wide open space, the outside cafeteria area quieter than normal since the burger place and the other two places that served food to the staff at SCBI didn't open until at least 10 a.m., so there was still some time before they were ready to serve customers with their various food options. Now the area had become a staging area where all the staff was being rounded up.

It was pretty cold as she drew closer to the multiple tables where a large group of people were sitting and talking, the looks on their faces showing they were not happy to be kept out in the cold. Lisa figured the Director of the National Zoo and the head of SCBI, Dr. Ashton, had probably asked everyone to come here since it was the only space big enough for all the staff that arrived this early to congregate. No offices in any of the buildings on the campus could hold what could be close to a hundred employees that arrived in the morning for their day at work.

Lisa noticed Frank standing around near the first open benches that marked the beginning of the Eatery's big communal area. As she drew close, he looked up from the conversation he was having with another researcher from the Cave, one Marcus Wright, who stood there sipping from what was probably not his first Redbull of the morning, and waved her over. Heading towards the duo, she felt many of the eyes of the gathered staff turn towards her and follow her. It was as if they knew some big, dark secret and she wasn't in on it.

That explains all the cars in the parking lot, Lisa thought as she walked towards the collection of various researchers, lab technicians, zoologists, biologists, conservationists and more that made up the bulk of the Smithsonian Conservation Biological Institute staff. In the half an hour that the first people had arrived and found out something interesting was going on, they had probably called all their buddies and work friends to get there as soon as possible so they wouldn't miss out on the intrigue. That's what happened in a close-knit environment like the SCBI, news and gossip traveled fast! Ignoring the stares of the various people, Lisa walked up to Frank and Marcus, greeting both as she did.

"Well, we've got a hell of a mess this morning it seems," Marcus said in his Southern drawl that Lisa had found to be quite endearing even if the young wildlife biologist could be an annoying pain in the ass sometimes. Of course the guy couldn't help it, that's just the way he was.

"Yeah, I heard there was a break-in at the Cave, do you know anything more?" she asked, looking from Marcus to Frank as she searched their faces for some clue that they could hopefully provide her with answers.

Her biggest fear was that the burglar had possibly broken into some of the labs and stolen electronics. That seemed to be a popular thing among break-ins in todays world. Computers and other hi-tech equipment was always a big draw for those looking to make a quick buck of a few minutes of robbing a place. That made Lisa worried.

She had most of her work saved on the computers around her office, and had a bad habit of backing the data up with the security protocols that had been put into place. A dreaded feeling crept into the back of her mind as she stood there, her fear that her work could have been destroyed or stolen making her even more curious as to what had actually taken place at Building Fifteen the night before.

"Wait, I thought they had security here at night?" Lisa asked.

"Don't know, but whoever was working last night if they do have a guard should be fired. They have one simple job to do and that's keep the buildings secure," Marcus muttered in between sips of his energy drink.

"Yeah but I think they only have one guard working the whole campus— that's a lot of buildings to keep an eye on," stated Frank as he looked around at the growing number of people that continued to show up and fill the tables and benches around the Eatery.

"Well they could at least have let us into to our offices first, I need to check my e-mail for some important correspondence I'm waiting on! Not to mention gathering us all up like we're a bunch of sheep and keeping us in the cold!" Marcus complained, and Lisa was immediately reminded why the young biologist got on her nerves.

Marcus Wright thought whatever project or research material he was working on was the most important thing going on at the entire campus, and while she did find some of the things he was studying regarding his latest collection of research on the wolf in folklore and legend, he was a lad in serious need of a reality check.

"Oh stop your whining, we've been out here for like twenty minutes and it's not that cold out. Besides, you have a jacket!" Frank informed the man.

It made Lisa smile, despite the worry she had regarding what was going on at the Cave to see Frank, a lowly lab intern standing up to the nefariously whiny Marcus and reminding him that he wasn't the only one being inconvenienced this morning.

Suddenly, Lisa spied Dr. Ashton in the company of a trim man with a shiny bald head and tense features who was wearing an expensive, custom-made black suit and a second man who was dressed up in all the furnishings of an Italian gangster, including a fedora that sat pulled down on his head, a cigar stub sticking out from his thin, down-turned lips. They looked like something out of a movie, but while the bald man seemed to overflow with authority and seriousness, the man next to him almost seemed comical.

Everyone gathered around the Eatery's eyes immediately turned their attention to the arrival of the three men. The group stopped near the front of the crowd and the bald man motioned for Dr. Ashton to stand back as he took center-stage and waited for the murmuring of the crowds to cease.

Once everyone's attention was on him and the people in attendance had silenced, the man with the straight, military posture and serious expression cleared his throat and introduced himself.

"My name is Special Agent Jim Poole with the Federal Bureau of Investigations out of Quantico, Virginia," he said loudly for all to hear. There was a quick rush of hushed mumbles as people questioned each other or made comments to their neighbor and the FBI Agent in the fancy suit waited for the noise to stop.

FBI— this is more than just a burglary! The FBI doesn't get involved in local burglaries do they? Lisa told herself as she watched the man continue speaking.

"You know the gentleman to my left, the head of SCBI, Dr. Wesley Ashton," he said nodding towards the Director standing there in one of his nicer suits tweed suits that still didn't hold up to the quality of the FBI Agent's impeccable dress.

He must be someone important to afford clothes like that.

Agent Poole then motioned to his right and the wannabe lead in a bad, television police drama stepped up next to the Agent and removed the cigar from between his lips and looked around the gathered crowd, his eyes squinting in the morning sun as he shifted his fedora down a little to better guard his face from the stream of light he was standing in.

"This is Lieutenant Garza of the Rockville City Police Department," Poole said gesturing to the 'gangster' standing with him.

Rockville City? So far these people seemed to have nothing to do with the local law enforcement agencies who Lisa would normally assume would handle some issue that arose out here in Front Royal. The FBI, I thought they handled things like domestic terrorism and crimes across state lines, things like that.

Then before she even realized it, she felt the warning feeling of dread coming over her again like it had when she first arrived. Why would the FBI be at SCBI? Maybe it wasn't just a break-in at the Cave, she pondered and then before she noticed, her mind drifted back to the call she had received from the officer on that task force in Maryland regarding the serial killer that she had seen on the news, and she began to think that something far worse than a burglary had taken place last night.

"I am here to inform you of the reason you have all been gathered, and no one has allowed you to enter your offices or other places of work here at this facility. At this point, the only information I can share with you is that a body has been found in Building 15. It is that of a security guard that was working last night. We are currently investigating, and we ask that you bare with us as we try to get you all into your offices and labs once every building has been cleared.

'There are officers with the Warren County PD, Virginia State Police, Montgomery County PD, Rockville City and Agents with the FBI. This is currently a serious situation, and I ask that anyone who works in the building mentioned, please see one of the officers posted around the campus or come to the main lobby of Building One so we can get some routine information from you. Everyone else, I ask that you remain here until your building has been given the all clear and you can at that point enter your offices and attempt to return to work. Thank you," and with that Agent Poole stepped back and the crowd of people began shouting questions and talking back and forth loudly.

Many of the staff who had been joking around and mingling absentmindedly just minutes before were now panicked. They began calling out, hoping to have their worries answered...

"Was the guard killed?

"Does this have to do with the serial killer on the loose?"

"Why can't we go to our offices now?

The questions continued to pour forth, but Agent Poole and Lieutenant Garza just turned and headed in the direction they had come from, the direction that went to Building 15.

Lisa turned to Marcus and Frank, seeing the pale look on Frank's face she patted him on the arm and told him he'd be okay. Then seeing the crowd of employees, angry that they were still being kept in the cold and upset that they hadn't been given any more information began breaking apart, people complaining and heading for their respective offices and labs to see if they could be let in. The gossip and theories were pouring out of people as they passed by. Lisa looked at Frank and just shook her head.

"Guess we better get going to the Cave— sounds like they have some questions for us," she said to the two standing before her.

"Yeah," was all Frank could mutter and Lisa felt her heart breaking a little at the terrified, young intern's look.

Then, all three of them made their way towards their offices, taking the small footpath that led over a hill surrounded by a grove of cedar trees and down to the backside of the Cave. It was the quickest way to arrive at the building, even though it wasn't the most scenic, as they cut through trees and bushes, eventually winding up at Building Fifteen. As the back entrance came into view, a police officer wearing a Warren County uniform looked up and hollered over at them as they trudged down a small embankment.

"Hey, you all aren't supposed to be back here. This is a closed scene!"

Lisa not bothering to stop, just walked straight for the man.

"We were told by the FBI Agent in charge to come to this building. We work inside," she stated, and the man quickly changed his tone towards the employees.

"Sorry, as you can see we have our hands full right now, and we've already had to run a group of curious employees out of here that belonged over at another building," the officer explained and as he talked, Lisa noticed the smashed window pane and the glass shards sprinkled all over the ground. Someone had certainly broken into the Cave the night before.

But why? What were they after? And, why kill someone— could it really have some tie to the serial killer assaulting Maryland's streets?

"If you'll just follow me," the Warren County Police Officer said, ushering them towards the front of the building, then as if to answer their stares he had seen go towards the back entrance and the smashed window, he said, "We can't use that door, we're waiting for the Crime Scene Investigators to start dusting for prints and process that area first."

Lisa couldn't believe this was happening. What started out as a simple trip to work had turned into her being dropped right into the middle of a major police investigation that the FBI seemed to be running. A man was murdered for God's sake! All thoughts of her work and the safety of her research seemed to drift away as she concentrated on the task at hand. She needed to find someone that could answer her questions as to what had happened the night before and why.

The officer led them around the building and making a left after the breezeway, they eventually found themselves at the main entrance. Lisa looked up at the statue that always stood watch over the Cave, the she-wolf and her 'babes', Remus and Romulus, and as she looked down, she caught sight of the bald Agent Poole and his comical sidekick with the perpetual bad attitude Lieutenant Garza. Garza seemed to be in the middle of yelling at a officer who was stringing up yellow police tape, directing the officer to make sure the entrance doors were still accessible, while Poole looked up and seeing the officer leading them towards the commotion, he took long strides, his square shoulders moving gently back and forth as he quickly covered the ground between them.

"Officer Robinson?" Poole asked as he came to a stop a few feet from the motley group the policeman was guiding. Lisa could feel Poole's eyes search each of them, quickly seeming to type and classify them like the profiler he probably was. Lisa imagined he was not only adept at judging people and seeing right through false facades, but was a master of the skill through years of interrogating some of the worst criminals in history. That's the type of person she guessed the fit, deadpan Agent was. He also seemed to be older than he looked, the lines in his face revealing that no matter how athletic and in-shape the man appeared to be, he had actually been around these scenes and handling these investigations for many years. It would explain the confidence he exuded.

"These three work here," Officer Robinson answered.

Agent Poole's eyes quickly scanned their faces again as if to confirm what the Warren County Police Officer had told him.

The three of them just nodded in agreement.

"Very well Officer, you can return to your assigned area, I'll take it from here."

"Yes Sir," Robinson said, and with a quick turn, he was heading back in the direction of the Cave's back exit.

Poole then turned to Lisa, seeming to have figured out she was the most senior person there, on top of being the oldest, said, "Now if you'll just follow me, hopefully we can get this matter straightened out as soon as possible so that you all can get to doing whatever work you are accomplishing here."

"We are studying many aspects of the North American Gray Wolf and actually preparing a pack of wolves to be transported from our facilities here, to the National Zoo in Washington D.C., where their new habitat will be open for the public in a few weeks," Lisa said as they followed Agent Poole out of the chill and inside the Cave through the double, glass doors that made up the entrance of the structure.

"Excuse me, but when will we be allowed back to our offices?" Marcus asked, the annoyance of this event having inconvenienced him sounding event in his tone.

The FBI agent stopped abruptly and Lisa almost ran into his back. Fortunately, she had been watching the man lead them through the corridor towards the West Wing, the opposite side of the building then their offices and lab space was located. Turning on his heels, he looked at Marcus with that hard stare and serious demeanor and Marcus shut his mouth before he could say anything else to annoy the man with the badge and gun.

As if acknowledging his surrender, Marcus raised his hands up in mock surrender and looked towards the ground as if he was a little child who had just been scolded by their parent. The way he had shut down Marcus' annoying questions before they had a chance to really start up amused Lisa to a massive degree.

"Once my team has had the time it needs to process the scene, then, and only then will you even be allowed close to your offices. For the time being, consider yourselves on a government granted hiatus, a vacation if you will from the pressing matters you have to attend to!" Poole stated with a hint of irritation coming through.

The look on Marcus Wrights face was priceless. The young biologist who thought his work was so precious and more important than everyone else's looked like his face had just been slapped. He was shocked at having been treated like a child by this stranger in a crisp, Italian-made suit, but worse of all, he had been put into his place and given a dose of reality that other than a few, the rest of the world didn't care about the breakthroughs in wolf myth and legend that Marcus was working on currently.

Lisa felt sorry for the man to have his pink cloud burst like that from under him, but glad that Poole had been the one to give him the important wakeup call. A smile formed on Lisa's face and Poole seemed to catch it out of the corner of his eye, but said nothing to embarrass or insult the man further.

God, if only this Agent could be around the remind Marcus of the real work being done around the Cave on a daily basis, and that the world didn't revolve around him!

"Now, can I get your names and the area of the building that you work?" Poole asked.

"I'm Lisa Davies, wildlife biologist and zoologist here at the Cave…er…Building Fifteen, and this…" she gestured towards Frank then Marcus, "…is Frank Elton and Marcus Wright. Frank is my intern assistant and works in the same lab as me, and Marcus is a few doors down in the same wing of this facility and also a wildlife biologist."

When she had mentioned her name, she noticed Poole had quickly become more intrigued in her and Frank than he had in the past.

"Well then, Mr. Wright if you'll just head back to the entryway of this building and follow the Montgomery County Officer's instructions that is posted there, I need to have a little chat with Ms. Davies and Mr. Elton," Poole informed them, looking straight at Marcus as he pointed back towards the entrance that they had just come from.

With a scowl on his face, Marcus turned, not bothering to argue and stormed down the hall. Lisa and Frank just watched him go, both of them wondering what the FBI could want with them. As if in answer to the question floating in both their minds, once Marcus was out of sight, Agent Poole said, "In case you are wondering why we needed to speak more privately, it was your lab that the killer seemed to be interested in last night."

"Wait what?" Lisa blurted out, unable to believe her ears.

Why would her lab be victimized, what was really going on? A man was dead, and it had something to do with her work?

The questions and apprehensive feeling she had experienced earlier was suddenly back, this time the accusing tone of her inner self seemed to be blaming her for the death of the security guard, yet she didn't know how she was connected to the event other than her lab being victimized.

It seemed like things were certainly about to get interesting.

"That Ms. Davies, was something I was hoping you could help me out with," Special Agent with the FBI, Jim Poole stated, his tone and expression reminding Lisa that the various law enforcement agencies present at SCBI this morning were just as in the dark as she was.

What is going on here— this doesn't make any sense!

Hopefully they could start piecing the clues together, and Lisa immediately thought of how strange a coincidence it was that right after a package is sent to her from Oregon, Tyler Suffux not only disappears, but days later when the box arrives with a possible scientific treasure trove of information and hard evidence to change the history books, her lab is broken into and a security guard is killed.

Could there be a connection? she asked herself as she thought about the odd similarities to everything that had happened in the last week or so.

Things seemed to begin to weave themselves together from there as Lisa added more to her theory, then looking into Agent Poole's hard, beady eyes she replied "I think this does have something to do with the serial killer."

Poole's eyes narrowed, his cool and calm veneer seeming to have been whisked away to be replaced by the serious and overworked form that lay underneath that rigid posture and nicely pressed Italian suit.

"Why do you say that Ms. Davies?" he asked.

Lisa then began explaining her role in the events of the last week to the FBI Agent, even mentioning that she had aided one, Detective Preston and a newspaper reporter on analyzing the bite mark photos they had brought in the other day. She also told him how she was the same expert someone from the task force had contacted in regards to aiding in the investigation as a source of familiar with predatory animal wounds.

As she continued to talk, Poole's eyebrows dropped lower and knit themselves together. The look of worry in his face becoming more pronounced.

As Lisa finished summing up the key points of her week so far, both Agent Poole and her assistant Frank just stood there, looking like their jaws were about to come unhinged. Poole was obviously aware of the help she had been providing the investigation recently, but hadn't seemed to know the bit about Aidan Preston or the reporter.

I hope I don't get them in trouble.

Lisa then finished up about the strange animal leg that seemed wolf-like but much bigger, and then she remembered the tracks that Detective Mack Jones had asked her about. She could picture the photos he had faxed over to her and the odd size and elongated nail impressions that had been left, like the nails were quite sharp and much bigger than normal, almost like claws.

That's when she realized that Special Agent Poole and her intern Frank both looked at each other and then their eyes fell back onto her.

Yeah, apparently they both seemed to think that things seem a bit too similar to be just a coincidence. What have I gotten myself involved in?

Chapter 36

As Aidan and Nick walked into Montgomery County Police Headquarters, their goal to speak with Detective Mack Jones about the events of the previous night, Aidan wasn't surprised to find that the task force had taken over most of the second floor offices and labs and that Homicide had been completely reworked to accommodate the extra staff and equipment. There were more tables, chairs and all the workings one would be expected to find strung about like computers and fax machines. One conference room had been turned into the tip hotline, where it appeared three to four officers were constantly maning the telephones in hope that a lead would come in from the public.

It certainly reminded him of the days in October, years prior, when the Beltway Sniper Shootings had taken place. That had been the first serial killing duo that Aidan could recall ever hearing about until now, except with the recent murders, they weren't sure exactly how many people were responsible but they knew it was more than one individual. Every other major mass murderer that he could recall had operated alone. Ted Bundy, Son of Sam, Zodiac, the list went on and on. Of course, the shootings had also been a first for many things that Aidan experienced. Not only had it became the largest manhunt in the history of the U.S., but it set a precedent for how various law enforcement agencies from multiple States and the Government could work together and reach a common goal.

It was that event that had led to the idea of a massive joint task force being a plausible plan, an unprecedented attempt to combine organizations and groups with differing operating strategies and obtain one final result, the end of the murder spree that had cost so many people their lives. Remembering how hectic everything had been in those days, seeing an operation that was as manageable as Special Agent Poole seemed to be running it was impressive.

There was order instead of chaos, and everyone seemed to have and know the important role they were playing in the investigation. Unfortunately, like any case, there was going to be an issue with the hierarchy. It was unavoidable. Certain people just couldn't stand the thought of being under the command of someone they were either unfamiliar with, or just wore a badge that was different from theirs.

Aidan looked around the Homicide Division's space, hardly recognizing it as the office he had spent so much of his time, the desk where he had compiled and studied all the information he had on a serious crime as he worked non-stop to solve it. Those were the days he missed and over this last week, having gotten a taste for the chase again, he knew he had to get back onto the force.

Being a Detective was his life, and he couldn't imagine having to find another occupation when being a police officer was who he was. This last year had been a painful reminder of the love he held for the job, and he wasn't planning on continuing with this leave of absence any longer than he had to.

I'll go see Dr. Harper in a few days, possibly tell him the nightmares have stopped. But, Aidan knew the psychiatrist would see right through him if he attempted to lie. There was just no getting around it.

As Aidan and his new, reporter of a friend Nick Haley stepped into the room that now housed the majority of the task force's resources and personnel, he noticed most of the eyes in the place turn to stare at him and Nick, a couple of people mumbling something about the appearance of the two. While Aidan didn't know everybody that comprised the task force, there were a few faces that he recognized. Detective Tim Melvin was one of those faces. He was currently on the phone, his conversation energetic as he wrote down some notes on a piece of paper. His anal-retentive obsession with keeping his work space pristine was something that Aidan had always joked about, but when it came to keeping track of notes, reports or details for any investigation, it was that obsessive-compulsive dedication that Melvin put into his desk and filing cabinet that provided a vast record of information on ongoing and closed cases, all easily findable for the man in a matter of seconds.

Looking around and not seeing anybody that seemed to be in charge, Aidan headed for Tim's desk, where the young Detective was sitting, finishing up his phone call and replacing his pen into his shirt pocket and straightening the paper in front of him. Everything on the tabletop was perfectly aligned as if the man used a T-square each and every morning when he arrived punctually for his shift. Aidan remembered that the man had a habit of always being on time, and if he wasn't in the office it was because he had orders from Chief Stone, he was at a crime scene or he was somewhere else in the building taking care of something important that needed to be done that second. Tim looked up as Aidan passed through the crowded room and appeared before him.

"Hey Melvin, how's it going?" Aidan asked.

Tim gave a smile and then quickly glanced around, his eyes searching the room before he answered, "You know that if Stone catches you in here, he's going to lose it, don't you?"

"Probably, but we're here to see Mack, it's important."

"Who's he?" Tim asked, nodding in the direction of Nick.

Nick didn't bother waiting for Aidan to answer. "Nick Haley— I have some information on the killings for the Detective," he said.

"Haley…Nick Haley…why's that name sound familiar?" Tim asked, slowly speaking the name over again. It took a moment, his view moving from Nick to Aidan and then back to Nick again, realization dawning on her face. "Wait a minute, aren't you the reporter covering the murders for The Informant? The "Midnight Massacre" story?"

"Yeah that's the one," Aidan quickly replied, hoping no one else had heard Tim Melvin speaking, and wanting to make sure Nick didn't answer.

Nick just stood there, quietly allowing Aidan to handle everything. Besides he had enough on his mind with Bo being killed along with his employee and the patrons of 'The Dancing Bear'. He was trying to remember as much as he could about the four guys he saw while freezing his butt off in his car the night before, waiting for the vehicle to warm up so he could head home. Nick knew that Aidan didn't want to stir up any issues with his boss, and coming into the station with a civilian was bad enough, but that civilian being a reporter who just so happened to be the one covering the serial killings that the joint task force was working to unravel, well that might cause the man to blow a gasket. That was the last thing either man wanted. As soon as Tim had said it though, he noticed things growing quieter on their side of the office, people once talking among themselves had stopped and were watching the scene unfold around them.

This isn't going to be good if anyone happens to tell Stone about my little visit, he thought. He remembered the last little conversation they had had in his office, and he wasn't looking for a repeat. Then thinking of the uptight, by-the-book boss, he realized that Chief Stone wasn't anywhere to be seen. In fact, it didn't look like Mack or even the 'Pit bull', Sergio Garza were around. He also didn't notice anyone that fit the general description of an FBI agent, a type that usually stood out in a crowd of various law enforcement types. Taking another look around the room, this time seeking out Andrea, he was disappointed to see she was nowhere to be seen as well. It seemed that everyone that had any importance to the ongoing investigation was missing from HQ, and that meant only one thing. They were at the murder site.

"Look Tim, Mr. Haley here is a possible eyewitness to the last known customers to enter 'The Dancing Bear', where everyone was murdered yesterday or early this morning. If so, then I was supposed to meet Mack here once they got back from the scene, and see if this man could give a description to a sketch artist of the four men he saw last night going into the pub as he was leaving," Aidan said, his voice a little louder in an attempt to get all the eyes that were staring at him off his back.

"Wait, you were at that bar last night?" Tim asked, spinning in his chair to face Nick. He seemed to have changed instantly from obviously thinking the guy was there to waste his time hounding him for a story to realizing why Aidan had actually brought him in.

"Yes I was there. I had been speaking with the owner Bo, or Bodham Choplinsky as he's legally known, and I even ran into Ted Hanson, the reporter for Channel 5 News before I left," Nick explained.

Now they had Tim's full attention.

He should have known I wouldn't do something as foolish as bring a journalist into Police HQ for nothing, Aidan thought as he glanced around and saw that most people had seemed to go about their work, only a few stole quick, little glances over their way.

"Okay, look Preston, I can set him up with the sketch artist and see what he can remember about any of the people you saw last night while out drinking at the pub," he said then turning to Nick, mentioned, "hopefully you didn't drink to much."

Nick just shook his head, confident that the faces he had been picturing in his mind all morning, even though he had only gotten a quick glance at them the night before, would be as accurate as possible. He was positive he hadn't had enough to drink to distort his vision enough to be wrong about the appearances of the individuals who might have been responsible for Bo's death.

"Sounds good to me," Tim said, looking at the pair of men standing before him.

Once again it seemed to him that the 'legendary' Aidan Preston had triumphed again in a case where almost two dozen police officers and FBI agents had been working nonstop for almost a week, but hadn't uncovered nearly as much as Aidan and his newspaper reporter had. There were even rumors going around that Mack had been revealing information to an outside source to get a second opinion, and knowing how long the two had known each other, Tim was pretty sure the person he had been speaking to was Aidan.

Then as if reading Tim's mind, Aidan asked, "So where is the lead on the case and Mack?"

"Oh I guess you didn't hear about the latest murder from last night?" Tim said getting up from his desk and motioning them to follow him. Aidan and Nick fell into line behind the Detective as they wove through the tangle of desks and people scattered from one wall to the other in the crowded room, their destination being the conference room with the Moonlight Massacre's tip hotline. Tim was looking for Tri Everett, one of the police sketch artists who was doubling as a hotline operator, fielding all the calls coming in from the public.

"We just said we were here because of that scene."

"No there was another site," Tim informed them.

Both Aidan and Nick looked at each other then at Melvin, their shocked expressions clear to the Detective as he just shook his head in confirmation, as if now the shock should be draining from the faces.

"Two places in one night? Where was the other attack?" Nick asked, his hand pulling a worn notebook from the bag hanging at his side, turned to a blank page with pen in hand and ready, he looked up at Detective Melvin.

Tim seemed hesitant to relay the information, already sorry he had let the news slip when he remembered that Aidan and him were in the presence of a reporter. Then again, it wasn't as if Aidan wouldn't have found out, and the way those two seemed around each other, working their own angle of the crimes like partners would, he couldn't see Aidan holding the information back from the man. Finally he glanced around and ushered them into the supplies office next to the conference room where they were working hard at fielding all the calls for the hotline, having the time-intensive task of weeding through the massive volume that was pouring in, he said, "Okay, but you didn't hear this from me— Turns out, that the second sight which was just reported this morning came from Front Royal, Virginia."

"Front Royal, wait, we were just there a couple days ago," Aidan informed Tim who took another look over his shoulder, to make sure they had the privacy he needed before continuing.

"Yeah well, apparently a research facility was hit. At first they thought it was a burglary due to the mess that was made of the back entrance, but then they found a lab broken into and the night security guard had been torn to pieces. Real sick shit!"

"What lab was it?" Nick asked, furiously writing down everything he could.

"Well I guess it's not so much a lab as it is more animal studies and 'save the animals' type things there. It was place called the Smithsonian Conservationist Biological Institute." Tim stated and as soon as he did, Aidan got that feeling in his gut again.

Something was wrong with this, there seemed to be a pattern that connected these not-so-random killings after all. If only he could see it, but as he closed his eyes and tried to focus, all he seemed to be doing was drawing a blank.

What was it about SCBI that tied these killings to it?

Are they not as innocent as we first assumed? Maybe they did have an animal escape and they were just covering it up, hoping to be able to stop it before it kills again. However, that didn't seem to be happening, people were still dying, and now the latest victim had led them straight to SCBI's front door. Aidan knew he needed to get over there and question the staff again, preferably sooner rather than later.

He could even kill two birds with one stone by meeting Mack there and having Nick give his statement to Mack Jones. He could also get some information to go towards the hunch he was starting to have about what was really going on these parts. Could the killers be actual employees of the National Zoo or was he just grasping at straws?

Yes, it was time to question the members of SCBI again. That much he was sure of.

Turning to Tim, he said, "Alright, can you get the sketch artist to work with Nick here, meanwhile I'm going to make a phone call."

"Okay, yeah let me get Trish. She's going to love you for providing her a break from the shit she's dealing with working on that hotline," Tim said with a smile and walked out of the supply office to get the woman.

Nick turned to Aidan. "What do you think?" he asked.

"I don't know, but I think there's something more going on at SCBI that we originally thought."

"Yeah, tell me about it. I don't believe in coincidences."

"Me neither."

"So who are you going to call?"

Aidan was already in the process of reaching into his jeans pocket to locate his cell phone. "I think it's time I had another talk with Lisa Davies over at SCBI," he said as he plucked the phone out and began scrolling through his contacts. Fortunately, he had the forward thinking to get the woman's number when he and Nick had visited her the last time.

"Okay, well I guess I'll see what I can do with this Trish woman," Nick said and just at that moment, a woman with short, spiky platinum-blonde hair made an appearance, the woman who didn't look like she should be working for the police, but rather belonged in a Gothic clothing store, selling teenagers their rebellious gear and wardrobes at discounted prices, was behind Detective Melvin as he came back into the room.

"Gentlemen, this is Trish," Tim said with the wave of a hand.

Trish Everett was short and thin as a pole, her eyes were hidden behind thick, tinted, prescription eyeglasses, and she seemed to have more piercings than would be allowed in a police facility or any government type work. Her eyes were covered in mascara and thick eye shadow, giving her a smoky look to her pale complexion, that was even more noticeable thanks to the black lipstick she was wearing. A small chest that was covered by a red, Sid Vicious t-shirt, with another long-sleeved, black shirt underneath that covered her forearms down to her bracelet overloaded wrists. Thin hips and a minuscule waist were covered in a pair of camouflage cargo pants with various patches of bands and slogans sewn onto the pockets and other parts of the material, and she had thick army-style boots with metal studs lining them.

Aidan had never met this woman before, and realized she was definitely an improvement over the stuffy, elderly woman they used to have as a police artist. Sharon something, was all Aidan could remember of the person who used to hold Trish's job now, and seeing the girl who he guessed had to be in her mid-twenties, he had to admit that she certainly knew how to draw attention.

Taking a look over at Nick, he could see the man's gaze indicated he might not be as open-minded as he thought, and the expression on his face almost made him laugh. But, he couldn't afford to, he had business to take care of.

"Okay, I'm going to make that call now, Trisha I leave him in your hands," Aidan said heading out of the office and making his way towards the hall.

Nick just watched him disappear and then Tim Melvin headed back to his desk, leaving the reporter in the hands of this Gothic rebel. He wondered if it was safe, and immediately thought that she was probably the type of girl who could chew him up and spit him out.

Imagining her doing just that, he looked away from the exit that Aidan had followed and turned to the young woman.

She just smiled, her perfect white teeth standing out against the black ring of makeup on her lips.

"Ready to have some fun?" she asked in a sexy yet terrifying way.

Nick swallowed hard, only able to shake his head yes.

Who had Aidan left him with?

Trish just smiled.

Her lab and office area were a mess, and Lisa didn't know where to begin in the attempt to clean up after the attempted burglary. She was restricted to her office since the lab area was still officially a crime scene. Even though they had removed the body over an hour ago, the technicians with the 'CSI' logos on their jackets were busily sweeping the area of the lab for evidence.

The other problem was that the massive amount of blood that had once been inside a human body, was spilled all over the floor and some had splattered onto the wall closest to where the main portion of the body had been found. There had even been some fleshy pieces of bloody pulp that she assumed had probably come from the guard and included sections of stomach and intestines. Lisa didn't know if she could stand being in the lab again after this.

When she had been accompanied by Agent Poole and a Detective Jones whom she had talked to on the phone twice before, they had already had the body moved so she was saved from having to witness that, but the blood told the story clear enough. This man had died horrendously and painfully, the same way that all those poor souls had throughout Montgomery County. She was grateful the media hadn't done the severity of the murders justice; people should not be exposed to this senseless violence.

Special Agent Poole had finished taking her statement, making sure she gave a detailed account of everything that had happened, printing out her correspondence with the missing Tyler Suffux and a detailed log of everything that had arrived and now appeared missing.

Even the Dire Wolf skull was gone. Having heard there was a break-in she had figured someone might have been after the lab equipment and machines, but if that was the case, they would have gone for the newer labs with their multi-million dollar pieces, not the ones she had rescued from being trashed. But, once she was brought into the sealed scene to help the investigators figure out was missing, she saw that her initial assumption was wrong. The burglary and the murder did seem to have been initiated as someone broke in and stole everything that had just arrived for her. They had even taken the samples she had put in her office freezer.

Why would they have broken into here all for a odd leg and a fossil that while rare, wasn't that rare?

It just didn't make sense. Unless, there's something about that strange specimen of an animals leg that someone didn't want her knowing about. Immediately her mind jumped to various ideas, thinking about them and then discarding them.

A rival research facility?...No. Maybe it was a genetic aberration...that would explain the deformities that she had witnessed in the leg's size and shape...No. Could someone be working on some genetic cloning program that had created a mutant species...then they lost track of the animal?...No.

No matter what she tried to think of, the answers all seemed to point to being either too fantastical, or just plain insane. She worked for the Smithsonian for heaven's sake! This wasn't the private medical sector or some major industrial field where millions of dollars for a simple breakthrough was possible. They worked off small grants, wrote papers that only found circulation in the scientific community and only when they made a big discovery did the public ever really seem to even notice their work.

Of course, if the remains were due to some illegal experimentation that a company was doing, and they lost a research subject, that might just be worth doing something drastic to cover it up. After all, history was full of companies that had done worse, much worse.

Lisa sat down in her desk chair, alone in her office, the room without a door looking into the lab area as multiple people scurried around, working on various tasks. She placed her head in her hands and let out a sigh. What was she going to do? Could Tyler Suffux's discovery and his disappearance really be related to the theft of the items and the murder that had taken place in her lab? It did seem like an odd coincidence, but the two events were separated by 3,000 miles, having occurred on the opposite coasts of the country. What did that specimen and fossil mean to someone?

Who would kill a man over something so infinitesimal? Lisa wondered, having a hard time trying to justify the murder. Then she thought of all the other murders that had resulted over the last week. Suddenly, she realized that if the same person was behind the murder at the SCBI campus, and the other deaths throughout Maryland, then you add in the time frame that the discovery was made along with Suffux going missing, it all seemed to fit somehow. Like the killer had moved from one coast to the other in the time it took for her package to arrive?

No, there was no way that was the piece that tied all this together!

Things seemed to be getting even more crazier than she had thought possible, and as she looked at the calendar on her desk, she began marking down dates as they corresponded with the known killings and all the other data she had. As she sat there looking at the red pen marks on the white boxes, she realized the first killing had happened almost exactly five days from the time she had lost contact with Tyler Suffux.

The right amount of time to cross the country for a killer?

Was there something that she found in the things that were sent that was not supposed to be seen? Was she in danger as well? The questions continued to pile up and her head began to hurt. Opening her eyes, she looked once out past her office and at the bloody lab area.

Dear God, what is going on?

As she looked away from the scene playing out just thirty feet away, she then realized that her computer was whirring softly as if in hibernation mode.

That's odd, I turned it off yesterday didn't I?

Reaching up and taking hold of the mouse, she moved it gently and watched the screen wake up. As it turned from black it revealed a message flashing down in the corner of the screen.

What the hell is that?

Clicking on the flashing icon, the message popped up and she read:

'PRINT JOB SUCCESSFUL'

What? Lisa knew she had definitely not left the computer in this condition. The last thing she had done before leaving yesterday to go meet up with her friend Morgan at the National Zoo was to respond to his e-mail confirming she would see him in about half an hour. Lisa felt a strange feeling tingling down her spine, a feeling like she had felt when she first walked into the office earlier. She felt like her privacy had been violated, that someone other than breaking into her lab had been in her office as well. There certainly was the possibility since there was no door separating the two. She had never seen the need for one up until now.

Knowing now that she hadn't been the last one on her computer, she checked the log to see what had been the last thing printed from the computer. It had been her e-mail to Morgan! The strange feeling grew tight and she felt like the walls were closing in on her. Pulling her legs into her chest as she sat there in her chair, she held her limbs tight, almost to the point of cutting off circulation, as if letting go would only make this nightmare continue. She wanted to just scream, but knew that would just draw the police back onto her with more questions and she wasn't sure of anything at this point.

Someone had accessed her computer last night, that much she was positive about. Someone had also checked her e-mail and found her message to Morgan about taking the samples over to her. Suddenly Lisa paled, her dark Hispanic complexion dulling as fear seeped into her.

Oh Dear God! she thought wildly.

Whoever had gone to the effort of breaking into the lab, killing and mutilating a guard, accessing her computer and printing out the last e-mail she had sent, now had the knowledge that there were still samples taken of the specimen that had been stolen and that those samples were with Morgan Lafayette over at the National Zoo!

Lisa felt dizzy as everything hit her, the unreal reality of everything going on was just draining her. She reached for her phone knowing that she had to call Morgan and warn him. He was in danger. Just as she was about to pick up the phone, it rang and jumped around on the receiver.

"Ahh!" she cried out, startled by the sudden phone call. Maybe it was Morgan…she hoped he was alright. As far as the FBI had told her, there had been another incident, but that had been in Rockville not downtown D.C., and he hadn't mentioned any other zoologists being killed when she was recounting her story. Of Course, now she realized her story had ended with the tests she had done here and the samples she possessed. She hadn't told anyone that she had involved a colleague over the the Zoo to help her get to the bottom of the mysterious piece of unusual leg. Now, the only people who knew were her and the killer!

The phone continued ringing and she grabbed it up.

"Hello?" she asked, her voice trembling, her nerves shot.

"Ms. Davies— this is Detective Aidan Preston of the MCPD, I was in there the other day with the reporter."

"Oh yes…how can I…how can I help you Detective?"

"Well that's just the thing, I'm not exactly sure, but I'd like to come discuss some things with you," Aidan said over the line.

This is my chance!

"Okay, can you meet me over at the National Zoo as soon as possible?" she asked quickly, her heart thumping loudly and the blood rushing to her ears.

Please Lord, let Morgan be okay!

"Sure, I can be there in probably thirty minutes— maybe forty-five depending on the traffic."

"Good I'll see you then, and please hurry… I think my friend is in danger," Lisa said and with that she hung up the phone and grabbed her car keys from her purse.

Within moments she was out of the Cave and heading towards the parking lot.

Please Morgan, please be okay!

However, the terrible feeling she had wouldn't go away.

Something bad was going to happen!

Chapter 37

Jeremy Wilkes continued surfing the internet's exhaustive and seemingly endless supply of websites and archives on everything he could find on serial killers. It was amazing how much information was available, accessible to anyone that had a computer, cell phone or media tablet like one of those IPad 2's or the many knock off brands that everyone seemed to be getting. He wished he had a media tablet instead of the crappy, old desktop computer that seemed to have been manufactured in the Stone Age. At least that was what he assumed of the dinosaur of a machine that his mom had given him a few Christmas's ago.

He had asked for a laptop like all his friends had gotten back then, but instead, he got this hand-me-down, piece of crap. His mother had tried to act like it was a perfectly fine piece of equipment, but other than surfing the web and using it for homework, it just wasn't cutting it. Jeremy needed something that actually seemed to have a decent graphics card so he could play the latest version of "Kill Or Be Killed", the hottest new computer game out. It was all the rage with his friends at school, even though lately his attendance had been lacking.

It wasn't his fault!

Jeremy just felt that there was no point in going to classes that were taught by people who seemed miserable with their station in life. How could he be expected to learn from them, if all they had amounted to in their lives was working in a high school, grading papers all day, and being ignored and made fun of by immature teens that hated being there to begin with. Instead, he decided that the best education he could achieve at this point in his life wasn't a free one provided by local government taxes, but the one he received by exploring life and what was out there.

Especially lately, since his best friend Tommy's older brother was working for the Zoo, or some branch that was related to them because Frank worked in Virginia and not downtown. Now that was some interesting stuff that the guy was doing! He was doing research on wolves and other animals, and got to actually spend time in the cages they put the animals in.

Frank had even suggested that they should come visit on Halloween, when they were moving the pack from their place in Virginia to the actual Zoo. Now that was going to be cool! The fourteen year old boy thought.

Yeah, screw school when there's so much more going on that can provide a person with an education they'll actually need. Like staying alive and surviving. Take the murders for example, he couldn't get them out of his head, especially after some of his sister Amy's friends were killed by the serial killers the other day. She had become withdrawn from everyone, and at first, Jeremy was worried she might be becoming a basket case.

That was the last thing he needed to be dealing with. It had already been hard enough lately with his failure of a father trying to get back into their lives. Why couldn't he just leave them alone, or why couldn't his mom stop him from coming by. He left her, not the other way around, so she should be the last person she'd want to see.

It was time she moved on. After all, he had heard his mom and Amy talking about some new guy in her life. Alright mom! Jeremy almost shouted as he thought about how stressful it had been around the house lately. Definitely when she had found out from that rat of a Guidance Counselor of his that he had been missing days from school. That no good Counselor just didn't understand how it was to be a teenager these days— it wasn't like she was in her mid-twenties or anything, she was like forty! No, no one understood what he was going through.

Jeremy just wished he was old enough to have his driver's license, then he wouldn't have to worry about all these people who felt like they were responsible for him having to keep an eye on him and question his decisions.

Finally, he pushed thoughts of school, parents and teenage life in general out of his head as he read through a digital edition of The Informant's latest paper. The title he had seen the other day had definitely caught his eye, and over the last day and a half, he had been pouring over every piece of information he could on serial killers and the murders that were continuing on throughout the city, and now it looked like across state lines.

No wonder the FBI's involved— these creeps are some bad asses and they still haven't been caught! They were up to over a dozen murders the press and police had linked them to, and it didn't look like they were slowing down.

He had read the latest story in the newspapers and believed that behind the 'Moonlight Massacres', there was something that didn't fit. It seemed to be tickling at the back of his mind, trying to get him to see the connection that everyone else seemed to have missed, but , his brain was drawing a blank when he tried to picture what it could be.

What is it about these killings that doesn't add up? he wondered as he scrolled through the various pages online, reading every article he could find on the murders. What was nagging him? It seemed like the answer was right there, but he couldn't put his finger on it. In the course of a week, thirteen people had been killed and it didn't seem to be slowing down. Every night a new person or group of people seemed to meet their end in some horrendous fashion, and most of the media seemed clueless. They were even reporting that the FBI task force that had been setup to investigate and catch the serial killers, had no new information.

Of course, he didn't know if he believed all that. After all, his mom was a cop, a Detective that solved homicides on a daily basis, and he had seen all the crime drama shows on television and knew that there had to be forensic evidence that the FBI was working on evaluating. With technology the way it was today, it didn't seem like anyone could get away cleanly from a scene without leaving some kind of evidence that they had been there and were responsible for the crime.

While Jeremy knew that they weren't as technologically savvy as they were on the TV, they weren't a bunch of country deputies that didn't know the meaning of the word forensics. He had heard his mom refer to all kinds of different terms over the phone when she was home, but still actively working on a case instead of relaxing for the night.

No, the police had to be onto some lead they weren't revealing to the general public, especially with his mom working the case alongside the FBI! So far, the only source of information he had seemed to find reliable and shedding light onto a different side of the massacres was that reporter from The Informant. Now he was asking the tough questions— getting to the bottom of the investigation and keeping the public informed of the latest headlines as they broke. That guy, Jeremy thought, was even the first to bring up the idea that there could be some tie to a wild animal or trained attack dogs being involved in the events! That was something none of the other papers had even mentioned until after The Informant ran the story.

In fact, it seemed like most of the information the media was covering had first come from the articles of that guy, Haley. Now he was a journalist! He was hitting the streets and coming up with the real answers to the questions being asked, and that's what Jeremy thought a reporter should be doing, not just leaving a bunch of questions for the public to ask themselves. If that was how everybody was going to act, then Jeremy imagined there would be a lot more deaths to come since no one would be using any common sense to solve the thing.

He had skipped school a few days ago to go with his friend Tommy, so they could make a trip over to the scenes of the murders, and check out each one for themselves. Both teenagers were intrigued by the serial killers, and while Tommy seemed to be one who would never allow Jeremy to see how scared he was of going to the places like Croydon Park and the abandoned quarry, and seeing where the massacres took place, Jeremy knew his friend wasn't comfortable going.

They had originally treated their idea like someone might plan a day of sightseeing around downtown D.C., visiting the various museums and other landmarks that made the Nation's capital so famous. Jeremy was excited, and wouldn't let his friend's obvious hesitation slow him down.

This was the first exciting thing he could remember happening around the area for years. While Tommy had seemed to share his excitement when the killings first started, the boy had quickly moved onto something else that had grabbed his attention, the latest fad for the week, but Jeremy was still engrossed in the subject of the "Moonlight Massacres".

He had made copies and cut out the various newspaper stories he had seen, tacking them up onto the wall above his computer desk with push-pins. Jeremy had even found a map of Maryland, with a little portion of Washington D.C., Virginia and Delaware visible on at the edges of the chart. Double checking the news reports, he had added red pins in the locations of the various murders.

So far he had recorded five sites that victim's bodies had been discovered, and from what the paper had said, they were mutilated almost to the point of being unidentifiable. Yeah, Jeremy thought these guys were sick, but there was also some fascination he held towards the story, a fascination that Tommy was beginning to tease, was a morbid hobby for Jeremy. Meanwhile, Jeremy had learned to just ignore his best friend's jesting, it was the fastest way to get Tommy to drop the subject and move onto something they both enjoyed.

Just then Jeremy saw the phrase in The Informant that he had wondered about earlier, "Clinical Lycanthropy". It was that diagnosis that the journalist had said was suspected to be behind the serial killer's motives.

Lycanthropy? Isn't that werewolves? Jeremy wondered, turning to the ancient desktop computer and pulling up his web browser. Did this story have some supernatural twist to it? While Jeremy wasn't so sure he was down with believing in men who turn into monsters at the full moon, he knew something was going on and he wanted to get to the bottom of it. Maybe he should do some more research. Bringing up the search engine toolbar on the page, Jeremy began typing in various information. As he did, he hit 'Enter', and watched as a batch of results appeared in answer to his inquiry. Scanning through the first few websites, he finally found one that looked promising.

Clicking on the page's link, he watched as the computer screen came alive and the sound of a wolf howling filtered out of his dusty speakers. He had forgotten to turn them off the last time he was using them and jumped slightly in surprise. The sound bite was just part of the page's layout, and Jeremy shook off his jitters and laughed at his actions. What an idiot! he muttered to himself in his head and looked at the webpage he was currently viewing. It was the page for what appeared to be the host of a popular, 'strange phenomena' radio show and internet site of the eccentric Lincoln Douglas.

From what Jeremy could gather, Douglas' program was called "Bump In The Night", and aired on more than 500 stations in the U.S., as well as Canada and Mexico, with a audience of nearly 3 million weekly listeners who tune in to hear the man nightly.

A media phenomenon, "Bump In The Night", deals with topics that range from UFO's, strange occurrences, ghosts and other unexplained phenomena. Anything that happened, from the supernatural to the unexplainable was covered on the late-night, radio talk show. It was this program and its unusual topics that had came up when Jeremy had searched for 'werewolves + unexplained murders'.

The page he was looking at had links to all the latest recordings of the show for the last month. Browsing through the individual topics and the short summaries next to the titles of each show, Jeremy was able to narrow his search down and finally found the link to the show that had aired over the radio the night before. It was this program that he found the reason the paranormal and strange phenomena geared radio show had came up under the internet's search engine's results. The host, Lincoln Douglas had apparently spoken to his listeners about werewolf related killings around the United States, and had been talking about the recent murders on the East Coast in Maryland and Virginia.

Choosing the link for the recording, Jeremy adjusted the computer speakers and waited while the .WAV file loaded. Sitting back in his swivel chair, he kicked his feet up onto the top of his desk, hearing a soft, classical piano tune drift out, the opening to the show, and let the low rumble of Lincoln Douglas' voice fill his tiny bedroom…

"Good evening America. It is time, once again, to shed some light on the things that do go bump in the night. This evenings show will be one of intrigue and mystery as we look to the natural and supernatural for answers to the topics of the night— so welcome and thanks for joining as we get into the first case we have scheduled. America, let's get ready to delve into the mysteries of this world, and the worlds we do not normally see…"

Jeremy leaned back a little more, his brain wrapping around the words the host was speaking, and he knew that Douglas' voice was probably one of the reasons he went into radio. He sounded like Vincent Price, his deep, cavernous sounding reflection giving Jeremy a chill as he listened to the man speak.

"Werewolves are a topic we have covered many times on this program over the years, but as always, when the beasts roam the night, there are always things to report. The werewolf is a monster that populates movies and books. When the word werewolf is mentioned, people typically recall the image of Lon Chaney Jr., the actor who played the role of Larry Talbot in Universal's "Wolfman", in 1941, however, the truth is— the creature has been a part of folklore and multiple cultures all over the world and for thousands of years. A werewolf has had many names over this time: Shape-shifters, Loup Garou and lycanthropes are just some.

'A werewolf is a human with the ability to change into the form of a wolf or wolf'like creature, either on purpose or due to having been placed under a curse. This transformation is often associated with the appearance of the full moon, as popularly noted by the medieval chronicler Gervase of Tilbury.

'Like I said before, their history has spanned many millenniums. Werewolves are a frequent subject of modern fiction, although fictional werewolves have been attributed traits distinct from those of original folklore. Werewolves continue to endure in modern culture and fiction, with books, films and television shows cementing the werewolf's stance as a dominant figure in horror, and with Halloween only three days away, the subject is ripe for study," Lincoln Douglas said.

Jeremy looked at the date at the bottom of the computer screen. It was October 30, tomorrow was Halloween. Confused for a second by Douglas' date for Halloween, he suddenly realized that the radio program had originally aired two days ago. Ah, that explains the comment about the 'three days', he thought, turning his attention back to Lincoln Douglas as he spoke.

"Werewolves are often attributed superhuman strength and senses, far beyond those of both wolves and men. The werewolf is generally held as a European character, although its lore spread through the world in later times. Shape-shifters, similar to werewolves, are common in tales from all over the world, most notably amongst the Native Americans, though most of them involve animal forms other than wolves, there are still those instances where a wolf is the chosen form of these skinwalkers. Although the idea seems preposterous, we cannot just dismiss the notion. To physically transform from a human being into that of a wolf, requires massive reshaping of bones, muscles and internal organs, not to mention the outer appearance of fur, claws and fangs. It is an idea that modern science has attempted to rule as fantasy.

'These scientists declared that werewolves were medically impossible hundreds of years ago, however, look at the breakthroughs that have occurred in the last few centuries. People in the middle ages and up through the Renaissance period, believed that a physical transformation of man into wolf was impossible, and decided that lycanthropy was nothing more than a psychosis of the brain, a hallucination that afflicted those who believed them to be werewolves. Yet, look at all we have discovered over the years that what back then seemed infeasible. We mapped the human genome, put a man on the moon, and have cloned animals. So as science continues to be tested and new revelations are revealed, is it so ridiculous to believe that some people under the right conditions, could turn into a wolf or wolf-like beast?" Douglas asked, his velvet voice perfect for the dark, macabre tone he was setting on his show.

As Lincoln Douglas continued to speak, Jeremy began scrolling through the "Bump In The Night" website, searching for more detailed information on lycanthropes. He discovered a sidebar that when he clicked on the heading labeled 'Werewolves', he was taken to a page that described 'how to tell if you have a werewolf in your area'. As he explored the various info, he heard the radio host mention something about Maryland. His ears perked up and he turned his attention back to the recorded file playing.

"...they are believed to be killers, maiming their victims and then eating them. Take for instance, the ongoing serial murders happening along the Eastern shore of this great country."

Jeremy sat up. Now they were getting somewhere!

Listening closely, the radio host described the murders that Jeremy had become so fascinated with.

Yes, now it was getting interesting.

Could werewolves actually exist?

Jeremy grabbed a piece of paper to take notes. He scribbled down everything he could as the host of "Bump In The Night", continued on the subject that had sparked Jeremy's curiosity.

Was the creature of folklore real?

Was it walking the streets of Rockville, preying on innocent victims like Amy's friends?

Jeremy knew he was going to find out. He wasn't sure how just yet, but he was going to get to the bottom of these murders!

That much he knew for sure.

Andrea looked incredibly beautiful in her thin, black dress and she knew it. That was the whole point of choosing the garment for this evening. She wanted to make an impression, one that Aidan Preston wouldn't soon forget. She couldn't believe how the man she had worked with for years had gotten so close to her emotionally over the last few days. It was like she was a young girl again, experiencing her first crush, and Aidan was the boy who had stolen her heart.

She knew it was ridiculous, they had only spoken a few times over the phone and seen each other twice, but that second time when he had stopped by her house, she knew something had clicked between them. There was an unspoken connection that even her seventeen year old daughter Amy had noticed.

Now, she found herself spending the time to do her dark hair into a bun, put on makeup, paying special attention to the dark eyeshadow and mascara she had applied that was bringing out her deep, brown eyes and finished up with a little blush and a dark red lipstick that she had made sure highlighted her shapely lips. Overall, she was quite happy with the final appearance.

Standing in front of a full length mirror hanging on the back of her bedroom door, she did a quick, final check to make sure everything was in order.

Her dress was a tight material that hugged her shapely figure, accenting every curve that she worked hard on maintaining, and it seemed to show off just the right amount of ample cleavage and her long, smooth legs. Yeah Aidan, come and get it! she thought, her image in the mirror smiling back at her as she brushed a loose hair away from her face and then grabbed her jacket off the bed. Her date would be there in a few minutes. As she opened her door and stepped into the hall, she ran into Amy who was on her way to the kitchen to scrounge up a snack. The girl gave a whistle, letting her mom know she looked great. Andrea turned and meet her daughter's eyes, her cheeks flushing slightly as she realized how much time and effort she had put into getting ready to go to dinner with Aidan. She was embarrassed.

"Looking good mom," Amy said with a smile, her eyes looking her mom over with a quick glance.

"Thanks sweetheart— I don't look too dressed up do I?"

"No. You're going to knock him dead though!"

Andrea smiled. She was glad her daughter seemed to be taking her going out on a date so well. Especially after the week they had all had. Between Amy's school friends being murdered, the investigation into the killings eating up most of her time away from home and the recent reappearance of her ex, Robert, Andrea felt that this would be a nice break from the hectic turn life had taken.

She hadn't dated anyone in months, and she had butterflies in her stomach at the thought of going out tonight. Not that she thought she was out of practice, it was just that Aidan Preston seemed to ignite some lost flame she hadn't felt in a long time. Probably since her and Robert had first gotten together. Andrea couldn't believe that was almost eighteen years ago. Where had the time gone?

"Well thank you sweetie. Now what are your plans for while I'm gone?" Andrea asked, hoping to change the subject from her own evening agenda to focus on her daughter.

Letting her mom shift the topic of the conversation away from her, seeming to sense the stress Andrea was going through at home and at work with the investigation, Amy just shrugged and said, "I don't know. I was thinking about renting a movie on cable, but I'm not sure."

"Well the '31 Days of Halloween' program still has a few good horror movies scheduled through the end of the month."

"Yeah, I already checked, but I've already seen most of the ones they have playing tonight."

"Oh, okay. Rent whatever you want, just stay away from the adult channels."

"Mom!" Amy said, surprise at her mom's joke, and a hint of embarrassment registering on her young face.

Of course it was a joke. Andrea knew that was not something she had to worry about with this child. Her brother on the other hand was getting to that age where she would have to look into the parental controls on the cable box. Jeremy was almost fifteen, and Andrea wasn't prepared for that phase of her child. He was already growing up too fast as it was, and x-rated movies was just the next phase of her motherly worries.

"I know, I was just kidding," Andrea said with a mischievous smirk.

Suddenly, there was a knock at the front door, and Andrea and Amy exchanged a look. Andrea didn't want to go rushing for the door and making a fool of herself in front of her daughter. No, she needed to play it cool. Waiting for the doorbell to be rang, Andrea sauntered over to the door, knowing her daughter was watching her. Acting like she wasn't giddy and excited, her words caught in her throat as she looked through the peephole in the door, the fish-eye view exposing Aidan standing on her porch, a bouquet of flowers in his arm.

Dammit, why does he make me feel like a young girl again?

What is it about this man that got to her so?

Letting out a breath, Andrea turned the handle and opened the door, revealing her date standing there, dressed in a pair of dark slacks and a dress-shirt instead of his normal attire of jeans and a t-shirt. He had shaved, his strong jaw smooth and clean, and Aidan had even seemed to have spent some time trying to get his messy, dark hair to lay down in a more manageable style.

Yes, Andrea thought as he saw her standing there, his eyes quickly looking her over, and a smile appearing on his impressed face, he is a handsome man!

Andrea smiled back and took the flowers from him as he handed them to her.

How did he know she loved orchids?

Chapter 38

Andrea Wilkes looked incredible, and Aidan couldn't believe he had never noticed this side of her over the last couple years that they had worked Homicide together. He knew that she was a strong, independent woman who was raising two teenagers by herself since her husband had walked out on them, and he had even found himself finding her fierce love of law enforcement a little admiring and intimidating at the same time, but the closeness and the comfort they experienced around the other and the obvious attraction they had found over the last week since they had begun seeing more of each other outside of work seemed to really be affecting him. The amazing sex appeal she possessed and the secret vulnerability she seemed to be experiencing was a side of her personality he had never seen before.

He was finding it hard not to think of her when he wasn't with her, even with everything else going on. This week had been a difficult one, but the investigation seemed to finally be making some headway. The description that Nick Haley was able to give Mack about the group of individuals he had seen near The Dancing Bear the night that the place was attacked, was the first break they had had in the case. That and along with a new criminal profile to go on, they had given the newspapers and television channels a detailed description of the suspects they were looking for.

Nobody could believe that the murderers could be four men, the average serial killer being a loner, usually committing their crimes solo and not with the aid of others, but there was a first for everything. Now though, Aidan wanted to erase the whole week of mutilated corpses and focus on the beautiful, dark haired woman sitting before him.

They had chosen a small restaurant called Ambrosia after the Greek mythology for which the place and menu was based. Ambrosia was the food and drink of the many gods and demi-gods, and the interesting meals and dishes that the establishment had all sounded quite delicious as Aidan perused the menu. Of course, he wasn't able to concentrate too hard on the various delicacies since his eyes kept slipping over to Andrea.

What a woman, he thought, and then began to question if he was indeed making the right decision by pursing a relationship right now.

He had a lot going on currently, and even though his psychiatrist Dr. Harper, had cautioned him on entering the dating world too fast, he was drawn to Andrea's adorable charm and sophistication. It was hard to resist the feelings she was drudging up inside him.

He knew from the last time they had talked that she hadn't been too serious with anyone since her ex husband, but there had been a few guys over the years, none that had amounted to anything and she was timid about jumping right into anything as well, but Aidan was not a womanizer and his record over the last few years of women he had dated casually had been right around Andrea's. The last serious relationship he had been in was with Naomi Cassidy, his college sweetheart, and that had been ages ago.

Pushing the thought of his last few flings with the various women he had seen in his life, Aidan turned his full attention onto the woman sitting across from him. Their chairs were set around a small, round table that fit the two of them comfortably, and sitting on the top of the quaint tablecloth, they each had a glass of wine and their plates of food, and sitting in the middle of the setting there was a glass vase holding two roses. While the date certainly had all the makings of a memorable, romantic evening, Aidan had to keep reminding himself to take it slow for not only Andrea's sake, but his own as well.

"So how has your daughter been doing? She seemed to be pretty cheerful earlier," Aidan asked as he ripped a piece of pita in half and dipped the bread into a dish of hummus.

"Amy's mood seems to swing up and down depending on her day. Overall, she's been adjusting to the news of her friend's deaths pretty well. That's not to say she's completely over it though," Andrea replied, the image of her daughter crying just last night during an emotional state of panic that had overcome the seventeen year old was fresh in her mind. As she twirled her fork around the assortment of food left uneaten on her plate, she stabbed the utensil into a small chunk of lamb and took a bite. She seemed surprised by how delicious it tasted, but then again, Andrea had never been to Ambrosia while he had.

"That's good, I'm sure it's been incredibly hard on her. It's not everyday a person finds out that four of their friends have been murdered."

"Tell me about it. Here we are, both Detectives working Homicide and I know I wasn't ready for this serial killer business."

"Well, one of us is a Detective currently, I'm still on administrative leave until I get cleared by the Medical Board," he admitted.

Andrea paused, unsure of what to say, having forgotten that he wasn't officially part of the investigation. She didn't want to offend him, but Aidan sensing her trying to tread lightly on the subject of his suspension just shrugged, lifting his hands up and palms open, displaying a gesture that seemed to say, 'oh well, what can you do?'.

"Don't worry about that topic offending me. I think I've had plenty of time to come to grips with the reality of my situation."

"And have you?" Andrea asked.

"Have I what?"

"Come to grips with being on administrative leave?"

"Yes," Aidan answered after a short pause, leaning back in his chair and setting the menu in his hands down. "At first it was hard, not doing the thing I love because I wasn't allowed to. It felt like one of my basic freedoms had been taken from me. I wanted to be out there investigating the serious crimes that were happening around the County, and it had almost driven me crazy having that task taken from me, but I guess I also needed the time to rest and recuperate."

"That's right, you almost died!" Andrea said, remembering the incident that had taken place a year ago. They had been working together at the time, but she wasn't involved in the call that Aidan had responded to when he was shot.

"Well, I don't know about almost dying, but taking a bullet to the chest certainly threw off my golf game."

Andrea just stared at Aidan, unsure if he was joking as he downplayed the seriousness of the injury. She had been there to see him at the hospital along with many other officers and detectives from both Montgomery County and the Rockville Police. It was a little more than just the flesh wound that Aidan was trying to make it sound like. He had been seriously wounded. Then seeing the smirk on his face, Andrea relaxed, and tried to push the horrid memories of a guy she had worked closely with for so many years, laying in bed from a botched judgment call going into a situation, and focused instead on how good Aidan looked now. He seemed to be fully recovered, but there was still something off about how he had responded.

Aidan seemed to have something bothering him, like there was something still haunting his nights and dreams. He had mentioned earlier about having some trouble sleeping, but was that it? Andrea wasn't sure.

"Just kidding— the closest thing I've ever done to golfing is hitting the local Putt Putt for a round of miniature golf!" Aidan admitted, and they both laughed.

Andrea remembered how Robert had been a big, golf aficionado, and was thankful that was one more thing that her ex and Aidan didn't have in common. So far the differences were clear cut. Where Robert was full of himself and arrogant, always thinking of his own needs and never those of Andrea or their kids, that had been proved when he cheated on her and then left, but Aidan was nothing like that.

So far, Aidan was as far from Robert as the two men could be, and that was definitely a plus in her book. Sure she had been married to the guy for years, but it had ended badly, and they still weren't on good terms after all this time, especially lately with him trying to worm his way back into her family. Aidan however, was someone she would like her kids to meet. Amy already seemed to have given the man her seal of approval, and while Jeremy would probably be less receptive to another cop in the house, Andrea knew he would come around and eventually warm to Aidan.

That was at least something she knew of the fourteen year old.

"So…" Aidan began, then after a short pause, he said, "…have you missed me around the office, or is being on this joint task force making up for the lack of my presence?"

Andrea took a sip of her fine, seeming to swirl the glass softly in her hand as her eyes met Aidan's, she swallowed the bit of Chardonnay and said, "I got to tell you, I loved working with you back in the day, I trust you and you can watch my back anytime, but being with this task force is something completely different from the daily routine of chasing down criminals. I mean, this whole case is strange."

Aidan smiled, his eyes narrowing as he took a drink of his own wine and then said, "Oh believe me Andrea, I would love to watch your backside anytime!"

Andrea felt her cheeks flushing as she caught on to Aidan's twist on her words. She found it humorous and intriguing all at the same time. She looked at him for a moment, then gave him a wink, her dark hair tossed over her shoulder as she leaned her elbows on the tabletop and drew closer to the man. Knowing her position was providing him with a glimpse at her cleavage, she kept her elbows propped on the table as she spoke softly, "Well, another couple of glasses of wine and you might just get lucky," she said, giving him a sexy look that curled the corners of his mouth up in an excited smile.

"Oh, and who said I was that easy?" he asked jokingly.

"No one, but you forgot, you're the one who came to my house to check on me and see if I was okay, brought me those beautiful orchids, took me out to this nice Greek restaurant, and now is subtly trying to seduce me with his good looks and sweet words," Andrea explained, ticking off the individual events with the fingers of one hand.

"So it's working?" Aidan asked, leaning in close to Andrea as she took another drink from her glass and seemed to mull over his question for a moment.

"Yes," she finally said, noticing that while Aidan had taken a quick glance at her chest area when she had repositioned herself for him, but his eyes had quickly returned to her own deep brown eyes, showing Andrea that he really was a gentleman.

Aidan couldn't believe how hot Andrea was making him. He longed to lean across the table, take her lithe, perfectly-shaped form into his arms and plant a long, passionate kiss onto those dark red and full lips.

Those lips, so plump and kissable!

Trying to reign his emotions back in, Aidan cleared his throat and took finished off his glass of wine. Andrea really was something else, and as they sat there just staring into each other's eyes, he knew he was falling for her hard. Not to mention that she seemed to be doing just the same towards him.

Yes, there was some deep magnetic attraction that having been pushed aside for so many years as they had worked together as professionals, and now that they had reentered the other's lives, it was hard to deny the strong, current like pull that was pulling them both together.

Aidan thought again of his initial concerns about getting involved with a co-worker, and decided to try and veer the conversation back to something a little less dangerous.

"So, what progress have you been making on the "Moonlight Massacres"?" he asked hoping she wouldn't be offended by the change in thought process.

Finishing her own wine, Andrea set the empty glass down and waited for the flushed feeling that had overcome her to cool down slightly. She seemed to understand he was trying to change the subject, and figured that maybe they had better calm down a little with the passion before they both did rush into something they weren't ready for. That was a worry for later, right now they needed to order and discuss the case. What happened afterward was to be decided then.

"Special Agent Poole of the FBI is the one running the show. Of course, good ol' Lieutenant Sergio Garza has been sticking to him like a pathetic underling that can't leave its master's shadow for fear of being abandoned and cast aside. Either way, Poole seems to have his act together. Must have been military before joining up with the FBI because you can tell he carries himself differently than the others. Then again, the other Agents that he brought along with him seem to be confident enough, if they'd just let us do our jobs without having to look over our shoulders," Andrea explained, leaning back a little in her seat, leaving her body clad in its tight, black dress available for Aidan to take a peek. However, he kept up his gentlemanly politeness, keeping eye contact with her the whole time she talked.

She's a doll, Aidan thought as he absorbed everything Andrea had to say, watching her mouth form the words slowly, the subtle hint of her perfume drifting over to him and he inhaled the sweet scene. It was lavender and lilac. A perfect combination of both that accented her own natural scent to get the blood rushing in his veins.

Sorry Dr. Harper, I don't know if I can slow my feelings for this goddess down!

Then Aidan suddenly realized he had been daydreaming, lost in his thoughts for a few seconds and he had drifted away from the conversation at hand as he thought of Andrea Wilkes, her fine figure and beautiful features wrapped up perfectly in the little dress she had worn. Aidan had realized he hadn't heard the last thing she had been saying until a name had entered his subconscious that Andrea had spoken.

"Wait, what?" he asked, trying hard to not look like he had zoned out for a moment.

"I said, at least Agent Cassidy has an actual profile we can work off of. Thanks in part to you bringing that reporter in this afternoon. Since then, we've had the suspect sketches playing constantly on the various local stations," she said, obviously not having noticed his lack in concentration a moment ago.

Aidan just nodded as she spoke. Had she really just said Cassidy? Could the criminal profiler working the serial killers investigation for the joint task force be the one and only Naomi Cassidy? Of course, it had to be. How many Agent Cassidy's could there be in the Bureau, let alone out of the Behavioral Analysis Unit at Quantico?

"Aidan?"

Aidan was sitting there, his mind a blur all of a sudden at the realization that the one woman he had let closest to his heart was actually in town, working for the FBI on the same case that he was following up on his own time. Naomi Cassidy, Aidan had always thought, was the girl he had let get away. Really, he knew that they had ended the relationship amicably, but he had definitely pined for her for a long while after they had broken up post college graduation.

"I...I'm sorry, just got lost for a second," but as soon as he said it, he knew Andrea hadn't bought it.

"No, it was something I said— what's the matter?" she asked, a look of worry mixed with a bit of curiosity etching itself onto her face.

"It's nothing, I just thought you had mentioned someone I might have known."

"You mean Agent Cassidy, that's who you're talking about isn't it? Andrea asked, the sound of accusation seeping slightly into her tone.

Aidan didn't know what to say. Could Andrea have sensed he was acting a little different now that the female FBI profiler had been brought up. He watched as realization seemed to dawn on her, her eyes narrowing as she leaned forward again, not bothering to attempt to move sexily or seductively now, her thoughts focused on the issue at hand.

"You guys used to be an item didn't you?" she asked out right, and Aidan could hear the tone of her voice.

Was that disappointment in her voice or jealousy?

Aidan wasn't sure how far to push the conversation, and what he needed to reveal. After all, there was no point in bringing up the relationship he and Naomi had shared in too much detail when he was out on a date with another woman. That would just be downright rude. However, she was the one that was asking about the other woman that had once been a significant part of his life.

Oh well, she wants to know— no point in lying.

"Yes we had dated, but that was years ago when we were in college," Aidan answered.

"Was it serious?"

"It was difficult. We were both physically attracted to each other, but in the long run, we just weren't compatible. The relationship had been too serious too fast. In the end we broke up, remained friends for a few months, but then lost contact. I haven't seen or spoken to her in years. To tell you the truth, she was a part of my life a long time ago, but not anymore."

"Okay," Andrea said nodding. She seemed to be content with his answer, and didn't pursue the issue.

"There's only one woman that I've found smart, interesting and attractive enough to even consider starting something with her, and I'm hoping that she feels the same way, or else I'm going to look like a fool," Aidan said, his gray eyes looking deeply into Andrea's.

Andrea blushed slightly, a smile appearing on her face. It looked to Aidan, like his answer was the one she had been looking for, but instead of just feeding her some line in an effort to get her into bed, what he had said had been real. She was an amazing woman, and since they had arrived at the restaurant earlier, he couldn't stop thinking about her, watching every little move and expression she made, and feeling like everything she did was tugging at his heart.

"Good answer Mr. Preston," Andrea said with a little laugh, the atmosphere in the air seeming to return back to the carefree attitude that had been there moments before the subject of Aidan's old flame was brought up.

"So did you want to order dessert?"

Andrea seemed to think about her decision for a moment before answering. "Why don't we just get the check and head back to my place. I know my daughter wouldn't mind if we took over the living room. We could watch a movie, maybe crack open another bottle of wine," she suggested.

Aidan knew where this was going, and he had to agree with her decision.

Yes, it was time to get the check.

Chapter 39

Conall was angry. How could their mission not be over yet? It should have been simple, and now they were too exposed here in this area, the deaths starting to stack up, and the law starting to become suspicious— more than suspicious. The murders had apparently caused quite a stir among the public in the Washington Metropolitan area, and to make matters worse, they had to lay low since the television had started showing composite sketches that someone had come up with of him and his pack. Who had seen them the night they had feasted on the flesh and blood of those worthless specimens in that shanty of a pub?

How the hell had they been so sloppy? Yes, he blamed himself. He was the alpha male, and the well-being of the pack was his sole responsibility. He already blamed himself for the failure to keep this incident isolated back West, and now the problems continued to stack up. Fillin was acting careless and if he continued on that path, he would do something regrettable. His blood-lust was becoming less controllable, and that was not allowed.

He needed to rein them all back in, put the leashes on those mangy dogs and get them to calm down. That bitch at the facility in Virginia had sent something that was as dangerous to their existence as silver was, was now out there and another person was involved. He needed to get rid of them both and collect the evidence that could damn them before it was too late.

Yes, that was what he needed to do, and he wasn't sure he trusted the others for what he had in mind. The danger of exposure was great, and he needed to be able to trust that everything went right this time so they could get out of this area and make their way back home. How he missed the forests of the West Coast. Those ancient Sequoia's that reached for the sky, and the vast expanse of land where they could run free, him and the rest of his pack, under the bright, watching form of the moon as they sped through the woods. He missed the hunt as well. The pathetic samples of the human species that they had slain so far were nothing more than appetizers to sate their hunger until they could get home and join with the rest of their brothers and sisters for the glory of the hunt.

Ah, soon…soon, he thought as he looked up at the overcast sky above and noticed the sun behind the gray cloud cover, struggling to break free. It reminded him so much of his inner-self. Contained in this form until their purpose here was served, and only then could he shed this mortal disguise and roam the Earth as the gods had made his kind to do all these thousands of years.

He dreamed of running wild in the massive forests of this continent, shedding this false skin and revealing his true self under the watchful eye of their female goddess, the moon. Such a strong pull he felt towards the heavenly body, sitting high above, its pull growing stronger the closer the Hunter's Moon came to completion.

Soon the moon would be full, and of all the glorious evenings— Halloween! Tomorrow night the moon would reach its apex, and the final culmination of his plans would be complete. He still had much to decide before then, for he must make his decisions in the best interest of the pack. His brothers deserved nothing less, even though they were less evolved than he. But, what did he expect. There were few who could trace their ancestry back so many ages to a time when their kind was known and feared. Conall Perterson's blood was as close to royalty as his kind came.

He was a direct descendant of Peter Stubbe, one of the most famous werewolves in history. A piece of Stubbe he kept with him at all times. He wore his ancestor's pendant, a talisman that had survived his families hideous persecution by the Church all those centuries ago in Germany. Even thinking of the story that had made itself known to history as the Church passed the tale on through the years, he knew the true account that those lies had fortunately hidden. It was in part that because of those sanctimonious bastards that his lineage had survived. Oh what fools! What bastards— waving their holy crosses as if they could protect them from the death that Conall and his kind had imposed upon them all throughout history.

Conall fingered the pendant around his neck, the gold pendant catching the little light that made its way through the clouds. Ah, to think that if only the judges who had tortured and murdered his ancestor Stubbe, had not believed everything the man had said. He was a devious wolf in sheep's clothing, and as they stripped his flesh with hot pincers, he had told them so much that assaulted their very sense of godliness. Those pious people, thinking that their methods were pure was the downfall of their plan to extinguish Peter Stubbe and all who could call him their kin. He remembered the real story, the truth that had been passed down among his family line over the centuries.

Peter Stubbe was thought to have murdered his only son, a nasty bit of trickery that he had spoken as he was killed was that he had ate the brains of this innocent boy while out in the woods. However, that was not how it had come to pass. The real story was that the child, a wolf like his father and his father before him, had actually taken him to the woods to teach him how to harness his inner beast. It was a lesson that Stubbe had went over for weeks and weeks until the boy fully understood his animalistic nature. It was then that they took the still live form of a boy from a neighboring village and after smashing his head in to disfigure his image, they sacrificed him to the moon goddess that night and ate of his flesh. It was this union, this holy communion that was to be the last that Peter's son saw of his father.

Shortly after, he was captured and imprisoned, but not before being able to pass the gift of their kind onto his son.

It was that and his ancient talisman from a forgotten age of man and beasts that had traded hands over the years until it found its way to its place around Conall's neck. Eventually, it would pass to his first born to continue the tradition, but not before he was able to teach that pup how to connect with his inner-wolf under the pale moonlight.

It was these moonlit nights that allowed his kind to reveal their true form and roam the ethereal world of the unknown, hidden from the sight of mankind due to their close-mindedness and inability to believe in the existence of their species.

Bringing himself to the task at hand, he let go of the pendant, its pentagram spinning as it nestled back in place against his chest and then he looked to the men behind him. Fillin, Tala and Fenris were as ready as he was. Turning his head back, he arched his body, throat stretched and mouth to the sky as he let out a deep, loud howl that reverberated through the night. He was followed by each of the pack members behind him as they too released their calls into the air.

It was time to hunt!

- -

When Aidan arrived at the National Zoo, he walked through the main gates and was reminded of the last time he had been to the local landmark. It seemed like eons ago, but really it had only been a few years, and he was surprised by how much the place had changed. They had expanded the grounds, renovating many of the exhibits and reworking some of the trails. The main path that wound all throughout the place, and where the individual trails to certain areas split off from was called Olmstead Walk. It was this paved, massive sidewalk that the majority of people traveled along every day that they visited the Zoo.

Branching off from the main walk, was the trails that led to themed trails like the Valley Trail and Asia Trail. The Valley Trail, in all its newly renovated glory, was a pathway that wound down through the Grizzly Bear, Red Fox and the old Mexican Wolf enclosures that had been removed during the construction of the state of the art Seal and Sea Lion exhibit.

As he traveled down the asphalt walk, he remembered hearing something about how the wolves had been moved from the valley area because they were being transferred a brand new Trail that hadn't been completed and opened to the public yet.

Aidan wondered what else the new Midnight Trail was going to hold other than the Mexican Wolves. He'd have to remember to ask Lisa when he had a chance. Andrea had told him about her son's latest fascination with the Zoo and the inner-workings of the Smithsonian Institute, and he thought it might be something he should know before he met the infamous Jeremy. Amy, her daughter, he had already met, and the girl seemed to have taken to him instantly. In fact, even Andrea had seemed impressed with the girls response.

Andrea, now there was a woman he found himself attracted to immensely, and after the night they had shared together, he found the beautiful brunette with her sharp, intelligent mind and sensually, firm body intriguing and entering her thoughts more and more. In fact, even though they had gone back to her place after their dinner at Ambrosia, and ended up spending the rest of the evening curled up on her couch watching some ridiculous horror movie that she admitted she adored in the genre, they had held each other tightly and passed the hours on the sofa together. They had both ended up in bed hours later, and the memories of that experience were fresh in Aidan's mind.

What a woman! He thought as he remembered the delicate curves of her body and the supple firmness of her breasts as they rose and fell as on her chest as they lay afterward, mixed among the covers and sheets that they had practically ripped from the bed with their passionate love-making. Aidan pictured her soft, naked shape in his mind, remembering what it was like to hold her in his arms after the intense hour they had shared, her lithe body pressed against his own bare form as they lay there panting softly and just enjoying the feel of the other's closeness. It was a feeling he hadn't experienced in many years, this white-hot passion and the mixture of wanting to move slowly being overpowered by the need to finish the night off right. They had both wanted to progress to this step of the relationship, and it just seemed fitting after the dinner and movie they had shared that they would eventually make their way into her bedroom.

The vivid images of their time together played out in his head, and for the first night in almost a year, the recurring nightmare that Aidan was afflicted by, hadn't caused him to wake up in a puddle of sweat. Yes, he had the dream again, but this time, whether it had anything to do with sharing the bed with Andrea or not, it hadn't seemed so intense. It had woke him up, his eyes searching the dark room quickly as he attempted to orientate himself to the alien surroundings, until he remembered that he was with Andrea and they were in her bedroom.

He was safe and so was she. Soft, dark curls lay against her tan cheek as she slept, fortunately his nightmare hadn't woke her up. It was bad enough having to relive the horrors he experienced in that dream with Dr. Harper, but he wasn't sure he was ready to tell Andrea how screwed up in the head he seemed to be. Although, he wasn't sure it would interfere with the mutual feeling of attraction they both held for each other.

Having parked in the staff parking lot when he arrived, Aidan now found himself traveling along the Olmstead Walk, the path winding along the various habitats and other branching trails that wound further from the main walkway, the entire grounds incorporated into and surrounded by the dense forest of Rock Creek Park. It was a lovely setup that the Zoo had managed, utilizing the natural environment to give the park a wild feel that many other organizations attempted to recreate by building replica wooded areas around their animal's enclosures and the various paths that wound through the National Zoo. It was all just part of the great location that the Zoo had maintained for so many years.

Looking up through the large maples and oaks above him, he saw that the sun was out, but due to the harsh wind blowing so fiercely along the ground, it felt as if the bright ball of heat was unable to warm the air at all. Winter was still supposed to be a week or two away, but Aidan knew that no matter what the official date was, the season was upon them. They were calling for snow later tonight and tomorrow after all. If that wasn't a wakeup call that the frigid months were here, then he didn't know what was. Pulling the stocking cap down on his head to make sure his ears were covered from the freezing lick of the wind as it whipped around, the gusts picking up in certain parts and dissipating as it wound through the closest tree line and animal safety barriers in each enclosure. Shoving his hands deep into his jean pockets, Aidan hurried along, passing the bear exhibit with a quick glance and saw that the cage appeared to be empty.

Probably already hibernating for the winter— at least he's got the right idea! Aidan hated the cold and the snow, wishing he lived in an area that wasn't so affected by the changing of the seasons and the cold touch of winter. Maybe he could move down to Florida or somewhere else that didn't seem to have to worry about the harsh wintry time of the year. Yeah, he could get a job working for a law enforcement agency down there. Miami and some of the other hot spots that drew large flocks of tourists each year to the Southeastern State were filled with violent crimes due to the many people who passed through their city limits every day. He could go down and set up shop with the local PD, and then possibly get Andrea to move down with him. Of course, she could bring the kids, although he still wasn't positive about that aspect of their relationship, and decided to work on it one step at a time.

The depths of their feelings towards each other were definitely worth exploring, and it wouldn't hurt to live in a warm climate, close to the equator, and not worrying about weather like Aidan was now experiencing. As he walked along the pathway, a strong gale picked up as he was hit with a powerful gust that almost knocked the cap off his head. As the nip of the cold air bit into him, he felt a painful throb in his upper chest, and the tendrils of discomfort seemed to be spreading across his shoulder and back.

It was his wound, and even though it had healed, completely, the cold seemed to make it ache from time to time, just like it was now. It was a painful reminder of the past that haunted him every day, along with the dreams that cause him to awaken in a tangle of sheets, almost screaming his head off in frustration.

What was he going to do? Then suddenly he felt the sharpness of the injury shoot a reminder of the level of discomfort that he was in straight to his brain. Reaching up, Aidan grabbed his chest through his jacket and tried to massage the area and chase the pain away with the palm of his hand. The only good he could see of the drop in temperature that was about to beset the area, and the possible chance of snow the radio had been mentioning was the hope that maybe the weather would provide a reason for the serial killers to not commit one of their atrocious killings tonight and tomorrow. However, it seemed like today, being October 31st, the chance that the murderers would strike again was incredibly high. So far weather didn't seem to be a deterrent. After all, the first victim had been killed during a torrential rainstorm the night she met her end.

Please, don't let anything happen tonight, he pleaded silently as he turned right and followed the Valley Trail to its end. The pathway stopped at a small gate, signs posted alerted him that he had reached the end of the grounds for all visitors to the Zoo. Beyond the gate lay the building he had come here for.

It was a small, stone and brick structure, sunk back behind the trees, the large bodies of a strand of evergreens blocking most of the building from view, but Aidan knew he had reached the facility that Lisa Davies had asked him to meet her at. Looking at his watch, he saw that he was right on time. It had only taken him thirty minutes to get through the lightly congested traffic of the Nation's Capital, and then a five minute walk from where he had parked his Challenger in the staff-designated parking area before he reached his final destination.

The building was just as Lisa had described it. It was a old-fashioned place, more cottage than actual research facility, set off the beaten path of the Valley Trail, and partially hidden by the thick growth of trees that each intertwining road of the Zoo's walkways was placed among. As he approached the old staple from an age that dated back to when the grounds were first constructed, this vast span of the woodland of Rock Creek Park built to become the Smithsonian Zoological Park for the Federal Government, became clearer and clearer.

Walking along the unpaved path that led to the front doors, he reached out and grasped the handle. Turning it quickly, the glass door opened on greased hinges, reminding Aidan that even though the building looked old, it had been modernized over the years to allow for the ever-expanding functionality of science in the present day.

Research and conservation was as much an important field in the scientific community as the actual housing and maintenance of the enclosures and the animals inside. The Zoo wasn't just a place where people could go to see a massive collection of animals from around the world, but it functioned along with its sister site, the SCBI, to truly discover everything the zoologists and wildlife biologists that worked at the individual sites and other locations owned and maintained by the Smithsonian Institute. It wasn't just about showcasing animals to them, but finding new information and learning how to conserve this multitude of species from facing endangerment of extinction out in the wild.

Stepping into the building, he was surprised to see the inside was as far from historic as the outside of the place suggested he would find. Sleek, white walls and a slick, polished floor covered the massive foyer, and three separate halls branched off from the main entryway he found himself in. Before he could guess as to which one led to the office of Morgan Everett, Lisa Davies appeared at the end of the first hall and waved him down.

"I thought I heard someone enter," she said, giving him a slight smile as he approached.

He could tell from the look in her eyes that she was scared, terrified of something and no matter how much she tried to hide the emotions, the more evident they seemed to be on her Hispanic looking face.

What has she so spooked?

Could she have something to do with the serial killers and the murder at her lab?

What was really going on? He wondered, then extending his hand he said, "Ms. Davies."

Lisa shook his hand, the worry that radiated from her seeming to dissipate some now that he had shown up. "Please, call me Lisa," she said, the terror that had been eating at her seeming to vanish, or at least be buried deeper by the woman. He was curious to get right down to the point of his visit.

"Okay Lisa, you mentioned on the phone that you had important information. I'd like to hear it, and then ask a few questions of my own."

"Yes, but first, let me introduce you to Morgan, he was just about to fill in some questions that had been bothering me as well. Maybe that will answer your questions as well."

Aidan nodded consentingly, following the exotic woman with the obvious Mayan heritage so evident in her features; into the office that she had first came out of when he had walked in. Looking around the room, he was surprised to find that the office of Morgan L. did not look like what he expected.

He imagined a stuffy old academic type crowded into a dusty, old office with bookcases filled by journals and other reading and research material, and the a big, antique desk where the old zoologist would be studying some intricate puzzle that would answer a question that researchers had been pondering over the last decade or so. However, that was all way off from the impressive lab before him.

Every inch of floor space seemed dedicated to scientific equipment, most of which Aidan had no clue as to its purpose or what it was called. He did recognize some fancy looking electron microscopes, computers with massive, black towers dedicated to hard drive space and even a DNA sequencer similar to the one they had at the forensics lab back at Police HQ. Overall, this room alone seemed to be holding sophisticated enough instruments to put the forensics lab back in Montgomery County to shame. How was it possible a research facility could have this much money to put into a place like this when the Federal Government was always complaining about budget issues and making cuts to essential things like emergency services.

"I see you are impressed with my lab," a high-pitched, heavily-accented voice called out from behind Aidan, and as he turned, he saw a older gentleman with a shock of white hair pushed back from a high forehead, and eyes that were set deep into a thin, almost emaciated looking face. The man walked with an odd, bow-legged gate, that was noticeable as he shuffled from the small recessed area where he had been and moved into the wider lab area to greet his new visitors.

"Dr. Lafayette?" Aidan asked, looking the thin form of the French Creole over.

He had obviously spent a large part of his life down in Louisiana, possibly Baton Rouge or New Orleans based on his dialect. Aidan had an ear for accents and was pretty good at guessing where someone was from or had recently been for a long period of time based on the reflection in their voices. It was a talent that he rarely needed to rely on when doing his job as a Detective, but it did come in handy when meeting new people.

"Ah, yeh, dat be me," the squirrelly man said, quickly nodding and reaching a wild hand over to grasp Aidan's. He seemed to be stuck on a constant caffeine rush, his movements hectic and far from fluid. It was like he was twitchy, or possible on edge, but as the man smiled, revealing a mouth of poorly maintained teeth, he could see the analytical way he was studying Aidan right back. He may seem like he was a little nuts, and he might be, but that didn't mean he wasn't highly intelligent.

"Baton Rouge?" Aidan asked as the man's eyes examined him from top to bottom, the movement of his gaze being the only slow action he made.

"N'awlins," he said, his grin widening and his eyes scrunching as he studied Aidan. "And, if I was ta guess, I'd say you was a police officer— not one of dem beat cops however, but a fella' with some sense in dem head, investigator-type right?"

Aidan nodded. "That's right," he said, then added, "I'm a Detective with the Montgomery County Homicide Division."

"Ah homicide, you be followin' dem murdas, haven't yeh?" Morgan asked, as he turned to Lisa and waved his out-stretched fingers towards her, saying, "Scary— bad juju dat be."

"Yes, I'd have to agree. So listen, while I appreciate you taking the time to meet with me…" Aidan said to Dr. Morgan Lafayette, who's wild motions now carried him over to a machine that was beginning to hum, and continued, "…I'd really like to be filled in with everything that seems to be going on with you and Ms. Davies here regarding anything you know that might help this investigation into the serial killers who have now added SCBI to the growing list of crime scenes."

"Course, course, Lisa be a doll and explain to dis man what it is that you've uncovered while I get a workin' on this," Morgan said as he stopped next to a machine that began spitting out copies of pages, printing the screen of the main DNA sequencer it was attached to.

Aidan turned and looked at Lisa for an answer. She seemed to be composing herself, that fear he had noticed earlier being dragged up again now that he was bringing the subject up. "Well," she began, her deep brown eyes looking from him to the floor as she attempted to find the right words to explain what was happening around her, and Aidan realized the hesitation was probably because she herself was having a hard time believing what was going on herself. "…I guess I should start at the beginning."

Lisa spent the next ten minutes filling Aidan in about everything that had happened to her, and retelling the story she had given to the FBI in charge of the joint task force. She told him about Tyler Suffux and his e-mails, how he went missing and even about the package that had arrived and now seemed to have been stolen from her office. She then informed him of her fears that her and Morgan could be in danger. Aidan listened patiently, putting the new information he had gathered together with what Lisa was supplying him with. Unfortunately, the more she gave him, even the wild assumptions; he found the pieces beginning to fit into the grand picture of everything going on.

Could these people have come from the West, and begun their killing spree all in an attempt to cover up the theft of this unknown specimen and the fossilized remains of an extinct animal?

It seemed farfetched to Aidan, but then again, weirder things had been the motive behind serial killer's actions.

Is it possible?

He just didn't know what to think at this point.

It seemed to be the only lead towards understanding why these killings had started up when they did, and it also explained why SCBI had been involved in the process of these bloody slayings. Could the crazed murderers who were waiting to stop that package and its contents from arriving have been just biding their time, killing to get their jollies while they waited, and then once it had arrived they went for it, maiming and mutilating a guard in the process?

Could Lisa Davies and Dr. Morgan Lafayette be the next possible victims lined up to join the same fate as the other fourteen murdered people? He wasn't sure of anything yet, but his gut instinct was telling him there was a distinct chance this could be the answer he had been looking for.

"You mentioned a way of possibly finding out if there have been other unsolved, large animal attacks across the country in the last week or two— how do we find out?" he asked.

"We would contact the Federal State and Wildlife Commission , they archive any wild animal attacks reported by State and Local Governments and keep the documents available online. Anything that seems suspicious is usually investigated by the police and then that information along with the coroner's report goes to the FSWC.

'The number of deaths from venomous and nonvenomous animals is reported annually to the US Department of Health and Human Services and published in Vital Statistics of the United States along with the data being available on the internet," Lisa said as she turned to Morgan and asked if she could use his computer. Agreeing wholeheartedly, the Cajun fully involved in the results he was studying from the computer program, he waved her off and pointed to an available computer sitting on a table near them.

Aidan followed Lisa as she sat down before the computer and began typing at the keyboard. Within moments, she had accessed the U.S. Department of Health and Human Services' site. Scrolling through a few pages, she entered a login once she reached the required access, and Aidan for one was glad he was working with a zoologist and one who knew what she was doing. It would have taken him ages to get to the point she was, and without an access from a scientific facility like SCBI, he wouldn't have been able to pull up the latest data that they needed. Sure the police could have, but there would be forms to fill out, and the bureaucrats never seemed to be in a hurry when it came to helping anyone but themselves.

"How recent does the data go through?"

"Give me a sec…it's done in categories and I have to go through the prior years. Let's see…okay, we have from 1979 through 1990. There were 1,882 animal-related deaths in the United States, 1,164 of those caused by nonvenomous animals and most deaths occurred among white males. From 1991 to now we have had 1,430 deaths so far, 870 from nonvenomous creatures. Those are the ones we are looking," Lisa stated as she continued moving through the data.

"And we're definitely looking for nonvenomous animals right?" Aidan asked.

"Yes," she said looking away from the screen and into his eyes. "There was no poison found at any of the scenes from what Agent Poole said to me about the murders, and the larger predatory animals that could possibly be attributed to the deaths that match the wounds and bites of the unknown animal that we're dealing with would mean that is a nonvenomous animals. The largest predators on the planet don't use toxins or venoms to immobilize or kill their prey, relying on either sheer power, speed or their teeth and claws to take down their meals."

"Okay, so what about recently for nonvenomous animals around the United States?"

"It looks like that over the last few weeks there has been a massive upswing in the data regarding those attacks, and of course this might not be all of them."

"Why not?"

"Because…," Dr. Lafayette interrupted, slipping next to Aidan with the printout in his hand, "…when dem animals kill, sometimes dey drag the carcass of dere kill away from the scene, or the person could'a been missin' and when dey are attacked, da bodies are never found so dere listed as missin'."

"I see, so this might not be exactly accurate," Aidan said, the annoyance in his voice sounding like it was building.

"Accurate to the exact numbers— no, but it will show us if there has been any unidentifiable attacks that have been reported. Like look here," she said, pointing to a list on the screen.

Aidan looked at the column and saw that it was the data that had been collected and that Lisa had been able to narrow down the search parameters. The column showed the locations of unknown animal attacks across the country, and as he read through the dates and places they occurred, Aidan began to feel his gut tightening.

"Oh Dear Lord," she muttered

Even Dr. Lafayette seemed surprised by the findings as he added a loud, "Well I'll be damned!"

There had been a rash of unsolved, large animal attacks that had been reported into the Health and Human Services over the past week and a half. These killings seemed to show a pattern, the data went up to the date of the first killing, the night that Sara Moulton was murdered. As Aidan studied the locations he was sure that Lisa was onto something. From Oregon across the country, attacks had been adding up, their grisly nature and single victims having not drawn any notice from anyone since they were so spread out, each happening further from the las, usually in a different county or State altogether. That's when Aidan noticed that if a person was to draw a straight line across the map, each killing fell into step among the dots that marked the killings.

This was not good— no, definitely not good!

That meant the fourteen deaths that had been attributed to this group of mass murderers was not the only ones they were responsible for, but instead there was at least half a dozen more locations all over the country where attacks had occurred.

And there could still be more that went unreported!

How long had these people been at work?

Suddenly Dr. Lafayette broke the silence that had ensued as Lisa and Aidan looked from the data and to each other. "I guess now'd be an appropriate time ta discuss da findings of da DNA sequencer, yeh?"

Aidan suddenly remembered that Lisa had managed to take samples from the specimen that Tyler Suffux had found and sent to her, and now Morgan Lafayette had spent the previous night and all the hours this morning, running the DNA and samples to figure out what it was.

"Yes, please tell us what the leg has to do with all of this," Lisa said before Aidan could respond.

Yes, why was this box of useless junk so important, Aidan wondered, unable to think of a reason that a fossilized bone and piece of a leg could be behind a string of gruesome murders all across the country.

"Well, why don't ya take a look," the scientist and head zoologist in charge of species taxonomy said.

He handed the sheet of printed papers to Lisa and she quickly began scanning the pages, and Aidan watched as her face continued to distort into confusion, and her eyebrows smashed together in concentration. Finally after she had finished going through the report, she looked up at Morgan and then at Aidan. There was something in her eyes that Aidan found he didn't like. "What the hell is this?" she asked, her voice not much more than a whisper as she held the paper to Aidan. "The results can't be right— there had to be some cross-contamination when we prepared the samples. This is almost the same thing I was getting in our lab before I asked for you help," Lisa explained to Morgan.

Aidan had shuffled through the pages, but found they didn't mean much to him. He wasn't a scientist and had no history dealing with animals other than a dog he had as a boy, so to him, the printouts looked like a mess of unintelligible gibberish. Sensing Aidan was clueless, Lisa took the papers back and began explaining the columns for the Detective.

"This first column basically tells us the scientific name that was matched to this type of DNA formation. So here you can see the largest percentage that is shown in the second column is that of Canis lupus, which means that 45% of the cells in the leg we found match that much of the Gray Wolves genetic makeup."

"So what are the other percentages?"

"Well that's where this gets strange— most of the time we see a match that is around the 99% range when testing for DNA typing, however the in the sample of tissue, blood and hair shows that it all came from the same creature, it just isn't all wolf!"

"I'm afraid you lost me," Aidan stated.

"This sample found matches to multiple animals that have had their DNA encoded and entered into the database. For instance, 23% of this creatures genes are not having a match found, but with the aid of computers these days we can get a close idea as to what it is closest matched to. According to this, we have genetic material that matches no other known animal on this planet, so it would seem this creature is closely related to the wolf species, but there are substantial differences. Its genus, family, order, class, everything is coming up as unknown. It would indicate that it is an unknown animal, never before discovered or possibly extinct. Either way, this animal had multiple DNA strands working through its body. I've never seen anything like it.

'There is a second unknown grouping of genes that is also unidentifiable at 5%, but there is nothing in the system to compare it to. Then the last and final piece of the sequenced DNA suggests that 26% of the host species that the leg came from was part Homo Sapien as well," Lisa explained.

"Wait— you mean human, don't you?" Aidan asked, knowing the answer was already there before him. The look she had on her face told him everything.

"Yes," she finally admitted, "the leg of the creature Tyler Suffux found is showing DNA markers that correspond to that of both wolves and humans."

"But that's not possible," Aidan blurted out, unable to believe what he was hearing.

"I ran dem twice!" Morgan Lafayette finally said, the entire time having been deathly silent while Aidan and Lisa had been talking. Now, Aidan remembered the old, wiry Cajun was in the lab.

What the hell does this mean?

Wolf and human— what the hell?

This case was just getting stranger and stranger.

Chapter 40

Nick Haley pulled his cell phone out of his pocket and dialed The Informant's newsroom. He was hoping Danielle would be at the main desk and pick up the call. By the third ring, her peppy voice answered and he felt a abundance of relief. Danielle had been crucial in helping him dig up information that he needed for his articles, and once again he needed the services of the attractive intern.

"Informant newsroom," she stated as she listened on the other end of the line.

"Danielle, it's Nick."

"Oh hey there! I was wondering when you were going to check back in."

"Well, I've been pretty busy down at the MC Police HQ."

"Police Headquarters? What did you do now?" the intrigue clearly visible as she asked.

Nick had a feeling the reason the young intern seemed to be interested in him wasn't because she found him attractive, but because she had figured out that by aiding him in his research and showing she had what it takes to be an investigative journalist, she was really just looking to advance her career. And, what better way then to get in good with the reporter covering the largest story The Informant had had in years. The numbers coming in on new subscriptions for the newspaper were ridiculous and even Marty was beaming. It was like Christmas had come early for the Editor in Chief as he sat back and continued to make sure Nick was getting his articles in by the deadline.

"Actually I had to go give them some information about the possible serial killers identities," he admitted.

"What? How did you come by that?" she asked, her soft voice rising in decibels at her surprise.

"It's likely that I saw them when they entered The Dancing Bear the night they murdered all the pub's customers and staff."

"Wow!" she exclaimed, then hesitantly she added, "You're being careful on this one right?"

Was that actual concern for his well-being? Could the adorable Danielle actually be interested in him for more than just her career?

"Yes, I'm watching my back, and I've got a new friend that works or at least did work for the MCPD, and he is dead set on getting to the bottom of this investigation, so I've got my bases covered. I'm being careful," Nick informed her.

"Good…I'm glad!"

There was that hesitation again. Was she really worried about him?

"So even though you checked in earlier with Marty, he keeps asking about you. I think he's worried you're stretched thin and might not get the latest on your 'Moonlight Massacre' piece in by the cutoff."

Good old Marty, always caring for the only thing that affects him and the paper.

"Don't worry, I'm actually almost there now. I'm in the car as we speak. But, I called because I need you to do something for me."

"Anything for you," Danielle replied, and Nick wasn't sure if it was just the favor she was referring to.

"Okay good. I need you to pull up anything you can find on the National Zoo, and any events they have that are coming up."

"Is there something in particular you're looking for, cause other than the Halloween thing they do every year, I know they moved up the Grand Opening for that new section they had been working on. It was in the Community section that Greg had just written in the paper the other day."

Nick froze, his body tensing and his hands tightened as he gripped his Oldsmobile's steering wheel. *Of course, how could I have missed it?*

"Wait, what was that you said about the event they do every year on Halloween?" he asked, knowing in his gut that this was the clue he had been looking for.

It all made sense. Aidan had said that his psychiatrist had talked about October 31st having some special meaning for the serial killers, an important date in history for some anniversary not well known to the general person. *What was it again? Somebody had died, that much he was sure of, but he needed to know exactly what was so important about tonight!*

"Every year down at the Zoo, they hold their annual Halloween celebration downtown. It's a big get-together, where they have all kinds of activities and various things happening. Normally the Zoo is closed by six every day, but for Halloween night, they stay open until midnight. The grounds are decorated for the holiday, and they have a haunted corn maze setup in one of the old animal enclosures with big hay bales making up the walls, kids crowd the walkways for trick-or-treating, the staff giving out candy to the groups who come, and this year was they were even having some contests and a performance by some local bands. It's a big thing to do in D.C., and pretty popular too. I went with some friends last year, and it was pretty fun, although this year I think I'm going bar-hopping with them, maybe looking for some good-looking guys to party with," she informed him, adding the last part in that seductive voice she was so good at portraying.

Yeah, she was definitely coming onto him, he was sure of it now. However, he had other things to worry about— things were heating up with these murders, and he had a feeling that the Halloween Event was about to have its party crashed by some unwanted, murderous guests.

It was the perfect place, a dark and scary night dedicated to people dressing up in all kinds of costumes and slinking around with the crowds, not realizing the danger they were putting themselves in tonight. Nick couldn't see how the killers couldn't pass up the chance, they definitely weren't shy about where they struck, and this event certainly seemed like their next victims were being served up on a silver platter.

"Okay, look— I need you to get me all the details you can on the event tonight. I'll be there in a couple minutes and I need that right away. Also, I need you to do some research and find me what you can about lycanthropy and any relation it has to tonight's date. It has something to do with someone who was killed hundreds of years ago, so you might have to look online instead of the archives," Nick said, letting his foot press the accelerator a little harder and sending his car speeding down the slick roadway.

"Okie Dokie! I'll see you when you get here cutie," she said, the flirtatious tone ringing through Nick's head as the line disconnected and he heard a dial tone on the other end.

Nick set the phone down and added a little more gas to the engine, his old car sputtering as it raced down the street. He hoped there were no cops out, since he was on his own deadline with the information he needed to put together. There was a murder to attempt to stop, and he now had an idea where it could take place. Hearing about the attack at SCBI was what put things together for him.

I sure am lucky, he thought as he realized how much this partnership he had solidified with Aidan Preston, suspended Detective with the Montgomery County Police Department, had come to be a real blessing for him. Yeah, he was certainly dancing around the big leagues with this story.

Pulitzer Prize here I come!

A light coating of frozen rain water had blanketed the street, and as Nick approached his turn to get onto Rockville Pike, he had to slow his car down to a crawl to avoid sliding out on a patch of black ice. The wheel shook slightly as Nick got the big beast of a car under control and rounded onto the Pike. He was only a few minutes away from The Informant's building now.

As he drove, he looked up at the sky and noticed that the gloom of cloud cover seemed to be rolling in, blocking out the sun as it was slowly sinking, in a few hours it would be dark due to the storm that was approaching.

Flipping on the radio, he scrolled through the stations until he found a station that was delivering the local weather forecast on the "8's". Listening to an old song from the early nineties start to dwindle down, he heard an upbeat announcer come on and begin to give the station's listeners the latest traffic and weather report.

"…that's right, for those of you in the Washington Metropolitan area trying to get around the Beltway this time of day, it seems like the lunch hour rush has become the time for people to call it quits early and head home from work. Traffic is backed up on I-495 right now heading North as commuters seem to be taking a half day this dreary, Friday evening. I-270 is not nearly as bad, but expect delays to start to build up in a bit as we have all these souls cutting out from their jobs to enjoy an extra long Halloween evening and weekend. And now for the weather— we have a storm front coming in from the West, cold pressures are building and meeting with the warmer weather above us, and it looks like we are in for the first chance of snow as this month comes to an end and winter is preparing to roll in hard!" the announcer said as Nick listened and took another glance up at the sky.

Snow, just great! It's not even November yet, he grumbled to himself as he saw that the dim glow of the sun had been hidden behind a snow cloud and he reached for the A/C knob. Cranking the heater up, he felt the warm air fill the car as he merged with traffic onto Rockville Pike and made the journey to his office. It took a little longer than he wanted as he fought the commuters driving home, and he had been in the car long enough to hear two older songs play on the radio, the last being a holiday-themed selection that he hadn't heard in ages. The 'Monster Mash'. Hearing the last notes fade as he pulled into the parking lot of The Informant's main building, the station started into commercials and he switched the radio off.

Once he was parked, he stepped out of his car and felt the cold wind whip around him, sending a chill through his clothes and down his skin.

Maybe come Christmas time when the weather really starts to get bad, I can take a couple weeks off and go to the Bahamas— get away from the winter snow! he dreamed, zipping his coat up and scooping up his work bag, he headed for the large, front steps that would take him inside and out of the chill. *Yeah right, like I can afford a vacation!*

As Nick neared the landing at the top of the wide, concrete steps that led to the glass entrance of the paper, his phone started ringing in his pocket. Answering it as soon as he saw the call was from Aidan, he paused at the top of the staircase and waited to enter the building.

"Hey, it's Preston," Aidan said as soon as Nick said hello.

"What's up, I was just about to head in and work on the latest article. My Editor wants the story on The Dancing Bear killings and the SCBI murder finished for tomorrow mornings paper, so I've got a lot to get done."

"Okay, well I won't take much of your time. Listen— I need you to try and come up with some information on some killings that have occurred across the country during the week before the murders started here," Aidan said.

"Wait, you're saying there have been other murders our boys may be responsible for? Why didn't anyone know anything about these other attacks?

"They were spread out in different Counties and States over the course of the week, and most of them were reported as just being animal attacks. Currently they're just unsolved cases with most of them being blamed on Bears or Mountain Lions, but I think there may be more to it. The MO is the same in most of them, but I need a little more info before I can take this to the FBI. Things here are already adding up to being some weird shit, and I don't want to cause those investigating the crimes to think I've lost my mind. I'm beginning to wonder if I have anyway," Aidan admitted.

"Where are you?"

"I'm at the National Zoo with Lisa Davies from SCBI, and a zoologist that works here who's helping us try to figure out what kind of animal these guys may be either using or mimicking the attack patterns on, but so far the data is looking off."

"Off how?"

"I'm not really sure how to say it, but according to the tests they've been running all night and today, they are getting DNA hits for completely different animals. According to Dr. Lafayette, who seems to me to be a big believer in the crazy, cult-like beliefs that surround New Orleans and its voodoo population, the killer we're looking for has Wolf and Human genes."

"What, is that even possible?" Nick asked in an incredulous tone, the rising of his voice seeming to indicate how preposterous he thought Aidan sounded.

"I don't know, I think there might have been some contamination in the samples that Ms. Davies had Dr. Lafayette test, that seems to be what they are hoping for as well, but I have some other hair samples that Mack found at the bar the night it was attacked, so I'm having them run those now for a comparison."

"Okay, well I'm just heading into the building now, so let me know what you find out. Oh, and what was the name of that guy who was killed on Halloween hundreds of years ago, the guy who confessed to being a werewolf?" asked the reporter, pulling his jacket's neck lining tighter around his throat as he leaned against the building trying to block the wind from hitting him.

"Stubbe, Peter Stubbe," Aidan answered quickly.

A little too quickly, Nick thought, like Aidan was having the same thoughts he was, and it was on the top of his brain like a problem being studied and worked out.

"Alright, I'm having the intern that works with me run some background into the story and see where that leads. Oh, and another thing Aidan…" Nick mentioned, "I don't know about you, but tonight being Halloween, I think that whatever has been happening is only going to get worst tonight. I'd ask the zoologist you're with there about the party they are having tonight, apparently the Zoo puts on this Halloween Bash every year, and I think it sounds like the perfect target for these serial killers to find a large population of possible targets to mutilate and dismantle!"

"Yeah well, I think the two people I'm with might just be in specific danger as it is."

Aidan then gave Nick a quick rundown of the ties to the unsolved animal attacks across the country, the story of the missing Tyler Suffux and how the items he shipped were the only things stolen during the break-in. When Aidan finished, Nick thought there was something else the man was leaving out, something bothering him, but he couldn't place what it was. As he and Aidan finished their conversation, Nick didn't bother asking the Detective what it was that had him so cautious with what he revealed, but Nick didn't pressure him. He knew he'd tell him when the time was right.

Hanging up with Aidan, Nick turned towards the doors that led into the building and entered into the large foyer, glad to finally be out of the harsh, heat-stealing winds that were flowing violently on the other side of the glass panes that made up the large lobby of the paper.

What hadn't Aidan told him?

Why was there something that seemed to be nagging at him about this story? Trying to add together everything Aidan had just told him, he headed for his desk to get to work on the story of his lifetime.

Everyone at the paper, Marty especially, was going to be leaning on him to pull this off, and Nick knew that he could.

Come tomorrow everyone would know his name as the one who first broke the juiciest details of these massacres, and with Ted Hanson out of the way due to him becoming one of those torn apart at the hands of these serial killers, he knew there was no one else holding any competition to his articles. Even the other papers seemed to be stealing their facts a day late from The Informant's pages. But, then with how fast everything was moving with these killings, a new murder or more each night, it was exhausting to try and be on top of all that was going on, however, if anyone could do it, Nick knew that person was him.

Now, it was time to see what Danielle had dug up for him!

- -

Mack listened to Detective Tim Melvin explain what that reporter friend Aidan had been hanging out with had supplied them with in his statement. He wasn't so sure that one of his oldest friends like Aidan Preston should really be spending so much time investigating these murders, especially since he was on administrative leave. All it was going to take was for Poole or someone else to mention that Aidan was in the station earlier to Chief Stone, and Aidan's career could be placed on the back burner for insubordination and interfering with an ongoing police investigation. And Mack knew that was the last thing an opinionated and by-the-book person like Stone would allow. He expected his officers to follow orders, not go gallivanting around with a freaking reporter for God's sake!

And, even if Poole didn't bring it up, now that Lieutenant Garza had gotten wind of the person responsible for helping them create sketches of the four men that might be involved in the killings, the 'Pit Bull' might just decide to inform the Chief. It was just something that rat bastard would do for the fun of it. He was definitely not one to be trusted, and was always looking for a way to prove himself in Homicide.

Aidan needed to be more careful, and as Mack thought about it, he realized the chances he had taken by involving Aidan in the investigation. He was playing it pretty close to the vest as it was himself. All he needed was for Poole or someone else to figure out that the information that Aidan and the reporter had learned about, and was making its way into the newspapers could cause him to get suspended. It was bad enough he had taken some of those hairs from the scene at the bar in the men's restroom. Detective Andrea Wilkes had almost caught him for Christ's sake! Yeah, he needed to watch his own back, while at the same time looking out for his old friend's back as well. Aidan deserved to be reinstated, and Mack just hoped he didn't step on anyone else's toes as he worked his angle on the case.

Mack needed to give him a call and see if he had anything new to report, but he figured he should probably wait until he was out of the office that the task force was working from. He didn't need someone listening in and hearing what he needed to talk to Aidan about. Ever since Aidan and the reporter came in to MCPD HQ earlier, some of the officers had been giving him a weird look once he got back from the scene at SCBI. Mack just shook his head in disgust and turned back to the report that was sitting on the desk before him.

It was a copy of the statement that Nick Haley had given Melvin earlier when he was working with Trish, the Goth sketch artist who seemed to love to push the boundaries of appropriate attire in Local Government. Not that Mack minded how free-spirited the girl was, he just wished she would just dress a little more normal. She was a little older than his first born daughter, and if his baby tried to leave the house dressed like Trish did, that girl would be grounded for a month.

Grounded for a month and I'd burn those clothes!

A smile formed on Mack's fat cheeks, and he imagined the look Trish would give someone if they attempted to remind her that their was a business-like dress code that County employees were supposed to comply with. Of course, even that is to lax, Max thought as he moved the reporter's statement aside and began reading all the notes and questions asked of the people at SCBI earlier. He had been busy making sure the offices and other facilities were swept by teams of officers before they could let the staff return to their work. They wanted to make sure the multitude of buildings were secure, leaving Agent Poole and Garza to interview Lisa Davies, the wildlife biologist about the scene at her lab and office.

He studied the typed transcript she had gave to the law enforcement agents, and found her story a little hard to believe. She thought all this was over a package that had been shipped to her from some guy who reportedly had gone missing right after? Mack wasn't so sure. Why would someone kill all these people over some stupid bones? Now that seemed like it was stretching it, but then again, this whole case had been an exercise in futility.

No hard evidence to tie anyone to the murders, half the forensics were either contaminated from what the lab boys were saying and there was so much material to sort through from each of the scenes that they were behind as it was, even though the forensic teams were working around the clock.

How lot of good that's doing! He thought angrily as he flipped through the typed conversation that Poole had Garza jot down from Lisa Davies, and he moved onto the actual case reports.

As he was reading, he saw Lieutenant Garza, dressed in that suit that Mack thought was fitting on a day like today. He looked absolutely ridiculous in his fedora and three piece suit with thin pin stripes, making the man seem to those who didn't know his over the top tastes, that the man had dressed for Halloween.

All he needs now is one of them old Tommy guns! Mack pictured the complete, gangster outfit in his mind and a big smile crossed his face. Watching Garza cross the room, his smile dropped as he watched the man come to Chief Stone's office and knock loudly on the door. Mack had seen this temperament before from the man, and he knew that something was up. Noticing the copy of this morning's edition of The Informant folded under Garza's arm, Mack felt a tingle move over his large frame. Garza was pissed about something as usual, but this time it looked like it might have something to do with Aidan's reporter buddy.

This can't be good, Mack noticed, watching the office door open and Stone wave Garza inside. As the man turned to shut the door behind him for privacy, he could have sworn that his shifty eyes had spied Mack watching him and narrowed.

What the hell is going on now? Mack wondered, but he knew something bad was going down.

He just hoped it wasn't about him or Aidan. That was the last thing he needed to be involved with at the moment.

Shit, what is Garza up to?

Chapter 41

As Nick opened his e-mail, he scanned through his new messages and noticed one in particular that caught his eye. It was from someone named Jeremy Wilkes. Nick tried to think of anyone he knew by that name, but he was pretty sure that even though the last name sounded familiar, he couldn't put a picture to the kid in his mind. And, it was definitely a kid from the look of the e-mail he had sent. Quickly reading through the message, he grinned as he realized it had to be some sort of joke. This Jeremy, whoever the hell he was, had apparently been following his articles in The Informant, and seemed to be giving him a fun little Halloween prank.

It's a little early still for trick or treating, Nick thought, but clicked on the link anyways.

As he waited for the page that he was redirected to load, he took a look around the busy newsroom, watching multiple people either rushing around the large room to fight to get their stories ready by the deadline, or people sitting at their desks and hurriedly typing away at their computers, trying to finish typing up their latest articles. Fortunately for Nick, he had worked the story over in his head a few times on the way in, so that by the time he arrived and had checked with Danielle on the information he had asked her to dig up, he was able to quickly knock the article out and get it entered into the system before Marty had the chance to start breathing down his neck.

In fact, the Editor in Chief seemed to have other things on his mind as he rushed about, struggling to keep the madhouse that was a newspaper afloat, and dealing with the guys working over in the new subscriptions detail who had messed up a batch of delivery addresses this morning and had a whole slew of people calling in, wondering where their paper was when it hadn't arrived by 8 o'clock.

There were even a few other issues that had sprung up since then, and Marty was going full-steam, wishing he could blow holes in anyone who pissed him off when he was already as irate as he was now. That was one of the incentives Nick had to get his article in on time. He didn't want Marty trying to strangle him for running right up to the deadline again.

That man is nuts, Nick thought as he watched the thin, balding man running about, and this time almost chasing down one of the guys from the Metro section over a piece covering the decline in real estate sales in the last month.

Apparently people who had been looking to move to the area had read or seen on the news about the latest crazed murderers stalking the County, and were dropping out of contracts, taking the hit on the fees that came from early cancellation of a sale. Real Estate Agents were pissed just as the public was that the police hadn't stopped the serial killers yet. He had even seen the sketches that he had helped the police come up with playing on the news channels on TV.

Marty informed him that the police had given him and all the other newspapers copies of the sketches to put into the next morning edition and Marty felt they would be a great addition to run under Nick's headline on the main page, then again that was always Marty, coming up with some way to get the circulation numbers higher. If there was one thing that could be said about the man who was storming around, chain-smoking like crazy, it was that he was truly dedicated to The Informant.

One of these days, that way that man treats himself and his high blood pressure is going to give him a stroke or heart attack, Nick thought as he watched Marty snatch a paper from Bert Nelly over at the Sports desk, and rip it in half, shouting some nonsense about "absolute bullshit"! Turning back to the computer screen before him, Nick went back to work looking through the internet page that had been sent to him from some fan of his who was following the story.

Kid probably believes in the bogeyman too, he laughed, reading through the page dedicated to werewolves and this guy Lincoln Douglas' radio program. This guys probably a quack, filling the heads of his listeners with a crap load of rubbish about out of body experiences and vampires rising from the grave at night. Nick shook his head, his long brown hair brushing against his shoulders as he stroked his smooth shaved chin and continued reading.

Just at that moment, Danielle appeared behind him, her tight body pressing into his back as she leaned over and dumped a pile of papers before him. The stack landed on his desk, and the young tease took her time pushing herself off him. Yeah, she was definitely interested in something about him. Nick wasn't sure what, but he hoped it didn't have to do with advancing her career and could end up with her going home with him after a few drinks at a bar.

He cringed slightly as he pictured Bo's ravaged body, lying in some metal cabinet in the Baltimore Morgue right now. He closed his eyes, trying to erase the image his mind was conjuring up. Even though the body had been removed by the time he and Aidan had gotten to The Dancing Bear, the bloody mess that had transformed the pub into a crime scene was everywhere. Pushing the thought form his mind, he turned slightly to see that Danielle was still leaning one tight, skirt-clad hip against the corner of his desk as she stared at the screen he had been studying moments before.

"You're really taking this lycanthropy thing to the extreme aren't you?" she asked, and Nick realized how silly the page must look to her.

He quickly reached over and minimized the browser, making the page vanish from the screen as he caught the smile on Danielle's lips as she looked from it to him. Those green eyes looked so ravishing and he pictured asking the intern out right at that moment. Shoving his silly boyhood crush away, he smiled in return.

"Actually a fan sent me over the link. The kid thought it might help me with my next story apparently," Nick admitted.

"Right, werewolves stalking Maryland— that seems a bit far-fetched! It'd be one thing if it was in Louisiana or something, you know the setting where that Sooki girl on that HBO series takes place. Now that's a creepy setting! All those old, rundown mansions and overgrown swamps stretching across the bayous. Maybe down there, but not in boring ol' MD!

"You know, most people believe the simplest answer is usually the right one," Nick mentioned, studying the elfin features of her small, sexy face and long blonde hair, and giving her a mocking smile.

"Simple— yeah like we just have a couple nuts running around killing people who have lost their marbles and are sick enough to be eating parts of their victims— gross!"

"Or if you look at the evidence the police have collected; paw prints, hair, saliva samples and more that aren't able to be typed or matched to a particular person or animal, one might be inclined to believe these Moonlight Massacre's are the result of the supernatural."

"Uh-huh, supernatural! Now I'm worried this boy has gotten to some hidden psychosis in your head, especially if you believe a monster is wandering the streets, barking at the moon," she said with a slight tease, her pixie-like nose wrinkling in amusement.

"You mean howling," Nick said.

"What?"

"Howling— you said barking, but that would be a dog, wolves howl."

"Oh whatever! I think whoever these crazy four bastards are that are doing this have a serious screw loose, but you keep talking like that and I might not be comfortable with you walking me to my car after dark. You might go for my throat."

"I just might, but I don't think it would be to harm you, you have the opposite affect on me," Nick admitted and caught the realization in the girl's eyes as her pupils seemed to dilate.

Was it him or were her cheeks blushing?

God she was sexy!

Taking a moment to recover from Nick's statement, a smile turning Danielle's firm lips up and the freckles around her nose and cheeks seemed to blend into the new coloring that had come upon her.

"I'll have to keep that in mind Nick Haley," she said in a low whisper that made his blood race.

"But first, you might want to take a look at all the research you had me doing," Danielle said, picking up the first few pages and handing them to Nick. "I think you'll find it pretty interesting."

Nick's mind was wandering, his head full of thoughts of Danielle and him, but he shoved them aside and looked at the papers she had handed him. The first was a flyer that she had printed regarding the annual, 'Boo at the Zoo' Halloween event taking place at the National Zoo downtown. He scanned the page, noticing the bold print where things like, "Lots of Treats, But Many Tricks Too" and "This is one Halloween party you won't want to miss!" rang out loudly from the face of the flyer. He continued reading, and began to think that as much fun as this tradition sounded, it had to happen on a bad night like this.

Nick had a bad feeling that something terrible was going to happen tonight, and he had to warn somebody.

They can't have all these kids and adults wandering the Zoo's grounds tonight, not while a group of mass murders is running around!

He looked down at the flyer again, reading carefully all the details and committing them to memory for future retrieval. For some reason he figured he would need to know exactly what to expect tonight at the event.

'Boo at the Zoo' seemed like just the place a group of serial killers could walk around, unnoticed by the general public as people would be dressed in all kinds of costumes and disguises, participating in the haunted trails, hay bale mazes, festive decorations and over forty treat stations where volunteers would be supplying the little trick-or-treaters with candy as their parents take them around for the activities.

That feeling that Nick couldn't shake was still bothering him as he flipped the page to the bottom of the stack and looked at the next paper Danielle had come up with. It was an article she had printed off the computer entitled, "The life and Death of Peter Stubbe".

That was it! Stubbe was the guy he was trying to remember!

This was definitely what he needed.

Nick looked up and gave Danielle an appreciative smile, which she matched, her brilliantly white teeth shining.

When this whole serial killer business was officially done and he was hopefully on his way to winning an award for his articles, he'd have to take Danielle out for a celebration dinner and drinks.

Maybe just drinks.

Then looking at the beautiful intern still perched on the end of his desk, Nick Haley wondered if he could persuade the enchantress to skip the drinks all together and go straight to his place.

Hey, he told himself, it could happen!

- -

Andrea Wilkes hung up the phone on her desk and leaned back slightly in her seat. She felt the back support in the chair was lacking in any actual aid to preventing her spine from being tortured after all this time she had been sitting, and she knew she needed to get up and stretch. Unfortunately, there still seemed to be a lot of work to do. She glanced at the report she was looking at and was confused. How was it that every saliva and other fiber than didn't seem to belong to any of the victim's could be degraded to the point that it couldn't be used to give a positive ID or even one of the killer's DNA?

It was one thing to think the rain had ruined the first scene, and that the elements could have screwed up some from the outdoor locations, but not the scene at the bar or the one in Virginia at the SCBI facility. Those had taken place inside. There shouldn't be anything to interrupt those forensic samples unless every last fiber and trace amount of anything collected had been left to throw them off. It had happened in the past. Killers thinking they were uncatchable and too smart for the law, would plant evidence to be discovered, either in an attempt to throw investigators off their trail, or even to point the finger right at them. That's how deranged some of these people were, especially the ones with their God complexes.

Pushing away from the desk, she let out a tired breath and stood up, reaching her arms over her head and stretching the stiffness from her limbs.

Oh that felt good!

As she felt the kinks work out of her spine, her mind turned to the eve before, the heavy and wanton actions she had experiences when she had been with Aidan Preston. The memories of the passionate night radiated in her mind and brought a heat that worked its way through her body as she finished stretching, remembering the details of their intimate evening.

Yes, it had been wonderful, the images of their arousing lovemaking so fresh and the tingle she felt rush through her as she recalled their time together.

Her heart raced a little faster as she summoned up the reactions she hadn't felt in so long, and she pictured exactly how it felt to have his lips meet hers, the light stubble on his cheek and chin scratching her skin lightly as their tongues explored the other's mouths. Then the excitement that had made her body go weak in his strong arms, the burning desire that had flooded her brain and let her release herself into his care as he explored every curve and area of her tight body.

Andrea felt her face flush as the previous nights actions played out in her head, her body warming as she twisted her waist and heard her back crack lightly, the muscles feeling a little less tight as she pivoted back and forth and finished stretching. Attempting to push the vivid images of her and Aidan's long hours of passion together aside, Andrea focused on the work at hand.

There was a group of serial killers out there, and no matter how amazing her time with Aidan had been, she had to push the thoughts from her mind and address the more serious issue. The unsure future of a relationship with a man who just might be back to working with her daily was something she did not need to think of at the moment since she wasn't sure where the feelings they had explored with each other were heading, so pushing it from her mind, she turned her attention to the files laid out on her desk.

Andrea knew that she wouldn't be leaving work anytime soon, and decided instead to follow up with the questions she had on the report. Fortunately, as a matter of keeping the entire task force's work in close proximity to itself and MCPD HQ, the bodies of the latest victims from The Dancing Bear, and the guard from SCBI in Virginia had all been transferred to their building at One Research Boulevard, where they were using a vacated forensics lab as a makeshift morgue for the time being. This saved them time from having to have everybody shipped off to Baltimore and the autopsies performed out of County. It also meant that if they had any questions regarding the Medical Examiner's findings or reports, he was just down in the basement, two flights below the main task force's command center.

Scooping the files up into her arms and stepping away from her desk, Andrea headed through the crowded room and took the stairs down to the temporary morgue. As she entered the room, where the scent of formaldehyde was strong and mixed with a potent chemical she wasn't able to name, but assumed was most likely ammonia, she found herself covering her nose with her hands as she walked over to a table where a jar of salve was sitting near the entrance to the next room. One of the other Detectives had left the container of Vick's VapoRub for anyone who might need it when entering the newly assigned lab area.

Dipping the tip of a finger into the cream-like substance she quickly dabbed some under each nostril and inhaled the strong odor of menthol and camphor, which cut down on the severity of the smell of death and decay that was now present on this level of the building.

She thought it was funny that even though most ME's and other pathologists who worked in a morgue all day long never used the stuff, the few times her and some of the other officers had to be around the victims for a short period of time they were putting the ointment on constantly. It just showed how ridiculous some people could be, then again, she had just put some on out of habit.

Oh well, she thought, stepping through the large, metal door that was before her and entering into the morgue that had just recently been setup. She was hoping that the Medical Examiner was in since he had already finished the latest autopsies, starting as soon as the bodies came in early this morning and spending most of the day working to cover the large number of reports needed to be compiled. As it was, Dr. Mohamed Taj Batra had spent almost seven hours with the help of two assistants, completing every single one.

Special Agent Poole had pulled some big strings to get the old, unused ballistics lab that was housed in the MCPD building's basement retrofitted to be usable as a place to house and store the bodies of the serial killer's victims, and where they could be properly autopsied. With a few phone calls from Poole and Chief Stone, two groups comprised of construction workers, electricians, plumbers and other professions had been contracted as a team, and then brought in and in less than twenty-four hours, the space had been converted into the place it was now.

Poole had decided after the man was found in the woods, that they needed to have easier access to the bodies until the case of the serial killer's was solved. He still had a hard time referring to the group as the Midnight Massacres, a name he continued to argue was just an excuse for the media to sell some papers. However, as much as Poole seemed to prefer just sticking with his unlabeled UnSubs, Andrea liked the name. It was catchy.

Either way, she was in the morgue now to speak with the ME about the discrepancies she had found in the various reports. She wanted to make sure they were right, before anyone headed off in the wrong direction because of an error that had just been casually passed over. That was where the Medical Examiner came in. Dr. Mohamed Batra was not what Andrea had expected when she first met him earlier that day. Poole had mentioned that he had worked with the man before on a few cases and even insinuated that the doctor was a genius. While Andrea wasn't sure what the man's IQ score was, and wasn't sure it mattered, she had seen from the autopsy reports he had furnished them with, that he had a larger grasp of scope when it came to the human anatomy and all things death related than the Baltimore ME had. It was no wonder Poole had brought the man into the folds of the joint task force, he was brilliant.

However, therein lied the problem. The conclusions this man had reached compared to the first autopsies showed a varying difference in medical opinion between the two doctors. While the Baltimore ME, Dr. Eugene Phillips, had seemed more focused on the wounds that could be explained away as just simple scavenger dog marks, this new guy seemed to be highly detailed in his study of the unexplainable markings, carefully making sure he did not disturb any evidence that could still be left on the body for him to test himself rather then send the results for analysis in the labs upstairs.

As she entered the next room, the main space of the old ballistics lab, she noticed how much work the contractors had put into the area. It looked completely different, and actually had become the spitting image of a permanent morgue, even though the makeshift room was just temporary. Hopefully, we won't need its services much longer, Andrea pleaded as she gave a silent prayer that these criminals murder spree would be brought to a swift end. Justice needed to be served, if not for the victims themselves, but for the general public that had been afflicted with the fear that these murders had first brought to Montgomery County and now the entire Washington Metropolitan area.

Dr. Mohamed Batra was younger than she would have thought, no older than forty, with dark eyes the color of obsidian and skin the shade common to men from India. He had jet black hair that was cut and gelled back in what Andrea assumed had to have been the work of an expensive stylist, and he wore a deep blue dress shirt complete with a matching tie and black slacks that went well with his skin color under the common Medical Examiner's uniform of a green, medical scrub-type shirt and pull over pants to protect his regular clothing from being contaminated during his work with the bodies.

Overall, he seemed quite fit and healthy, a far cry from the usual form of the older Dr. Phillips that she was used to dealing with through the Baltimore County Morgue. Since Agent Poole had gotten permission to setup the makeshift autopsy room in the basement of police HQ, and brought Batra on board, she had gotten to know a little more about the man.

Mohamed Batra was born in India, and had worked hard to achieve the place and status he held in the medical field. He had come over to America ten years ago at the insistence of the FBI, to aid them in a serial killer case that he had been asked to consult on. Ever since then, he had made the United States his home, and after gaining citizenship, he came to work on many murder investigations for the Government.

From what Poole had told her of the man, he seemed to be called in on all the strange cases where they needed his trained eye and vast intelligence to pick up on things that another ME might miss. That was the main reason that the FBI had furnished Poole and his joint task force with the man's invaluable assistance.

As Andrea heard the door close behind her, sealing herself in with the four bodies that were laid out on cool, steel tables under strong fluorescent lighting that revealed the mutilated corpses even more, she noticed Dr. Batra was sitting in a chair before a computer monitor that was stationed in one corner of the room.

He was busy going over some data that Andrea had never seen before, the coded sequences of what appeared to be DNA strands displayed on the screen, obviously magnified to many times the normal resolution to be able to be seen by the naked eye. When Andrea approached, her glance around the wide-open room taking in everything she could, Dr. Mohamed Batra swiveled around in his chair and stood to welcome Andrea into his domain.

"Good afternoon Detective, is there something I can help you with?" he asked, his original accent almost completely gone from his speech other than the emphasis he put onto certain words being obvious.

He had obviously lost most traces of the inflection he put on most sentences from the years he had been in the country, reminding Andrea that the reason he had come to the U.S., in the first place was because of how ingenious his medical methods were and the care he put into studying the depths of damage that could be inflicted onto the human body were. He also brought a much needed expertise and fresh perspective to the investigation of the Midnight Massacres, and for that Andrea was glad that the young Indian ME was here.

"Actually, yes there is Dr. Batra. I was hoping you could help me understand something in your reports here," Andrea replied, tapping the folder under her arm with her left hand.

"Of course my dear, how may I be of assistance?"

"Well, as you put in the last few autopsy reports, the only ones you fully were responsible for handling since the Baltimore ME took care of the first ones, it seems that you are leaning more towards the majority of wounds being actually inflicted by an animal rather than a human. In fact, all your reports seem to suggest that they are wounds distinctive to a large predatory animal instead of a serial killer possibly attempting to mask his actions in the guise of a bear or other large beasts attack. Could you please help me understand that?"

"Yes, it would be my pleasure," Batra said, the leading Andrea towards one of the steel tables where the body of the guard was positioned under the lights, his sickly grayish blue skin showing signs of massive blood loss along with the obvious mutilation that appeared on the body.

"Here we have Jesse Vaughan, aged twenty-four. He appears to be a well-developed, well-nourished adult male, whose appearance is consistent with the reported age of the victim. There are no readily identifiable surgical or traumatic scars, and no apparent tattoos or piercings," he said, motioning to the body laid out as he slipped a pair of latex surgical gloves onto his hands in preparation for touching the body.

Andrea looked at the deep cuts and wounds that appeared to be large bite marks that were evident all over the man's flesh. His thighs were the most gruesome part, with sharp puncture wounds from a knife or possibly claws having torn through the skin and pierced down to the bone while practically filleting the legs, their ripped skin and muscles dangling from the large, ragged holes. This man had lost a tremendous amount of blood while he was still alive, and Andrea could only hope that he had passed out from the loss of liquid or the pain, before the rest of the wounds covering his upper torso, neck and head were inflicted.

No human life deserves to be mutilated and then discarded like this!

Dr. Barta continued the recap of his autopsy examination, pointing out the various locations and marks as he spoke.

"The reason I put into my report that the evidence of injury did not appear man made, but looked, in my opinion to have been inflicted by a large predatory animal is because I have seen and performed autopsies on multiple people who had been attacked and killed by tigers over the course of my time as a coroner in India, and I am quite familiar with the resulting wounds of such a big creature. The bodies of each one of the victims that have been discovered, including the ones that Dr. Phillips autopsied earlier this week, all show signs of the cause of death being from blunt force injuries of the head and neck, upper and lower extremities and the torsos, consistent with a large predatory animal."

Andrea meet Dr. Mohamed Batra's gaze as she looked from the body to him, his head nodding up and down slowly as she realized how serious he was. He then began explaining the injuries. She noted that there were multiple puncture wounds to the head, neck, upper torso, extremities like his arms and especially his legs.

"On the posterior scalp is a 1-3/4 inch horizontal laceration, extending from the midpoint of this cut is a vertical 3/4 inch laceration creating the shape of a "T". A 1-1/2 inch cut is also on the left posterior inferior scalp.

'The scalp is avulsed with an 11 inch laceration which extends from the frontal vertex of the head, extending roughly to each mastoid area and to the nape of the neck, with a depth deep enough to expose the skull," he said, using a finger to move the torn skin away from the area at the base of the man's head and revealing the white bone underneath.

"Jesus!" Andrea muttered as she realized that the cut had been performed by something sharp enough that it had actually cut into the bone, leaving a line running the length of the wound. She felt nausea running through her stomach, and was glad that the VapoRub she had applied earlier was cutting into the stench coming off the body. Dr. Batra, who didn't seemed phased at all by the gruesome sight before him or the smell, just continued explaining the injuries for Andrea's benefit.

"On the right neck, below the inferior attachment of the right ear is a 1/2 inch by 1/2 inch puncture wound, and below the right angle that is formed are a pair of puncture lacerations each below the angle of the jaw, measuring approximately the same as the mark mentioned before and separated by a space of 2-1/2 inches. Another pair of similar lacerations is below the midshaft of the right jaw, measuring 9/16 inch by 5/16 of an inch for the more superior puncture and separated by 3 inches spacing. This pattern repeats from the anterior to the posterior of the neck, ending on the left of the neckline. Multiple red linear abrasions are on the neck, under the chin, and some extending from the puncture marks, all ranging in size from 1/8 inch to 3/4 inch. Interspersed among the the injuries I just described are multiple contusions ranging in size from 1/2 inch by 1/2 inch to 4 inches by 1 inch.

'The skull is exposed and has multiple, intersecting horizontal linear scratches ranging in size from 1 to 3 inches, mainly on the occipital area of the skull. A portion of the left parietal skull is absent and surrounded by comminuted fractures, the left dura is lacerated, while the left temporal region of the brain is disrupted due to the skull being broken apart.

'The left side of the brain, mainly on the left frontal and parietal lobes has subarachnoid hemorrhaging in this area and the brain stem of the skull. There is evidence of hemorrhaging in the bilateral diagestric muscles and in the surrounding soft tissues of the neck, while the cervical spine has a fracture between the fifth and sixth cervical vertebrae."

Sensing Andrea wasn't following as well as he would have hoped, he stopped for a moment to allow her to process everything he had been showing her. This allowed her a chance to ask him a question that had been forming in her mind as he had shown her the varying degrees with which the head and neck had been mauled.

"So you're saying that these wounds aren't consistent with a person who could have been armed with a knife or some other sharp weapon?" Andrea asked.

Dr. Batra studied her for a moment, an amused looking glint appearing in his eye as he smiled slightly and shook his head, no.

"In my professional opinion, this man was not killed by a human wielding any form of known weapon. He was killed by a dangerous predatory animal of some kind. His wounds are consistent with that of teeth and claw marks of something quite large to inflict the size of punctures and lacerations that are seen here. I was able to take trace forensic samples which I am testing now of saliva that was found at the wounds, and coarse black hairs that are not the victim's, but were left on the body and clothing. The results should be finished analyzing in a few hours and I'll be able to tell you for certain what kind of animal was used to kill these people.

'I physically examined and observed the deepest wounds and the grooves carved into the skull and other bones of Mr. Vaughan here…" he said, gesturing to the naked and mutilated body before them, "…and looking at the areas with the help of a electron microscope I was able to see the scratches in as high a resolution as possible, and I am confident that due to the residue left over by the friction of the killer's claws and teeth as opposed to what one would see had a knife nicked the bones, that this was definitely the result of some creature— not a man made weapon."

Andrea felt a shiver run down her spine, and she suddenly realized that although Dr. Batra had answered the confusion she faced when she had read his report, there was now something even worse bothering her. That reporter Aidan had been hanging around with that was covering the story in The Informant, had mentioned the possibility of the killer's using a trained animal of some kind to attack their prey first since some of the wounds on all the victims had happened before they died based on the autopsies. This meant that Aidan Preston and Nick Haley's theory had been right from the beginning.

But what kind of animal were they dealing with?

Although, she couldn't answer that question right now— she knew she wouldn't like what she found when she did.

What the hell could be responsible for such death and destruction?

That feeling that coursed through her body, sending a shiver through her was back.

This was far from over.

Chapter 42

Lisa Davies watched the Detective pace around the lab, his hands in his jean pockets as they waited for Dr. Morgan Lafayette to finish running the results of the DNA sequencer again. Looking at the clock on the wall she saw that it was almost 6 o'clock. That meant she had very little time before Dr. Ashton expected her to show up at the main administration building of the National Zoo, where staff and volunteers from FONZ, Friends of the National Zoo, were to meet and prepare the activities for the Boo at the Zoo event that would be starting at around 7 when the sun was supposed to set.

The annual Halloween tradition was a great community service project that the Zoo put on each year, along with the other holiday activities like the 'Zoo Lights' festival during Christmas and the New Years Eve 'Zoo Spectacular' that fell upon them right after that. Being the resident wolf specialist and wildlife biologist, Lisa was expected to help host the "keeper talks" segment at the Valley Trail, where various zoologist stationed at the different trail entrances and along the Olmstead Walk path were to help explain to the kids about the various animals that were in the enclosures along their different sections of walkways.

Lisa had the same assignment last year, and enjoyed giving back to the community during special events, however, tonight she was more worried about her and her friend Morgan Lafayette's safety and what could happen rather than making sure the various kids out looking for candy had their Zoo issued, reusable bags filled with treats. Someone or according to the first batch of results the head zoologist came up with when testing the hairs Aidan had supplied her with, something, was responsible for the death of the guard at SCBI and the multiple other killings that encompassed the surrounding area of Maryland and Virginia.

As Lisa watched Aidan walk back and forth, she saw his hand reach up to his left arm and move his shoulder in a circular motion, as if he was trying to work out a spasm or other pain. Coming to a stop before a small water cooler in the corner of the room, she watched him take an empty cup from the stack on the counter near the cooler and fill it full of water. He then pulled a prescription bottle out of his pocket and shook some pills out into his palm. Tossing his head back and gulping the cup until it was empty, he swallowed the medicine and replaced the bottle in his pocket. She wasn't sure what he had just taken, but had a feeling it had something to do with the pain he seemed to be trying to ignore in his upper chest. When he noticed her watching him, he quickly turned and walked away from the corner, a look of annoyance or possibly shame crossing his handsome and dangerous features.

Lisa could tell that this man had his secrets, and he obviously didn't want to share them with strangers. She wondered what he had just taken, but quickly ignored her analytical mind, just telling herself she was paying attention to details that didn't matter in the grand scheme of things going on tonight.

It's none of my business, she thought, but then she began wondering if that was true. Why had she called him to meet her here at the Zoo? Why did she choose to trust in him to tell him about the possible threat on her and her friend's lives? It's because you feel safe around him— he's a cop after all!

But, was that it, or was there something more?

Why had she called Detective Aidan Preston to come be here with her and Morgan at their time of possible need? It wasn't just because he was a police officer, no, it was because from the moment she had met him, she knew he was open-minded enough to look at the evidence that she had found regarding everything that was happening, and not just jump to conclusions based on the truth having to match reality. After all, the reality was that something was very wrong with the results they were getting, and there was a sinking suspicion growing in her stomach that pointed to it not being because the hairs and blood they had tested before were contaminated or degraded by an outside source.

No, that wasn't it. It was because she knew in her heart that the DNA typing and matching she had done with her assistant Frank before, and now the tests Morgan was performing on the hairs Aidan had provided from his friend in the task force was pointing to something she couldn't explain. Something unseen before in science— a crossbreed of genes that had mixed and formed some hybrid like aberration. Yet, was that really what it was? Or was this something that had just never been discovered before by humanity. Of course it had been discovered before, there were tales and stories that went back to the creation of the written language that spoke of these things, but it was a word that her zoological background that relied on science to explain things rationally, wouldn't allow her to utter.

Was it really possible?

Had they stumbled upon the beasts of myth and legend?

No matter how much she tried to deny the absurdity of the notion, she couldn't explain away the data they had already come up with. The data didn't lie.

As she watched Morgan studying the screen of the DNA sequencer, checking the genetic markings and comparing them to matches in the database, he turned to her and gave her a knowing glance.

The hairs from the crime scene Aidan had brought were the same as those sampled she had collected off that weird, misshapen piece of leg.

The samples matched— they were looking at evidence of a wolf-human genetic mixing.

They were dealing with a Werewolf!

- -

Aidan answered his phone on the third ring. The caller ID showed that it was Chief Stone. As he put the phone to his ear, he let out a breath as he realized this was one call he wasn't looking forward to.

"Preston," he said in a dry tone, waiting for his straight-shooter of a boss to tell him what the problem was.

"Aidan, we need to talk," Stone said without wasting time with formalities.

"What's the problem?"

"Oh, I think you have an idea as to what could be the issue. It's about a certain Detective on administrative leave and the possibility of information inside the current investigation into the Midnight Massacres, as the media has dubbed them. Lieutenant Garza has made some accusations regarding inappropriate conduct perpetrated by members of my department, and I'm going to get to the bottom of this immediately. Does the name Nick Haley ring a bell?"

Dammit Garza! Just couldn't take his nose out of other people's business!

Aidan realized there was no point in denying it, Stone wasn't one for bullshit, and could sniff it a mile away. He responded, gripping the phone tight in anger at what was happening, "Yes Sir, the name is familiar. He's the reporter for The Informant."

A silence on the other end of the line, then the Chief finally spoke.

"Yes, the reporter, and according to the information he's gleamed from an investigation that is supposed to be closed to the public, he is writing all kinds of details in that crap of a paper and making us all look bad. I just got off the phone with the Mayor and he's pissed as well at the progress we're making, and this news hound digging into our case, isn't helping the cause!"

Aidan had expected that his working the case unofficially would come out, but he had hoped it wouldn't have been Stone finding out so much about the personal time he was involving himself in the case. Thanks a lot Sergio! He could feel the anger at the Lieutenant rising, and then when Stone spoke next, the thing he said took the wind out of Aidan's sails.

"I've suspended Mack Jones, and he is no longer involved in the case."

"Wait, what? How can you do that?" Aidan asked, his fear that he would be risking his own reinstatement disappearing as he realized he had screwed Mack over by including him in his personal obsession.

"Don't question my motivations here son, you've got enough to worry about as it is. I expect you in my office within the hour. If you're not here by 7 sharp, you can forget about the Medical Board testing coming up, because you will be formally brought up on charges for interfering with a police investigation. I mean it Aidan, 7 o'clock and not a minute later. I suggest you drop what you are doing and get over her immediately," Stone said, and without waiting for Aidan to respond he hung up the phone, the sound of a dial tone echoing in Aidan's ear.

What the hell was he going to do? He couldn't let Mack take the fall for his actions— he had to fix this! But how?

Ending the phone call from Stone, Aidan quickly scrolled through his contacts until he reached the number he was looking for. Dialing Nick Haley, he knew he had to get over to headquarters immediately. Especially if he was going to catch Mack before he left.

"Hello?" Nick said as he picked up.

"Hey, I need you to do me a big favor!"

"What's that?"

"Are you doing anything right now? I need you to babysit someone for me," Aidan explained.

"Babysit...what?" the confusion in Nick's voice was prevalent.

"I need you to get over to the National Zoo and watch over two of the zoologists here. It's Lisa Davies and her friend Dr. Morgan Lafayette," Aidan said.

"What's going on?" Nick asked, worry now taking over the confusion.

"I think they are in danger, and I need you to keep an eye on them tonight. I have to get over to the MCPD headquarters by 7, or else I will have cost a man his job possibly by involving him in our private investigation."

Nick exhaled loudly then said, "Okay, I can leave now and should be there in a little while. Maybe fifteen minutes— will that work?"

"Yeah, and I'll fill you in on everything once you get here, just hurry!" Aidan said, and with that he ended the call.

He turned to Lisa and Morgan who were just standing there looking over the results of the DNA analysis that had just begun printing out. There attention had turned momentarily to Aidan as he began to explain what he had to do. At least he didn't think he needed to worry about something befalling one or both of them with Nick keeping an eye on them. And, if anything did happen tonight, Nick could call him and he'd be there in no time.

Aidan wished he didn't have to leave them here with everything going on, but he also couldn't idly by while his friend of many years lost the one job that he was good at because of something Aidan had done.

That's when Lisa turned to him, the printout in her hand and a grave expression on her face.

"What is it?" he asked, but knew what she was going to say.

"It's a match," she said, the look in her eyes telling him everything.

"Shit!"

The hairs Mack had taken from the crime scene at the bar were almost a direct match to the wolf-human genetics of the leg that the man in Oregon had discovered and sent to her. That specimen that caused her lab to be broken into and someone to erase all record of the items having arrive. Unfortunately, the last piece of evidence to be taken to destroy any trail of this weird creature was in the lab he now had to leave, the people who's lives might be in danger, having to pray nothing happened while he was gone.

However, Aidan wasn't sure their prayers would be answered. Something evil was on its way to the Zoo, and of all nights for this whole thing to come to an end, it was not only October 31st, Halloween night, but the Hunter's Moon was beginning to send its ghostly light down upon the Zoo from the sky as the sun began to disappear below the horizon. It would be brightly visible soon, once the sun was gone, and the full moon was high above as if it was a portent for the horrors to come.

Yes, something wicked was coming this way, and Aidan just hoped he was back in time to do something about it.

- -

Jeremy hadn't received any response from the e-mail he had sent to the reporter, Nick Haley. He had gotten his contact information from The Informant's website, having looked through the pages until he found the investigative journalist listed under the Crime section. He had hoped the guy would have gotten back to him by now, but undetermined, the boy began working on combing through the internet, looking through everything he could find on werewolves. He was amazed at how much history there was on the subject. He knew they had become more and more popular thanks to those teen romance novels like Twilight, and even though he had never read one of the books, he had seen one of the first movies at the local cineplex.

According to some of the data he had collected and saved, even taking the time to print out some of the more relevant articles that dealt with lycanthropy as an actual reality, not the fantastical beliefs that perpetrated the myths and legends, he had a pretty good idea of the types of things that separated the two ideas circling the internet regarding real werewolves.

He knew for certain that the creature had the ability to shape-shift into a wolf-like creature and it looked like from the attacks that had already killed so many people, that the full moon had nothing to do with it since they had killed every day of the last week it seemed. It did seem likely however that during the phase of the full moon, they were probably at their strongest. And, while there were many arguing theories online talking about the powers that such a beast could have, the basics seemed pretty possible.

It would have enormous strength, uncanny reflexes, speed, agility and endurance. Werewolves would also have heightened senses and excellent tracking skills due to them being part wolf. It didn't really matter how a person came to be a werewolf, whether it was a curse, being bitten by another werewolf, a magic belt or the wearing of a wolf skin and rubbing a special ointment onto one's skin, what really mattered was that they existed, he was sure of it, and more people were going to die!

Jeremy found some of the other legends and methods to be absurd. These methods could be done accidentally or intentionally to become a werewolf. He took a pen to the list he had printed out of possible ways he had found to become a werewolf; Being born on the winter solstice, being born on a full moon that occurred on a Friday, being conceived under a new moon, being the seventh son born of the seventh son, being born on Friday the 13th, not going to confession for 10 years, attaching Lycanthropic-related flowers to your shirt on a full moon or eating those flowers, and sleeping at night on Friday while the light of the full moon shines in your face.

As he continued crossing out the most ridiculous reasons a person could be subjected to lycanthropy, he soon found himself with a list of three main conditions that the majority of the literature and old myths seemed to focus on. In most old legends the human became a werewolf by either being born under the curse or by being infected from the bite or scratch from another shape-shifter.

There were also rituals that could be performed at certain times and under the right conditions that allegedly turned the sorcerer into a werewolf. Jeremy favored the most old-fashioned one he was familiar with, being bitten by the creature and having its curse infect a person. However, from the accounts he had read, a person's chances of not dying from the bite was incredibly slim.

Just look at all the people that have died in the last week, he thought.

He opened a second tab on his web browser as he selected another link he had saved from Lincoln Douglas' site. Reading over the part he had bookmarked the page for, he began reading the highlighted paragraph to himself, his voice low so his sister wouldn't hear him. "Cursed werewolves are subject to natural phases of the moon's lunar cycle. Once the subject has changed into wolf-form, the subject's mind blacks out and they will not remember much, if anything, of the details of the night before. The instincts of the animal take over and control the actions of the beast."

So according to this and the newspaper article he had read from The Informant, Clinical Lycanthropy could be the psychological part to these crazed beasts, but because society disregarded the idea that man could turn into beast, they assumed it was all in their head and nothing more than a vivid hallucination.

Continuing to read, he was surprised to find how many cultures around the world had stories and ancient tales passed down from generation to generation regarding these beasts. The wide range of different cultures, many having been separated from each other for thousands of years all told of these animals, the most concentrated accounts coming from Europe, Canada and America, but almost every society, no matter how isolated, had tales of such things.

It makes sense that such a wide-spread belief would point to there being some truth behind the fiction! Jeremy was excited, a rush of adrenaline coursing through him as he finished clicking on a few more links and sent some of the pages to his printer. As they slid out of the machine, he picked up the top one and studied it. The main thing he was interested in if there was a werewolf or pack of wolves loose and killing off people, was how to kill the creature.

There seemed to be two main items that the tales and legends agreed upon being able to stop a werewolf. They were pure silver and Aconitum. Clicking on a website that would give him a better idea of what the flowering plant known as wolfsbane was. As he read, he learned that it was a highly toxic, belonging to the buttercup family and that there were over 250 species of Aconitum. It is a native of the mountainous parts of the northern hemisphere, growing in moisture retentive but well draining soils on mountain meadows.

Well there goes having access to wolfsbane, he thought as he switched the site he was on to one about silver and the aversion werewolves have to the precious metal. A soft, white lustrous transition metal, silver has the highest electrical and thermal conductivity of any metal and occurs in minerals and in free form.

He found that the metal was used in coins, jewelry, tableware and even photography. He continued reading and found that pure silver also has the highest thermal conductivity, whitest color, the highest optical reflectivity, and the lowest contact resistance of any metal. The metal is stable in pure air and water, but does tarnish when it is exposed to ozone, hydrogen sulfide, or air with sulfur in it.

Silver had been used for thousands of years for ornaments and utensils, for trade, and as the basis for many monetary systems. Its value as a precious metal was long considered second only to gold. In Ancient Egypt and Medieval Europe, it was often more valuable than gold, but that still didn't explain why a werewolf would find the metal harmful.

What is it about silver in all these stories?

In answer to his question, he began to reach a paragraph that was exactly what he was looking for.

Now we're getting somewhere!

Associated with the moon, as well as with the sea and various lunar goddesses, the metal was referred to by alchemists by the name luna. One of the alchemical symbols for silver is a crescent moon with the open part on the left. Silver itself is not toxic but most of its salts are poisonous and may be carcinogenic. Compounds containing silver can be absorbed into the circulatory system and become deposited in various body tissues leading to the condition called argyria, which results in a permanent grayish pigmentation of the skin and mucous membranes. Although this condition does not harm a person's health, it is disfiguring. Ingestion of colloidal silver and silver compounds can lead to argyria.

Jeremy realized he was onto something now. Could this be why the metal had such a negative response to this element?— after all it was the only steady constant in all the myths and legends for dispatching a werewolf!

Then he seemed to hit the money load! As he scrolled down to the next page, he learned that silver has germicidal effects and kills many microbial organisms in vitro without causing noticeable harm to more complex life-forms. Hippocrates, the father of modern medicine, wrote that silver had beneficial healing and anti-disease properties. Various kinds of silver compounds are sold as remedies for a variety of diseases. Silver compounds are used to accelerate healing in burn victims. Silver-ions and silver compounds show a toxic effect on some bacteria, viruses, algae and fungi because of the oligodynamic effect which is typical for heavy metals. Copper is active against algae while silver is active against bacteria primarily due to silver's activity in the absorption of oxygen causing bacteria to oxidize on contact.

This must be why it is so lethal to werewolves! he realized. Whatever type of virus or infection caused a person to become a lycanthrope, or however they were able to biologically turn from man to beast, silver seemed to have a negative and deadly effect on them. He smiled as he printed out the latest pages that he had just read, deciding to add them to his wall, where his map and other newspaper clippings were hung.

"Score one for the good guys!" he whispered, remembering that his sister was just down the hall in her room and the last thing he needed was for her to come storming into his room and seeing what he was up to.

Suddenly there was a soft ding from the computer and Jeremy noticed he had a new message. He was logged into his Facebook account and someone was trying to contact him. Minimizing the page he had been studying, he pulled up the small window on the social networking site and saw that his friend Tommy had contacted him.

> **TDawg1: Are u almost ready?** The message said.
>
> Jeremy quickly typed in a response.
>
> **JeremyW: Ready for what?**
>
> **TDawg1: My brother was going to take us over to the Zoo, they're having some Halloween gig 2nite.**
>
> **JeremyW: Oh OK, sounds good. I was wondering what we were going to do tonight.**
>
> **TDawg1: Frank said he'd take us over to the new cages they built. The trails not open to the public yet, but we can check it out! Get a behind the scenes tour before ne1 else!**

Jeremy felt a sense of intrigue at the mention of seeing the new exhibits before they were open to the public. It would be neat to check it out, and especially on Halloween.

JeremyW: You mean the Midnight Trail?

TDawg1: Yeah, so u down?

JeremyW: Definitely! I can be ready in about 20.

TDawg1: Gotcha, well we will be there then, so hurry up and get ready. It's freaking cold out tonight!

JeremyW: C U then

Jeremy quickly minimized the screen and headed for his closet. He looked at his watch and saw that it was almost 7. He'd have to hurry if he was going to be ready in time to sneak out. His mom had definitely not seemed to happy learning about his recent absences from school and had told him he was grounded. Luckily his bedroom window was on the ground floor of their townhouse and it faced the small back yard they had. Unlatching the window, he walked over to his closet and began pulling out his jacket and other clothes to prepare for the cold.

He couldn't wait! The Midnight Trail was going to be awesome tonight with all the Halloween decorations that were set up around the grounds of the Zoo, and it would be perfect to check out the dark and spooky path at night. Frank had told him there were hidden speakers along the trail that mimic wolves howling, bats squeaking and other ambient sounds as visitors walk the trail once it was open. He felt like a VIP, getting backstage access to the new area since Tommy's brother was taking them.

It was going to be so cool!

Grabbing the pages he had printed from his printer, he slipped he papers into a folder along with other research he had pulled up and decided he would show Tommy and Frank all the crazy research he had done. He knew Frank would be impressed, and that was what mattered. Tommy would probably think it was lame, but Jeremy knew he was onto something and that the killings that had been happening around the area didn't seem to be stopping anytime soon.

As he looked out his bedroom window at the dark night, he realized the moon was shining high above, its face full.

Perfect! What a night to check out the new Midnight Trail— a full moon with a werewolf on the prowl!

A tingle of excitement coursed through the fourteen year old.

Now all he had to do was sneak out with no one knowing.

This was going to be a night to remember!

Chapter 43

Nick sat on one of the chairs around a lab table, watching the beautiful wildlife biologist moving about, her black hair swinging against her shoulders as she finished getting her winter coat on and a knit cap in place over her head. The temperature outside the building had definitely dropped with the strong wind making the air feel like it was around freezing, and if she was going to be stuck outside for a few hours handing out candy at her assigned station, then she needed to be dressed warmly.

He couldn't believe she was being so stubborn and had said that she would still be going through with her volunteering for the kids that were coming to the Zoo's event. Her life could be in danger, and she was acting like she wasn't going to let some faceless threat stop her from living. Oh well, at least they were serving hot chocolate and coffee as well, since he was planning on going with Lisa until Aidan got back. Nick couldn't believe how cold it had gotten since the sun had dropped out of view, replaced by the pale white of the perfectly round orb. The moon was bright tonight and had taken on a slight red-tint that reminded him that it was the Hunter's Moon this Halloween and he couldn't shake the feeling that there was something dangerous out there, stalking the Washington Metropolitan area for prey.

He was also dealing with the crazy information that Aidan and Lisa had filled him in on when he arrived. Werewolves— seriously? He was worried that everyone around him was losing their minds. Was he really the only sane and objective one present among these people who were supposed to be brilliant scientists? Nick wasn't sure what to think. He had listened to them relate everything that had happened, including the unsolved murders that had seemed to follow the package across the country, but werewolves? Come on! He finished zipping his own jacket up tight around his neck, wishing he had thought to bring a pair of gloves or a hat. Leave it to him to have everything he needed in his work bag except what was essential to keep from freezing his ass off.

Lisa turned to him and asked, "Are you ready?"

Rubbing his hands together in preparation for the chilling weather he was about to be in, he nodded his head. "All set— might as well get going."

"Okay…," she said, then turning to the strange and slightly pecliar form of Dr. Morgan Lafayette who had continued to attempt to convince them he would be fine in the building by himself, said, "…make sure you lock the door behind us. It would make me feel a lot better if you humored me and I don't have to worry about your well-being."

"Of course, my dear. Dere ain't no point in stayin' with me. Nobody's gonna be botherin' me here," Lafayette said, giving her a reassuring smile, but from the look on Lisa's face, Nick knew she was still contemplating staying.

"Alright, time to rock and roll," Nick said as he and Lisa headed for the exit.

Lisa paused one more time in the doorway and gave her old friend one last look, then following Nick, they headed into the hall and towards the glass doors that would lead them in the direction of the Valley Trail. Their plan was to cut through the small wooded section that surrounded the old, stone structure that housed Morgan's lab, and to check in first at the administration building and then make their way to the area Lisa was supposed to be manning.

It was a short walk following Lisa Davies over the various paths and trails that inter-crossed over the vast, downtown grounds of the National Zoological Park. With his jacket zipped up and his collar turned up against the chilling wind, Nick wasn't sure that many people would be coming out tonight for the 'Boo at the Zoo'.

It seemed like a bad idea for parents to not only drag their kids out in this freezing weather, but to walk them around this wooden destination on Halloween while a group of murderers were killing people all over the surrounding Counties just for some candy made him question people's parenting decisions. There was a reason he hadn't had any children yet even though he was already thirty-five. Other than the fact that he hadn't found Mrs. Right, his job was demanding and he just couldn't see him settling down anytime in the near future.

Kids at this point in my life— Who has the time or the patience?

At that thought, Nick's mind focused on the two women he had found quite irresistible recently. The first was Danielle, the intern working at The Informant for the last few months. There seemed to be something there that could lead to them at least getting drinks after work, and then he could see where one thing led to another. Then there was the stunning visage of Lisa Marie Davies, the woman who had been left in his care while Aidan had to drive into talk to his Chief at MCPD headquarters.

He found her name alone to be endearing. Lisa Marie— her mother must have been an Elvis fan, he thought as he watched the beautiful, Hispanic woman dressed warmly in her winter parka with fleece lining the hood and interior of the jacket, which he thought was a must for a wildlife biologist who worked on conservation efforts. He couldn't imagine a zoologist sporting a fur coat or animal lined jacket. Now that would be ridiculous!

With her striking facial beauty, fit body, long legs and curves that were obviously a gift from her ethnic heritage, Lisa Davies was definitely a looker. Being in her presence he could hardly remember what Danielle looked like. Then again, that was always his problem. Settling down and the thought of monogamy were something he wasn't sure mankind was supposed to choose.

He sometimes thought that the animal kingdom had it right in the regard of taking various mates throughout a lifetime. After all, there were only a few species that mated for life, and the way Nick's interest was drawn to all kinds of women he was introduced to in his course of his daily life, he knew even though he would never cheat on a woman that he was involved with, he would certainly let his eyes and mind wander.

He didn't think that made him a bad person, he was just a visual person, and right now he had his sights set on the rear end of a certain zoologist as she walked briskly out of the administration building, having checked in with the volunteer in charge of the 'keeper talks' stations and they headed back towards the Valley Trail.

The large folding table that had been setup on the edge of the trail next to the Bear habitat was where she was scheduled to work for tonight's event. By the time they had reached the station, they had just enough time to get the thermoses of hot cocoa ready and the bowls of candy that she was to hand out to the various trick-or-treaters set out on the table. Even Nick had taken a bowl into his arms, deciding to help her out since he was stuck out here babysitting as it was. At least the view was incredibly pleasant, Aidan could ask him to protect her any day.

Lisa Marie Davies, what is your story? He wondered as he watched her pour bags of mixed, wrapped candy into a big Tupperware serving bowl. There was liveliness in her movements, and even with everything going on, the thought of being out here with the children coming seemed to lighten her mood. She wasn't nearly as stiff as she had been when he first saw her tonight when he had arrived to take over for Aidan while he ran his errand.

It took no more than five minutes from the time they had the station set and ready for the crowds that would be flocking to the zoo on this cold Halloween night, then the first children dressed in matching costumes arrived, heralded by their parents who were pushing a stroller that would eventually hold the two children once their sugar highs caused them to crash and their parents were forced to wheel them home for the evening.

Nick had to admit, the amount of time that the National Zoo had put into the decorations and other aspects of the holiday festivities was pretty neat. He was surprised he never made it out to the downtown park any year before this, but then again, it wasn't like he had a kid to bring to these types of things. Maybe one day he would, but for now, his usual holiday traditions of getting drunk at a bar, alone, would just have to do. Of course, with that thought process working through his mind, he immediately focused on his friend Bo's death. That was a terrible blow to him when he had first heard the news, and it was also something he just couldn't shake from his mind. He silently prayed that Bo had met his end quickly and without too much pain.

Nick turned his attention to the groups of people slowly wandering down the trail from different ends, stopping at each station along the route and collecting candy in their treat bags and getting fun-filled information told to them by the zoologists and volunteers working each table. He could hear Lisa explaining something to the group that had arrived in costumes, but he was too busy dispensing candy to the children to pay much attention to the details and facts she was relating to all who were listening. Nick noticed how well she captivated her audience, and found himself paying more and more attention to the woman, watching her thick lips forming each word as she spoke.

"…and the Grizzly Bear and Black Bear are actually commonly misidentified and easily confused for the other," Lisa was saying to the young girl and boy who had eager, wide eyes as she spoke to them. "The color of a Grizzly Bears fur varies from blonde to black. They are most commonly medium to dark brown. The long guard hairs often have a lighter tip, giving the bears their 'grizzled' appearance. Black bears exhibit a great variation, ranging from black to light blonde. Cinnamon-colored black bears are quite common in the west. Many black bears have a light patch on the chest. The snout is usually light in color, even in black bears."

Man she really knows her stuff, he thought as he was learning a thing or two from the brilliant wildlife biologist that had just entered his life thanks to the story he was working on. If not for these killings he would have never had the chance to meet Lisa, and he was hoping that he might get to know her better once this was all over.

"…both bears vary greatly in size, many male grizzlies averaging around 500 pounds. Large grizzlies can tip the scales at 800 pounds. Black Bears however, average 110 to 330 pounds, with large males topping 400 pounds. The claws of a grizzly have a formidable reputation. Very long, between 2 to 4 inches and are often clearly visible in the tracks. They may also be visible from a distance. Black bear claws are much shorter than those of grizzly bears, usually around 1-1/2 inches. They are less visible from a distance and are another way to distinguish between the two bears."

As he listened to Lisa discuss the differences between the two bears, he wondered if there was a chance they had overlooked something and these killings weren't the result of some crazed maniacs using trained animals to attack their victims. It seemed to be less likely the further his and Aidan's investigation went on, but to admit to the other option was just plain lunacy.

The four men he had seen disappear into The Dancing Bear that night had to be involved, but who was to say they couldn't have had a pack of large dogs with them that they let loose onto those who had fallen prey to their disturbed actions?

There was just too many questions he had that he couldn't seem to put answers to, too many variables that weren't adding up. To believe there was some wolf-like beast the size of a large man hunting down and mutilating people seemed to be just a little too much like fiction for him to jump on board with the others regarding the werewolf theory, there was something that just wasn't adding up. Just then, as he was picturing the four possible suspects the night he saw them from his car, he could remember seeing a tattoo on the shorter one's forearm. Even though it had been cold that night, he could recall that none of the four had been wearing jackets or any other warm clothing.

As he tried to remember the mark he had seen on the one suspicious character, he turned and watched the crowds of children dressed in Halloween costumes gather around the table, listening intently as Lisa spoke of the bears that were in the enclosures behind them. There were little pirates and ghosts, Disney princesses and even a few costumes to go with the Zoo theme as parents had dressed their children as various animals like panda bears and even a little werewolf. Nick just automatically doled out the candy into the eagerly waiting bags and pails on the opposite side of the table, thinking back to that awful night when Bo had been killed. Then he remembered it!

The tattoo— It was that of a pentagram! Suddenly Nick knew without a doubt that these four were responsible for the multiple killings that had taken place all over Maryland and then in Virginia. Each person had that design carved into them, the locations varying depending on the victim and their wounds, but it was a constant that was involved in every scene. Setting the bowl of candy down and letting Lisa take over the job of dishing the treats out to the kids as they came up in between her lecturing, he pulled his phone out of his pocket and dialed Danielle's cell. He was praying she hadn't gone out yet for the night, and was hopefully available to recall some of the information he had her research.

"Hello?" her sweet, sultry voice drifted into his ear as a cold blast of wind whipped around him, causing him to squeeze his arms tight against his body against the air currents.

"Danielle, it's me— Nick!" he yelled, raising his voice as another gust rocketed past him.

"Oh, hey! I'm glad you called, I was just getting ready to go out. Are you looking for somewhere to grab a drink, maybe have a little fun?" she asked, the hint well received and he could just picture her getting ready, dressed in a short outfit that showed off her sleek, runner's body as she prepared to go and hit the streets tonight with her girlfriends.

"Unfortunately, I'm a little busy this evening, but I did have a question for you."

"Um, okay— shoot," she said, and Nick could hear the disappointment in her voice.

Oh why did I have to get stuck babysitting! He thought, then looking at Lisa standing there, her hands moving animatedly as she handed out treats to the various costumed children and was still filling the time with all kinds of facts and information that had the kids begging for more, he figured at least he was stuck spending his time with another highly attractive woman. Maybe, I'll get lucky and both of them will say yes to a date! You never know when you might need a backup plan!

"Do you have any copies of the files you printed out on all those topics I asked you about looking into?"

"I have some of it, the rest I can pretty much remember of the top of my head, why?"

"I needed to know what you remember about the symbol of the pentagram."

"Ah, the good old Devil's Mark, yeah sure I can recall all that," Danielle said with a laugh, then started reciting from what she could from memory, "The pentagram or druid's foot is used as either an invocation or a protective ritual. This ritual is used to develop the magical capabilities of the human personality.

'In ancient times it was sometimes associated as a symbol for health. In the Middle Ages, it was used in magical formulas to gain power over elemental forces. It was known as the "druid's foot", because it was thought to protect against the evil forces associated with witches and druids. It was worn as an amulet to ward against witchcraft, and as a talisman, it activated the inner powers of a person to attain a certain goal."

"Wait, what did you call it before?" Nick asked, trying to remember the phrase she had used when he first told her he needed the information on the pentagram.

"You mean the Devil's Mark?" she questioned.

"Yeah, why did you say it like that? he said, wondering if it was a coincidence that the sign was attributed to a beast of some sort. And, of course Danielle wouldn't understand how the pentagram fit into the puzzle because that was one piece of information he had not revealed in any of his articles. Aidan had suggested he keep that grisly bit of news to himself so it didn't affect the task force's investigation with the general public knowing everything.

What is it about the pentagram?

"Oh well, that's just another name for the pentagram, at least in folklore and some of the old stories and movies about werewolves. It was kind of a joke since you were acting so weird earlier about that topic. What with you looking it up on the work computer and everything. I thought the murders had you cracking under pressure, because of the whole lycanthropy angle."

"No, no, I'm fine, but tell me what you discovered about this mark?" Nick said, desperate to fit the pieces together as they were given to him, and for some reason things were looking a lot clearer the closer he seemed to be getting to the inside truth of the story. He just hoped he was on the right path!

"Well the "Devil's Mark" or the "Mark of the Werewolf", as I've found it also called was a symbol that ancient beliefs held could be found on a werewolf because they were thought to be cursed. They thought that the sign of the pentagram, a five-pointed star was usually found on the chest or palm of the accused. It was also believed that the mark would appear on anyone who survived a werewolf attack at the first full moon officially marking them as cursed.

'Apparently, it got so bad that people back in the dark ages would cut off moles and other birthmarks and cover up bruises and scars so that people wouldn't see the deformity and assume they were really a wolf hiding in the guise of a man. Basically any skin deformity found on the butt, back or upper thighs could be the Devil's Mark. So you better watch out Mr. Haley, cause if you see someone with a skin irregularity such as a scar or mole in these areas, you may be in the presence of a werewolf!" Danielle said with a laugh.

"Haha, very funny! I didn't know you were a comedian."

"Thank you, thank you…I'll be here all week!" she continued.

It was good to have a little break from the tense feeling of foreboding that seemed to be settling over him the longer they were outside in the open, here at the National Zoo, just waiting to see if something was going to happen, it helped to laugh. He looked to Lisa who had just wrapped up one of her speeches, the children with their bags full of candy heading off down the Valley Trail to the next table about fifty yards away where a volunteer was explaining the benefits of Owls in society and their nocturnal brethren.

Then looking up at the dark sky above, the white moon with its off-color tint reminded him that tonight there were other things to be worrying about then enjoying a phone conversation with Danielle.

"Is there anything else in the stuff you pulled up about the symbol, anything more in depth?"

"Um, yeah, hold on..." she said and Nick could hear what sounded like her shuffling through papers on her end of the line. "Yeah, here it is, you ready for this?"

"Lay it on me," Nick replied, slipping his trusty notebook from his pocket and jotting down what Danielle had already told him. He was always prepared, something he had learned in Boy Scouts as a child, and never went anywhere without a pad of paper and a pen.

"Okay, it says that there are a lot of theories about werewolves and pentagrams. Some say that you can spot a werewolf by seeing if they have the sign of a pentagram on their forehead or on the palms of their hands. However, because werewolves are very hairy creatures, even when in human form, this might be a little difficult to check. Another theory regarding werewolves and pentagrams is that werewolves can spot their next victim because it's the victim that shows the sign of the pentagram on their forehead. However, this theory probably came mostly from the movie The Wolfman. Wait, I don't remember that part from the movie..."

"That's because it's not talking about the newest one with Anthony Hopkins. Geesh, don't people your age watch any of the classics?" Nick joked.

"Oh now who's being the comedian? You better watch it bub, there's a few things I can think of that I'd like to do to you that would drive you crazy!" Danielle whispered.

Nick felt that flush of heat again and his heart started racing. There was that flirtatious side of the girl again. Oh how he'd love to take her up on her offer of going out and getting some drinks with her friends! But, he had a job to do, and this story was going to make his career! He had to keep focusing on that, and not on what Danielle was doing to him emotionally and physically.

"Okay, okay, I relent! Now keep going with what you have there," he said, turning his attention back to the notes he was writing.

"Alright, well it says that the whole take on werewolves and seeing the pentagram on future victim's skin was probably a liberty the movie's writers took with the film's script and not actually based in folklore. Anyways, there are other references to the pentagram and werewolves or at the very least some symbol that marked the beast for people to distinguish the creature from that of regular humans, but there is also a lot on how the sign relates to other areas of magic and witchcraft," Danielle informed him.

"Like what?"

"Well, in a lot of tales, the pentagram or pentacle symbols show up and it's mostly used as a sign of evil or Satan worship. There's also some stuff here about the five points on the pentagram and what they mean. These five points are supposed to represent elements of the Earth and spirituality. The five points actually represent: Earth, Wind, Fire, Water, and Spirit. It also shows up in many Biblical references and some churches and religions even use this symbol in place of the cross."

"Wow, okay— sounds like you did your homework. I own you one," Nick said, finishing jotting down in his quick scrawl the information Danielle had just given him.

"I'm going to hold you to that, just remember you said it!" she said, that teasing hint of playfulness still in her voice.

Nick double checked his notes and then decided to let Lisa know what he thought. He thanked Danielle and after promising her he'd take her out for drinks later this week, they hung up and he turned to the wildlife biologist who was looking at him curiously, those dark brown eyes seeming to look into his soul and he felt himself incredibly attracted to her as well.

What was he doing to himself? He needed to cool it, before he ruined his chances with either of them. Keep it cool Haley, he muttered in his head as he looked at Lisa and smiled.

"What's up?" she asked, setting her bowl of candy down and rubbing he hands together for warmth.

Looking up at the dark void above, the flickering of stars high in the heavens and the Hunter's Moon just hanging suspended above them, he realized it was starting to snow, the soft flakes drifting down from the night sky and onto the Earth below.

Well I'll be damned— the weather report was right for once!

Chapter 44

"What the hell is wrong with you Aidan?" Stone demanded, the anger in his low gravelly voice quite clear.

Aidan was sitting in the Chief's office, Stone sitting behind his large desk, his hands squeezed into fists and sitting on top. Everything was organized with military precision, his nameplate and the various folders all arranged neatly, each one labeled with the name of the various victims of the serial killers rampage through Montgomery County and now Virginia as well. Even though Special Agent Poole of the FBI was in charge of the investigation, it was Stone's precinct, his Homicide Division and his building that were being utilized in the massive manhunt that would hopefully bring these murderers to justice. However, he was still under the impression that the suspects they were looking for were ordinary people, albeit serial killers, and Aidan was beginning to question that assumption.

After everything he had seen over the last week of the various crime scenes and autopsy reports, and now the data that Lisa Davies and Dr. Morgan Lafayette had analyzed in their labs, he was beginning to wonder if his recent belief in the supernatural wasn't unfounded. Something was surely going on, something that normal science might not have the answers to explain away, and the further he followed this case on his own, the more convinced he became that he was dealing with an evil that modern society had relegated to folktales and legends. He just wasn't sure if he could convince Chief Stone that he hadn't completely lost it.

A lot was riding on this meeting right now. Mack had already been taken off the case, suspended with pay until Internal Affairs could decide if his actions were to be considered misappropriate conduct or not. It seemed that Lieutenant Garza had blown the whistle on their unofficial, side investigation, and Stone was not happy. When Aidan had first arrived he told him that he was to cease and desist with any "vigilante-style work", and that he was lucky he was already on administrative leave or else his reinstatement could be in jeopardy. Unfortunately Mack was getting the brunt of the disciplinary action that Stone could dish out because he was a part of the joint task force and Agent Poole was pissed that so much had been given to the media as well. No matter how much Aidan tried to take full responsibility for The Informant's in depth articles, the Chief wasn't buying it.

The problem was that Garza had two different crime scenes he could use as examples where Mack and Aidan had been conferring with each other, and the second one was when they had first met Nick Haley. That was all the fuel Stone needed for his fire. He was not a happy camper. Aidan wished there was something he could do for Mack, but right now Stone seemed to only be focusing his attention on him.

Now, Aidan wasn't sure if his boss was going to think he had completely gone off the deep end when he started telling him about the analysis of evidence from The Dancing Bear that he had Lisa and Morgan run at the Zoo. There was one thing he did know for sure, and that was that if someone had told him what he was about to tell Stone, he'd sure as hell think they'd had a couple screws loose. Aidan just hoped that his boss didn't think he had completely stepped off the deep end and recommend him for more intensive, psychological evaluations. Seeing Dr. Harper weekly was bad enough, but he knew he was risking everything by what he was about to reveal.

"Chief, there's something I need to tell you about this investigation. Something I think that you need to seriously consider, because I believe there are two people who's lives are in danger and need police protection," Aidan said, watching Stone's face to see how he would react.

"I assume you're talking about the scientist who works for the Smithsonian?" he said, the expression on his face remaining grim, the lines in his face hard and set.

"Yes, Lisa Davies, the wildlife biologist from SCBI. It was her office that was broken into and where the guard, Jesse Vaughan was killed."

"I have already spoken to Agent Poole regarding the possibility that she could be targeted, however, he agrees with me that there is not enough information to suggest that any of the murders have been targeting to specific individuals. It seems like the break-in was just a single occurrence that was the result of these people being there at the time. I'm sure the motive behind the killings is far from something as simple as the stealing of some old bones."

"Sir, I disagree with that assessment," Aidan said, feeling the tension in the room growing as he contradicted his superior officer's decision.

"Oh, is that so? Let me remind you that any decision made regarding this investigation is not something you are a part of. You are on thin ice as it is with your disregard for my orders, and while I'd hate to lose a Detective in my Division over something so ridiculous as you going off half-cocked and acting like one of the damn Hardy Boys, I will remind you that you still need to go before the Medical Board and have a review of your file by me in regards to you being allowed back to work. The way it looks now, you are not going to be receiving high marks due to your recent actions— if you're even brought back!" Stone yelled, for once his solid expression broke, and for the first time, Aidan heard the usually reserved man truly angry.

Aidan sat there, his hands gripping the armrests of his chair. He breathed out and tried to think of what he needed to do to get the man to understand how much danger he thought could be heading to the Zoo. He looked out the window, through the half closed blinds and saw that it was already dark, the sun having disappeared fully and the pale moonlight filtering into the office.

Damn it, I should be back there now! he thought, angry at so many things right now. He didn't need to be sitting here, listening to Stone threaten him and his job, he needed to be at the logical place that the killers would strike next. He had no doubt that this had all started over a secret being sent across the country, a secret that people were willing to kill for. As he sat there, his eyes moved from Stone's and he looked at the desk before him. Laying there, on the top of one of the folders was the composite sketches that Nick Haley had come up with of the possible suspects that the FBI and police were scouring the Washington Metropolitan area for right now. He studied the faces of the drawings, all four pictures side-by-side on the same page.

If it wasn't for his vigilante actions and disobeying his Chief's orders, they wouldn't be as close to discovering who these men were. If it wasn't for him bringing the reporter that Stone and Poole had such an issue with, into the station to report the people he saw that night as he left the bar, they would be flying blind. But, how could he get this man to see that. He let out another breath, trying to calm his nerves as he tried to decide on his next course of action. Should he tell Stone what he really thought was behind these killings? So far the task force led by Agent Jim Poole of the FBI was under the assumption the victims had also been attacked by trained dogs that one or all of the suspects controlled. How absurd was that?

Looking at the pictures once more that was laying on Stone's desk, he decided right then and there that he wouldn't mention the possibility of a wolf-like creature being really responsible for these murders. He just needed Stone to get on board with the realization that the two people at the Zoo that he had left under Nick's care, were in danger. Glancing at the light coming in through the window once more, the full moon almost appearing blood red, he reached his decision. No more playing it safe, he needed to speak up now!

"Chief, I don't care what you do to me or my career over this case— I just need you to understand that I believe there is sufficient evidence to warrant that Lisa Davies and Dr. Morgan Lafayette are at the National Zoo right now and that they are in danger. A danger that, while I don't know how severe and insane sounding it might be, needs to be stopped. I believe the killers have targeted this woman for the items she received at her office in Virginia, and it is because of that package that they need to be protected!" Aidan said, his anger welling up and releasing as he sprung out of his chair and banged his fists onto the Chief's desk.

Stone just sat there, his eyes widening slightly, and Aidan noticed a little tick above one. The muscle seemed to be twitching, the only movement in the set expression that the man wore daily.

Aidan watched him shift in his chair, the after waiting a moment for Aidan to have said what he needed to, he rose from his seat as well, his hands splayed out on his big desk as he leaned forward, his weight held up by his arms and looked Aidan straight in the eye as he said behind grinding teeth, "Detective—

'It is because of the years you have served this County in my Division and your exemplary record that I don't have you arrested right now! I took your advice into consideration and even though Special Agent Poole disagreed, I sent two officers over to the Zoo right before you arrived, just to be on the safe side…"

Aidan couldn't believe Stone had listened to him. It gave him a whole new attitude towards the man he called his boss. He relaxed his aggressive posture a little and leaned back some from being face to face with the Chief as he let the man continue.

"…However Preston, if you ever speak to me like that again, I will have your badge and gun so fast, you'll think you were mugged by the Flash before you even realize they were gone!"

McGuire and Street, the two Montgomery County officers that Stone had sent to the National Zoo, walked through the crowds of adults and children running around in costume with bags of candy dangling from their hands, both annoyed that Chief Stone had sent them out to freeze their asses off on a security detail. It was bad enough that it was freezing, but now there was snow falling from the sky, flurries dusting across their shoulders as they made their way down Olmstead Walk towards the split where the Valley Trail supposedly started.

"This is ridiculous— freaking babysitting when we should be out looking for the serial killers who are probably at this minute racking up more of a body count!" McGuire complained, the well-built rookie officer swiping snow off his shoulders and pulling his cap further down on his head.

"Oh stop your whining and just deal with it. Besides, it beats having to run around on call, responding to who knows how many asinine situations people are calling us for because of this storm," Street responded. Tom Street, who almost had his twenty-five years in with the County and was looking at retirement in a few months, was certainly not as gung-ho as his partner. He wished McGuire, "the Kid", as he liked to think of him, would just relax. He would have plenty of years to worry about shootouts, robberies and all kinds of other shit without having to drag him into it.

Three more months, he muttered to himself, counting down the days until he would officially be done with this whole 'serving the public' routine. In fact, he was tired of the weather in Maryland as well.

He wasn't the type that needed to see the trees changing colors every fall, and then having a humid and miserable heat wave in the summers. He had already looked into buying a boat and possibly heading down to Florida with the Missus once he finished up with the police. After all, his kids were grown and starting families of their own, there wasn't anything to tie him down to this State any longer than he needed to be.

"All I'm saying is that there are obviously more important things going on tonight that we could be handling," McGuire groaned.

"Jesus Kid, give it a rest…" Street mumbled, sticking his hands into his pockets in an attempt to warm them. He really didn't need this shit right now. With his luck, he'd get pneumonia or something from being out in this weather. "…Besides, from what I heard through the grapevine— this woman we're supposed to find and keep an eye on might be involved in some way with the killings that have been going on around the County."

"What, really?" the younger officer asked, the look of intrigue that lit his blue eyes up like Christmas lights caused Street to just shake his head at his partner in mock disgust.

"Son, don't expect any excitement on this job. Besides, you'll have plenty of time in your career to make a name for yourself," the older Street mentioned as he watched the light in McGuire's eyes dim a little, then to not disappoint the man anymore, added, "now I know you'd put Dirty Harry to shame, but you don't got to go livin' life so quickly."

Did he really act like that when he was a rookie— all green-eared and ready to take on the world? Truth was, he couldn't remember, it had been so long ago when he had first went through the academy and joined the force, that nowadays he didn't even bother trying to remember the olden days.

Just then the radio clipped to his belt crackled to life.

"Patrol 2314 this is Base, Street you there, over?"

Unhooking the big, bulky unit, he pressed the button and responded. "Yeah Base, this is Street— go ahead."

He could tell that the voice on the other end belonged to Wilson, the sloth of the precinct. He was probably sitting there munching donuts, giving every guy with a badge a bad name.

"We were able to contact the National Zoo's Head of Security, and let them know you were over there. Once you locate the woman, get her over to the admin building. They said they'd be more than happy to keep an eye on her for the night." The voice on the other end chuckled.

"Roger that Base— we'll drop her off with Metro and let them babysit."

"Okay 2314, radio in when you're on your way back…Base out," Wilson said and the radio silenced with a beep, letting Street know the channel was clear.

He turned to McGuire who was breathing into his hands, trying to warm them some as they slowed down a bit, approaching the entrance to the Valley Trail, a small street sign announcing the intersecting path that led off Olmstead Walk.

"Well at least we won't freeze to death being out here for too long," Street said with a shrug.

"Yeah, well nobody can be as toasty as that slob Wilson, probably stuffing his face and sitting there sweating up a storm due to the heat being on back at HQ."

"Fucking Wilson."

They came to a stop right at the beginning of the path, letting a group of kids and their adult chaperone's rush past.

"Reminds me of when my two kids were little," Street said with a sigh. "Where does the time go?"

"Hey, not all of us are counting down the clock until retirement. Just remember that you were just beaming earlier when you realized that you were down to three months," McGuire reminded him.

"Yeah," Street said, "But still, memories of the good old days come creeping back now and then."

"Some of us don't have to worry about Halloween being that big of a deal."

"That's right, you don't have any kids do you?"

"Nope, proudly single. Bachelor for life— long as I can help it," McGuire said with a big smile, the wild ways of youth still running its course through their veins.

Suddenly Street froze, the strange look on his face obvious to the rookie. "What's the matter?" he asked.

The two of them looked just like the sketch that had gone around the office, he was sure of it. At least he was pretty sure. Tim Street had a way with faces, and that was something that hadn't faded with age.

"I think that's them," he said loudly, raising a finger and pointing it down the path.

McGuire followed Street's hand, trying to figure out what his partner was talking about.

"Them who?" he asked.

"Two of the guys from the picture…the suspects wanted in question with the murders."

"What—where?" McGuire stated, looking at the various people walking along the Valley Trail, many seemingly just regular people bringing their kids around for the candy and other free knickknacks that were being handed out at the various tables spread along the sidewalk. He couldn't see who Street was pointing out, but he had learned in the short time he had been partnered with the man, that his instincts were dead on.

Before he could say anything, he saw Street place his hand on the butt of his gun and dash down the trail.

"Wait, Street!" he called, but the man was already in pursuit.

"Hey, hey you— hold up a minute!" he was yelling, not paying attention as he left his partner in the dust.

Tim Street knew he was right about this. There was no question in his mind that these were two of the four possible killers, here and now. He was working on instinct now, skills he had honed over almost twenty-five years of law enforcement work. With one hand on his Glock and the other quickly bringing his radio to his lips, he pressed the button while keeping his eyes on the two individuals slowly making their way through the crowd.

As far as he could remember, they had been told that Lisa Davies, the woman they were supposed to be finding and escorting over to the Zoo's security force that was comprised of Metro Police, was close to the middle point of the trail, the third volunteer station set up from the intersection of it and Olmstead Walk. That meant the suspects were almost to the woman's location.

He had to warn her!

"2134 to Base, 2134 to Base— Wilson come in!" he yelled as he hustled down the paved sidewalk, his boots smacking against the asphalt as he weaved past a few small children and unknowing adults.

He knew there was no way that he could draw his weapon and open fire if the suspects were armed here out in the open. There were too many civilians around. Damn it! Street cursed silently, his mind running the different scenarios over in his head as fast as he could think them. His best bet would be to corner them during the next break in foot traffic, he just hoped he got there fast enough.

Please Lord Jesus, give me the strength I need, he prayed, feeling a little sweat on his brow that seemed to freeze in the cold air as he ran.

"Patrol 2134 this is Base— what's up?" Wilson finally asked, his voice a little muffled and Street knew he had been too busy eating to respond quickly.

"Goddamn it Wilson, put down the damn donut and call get dispatch to send backup!" he shouted into the radio, the anger rising in him as he hurried along. "I have two of the suspects wanted in the Moonlight Massacres here at the Valley Trail branch of the National Zoo— I repeat, send backup!"

At that moment he noticed the younger and more fit McGuire had caught up to him, his breath coming out much more controlled than the panting and huffing that was Street's own.

I need to work on that! Maybe start running everyday again, Street thought.

"Where?" McGuire asked as he ran alongside his partner, his stride making it look so easy that Street silently cussed at the young officer.

Not bothering to speak, afraid that it would interfere with the breath he was already trying to pull into his lungs, he just pointed again, this time the suspects were only twenty feet ahead and the Kid seemed to finally see them. The realization that struck in his eyes as they ran was enough to cement the certainty that Street had felt regarding the suspects identities. How many other pairs of guys were walking along together that looked like one of the four from those sketches? Street was willing to bet that the chances were slim to none.

"I see them!" McGuire called out, and before he knew it, the younger cop was pulling away from him, leaving him in his dust as he broke out in a full-on sprint towards their targets.

"No, Kid— wait up!" he called, but it was no use, the rookie officer was already almost upon them.

Dammit McGuire!

Of course, by the time they hit the small break in the crowd, the walkway clear for about thirty feet to the next station, the one where Lisa Davies was supposedly working, all the scenarios that Street had been running in his head were tossed out the window. Nothing he had presented himself with could prepare him for what he saw before his very eyes.

Holy shit!

Aidan was in his car, the Challenger tearing down the road as he ignored the speed limit, traveling twenty miles above the posted signage as he rushed down Connecticut Avenue, the downtown location of the National Zoo only ten more minutes away. His mind was awash in feelings of failure and the possibility that he was too late to do anything, and he kept reviewing the last few minutes he had been in Stone's office over and over in his head.

What the hell did I do? I'm probably looking at the end of my days as a Detective in Montgomery County!

The way the meeting he had with the Chief had gone went better than he had expected. He had thought his career was through when he had gotten the call to come in, but it turned out that other than seeing Stone reach his near-boiling point, and hearing him lose his temper for the first time that he could remember in all the years he had worked under the Chief of Detectives, Aidan was surprised to hear the man had actually heeded his warning and sent a patrol car over to keep an eye on Lisa Davies at the National Zoo. Still, Stone had been pissed.

Aidan had been a Detective for the Montgomery County Police Homicide Division for over ten years, and the only thing he could remember the controlled and unmovable, Chief Stone, ever seeming to be affected by in all that time was the rare occasion when they had lost an officer in the line of duty.

That was a hard time for everyone on the force when something that tragic occurred. However, even then his boss had never out right lost his temper like he had just moments before. Instead, he had always seemed to become more withdrawn into the job, pushing his Division to excel and continue to pull in outstanding rates for closing cases. The blowup he had witnessed, Aidan knew was a result of the stress that the political machine of the Washington Metropolitan area churned out when dealing with such high-profile cases like the Moonlight Massacres.

It was a big deal to all concerned, and with the joint task force taking the lead on the investigation, it wasn't as simple as just letting the FBI take the fall for any lack of progress made in ending the killings.

It was bad enough that while they were able to do nothing but wait for the next bodies to be discovered, still having no definitive suspects other than a general police sketch that a reporter had given them. The same reporter that was following the story of the murders in the newspapers that had the public eating up everything about the case that they could. The public was in a panic, and it fell onto Chief Stone to come up with results. The problem was, with new victims turning up daily, they were still no closer to discovering the identities of the men from the pictures, no matter how constant the TV stations and the daily newspapers were showing the sketches and asking the public to call in to the hotline.

The look on Stone's face when the phone on the desk began jangling off the hook and his boss picked it up, and then the ensuing conversation was one that was seared into Aidan's mind as he drove. With the speed he was going, even though it was probably not that safe due to the roads starting to get slick from the snow sticking to the street, the one-sided dialogue he had heard sitting in that office earlier had him press his foot down even harder onto the gas pedal, the car going even faster as he flew towards his destination.

"This is Stone," the Chief had said, leaning forward over his large desk, his gaze moving from Aidan then away as he listened to whoever was on the other end of the call.

Aidan sat patiently, watching the man, and even though he was unable to hear the conversation, he could gauge from Stone's expression that something was wrong.

Had they found the latest victim or victims of the killers? Or, was it something else entirely. That feeling of foreboding that Aidan had became stronger as the seconds ticked by.

So far, there had been no reported severely heinous crimes or murders where mutilation or a pentagram carved into the bodies had been discovered for the previous night.

Could they have hopefully stopped, or felt the pressure of the task force looking for them and gone into hiding? No, Aidan knew better than to believe in those possibilities. They were useless hopes. Stone continued asking questions as he sat there, his mind trying to piece together what the issue could be from his bosses reactions.

"What the hell are you talking about— have you regained contact with them?"

Suddenly Aidan realized this phone call had something to do with the patrol Stone had sent to the Zoo.

Dear God, had the killers already made their move? No, Nick would have called me! he told himself, but a sense of terror filled him as he pictured the many visitors walking the grounds of the park, children of all ages being in abundance at the Halloween event. A sick feeling went through his stomach and he knew something was not right, but instead of demanding what was happening, he sat anxiously listening to his bosses conversation.

"Alert the task force…what, okay good— let D.C. Metro in on it! I want that place locked down NOW! No one goes in until Agent Poole or myself authorizes it!" and with that Stone hung up the phone, the look on his face, that haunted expression in his eyes more than Aidan could take.

"What's wrong?" he asked, not wasting a moment.

Something is definitely wrong!

"We've lost contact with the two officers I sent out to the Zoo, and 911 Dispatch is fielding calls from all over that place that there's some kind of animal loose. Apparently, we have reports that we have officers down, and Metro PD is unable to secure the situation!" Stone said, pushing himself away from his desk and standing.

Some animal loose? How unlikely was it that it was just some escaped animal, Aidan thought. He knew that the confusion coming in from the Zoo was because nobody there knew what the hell they were dealing with— probably because this was going to be one for the history books!

Before Stone could object, Aidan was out of his chair and headed for the door.

"Where the hell do you think you're going?" he yelled.

Aidan just spun quickly at the door, looking Stone straight in the eyes. "I am going to go do something about this and put a stop to these senseless killings!" he responded and without waiting for another word from the Chief, he was gone from the office, leaving his boss just standing there speechless.

That had been no more than ten minutes ago, and Aidan knew from the intuition he he felt in his gut that he should never have left the Zoo. Even having called Nick to keep an eye on Lisa and Stone having sent a uniformed patrol to the Smithsonian's Zoological Park, something had gone wrong.

Please let me not be too late!

His grip tightened on his steering wheel, his hands turning white as the blood barely circulated through the strong hold he had on the leather. Relaxing one hand enough from the wheel, he pulled an emergency police light from his glove box and plugging the cord in with the car's lighter attachment, he cracked his window enough to slap the magnetic globe onto the roof of the Challenger and flipped it on. The light flashed with a bright, strobing blue glow as he slowed just enough as he came to a major crossroad and made sure the other vehicles had slowed or stopped to allow him to breeze through the intersection. Laying on the horn, he pulled through and pushed the accelerator down to the floor again with his foot.

At this rate, Aidan figured he would be at the Zoo in no more than five minutes. Keeping his eyes on the road as he weaved past a few other vehicles traveling down the four lane roadway, he pulled his phone from his pocket and began dialing Nick Haley's cell phone number. He just hoped the reporter picked up. If they had been harmed in any way, Aidan would never forgive himself.

The sensation of helplessness was strong and Aidan tried to push it from his thoughts. He wouldn't allow that to affect him as long as he could stay focused on the task at hand, but the feeling kept coming back to the surface.

Maybe his psychiatrist was right about the nightmares being about him not having control over the outcome of events in his life. Had Dr. Harper touched on the meaning of the dreams that Aidan was grappling with overcoming? Was it all about his being powerless to do what he knew he had to? It was a weakness that subjected and exposed him to a raw sensation he had never experienced before up until a year ago when his decision had cost a little girl her ability to walk for the rest of her life.

He was vulnerable and he could not live that mistake down no matter how hard he tried.

Is that my problem— I feel I failed that girl all those months ago, and now I have failed all the people who could be in danger at the Zoo?

The picture of little boys and girls dressed in costumes of their favorite characters, having fun and running about with their parents with bags full of candy, entered his mind's eye. He could see the young, innocent children being slaughtered like the other victims that had turned up this week. Then he saw the image of Nick Haley, Lisa Davies and Morgan Lafayette, people he had sworn to protect being butchered by some unknown evil, their bodies mutilated and the symbol of a pentagram carved into their flesh.

No, no, no! I won't let that happen!

Aidan knew he had to do something.

I just hope I'm not too late!

Chapter 45

Nick had been preoccupied in his thoughts when the screaming began. He and Lisa turned in the direction of the yelling and saw adults rushing with their children towards them from all directions as the crowd scattered about thirty yards away from their current position at the Halloween volunteer station. The screams of terror were then punctuated by the sound of gunshots, and as the crowd rushed past them, tears in children's eyes and looks of shock and expressions of grim horror on the adults, he saw what had caused all the chaos.

There was a uniformed police officer laying on the ground, his throat torn out from his lifeless body as blood flowed across the paved walkway of the Valley Trail, staining the snow-covered ground red. Standing above the cop's body was another man, one that Nick recognized all too well. He was the same short, muscled creep with the feral look in his eyes that he had seen entering The Dancing Bear just the other day, and even with snow falling and obscuring most of what was happening, he could still see the sleeveless shirt that exposed the pentagram tattooed arm that he had seen the night Bo and all those other people had died.

"Oh shit!" he muttered and then heard the gunshots from the second officer.

The police officer that appeared to be much older than the young man who was already dead, was crouched on one knee, his arms extended out in front of him and a Glock was trembling in his shaking hands. Nick looked to the target that the cop had opened fire on and saw a second face that looked familiar. He watched as bullets tore into the man, holes opening in his chest as blood oozed from the wounds, yet the shots didn't seem to be stopping the man, just slowing him down.

What the hell? He wondered as a strong gust of wind blew past him, sending the smell of cordite in the freezing air right past him and Lisa.

"We need to get out of here!" he yelled over the screams and gunshots, looking towards Lisa who was standing there frozen in place. Her terrified eyes widened even more as her mouth flung open and she pointed to the scene behind Nick. Turning his head quickly, he saw what had stopped Lisa dead in her tracks.

The man who had been shot grabbed hold of his bloody shirt, ripping it down the middle and flinging the dirty garment to the side as a deep roar echoed out of his throat. The police officer who was down on one knee was struggling to get up, seeming to want to add some distance between him and the suspects before him. The second man who had finished off the cop's partner reached down into the gaping ragged hole in the dead officer's neck and grabbing hold of the exposed spinal column, he tore the head clean off with no visible effort, holding the bloody stump in his hand, a delighted smile appearing on the man's evil face.

Lisa gasped from behind Nick and he stood glued to the spot as well as he watched the still living police officer turn slightly and begin emptying the rest of his clip into the second bad guy, the one holding his partner's dangling head in his tight grip. That's when Nick saw something that would haunt him for the rest of his life, the many things he had seen and written about in his long career as an investigative journalist still not able to prepare him for what he was witnessing.

The first suspect, the one that had at least six bullet holes in his naked chest let out another roar, this one turning into a wicked howl-like cry as his neck leaned back and he looked to the moonlit sky. His arms opened wide as if embracing some invisible force from the heavens, and Nick saw even from the distance he and Lisa were from the scene that the man was changing!

The man's dark eyes once an unrecognizable color from the thirty yards separating them from the killers seemed to almost glow with a effervescent and inhuman glow. It reminded Nick of the reflective shine a person saw on a cat or raccoon at night when a car's headlights shone across them. Or, possibly just like a wolves! Nick realized as the strangeness didn't end there. The killer's body was shifting around with odd, jerky movements, almost like a barely-controlled seizure racked his torso and limbs, causing him to grimace for a second or two, then his head shot up, his eyes glued to the police man who had shot him and was desperately trying to reload his gun as the two men closed the distance between them and their assailant. That's when Nick saw the other man's eyes begin to glow with that supernatural tint just like his comrade.

Then right before his eyes, Nick saw the two men, their bodies shifting, the bones snapping and rearranging themselves under the skin, stretching as they changed shape and they began sprouting wiry, dark hairs that began thickening along with the other terrifying transformations affecting them. Their faces, ones that Nick himself had helped plaster all over the place for the public to be on the lookout for, began to elongate, their heads stretching along with the rest of their appearance as they grew taller and thicker, the muscles growing and the pigmentation in their skin darkened. As they continued to change, the whole process happening so quickly, Nick felt Lisa grab his arm.

"We need to get out of here now!" she said, snapping him out of the trance he had been in.

Werewolves— freaking werewolves!

He turned towards her, tearing his eyes from the horrible amazement that was happening down the trail from him, and meeting Lisa's gaze he nodded in agreement. They had to move before the killers-turned-beast were no longer distracted by the still alive police officer, who Nick knew wouldn't be for much longer.

"You're right, go!" he yelled, grabbing her shoulders and pivoting her around. He then pushed her forwards and they took off, not bothering to look back no matter what they heard or how badly they wanted to look.

- -

As she checked the messages on her answering machine, Andrea found that Robert had called again today while she was at work. When was he going to get the hint and realize they didn't need him just showing up in their lives after all this time? It was bad enough that he acted like it was because he was really worried about the kids after Amy's friends from school had been murdered, but had heard from a friend that Robert Wilkes had actually just broken up with his latest female conquest, and while she had done the dumping, it looked like he was probably trying to get back into the picture because he was looking for some kind of sympathy from Andrea.

Fat chance in hell! She thought as she deleted the message and headed down the hallway towards her bedroom. Aidan Preston's face slowly replaced that of her ex husband as she neared her room, the memories of the passionate night they had just shared making her feel more alive than she was used to. He had been kind and caring the entire evening when they had gone out for dinner, and then afterward, the time they spent curled up on the couch in her living room, watching a movie and just holding each other was something she had almost forgotten could be missing between two people. It had been so long since a man had held her, the comfort and security she felt as he wrapped his corded, athletic arms around her, keeping her tight against his muscled chest. She recalled what it was like to hear his chest rising and falling slowly, her head pressed firmly against him as he breathed, their breaths seeming to fall in time with each other.

Yes, she was certainly falling for Aidan, a man she had known for a few years when they had once worked together, and they had even gone to bed together after the wonderful date they had. That intense, hot couple of hours spent exploring the other's body and bringing a final release of pent-up energy and feelings to a climax. Yet afterward, when they were just lying there, the sheets wrapped around their glistening forms, once again Aidan just holding her in his arms, she realized how much she still didn't know about the man. What was it about him that had changed in the last year? She knew there had been some form of attraction and flirting even when side by side in Homicide, but they had always kept it professional, never crossing any boundaries that could lead to the feelings they were experiencing now.

Maybe it was because they had been partners back then when certain cases brought them together, needing each other to play their part in the collaboration to solve a certain violent crime, that they never followed through with those emotions buried just under the surface. Or, it could be because Aidan had not been with the department for the last year, and seeing him so infrequently, those feelings never had a chance to resurface. Was that it? Then again, Andrea knew that the situation that had led to Aidan taking time off from work had been a brutal one. Some officers never could make it past such an event, and Andrea wasn't sure that Aidan had either.

There was something haunting him, a look that seemed to be hidden behind his striking gray eyes, one that only became visible when he was truly open with himself and others. It was that look that Andrea had glimpsed a part of the night before. After they had taken care of each other's more physical needs, Andrea remembered that they had both started to slip off into an exhausted dream-like state, but shortly into that period when the first light of dawn was only a few hours away, Aidan had struggled in his sleep with some nightmare.

She could envision how his body had tensed so rigidly, how his eyes moved around hectically behind closed lids and his teeth grinding together as he clenched his strong jaw. It was this movement that had woke her up, it having been so long since she had shared her bed with someone else, the uncomfortable actions Aidan experienced making her look to him in alarm.

Then he had shot up, pushing the covers off his body and gasping loudly. She had asked him what was wrong, but he just tried to push the incident to the side like it was no big deal. Maybe it was something he was used to happening nightly so that it wasn't an issue for him, but after the connection they had shared, Andrea was worried. After he had just brushed the nightmare aside, she watched him get up from the bed, sliding into jeans that hung low on his lean hips, his abdomen trim and lightly muscled, and then Aidan had gone into the bathroom to throw some water onto his face. She had the assumption that this was a nightly routine that he followed, and although she didn't want to tread anywhere he wasn't ready to go with her, she was still worried.

The image of his athletic form walking away from her to go into the small bathroom that was attached to her master bedroom stuck in her mind, a few scars were apparent on his otherwise unblemished skin, most old, but then of course there was the larger, most recent one that was on his upper chest, the one that Aidan had reached up to and touched unknowingly when he first woke up from the nightmare.

That was the one that was a constant reminder of the shooting that almost robbed him of his life and had the unfortunate effect of paralyzing a young girl for the rest of her life. As Aidan had stepped into the bathroom, she remembered him reaching into his pants pocket and pulling a prescription bottle out. He had downed a handful of the pills, what they were Andrea couldn't say, but she assumed they had been something for anti-anxiety.

It was common for people that had been in a stressful, almost life-threatening environment to be on some form of medication, and Aidan had been up front about being made to see a psychiatrist as part of his rehabilitation to get his job on the force back.

So why did she feel like there was something more behind Aidan Preston and his ruggedly handsome features than just the occasional anxiety and bad dreams? Andrea wasn't sure, but she figured they had the time to cover that part as they continued to explore where this relationship was taking them. In fact, Aidan was supposed the be coming over tonight, and she decided that she needed to go change into something a little less work-related than the slacks and button-up dress shirt she was wearing.

As she passed her son Jeremy's room, she decided to check on the fourteen year old and see how he was doing. She had grounded him for a week due to his absences from school, and even though she had told him he was not allowed to use the computer to surf the web, she hadn't gone through the effort of unplugging the machine and taking it out of his bedroom. Since she was going right by, Andrea figured she might as well see what he was up to.

"Jeremy?" she asked, knocking lightly on the closed bedroom door with her knuckles.

There was no response.

He couldn't be sleeping, she thought as she waited outside his door. Calling his name again and knocking a little louder, she waited a moment then grabbed the brass handle and tried to open the door. It didn't turn. Dammit, why is his door locked?

"Jeremy, why is your door locked?" she called out, louder this time.

After receiving no response she went into the kitchen and grabbed a thin pin that would slip into the round hole that each of the bedroom doors had in them. Walking back, the small pin in her hand, she crouched down in front of the door and slipped the metal key into the handle. Jiggling it around, she heard a pop sound as the lock disengaged and the handle turned. Opening the door, she called his name one last time and entered.

Jeremy wasn't there! Looking around the boy's room, Andrea was surprised that he wasn't inside. To secure the door, a person had to lock it from the inside, so he should have been there. But, he wasn't. Where the hell was he? Andrea glanced around the room, her eyes traveling across his messily made bed, and then stopping on the wall where he had all sorts of maps, computer printouts and newspaper articles stuck up with push pins.

What the hell is this?

Walking up to the far wall where the computer was set up on his desk where he did his homework and read, she scanned the pages and stories. They were all related to the Midnight Massacre killings. What has he been up to? she wondered, looking at the map of Maryland and seeing that he had marked all the places that a murder had taken place. It was like he was following the killings with some morbid fascination. Just like a fourteen year old boy, to find something so horrible entertaining. She'd have to have a talk with him, but of course that meant finding him. Where could he have gone?

Then she saw that his computer hadn't gone into sleep mode yet, the screen still glowing with life. Wherever he was, he hadn't left too long ago. She knew his computer was set to go into the screensaver after twenty minutes of not being used, so he had to have just left.

Pulling the rolling chair away from the desk, Andrea plopped down in the seat and grabbed hold of the computer mouse. Moving it to the bottom of the screen she saw that he had multiple pages that he had left open, having just minimized them instead of closing them out. She clicked through them, seeing they all had to do with lycanthropy and werewolves. Jeremy really was getting into this case. She knew from the newspaper and the television news stories that many people were going off that one reporter from The Informant, and following his Clinical Lycanthropy motive and reasoning behind the killings. It wasn't as if it was too crazy of an idea, even Aidan had told her that it was his psychiatrist who had thought up the connection that the news was running. Still, where had her son gone?

As she opened the last page, she saw that Jeremy had left his Facebook page on and the chat box at the bottom was still open. He had just been talking to his best friend Tommy. Reading through the conversation, Andrea grew angry as she discovered he had sneaked out to go hang out with Tommy and his brother Frank. Dammit, that boy was just asking for a beating! Andrea thought, knowing that while she would never lay a hand on one of her children, she could still ground him for life!

Looking at the clock on the bottom of the screen, she saw it was a little after 7 o'clock. She would have to call Aidan and tell him that she'd have to cancel their plans for him to come over again and have dinner at her place since Jeremy was now MIA. That boy was just causing all sorts of problems. She hoped that Aidan wouldn't read too much into her canceling their plans for the night, since it definitely had nothing to do with him being the reason she had to postpone their evening, but that her son was cruising for trouble.

Reaching into her work pants, she extracted her cell and called Aidan.

He picked up on the third ring and from the loud noise in the background, she knew he was driving, and from the sound of it, fast.

"Preston," he said, his strong masculine voice sending a chill of excitement through her.

"Hey, it's me— I just wanted to let you know that tonight's actually not a good night for you to come over. It looks like my son Jeremy took off with some friends for the Zoo," she said, hoping he didn't think she was blowing him off.

"Wait, the Zoo?" Aidan yelled, his shocked tone surprising her.

What could be wrong with the going to the Zoo on Halloween, they are open late due to the holiday? she pondered and replied, "Yeah, the National Zoo down in D.C., why?"

"Shit, is he already there?"

"I don't know, I just found out that he must have sneaked out his bedroom window and is gone. What's the problem?" Andrea asked, a sense of worry tearing at her stomach all of a sudden.

"There is a problem at the Zoo, Poole and Stone have gave orders to seal it off! Apparently, the killers were spotted there, and from what I've heard, they took out two officers sent to pick up a woman there and place her into protective custody!" Aidan said.

Andrea's stomach tightened and that feeling in her gut grew worse. Her only son was at the Zoo, and the possible suspects in the Moonlight Massacre killings were there as well?

Oh shit!

Jeremy was probably at this moment right in the middle of danger. Her surprise at Aidan's words turned shock to despair in the span of a breath. She reached out to steady herself on her son's desk, the blood feeling like it had flushed out of her system.

This can't be happening, she told herself. Yet, she knew it was. The dire situation, the extreme danger her son was in, it all hit her like a sledgehammer. Her knees were weak and she sat back down in the chair before she collapsed.

"Andrea are you there?" Aidan asked.

After a moment of silence, her mind reeling, she responded with a hushed whisper, "Yes." Her throat seemed to have gone dry and she couldn't speak.

"Listen to me— I'm almost there now— I won't let anything happen to your son!" Aidan stated, the sound of him laying onto his car horn ringing in her ears.

Oh my God, what is going on?

"Andrea— I promise you!"

Jeremy and Tommy followed Frank up to a closed fence that had been erected at the entrance to the Midnight Trail, to keep the Zoo's visitors from entering the area before the grand opening. It was obvious that the construction crews were still busily working to prepare the new walking path and animal enclosures in time, equipment and pieces of supplies were littered around the ground past the entrance. As Frank opened the latch on the gate, the three of them quickly hurried in, the beginning of the new Midnight Trail stretching out in front of them for as far as the eye could see.

Of course it was hard to see much of anything too far away with it being dark and the powerful lights jerry-rigged along the path were currently off since no one was working tonight in the closed-off space. Jeremy watched the flakes of snow which had been falling ever since they arrived begin to fall faster and in larger amounts. It seemed like this storm they had been hit with before winter was definitely winding up to be a biggie. The dark sky was full of thick clouds, yet the pale orb of the moon was still able to break through them and cast enough light down onto the ground to see where they were going.

At least the snow and moonlight adds to the creepy atmosphere of this place, Jeremy thought as he looked around him at the architecture and landscaping that had gone into the trails design and layout. It was certainly a neat place, and even though the construction wasn't finished, the hidden speakers throughout the trail were playing various sounds and noises from a soundtrack of animal calls that added to the intriguing depth of the dark trail.

There was almost an ominous, scary quality to the place as the screech of bats and the howl of wolves echoed out of the speakers. Jeremy was fascinated by the place, aided by the thought of how they were technically trespassing in the new area well before any of the general public would get to see it.

The howling of the wolves that was coming from the hidden equipment along the trail brought a chill to his spine as he listened to how realistic it sounded. They had even added what sounded like low screams that were mixed in. Jeremy was surprised by how intense they had made the audio soundtrack. Then as a louder howl sounded, Jeremy thought of the Moonlight Massacre killings that he had just been researching right before he had slipped out his bedroom window and met up with Tommy and Frank.

I wonder if a real werewolf would sound that ferocious as it howled on a night like tonight, Jeremy thought as he looked up at the round and full moon shining through the snow clouds.

Lycanthropes were definitely on his mind, the large, wolf-human hybrids from the ancient tales where the beasts stalked and killed, making themselves into bona-fide legends that scared peasants and even kings into believing the beasts were of the devil. Their wicked, blood-thirsty

"That's odd," Frank mentioned and both of the younger boys looked to him for an explanation.

"What's that?" Jeremy asked.

"I don't know— it's just weird that the Smithsonian would be playing an audio tape like this."

"Maybe it's just for Halloween," Tommy suggested.

Then the howling stopped and the speakers began with the bats screeching again. However, as the wolf vocalizations faded and the new track started, the screaming didn't.

"What the hell?" Frank muttered, looking around.

"What now?" Tommy asked.

"That screaming isn't coming from the tape!"

"What are you talking about?"

"Shhh, listen!" Frank said, quieting the other two as he put a finger to his lips.

Ahhwwoooooohhhhhhlll!

The howling commenced and all three of them looked at each other as they realized Frank was right. The screaming wasn't part of the Zoo's soundtrack that was pumping through the Midnight Trails hidden speakers and neither was the howling

What is happening— why are people screaming?

"Could it have something to do with Halloween? You know, maybe they've got something special going on for the event tonight," Tommy offered.

"No, that's not coming from speakers, there's none of the usual static feed that comes through when they play annoucements or anything. The Zoo's PA system and audio equipment is pretty old, and you can tell when a recording is playing," Frank informed them.

Shit, that means people are actually in trouble!

"So where's it coming from?" Tommy asked as he looked up and down the trail, the quiet dusting of snow being the only movement they could see as the winds blew flurries around on the ground and through the trees.

"Um, guys!" Jeremy said, and both Frank and Tommy turned quickly towards the youngest of their group.

Jeremy was pointing towards the entrance they had come through a little while before, and through the line of trees that was past the gate, they could see a little bit of the back end of the Bear enclosure and a partial piece of the Valley Trail. Frank and Tommy stepped up next to him as they all looked past the trees. They could see people, adults and children alike running for their lives.

Why? What is going on? Are we in danger? These were just some of the questions flooding Jeremy's mind as they began making their way out of the Midnight Trail to seek answers to their questions.

What the hell was going on and why were people screaming for their lives?

Jeremy had a bad feeling about this, and slowed a bit as they neared the gate.

He wished he was home right now— prayed that he hadn't slunk out his bedroom window to come here— wondered if he'd ever see his mom and sister ever again.

The screams continued and then there was another howl that sent a shiver coursing through his body, the cold winds with winter temperatures rocked right by them, adding to the uncomfortablness he felt as they slowly approached the fence that seperated them from the rest of the Zoo.

"Do you think we should go out there?" Tommy asked, the fear of the unknown terror that was going on no more than 150 yards away causing his voice to rattle with fear.

Jeremy looked back at the boy as he stood there shaking.

There was only one way to find out!

Jeremy headed for the gate.

Chapter 46

As the main front entrance came into view for Aidan, he could see it was a certifiable nightmare at the large gates that led into the Smithsonian National Zoological Park. There were people everywhere; visitors to the Zoo, some adults and children in costume, others just curious bystanders, Smithsonian security guards, D.C. Metro PD and Agent Poole's joint task force comprised of his FBI Agents, MCPD and the Rockville City PD. The entire entryway had been closed off, the gates closed from the outside as officers directed pedestrians out through a small side door near the large wrought iron fence with its massive bars. Two large, stone statues of lions, each bigger than a car were sitting there like immobile guards, one on each side of the entrance courtyard off of Connecticut Ave as if just watching the mayhem unravel.

There were emergency vehicles everywhere, encircling the street while others were parked on the grass and sidewalks that led into the Zoo. Ambulances, police cruisers, a SWAT team armored truck and the MCPD mobile command center were all there. Aidan estimated there had to be at least two dozen vehicles, all of them with lights flashing across the crowds of people and armed officers flooding the street and sidewalks.

The main cobblestone walkway that ran from the four-lane street and through the Zoo's gates was comprised of a beautifully sculptured botanical garden with a stone sign that was made up of massive, stone-carved letters that said 'ZOO'. Any other day it would have been a beautiful and impressive site as a person walked onto the grounds.

From what he could see, it looked like they had actually gotten the entrance secure and he had a feeling that Agent Poole had already put patrols and cars into place to guard the other exits and any other ways in and out of the urban park. It was as closed down as a massive location such as the National Zoo could be, however, that still left a lot of places that could be accessed by someone able to slip through the woods and climb the tall stone walls that made up the outer security fence for the whole compound.

Overall there was a massive amount of uniformed presence there, all set back a bit in the staging area. Aidan pulled his Challenger off onto a curb and hopped out. He didn't bother unhooking the flashing police bubble on the roof of his car, hoping it would keep them from trying to tow the vehicle as they attempted to clear the area of civilians.

This was an official police matter now and it was certainly being handled as seriously as possible from what Aidan he see. Aidan passed a group of officers standing off to the side and headed for the mobile command center where a tactical team was in the beginning phases of setting up their gear to be ready when called upon. This was obviously Special Agent Poole's show, and that meant he would be in the command center for the time being, so that's where Aidan headed straight towards.

The mobile command center was a large, thirty-one foot vehicle, built on a new, Freightliner MT-55 Chassis and equipped landline, cellular and satellite phone service, cellular and satellite internet/intranet systems and satellite television. It also has multiple 42 inch video monitors that have their own video selector switch, capable of selecting any video input available in the vehicle like On Air Television, Helicopter Video Downlinks, Satellite Television and more. The hybrid telephone system installed in the command center is capable of operating on landline inputs, Tellular, or satellite service, along with a complete .96cm Ku-band satellite system and four Panasonic CF31 Laptop Toughbook computers, each installed at their own workstations.

It was a vehicle that Montgomery County procured after the 2003 Sniper Shootings, when the department realized that the functionality and usefulness of having a command center that could be taken to any crime scene necessary. It also provided ample storage and workspace for crime scene management, evidence collection, communications workstations and mobile conference rooms that can accommodate a host of add-ons for area surveillance, communications and mission critical equipment.

With the mobile command center at his disposal, Poole could run the entire situation from the comfort of the inside of the vehicle, but having heard what the man was like, Aidan knew he would probably be out in the cold weather with every other officer until this was over. He just didn't seem to be the type to hide away inside the warmth of a command center if he could be out in the mix of things, barking orders and coordinating all the various aspects of this incident.

They had an unknown amount of possible hostages in danger and reports of two officers having been killed based off eyewitness interviews conducted on some of the visitors who had fled the scene and been rounded up at the staging area just forty yards from the Zoo entrance.

The suspects were considered armed and dangerous with multiple civilians still trapped inside the gates and in multiple parts of the urban park. There seemed to be strange reports of some kind of costumed killings where one of the suspects might be either dressed up for Halloween, or they had an actual animal loose in the Zoo. That or the killers were using the animal they had set to attack the other victims in their bloody killing spree, but there was no positive ID on what kind of creature it was. Reports were mixed and witnesses were hysterical.

Some seemed to even be claiming there was a werewolf loose as they were treated by paramedics and police officers for shock and minor injuries from people rushing about and knocking into each other.

As Aidan approached the command post, he saw Lieutenant Garza and a bald man wearing a sharp, tailored suit locked into a heated debate about the best way to get into the Zoo with tactical teams and suppress the threat. Garza seemed to be all about rushing in with guns blazing, while the FBI Agent that Aidan assumed was Jim Poole based on the description he had received from Mack the other day was stressing the importance of getting in quickly but quietly so that nobody else was hurt in the ensuing raid. There were still many civilians considered to be trapped inside, and with there seeming to be conflicting reports of what they were facing, Poole was playing it slightly close to the vest.

A short, gruff man with a buzzcut and deep set eyes that made his face seem hollow was standing there, his solid frame decked out in tactical gear and Aidan recognized him as Captain Jeffrey Palmer, the head of the SWAT team for Montgomery County. Apparently with this being tied to the killings that had first started in Maryland, the Washington D.C., Metro PD was letting Stone's boys have the lead while they provided any needed support to the joint task force. Palmer's team and the Police Commissioner for D.C.'s MPD, Phillip Andrews, were also present standing outside the mobile command center vehicle. The expression on Andrews face seemed to point to him not liking his subservient role in the situation, or him being out in the middle of this cold, snowy night when the command vehicle was right there. Palmer on the other hand could care less. He was one tough SOB, and Aidan had remembered working with him once or twice on hostage negotiations that had occurred in his time with the force.

"Aidan Preston, long time no see," Palmer muttered as Aidan walked up.

"Palmer," Aidan replied with a shake of the strong man's hand.

"What are you doing down here?"

"I need to get in there," Aidan said, nodding his head towards the large, closed gate.

"Not going to happen!" a voice boomed from behind them.

Aidan turned and came face to face with Special Agent Poole of the FBI. He was a few inches taller than Aidan, and even though he was older by at least fifteen years, the man looked like he was in excellent shape and could handle himself in any situation. He also had the tell-tale sign of sleep deprivation, a look that Aidan was all too familiar seeing on the people who had been working the Moonlight Massacre investigation.

"I'm Special Agent Jim Poole…" the bald, imposing man said quickly and then without offering his hand as a formality said, "…and you must be the Homicide Detective I've heard so much about."

"Well, that depends on what you've heard," Aidan stated.

"I assure you it is enough details to make me question why you are here, Mr. Preston," Poole stated, conveniently leaving off the title of Detective when he said Aidan's name.

"I'm here because there are people in there who are in danger, and I'm either going in there alone or with your team, but we need to act fast."

"I'm afraid that is out of the question," Poole informed him. "Nobody is going in or out until we know exactly what kind of situation we are dealing with. I will not be responsible for any more lives ending tonight while I'm in charge, so that especially means you."

At that moment a helicopter flew low overhead, the rotating blades stirring up the powdered snow on the ground and sending winds and flurries swirling around like mini tornadoes. The police helicopter was circling over the Zoo, using a spotlight to report back to the command center what they were seeing.

The radio crackled to life:

"Command this is AirHawk1847, repeat, this is AirHawk1847— we have a visual on possible survivors near an enclosure on the West side of the property. We are moving in for a closer look— Over," the pilot called out over the airwaves.

Poole turned to Palmer and nodded to the man, shielding his eyes as another powerful spotlight passed over them, illuminating the ground below as a second helicopter flew overhead. Captain Palmer reached up to the radio attachment hanging from his uniforms shoulder lapel and talked quickly into the black walkie. "Roger that 1847— let us know once you have done your full sweep of the grounds— we have visual that AirHawk 447 has arrived and will be handling the aerial video surveillance, over."

It was a few seconds before the helicopter responded, and Aidan could see that it was tilting to the side as it swept lower to the ground, making a quick rotating sweep and sending more snow flying up as the blades stirred up everything on the ground below the sleek, black chopper.

"Copy that Command— AirHawk 1847 out," the pilot said, and with that, all attention was focused on the task at hand.

Poole stood there sizing Aidan up, while the unofficial Detective said, "Look, I was just in this there earlier, I'm familiar with the layout and I know the location where the people that these killers are after are located. I need to get in there right away…just send a team in with me, and I can lead them to the area."

"Not going to happen," Poole said, shaking his head in denial of Aidan's plan. "The entrances and exits are sealed, and until our intelligence is updated and we have a grasp on the situation, nobody is going in through those gates."

Try and stop me, Aidan thought as he stood there attempting to convince the Agent of how serious the dilemma was.

Then suddenly there was a commotion at the gate. All eyes turned to see a group of people standing on the other side, yelling and screaming to be saved from the "monsters"! Aidan took this as his cue to go. He headed straight for the small access door that was guarded by two SWAT officers on the street side as emergency personnel and two others members of the tactical team rushed to the wrought iron fence and began aiding the people as they moved them through the gate and into the care of paramedics.

Aidan ran, and as if having sensed his plan, Poole suddenly shouted to the two SWAT officers guarding the gate, "Stop that man!"

However, before they could realize who the FBI Agent was talking about as the crowd of survivors poured out of the Zoo, Aidan was sprinting past, knocking into the man who attemped to step in front of him, and sending him falling back onto his butt as Aidan reached out and snagged the man's radio from his belt and continued running until he was through the gate and heading down Olmstead Walk towards the Dr. Morgan Lafayette's building that was ensconced by woods at the far end of the Valley Trail.

As he began to slow, taking a look behind him to make sure no one had followed him into the Zoo, Aidan came to a stop, attempting to catch his breath. His shoulder and chest were aching slightly from the collision with the SWAT team member, the old bullet wound seeming to spur to life from the action he had just put his body through. He grimaced slightly as he continued walking, rubbing his chest with one hand as he pulled his Glock out of his holster and cocked it, a .40 caliber bullet nestling into the chamber.

Aidan hoped he wouldn't need the gun as he attempted to save the people who were trapped in this massive maze of animal enclosures and wooded pathways, but he knew that was probably not going to happen. If he had the chance and ran into one of the "monsters", that the latest group of civilians had mentioned when they had made it to the main entrance and were escorted into the safety of police protection, he would use the gun to end this nightmare. Too many people had died so far, and Aidan wasn't going to let Lisa, Nick, Morgan, Jeremy or any other adult, teenager or child that was stuck inside the Zoo down.

This ends here and tonight!

Suddenly the radio he had clipped to his belt sputtered to life. "Dammit Preston, this is Chief Stone! What the hell do you think you are doing in there?" Stone demanded.

Obviously he had finally arrived at the command center, and Aidan had no doubts that it was probably Lieutenant Garza who had told the Chief about his recent actions to storm into a closed down crime scene and hostage situation. Oh well, this was a long time coming, he thought as Stone spoke again, his voice irate and pissed, "I have had it with the insubordination and interference in a police matter— You are under arrest!"

Aidan unhooked the radio and brought it to his lips. "Chief, you can go fuck yourself and this job, I have lives to save," and with that Aidan turned the radio off and replaced it on his belt. There was no telling when he might need it again, but he knew he didn't need the blaring equipment giving up his position as he walked quickly towards the Valley Trail, careful not to make too much noise and alert the killers to his presence just yet. He was relying on the element of surprise if this was going to work, and he still didn't know the extent of what he was dealing with. Monsters? Werewolves— would regular bullets even work on them? Aidan didn't know, but keeping a tight grip on his gun, he knew he was going to find out.

He was certainly going to find out!

Here goes nothing, he thought as he turned off Olmstead and onto the beginning of the Valley Trail.

It was now or never!

- -

Dr. Morgan Lafayette had at one point in his life, served in the army as a grunt. He had gone to and lived through Vietnam, taking an honorary discharge once he had ten years into the service, and following through with his schooling and interest of wildlife, becoming a permanent member of the Smithsonian National Zoological Park almost twenty years ago. Ever since then he had moved from Louisiana to work at the Washington D.C. location, he had dreamed of coming across some proof of the kind of crazy stories of the Loup Garou that he had grown up listening to as a child in New Orleans.

There was a strange, supernatural side to the city. One that thrived on ancient beliefs and a mixture of cultural reactions that formed the many religions that made up the Cajun Country. Things like Voodoo with both African and Haitian influences, Gris-gris, Sangria, Paganism Catholicism, Christianity and many other faiths were common in the melting pot of culture that was found in Louisiana.

The French-Creole mix that set the State of Louisiana apart from every other place in the United States, and created a timeless vision of the odd and mystical world that was found all along the bayous and forests of the deep South.

It was there that Lafayette had first grew to learn about the supernatural world that so many people just ignored around them. It was like a living, breathing thing and that was Morgan's first experience towards the beliefs that would lead him to believe the possibility of what he was encountering now. Werewolves were real— they had just remained hidden in the shadows of this world until now. Born and raised Catholic, he made the sign of the cross over his chest as he set to finishing the task he had begun over an hour ago.

All those years in the army seemed to lead up to this moment. Utilizing that training had kept him alive through Vietnam, and now he hoped it would do the same here. If not, he wasn't going to go down without a fight. He picked up the hot metal with a pair of tongs and pried open the hot mold over the utility sink he had in his lab. As he smacked the mold against the bottom of the tub, six shining objects jangled around the bottom of the basin, rolling around until they came to a stop. Picking up one of the metallic objects, Morgan held it in his hand, studying the item under the fluorescent lights that lined the ceiling above. Having used the old mold he had kept since his days in Vietnam, Morgan Lafayette had cast silver bullets.

The pure metal glimmered, catching the light of the lab and reflecting it against Morgan's glasses. They were perfect he noted as he studied them. Setting the M1911, semi-automatic pistol down on the counter, he collected the bullets from the sink and wiped them down with a rag. Polishing the rapidly cooling .45 caliber bullets, he began slipping them into the clip of the pistol, a gun that he had used more than once in the heat of war on that far distant battlefield amid the rice paddy fields, jungles and swamps of Vietnam. He only hoped that the stories had some truth to them and that pure silver would do the trick.

After searching through his lab for the large Catholic crucifix he had once had hanging from one wall of his office, years ago before his faith had started to waver, Morgan now considering himself an agnostic, had found the cross and melted it down to create the ammunition he needed for his automatic handgun.

Having completed the analysis of the samples, and performing the tests twice to validate his findings, Lafayette had discovered a possible reasoning for the werewolves existence. It seemed to be a virus that was responsible for the continuation of these creatures.

The transmission of the disease was spread through the bite, and Morgan was under no false beliefs that most people never survived the beasts attack. He just had to look at the recent rash of murders that had afflicted the Washington Metropolitan area to know the chance of survivors from a werewolf attack were rare. Yet, his mind still struggled with the scientific ramifications of these beasts actually having been real. He remembered the tales from childhood, and had never once assumed he would actually come face to face with the very real threat of a lycanthrope.

Finishing slipping the last bullet into the clip, the cartridge holding a full seven rounds of pure, silvery death in the magazine. The M1911 was a single-action, semi-automatic, magazine-fed, and recoil-operated handgun chambered for the .45 ACP cartridge. John M. Browning designed the firearm which was the standard-issue side arm for the United States armed forces from 1911 to 1985.

Lafayette knew that the M1911 was still carried by some U.S. Forces, even though it had its most varied use in World War I, World War II, the Korean War and of course, the Vietnam War. Morgan had kept his service piece after he had left the army, keeping very few things from that point of his life, but the handgun was one of those that he cherished and always kept near him. Even with war being far from his daily activities as a curator for the National Zoo, he still had the gun, a box of regular, full-jacketed ammunition and the old bullet molds locked in a safe in his office.

Lafayette was a firm believer in the Second Amendment and his 'right to bare arms', and nobody would keep him from that right, especially any snot-nosed academia who had never seen battle in their life, their only comfort coming in the form of a scientific textbook and working for the Smithsonian. While Morgan loved his job, he would always keep the gun for protection, locked away in his safe, in case he ever needed it again. And now, it looked like that time had come.

As he pushed the magazine into the base of the pistol, he pulled the slide back and let a bullet slip into the chamber. Lisa had warned him about the danger that she inadvertently had involved him in, and while he didn't know if the beasts would actually come looking for him or not, he would be ready. Silver bullets or not, the M1911 would hopefully stop anyone or anything dead in its tracks. Morgan knew from experience in Vietnam where the pistol semi-automatic had saved his life more than once.

Then when Dr. Morgan Lafayette had heard the screaming begin somewhere outside his building, most likely the Valley Trail since it was the closest walking path to his lab, Morgan had used a Bunsen Burner and other equipment he had in his laboratory and office, to melt down the cross and make the bullets. The crucifix had been a gift from his late mother, a woman ever strong in her Catholic beliefs that had given him the solid silver cross, an old family heirloom, when he had first joined the army and been deployed out of the country.

Setting the loaded gun down at his workspace, Morgan took the slide of blood that Lisa had brought him and slipped it under the microscope that sat in front of him. He adjusted the knobs, bringing the sample into focus and lifting his glasses onto his head, he peered through the eyepiece and studied the dark smear of crimson liquid.

Looking through the lens, the white and red blood cells became visible and focused in on the bodily fluid. As he jotted down his perceived findings, he realized that there was something about the blood that answered his question about the transmission of the werewolf curse. The disease was definitely a virus. That much he was sure of, but he wondered what kind. By figuring out how the virus enveloped the host cell membrane and initiated the infection process, he could hope to reverse engineer the blood and come up with an answer.

He decided that the best way would be to compare healthy blood to that of the virus, and then by allowing the infected sample access to a fresh, untainted source like his own. Morgan picked up a clean slide and pricking his finger with a pin, squeezed the thumb and let a drop of his blood fall onto the glass. Sticking a clear cover over his uninfected sample, Morgan was ready to see what would happen when the tainted, werewolf blood came into contact with his own. Getting the electron microscope he had sitting on a table ready, he took a small swab and mixed the two samples together. Then putting the cover back on, he placed the slide under the lens of the microscope and making the image crystal clear for his weak eyes, he magnified the sample so that he could examine the ultrastructure of the virus as it attacked his normal cells.

Watching the capsule-shaped healthy cells begin to be absorbed by the infected cells, the particles with their bullet-like shape were penetrated by the main, diseased blood and they began to change, translating by way of synthesizing the structural proteins and processing/producing a new assembly of genomic RNA strands from the intermediate strand, they began budding together, forming completely new virions.

As Morgan watched the rapid process, he realized that the incubation period was probably amped up due to the full moon tonight. He assumed that a normal gestation period for the virus, the time between the infectious bite and the appearance of symptoms would probably last for weeks to months. His experiments time frame was sped up due to the virus not being normally introduced from a bite into a muscle from the infecting creature, and instead, the blood being mixed directly by his actions since it would usually take time for the virus to work its way from the saliva of the attacking animal into the bloodstream.

In fact, Morgan realized, this virus was similar in many ways to rabies! The way it broke down and absorbed the host cells, transforming them into the new mix, had been so familiar to that disease that affected so many species in the wild, that being a zoologist, Morgan Lafayette knew he had seen something similar if not much slower than the results he had just reached.

Suddenly there was a commotion in the hallway outside his office, and not even thinking about it, he moved away from the electron microscope and picked up his pistol, training the M1911 on the doorway, ready for whatever may be coming in.

His finger was balanced lightly on the trigger of the weapon, his only needing to apply a little more pressure to the hair-fine pull and the semi-automatic would go off, hopefully taking out whatever was on the other side of his laboratory door. Then a familiar voice called out from the hallway, and Morgan removed his finger from the trigger and let the gun fall to his side.

"Hey, Dr. Lafayette— are you in there?" the Detective's voice called out.

It was fine; it was only Aidan Preston, back from police headquarters. Morgan relaxed and headed to unlock the door. He prayed that Aidan would have some news about what the hell was going on in this place. Ever since the screaming had seemed to come to an end about ten minutes before, everything had grown creepily silent. Turning the latch on the handle, he unlocked and opened the door to reveal the form of Aidan, his own weapon in his hand, and he seemed out of breath.

"Dear boy, what's de problem?" Lafayette asked, his Cajun accent clipping his words off at the end with a honey-like drawl that Aidan knew was so common down South and especially among those who had spent any number of years growing up in New Orleans.

Before Aidan responded he looked around the large lab space. "Ms. Davies and Nick aren't back yet?" he asked quickly, the look of worry evident in Aidan's eyes.

"No, I'm 'fraid not— what's goin' on out dere?"

"Lisa was right, the FBI and police have sealed off the Zoo's entrances and exits because the killers are here!" Aidan said, as he looked down and saw the gun in Morgan's grip.

"Dat explains the howlin' I heard, oh and let me show ya somethin'," the odd zoologist said, raising his arm up and holding the gun out for Aidan to take it.

Slipping his own handgun into its holster, Aidan took the old, model M1911 and studied it in his hands. It was a beautifully maintained weapon, one that Aidan had never had the pleasure of firing, but he wasn't sure what Lafayette was getting at. "I don't understand. What's so special about it?" he asked.

"Eject de magazine," Morgan responded with a mischievous smile.

As Aidan did, he saw the glint of light reflecting off the first bullet in the clip. Realization dawned on the Detective's face as he pulled the top round out and studied it in his hand. "Is this what I think it is?"

"Yeh, pure silva," the Cajun said, his smile growing wider.

Aidan shoved the bullet back into the magazine and studied the gun. It held seven rounds, six in the clip and one in the chamber. Morgan had already chambered a round, so the gun was at its fullest capacity.

"Amazing," Aidan muttered, looking towards the counter where the bullet mold was sitting and seeing that Lafayette had made as many bullets as he could, there being at least half a dozen more laying on the tabletop. "Do you think they'll work?"

In response, Morgan shook his head up and down, his smile unfading as he walked in that strange gait of his, ushering Aidan to follow him. They walked over to a large electron microscope that the zoologist had set up and motioned for Aidan to take a look. He gave Lafayette a quizzical look, then setting Morgan's pistol onto the table, he leaned forward and looked through the eyepiece. He could see the cells magnified to the point where they were highly visible, but he was a Detective not scientist, so he wasn't sure what exactly he was looking at. "What is it?" he asked.

"De virus that is active in de Loup Garou's blood. The werewolves as you call dem, transmit dis infection, dis disease onto those that dey bite. Look at how the host cells are bein' attacked."

Dr. Morgan Lafayette then broke into an explanation, trying to dull it down so that he wouldn't leave the police officer behind as he explained how the disease known as rabies worked. He told Aidan how, rabies was a viral disease that caused acute encephalitis, or inflammation of the brain in warm-blooded animals. It is transmitted by animals, most commonly by a bite from an infected creature. It is invariably fatal, if treatment is not administered right away, infecting the central nervous system, ultimately causing disease in the brain to form that effects the functionality of the organ and then death.

The early symptoms of rabies in people are similar to that of many other illnesses, including fever, headache, and general weakness or discomfort. As the disease progresses, more specific symptoms appear and may include insomnia, anxiety, confusion, slight or partial paralysis, excitation, hallucinations, agitation, hyper-salivation, difficulty swallowing, and hydrophobia. Death usually occurs within days of the onset of these symptoms.

The incubation period is usually a few months in humans, depending on the distance the virus must travel to reach the central nervous system, traveling to the brain by following the peripheral nerves. Once the virus reaches this system and the symptoms begin to show, the infected patient reaches the final stage, experiencing periods of mania and lethargy, eventually leading to coma and then death within a few days. It is because the salivary glands receive high concentrations of the virus that allows further transmission to other targets. Rabies kills around 55,000 people a year, mostly in Asia and Africa, and there are only six known cases of a person surviving symptomatic rabies after the illness began.

Any warm-blooded animal, including humans, may become infected with the rabies virus and develop symptoms. Three stages of rabies are recognized in dogs and other animals. The first stage is a one to three-day period characterized by behavioral changes and is known as the Prodromal Stage. The second stage is the Excitative Stage, which lasts three to four days. It is this stage that is often known as furious rabies for the tendency of the affected animal to be hyper-reactive to external stimuli and bite at anything near.

The third stage is the Paralytic Stage, and is caused by damage to motor neurons. Uncoordinated movements is seen owing to rear limb paralysis and drooling, and difficulty swallowing is caused by paralysis of facial and throat muscles. Death is usually caused by respiratory arrest.

It was this type of infectious characteristics that Dr. Morgan Lafayette believed caused the werewolf viral transmission to occur, possibly causing the line of creatures to continue surviving through the ages. While Morgan would have to do more research and could use better samples than the degraded ones from the leg that Lisa had brought him, he was pretty sure that this was why the silver would also work on killing the animals, just like the old folktales spoke of. It was the anti-bacterial properties of silver and its compounds that gave the metal germicidal effects that could kill many lower organisms.

Morgan then explained to Aidan that silver nitrate has antiseptic properties. A very dilute solution had been dropped into newborn babies' eyes at birth to prevent contraction of gonorrhea or chlamydia from the mother. Fused silver nitrate, molded into sticks, was traditionally called "lunar caustic". It was used as a cauterizing agent. Morgan then told him that Hippocrates, the father of modern medicine, wrote that silver had beneficial healing and anti-disease properties.

The Phoenicians used to store water, wine, and vinegar in silver bottles to prevent spoiling. Prior to antibiotics, colloidal silver was used widely in hospitals as a bactericide. In the early 1800s, doctors used silver sutures in surgical wounds with very successful results, and even in World War I, silver compounds were used successfully to prevent infection in World War I before antibiotics were discovered. By 1940, there were approximately four dozen different silver compounds on the market being used to treat every known infectious disease.

Silver and compounds containing silver, like colloidal silver can be absorbed into the circulatory system and become deposited in various body tissues leading to a condition called argyria which results in a blue-grayish pigmentation of the skin, eyes, and mucous membranes. Although this condition does not harm a person's health, it is disfiguring and usually permanent.

Argyria is rare and mild forms are sometimes mistaken for cyanosis. Silver Ions and silver compounds show a toxic effect on some bacteria, viruses, algae and fungi typical for heavy metals like lead or mercury, but without the high toxicity to humans that is normally associated with them. Its germicidal effects kills many microbial organisms in vitro. The exact process by which this is done is still not well understood, although several different theories exist.

Jesus, this could actually work! Aidan pondered.

"It's dese properties that I believe will cause the virus in the Loup Garou to have a serious adverse effect from de silver and could actually poison dem!" Lafayette declared.

"If you think they'll work then that's good enough for me," Aidan said, thinking of all the information the zoologist had just given him.

It did seem possible that there wouldn't be all these stories through the ages about killing the damn things, with silver bullets being the main source of weapon chosen for monster hunters, if the metal didn't work. But, there was only one way to find out.

"Take dis and find our friends," Morgan said, picking up the M1911 and placing it into Aidan's hand.

"I will search this place until I either find them, or send the beasts that could have caused this are sent back to hell!" Aidan said and with that he scooped the extra bullets up from the counter and stuffed them into his pockets.

Ready or not, here I come, he thought as Lafayette nodded to him and he headed for the door.

He was not going to let the people he knew die on his watch!

And with that, he was out of the lab, reminding the zoologist to lock the door behind him, just in case.

It's time to hunt some werewolves!

Chapter 47

Nick pulled Lisa by the hand, dragging her through the wooded area that ran up near the Asian Trail. They had been running for what seemed like ages, but really they knew it had only been a minute or two. As the beasts had descended on the last of the police officers over where they had just been minutes before, handing out candy to the various children and adults passing through their station, the fun, celebratory Halloween event, Boo at the Zoo, being a big hit with the crowds that had shown up despite the weather.

No, not beasts— werewolves! Nick had to remind himself. No matter how much he wanted to deny what he had witnessed, he had seen with his very eyes the two men he had witnessed entering the pub from the other night, turn into ravening monsters.

They had been at least a foot taller than an average human normally was after their transformation, and once finished morphing into their new guise, Nick had watched along with other bystanders and the still breathing police officer, as they set upon the man who was causing them pain.

The officer who had emptied his entire magazine of his service revolver into the men's chests, barely slowing them down as they attacked him, powerful jaws ripping into the screaming man's body as lethal teeth and claws ripped him apart piece by piece. It was something that Nick would never forget. Watching as the two werewolves, their powerful, dark fur-covered bodies lifted their bloody snouts from the innards of the corpse they were crouched over and let loose a duo of deafening howls that was met with another animalistic cry from somewhere further away in the Zoo.

Nick knew that it wasn't just a regular Gray Wolf meeting their eliciting vocalizations, since Lisa had told him that the wolves that the Zoo normally had exhibited at the urban park were still being kept temporarily at the SCBI facility's holding pens until the newly remodeled walking path and recently-constructed enclosures of the Midnight Trail were to be opened to the public. That grand opening was still weeks away, which meant that the howl that had responded to the two feral creatures only thirty yards away from them had come from another beast, a creature like the ones savagely tearing into the dead body of the police man. That's when Nick and Lisa had run for their lives, heading down the trail, and cutting up through a wooded area that ran behind the Grizzly Bear exhibit.

They hadn't bothered looking back, knowing all too well that the one beast's shinning eyes had met theirs and seen them take off. Nick had no illusion that these creatures weren't here for Lisa, but he would not let them get to her without a fight. Suddenly the story that had seemed so far-fetched when Aidan and Lisa had told him it just an hour earlier was pounding through his head.

These wolf-like creatures were here to tie up an apparent loose end that had come from one man, 3,000 miles away, that this man Suffux, had started by discovering an ancient bone yard on his multiple acres of property. His finding had probably cost him his life, and who knew how many other unfortunate victims across the country as this pack had traveled the distance, and once arriving in the Washington Metropolitan area, set loose and created a public nightmare or killings that plunged the surrounding Counties into a week-long terror.

If he survived this, Nick knew he was going to definitely have a story for the ages, one that would certainly win him that Pulitzer he had been chasing, but his thoughts right now were on survival. He had to get him and Lisa Davies, the beautiful wildlife biologist who had been unknowingly thrown into this situation, out of the Zoo alive. That was his goal, and by God, he would die trying if that's what it took to save the stunning woman who was right on his heels.

Snow continues to fall, pouring from the dark sky. The only light coming from the pale glow of the Hunter's Moon, lighting the forest as they stumble through, branches snagging their clothes and feeling like it could be a clawed hand reaching out from the darkness and catching hold of them. This is the thought churning through their minds as they run, their feet slipping on the slick, wet ground and causing them to slow as they make sure their footing is secure.

Where the hell are we going? Nick wondered, realizing he was leading their small group of two, and he had no idea where they were or where they were headed.

"Where to?" he finally called back to Lisa, her breath sounding just as ragged as his, except his lungs felt like they were going to explode from years of smoking. That's all he needed at this moment— to have his lungs burst as he falls to the ground, just lying there as the image of the slobbering jaws of the werewolves chasing them enters his brain.

No, must keep going— can't stop now!

"Up ahead..." Lisa yelled, "...there's a turn coming up...we'll be near the new construction area! It's closed off...with a fence!"

Nick saw where her idea was headed. Yes, they could hide out somewhere along the Midnight Trails newly built stone walkway that wound through a new stretch of Rock Creek Park, possibly steal away into one of the new animal habitats that were empty, or even lock themselves into one of the new buildings that had been erected off the main trail.

Yes, the Midnight Trail— that's where they needed to get to!

"Okay…how far?" he said, pulling a shallow breath into his body as the cold snowflakes whipped around them, stinging his face in the freezing air.

If I make it out of this, I'm giving up cigarettes for good!

"Not much further!" her soft voice, almost as ragged as his in this cold, being assaulted by harsh winds and another steep hill that tested their endurance as they headed towards their destination.

"Just a little more!"

That would have been music to his ears, hearing that as he felt like he was about to pass out from exertion, but then the sound of something large coming up through the woods behind them could be heard over the wind.

Branches snapped and footsteps crunched against the ground!

It was growing closer, and Nick knew that if he looked back, he would see the glowing red eyes of the wolves chasing them.

Who knew how close they were, but there was one thing Nick knew for certain…

The blood-thirsty beasts were gaining on them!

Aidan hurried out of the building and headed down the Valley Trail. He had seen the devastation he had passed when he first came down this way to find Lafayette. Folding tables were turned over, candy and other treats scattered all over the ground while bags and even empty children's strollers had been discarded as the owners of the items had obviously ran for safety. However, there were the two mutilated bodies, ones similar to the multiple victims that had first put Aidan onto this case, and the gruesomeness of what he saw was almost too much to bare.

His goals were ticking by in his mind as he passed the two dead police officers, their chests and throats were torn open and there was blood everywhere, staining the pristine snow a crimson red color. He had to find not only Nick and Lisa, but locate Jeremy Wilkes, Andrea's son and his friends somewhere on the massive grounds of the National Zoo, a place where the layout wasn't exactly small, and there were multiple places a person might be able to hide. Not to mention that there were homicidal killing machines running about that weren't exactly human. He certainly had his work cut out for him, that much he was sure of.

Brandishing the M1911 that Lafayette, that crazy, New Orleans native had given him and the pocket of rounds clinking together in his pocket, Aidan wondered for the millionth time if the bullets would even work. Sure, in all the horror movies he remembered seeing growing up, it was always silver that the hero or heroine used to thwart the hideous beasts of the night, but those were fictional movies and television shows, and as much as he hated to admit the absurdity of it all, this was real life! He just hoped the silver bullets would actually stop these beasts dead cold. He still hadn't seen one, but he was intimately aware of the devastation they could cause. Aidan had seen enough bloody corpses in the last week to last him a lifetime, and whatever he did, he did not want to be on the receiving end of those claws or teeth.

Hoping that Lafayette would heed his warning and keep himself locked in his office until this was all over, Aidan noticed a set of various tracks that led up away from the mess, the trail that the footprints in the snow made was going the complete opposite direction that it seemed most of the other patrons of the Zoo ran.

This had to be the way that Nick and Lisa had gone since they weren't in any of the groups of people on the other side of the gates where Agent Poole and the joint task force was set up, deciding how to get onto the Zoo's grounds without the killers taking any hostages. Little did they know what they were actually up against was something none of the highly-trained tactical units Poole had at his disposal had ever trained for. Werewolves, Aidan was pretty sure, wasn't textbook training that they went through at the academy.

Noticing a bloody track as he headed for the woods, Aidan saw that it wasn't a human track at all, but a large wolf-like print in the snow. Droplets of blood were mixed into the dirt in the middle of the print, and Aidan knew right away that the blood belonged to one of the officers who had lost their lives earlier that evening.

Dammit, more lives wasted because of these Goddamn beasts!

Aidan realized the tracks were following the same course as the prints he assumed were Nick and Lisa's. That meant they were being chased!

Hold on— I'm coming for you!

Running up the hill, he entered into the dark woods, the tall trees blocking out most of the light from the moon, but what little glow did get through was hardly enough for him to know that he wasn't walking into a trap. Taking the first few steps into the thick forest that was comprised of evergreens and large oaks, Aidan took his time as he glanced around into the darkness, trying to listen to see if he could hear rather than see anything ahead of him. As he controlled his breathing and let the night grow quiet around him, he could hear the various animals in the exhibits up ahead making a terrible raucous. Apparently the wild animals that called the National Zoo home, weren't liking the new arrivals either.

Aidan pushed aside his fears and ran up the hill, the snowy ground making his travel at time slick and dangerous, but nothing was as terrifying as the thought of what lay ahead. The darkness opened up as he entered a small patch of clearing. It seemed like a feeding area for the local white-tailed deer that called the Rock Creek Park home. In the effort of wildlife conservation, the Zoo seemed to have spared this section of woods from their ever-expanding urban park, and the moonlight filtered down onto the spot, allowing Aidan to see further ahead. He stopped cold.

Holy shit! he thought to himself, unable to utter the words for fear of being heard.

About fifty yards in front of him, he could see the backside of a large furry creature, it's wiry black hair and sleek, muscular body illuminated by the full moon. It seemed to be hesitant, the long ears on the top of its head seeming to be perked up and listening to the air for something. Aidan had no doubt that it was probably trying to pick up the sound of Nick and Lisa who obviously were still evading the beast since he hadn't come upon their bodies yet.

Keep running, he told them silently, hoping they made it past this evil Halloween night. As he stood there, trying to let his breathing calm and be as silent as possible, he lifted the semi-automatic in his hand and made sure a bullet was ready in the chamber. It was now or never! Taking another step forward, he heard the snap of a branch under his foot and wide-eyed he let out a small gasp and looked back up towards the creature. It was gone!

Aidan quickly spun around, making sure the beast hadn't gotten around him somehow. The last thing he needed was it to sneak up on him. He had no idea how easily and stealthily the animal could travel through the woods, but then he remembered the hunter that had been found a few days ago near the beginning of the Appalachian Mountains. It had been discovered that the man was an knowledgeable hunter and possible poacher who knew what he was doing out in the forest around dangerous animals. Probably more so than Aidan did. That sent a chill down his spine as he brushed a few flaked of snow away from his eyes, and scanned the trees all around him.

Where the hell had it gone?

Suddenly from no more than twenty yards away, the werewolf burst out from behind a strand of bushes a little off to Aidan's left and came rushing down the hill towards him. It traveled quickly, running on long, bipedal legs that were dark-skinned and ended in furry paws with sharp talon-like claws that glinted in the light trickling through the canopy above. Aidan had just enough time to react and raise the handgun in his hands, taking a defensive stance as he braced his right hand with his left and took aim.

The report of the gun firing echoed over the small hills and the clearing, sending a flock of birds that had found their home out of the storm, sheltered some hundred feet off, flapping their wings and scattering into the night air.

Meanwhile the werewolf that had been barreling down the hill towards him had closed the distance down to ten yards by the time Aidan was able to squeeze off the three rounds as fast as his finger would pull on the cold, metal trigger.

The beast stumbled slightly, the bullets having all met their mark directly into the center of the animal's muscled chest, the black fur that sprouted from the middle of its chest seeming to expand as the rounds punctured the creature's torso and it came crashing down to the ground. It's elongated maw with the row of long, razor sharp teeth hit the snow-covered dirt, and Aidan watched as blood spurted from its throat as the creature came to a halt, writhing on the ground as the sound of flesh sizzling came to Aidan's ears.

The silver was actually working! All three rounds had hit the creature and stuck into the chest, hopefully destroying vital organs enough to cause the creature to fall in surprise. Aidan wasn't sure if a werewolves' facial features could show surprise, but he thought he had seen it at that last moment when he opened fire on the creature before it was upon him. The sight of the gun hadn't slowed it in the least, and Aidan recalled the sight of the two police officers that had been murdered, and remembered the empty shell casings that were scattered about on the ground around the bloody victims. Obviously, the beast with whatever human recognition it still had operating under the wolf-like visage of the creature had thought he had a gun with regular bullets in it. It's assumption had been Aidan's saving grace.

Thank you Lafayette! he prayed, opening his eyes as he stared down at the creature that was still kicking about helplessly. It was the first, up close look he had had of the animal responsible for so many deaths in the area he called home. The place he had sworn to protect as an officer of the law. It didn't matter that he had been on administrative leave at the time that the killings had started, or that he was probably permanently removed from Homicide if not the force for his actions earlier and the way he had talked to Stone, but he had made a promise that his obsession with finding the serial killers who were responsible for the killings known as the Midnight Massacres would lead to him stopping the suspects responsible. And now, as he looked down at the creature at his feet, watching the eyes roll up into it's head as it's bloody jaws snapped one last time at him, he knew he was one step closer to ending this nightmare tonight!

Jesus, he thought, as he studied the creature, then realizing he knew nothing about the physiology of this beast, he raised the pistol once more and added a round right in between the wolves fiery, red eyes. The bullet entered just above the lupine snout, and he heard that sizzling noise again and then there was a terrible stench that smelled like burning flesh as a little smoke trickled out of the oozing hole.

Now, he needed to find this creature's friends before they found Nick and Lisa. He only hoped he wasn't too late as he took off up the hill, leaving the body just laying there smoking.

One down, three to go!

Nick and Lisa had made it to the tall fence that was blocking their entry into the area of the Midnight Trail. The linked barrier ran the entire length of the newly constructed exhibits, and they had already covered three minutes of half-running, half-jogging as they struggled to keep pushing each other not to stop as they looked for the gate that would allow them entry into the abandoned space. They had heard the gunshots that had sounded out through the Zoo, and they were afraid another soul had met his demise to the horrendous beasts.

The only good that had come from the shots had been that they gave Nick and Lisa some idea of the location that they had come from. It sounded like the action had come from a ways off, but then again, Lisa knew that the sound traveled strangely over the wide open spaces of the Zoo's grounds, sometimes noises seemed to come from a great distance and sometimes they sounded like they were right behind them.

Even the animal enclosures they had circled behind, the animals crying out as they seemed aware that their surroundings had been violated by some beastly hellions, had added a great ruckus of noises to the night's eerie atmosphere. It was like a chorus sounding out, among the many animals that called the place their home, the various primates climbed about screeching, elephants trumpeting with their trunks high in the air as they stirred about, lions and other great cats prowling around their cages, roaring from their own habitats. It was a strange cacophony of various alarms that Lisa had never heard before over the many years she had worked for the SCBI and through their affiliation with the Smithsonian, here at the National Zoo.

She was scared, no, it was more than that, but even though she was literally shaking in her boots, she tried to act strong for the man she was with. While the reporter had seemed interested in her from the moment they had met, even she had noticed the attraction being unanimous, she wasn't sure that there was anything between them to pursue. That didn't mean though, that she wanted him to see her acting like a terrified child.

No, she had more dignity than that, and even though she was worried that they wouldn't make it past this night, she would put on a strong front and push herself for as long as she could.

Everything was so screwed up! What had started out as a normal week for her, had led to her now being chased around the National Zoo in Washington D.C., by a pack of raving animals with one goal on their mind— to kill her and those she was with. She hoped that Morgan was alright, if he had met his end because of her, she would never be able to live with herself. After all, it was her fault that he was now involved in this madness. The poor man who had always been so kind to her over the years, and this was how she repaid him? By getting his life threatened by werewolves!

No, she had to make sure he was okay, but first, she had to make sure that her and Nick survived.

When they reached the gate that would lead them into the supposed safety of the Midnight Trail, she waited for Nick to take the lead, a position he had gladly taken like it was his manly duty, one that she didn't need to argue with as she kept her eyes open and scanned the ground they had just covered. So far it didn't look like they were still being followed, but she couldn't be positive. They had traveled a long ways through woods and over the various paths intersecting the Zoo's grounds, and the entire time they had been running along the fence line looking for the gate, she had kept expecting a hand to reach out and grab her, but none ever came. Now there didn't seem to be anything behind them, however as she looked and listened, waiting for Nick to get the gate open, she heard something upset the animals near the Primate House.

Great apes and monkeys began hooting and hollering from inside the building that was back about 200 yards from them. It was just beyond the bend in the fence and Lisa knew what it was that had set the primates off— the werewolves were coming. Nick seemed to have finally gotten the gate open and they quickly slipped inside. The reporter took a moment to slip a piece of wire into the locking mechanism on the gate and he twisted the piece of leftover construction debris that he had picked up from a pile of supplies through the bars. Grunting and putting his exhausted back into his actions, he finally got the wire to bend, causing the gate to be locked shut from their side.

"I hope that's enough," he said, grabbing the gate and testing the strength of the chainlink fence.

"It'll have to do," Lisa said, reaching out and placing a hand on his shoulder. Nick turned and looked at her, his long, brown hair covered in powdery snow, his cheeks and nose looking as red and cold as hers felt, and she added, "Are you ready?" Nick nodded his head, and taking one last look at the jerry-rigged gate, they turned and looked down the darkened Midnight Trail.

"Alright, let's go— we can try and make it to the new wolf enclosure, they built a new building down there that we might be able to barricade ourselves into until help arrives," Lisa stated.

"Okay," was all Nick said, and each of them taking a deep breath, they started running down the trail.

They kept running and seemed to have a sense of escape rolling through them until they heard a loud clattering noise behind them. Something had smashed into the fence and was working at tearing at the gate with a frenzy— that meant it was close, and that simple, temporary barrier that the construction company had put up was only going to slow them down. Nick looked at Lisa and she watched him more mouth the words than actually say them, "Run!".

The two of them took off, their lungs and legs burning again as they tried to put some distance between them and the pair of beasts that were after them. Lisa suddenly realized that with the creatures being part wolf, they probably had most of the characteristics that were common among the species. Heightened senses being something that they might be able to use to their advantage. If only they could make it to the new wolf enclosure in time. Her mind worked a mile a minute as they ran, the finally sound of metal being wrenched open drifting loudly from behind them. They had to keep going. The building that was to be the new Wolf House, dedicated to the Gray and Mexican Wolf conservation efforts to save the species, being their only possible safe haven now.

They had to get there!

The sound of one of the creatures howling echoed through the air, and they both her and Nick looked at each other, the fear in their eyes evident.

No, she told herself as their feet tore down the paved walk.

We are not dying here tonight!

Chapter 48

With the snow falling heavier, it was easier to follow the tracks on the ground. Aidan could make out two human prints, shoes that were the size of a man and woman's— it had to be Nick and Lisa. Then of course there were two other prints. Those were the same paws that he had been following for the last ten minutes. There were two of them, and as Aidan followed the trail, he wondered if he would be able to face two of the beasts at once. The last one, he figured, he had gotten lucky with, and he wasn't sure he would get the same chance with two of them still to come. Of course there was also one more left somewhere in the massive grounds, and so far he didn't think that Poole and his team had entered the park yet.

He had turned on the radio a few minutes ago, trying to see if he could get an update on the situation from outside the main gates, but so far there had been nothing but radio silence. That meant that Special Agent Poole was probably playing it safe and hadn't sent anyone into the Zoo before he had a clear idea of what was actually taking place.

Dammit Poole, get your men in here before anyone else dies tonight!

While he knew that regular bullets from the dead police officers service revolvers hadn't stopped the werewolves, Aidan could only hope that bigger firepower like that which the SWAT and other tactical teams were furnished with could possibly stop the lycanthropes in their tracks.

He knew that the massive task force was treating this as a possible hostage situation, but they couldn't be further from the truth. Yes, there were innocent civilians still trapped in the Zoo, but there was also an evil that Aidan couldn't allow to escape from this place. He had to end this tonight. No more murders would be on his conscious when he had the chance to do something.

Then of course, there was also Andrea's son to think about. Jeremy, her fourteen year old boy was somewhere in this place as well. He had to find him and get him to safety along with every other person that was still stuck in the downtown urban park.

First though, he had to find Nick and Lisa. They were somewhere close judging from the footprints. They had seemed to stop, the markings in the snow pointing towards them probably slowing at this point and deciding where to head next. That meant they were at least aware of the creatures following them. That mattered, and it explained why they had been running.

Aidan took a moment to let his heart rate decelerate, leaning over with his hands on his knees as he breathed in deeply. He wasn't used to all this exercise, and realized that he needed to get back in shape after all the months of doctor ordered bed-rest that he had been under. At least he had been more active over the last couple weeks, really working to get all the kinks and stiffness out of his joints that he had earned from the recovery period after he had been shot.

Now, he wished he had gotten back into his old routine of running daily as his breath rattled through his exasperated lungs. Yet, he had a mission to accomplish, and he wasn't about to give up. He picked up on the trail that he was following and started into a light jog, working his was faster and faster as he made his way along the construction zone that was marked by a tall fence that ran for as long as the eye could see, finally disappearing around a bend that a hill and trees blocked from his view.

His legs churning, the muscles threatening to cramp up on him, Aidan kept going as he heard another furious sounding howl erupt from up ahead. As the werewolf's howl subsided, he heard the sound of metal scraping across pavement, and knew he was almost upon them. He just had to keep going, not letting anything enter his mind and distract him from his goal.

Just a little further, he told himself as he ran, the loud noises of a gate being ripped open drifted towards him as he kept going, weapon in hand.

He took this time as he charged along the fence line to reach into his pocket and extract a handful of bullets. Popping the magazine out of the pistol, he stuffed the gun into his jacket pocket and began loading the clip. He had used up four rounds on the last wolf, so doing a quick calculation in his head as he topped the magazine off, he knew that he was down to about a dozen remaining from the original batch Dr. Lafayette had made. He would have to make sure that every shot counted, knowing full well that he couldn't make it back to Morgan's lab to get anymore silver bullets.

Have to play it safe— make sure every round lands on target!

Luckily, Aidan was a pretty good shot and felt confident that he wouldn't need anymore rounds than he had. Then again, he had learned the hard way not to assume anything when dealing with an unknown situation, and this was definitely one of those!

Pulling the M1911 out of his jacket, he slapped the magazine home and racked the slide, chambering a round in preparation of what was to come

Four rounds a piece for the remaining beasts.

It would have to be enough.

The Wolf House was a large, stone structure that sat directly off the trail and was located between the outdoor enclosures that would soon house the Gray and Mexican Wolves. It was an indoor exhibit, located on the Midnight Trail, a little ways past the bats and other 'nocturnal creatures' exhibits. It was comprised of an original looking, stone facade that fit with most of the other animal houses that were spread out through the Zoo's grounds. Once inside visitors would be immersed in new multimedia features and stations, colorful graphics and hands-on objects that would spotlight the fascinating world of the wolf. It would set the mood for discovery and wonder, while educating visitors about conservation issues.

The original goal was to create a building that looked like it's architecture dated back to the original construction of the buildings that were all throughout the historic urban park, while having inside, a thoroughly modern exhibit that would make the Wolf House as popular as the current Primate and Reptile Houses. There was even glass, viewing areas that allowed curious patrons an unobstructed view of the colorful, habitats of the two enclosures on either side of the building, and let people see into the woodsy landscape and rolling hills, waterfalls and vast open spaces that made up the wolf habitats. It was the only building close enough to their location that they could try to hide in.

Lisa and Nick reached the Wolf House just in time, but as they reached the thick glass doors with their reflective, window tint, they found the building was locked from the inside.

"Shit," Lisa muttered, desperation showing in her eyes.

"Is there another way in?" Nick asked, looking behind them for the creatures following them. So far the trail looked clear, but they both knew it wouldn't be for long.

The werewolves were fast, that much was sure, and they didn't seem to be tiring out as much as Lisa and Nick were from all the running they had been doing.

Nick slammed his shoulder into the door, the solid metal frame holding under his attack. Then looking at Lisa he said, "There's got to be another way in!"

"I don't know— there should be a side entrance, but I'm not too familiar with the building's layout. I've only been inside twice before after they finished construction on it," she admitted.

It looked like they were running out of time. Nick hit the door again with his shoulder, the locked access point still unmoving under his effort. Lisa smacked her hand against the metal, looking around frantically as she tried to remember if the Wolf House had a separate entrance for staff members.

"Wait, it's around the South side!" she declared and they took off, with Lisa in the lead and Nick right on her trail.

They could hear another loud howl from behind them, the ferocious cry seeming to be calling out for its other kin. Lisa knew that there were specific vocalizations that wolves used in their regular routine of daily life— the list included sending up a locating howl that would allow the other werewolves to know there location. It was calling to the other members of the pack and most likely calling them to it.

This was bad! Soon they would have more than the two creatures that were following them. The only saving factor that gave Lisa some hope was that as the creature cried out, there didn't seem to be a response from anywhere near them. She took that as a good sign as they made their way around the structure and found the staff entrance.

Quickly running for the door, Nick was the first to reach it this time and gave the handle a hard push. The door moved back slightly, but wouldn't open fully. It was like something was blocking the door from opening all the way.

"Help! Is anybody in there?" he yelled, hoping that the door being like this meant that there were others inside, but there was no response to his inquiry. "Come on, help me push, there's something on the other side!"

Lisa came up next to him and they shoved with all their might. After what seemed like a full minute of pushing, their shoulders hurting as they leaned their weight into the heavy, double doors, finally they heard a sound of something falling over on the other side and the door swung open. Looking at each other quickly, they realized this was their only hope. They rushed inside and as soon as they were into the safety of the building, Nick slammed the doors shut behind them and began stacking the heavy items that had been blocking the entrance back up. Someone had piled a bunch of crates and other leftover construction materials against the door as if they had barricaded the entrance, but who?

Nick worked fast, pushing crate after crate into place until he felt that the doors couldn't be opened from the outside. He looked from the pile he had created to Lisa, and gave her a smile, even though he was breathing hard through his mouth, his shoulders slumped in exhaustion, they had a moment where they just stared at the other, that mutual attraction seeming to take their minds off the fact that they were being hunted down and could possibly end up dead before the night was over.

With Lisa's help, Nick rolled two large steel drums over to the blockade and set them up at the back of the pile to add to the strength of the door. Hopefully nobody or nothing would be able to get through that door, but they still had to check the rest of the doors to make sure they could make them as sturdy as they had this entrance.

"We need to barricade the other areas," Lisa said, tearing her eyes from Nick, and looking around the inside of the building. It was a large space, with multiple learning centers erected that kids and adults alike would be able to learn different subjects on the Gray and Mexican Wolf conservation projects.

Nick looked towards the main door, and saw a chain had been looped through the handles and tied together.

What the hell? He pondered, wondering how the doors could have been locked and barricaded from the inside. Somebody had to be inside!

Just then Lisa let out a scream and Nick turned quickly on his heels, grabbing up the first thing he could find as a weapon, ready to throw himself at her attacker. Yet, instead of there being a large, wolf-like creature attempting to tear her to pieces, he watched as three young guys stepped out from behind one of the cubicle like learning stations where they had been hiding.

"Oh my God, Lisa, I thought I heard your voice!" the oldest of the three said, and Nick watched as Lisa ran to him and gave him a hug.

Who the hell are these people?

Then as if Lisa could read the question in Nick's mind, she gave him a smile and looked at the pipe he had picked up to defend her.

"It's okay Nick, this is Frank, my assistant at SCBI," she informed him.

That's where I'd seen him before, Nick realized. It was the day he and Aidan had gone and first met Lisa in her lab. A time that seemed like it had been years ago after everything they had been through in the last few days.

"What are you doing here?" Lisa asked, turning towards her intern and the two teenage boys with him.

"I was going to ask you the same thing, but after watching you rush through here and pile all that stuff up against the doors, I think we might be hiding here for the same reason," Frank informed them.

He then went about explaining how he had brought his younger brother Tommy and their friend Jeremy to the Zoo to check out the Midnight Trail before it was open to the public. They had only just gotten there when they had heard screams coming from somewhere in the main grounds. That's when they had seen the werewolves and rushed to this building to hide.

Frank then told them how Jeremy's mom was a cop and that he had been following the serial killings all around the Washington Metropolitan area and they had spent the time locked inside the building, discussing everything each of them had learned. Frank had told the two younger boys about the specimen they had been studying the other day, and they seemed to have pieced two and two together.

That's good, Nick thought, Means we don't have to waste time explaining what's going on to the new members of our growing party.

"Okay, we need to secure this building completely," Lisa said, "Those creatures are somewhere outside and they are looking for us. We need to keep quiet and make sure they can't get in here. Everyone understand what's at stake?"

All four of the others nodded.

Yes, they certainly had their work cut out for them if they were going to survive this.

"Good, let's get started."

- -

Morgan Lafayette had been working on trying to figure out another way to even the odds in their struggle against the supernatural beasts when he heard the main door of the building smashed off its hinges.

He had company!

"Oh Lord!" he muttered, scuttling over to one of his lab benches where he had been hard at work putting pieces he had found together to form a makeshift weapon. He had scavenged pieces from all over the lab, dismantling a few pieces of expensive equipment to begin work on something he could us to even the odds against these blood-thirsty creatures.

"Let's see how dey like dis!" Morgan mumbled, turning his attention to the sounds happening in the hall outside his lab. Fortunately he had heeded Aidan's advice and locked all the doors in the building that led to his work area, but from the sound of the main door coming off, he wondered if he really had a chance.

Lifting the heavy piece of equipment off the table where he had assembled it, he reached out and turned the handle on a large oxygen tank he had sitting on a Dolley next to him. Running from the tank was a tube that attached to the front end of his weapon, and another tube that ran from a separate source into the back end of the handle and device he now brandished in his arms. Combining one of the fire extinguishers that were stored in every lab for emergencies, various plumbing parts consisting of tubes and gaskets, 8 liters of petrol fuel that he kept around for some of the more interesting experiments he amused himself with, and a nozzle from one of the spare tanks he had dismantled, he had made a flamethrower. It was a quick and basic design, but it would do the job. He figured that with the 100 psi of pressure that the extinguishers could give out per load, it would give him a range of thirty feet.

Dey ain't gonna like dis too much! he thought as he scooted the cart with his reserve extinguishers and oxygen tank along behind him and headed for the door. If anything happened, he would be prepared!

Cradling the homemade flamethrower, he listened quietly for any more noise coming from the hall. As he stood there, he could hear a raspy, deep breathing coming from the otherwise silent hallway outside his lab. It was here in the building with him, he was positive. Twisting the knob that attached to the one tank, he lit the one tube's end and the highly concentrated gas pouring out ignites in a manageable flame. It was all set.

"Ready or not, here I come!" he shouted out, just as the door to his lab came flying inward, the metal bolts bending and snapping as a horrendously large creature appeared on the other side. Saliva dripped from the jaws, as burning, red eyes looked through the wreckage of the door frame until they located Morgan standing back in the middle of the room. With a snarl and snapping of its teeth, the creature ducked slightly under the top of the door post and stepped into the room, its clawed hands grabbing hold of the pieces of wood and steel that was in its way and flinging them to the side.

Morgan stood there, wide-eyed and frozen for a moment as he watched the creature enter from the darkened hallway and be revealed fully in the light of the flourescents hanging from the ceiling. It's amazing, he thought just as he grabbed the fire extinguishers handle and pulling the safety pin, he slammed his free hand down onto the nozzle and a jet of flame leapt through the air and covered the wolf's massive and deadly form.

"Raaaahhhrrrrr!" it cried out startled and in pain as it moved towards him, the powerful odor of burning hair and flesh stinging Morgan's eyes and nose as it kept moving forward with uneven steps.

"Die yah SOB!" his Cajun accent declared as he hit the nozzle again, holding the trigger down for the full ten seconds of pressure that was left in the tank.

Flames licked across it's body as it fell to the ground and rolled about, its cries of agony reaching his ears, and he almost felt sorry for the creature. It was a weird feeling to be killing something after all these years since he had retired from the army, but it was also something a person did not forget how to do. He was going to show this murderous beast that it had messed with the wrong zoologist!

As the werewolf rolled about the ground, clawed hands reaching out and smacking into lab equipment, knocking things all over the place as it's legs kicked against solid steel tables and sent other pieces of expensive Zoo property shattering on the ground. Morgan had hoped that it would only take one extinguisher's worth of pressure and content to end the beast's life, but as he watched the flames starting to die out, the creature rose up on its hind legs, acrid smoke pouring off its body as it attempted to roar in a mixture of anger and pain.

It's flesh was darker, almost charcoal-colored and most of the hair had burned off the animal's body, it's skin gone in some spots, and like a burn victim who just woke up and realized what had happened to him, the creature's eyes found Lafayette, and on wobbly legs it started towards him.

Oh shit! he realized as he quickly went about trying to hook up the second fire extinguisher to his flamethrower. The animal was almost upon him by the time he got the contraption ready to go again.

The smell was so much stronger now with the beast being only a few feet from him, and as he raised the nozzle and squeezed the trigger, sending another long burst of liquid fire out of the end of the weapon, the werewolf howled violently, it's body jerking back as the flames licked across him and he went for Morgan in one last lunge. Black fumes caused Lafayette to gag and cough as the obnoxious stench of burning hairs assailed him. However, as he continued shooting the last of the flamethrowers content onto the creature, he watch as a hairless arm, the fur having been melted off, came through the large flames roaring up in front of him and a clawed hand took a powerful swipe at his midsection.

He felt the sharp pain explode through him as he looked down in surprise at his stomach, a bloody gash opening up as his skin parted and he could see his intestines beginning to uncoil and fall across the ground.

"Ughh!" he groaned as he fell backwards, his eyes never leaving the flaming form that stumbled towards him and then dropped to the ground with one last cry of pain. Blood bubbled out of the crinkled, blistering flesh and steamed from the heat that was consuming the creature.

The fire continued to roil up through the lab, and as Morgan laid there, he knew he would not be walking out of this place tonight. He would die in the midst of this fiery inferno that had spread from the dying werewolf's smoldering corpse and was beginning to creep up the walls of the lab. Various tanks and equipment exploded as they were engulfed in flames, and Morgan took one last look at his stomach, his insides hanging out by his feet as his eyes began to close against the intense heat and smoke that was rising up around him.

He had done it though— he had killed the beast, sending it back to the fiery pits of hell from whence it came!

As he lay there, the flames crawling across the floor towards his dying self, he knew it would be a matter of seconds before they were upon him and reached the tanks that he had rigged up to use as his defense. Perhaps it wasn't his best idea, but it had worked! There was one less wolf, and that meant that Lisa and the others had a chance to survive. His sacrifice had given them that chance.

Closing his eyes as the fire began to make its way up his legs, the intense heat causing him to sweat profusely as he lay there, one arm on his wound and the other around the oxygen tank, he pulled the dolly with all the strength left in his dying body and let it roll into the center of the inferno.

Flames engulfed the tanks on the cart and suddenly he watched as he heard the metal hissing and then there was a large, deafening explosion and Dr. Morgan Lafayette knew no more. His pain ceased and he was gone in the powerful blast.

The lab continued to burn, smoke filling the space as the fire spread over every inch of the building. Support beams cracked and weakened due to the intense heat and the plaster walls began peeling as the structure began to crumble. It took no more than a few minutes before the entire building was lit, flames erupting from every office and room, the entire laboratory shaking as explosions erupted from all over the once whole work space.

Morgan Lafayette's remains would never be found as multiple, violent shock waves erupted from all over, shattering and blowing apart the last of the old, stone edifice.

The flames shot up into the night, brightening the dark sky as snow began falling down onto the burning remains of the structure, the wet flakes causing the inferno to subside as more and more snow covered the destroyed remnant of a lab. Dark smoke poured into the air, like a giant funeral pyre that was beginning to be extinguished.

The destruction and devastation that remained would forever remind future generations of what had happened at this spot, like an everlasting flame had been lit on Morgan's grave site.

He was gone, but he did not die in vain!

Andrea Wilkes arrived at the mobile command center that had been situated outside the main gates of the National Zoo earlier. Special Agent Poole was busy having officers rushing around, and he and three other people, one she recognized as the SWAT Commander, the others she could guess from their uniforms.

It appeared that the older man wearing a Metro PD coat with stripes identifying him as a Captain was spreading out a map of the Zoo's grounds on top of a police SUV's hood, while the others looked over his shoulder at the layout of the grounds where the situation was taking place.

Andrea had been to the Zoo multiple times as her kids grew up and she knew it was a lot of area to cover, especially with it now being dark and there being multiple threats inside the sealed off zone.

She had raced over to be here after she had spoken to Aidan on the phone and realized that her son Jeremy was inside the cordoned off zone. Thoughts filled her head as she walked through the crowd and approached the command area that Poole was operating from. Andrea also noticed that Chief Stone was stepping out of the mobile command vehicle and she caught his eye. Waving her over, she stepped past a group of tactical officers who were busy getting their gear and weapons ready to storm the grounds when ordered, and headed for her boss.

She was so worried about her son, but deep down she knew he was a tough kid and had shown her before that he could handle himself. He had gotten that toughness she knew from her, his father Robert being far from a brave and competent man when it came to dangerous or difficult instances. She just had to look at the end of their marriage to see that he was one to bail whenever something got too tough, but Jeremy was different and she was glad for that.

However, she still couldn't help being terrifyingly worried for the fourteen year old boy, especially after the talk she had with Aidan on the phone earlier when he told her what was going on. She could still remember the words he had said to keep her from worrying too much, promising to get inside and save Jeremy and the others he had come for.

At least he had made it in. That much she had learned from a few officers talking near her car when she had first arrived. They had been talking about some ex cop who had disobeyed a direct order from his superior and rushed into the Zoo, knocking his way past some of the tactical team who were guarding the gates.

"Please bring my son back to me Aidan," she whispered as she headed for the Chief's location. Everybody around looked like they were miserable out in the freezing winds and it didn't help that a storm had blown into the region and that snow was coming down hard, the full moon still holding the slight red-tint that gave it a bloody appearance. It was like a portent to the night that was to come. Blood would no doubt be shed, and from what Andrea had gathered from bits and pieces of conversations from groups of officers as she walked by that there had already been multiple kills confirmed and more to come if the entry teams didn't get in there soon.

"Detective Wilkes," Stone called, waving her into the mobile command center. As she walked up the aluminum folding steps that led into the large vehicle, she was met with a rush of warm air being pumped into the center from powerful heaters that were attached to the walls near the floor. These command centers were certainly not missing any comforts when it came to their use at any one of the brutal crime scenes they might need the mobility for.

As she stepped up onto the ladder, her hand grabbing the cold handrail as she moved inside, she caught Lieutenant Garza giving her a perturbed look, obviously upset that the Chief had invited her in, while he was stuck out in the elements. A smile crossed her face as she stepped into the vehicle, glad that Garza had seen her invitation, and seeing him pissed about it. Serves that prick right, she pondered, but pushing Sergio 'Pit Bull' Garza out of his mind, she followed Stone into the main communications section of the vehicle.

"We have a serious problem Andrea," Stone said, not wasting time with pleasantries which was just fine with her.

"What's the update on the situation?"

"Metro PD was able to pull the flats for the Zoo grounds, but the plans are slightly older and the latest additions they've completed are in City Records, but the idiots over there can't seem to locate the most current maps. That puts a cramp in the information we have gathered, and with the help of our air support, we have been able to figure out where the majority of everything going on is happening." Stone informed her, watching her intently as she took in everything going on in the mobile command vehicle.

Technicians were working at small tables, their counter space littered with a never ending supply of updates that were coming through secured phone lines and fax machines. Meanwhile two of the FBI Agents that had just arrived from Poole's team were busily speaking in hushed voices on private phone lines to people in authority, possibly trying to get the go ahead to storm the grounds of the National Zoo. With it being a National Landmark, Andrea knew that they had plenty of red tape to get around before they could be authorized to go in with guns blazing. She just hoped that Aidan was faring better than the task force seemed to be doing. At least he was inside, working on getting to the survivors, who, Andrea hoped Jeremy was a part of. She couldn't bare the thought of losing her only son.

It was bad enough that she had to leave Amy, her daughter in the care of Mrs. Neely, their next door neighbor tonight. It was bad enough that Amy had been going through a lot lately since the murder of her classmates, but when she had heard the tail end of her conversation with Aidan about Jeremy having run off to the Zoo, Amy had paled and Andrea was worried for the girl. Even though she was seventeen, she didn't want to leave her alone in their townhouse, so she had asked Mrs. Neely to keep an eyes on her until she got back. The elderly neighbor didn't mind and Andrea knew that Amy liked the older woman, even if she was insulted that her mom thought she needed a babysitter.

Oh well, she had enough to worry about right now, than to have her daughter's well-being concerning her and distracting her from what she needed to do.

Please let Jeremy be alright! Aidan, I know you'll keep him safe...

Suddenly there was a loud explosion that rocked the command vehicle and she could hear yelling and shouting from outside.

What the hell was that?

Without wasting any time, Andrea spun on her heels and pushed open the door that led outside the massive command center. Running down the folded-out steps, the wind chilling her to the bone as she wondered what that loud boom could have been. She had a bad feeling in her gut, that noise meant something wrong had happened, but what?

Chief Stone was out right behind her and as he landed on the slick ground beside her, he was about to yell for an explanation, when he realized all eyes were focused on a bright glow that was filtering through the trees from far off in the middle of the Zoo. The light was bright and colored the sky with orange and red flames, black smoke pouring up from the spot and twisting around into the night like a snake drifting up from the ground and into the air.

"What was that?" Agent Poole shouted to the tactical Commander who just shrugged.

"Wasn't any of my teams. My guys aren't carrying explosives for this situation. I'd say something exploded inside the park, but what it is, I couldn't say," Captain Palmer said quickly, turning his eyes back onto the flames that were leaping up from deep in the Zoo.

"I told you we should have already been in there!" Lieutenant Garza complained, his gruff, New York accent making his statement all the more demanding and annoying.

Apparently it had the same effect on Poole, who turned to Garza, his face turning red as he said, "Lieutenant, that is the last time you question how this situation is being handled. We still do not know the extent of what we are dealing with and I there is no number of casualties that will be considered acceptable due to improper planning when we go in! Is that clear?"

Garza's eyes dropped to the ground, his fedora shading his face from all the onlookers and the falling snow and he just nodded his head, adding a weak, "Yes Sir," after an momentary pause.

"Special Agent Poole!" a voice called out in the commotion and everyone turned to see Metro PD, Commissioner Phillip Andrews heading towards them with a rolled up set of blueprints waving about in his hand. "City Planning just found the new plans and rushed them over. Fortunate for us, their offices are only a few blocks down the street so as soon as they located the latest flats, they ran them over here."

"Excellent— let's see what we've got to work with," Agent Poole said with a smile finally breaking on his tense face. It seemed to Andrea that this was the first good news he had received all night.

"Oh and we were able to get confirmation from Airhawk 447, in regards to the explosion and the flames we are seeing. According to them, one of the buildings located a little ways off the Zoo's Valley Trail just blew sky high! On one of their last passes, they had noticed smoke and flames coming from the laboratory wing of the structure and by the second pass, it just took off and was engulfed in flames," Andrews said.

Agent Poole seemed to measure this information for a moment, raising his hand to interrupt the next person from speaking. He looked around and met everyone's eyes that were in attendance around him. Letting out a deep sigh, his breath visible in the crisp air, he breathed in once more and gave the order.

"I want three teams sweeping the Zoo in overlapping search patterns. We're not leaving a single stone unturned. I don't know how that building blew, but this thing has escalated for far too long. Captain Palmer— I want your teams locked and loaded, we are going in hot!" Poole commanded and the various officers began dispersing to ready for their roles as they prepared to storm the Zoo.

Andrea had heard enough. Her son was in there, along with multiple other people who were trapped with at last count, four deadly, serial killers. No, going in like Poole had planned could force the murderers into a shootout and hostages could be involved. That wasn't acceptable, not with Jeremy and Aidan somewhere possibly fighting for their lives.

"Sir.." Andrea called out, catching Poole's attention as he was about to head into the mobile command center and gear up. "I don't think this is such a good idea!"

For the first time, Special Agent Jim Poole seemed to really study her, taking a moment before responding. "Listen Detective, you may not agree with my decision, but you are a sworn officer of the law and as your commanding officer, you don't have to like my orders— you just have to follow them!"

Andrea felt her face flush, the cold snowflakes landing on her skin as they fell from the sky sending small jolts of cold across her burning features.

Aidan, keep Jeremy safe— I'm coming! she thought, and not bothering to dignify the FBI Agent with a response, she decided it would be best if she went Aidan's route and attempted to sneak in.

Of course, now it would probably be easier, and Stone didn't have to know. After all, everyone was running around preparing for the next phase of the situation, what was one missing woman in the grand scheme of things? She had to do it for those she loved. Her son was in there, and then of course there was Aidan. Her thoughts of Aidan and the way she made him feel when they were together caused her cheeks to flush again, but this time for an entirely different reason.

While it was too early to say if she loved the man or not, she knew that she needed him alive and around to get to the bottom of their relationship and see if it was possible.

Looking around at the mayhem and confusion going on all around the staging area, she decided now was the opportune moment.

It was time to find her loved ones!

Chapter 49

They had just finished moving two large tables in front of the main entrance that Frank had already bolted lock with a thick chain he had found in the renovated area that when finished would be the Wolf House's main exhibition floor, when something hit the doors with the strength of a truck.

"Holy crap!" Frank cried out as they all jumped back from the entryway.

Tommy had tripped over a bucket of screws that was laying out in the middle of the floor and he fell with a cry, the container spilling over and sending the contents scattering across the ground.

Nick turned and grabbed Lisa, pulling her back as the frame of the entrance shook again from another powerful blow that would eventually rip the double doors from there foundation. So far the tables and chain were holding, but there was no guarantee that it would last. As another violent blast shook through the front of the building, they realized a second attack was occurring at the other entrance, the ones they had piled as much stuff in front of as they could.

"Guys— there hitting both doors!" Jeremy yelled as the doorways continued to be rocked by powerful hits from the other side.

The werewolves were desperate to get in and finish this game of cat and mouse!

"We have to do something," Nick cried out, but as he looked around them, the mess of the renovations leaving all sorts of tools and supplies piled up along the edges of the floor, he saw that there wasn't much in the way of weapons that they could use.

"There's nowhere to really hide in here, we already checked," Frank mentioned as their group all huddled together in the furthest corner of the room as the onslaught on the entryways continued.

"There's got to be something we can do," Nick said, angry that he was unable to come up with a plan.

As they stood there arguing, Lisa began looking around at the half-built stations and the array of electronics and various equipment that had been moved into the Wolf House already in preparation for the final weeks before the opening. There has to be something we can use, she thought as she went over everything she had been thinking of earlier in regards to wolves and a possible weakness they could use to their advantage. She just wished she knew more about the physiology of the creatures as opposed to their relation to regular wolves.

Picking through some of the electronics that had yet to be installed, she found a pair of portable speakers that were similar to the ones that her and Frank had been using for her vocalizations experiments back at SCBI. Maybe some of this stuff could work to aid them in coming up with something to assist them. The only problem was she wasn't sure of what she could do with it all just yet. Think Lisa, think! she demanded of herself, her eyes scanning the array of bits and pieces that were piled up. If these creatures had the same basic senses, maybe, just maybe she could use something here to their advantage.

"What are you thinking?" a voice called out, and Lisa turned to see Nick standing there, a worried look on his face as the pounding continued to echo through the small building.

"I don't know," she admitted. "But, there's got to be something that we can do, maybe with some of this," she gestured to the mess of equipment.

The look on Nick's face seemed to show he wasn't so sure of her plan, but she wouldn't let that deter her. She was the wolf expert, if anyone could find a flaw in these beasts plans, it would be her!

Suddenly Frank came up to them and noticed what Lisa was doing. "Hey aren't those the same style of outdoor speakers we use back in Virginia?"

"Yeah they're similar. I was just trying to figure out if we had all the components here to make them work. Do you think you could take a look?"

"No problem," Frank said and got to work scavenging through the equipment, pulling various pieces out and setting them onto the floor next to him.

"You're going to have to explain to me what speakers are going to do to help us in this situation," Nick admitted, and Lisa just smiled at the handsome reporter who had been there every step of the way with her, ready to give his life to protect her. Maybe there was something more than just a physical attraction between them. God, she hoped they survived tonight to find out! Then, pushing the thought from her head, she focused on Nick's last question.

"Wolves have heightened senses compared to you or I. Their sense of smell and hearing are especially refined, their power of smell being the most acute sense the wolf fas next to their hearing. We believe that the range of a wolf's hearing is upwards of 80 kHz, where as humans only reached 20 kHz. It is stated that a wolf can hear up to 6 miles away in forest and 10 miles in open areas, including the high-pitched sounds that even a human can't hear, in the range where bats and porpoises produce sound. Even when it sleeps, a wolf's ears stand straight up so it can catch sounds made by other animals at all times.

'This helps the wolf catch prey, and lets it know when danger is near. In other words their ears are like directional satellite dishes, able to pick up something as simple as a field mouse moving under a bank of snow or a larger animal that is burrowed in their den under the ground.

'Back at SCBI, we were doing experiments with vocalizations, altering the frequencies that the speakers were able to output to reach the ranges that us, as humans cannot hear. They are ultra-sonic to us, but to dogs and wolves, they can hear them since their so in tune with those higher levels. If we can get these speakers powered up and producing a high enough frequency, we might be able to effect their hearing and equilibrium. It would be almost like the non-lethal, sonic guns they are using on tankers and other large ships to send loud noises that deafen a small craft of pirates temporarily without actually causing them permanent harm when they try to raid a ship," Lisa explained.

"And you think you could do that with this equipment here?"

"I think so, yes."

"Well then, what do you need me to do?" Nick asked quickly, just as the main entrance doors shook violently again, this time the frame cracking loudly.

They were running out of time.

"We have to hurry!" Nick states and turned to Frank.

"Okay, take these speakers here and run them down towards the entrances. We need to keep them wired to give them as much juice as we can."

As Nick took one and the boy, Jeremy, grabbed the other, they headed towards the doors, each carrying one of the large units, while Frank was busy hooking wires to the power box and running them into the exposed back of a computer that he had opened up. Lisa figured that the Smithsonian wouldn't mind if they used the expensive multimedia computers for parts, especially with everything else that was going on at the Zoo.

"So how are we going to get these working?" Lisa asked.

"Well, the problem with these high-end speakers is that they are usually used in sound-stage performances and concerts. They don't connect directly to a sound receiver, but use power amps, which are then hooked into an audio mixer. We don't have an audio mixer, but we have the amps here, so I'm going to see if I can use one of these computers and make a basic mixer out of it. In theory, it should work," Frank said.

The look on Nick's face as he was walking back from setting up the large speaker was one of worry. Lisa knew that he wasn't so sure this was going to work, especially with Frank's exact words being, "it should work". It was definitely not the most comforting thought to know they were relying on this one idea to save them, and it wasn't even a foolproof one. *Damn it— we need a backup plan!*

Jeremy watched Tommy's brother Frank working away at trying to strip the various motherboards and wires from two of the computers, trying his best to create a system that would operate the speakers for their needed purpose. As he looked on, he saw Frank plugging a quarter-inch cable into the 'In' port on the power amp. He then connected a second cable into the 'Out' port. He then grabbed the other ends and looked to him. Jeremy knew what to do and nodded.

Grabbing the cords from Frank, he took off and ran to each of the speakers, plugging the cables into the corresponding ports on the professional speakers. It was similar to hooking up the small computer speakers he was used to using at home, so he knew how to feed the cables into the correct slots. However, as he finished, he looked back over to Frank and didn't envy the older boys job. The guy was smart, but he was also rushing to build an audio mixing board that he could control through the last intact computer and monitor.

In the meanwhile, the reporter Nick Haley, who he was surprised was this in depth with the story he had been writing and that Jeremy had been following, was working on pushing more items against the growing pile of stuff barricading the doors, the same entryways that were slowly being ripped from their hinges. The reporter for The Informant— who would have thought. It seemed to be a small world, and one that could shortly end if they didn't finish this work now.

Shit, he hadn't even gotten a chance to kiss a girl yet! Damn, this sucks, he thought as he looked around the room and realized Tommy wasn't anywhere to be seen.

"Um, guys...where'd Tommy go?" Jeremy asked loud enough to stop everyone else in their tracks.

Frank's head jerked up, his eyes scanning the room quickly for his younger brother.

Where had the boy gone? He was just there, but Jeremy couldn't remember the actual moment he had last seen his fifteen year old, best friend.

As Frank stopped his work on the speaker system, having bypassed the need for the them to run wireless with their built-in receiver and powering them straight from the amp, he stood from the pile of electronics he had scattered around him and began looking around for Tommy.

No, we don't have time for Frank to be stopping! he thought as he took in all the main exhibition floor that they were in, listening to the noise of the metal doors being worked on savagely by a force that would put just as much effort into disemboweling them!

"When is the last time anyone remembers seeing him?" the pretty woman, Lisa asked.

Jeremy just stood there clueless. It wasn't that big of a place, so where was Tommy?

Finally Nick answered. "Okay, he was here only a moment ago, he couldn't have gone too far..."

"Tommy? Tommy— where are you?" Frank yelled out, no longer seeming to care who heard him.

Up until that point, they had all been trying to keep their voices down although Jeremy wasn't sure exactly why. It wasn't as if the werewolves on the outside didn't know they were there.

"This is insane!" Lisa said and began heading for the small hallway that led to a area that once the building was open, would be accessible to staff only.

Jeremy rushed up from behind and found himself following her down the corridor, checking each office and room that was there. The missing boy didn't appear to be in any of them. As they reached the last one, Lisa was just about to call his name again when Tommy stepped out of the little supply room and startled them. He looked wide-eyed and scared, but in his hands he held a small rifle and a small zippered case containing tranquilizer darts.

Holy shit, where did he find a gun!

"Oh my God, you scared us!" Lisa was saying, but Jeremy's eyes were glued to the rifle.

Suddenly there was movement from right behind them, and they heard Frank and Nick coming, Frank saying in an terrified tone, "He's not down in the other side of this place— we just checked, I don't..." then he saw his younger brother and the worried tone disappeared, "...oh thank God!— where the hell have you been?"

Tommy said nothing but just raised the rifle up in both hands to display his find.

"Yes, now that's what I'm talking about!" Nick cried out, walking over to the boy and clasping him on the shoulder. "Good job kid," he added, taking the case from him and unzipping it.

There were four tranquilizer darts inside.

"Of course, we're at the Zoo, they must have these at all the animal enclosures in case of emergencies, right?" Nick asked, directing his gaze towards Frank and Lisa.

They both stood there, still shocked at the recent turn of events, and then Lisa nodded.

"Yes, ever since that tiger escaped in California a few years back when that young man was mauled to death, Zoo policy was to have tranquilizer guns accessible to the staff in all the exhibits where animals are considered to possess a dangerous side to the the public if they got out. I think that's why the creatures outside have been concentrating on the doors and haven't tried breaking in through the glass windows that look out onto the two empty habitats."

"Wait I don't see the correlation," Nick interjected.

"The windows that are a part of every animal House, and look in on the various enclosures are made up of reinforced glass to keep a visitor to the Zoo from breaking the glass and letting an animal out. There as hard as steel, so the wolves outside would have an easier time trying to get through the stone walls of the Wolf House than coming in through that glass," Frank added.

"Well at least these will help if they do get in," Nick said, hefting the container of darts in his hand. "But I think we should probably get back to working on that radio, or whatever you want to call it."

"Right, I'm on it!" Frank said, his worries for his brother's safety now subsiding, he rushed back to the speakers and wiring he needed to complete.

In the meantime, Jeremy and Nick checked out rest of the rooms along the hall to see if there was anything else that they could make use of, while Tommy and Lisa headed back with Frank to check on the barricades and make sure they were holding.

"So you're the reporter right?" Jeremy asked once they were alone in the room that Tommy had found the rifle in.

"I prefer investigative journalist, but "reporter" works just as well usually," Nick admitted with a shrug.

"I thought so— you know I had e-mailed you earlier about the Midnight Massacres. I've been following everything you'd written over the last week"

"Oh yeah? Wait a minute…" Nick seemed to be putting Jeremy's name with the new information together, "…you sent me that link to the paranormal guy's website right? What was that program called again?"

"Bump in the Night with Lincoln Douglas," Jeremy added sheepishly.

"Well, I've got to admit Jeremy, but I thought you were just pulling my leg with all the werewolf stuff in your e-mail, but it looks like I was wrong."

"Hey, I didn't think this could be real at first either, but I guess I got my curious side from my mom, she's a Detective."

"Werewolves, who would have thought, you know?"

"Yeah, I definitely didn't start the week believing in them."

"I know what you mean."

Nick watched as Frank finished rigging up his makeshift audio mixer to the computer console that was looped to the speakers. He was able to log into the Zoo's internet Wi-fi access and download the audio drivers and other programs he needed to make the contraption work. Everyone had their fingers crossed as he began installing the software.

At that moment, the main entrance's double doors bent inward slightly and a massive muzzle with flecks of foam and saliva dripping from the open jaws appeared in the small hole. Luckily the chain was still holding the majority of the doors closed. The werewolf had actually punched through the steel at the top, buying them a little more time as its furry, claw-tipped arm replaced its face and began reaching for the chain, attempting to rip it off.

"Give me the gun!" Nick yelled to Lisa who just ignored him and headed straight for the creature that was attempting to get inside. So far the other entrance was holding, but it probably wouldn't for much longer if the other wolf's progress was any indication. "What do you think you're doing?"

"I'm a wildlife biologist and zoologist— have you ever fired a tranquilizer gun before?" Lisa called out as she slipped a dart into the chamber and slid he bolt into place.

"Well no…" Nick admitted, realizing that his macho show of masculine protection towards Lisa was at this moment unneeded. The woman was strong, and appeared to be used to fending for herself. But, that still didn't keep him from feeling like he had to protect her. It was just a part of who he was, and he felt responsible for the well-being of everyone trapped inside the Wolf House with him.

By the time she had the rifle ready and was within a close enough distance to make sure her shot hit the target, the wolf's arm disappeared from view. Damn it, where'd you go? She kept the rifle braced against her shoulder, her line on sight trained on the hole that the creature had made in the upper part of the double doors, waiting and ready for her chance. Her finger was poised under the guard, the digit barely applying pressure on the trigger until she had a clear shot.

Suddenly the beast reared up and it slammed its clawed fists into the door, weakening the chain wrapped around the handles even more. She needed to get to it and make sure it was sturdy enough to hold, its separating links needed to be wrapped tighter through the looped bars to make sure they didn't have too much force plying them apart. The only problem was that the werewolf was right there, its snapping jaws coming through the hole it had forced between the doors, anger and desire shining in its evil, burning eyes.

Lisa realized this was her chance!

Here we go!

Bracing the stock of the tranquilizer gun tight against her shoulder, she raised the rifle up, and without wasting a moment to calm herself, she just squeezed the trigger and heard the following crack of the rifle echo through her ears. The wolf, it's head still pressed through the opening, suddenly let out a cry of pain as the dart fired directly into its eye, the colored plume of feathers on the end standing out in sharp contrast to the dark body of the beast.

"Yes!" she heard some of her group call out from behind her, but she was too busy reloading for another shot to pay much attention to them.

There was no telling if the powerful sedative would even work on these creatures, so she decided to hit it with another. Just as she had the rilfe reloaded, the creature disappeared from the hole in the entrance, and they could hear a muffled whine, like one would hear when a dog had injured its paw or something.

Well at least it hurt it! she thought, a smile forming on her face as she felt Nick walk up behind her, his hand brushing past her dark hair and resting on her shoulder. "Nice shooting cowboy," he said, and as she turned to face him, she saw he was smiling as well.

Before she could say anything in return, Frank called out, "I've got it!"

All eyes turned to the young lab assistant. He stood up and began typing away at the computer terminal before him, and as he connected the last wire and powered up the amplifiers, a hum was elicited from the two speakers that were sitting close to the two entryways. He had gotten it just in time, because as he fired the speakers up and started adjusting knobs on the mixing board, the second doorway that would normally have been the staff entrance creaked open, the heavy pile of items pushed against it, starting to fall to the sides and scatter across the floor.

With one last shove, the doors parted a good two feet and the werewolf that had been assaulting them came into view. They all gasped as the size and features of the demonic creature as it's head and upper torso began tearing at the blocked doorway and it tried to fit it's massive shoulders through the smaller space. It let out a loud roar that caused everyone indoors in the Wolf House to back up slightly, fear radiating from them all as they watched the beast continue to frantically push through the blockade.

Oh no, we're too late! Lisa thought as she watched in horror as the lycanthrope tore apart the blockade, it's powerfully muscled limbs throwing crates and buckets of plaster, paints and other heavy construction materials that they had pushed against the doors.

Though I walk through the valley of the shadow of death, I will fear no evil… Lisa began reciting in her head, noticing that while the two teenagers, Tommy and Jeremy stood petrified in their spots, Nick appeared to also be whispering some unintelligible prayer.

Frank began typing as fast as he could at the keyboard, trying to get the speakers to begin their ascent through the various frequencies, while Lisa aimed the tranquilizer rifle at the new threat. As soon as she fired the first round, the dart slammed into the creature's chest and she was already reloading for a second shot. Meanwhile, Frank keyed in the last command and grabbing hold of the main knob on the mixing board, he twisted it violently, a loud blast of sound erupting from the speakers as they vibrated on the floor.

It was more than just loud, and everyone had to cover their ears as Frank worked the volume up higher into the frequencies that were not recognizable to the human ear. As he did so, the speakers stopped blasting out the loud pitched noise they had been, and just began to hum and shake. Everyone uncovered their ears, the ringing from the first, massive explosion of decibels causing everyone's head to hurt.

Lisa knew that the decibel level for which sustained exposure may result in hearing loss was 90 to 95 decibels. Pain begins at 125 dB, at 140 dB even short term exposure can cause permanent damage and 180 dB is when a short period of of exposure to these levels causes tissue death. High frequency sounds of 2 to 4,000 Hz are the most damaging. Frank had the speakers humming, the sound level no longer in the human hearing range. As she watched him continue to turn the knob, the levels reaching a powerful range that the werewolf still clawing, and pulling itself into the room suddenly stopped. It's head whipped upwards and it's jaws widened as it let out a howl, the creature seeming to be confused and striking out at the air with it's deadly claws.

The speakers continued to vibrate on the floor, and everyone's eyes were glued to the creature that was halfway through the door now. Now that the speaker's blaring levels were beyond hurting human ears, Lisa raised the gun again and fired a second dart into the wolf's furry neck. The animal was swaying back and forth, and Lisa wasn't sure if it was due to the powerful anesthetic taking effect or the lycanthrope's equilibrium being altered, the balance it had on it's back legs causing the creature to struggle as it tried to push itself back out the hole it was coming through.

"Yes— its working!" Tommy shouted and they all shared a silent breath of hope. They just might make it out of this. However, the darts and the blaring dB's coming out of the speakers were still non-lethal alternatives. They needed to figure out something to finish the beasts off.

"Look it's trying to pull itself out and retreat," Jeremy said with a hint of glee in his voice. Everyone's confidence had been elevated until suddenly there was a loud explosion from outside and the power seemed to flicker momentarily.

"What the?" Nick cried out, and suddenly the speakers fizzled and shorted out and the room was plunged into darkness. "Shit!"

One of the creatures must have blown the circuit breaker or tore the electric cable from the ground that led into the building. Now they were defenseless and in the dark. There didn't seem to be any backup generator installed to kick on once the building lost power, and they all huddled together, Lisa loading the last tranquilizer dart into the rifle with shaking hands.

Oh no, oh no, oh no, Lisa muttered as she was able to get the dart into the chamber and slip the bolt closed. It took her a moment to get her emotions under control and then she let out a startled scream as the main doors suddenly rocked open with a violent blow, the chain snapping and the links clattering to the floor as the wolf she had shot in the eye with the rifle tore through, its head swinging back and forth as if it was trying to regain it's footing and composure from the deafening audio attack it had just gone through the aftereffects still messing with it's equilibrium.

She raised the gun just as she saw the light from the moon pouring in and revealing the second beast filing in right behind the other. A powerful drift of snow blew in, spreading the think flakes all over the ground and the tumbled barricade that the wolves were pushing through.

There was only one dart left, and even though the second wolf seemed to be stumbling around more than the first, the drugs weren't working as well as she had hoped. With the amount of tranquilizer in those darts, two hits should have laid a full-grown, adult lion out, but the werewolves kept coming.

One dart— two targets!

Lisa knew that they were done for.

There was nothing more they could do now that the beasts were inside the Wolf House. God help us! she thought, but she knew there was no one looking down on them from above.

No, they were alone in this situation, left to their own devices, and they didn't seem to have a chance in hell of getting out of here alone!

Oh well, they had put up a good fight…

Chapter 50

Aidan had just reached the building labeled the Wolf House, and from he could see, he was just in time. The two werewolves had just broken through the front doors into the dark main lobby space within. Without wasting a second, he raised his gun and fired off two rounds towards the backside of the wolf closest to the door. It was a strange sight watching the creature as it stepped into the building just as he fired. It looked wounded somehow, the way it was walking drowsily and misstepped, its footing almost slipping as it went forward. Then the bullets sunk into the beasts back, eliciting a cry of pain as the creature whipped around to see where the sudden torment had come from.

Spying Aidan standing there with his gun focused on it, it let out a roar and charged towards him. As he fired again, the creature was fast enough to leap to the side, the bullet hitting a small snow bank that had formed on the ground and sending a pile of the white flakes up into the air.

Pffft

Shit Aidan, aim— can't waste these shots! He told himself as he focused on the creature coming at him. However, before he could fire again, the creature struck out with a long, furry arm, the clawed hand catching his jacket and flinging him off to the side. Aidan lost his balance as he flew into the stone building, his shoulder slamming forcefully into the hard exterior, but he was fortunate that he hadn't lost the gun in all the commotion.

"Ughh!" he cried out as he slumped to the ground, the pain in his right side throbbing deeply as he realized he had dislocated the shoulder. Spinning to his side, he dropped the gun into his left hand and raised it up just in time as the beast, it's clawed hands flexing and it's jaws opening and closing in anticipation of the meal it was about to have, came at him.

That's when Aidan saw the two darts sticking out of the beast's body. One was stuck in the neck and the other standing straight out from it's gut. Who the hell had shot it? And with tranquilizer darts no doubt! He realized that was probably the reason the creature hadn't ripped him to shreds already. It was drugged and sluggish, and then he saw the dried blood that had leaked from it's long, furry ears. It was almost like whoever was in the Wolf House had punctured the animal's eardrums. That explained how he was able to catch up to it and shoot it from the back without it having heard him coming.

Maybe there is a chance of turning this around!

Aidan slid onto his back, gun in his left hand and ignoring the pain as his dislocated shoulder pressed into the hard ground, he pulled the trigger. He didn't stop shooting until the firing pin clicked and he realized he had emptied the entire clip into the animal. It stood there for a moment, dark blood drizzling out of the multiple holes he had inflicted into the creature's chest, one bullet even piercing the fleshier part of the beast's throat. It tried to open its mouth as if it was about to say something, or possibly howl out in pain, but only blood and a line of smoke poured from it, the crimson liquid trickling across the scuffed up snow at its feet.

The dark, wiry pelt of fur that sprouted from its head like a mane, ran down it's muscular back to its tail, and across it's chest, the fur growing less and less as it ran down to its crouch where a patch of fur covered it's privates. With there only being a little fur on the black, muscled skin, Aidan could see that the multiple bullet wounds weren't attempting to close up, the silver inside them stinging the flesh as it seemed to poison the bloodstream. Then, the creature attempted to take one mistimed footstep and it came crashing down face-first into a pile of the white, snowy powder. The two original bullet holes in it's back already showing traces of poisoning from the silver he had shot it with. Gray, spidery veins crossed under the dark skin, extending outward like a cracked windshield would from a tiny hole over time. Yes, the silver had certainly finished the beast off.

Sitting up, Aidan popped the clip out and began slipping the last of the bullets he had in his pocket into the magazine. During the scuffle, it seemed like he had ripped his pocket somehow when he was thrown and now he only had four bullets left. Pushing the clip back into the M1911, he pushed the slide back and chambered one of the four remaining rounds.

Great, four bullets left— well, so far luck has been on my side.

Although he didn't think that was going to be holding for much longer. He pushed himself up and crawled to a standing position. He looked down at the dead wolf at his feet, the one that only moments before had been about to rip him open and end his existence as he knew it, but fortunately someone up there must have been looking out for him.

He glanced to the heavens and saw the full moon shining down upon him. The pale light reflected off the snow and made it slightly brighter outside, but it also had a strange effect on the blood that was lining the ground—it appeared almost black. The Hunter's Moon— what a name, he thought as he started towards the Wolf House just as the sound of a rifle discharging broke through the air and it was followed by a terrible howl.

The survivors were still alive and inside the building. He had to save them. He couldn't sit idly by and watch helplessly as the occupants of the structure were slaughtered. His feet shuffled through the snow, passing by the dead wolf with the multiple bullet holes smoking from the silver infecting the bloodstream and causing the creature to stay down and dead. Thank God!

As Aidan reached the torn open entryway, metal having been ripped apart and the double doors stripped from their frame, he quickly entered into the building just as a scream reached his ears. Peering through the dark, he could see the largest of the wolves he had to deal with so far, had grabbed Lisa Davies up by the throat, a rifle in her hands dropping casually to the ground.

He hesitated, unable to take aim for fear of hitting her or anyone else. He wouldn't let that happen again! No one would be paralyzed or killed from him not thinking before he acted, but he had to do something or else the wildlife biologist's throat would be torn open in a matter of seconds.

Then a second form came out of the dark, a pole of some sort being brandished like a club, and Aidan recognized the sight of Nick Haley rushing to save Lisa. The werewolf unfortunately seemed to see what he was doing as well and threw the woman to the side, discarding her like a meaningless rag doll and it reached out for him with it's long, powerful arms. Nick ducked just in time and slammed the metal pole hard into the beast's side, causing it to back up away from the group of people that Aidan could now see cowering behind him. That's when he noticed not only Lisa's intern Frank, was present, but Jeremy Wilkes was there as well.

He had found them all, and they were alive!

As soon as Nick went to step back, the creature lashed out with a strong kick that connected directly with the reporter's chest, sending him sprawling backwards into the group of onlookers. He hit into them with a collision of limbs flying and as he came to rest, Aidan could see where the beast's claws had cut into Nick's chest. Blood was seeping out, and Lisa rushed over to apply pressure to the wounds while Jeremy, Frank and even the cowardly form of the last teenager stepped forward to block the path of the murderous werewolf from getting to the injured adults behind them.

The wolf cocked it's head as if studying them in amusement, then took a step towards them, it's jaws opening wide and saliva spraying out as it howled in anger, it's intent to rip each of them to pieces all too clear.

"Hey fuzzball!" Aidan yelled, taking the moment now that there were no innocent bystanders in the way, and getting the beast's attention.

It spun around quickly and Aidan noticed that it's left eye was milky-white like Lisa had shot it with the gun earlier that she had been brandishing. That or maybe someone else was able to get close enough to hurt it before it got inside the building. Either way, his line of sight was clear of people, and Aidan raised his gun to fire, reminding himself once more that he only had four shots.

The creature, seeing the gun in Aidan's weak left hand, his right unable to hold the pistol upright due to the damage of his shoulder, charged at him, closing the gap between them in a matter of seconds. Aidan squeezed off a round that hit the creature in the leg, but the momentum it had behind it, caused it to crash into Aidan and they both went barreling out through the destroyed barricade and into the hard, frozen earth outside.

Aidan tried to roll out from under the beast, but it had him pinned and it's jaws struck down at him, it's hot, stinking breath smelling like rotten meat. Twisting his neck out of the way, the teeth just missed his jugular, barely tearing the skin on the side of his neck as its muzzle dug into a pile of snow. Aidan used the leverage of the animal's lunge to get his feet under it, his shoes braced against its hips, and as he pushed with all his might, he was able to just barely fling the wolf off him. The creature landed as easily as a cat, but the bullet hole in its leg caused the weight it placed on it to make it drop to its knee.

It was injured, the silver poisoning it somewhat, or was it the tranquilizer darts that Lisa had been using? Aidan didn't know and he didn't care. Rolling up into a shooting stance, he was about to fire when the wolf jumped forward, knocking into him again and sending the gun flying into a mound of snow. He tried to keep his eyes on the beast's slobbering jaws, not wanting those razor sharp teeth to find purchase in his skin, but he was also reaching around wildly trying to feel for the weapon.

Everything was just happening too fast and he had too many things to worry about. Suddenly an even worse pain than the dislocated shoulder erupted through him, and his head twisted to the side to see long, black claws gripping part of his chest and his collar bone. The nails were puncturing through his skin, and he could feel the hot blood flowing out of his chest, the same area he had just recovered from being shot a year before.

"Ahhh!" Aidan yelled as he felt his head going woozy, his vision disorientated as his blood flowed freely through his ripped open skin. He could even feel the wolf's nails scratching across the bones under his flesh, digging deeper as they explored his injury with enjoyment. It seemed the werewolf was enjoying inflicting so much pain on him since he had done so to the animal's fellow pack mates.

As Aidan began to think he was going to pass out from either a loss of blood or the creature ripping out his heart while it was still beating, he realized that mixed in the dark fur around the beast's neck was a gold necklace with a pendant of a pentagram. Just as he realized this, he reached his hand up through the oily, stinking fur and grabbed hold of the jewelry. With a strong tug, he felt the chain snap and he pulled it to him. This action seemed to enrage and distract the wolf as it's claws tore out of his chest and it reached with it's bloody, padded hand and it's wicked, gory claws, for the necklace in Aidan's grasp.

With the werewolf sitting up on his chest, the foul stench of it's body assailing Aidan's nose, he turned his head and flung the golden necklace as far as he could. The creature jumped up, the weight on its one injured leg still bothering it, and once it was clear or Aidan's beaten and bloody form, he watched as it reached into the snow to pick up the pendant, holding it up in triumph in one massive, bloody paw.

Just then the report of gunshots echoed through the air and Aidan watched as the werewolf's body was rocked back and forth, with the bullets smashing into its chest and gut with a fury. He had lost count after twelve and quickly pushed the pain from his mind, and reached out for the pile of snow that his gun had disappeared into. Once his hand closed on the semi-automatic that Lafayette had given him, it still holding three silver bullets left, then and only then did he turn to see who had just emptied an entire 17 round magazine into the creature to buy him time to get out of the way.

Standing there with her arms extended in a perfect firing stance was Andrea, the gun in her hand smoking and the smell of cordite filling the air around them. Aidan's eyes widened as he shook his head back and forth to clear his vision and realized that he really was staring at the woman of his dreams.

"Get up Aidan!— And what the hell is this thing?" she yelled.

A million questions entered his mind, like: Where did she come from? How did she find us? Am I just dreaming this? Yet, he shook the temporary paralysis off and realized that even though she had just filled the werewolf with enough rounds to drop any human, this thing was anything but human.

The wolf rose to it's full height, a massive 7' tall from its clawed wolf-like paws to the head that with its deadly jaw stuffed with razor sharp teeth and the pointy ears that stuck up on its head. The elongated, lupine muzzle with its pointy nose stuck out it's face and with one opaque, blinded eye and one dark pupil with streaks of blood-red flecks spreading throughout it, it arched its back and let out a deafening howl towards the moon, the multiple bullet holes in its chest and stomach seeming to already be healing. The regular shots comprised of full-metal jacketed hollow points having little to no effect on the supernatural-like creature.

And, while this largest of the wolves he had fought appeared different from the others. He had less of a pelt of fur covering his chest and body, the skin pigment having blackened even more, but the wiry hair that sprouted from its head and neck descended down it's back and the chest until it reached between its legs and joined the long tail that swung behind it.

The other noticeable difference was that while all the other wolves that Aidan had fought had black, matted hair, this last one seemed to have a grayish tint to its fur. Almost as if it was older than the others. Aidan wasn't sure if that made a difference, but he could have sworn that it seemed like the once fully-dead eye had started to regenerate faster than normal. It had something to do, he assumed with it probably being unfortunate enough to be having this fight to the finish smack-dab in the middle of a powerfully calling full moon, the pale reddish-white globe looking down to the Earth from its celestial place.

"Andrea you have to get out of here!" Aidan yelled as he stumbled slightly and backed up towards her, keeping himself in the between her and the beast.

"I'm not leaving you…" she protested, slapping a fresh clip into her Glock and chambering a round.

"Listen to me— I can handle this…" Aidan was saying, but he knew her eyes were moving back and forth from his bloody and injured body, to that of the werewolf who had stopped howling and now looked towards her with a blood-thirst she had never seen before in any creature's eyes. "…Jeremy is inside the Wolf House, he's safe. Now go to him and the others. Call Stone on the radio I dropped inside and get those tactical teams in here now!"

"No!" Andrea said defiantly as Aidan, surprised at her outburst took his eyes off the wolf standing twenty feet away that was busy digging at its leg with a clawed finger, wincing in pain as it tried to remove the silver bullet before its infection spread to other parts of its body. "I hate to tell you this, but I'm stuck with you— here and now!" she said, and then making sure the safety was off on her pistol, she pivoted and opened fire on the creature again.

However it was much faster this time, jumping out of the way before a single shot could score a direct hit, with one stray round glancing off its shoulder blade and the others nowhere near where they needed to be aimed.

"Keep it distracted!" Aidan yelled as he circled around to the side of the building that the lycanthrope had disappeared towards, the tall concrete fence with the razor wire at the top marked the ending of the Wolf House and the start of the vacant Gray Wolf habitat.

"Where the hell are you, you mangy mutt?" he cried, his left hand tightening on the gun in his hand.

If he was lucky, he would be able to stop this thing before it escaped, never having to worry about if it harmed another soul again. He knew in his gut that this was the last one. Even though he only counted two that he knew were dead, and the leader made three, and he was looking for him right at this moment, but something told him that the last unaccounted werewolf had met its match elsewhere.

Perhaps it had something to do with that large flare up and explosion he had seen earlier. Well, whatever it was, once thing was for certain.

This ends tonight!

Looking through the darkness, the moonlit night adding enough illumination to see where he was walking to, and he knew that somewhere in the deep recess in between the building and the wolf enclosure, there had to be multiple places for a creature the size of a huge man could hide, but where? Aidan just wasn't sure.

Suddenly he heard a crunch of snow directly behind him and he spun quickly, gun aimed with both arms to steady his shot, yet it was only Andrea. Holy shit, I had almost taken her out from being too jumpy! He would have to work on that as her surprised smile calmed him down just enough and he began using his head as he searched through the darkened area, snow continuing to fall all around him and wash out exactly how far he could see ahead of him. The storm was definitely getting stronger.

"Come out, come out, wherever you are!" he called, wiping his sweaty palms off on his pants as he switched the gun from his left and back to his right hand. Dislocated shoulder or not, he needed to be able to shoot as accurately as he could, and unfortunately that meant using his injured arm.

"Aidan— look out!" Andrea called and from behind a tree on the far side of the paved walkway, the werewolf had stole out from the darkness, it's leg a mangled mess from it ripping into it's own flesh and muscle to remove the poisonous bullet Aidan had shot it with minutes earlier.

"I see it," Aidan said, training his gun on the creature, feeling the inflamed burning from his ripped open chest and his hurting shoulder as his eyes never left the beast's own.

Aidan still couldn't believe that Andrea was there. The moment he realized she was, and that he hadn't been dreaming, his heart had begun pumping even wilder, his chest feeling like it would burst from everything he was dealing with at the moment. Images of their lips meeting, bodies intertwined together when this was all over and Aidan got a professional to look at his injuries, filled his mind. Yet, this time, he had a feeling Andrea would be spending a lot more time at his bedside in the hospital.

He was glad she was there, yet mortified at the same time. He loved seeing her, knowing that he was doing all this to keep her, her son and the others alive and to end this living nightmare, but he also knew that if he failed, they would be the next targets to meet their demise. Aidan wouldn't allow that!

Now that he had her in his life, he wasn't going to lose her like that. Standing there with the snow landing on his head and shoulders, blood dripping down onto the ground from his injuries, Aidan watched the creature's eyes lock on him with intense hatred. The hairs on the back of his neck bristled. Just then he realized the wolf had dropped to all fours and was charging at him, with incredible speed.

The creature had leapt into the air as Aidan fired his weapon at it, but it was moving too fast. It landed up on the top of the enclosure, hanging from the fence by one clawed hand as his bullets tore past it and embedded themselves into the concrete foundation where the beast had just been. As he tried to move his arm to realign his shot, the werewolf sprang from the top of the wall, it's jaws opened and spittle dripping from them, clawed arms outstretched towards Aidan as he watched the scene seem to slow down before him like it was a movie playing in slow-motion.

The ferocious werewolf was coming straight at him and Andrea, it's body soaring through the air like a missile coming falling to earth, it's target the two of them standing there in the open as snow fell around them, the fresh blanket covering his blood as if it was a blanket wiping the scene clean— like a fresh new beginning. Was this the end he had always knew was coming? No, he would not allow Andrea to be hurt— no matter what!

Then, as if he was moving on auto-pilot, his arm raised on its own, the gun feeling weightless in his grip as if gravity no longer held any limitations on him. Years of habit and training had him looking down the sights of the pistol, his mind telling him he only had one shot left, and his finger wrapped around the trigger as his left hand reached over and steadied his injured right arm as he pulled the trigger, the recoil kicking back and sending pain shooting through his dislocated shoulder. He watched as the bullet hit its mark, the wolves head snapped backwards as the body sailed through the air, and he saw a stream of blood explode out the back of the cranium.

That's when everything seemed to return to normal speed, his heartbeat and breathing speeding up and he remembered shoving Andrea out of the way. He watched as her body went skidding to the snow-covered ground, her rolling away from him just as the force of the beast connected with his body. Pain shot through him as he flew back, hitting the hard, cold ground with a thud and skidding a few feet across hard gravel. His head slammed into the paved ground and an explosion of light and sound blinded him for a moment as his sense were assailed by the large body of the beast that had crashed into him.

Pain was shooting through his body in multiple spots as he attempted to look down at his torso and limbs, but the large, furry form of the werewolf lay upon him. He felt a sharp throbbing feeling that seemed to be coming from all over his body as he tried to push the heavy weight of the creature off him. As he rolled the dead beast to the side, he was able to prop himself up on shaky arms, his eyes not bothering to look to his own wounds, but instead searching the area around him for Andrea.

Where is she— where's Andrea? He panicked, shoving the pungent, sleek-haired body further off him and pulling his legs out from under the lycanthrope. Then he saw her. She was climbing to her feet, no worse for wear other than a few scratches on her palms and knees. He couldn't believe the feelings coursing through him and as he stood, he stumbled forward on sore legs and rushed towards her.

He couldn't speak, his body tense and bleeding as he wrapped his injured shoulders around Andrea and squeezed her tight. He saw the tears in her eyes, and he knew that they were tears of joy. She had almost lost him, yet here they were. They had survived. He held her tighter, ignoring the pain that was radiating from all over and he locked eyes with her and their lips met.

They stood there, mouths locked together as they kissed passionately, each thankful that the other was still alive and well. While it was still too early to know how the hell they were going to explain everything that had happened this night to the many people who were going to be questioning them soon. Right now, it didn't matter though. All that was important was that they everyone in the Wolf House was now safe including Andrea's son, Jeremy, and that was all Aidan could ask for. As he held Andrea to him, he looked up at the sky, taking a look at the full moon over head, and watching as snow poured down from the heavens, cascading around and swirling in the cold winds that whipped past. By morning all the blood that had been spilled tonight would be covered, but for now they were just glad to be alive.

"Are you alright?" Andrea asked, leaning back a bit to look him over.

Aidan just smiled, his lip bleeding like many others parts of him and said, "I've seen worse."

"Yeah right, we'll from now on you're going to be taking it easy, no more playing hero."

"I think I can handle that," Aidan admitted, his eyes taking in Andrea's beautiful features as flurries coasted past them, some collecting in their hair and on their shoulders.

Aidan knew this was certainly going to be a night none of them forgot, and holding Andrea in his arms, he knew he had certainly came out the victor. After all, not only had he saved the day, but he had got the girl in the end as well!

"Let's go home," Andrea finally said, breaking the silence that had ensued for a moment as they just looked deep into each other's eyes.

"My place or yours?" Aidan asked.

"We've been to my place, how about we try something new and head to yours just for tonight."

"Sounds good to me," Aidan said.

He placed his good arm around Andrea's waist, holding her tight as he limped slightly and they made their way towards the others who had begun filing out of the Wolf House.

Jeremy seeing his mother, ran to her just as Aidan let her go, and she enveloped him in a tight hug. It seemed like the night was finally over.

Sure there would be a lot of questions to be answered over the next few weeks, but the Moonlight Massacres were over, and that's all that mattered to Aidan. There would be no more horrific deaths to plague the Washington Metropolitan area. The culprits were dead, and looking over to Nick who had an arm over Lisa's shoulder, he knew the man had one hell of a story to tell. Of course, it was still to be seen if the public would believe what had happened this Halloween Night at the National Zoo.

If Aidan and the other survivors hadn't been there, he knew they would have never believed that they had come under siege by a group of werewolves! No, who in their right mind would believe that? Yet, as Aidan pondered that question, he felt all eyes moving from the fallen beast to him, and he knew that at least he wasn't alone. Others had witnessed the horrors of this night, an evening where the Hunter's Moon loomed high above, watching everything that had transpired from the safety of it's heavenly home in the stars.

Yes, a lot of questions would be asked, but for now, as Andrea's arm wrapped around his torso and she helped him towards the Wolf House, planning on getting him out of the weather and tend to his wounds, he took one last look at the dead beast laying on the ground in it's own pile of blood.

Werewolves— who would believe it?

Suddenly there was a commotion from the right side of the trail and as they all looked in that direction, SWAT officers melded out of the darkness, assault rifles at the ready, and leading the band of men was Special Agent Jim Poole, his eyes taking in the entire scene of blood and carnage that had been spread over the once, pure white snowfall.

"Detectives," he said as he approached Aidan and Andrea. "Are these the only survivors with you?"

Their group of seven, some wounded, the rest just trying to make sense of all the horrors they had just encountered together, just nodded in agreement. Lisa had bandaged Nick's chest with That's when a second unit of armed officers, this one comprised of familiar faces like Mack Jones and Tim Melvin appeared, the bulletproof vest around Mack's chest fitting snug and not covering part of his large waist.

"Mack!" Aidan cried out, Andrea helping him over to the recently arrived group of FBI, MCPD and Metro PD.

The tactical unit spread out, four officers checking inside the Wolf House for any other civilians, while the others encircled the building's outside walls, searching the grounds and creating a protective circle around the civilians.

Meanwhile, Poole and two other Agents from the FBI stood over the carcass of the wolf, it's body still warm, gray veins pulsing underneath it's dark skin as the internal poisoning from the silver bullets worked through its bloodstream. The ragged hole in its head had finished trickling blood onto the ground, the wound looking raw and inflamed, and in it's almost human-shaped hand, it still held the golden necklace with the pentagram dangling from the broken chain.

"Well, you two are a sight for sore eyes," Mack said to Aidan and Andrea, his chubby cheeks red from the cold winds blowing about them as he looked their group over, then pulling a radio from his belt, he called in emergency services. "I need paramedics and a two of the biggest body bags you guys can find over to the new construction site called the Wolf House."

"I thought you were suspended?" Aidan asked, looking at his friend once he finished his call.

"It seems that Agent Poole there, pulled rank on the Chief and after I had filled him in on the severity of the situation from what you had told me when you called, he reinstated me temporarily to go in and lead the second assault team. Stone wasn't too happy, but then again, he isn't one to argue with the Feds," Mack said, his eyes glancing to the dead corpse of the beast. "Looks like you were right all along."

"What phone call?" Andrea asked, looking to Aidan confused.

"I called Mack after the first wolf I took down. Fortunately my phone has a built-in camera and I was able to send Mack a picture-message to help him convince Poole," Aidan explained.

"Oh."

"Yeah, it was the only way I thought that Mack would have a chance of getting Poole to believe him about what we were dealing with."

"Well, that was quick thinking," Andrea admitted.

"Hey, it was you who saved me, remember?"

Andrea's cheeks seemed to flush lightly beyond the color her cheeks had from the cold, and she shook her head. "No, I just distracted it. You saw how effective my bullets were on that thing, they barely slowed it down."

"But, it did slow it down, and that gave me enough time to react and get my weapon back. Speaking of which…" Aidan said looking from Andrea and back to Mack. "What happened to Dr. Lafayette? He's alright isn't he?"

At the mention of Morgan's name, Lisa and Nick came walking over to their small conversation, adding the size of the group.

"Yes, is Morgan alright?" she asked.

Mack stood there for a moment, Aidan recognized the look the man got when he had bad news to relate to next of kin and such, and answered for him. "He's dead isn't he?"

"Yes. He appears to have taken out the fourth werewolf when it broke into his lab, but he was able to kill it with what the investigators found in the debris and think was some homemade flamethrower. Unfortunately, it set the entire building on fire and it went up quick. The pathologist over there with the team investigating the fire thinks that at least that he died quickly. I'm sorry for your loss," Mack said meeting Lisa's tearing eyes.

Lisa just nodded, the feeling of loss weighing heavily on her. After all, she was the one to involve the Cajun zoologist in this whole mess. Then again, who could have seen it ending like this!

"He died taking out down one of those creatures…" Aidan said after giving Lisa a moment to wipe the tears from her eyes, "…I'd say that makes him one hell of a hero!"

"Yes," the rest of the group agreed, and Andrea and Frank placed their hands onto her shoulder, while Nick Haley caught her eye and gave her a smile. Breathing out carefully, she returned the smile, sniffling away her tears and wiping her nose on her jacket sleeve.

Aidan at that moment turned towards Andrea and he took her into his arms again, holding her tight even though his wounds shot pain through him and wracked his brain with waves of nausea. Andrea was okay, so was everyone else, he hadn't failed. Sure he was in for one hell of a hospital stay, his chest and shoulder seriously injured, his chest especially needing a good many stitches and surgery for the blood loss he'd suffered.

Looking deep into Andrea's endless eyes, he asked, "You think we can reschedule that dinner and a movie we had planned for tomorrow? He asked with a smile curling his bruised lip up at the corners of this mouth.

"For you, anything! Now let's get you looked at," she said, and with that Jeremy hooked his arm around Aidan's waist with a slight, approving smile, and they began walking down the Midnight Trail, there time with the behind the scenes access to this place over for all concerned.

The National Zoo was sure going to have one hell of a cleanup to get the new exhibit area ready for its grand opening, but that was the farthest thing from any of their minds.

They had just survived the most trying and deadly night of their lives, and this was one Halloween they weren't likely to forget.

Hell, it looked like Nick Haley got his story after all, Aidan thought as they all began filing away from the Wolf House.

In fact, they all were going to have one hell of a story to tell!

End.

"There is a beast in man that needs to be exercised, not exorcised."
        Anton LaVey

"Even a man who is pure in heart,
And says his prayers by night
May become a Wolf when the Wolfbane blooms
And the the Moon is full and bright"
        'The Wolfman'

"If depression is creeping up and must be faced, learn something about the nature of the beast. You may escape without a mauling."
        Dr. R. W. Shepherd

Made in the USA
Charleston, SC
20 May 2013